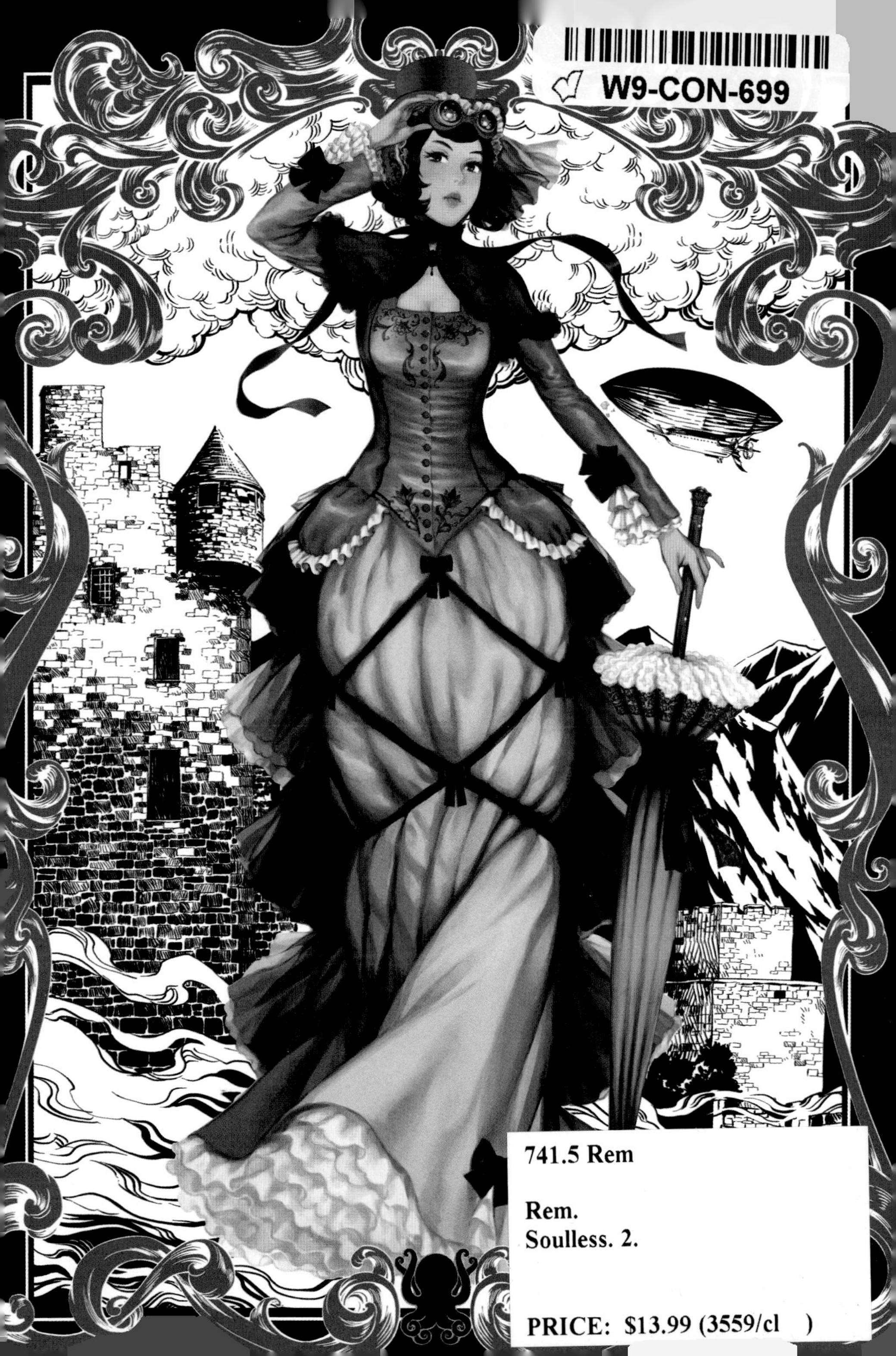

SOULLESS

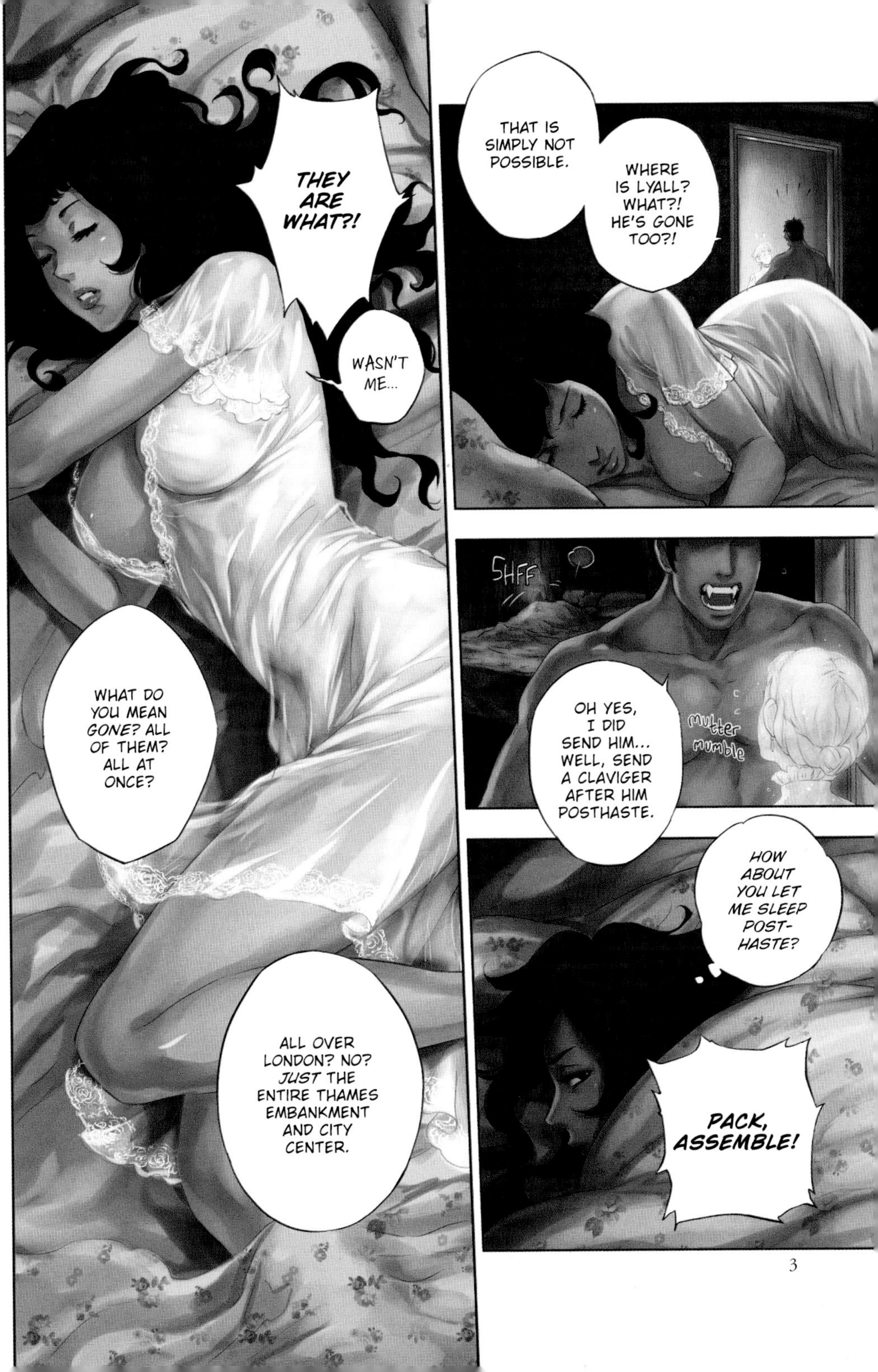
THEY ARE WHAT?!
WASN'T ME...
WHAT DO YOU MEAN GONE? ALL OF THEM? ALL AT ONCE?
ALL OVER LONDON? NO? JUST THE ENTIRE THAMES EMBANKMENT AND CITY CENTER.
THAT IS SIMPLY NOT POSSIBLE.
WHERE IS LYALL? WHAT?! HE'S GONE TOO?!
SHFF
OH YES, I DID SEND HIM... WELL, SEND A CLAVIGER AFTER HIM POSTHASTE.
mutter mumble
HOW ABOUT YOU LET ME SLEEP POST-HASTE?
PACK, ASSEMBLE!

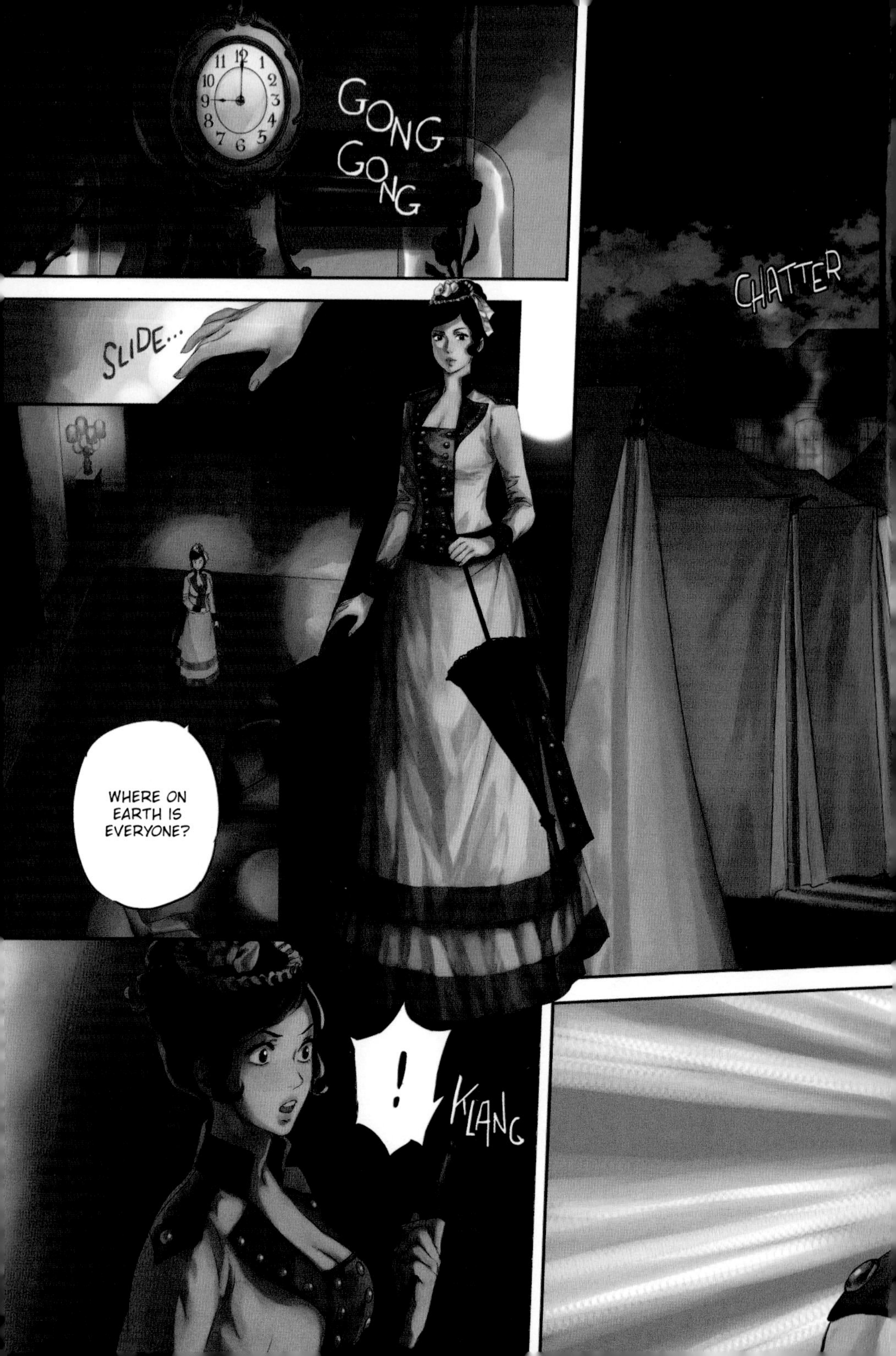
GONG GONG
SLIDE...
WHERE ON EARTH IS EVERYONE?
CHATTER
!
KLANG

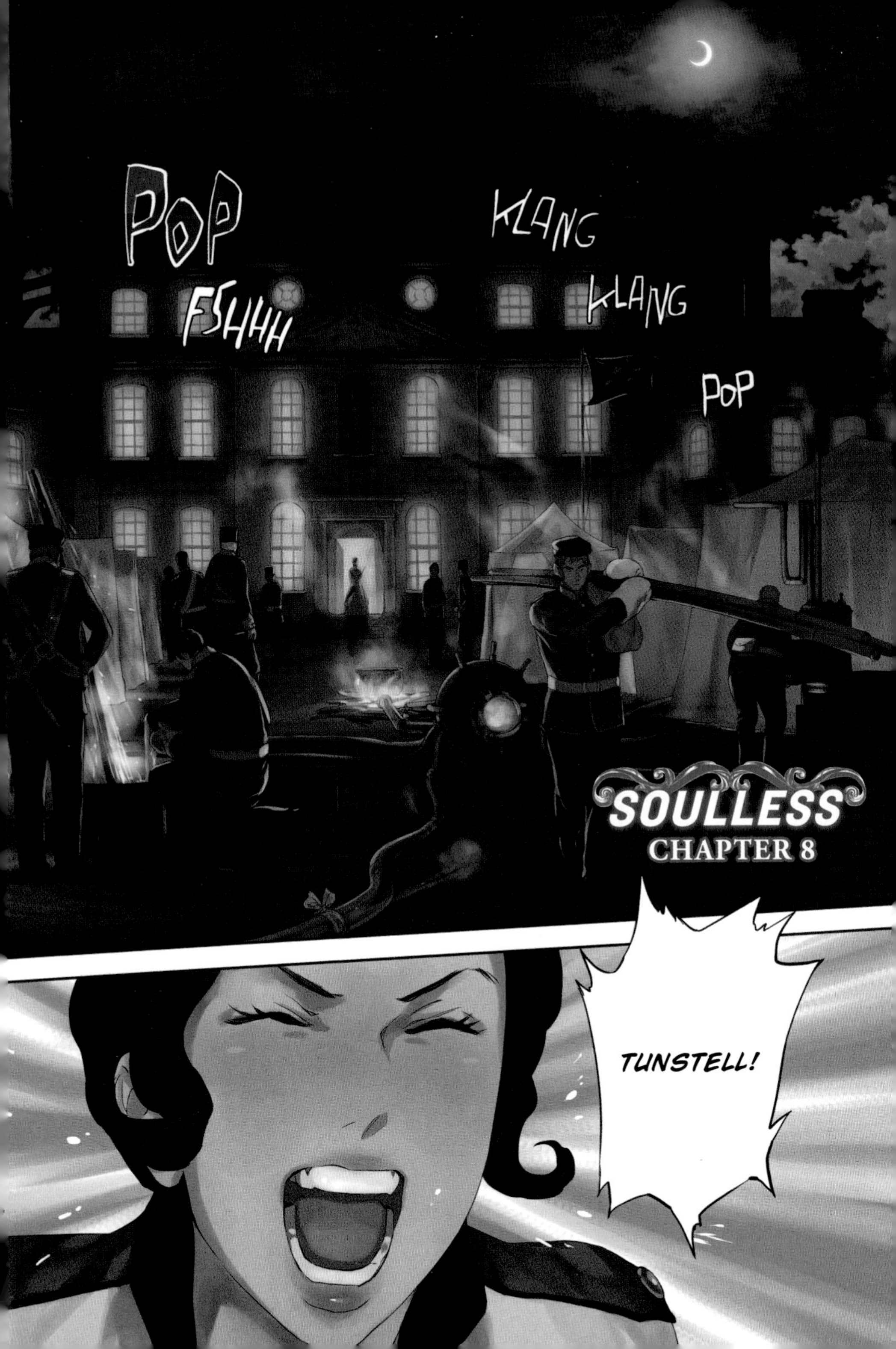
POP
FSHHH
KLANG
KLANG
POP
SOULLESS
CHAPTER 8
TUNSTELL!

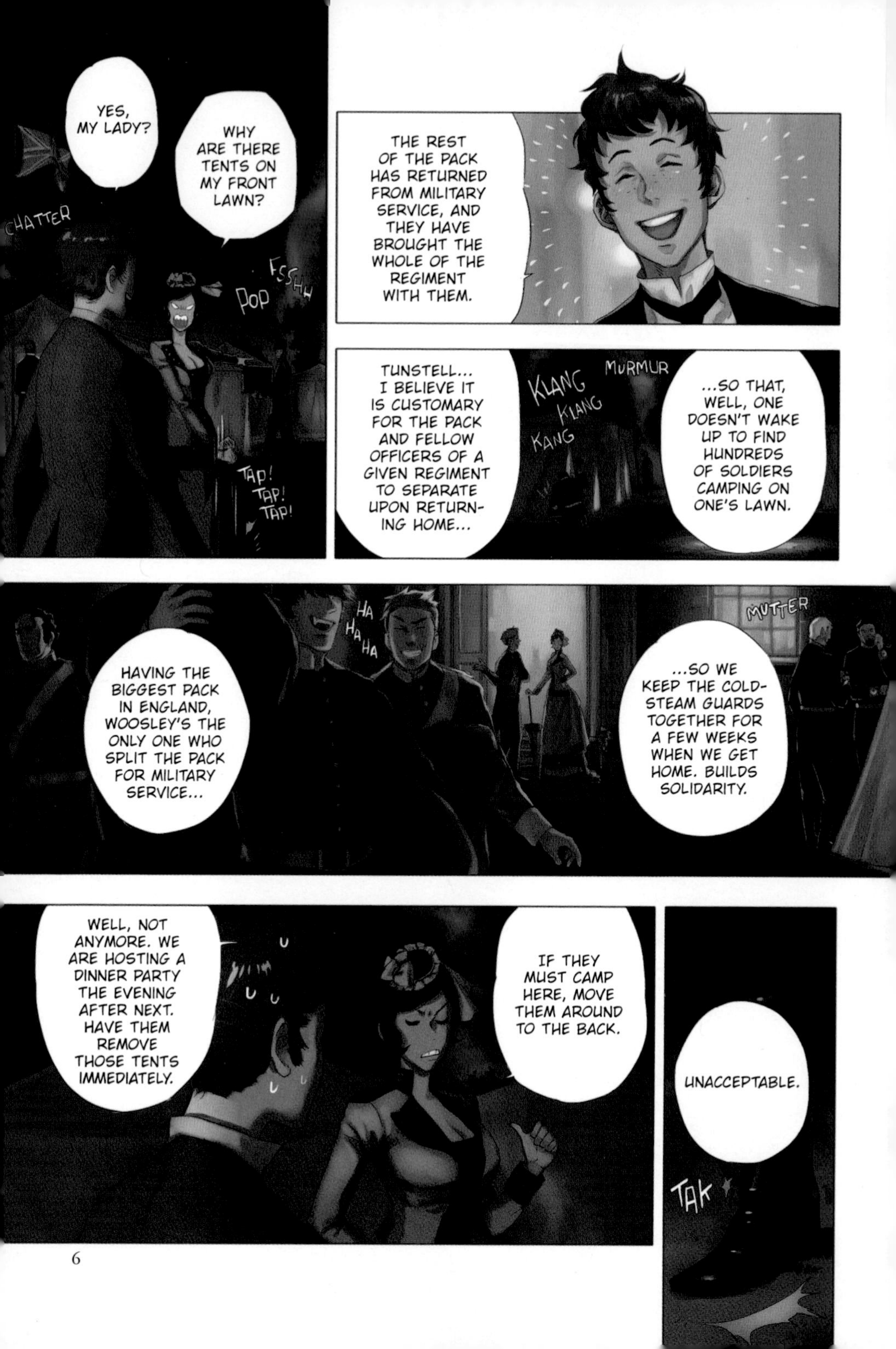
YES, MY LADY?
WHY ARE THERE TENTS ON MY FRONT LAWN?
CHATTER
FSSHH
POP
TAP! TAP! TAP!
THE REST OF THE PACK HAS RETURNED FROM MILITARY SERVICE, AND THEY HAVE BROUGHT THE WHOLE OF THE REGIMENT WITH THEM.
TUNSTELL... I BELIEVE IT IS CUSTOMARY FOR THE PACK AND FELLOW OFFICERS OF A GIVEN REGIMENT TO SEPARATE UPON RETURNING HOME...
KLANG KLANG KANG
MURMUR
...SO THAT, WELL, ONE DOESN'T WAKE UP TO FIND HUNDREDS OF SOLDIERS CAMPING ON ONE'S LAWN.
HAVING THE BIGGEST PACK IN ENGLAND, WOOSLEY'S THE ONLY ONE WHO SPLIT THE PACK FOR MILITARY SERVICE...
HA HA HA HA
MUTTER
...SO WE KEEP THE COLD-STEAM GUARDS TOGETHER FOR A FEW WEEKS WHEN WE GET HOME. BUILDS SOLIDARITY.
WELL, NOT ANYMORE. WE ARE HOSTING A DINNER PARTY THE EVENING AFTER NEXT. HAVE THEM REMOVE THOSE TENTS IMMEDIATELY.
IF THEY MUST CAMP HERE, MOVE THEM AROUND TO THE BACK.
UNACCEPTABLE.
TAK

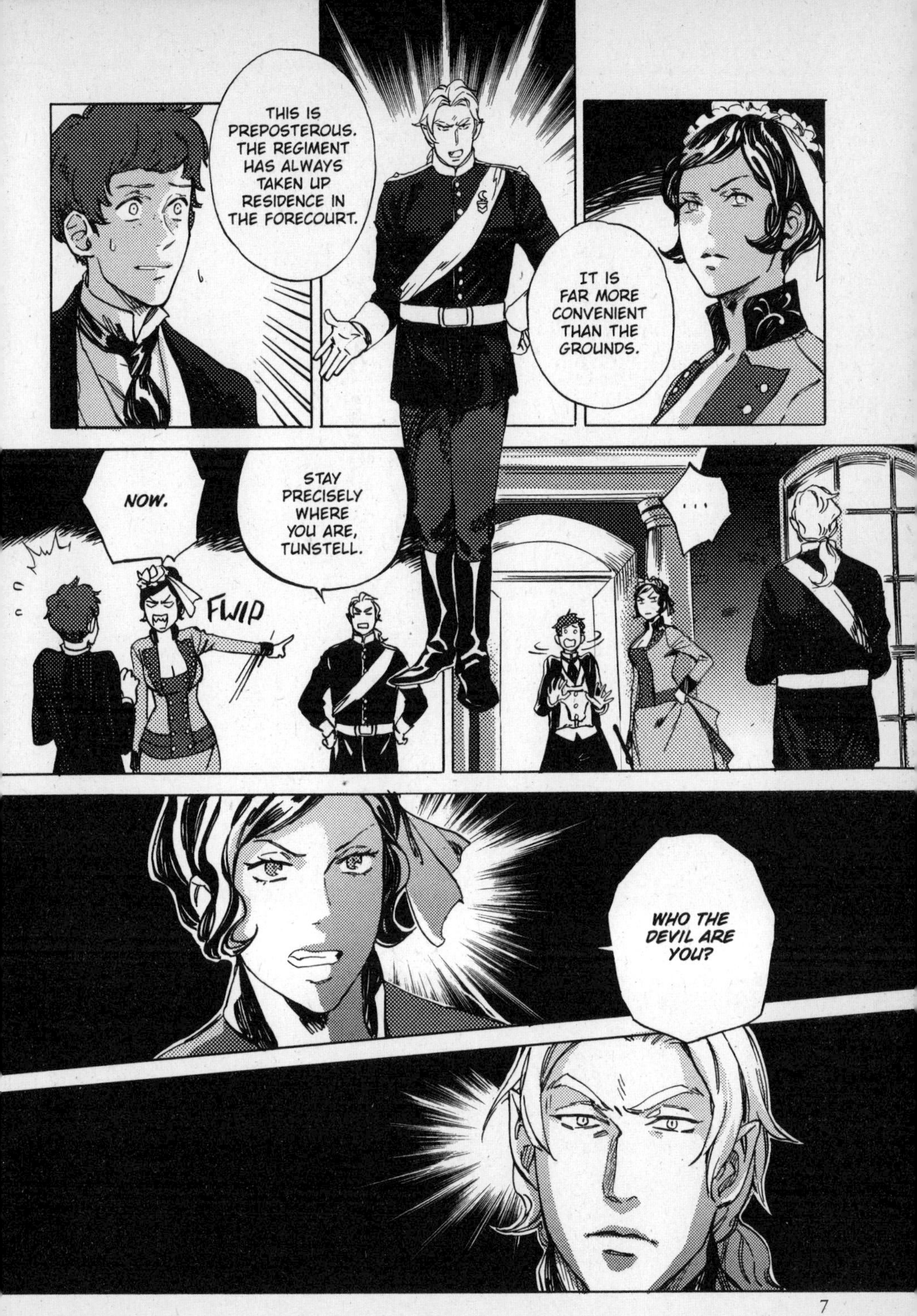
THIS IS PREPOSTEROUS. THE REGIMENT HAS ALWAYS TAKEN UP RESIDENCE IN THE FORECOURT.
IT IS FAR MORE CONVENIENT THAN THE GROUNDS.
NOW.
FWIP
STAY PRECISELY WHERE YOU ARE, TUNSTELL.
...
WHO THE DEVIL ARE YOU?

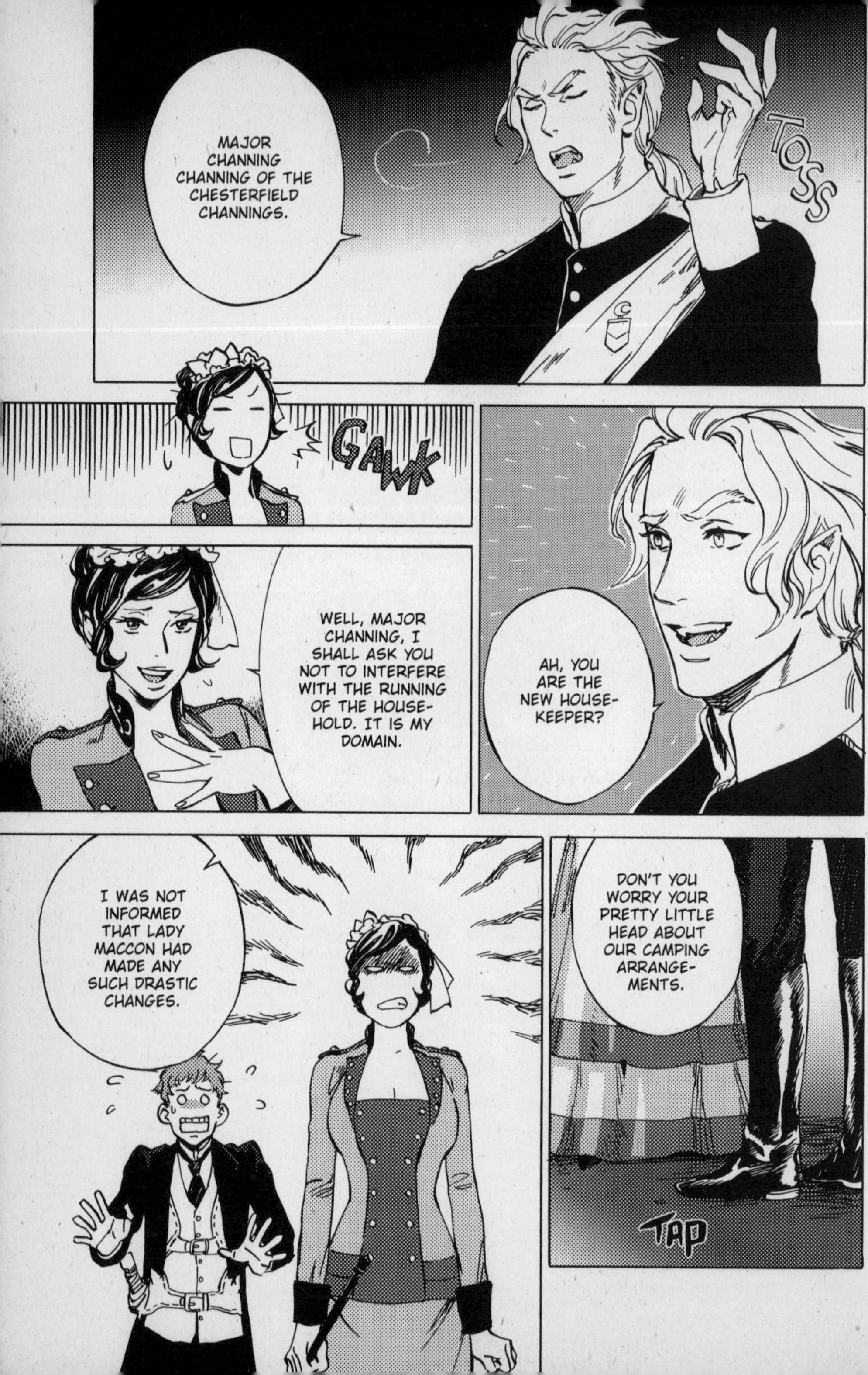
MAJOR CHANNING CHANNING OF THE CHESTERFIELD CHANNINGS.
TOSS
GAWK
WELL, MAJOR CHANNING, I SHALL ASK YOU NOT TO INTERFERE WITH THE RUNNING OF THE HOUSE-HOLD. IT IS MY DOMAIN.
AH, YOU ARE THE NEW HOUSE-KEEPER?
I WAS NOT INFORMED THAT LADY MACCON HAD MADE ANY SUCH DRASTIC CHANGES.
DON'T YOU WORRY YOUR PRETTY LITTLE HEAD ABOUT OUR CAMPING ARRANGE-MENTS.
TAP

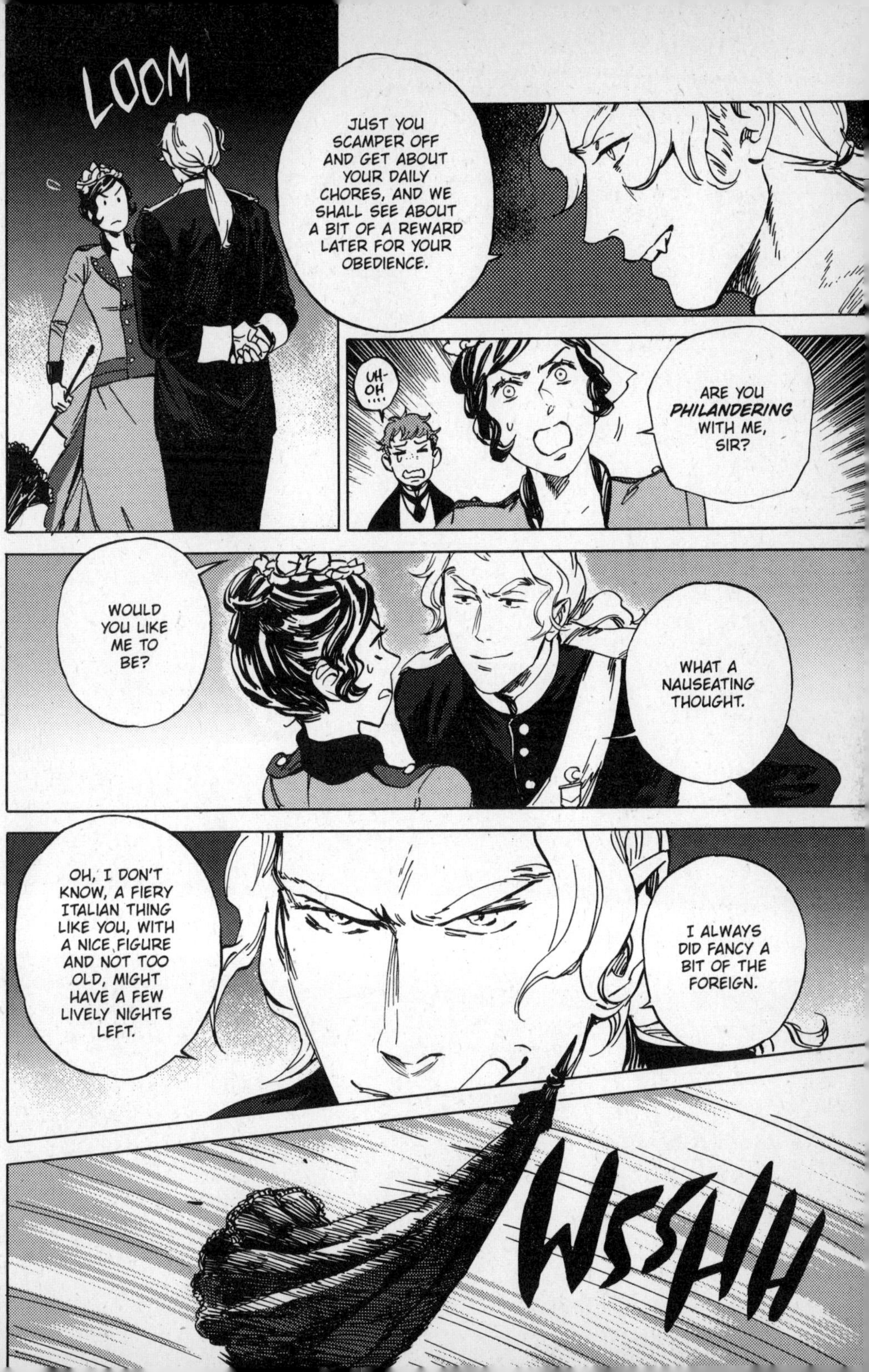
LOOM
JUST YOU SCAMPER OFF AND GET ABOUT YOUR DAILY CHORES, AND WE SHALL SEE ABOUT A BIT OF A REWARD LATER FOR YOUR OBEDIENCE.
UH-OH ....
ARE YOU *PHILANDERING* WITH ME, SIR?
WOULD YOU LIKE ME TO BE?
WHAT A NAUSEATING THOUGHT.
OH, I DON'T KNOW, A FIERY ITALIAN THING LIKE YOU, WITH A NICE FIGURE AND NOT TOO OLD, MIGHT HAVE A FEW LIVELY NIGHTS LEFT.
I ALWAYS DID FANCY A BIT OF THE FOREIGN.
WSSHH

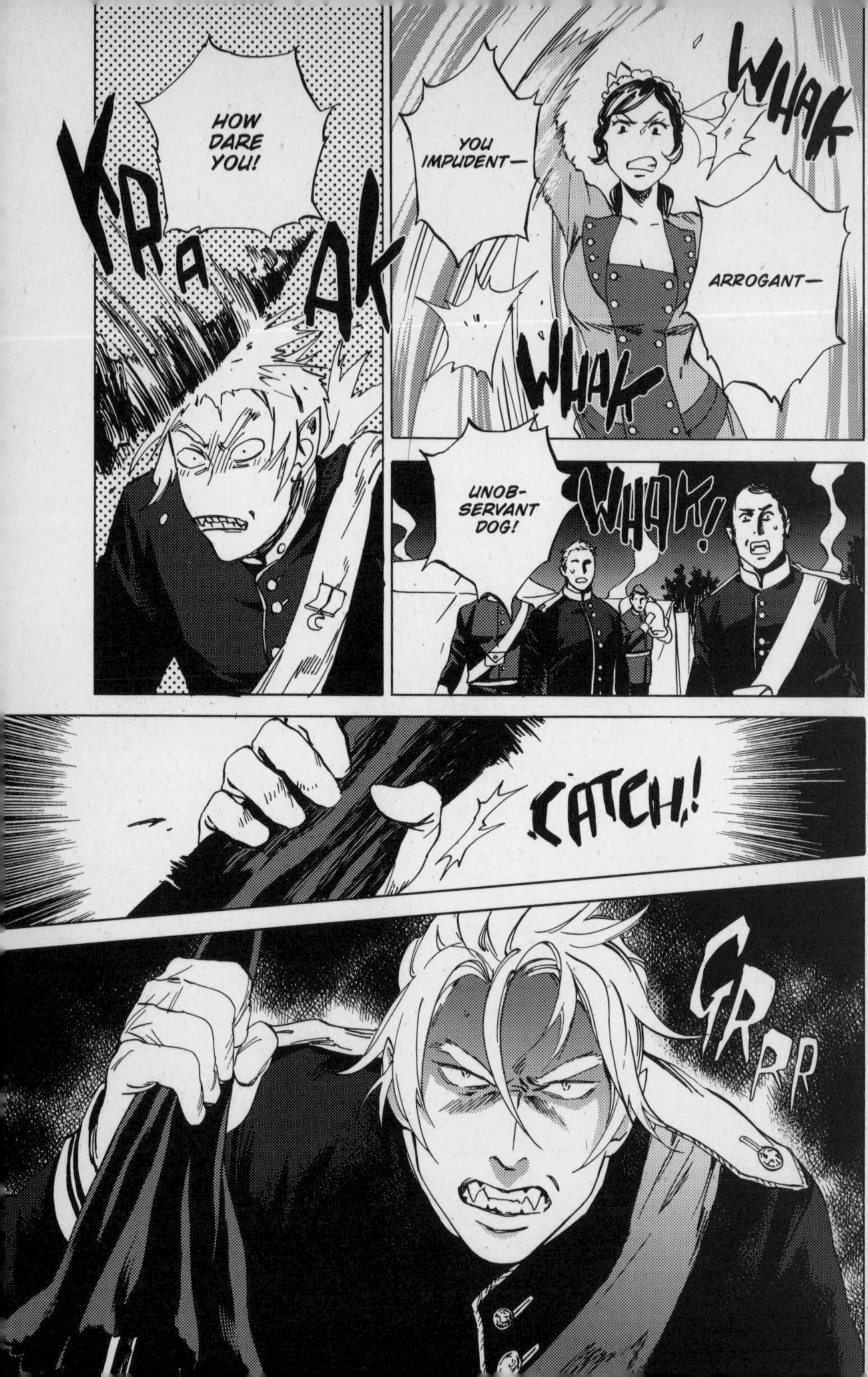
HOW DARE YOU!
KRAAK
YOU IMPUDENT—
WHAK
ARROGANT—
WHAK
UNOB-SERVANT DOG!
WHAK!
CATCH!
GRRR

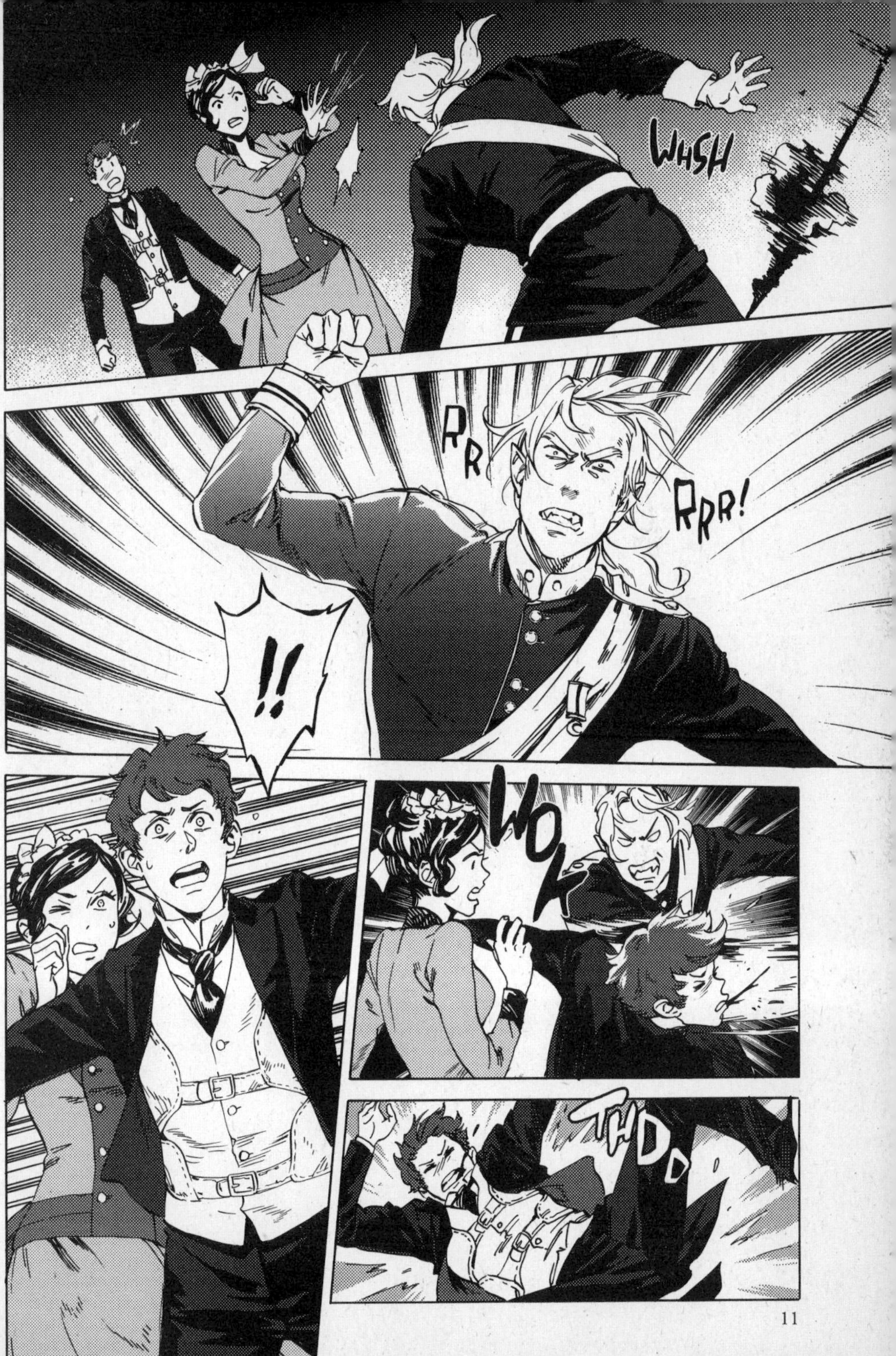
WHSH
RR
RRR!
!!
WOK
THDD

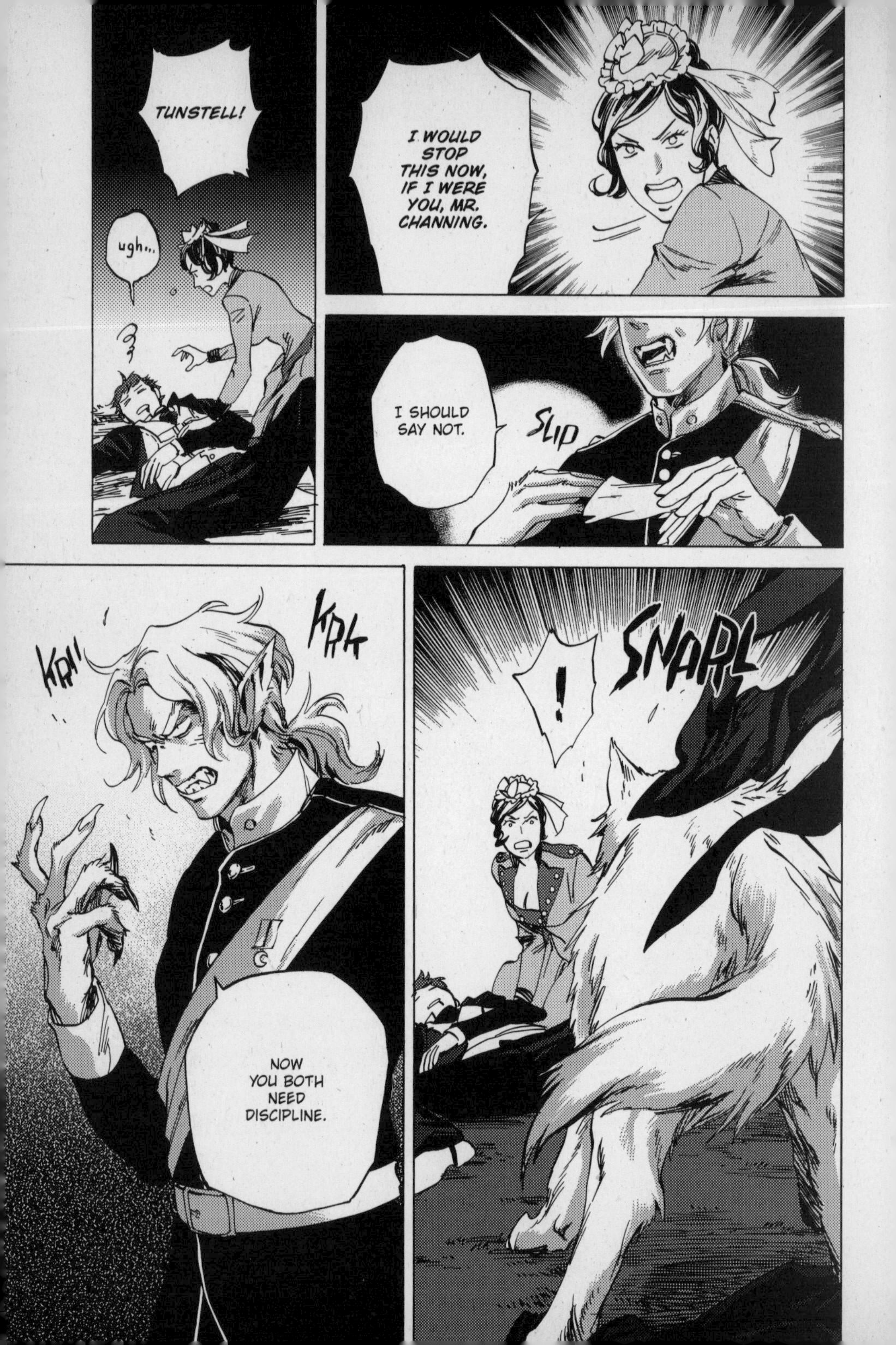
TUNSTELL!
ugh...
I WOULD STOP THIS NOW, IF I WERE YOU, MR. CHANNING.
I SHOULD SAY NOT.
SLIP
KRA
KRK
NOW YOU BOTH NEED DISCIPLINE.
!
SNARL

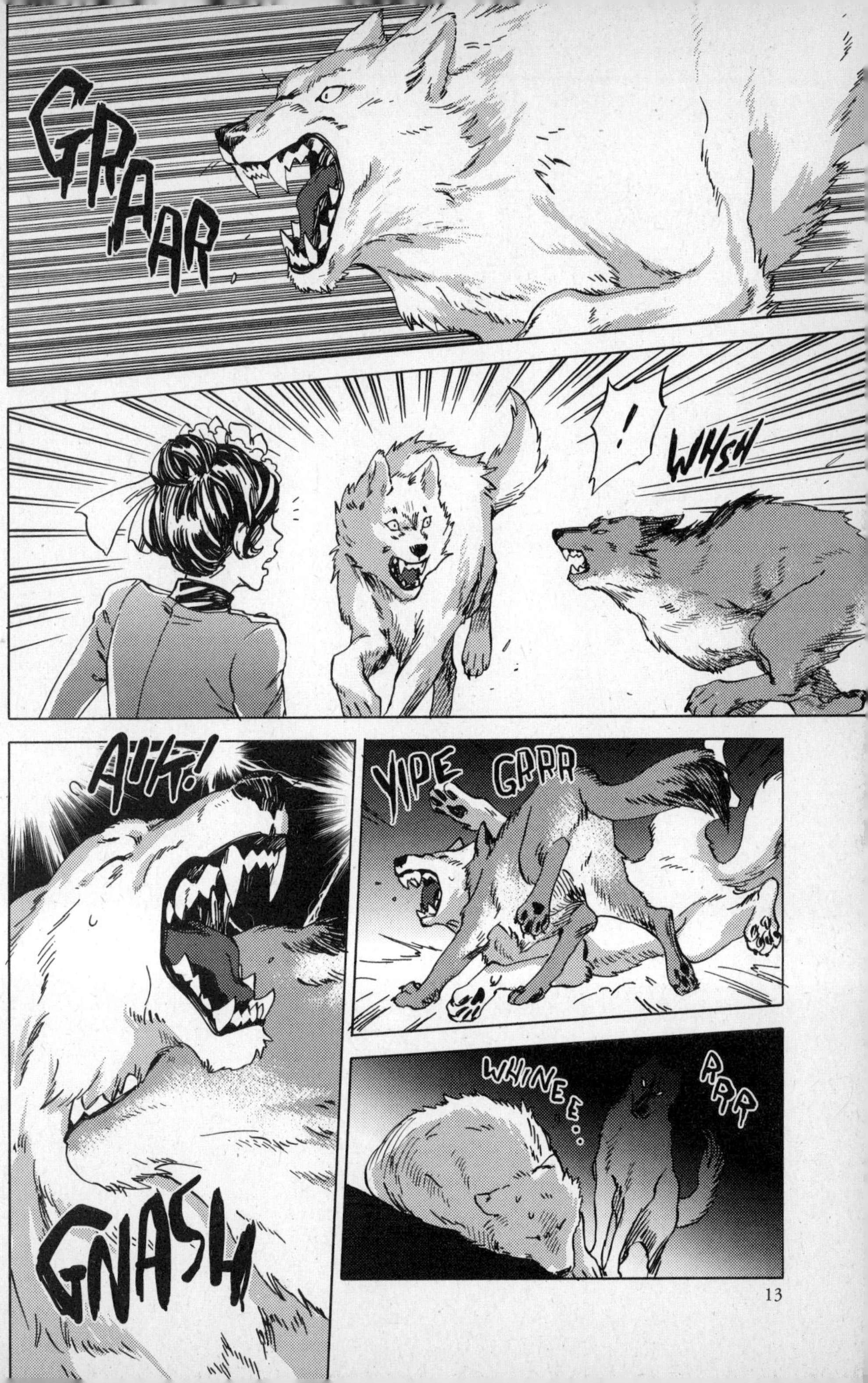
GRAAR
!
WHSH
AUK!
GNASH
YIPE
GRRR
WHINEE...
RRR

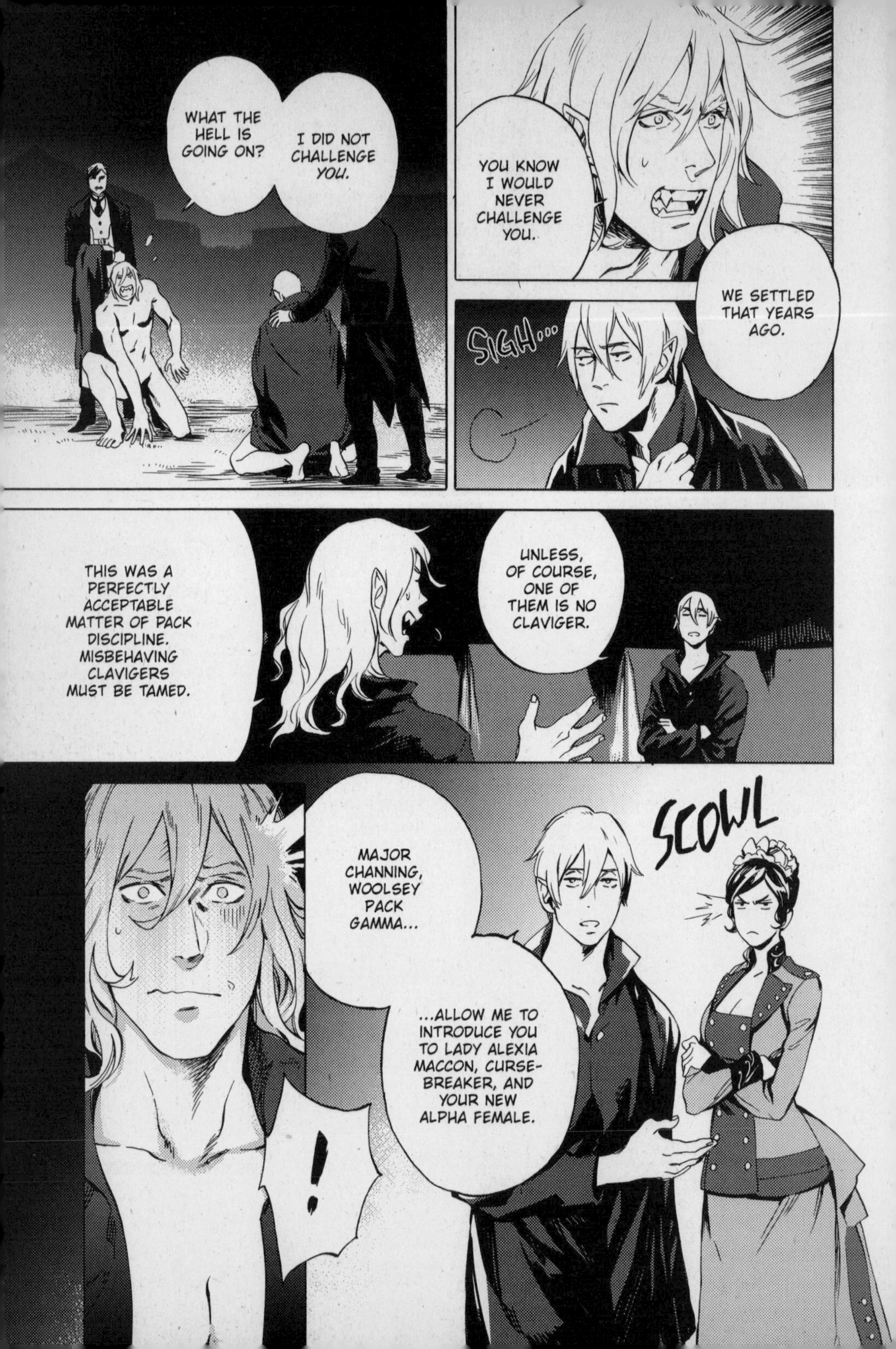
WHAT THE HELL IS GOING ON?
I DID NOT CHALLENGE YOU.
YOU KNOW I WOULD NEVER CHALLENGE YOU.
WE SETTLED THAT YEARS AGO.
SIGH...
THIS WAS A PERFECTLY ACCEPTABLE MATTER OF PACK DISCIPLINE. MISBEHAVING CLAVIGERS MUST BE TAMED.
UNLESS, OF COURSE, ONE OF THEM IS NO CLAVIGER.
!
MAJOR CHANNING, WOOLSEY PACK GAMMA...
SCOWL
...ALLOW ME TO INTRODUCE YOU TO LADY ALEXIA MACCON, CURSE-BREAKER, AND YOUR NEW ALPHA FEMALE.

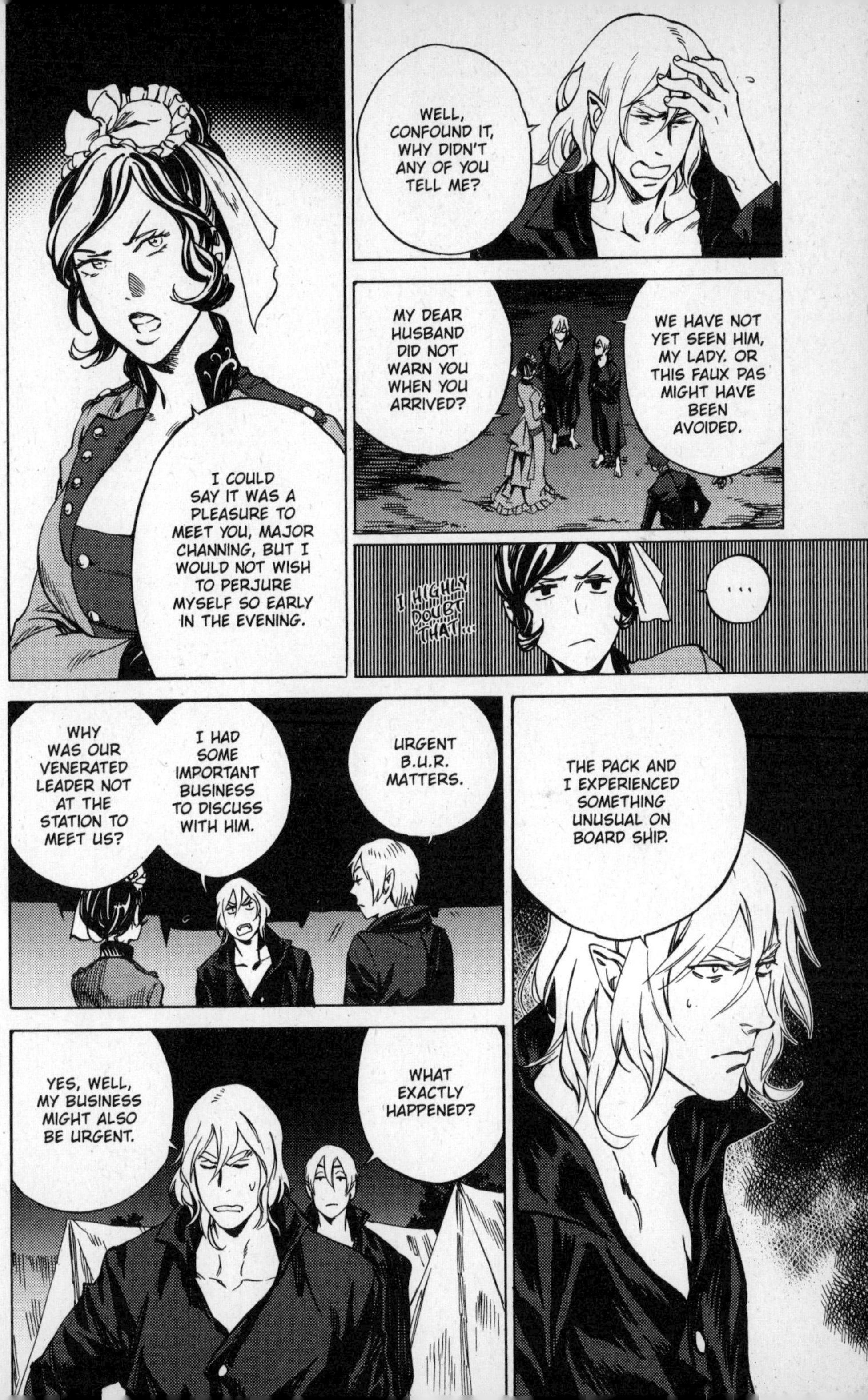
I COULD SAY IT WAS A PLEASURE TO MEET YOU, MAJOR CHANNING, BUT I WOULD NOT WISH TO PERJURE MYSELF SO EARLY IN THE EVENING.
WELL, CONFOUND IT, WHY DIDN'T ANY OF YOU TELL ME?
MY DEAR HUSBAND DID NOT WARN YOU WHEN YOU ARRIVED?
WE HAVE NOT YET SEEN HIM, MY LADY. OR THIS FAUX PAS MIGHT HAVE BEEN AVOIDED.
I HIGHLY DOUBT THAT...
. . .
WHY WAS OUR VENERATED LEADER NOT AT THE STATION TO MEET US?
I HAD SOME IMPORTANT BUSINESS TO DISCUSS WITH HIM.
URGENT B.U.R. MATTERS.
YES, WELL, MY BUSINESS MIGHT ALSO BE URGENT.
WHAT EXACTLY HAPPENED?
THE PACK AND I EXPERIENCED SOMETHING UNUSUAL ON BOARD SHIP.

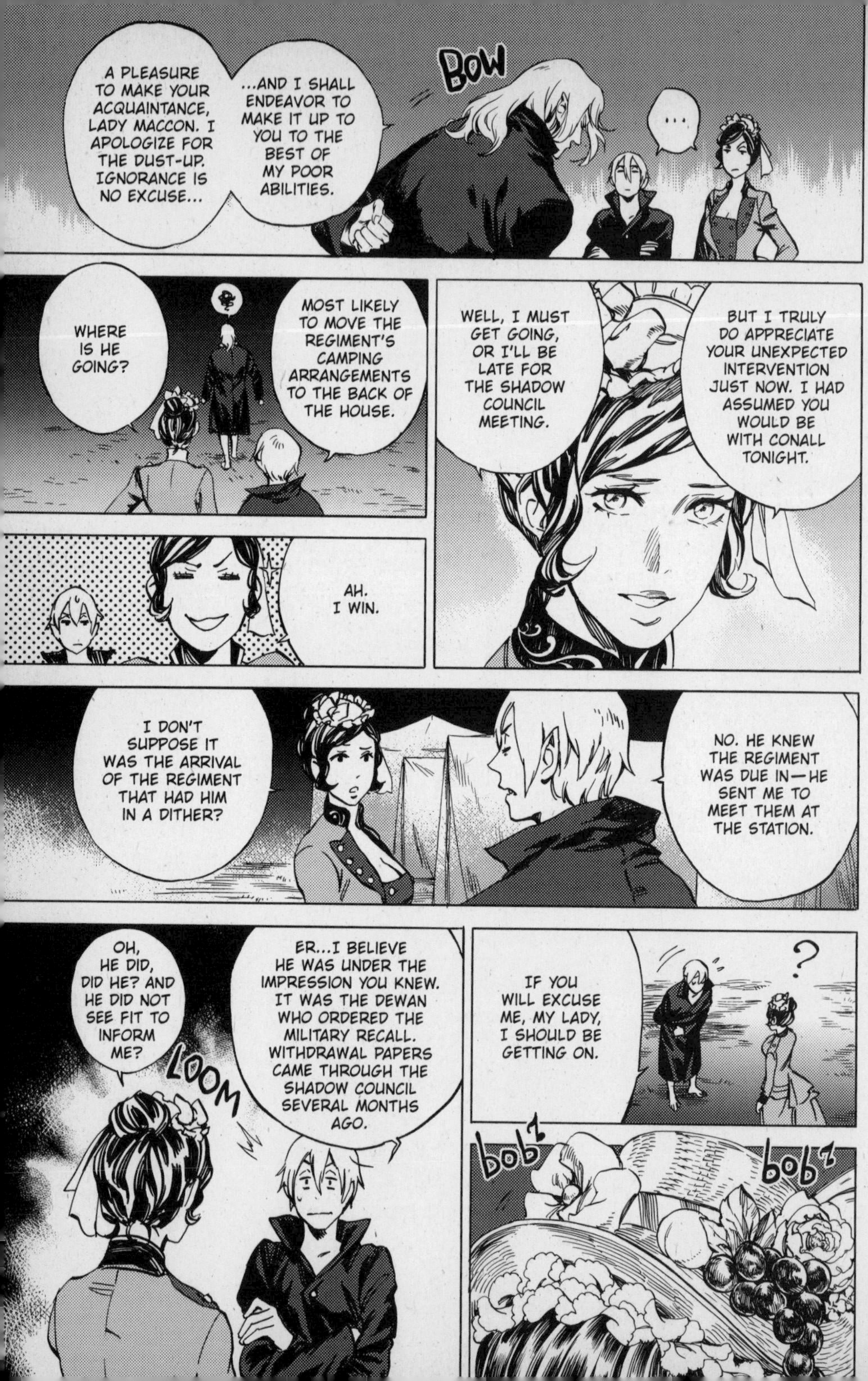
A PLEASURE TO MAKE YOUR ACQUAINTANCE, LADY MACCON. I APOLOGIZE FOR THE DUST-UP. IGNORANCE IS NO EXCUSE...
...AND I SHALL ENDEAVOR TO MAKE IT UP TO YOU TO THE BEST OF MY POOR ABILITIES.
BOW
...
WHERE IS HE GOING?
MOST LIKELY TO MOVE THE REGIMENT'S CAMPING ARRANGEMENTS TO THE BACK OF THE HOUSE.
AH. I WIN.
WELL, I MUST GET GOING, OR I'LL BE LATE FOR THE SHADOW COUNCIL MEETING.
BUT I TRULY DO APPRECIATE YOUR UNEXPECTED INTERVENTION JUST NOW. I HAD ASSUMED YOU WOULD BE WITH CONALL TONIGHT.
I DON'T SUPPOSE IT WAS THE ARRIVAL OF THE REGIMENT THAT HAD HIM IN A DITHER?
NO. HE KNEW THE REGIMENT WAS DUE IN—HE SENT ME TO MEET THEM AT THE STATION.
OH, HE DID, DID HE? AND HE DID NOT SEE FIT TO INFORM ME?
LOOM
ER...I BELIEVE HE WAS UNDER THE IMPRESSION YOU KNEW. IT WAS THE DEWAN WHO ORDERED THE MILITARY RECALL. WITHDRAWAL PAPERS CAME THROUGH THE SHADOW COUNCIL SEVERAL MONTHS AGO.
IF YOU WILL EXCUSE ME, MY LADY, I SHOULD BE GETTING ON.
?
bob
bob

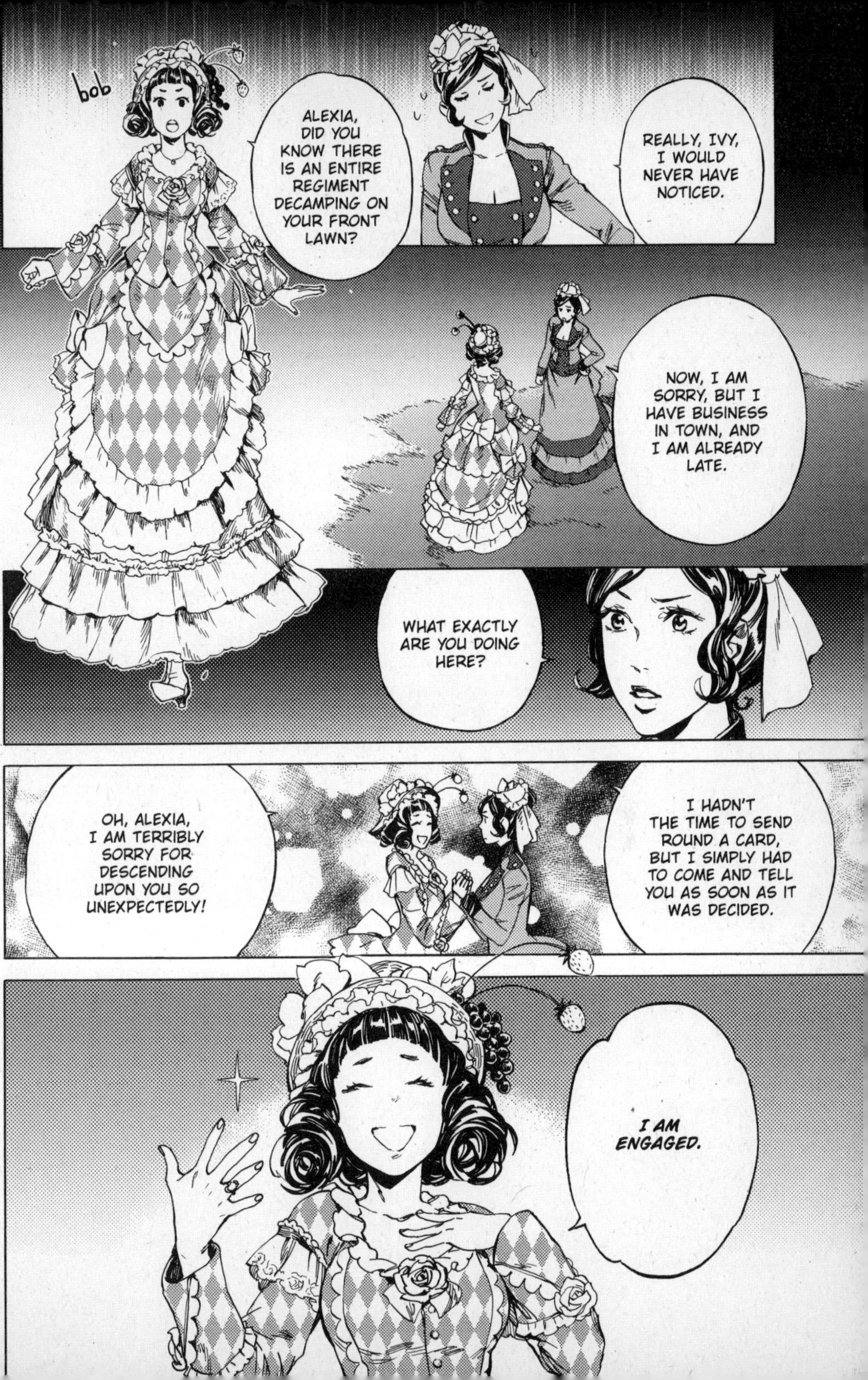
bob
ALEXIA, DID YOU KNOW THERE IS AN ENTIRE REGIMENT DECAMPING ON YOUR FRONT LAWN?
REALLY, IVY, I WOULD NEVER HAVE NOTICED.
NOW, I AM SORRY, BUT I HAVE BUSINESS IN TOWN, AND I AM ALREADY LATE.
WHAT EXACTLY ARE YOU DOING HERE?
OH, ALEXIA, I AM TERRIBLY SORRY FOR DESCENDING UPON YOU SO UNEXPECTEDLY!
I HADN'T THE TIME TO SEND ROUND A CARD, BUT I SIMPLY HAD TO COME AND TELL YOU AS SOON AS IT WAS DECIDED.
I AM ENGAGED.

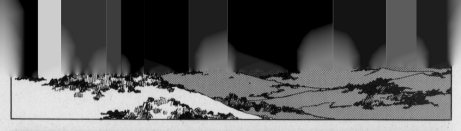

TROT

TROT

I WONDER IF ALEXIA FINDS ME MORE ATTRACTIVE AS A WOLF THAN A HUMAN.

TAK!

OOM

I WILL HAVE TO ASK HER ABOUT THAT.

hf

HMM... THEN AGAIN, PERHAPS NOT.

huff

haff

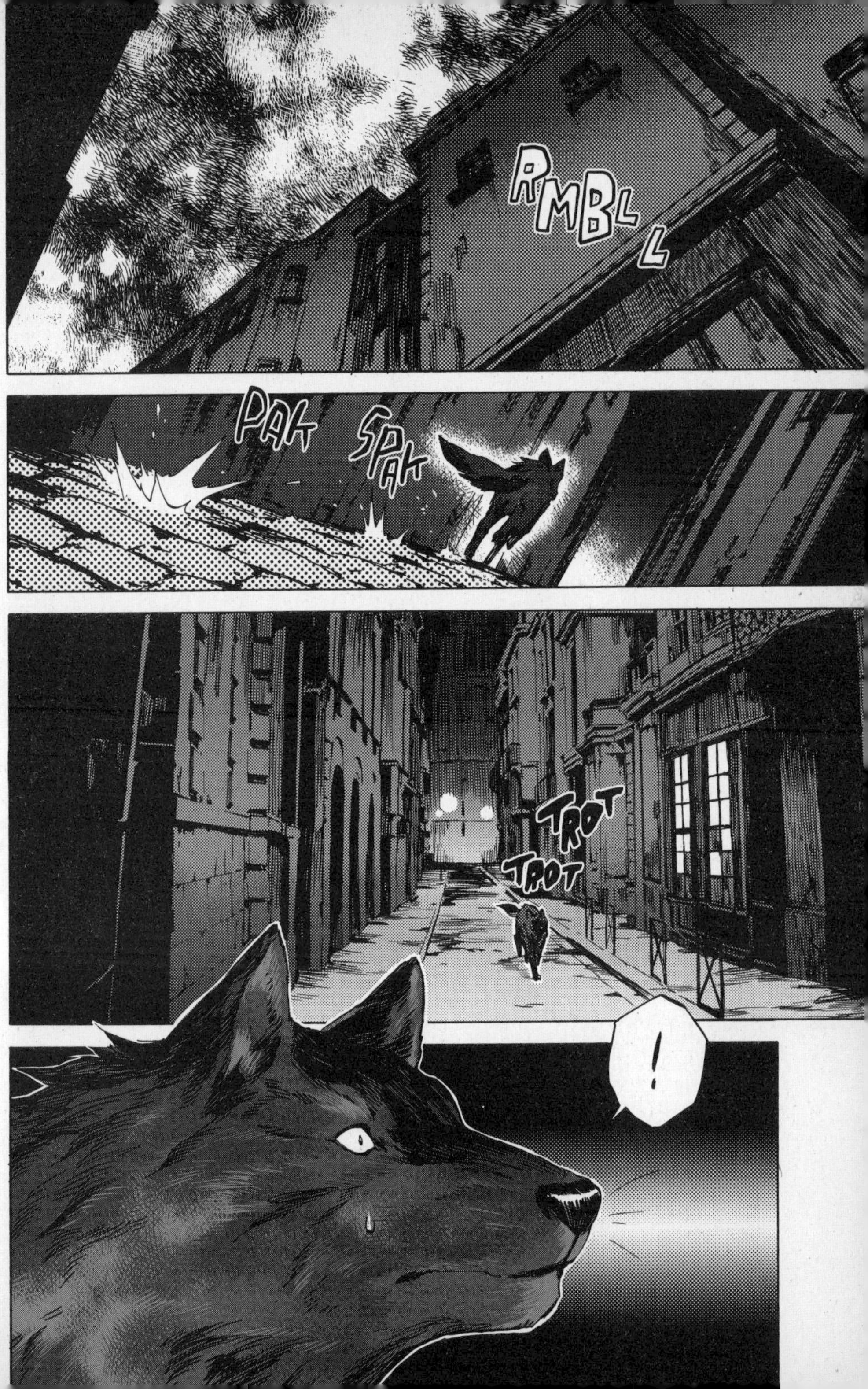
RMBLL
PAK
SPAK
TROT
TROT
!

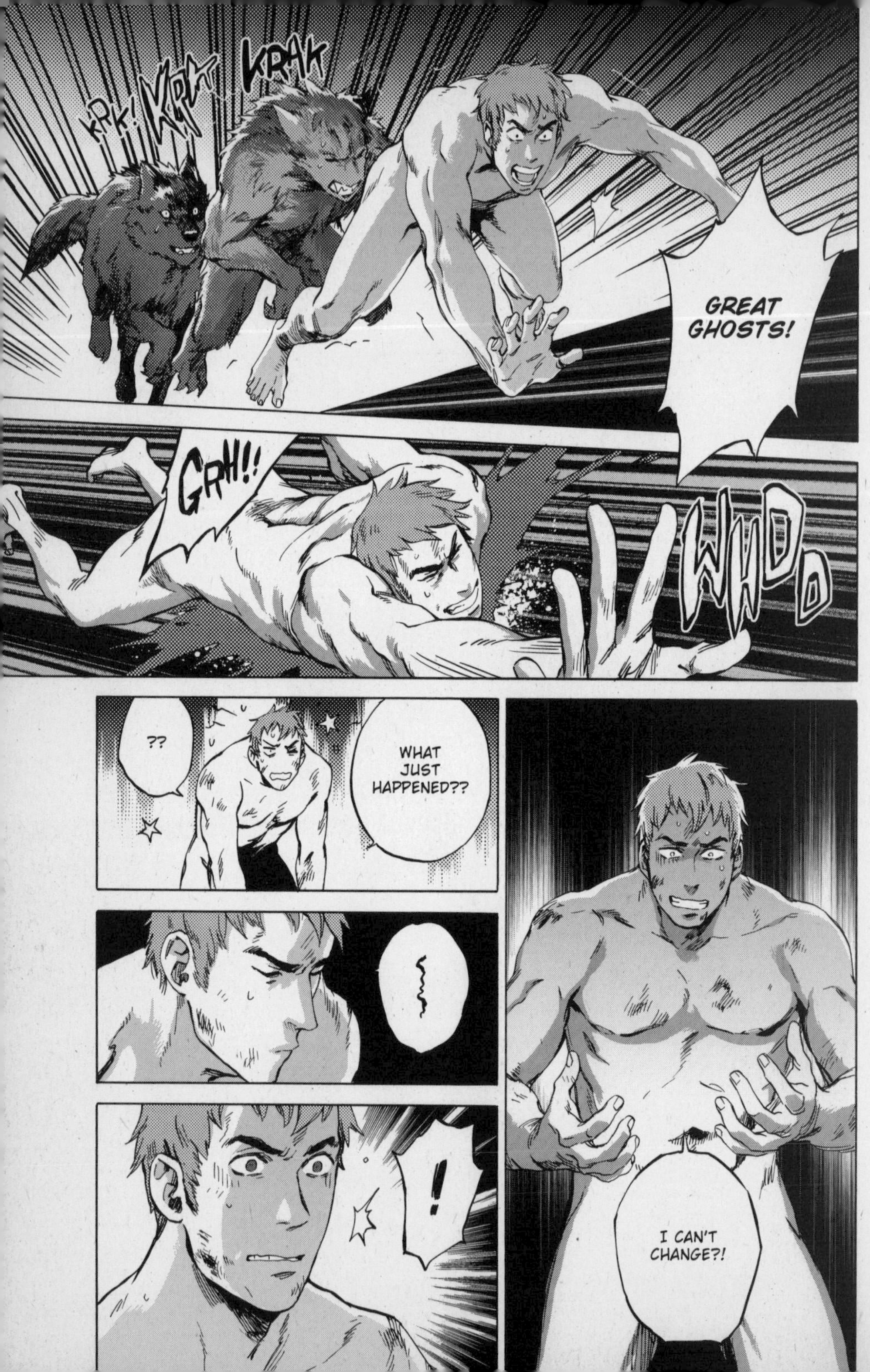
KRK!
KRAK
KRAK
GREAT GHOSTS!
GRH!!
WHDD
??
WHAT JUST HAPPENED??
...
!
I CAN'T CHANGE?!

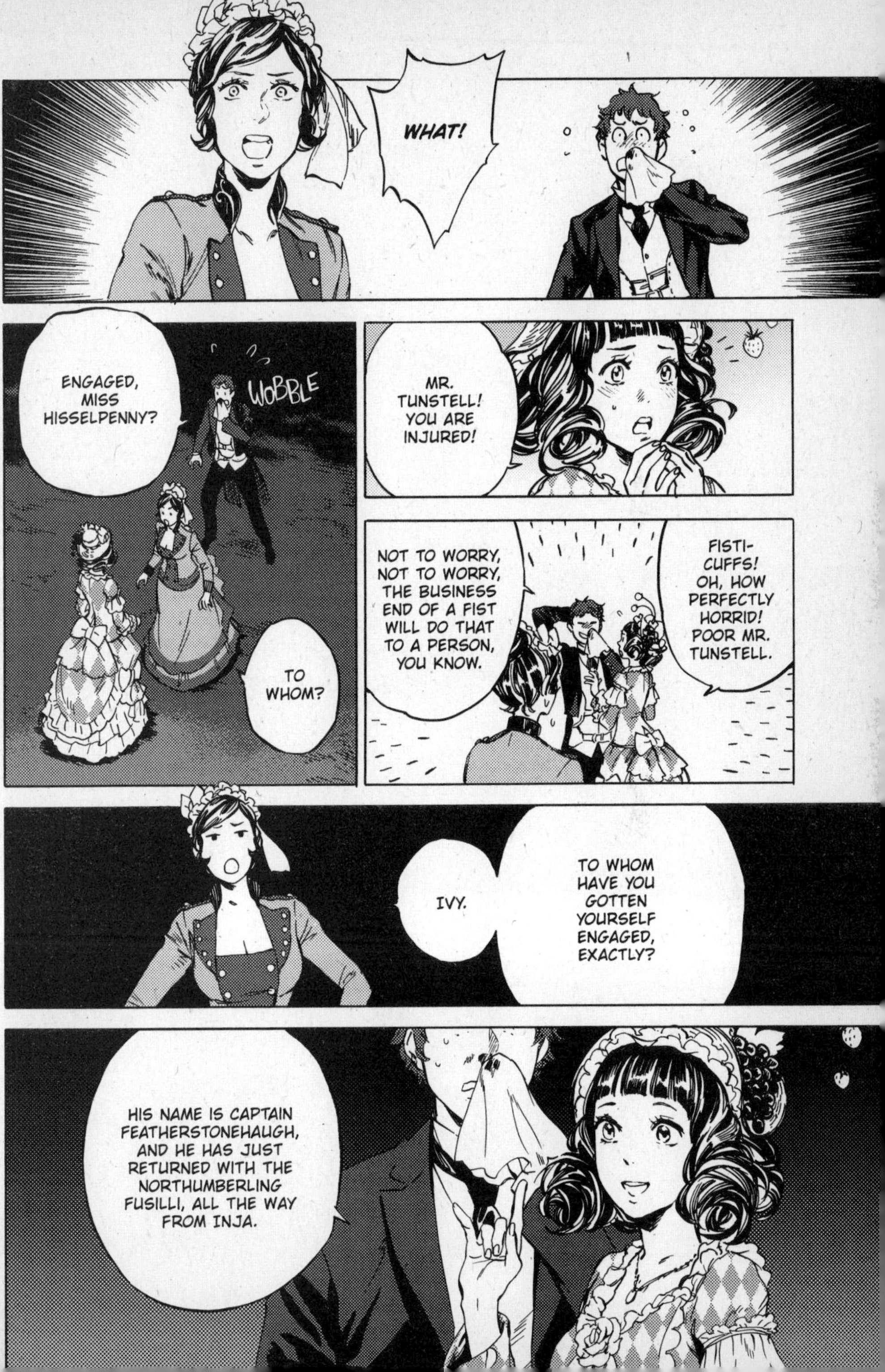
WHAT!
ENGAGED, MISS HISSELPENNY?
WOBBLE
TO WHOM?
MR. TUNSTELL! YOU ARE INJURED!
NOT TO WORRY, NOT TO WORRY, THE BUSINESS END OF A FIST WILL DO THAT TO A PERSON, YOU KNOW.
FISTI-CUFFS! OH, HOW PERFECTLY HORRID! POOR MR. TUNSTELL.
IVY.
TO WHOM HAVE YOU GOTTEN YOURSELF ENGAGED, EXACTLY?
HIS NAME IS CAPTAIN FEATHERSTONEHAUGH, AND HE HAS JUST RETURNED WITH THE NORTHUMBERLING FUSILLI, ALL THE WAY FROM INJA.

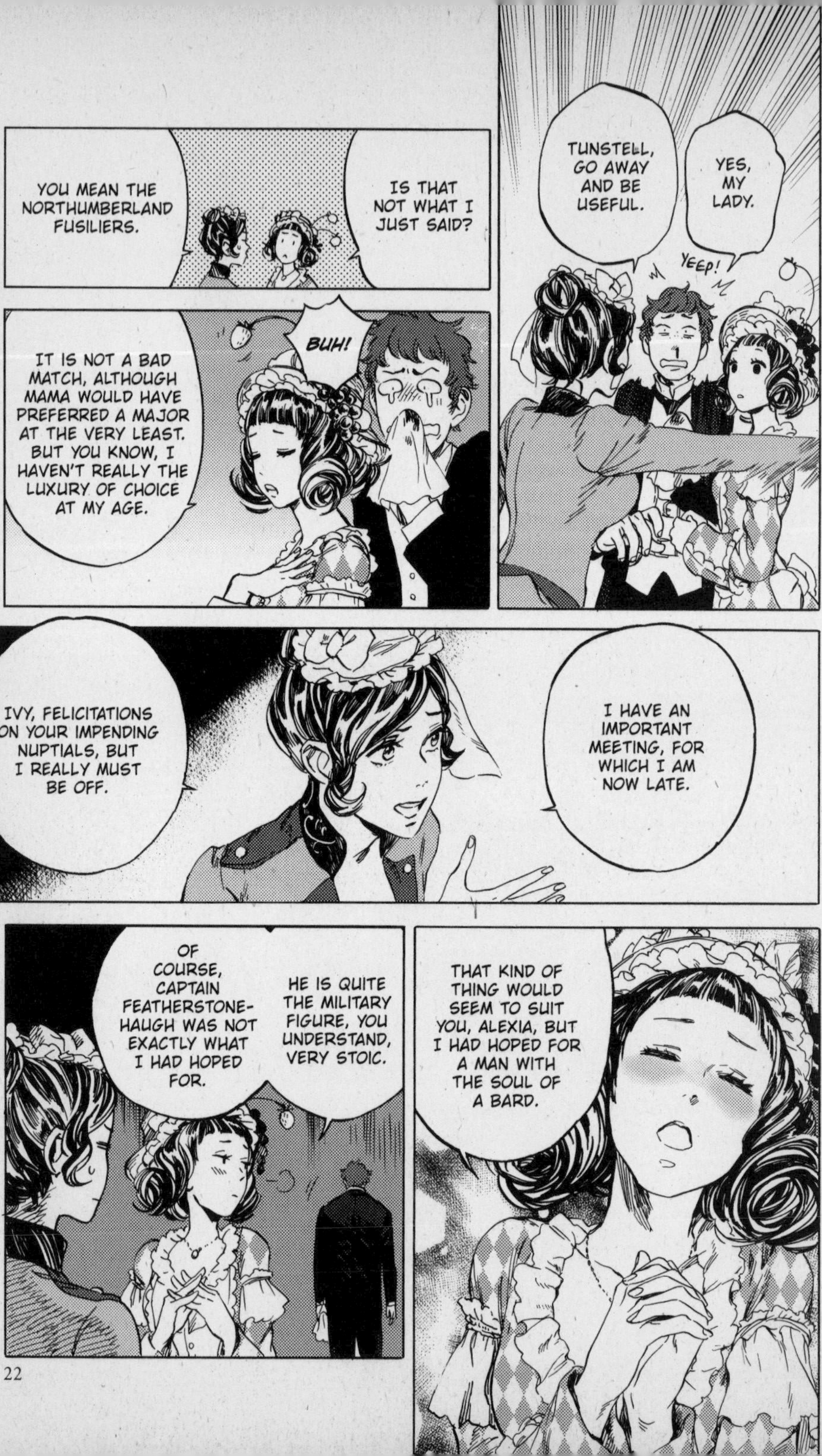

YOU MEAN THE NORTHUMBERLAND FUSILIERS.
IS THAT NOT WHAT I JUST SAID?
IT IS NOT A BAD MATCH, ALTHOUGH MAMA WOULD HAVE PREFERRED A MAJOR AT THE VERY LEAST. BUT YOU KNOW, I HAVEN'T REALLY THE LUXURY OF CHOICE AT MY AGE.
BUH!
TUNSTELL, GO AWAY AND BE USEFUL.
YES, MY LADY.
YEEP!
IVY, FELICITATIONS ON YOUR IMPENDING NUPTIALS, BUT I REALLY MUST BE OFF.
I HAVE AN IMPORTANT MEETING, FOR WHICH I AM NOW LATE.
OF COURSE, CAPTAIN FEATHERSTONE-HAUGH WAS NOT EXACTLY WHAT I HAD HOPED FOR.
HE IS QUITE THE MILITARY FIGURE, YOU UNDERSTAND, VERY STOIC.
THAT KIND OF THING WOULD SEEM TO SUIT YOU, ALEXIA, BUT I HAD HOPED FOR A MAN WITH THE SOUL OF A BARD.

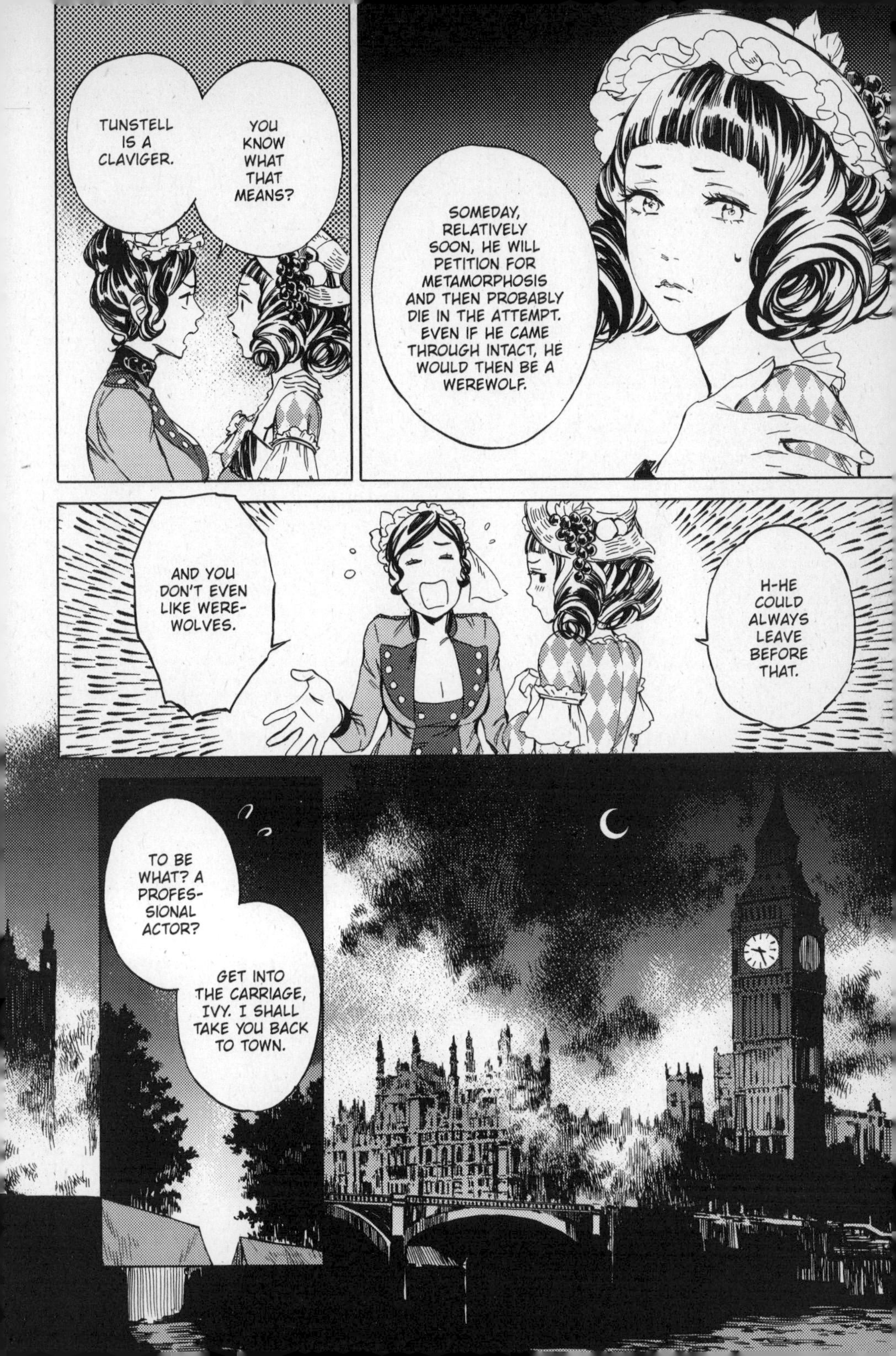

TUNSTELL IS A CLAVIGER.
YOU KNOW WHAT THAT MEANS?
SOMEDAY, RELATIVELY SOON, HE WILL PETITION FOR METAMORPHOSIS AND THEN PROBABLY DIE IN THE ATTEMPT. EVEN IF HE CAME THROUGH INTACT, HE WOULD THEN BE A WEREWOLF.
AND YOU DON'T EVEN LIKE WERE-WOLVES.
H-HE COULD ALWAYS LEAVE BEFORE THAT.
TO BE WHAT? A PROFES-SIONAL ACTOR?
GET INTO THE CARRIAGE, IVY. I SHALL TAKE YOU BACK TO TOWN.

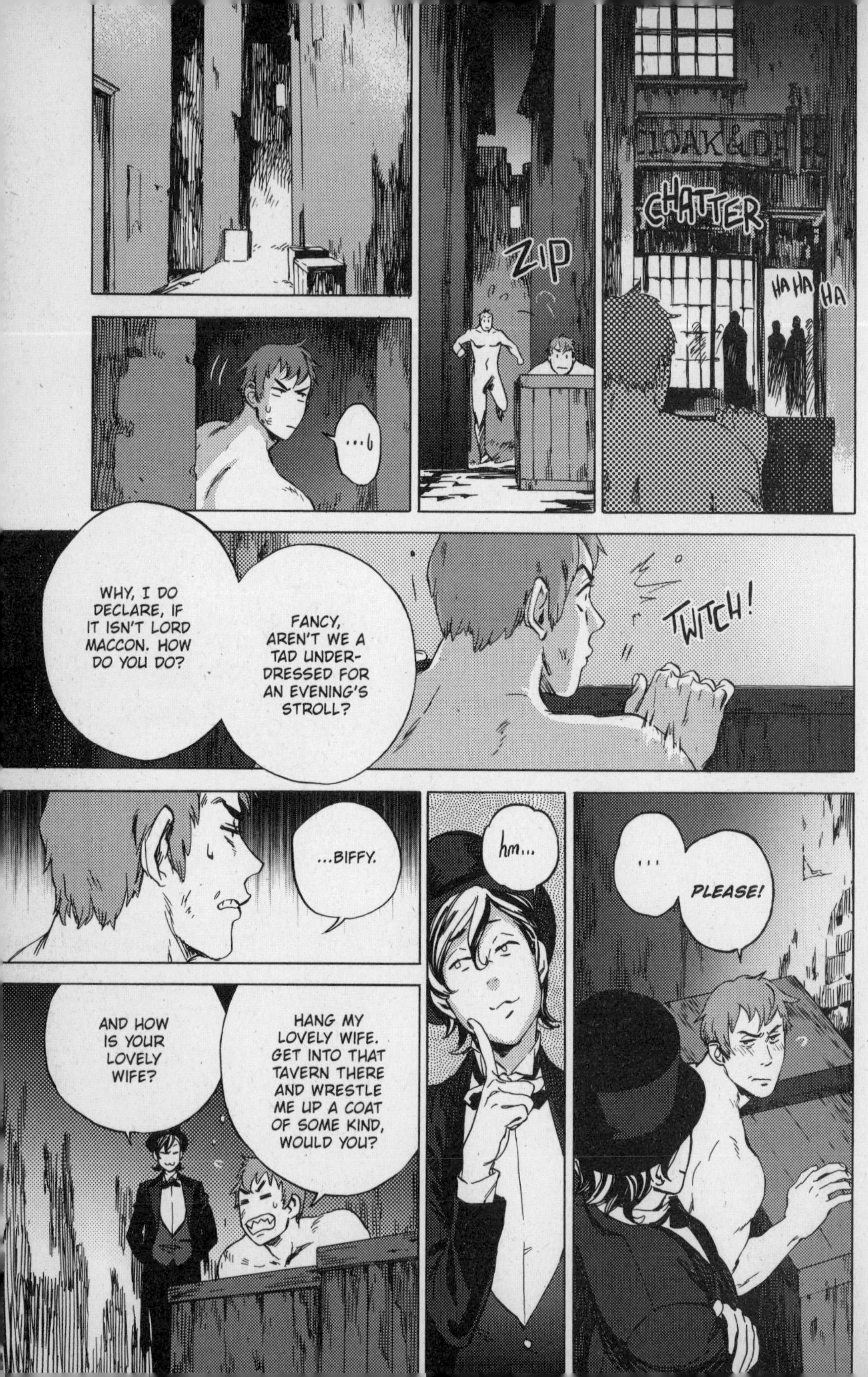
...!
ZIP
CHATTER
HA HA HA
WHY, I DO DECLARE, IF IT ISN'T LORD MACCON. HOW DO YOU DO?
FANCY, AREN'T WE A TAD UNDER-DRESSED FOR AN EVENING'S STROLL?
TWITCH!
...BIFFY.
AND HOW IS YOUR LOVELY WIFE?
HANG MY LOVELY WIFE. GET INTO THAT TAVERN THERE AND WRESTLE ME UP A COAT OF SOME KIND, WOULD YOU?
hm...
...
PLEASE!

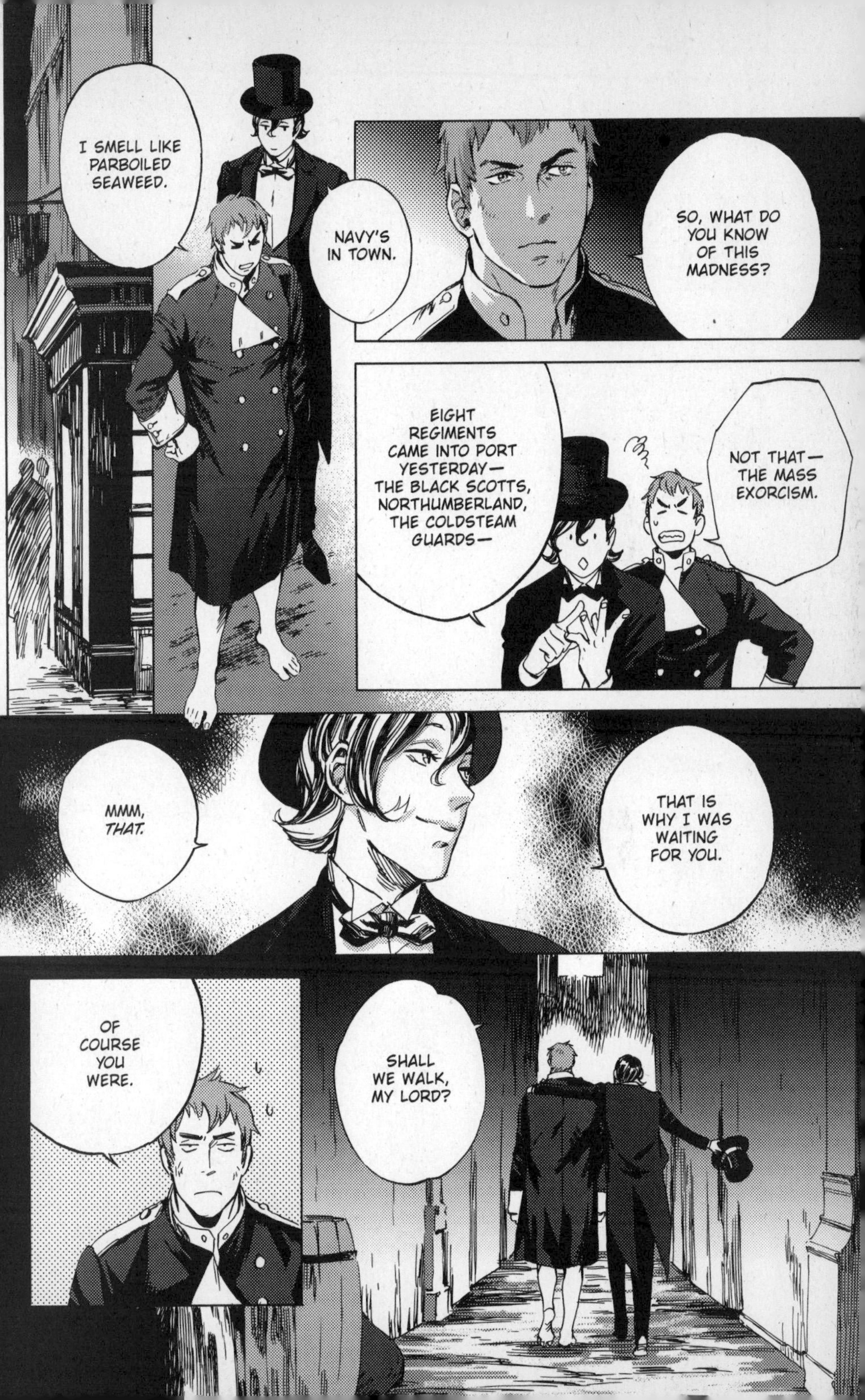
I SMELL LIKE PARBOILED SEAWEED.
NAVY'S IN TOWN.
SO, WHAT DO YOU KNOW OF THIS MADNESS?
EIGHT REGIMENTS CAME INTO PORT YESTERDAY—THE BLACK SCOTTS, NORTHUMBERLAND, THE COLDSTEAM GUARDS—
NOT THAT—THE MASS EXORCISM.
MMM, *THAT.*
THAT IS WHY I WAS WAITING FOR YOU.
OF COURSE YOU WERE.
SHALL WE WALK, MY LORD?

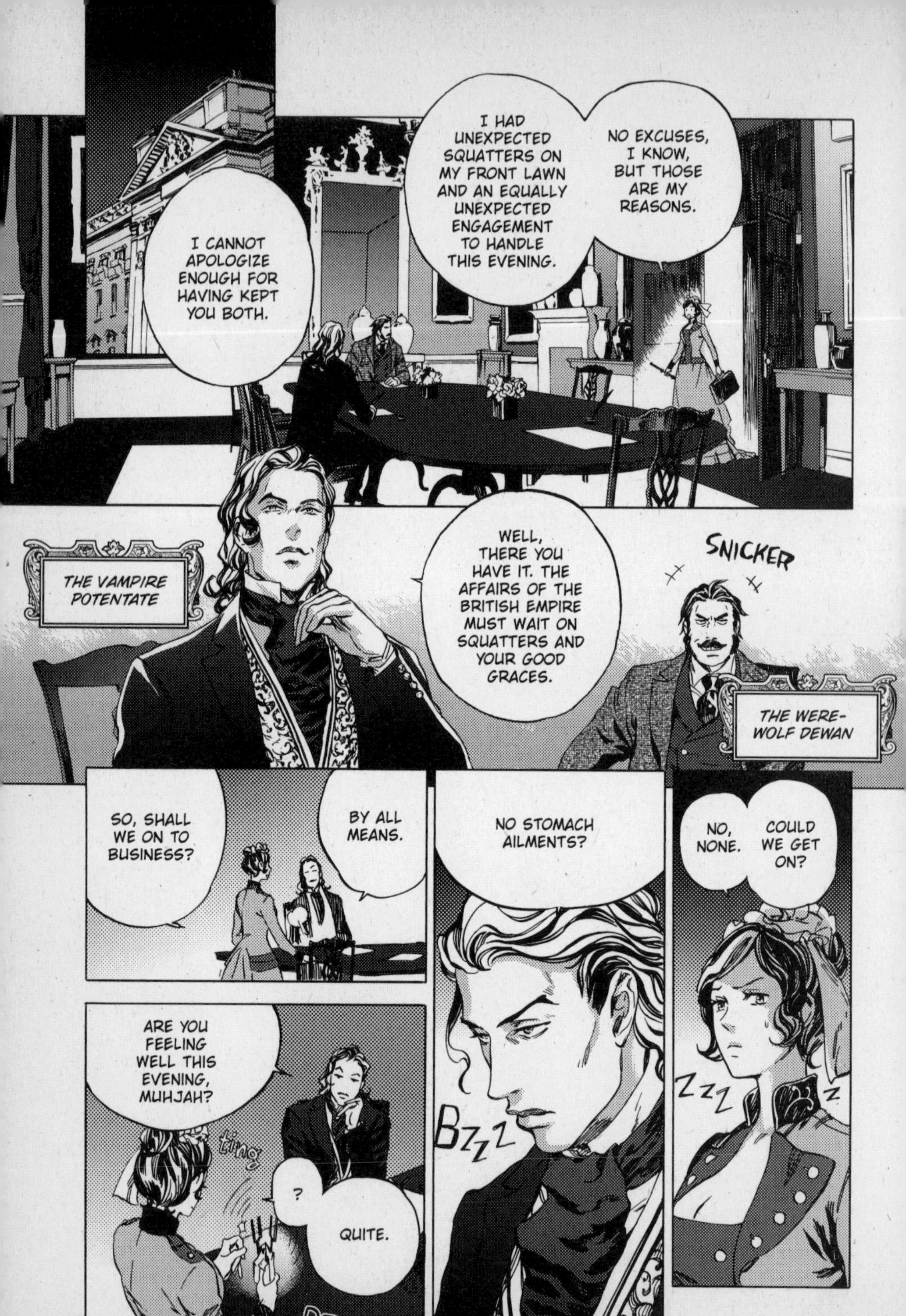
I CANNOT APOLOGIZE ENOUGH FOR HAVING KEPT YOU BOTH.
I HAD UNEXPECTED SQUATTERS ON MY FRONT LAWN AND AN EQUALLY UNEXPECTED ENGAGEMENT TO HANDLE THIS EVENING.
NO EXCUSES, I KNOW, BUT THOSE ARE MY REASONS.
THE VAMPIRE POTENTATE
WELL, THERE YOU HAVE IT. THE AFFAIRS OF THE BRITISH EMPIRE MUST WAIT ON SQUATTERS AND YOUR GOOD GRACES.
SNICKER
THE WERE-WOLF DEWAN
SO, SHALL WE ON TO BUSINESS?
BY ALL MEANS.
ARE YOU FEELING WELL THIS EVENING, MUHJAH?
?
QUITE.
BZZZz...
NO STOMACH AILMENTS?
BZZZ
NO, NONE.
COULD WE GET ON?
ZZZ
Z

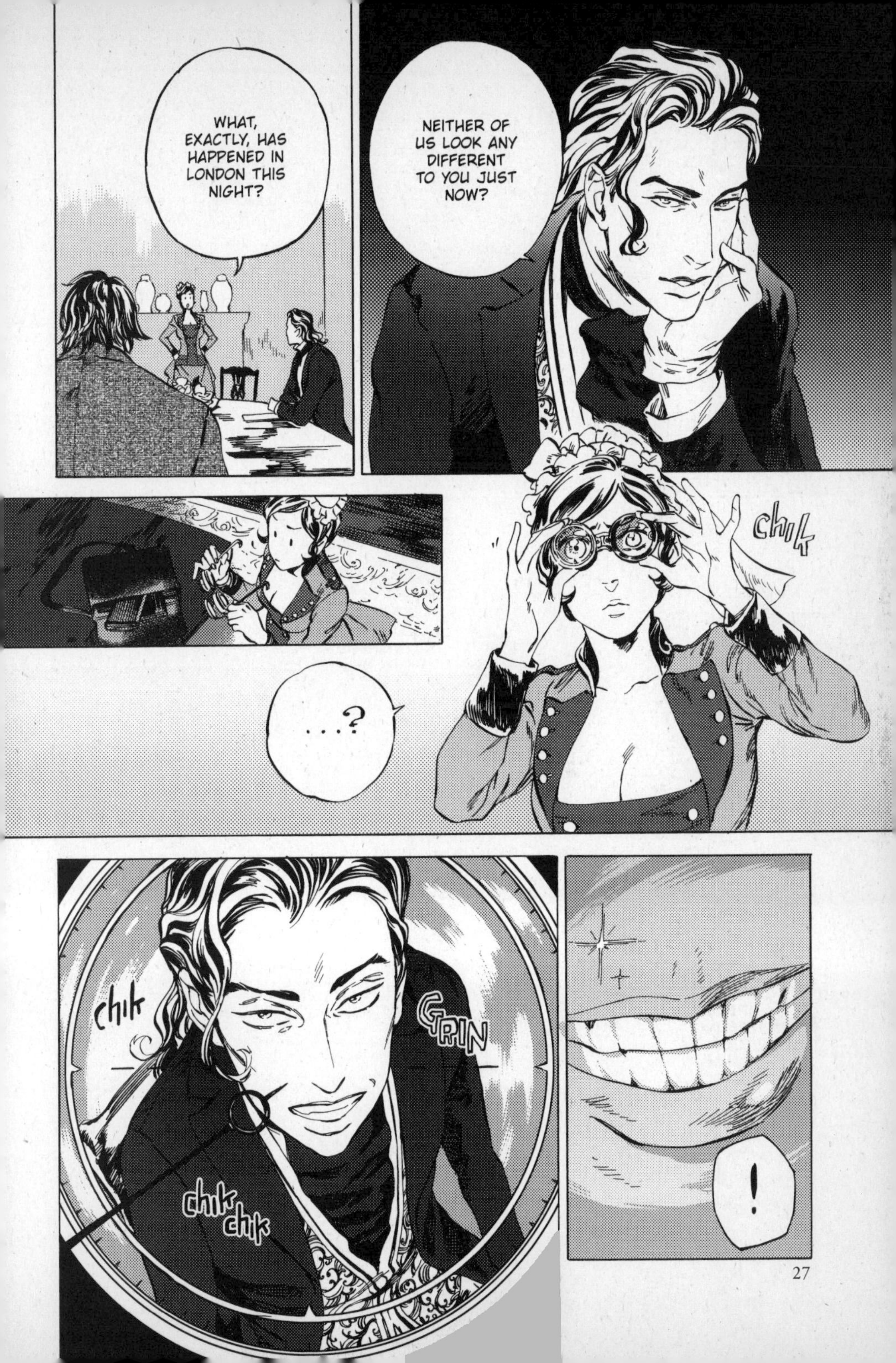
WHAT, EXACTLY, HAS HAPPENED IN LONDON THIS NIGHT?
NEITHER OF US LOOK ANY DIFFERENT TO YOU JUST NOW?
chik
...?
chik
GRIN
chik chik
!

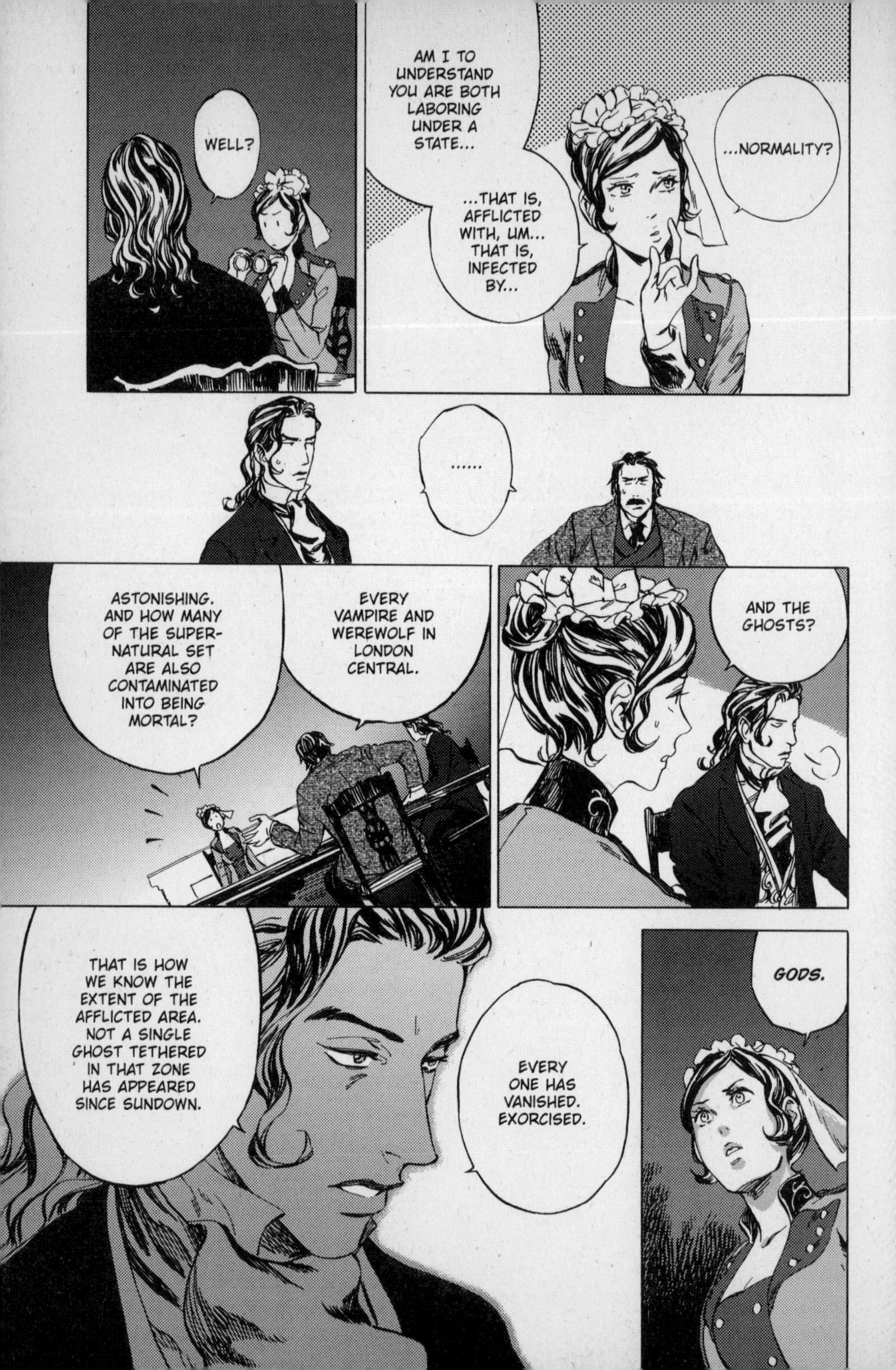
WELL?
AM I TO UNDERSTAND YOU ARE BOTH LABORING UNDER A STATE...
...THAT IS, AFFLICTED WITH, UM... THAT IS, INFECTED BY...
...NORMALITY?
......
ASTONISHING. AND HOW MANY OF THE SUPER-NATURAL SET ARE ALSO CONTAMINATED INTO BEING MORTAL?
EVERY VAMPIRE AND WEREWOLF IN LONDON CENTRAL.
AND THE GHOSTS?
THAT IS HOW WE KNOW THE EXTENT OF THE AFFLICTED AREA. NOT A SINGLE GHOST TETHERED IN THAT ZONE HAS APPEARED SINCE SUNDOWN.
EVERY ONE HAS VANISHED. EXORCISED.
GODS.

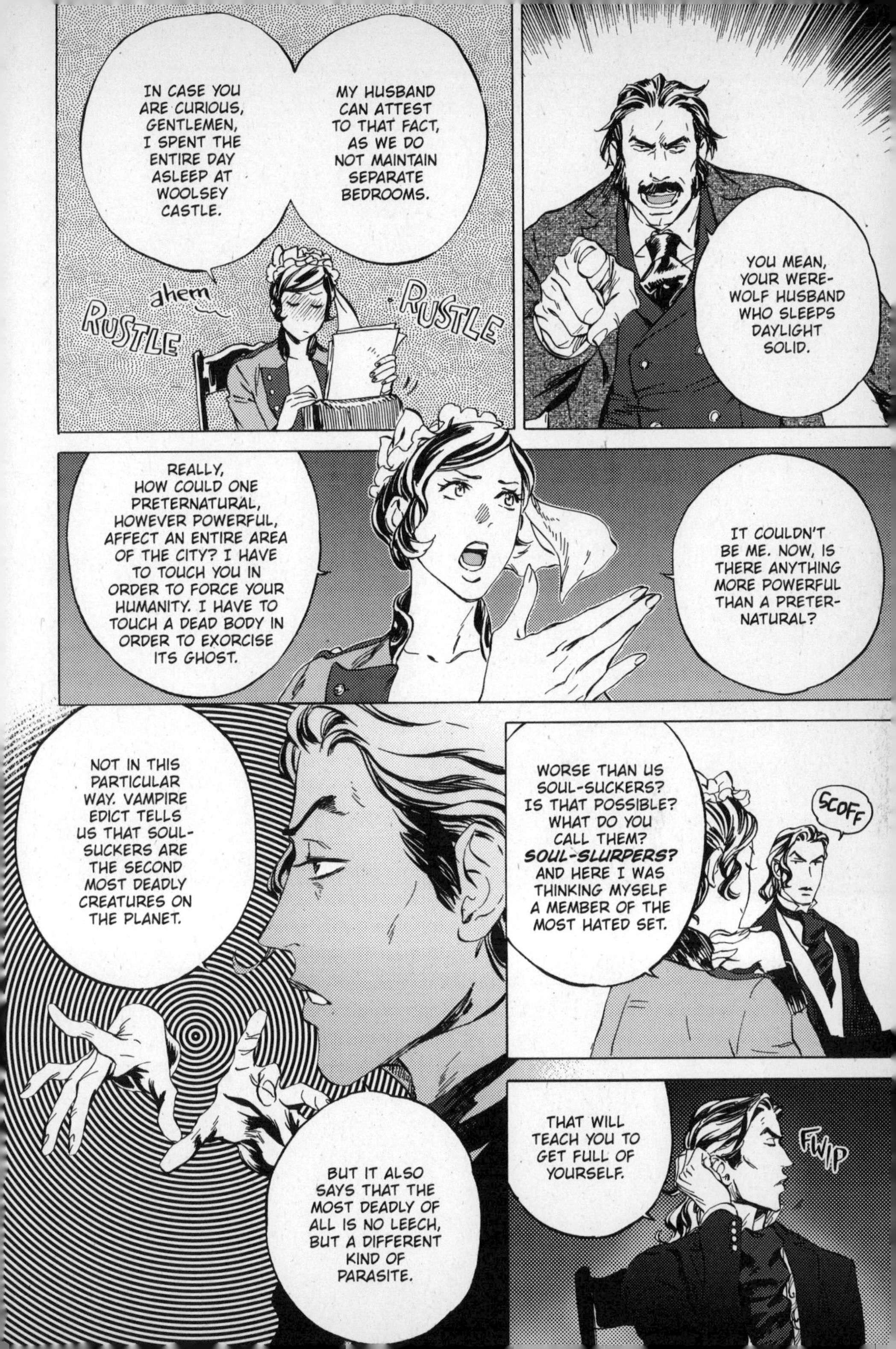
IN CASE YOU ARE CURIOUS, GENTLEMEN, I SPENT THE ENTIRE DAY ASLEEP AT WOOLSEY CASTLE.
MY HUSBAND CAN ATTEST TO THAT FACT, AS WE DO NOT MAINTAIN SEPARATE BEDROOMS.
ahem
RUSTLE
RUSTLE
YOU MEAN, YOUR WERE-WOLF HUSBAND WHO SLEEPS DAYLIGHT SOLID.
REALLY, HOW COULD ONE PRETERNATURAL, HOWEVER POWERFUL, AFFECT AN ENTIRE AREA OF THE CITY? I HAVE TO TOUCH YOU IN ORDER TO FORCE YOUR HUMANITY. I HAVE TO TOUCH A DEAD BODY IN ORDER TO EXORCISE ITS GHOST.
IT COULDN'T BE ME. NOW, IS THERE ANYTHING MORE POWERFUL THAN A PRETER-NATURAL?
NOT IN THIS PARTICULAR WAY. VAMPIRE EDICT TELLS US THAT SOUL-SUCKERS ARE THE SECOND MOST DEADLY CREATURES ON THE PLANET.
BUT IT ALSO SAYS THAT THE MOST DEADLY OF ALL IS NO LEECH, BUT A DIFFERENT KIND OF PARASITE.
WORSE THAN US SOUL-SUCKERS? IS THAT POSSIBLE? WHAT DO YOU CALL THEM? ***SOUL-SLURPERS?*** AND HERE I WAS THINKING MYSELF A MEMBER OF THE MOST HATED SET.
SCOFF
THAT WILL TEACH YOU TO GET FULL OF YOURSELF.
FWIP

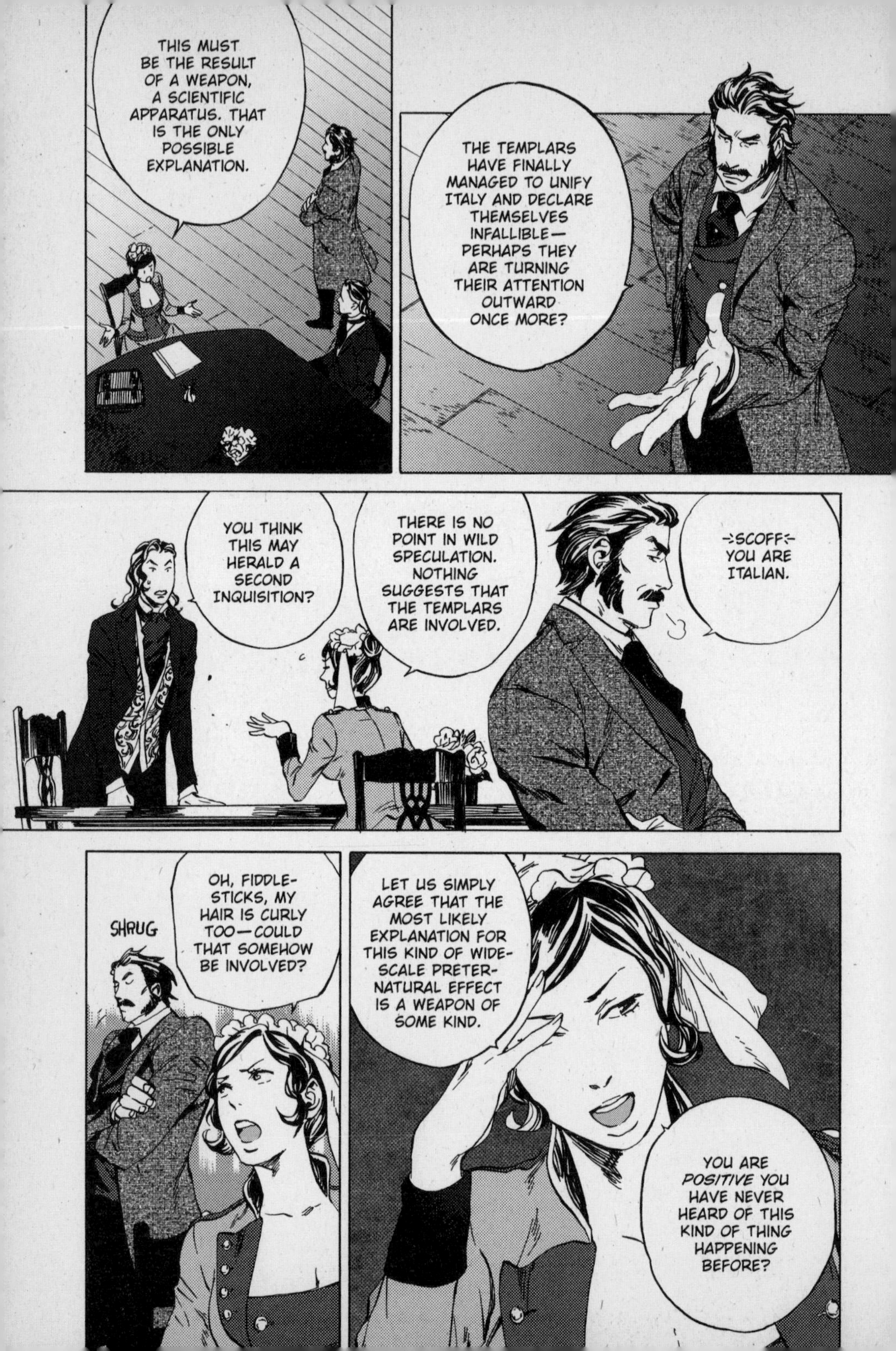
THIS MUST BE THE RESULT OF A WEAPON, A SCIENTIFIC APPARATUS. THAT IS THE ONLY POSSIBLE EXPLANATION.
THE TEMPLARS HAVE FINALLY MANAGED TO UNIFY ITALY AND DECLARE THEMSELVES INFALLIBLE—PERHAPS THEY ARE TURNING THEIR ATTENTION OUTWARD ONCE MORE?
YOU THINK THIS MAY HERALD A SECOND INQUISITION?
THERE IS NO POINT IN WILD SPECULATION. NOTHING SUGGESTS THAT THE TEMPLARS ARE INVOLVED.
SCOFF
YOU ARE ITALIAN.
SHRUG
OH, FIDDLESTICKS, MY HAIR IS CURLY TOO—COULD THAT SOMEHOW BE INVOLVED?
LET US SIMPLY AGREE THAT THE MOST LIKELY EXPLANATION FOR THIS KIND OF WIDE-SCALE PRETERNATURAL EFFECT IS A WEAPON OF SOME KIND.
YOU ARE *POSITIVE* YOU HAVE NEVER HEARD OF THIS KIND OF THING HAPPENING BEFORE?

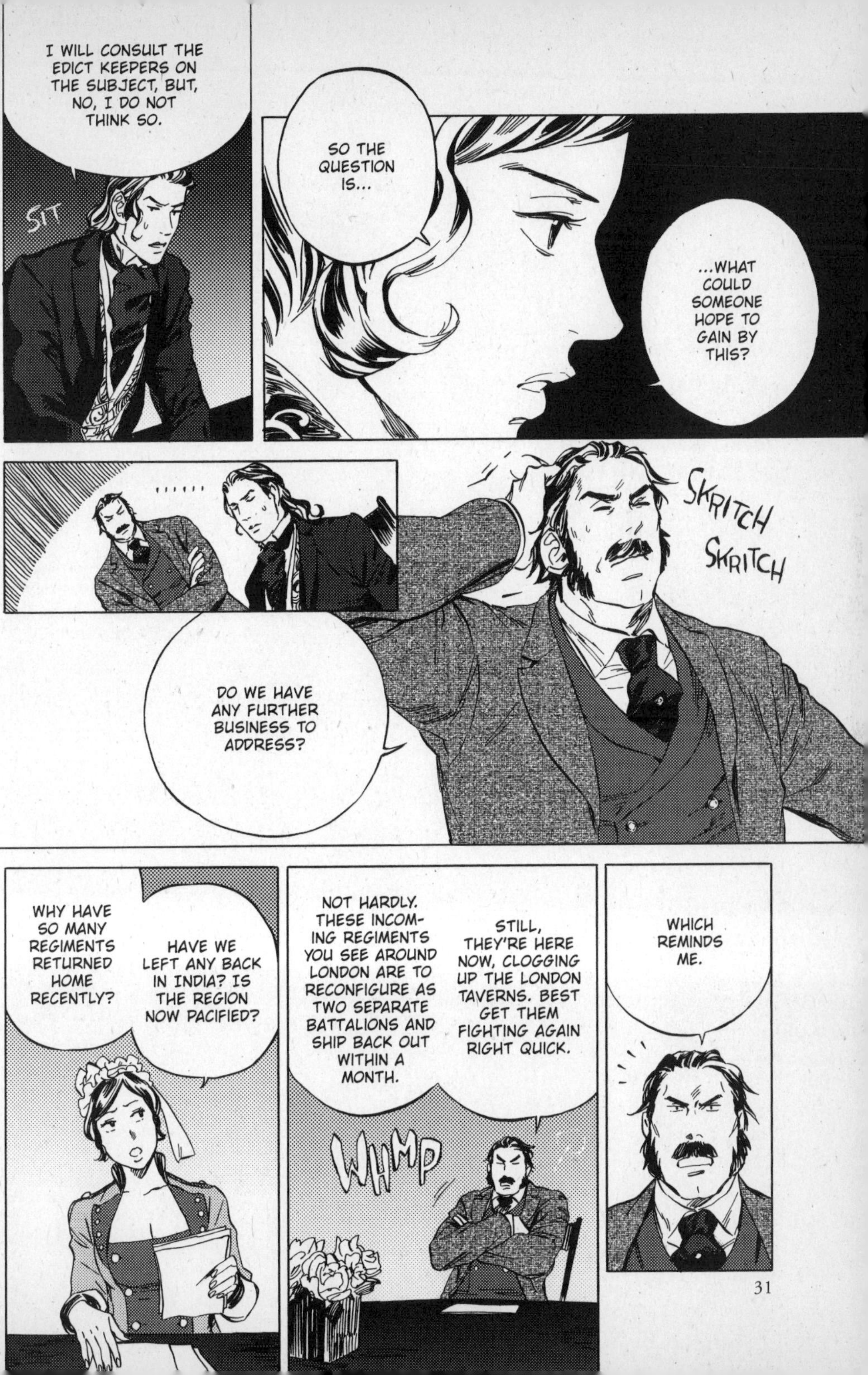
I WILL CONSULT THE EDICT KEEPERS ON THE SUBJECT, BUT, NO, I DO NOT THINK SO.
SIT
SO THE QUESTION IS...
...WHAT COULD SOMEONE HOPE TO GAIN BY THIS?
......
SKRITCH
SKRITCH
DO WE HAVE ANY FURTHER BUSINESS TO ADDRESS?
WHY HAVE SO MANY REGIMENTS RETURNED HOME RECENTLY?
HAVE WE LEFT ANY BACK IN INDIA? IS THE REGION NOW PACIFIED?
NOT HARDLY. THESE INCOMING REGIMENTS YOU SEE AROUND LONDON ARE TO RECONFIGURE AS TWO SEPARATE BATTALIONS AND SHIP BACK OUT WITHIN A MONTH.
STILL, THEY'RE HERE NOW, CLOGGING UP THE LONDON TAVERNS. BEST GET THEM FIGHTING AGAIN RIGHT QUICK.
WHMP
WHICH REMINDS ME.

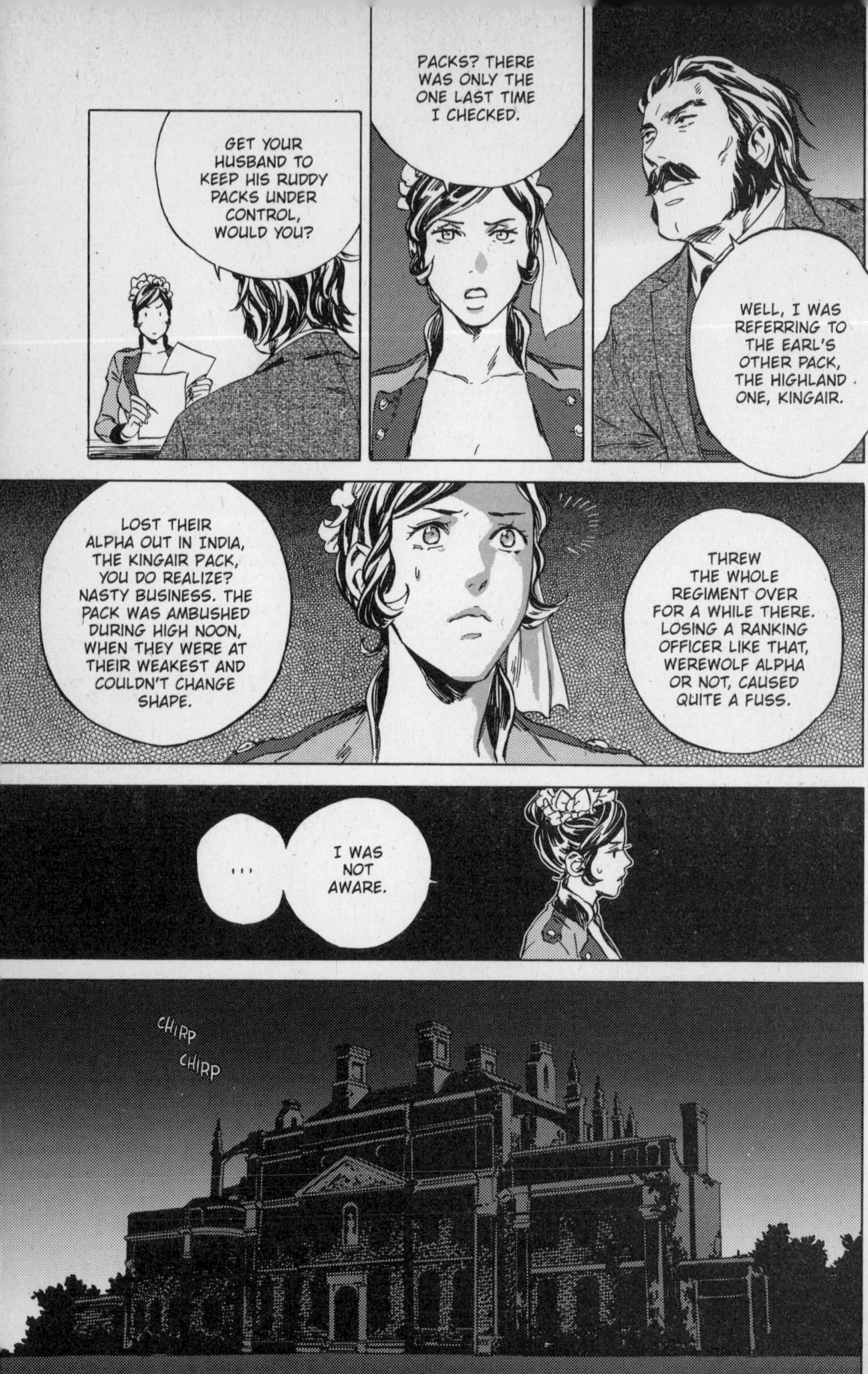
GET YOUR HUSBAND TO KEEP HIS RUDDY PACKS UNDER CONTROL, WOULD YOU?
PACKS? THERE WAS ONLY THE ONE LAST TIME I CHECKED.
WELL, I WAS REFERRING TO THE EARL'S OTHER PACK, THE HIGHLAND ONE, KINGAIR.
LOST THEIR ALPHA OUT IN INDIA, THE KINGAIR PACK, YOU DO REALIZE? NASTY BUSINESS. THE PACK WAS AMBUSHED DURING HIGH NOON, WHEN THEY WERE AT THEIR WEAKEST AND COULDN'T CHANGE SHAPE.
THREW THE WHOLE REGIMENT OVER FOR A WHILE THERE. LOSING A RANKING OFFICER LIKE THAT, WEREWOLF ALPHA OR NOT, CAUSED QUITE A FUSS.
...
I WAS NOT AWARE.
CHIRP
CHIRP

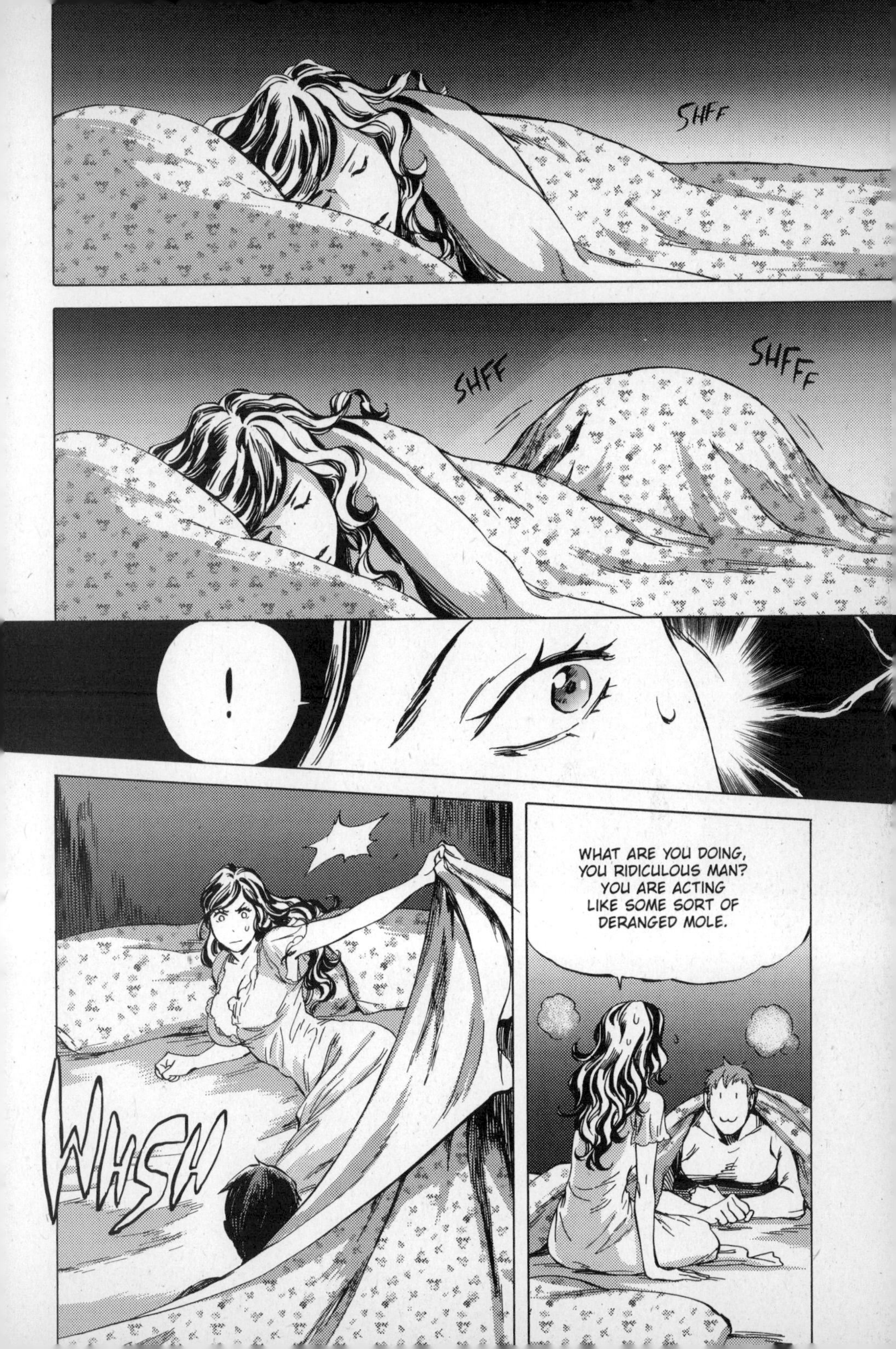
SHFF
SHFF
SHFFF
!
WHSH
WHAT ARE YOU DOING, YOU RIDICULOUS MAN? YOU ARE ACTING LIKE SOME SORT OF DERANGED MOLE.

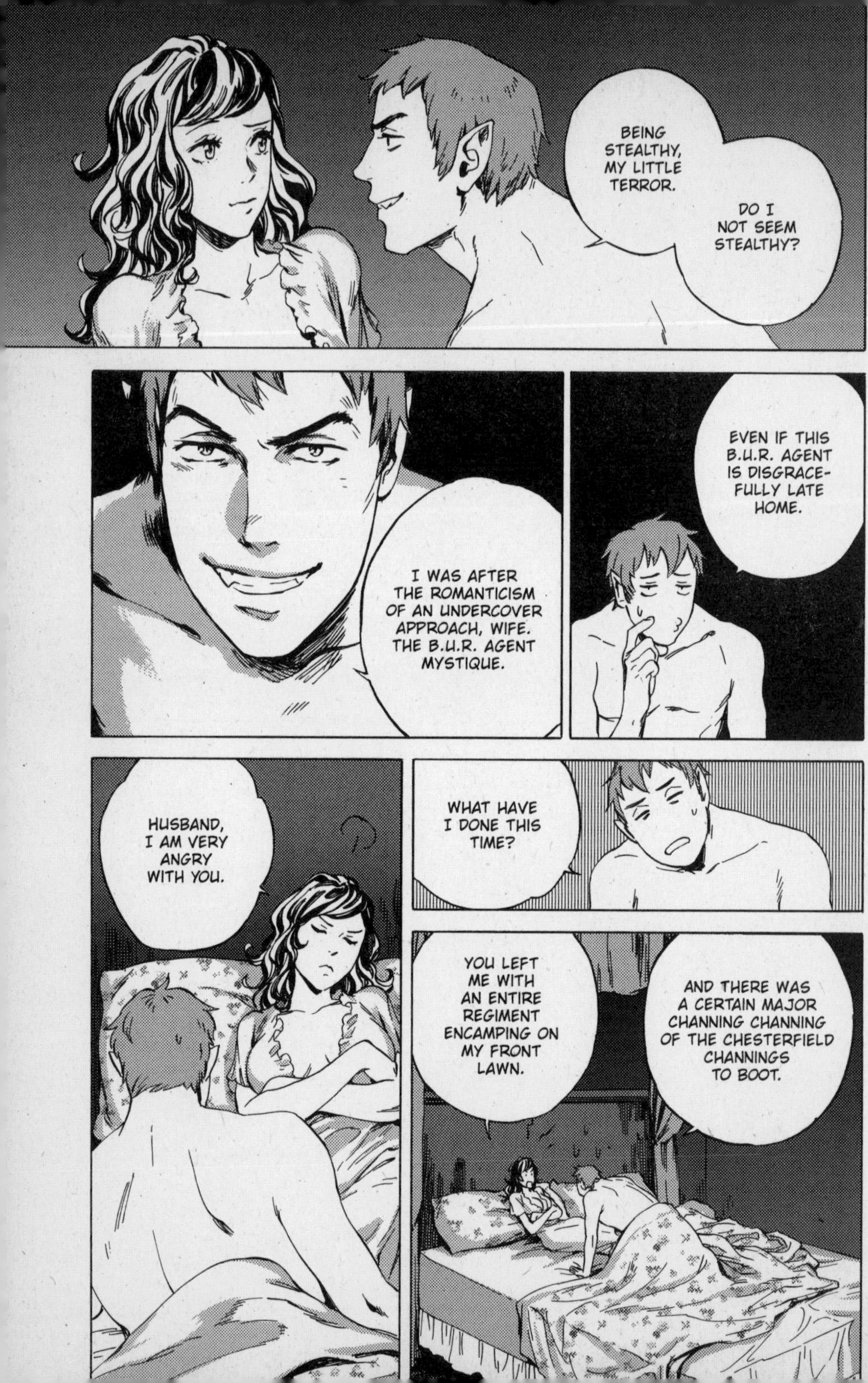
BEING STEALTHY, MY LITTLE TERROR.
DO I NOT SEEM STEALTHY?
I WAS AFTER THE ROMANTICISM OF AN UNDERCOVER APPROACH, WIFE. THE B.U.R. AGENT MYSTIQUE.
EVEN IF THIS B.U.R. AGENT IS DISGRACE-FULLY LATE HOME.
HUSBAND, I AM VERY ANGRY WITH YOU.
WHAT HAVE I DONE THIS TIME?
YOU LEFT ME WITH AN ENTIRE REGIMENT ENCAMPING ON MY FRONT LAWN.
AND THERE WAS A CERTAIN MAJOR CHANNING CHANNING OF THE CHESTERFIELD CHANNINGS TO BOOT.

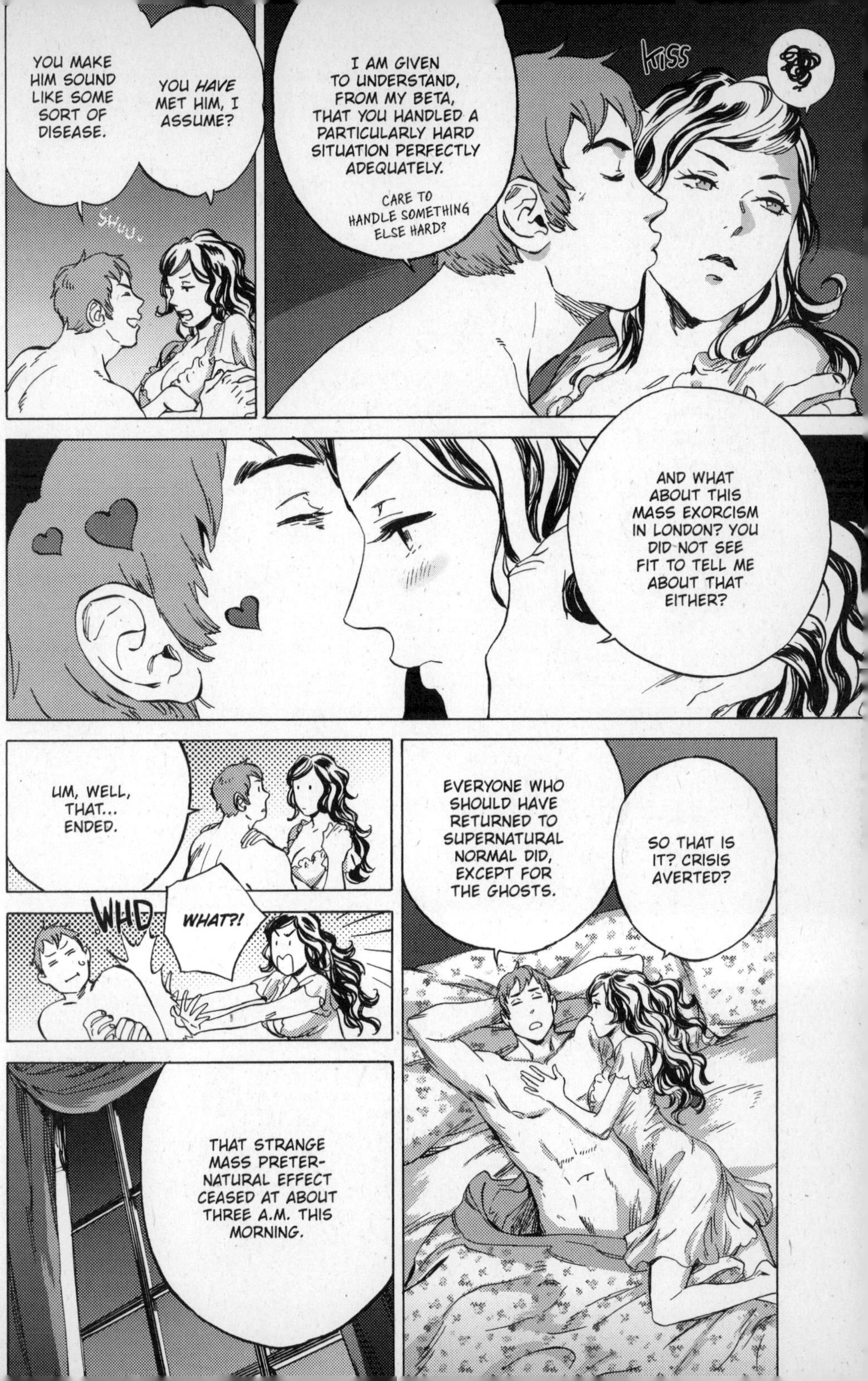

YOU MAKE HIM SOUND LIKE SOME SORT OF DISEASE.
YOU *HAVE* MET HIM, I ASSUME?
SHUU
I AM GIVEN TO UNDERSTAND, FROM MY BETA, THAT YOU HANDLED A PARTICULARLY HARD SITUATION PERFECTLY ADEQUATELY.
CARE TO HANDLE SOMETHING ELSE HARD?
KISS
AND WHAT ABOUT THIS MASS EXORCISM IN LONDON? YOU DID NOT SEE FIT TO TELL ME ABOUT THAT EITHER?
UM, WELL, THAT... ENDED.
WHD
WHAT?!
THAT STRANGE MASS PRETER-NATURAL EFFECT CEASED AT ABOUT THREE A.M. THIS MORNING.
EVERYONE WHO SHOULD HAVE RETURNED TO SUPERNATURAL NORMAL DID, EXCEPT FOR THE GHOSTS.
SO THAT IS IT? CRISIS AVERTED?

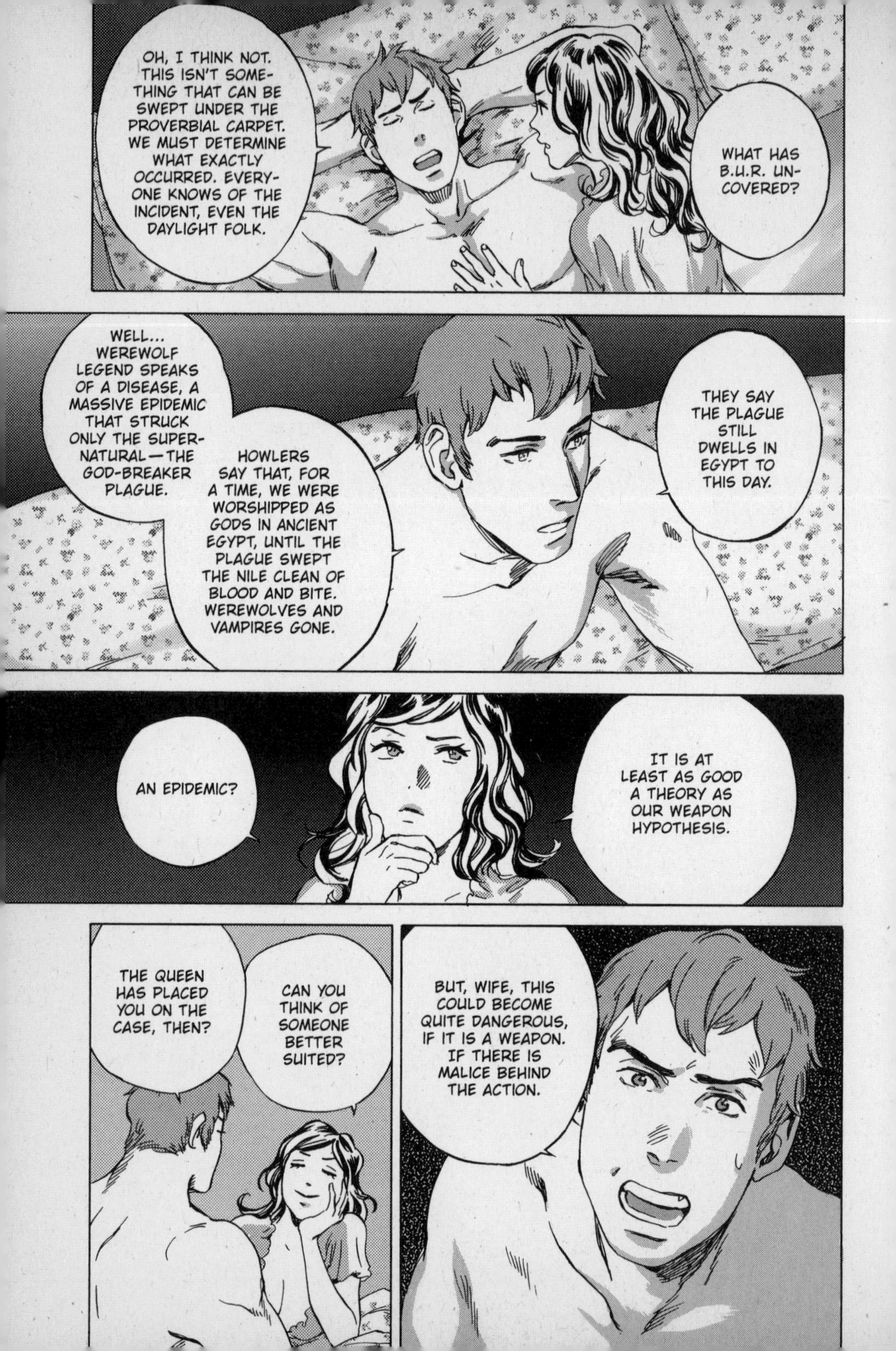
OH, I THINK NOT. THIS ISN'T SOMETHING THAT CAN BE SWEPT UNDER THE PROVERBIAL CARPET. WE MUST DETERMINE WHAT EXACTLY OCCURRED. EVERYONE KNOWS OF THE INCIDENT, EVEN THE DAYLIGHT FOLK.
WHAT HAS B.U.R. UNCOVERED?
WELL... WEREWOLF LEGEND SPEAKS OF A DISEASE, A MASSIVE EPIDEMIC THAT STRUCK ONLY THE SUPERNATURAL—THE GOD-BREAKER PLAGUE.
HOWLERS SAY THAT, FOR A TIME, WE WERE WORSHIPPED AS GODS IN ANCIENT EGYPT, UNTIL THE PLAGUE SWEPT THE NILE CLEAN OF BLOOD AND BITE. WEREWOLVES AND VAMPIRES GONE.
THEY SAY THE PLAGUE STILL DWELLS IN EGYPT TO THIS DAY.
AN EPIDEMIC?
IT IS AT LEAST AS GOOD A THEORY AS OUR WEAPON HYPOTHESIS.
THE QUEEN HAS PLACED YOU ON THE CASE, THEN?
CAN YOU THINK OF SOMEONE BETTER SUITED?
BUT, WIFE, THIS COULD BECOME QUITE DANGEROUS, IF IT IS A WEAPON. IF THERE IS MALICE BEHIND THE ACTION.

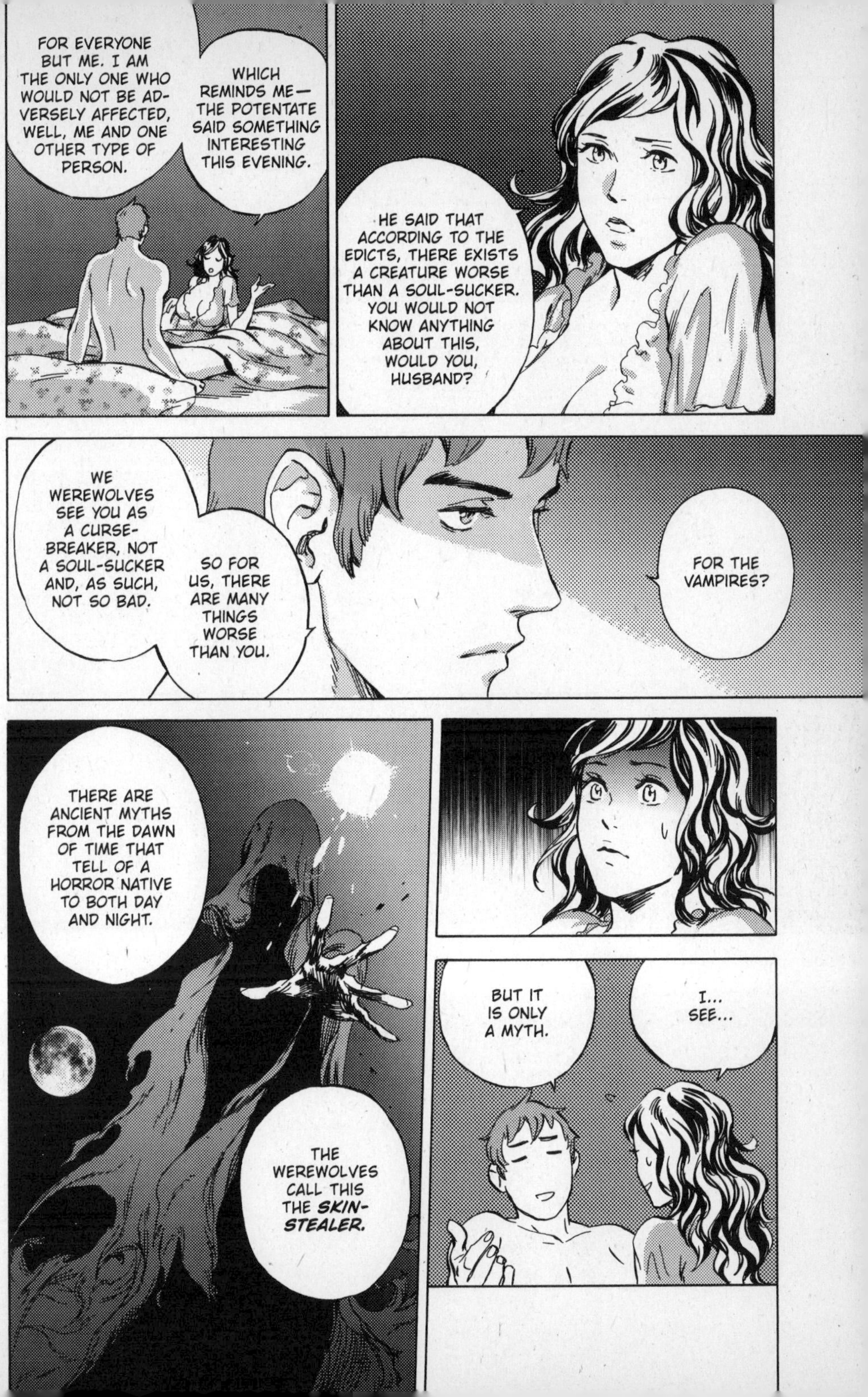
FOR EVERYONE BUT ME. I AM THE ONLY ONE WHO WOULD NOT BE ADVERSELY AFFECTED, WELL, ME AND ONE OTHER TYPE OF PERSON.
WHICH REMINDS ME— THE POTENTATE SAID SOMETHING INTERESTING THIS EVENING.
HE SAID THAT ACCORDING TO THE EDICTS, THERE EXISTS A CREATURE WORSE THAN A SOUL-SUCKER. YOU WOULD NOT KNOW ANYTHING ABOUT THIS, WOULD YOU, HUSBAND?
WE WEREWOLVES SEE YOU AS A CURSE-BREAKER, NOT A SOUL-SUCKER AND, AS SUCH, NOT SO BAD.
SO FOR US, THERE ARE MANY THINGS WORSE THAN YOU.
FOR THE VAMPIRES?
THERE ARE ANCIENT MYTHS FROM THE DAWN OF TIME THAT TELL OF A HORROR NATIVE TO BOTH DAY AND NIGHT.
THE WEREWOLVES CALL THIS THE ***SKIN-STEALER.***
BUT IT IS ONLY A MYTH.
I... SEE...

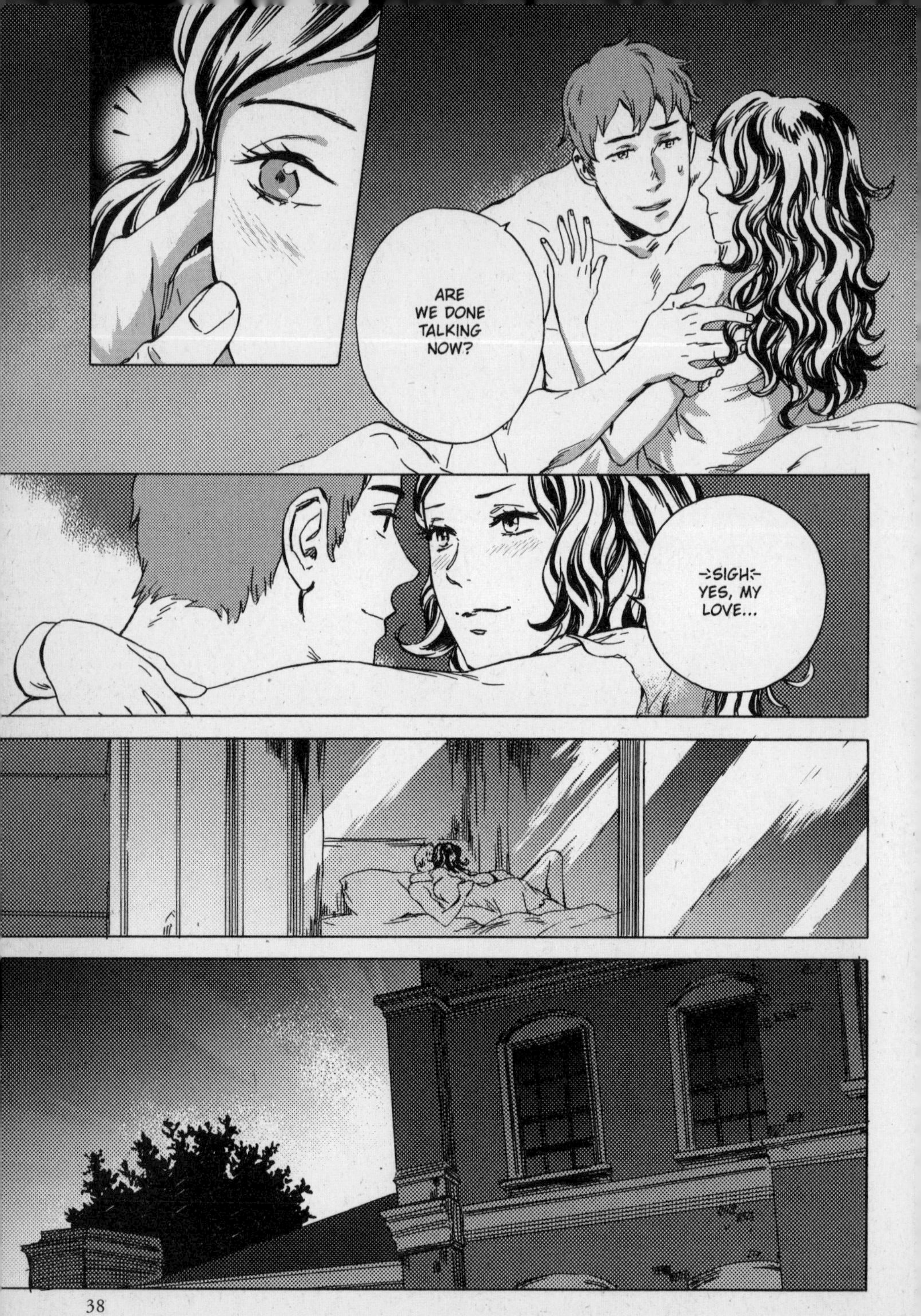
ARE WE DONE TALKING NOW?
-:SIGH:- YES, MY LOVE...

SOULLESS

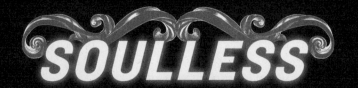

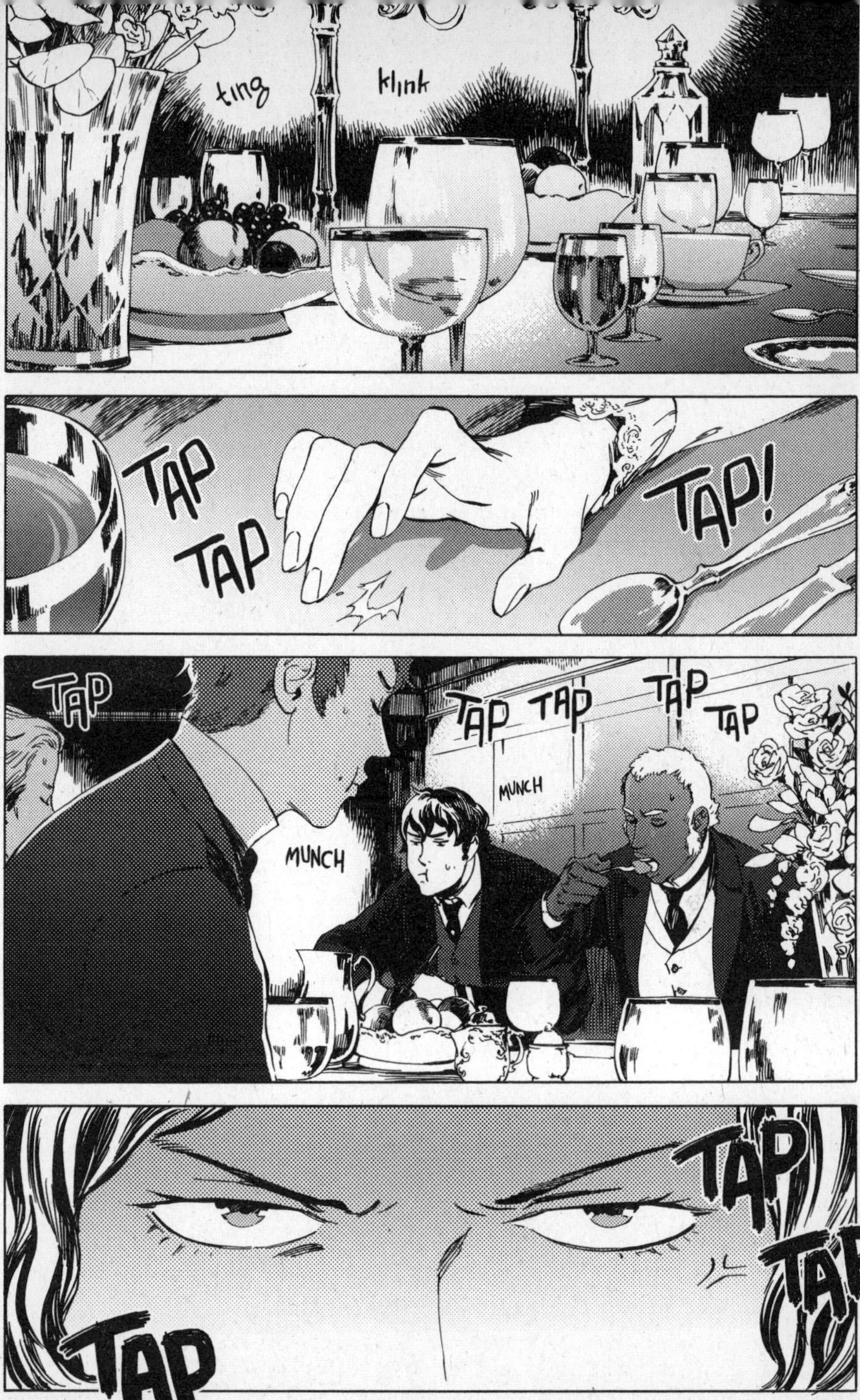
ting
klink
TAP
TAP
TAP!
TAP
TAP TAP
TAP
TAP
MUNCH
MUNCH
TAP
TAP
TAP

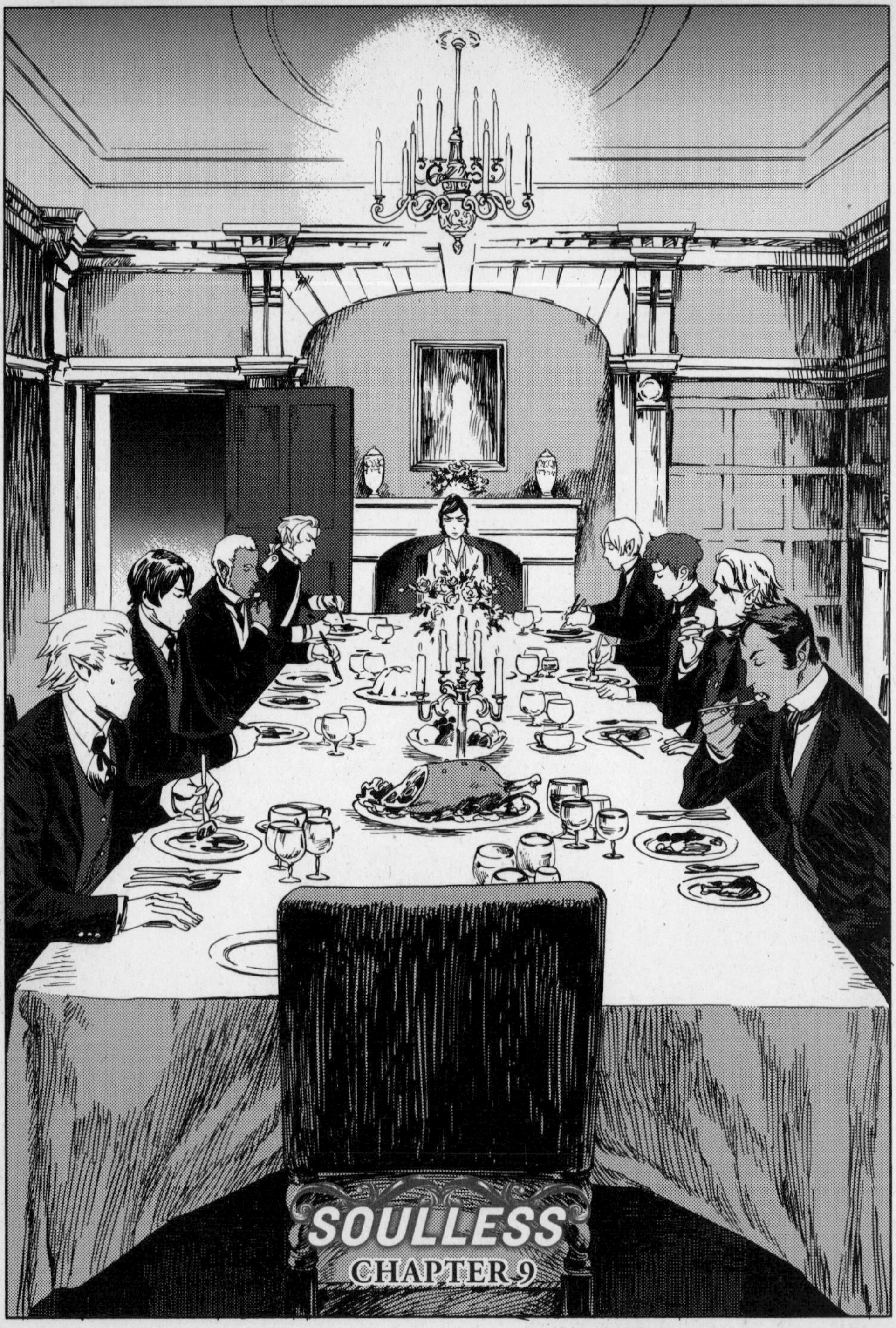
SOULLESS
CHAPTER 9

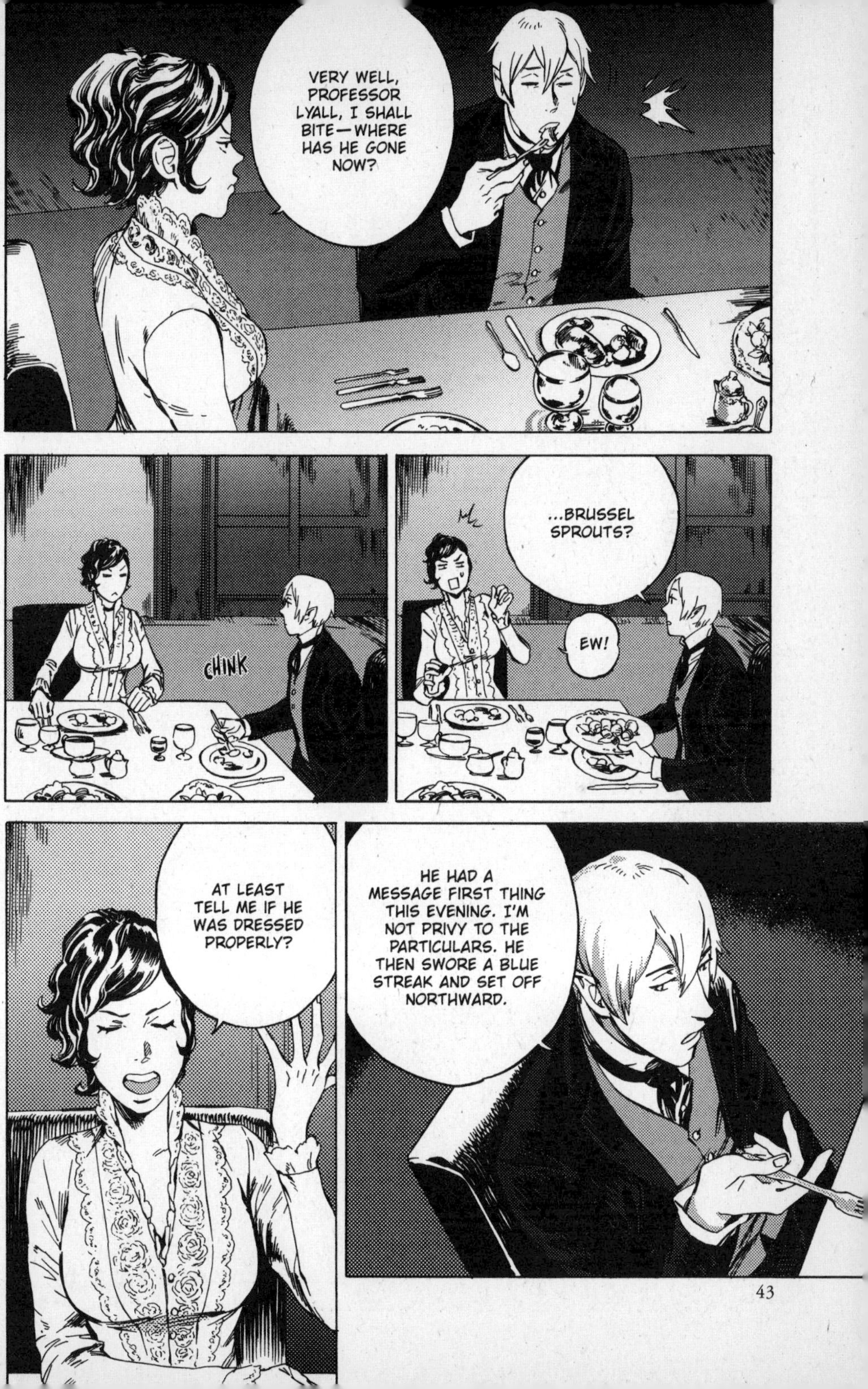
VERY WELL, PROFESSOR LYALL, I SHALL BITE—WHERE HAS HE GONE NOW?
CHINK
...BRUSSEL SPROUTS?
EW!
AT LEAST TELL ME IF HE WAS DRESSED PROPERLY?
HE HAD A MESSAGE FIRST THING THIS EVENING. I'M NOT PRIVY TO THE PARTICULARS. HE THEN SWORE A BLUE STREAK AND SET OFF NORTHWARD.

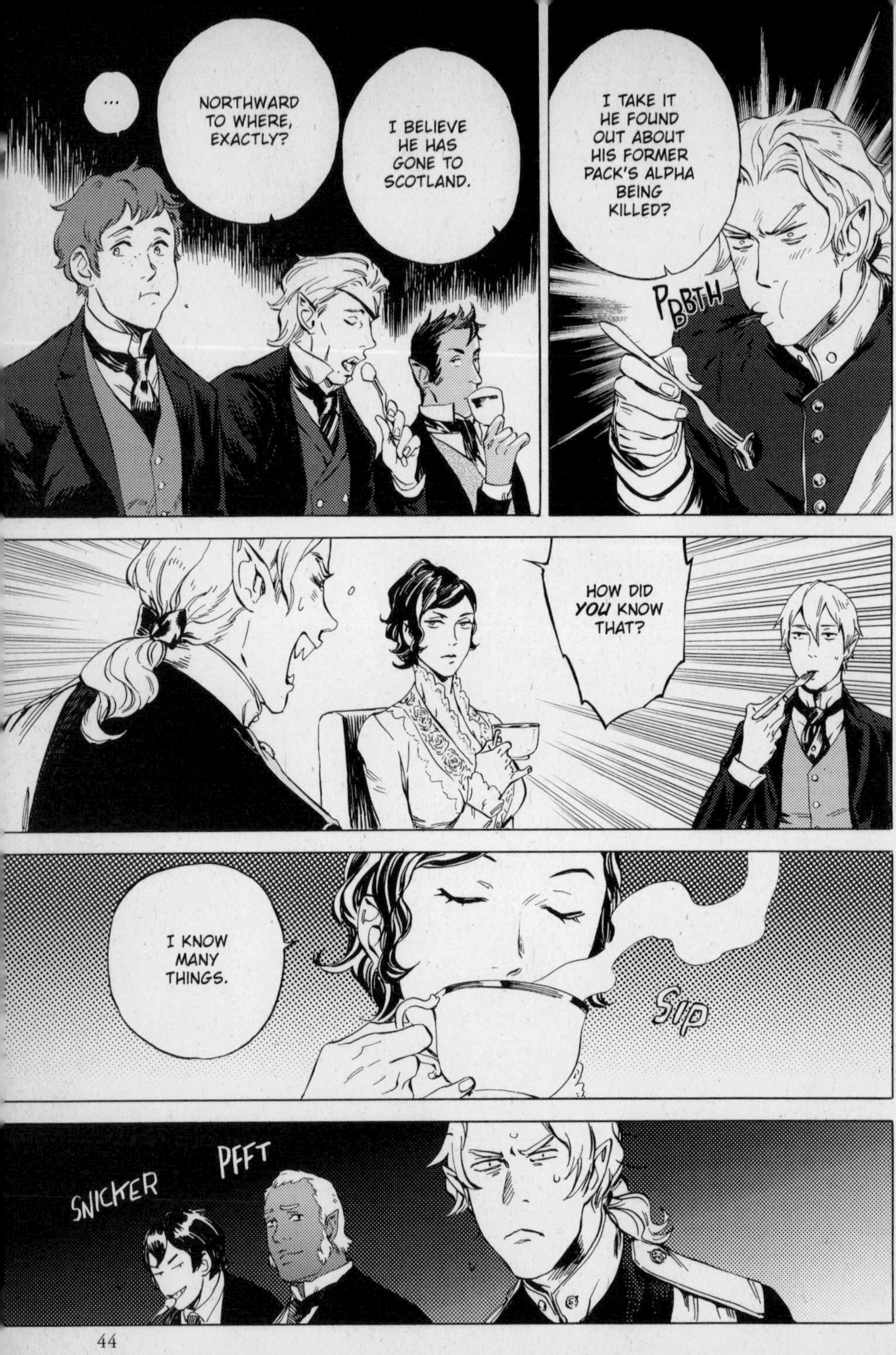
...
NORTHWARD TO WHERE, EXACTLY?
I BELIEVE HE HAS GONE TO SCOTLAND.
I TAKE IT HE FOUND OUT ABOUT HIS FORMER PACK'S ALPHA BEING KILLED?
PBBTH
HOW DID *YOU* KNOW THAT?
I KNOW MANY THINGS.
SIP
SNICKER
PFFT

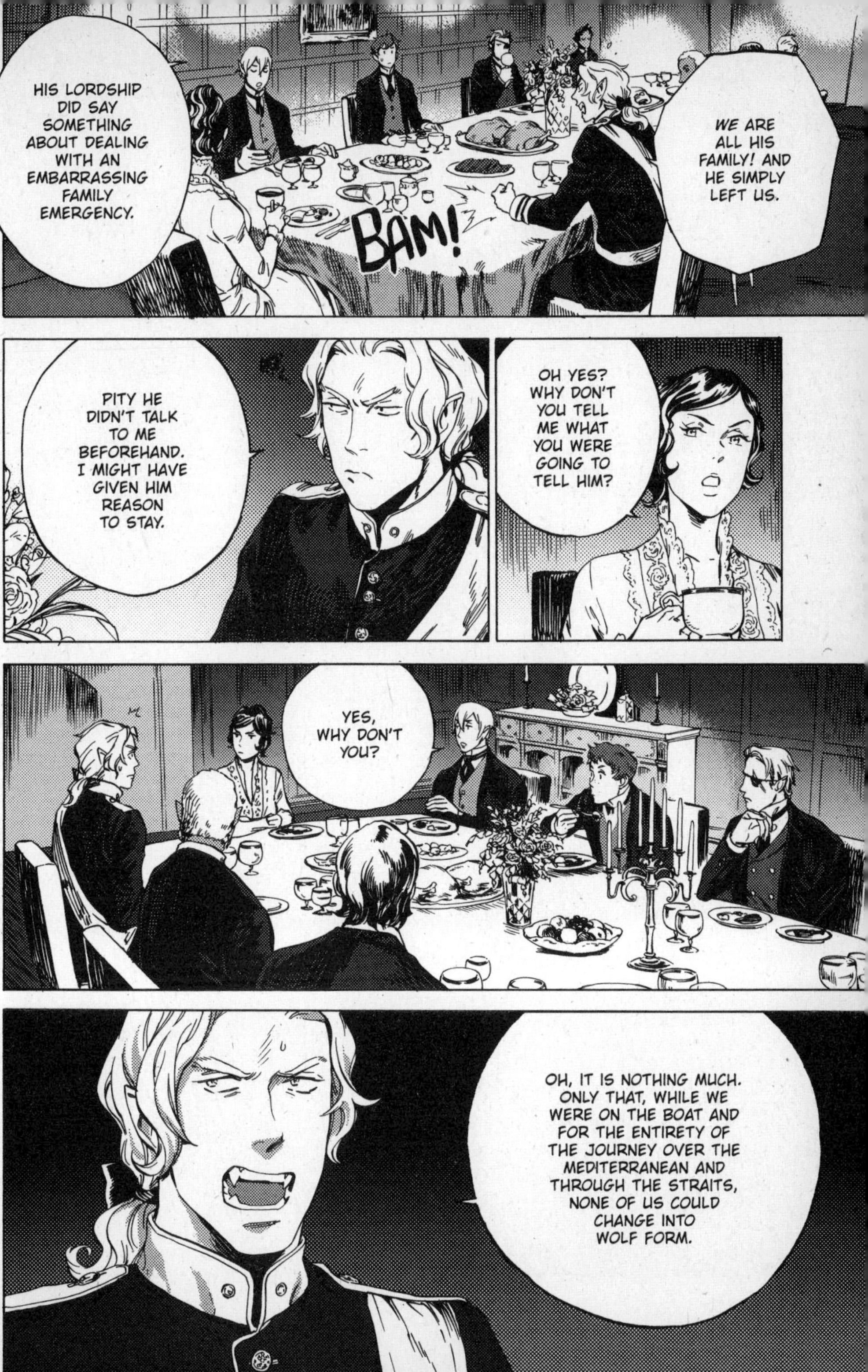
HIS LORDSHIP DID SAY SOMETHING ABOUT DEALING WITH AN EMBARRASSING FAMILY EMERGENCY.
BAM!
WE ARE ALL HIS FAMILY! AND HE SIMPLY LEFT US.
PITY HE DIDN'T TALK TO ME BEFOREHAND. I MIGHT HAVE GIVEN HIM REASON TO STAY.
OH YES? WHY DON'T YOU TELL ME WHAT YOU WERE GOING TO TELL HIM?
YES, WHY DON'T YOU?
OH, IT IS NOTHING MUCH. ONLY THAT, WHILE WE WERE ON THE BOAT AND FOR THE ENTIRETY OF THE JOURNEY OVER THE MEDITERRANEAN AND THROUGH THE STRAITS, NONE OF US COULD CHANGE INTO WOLF FORM.

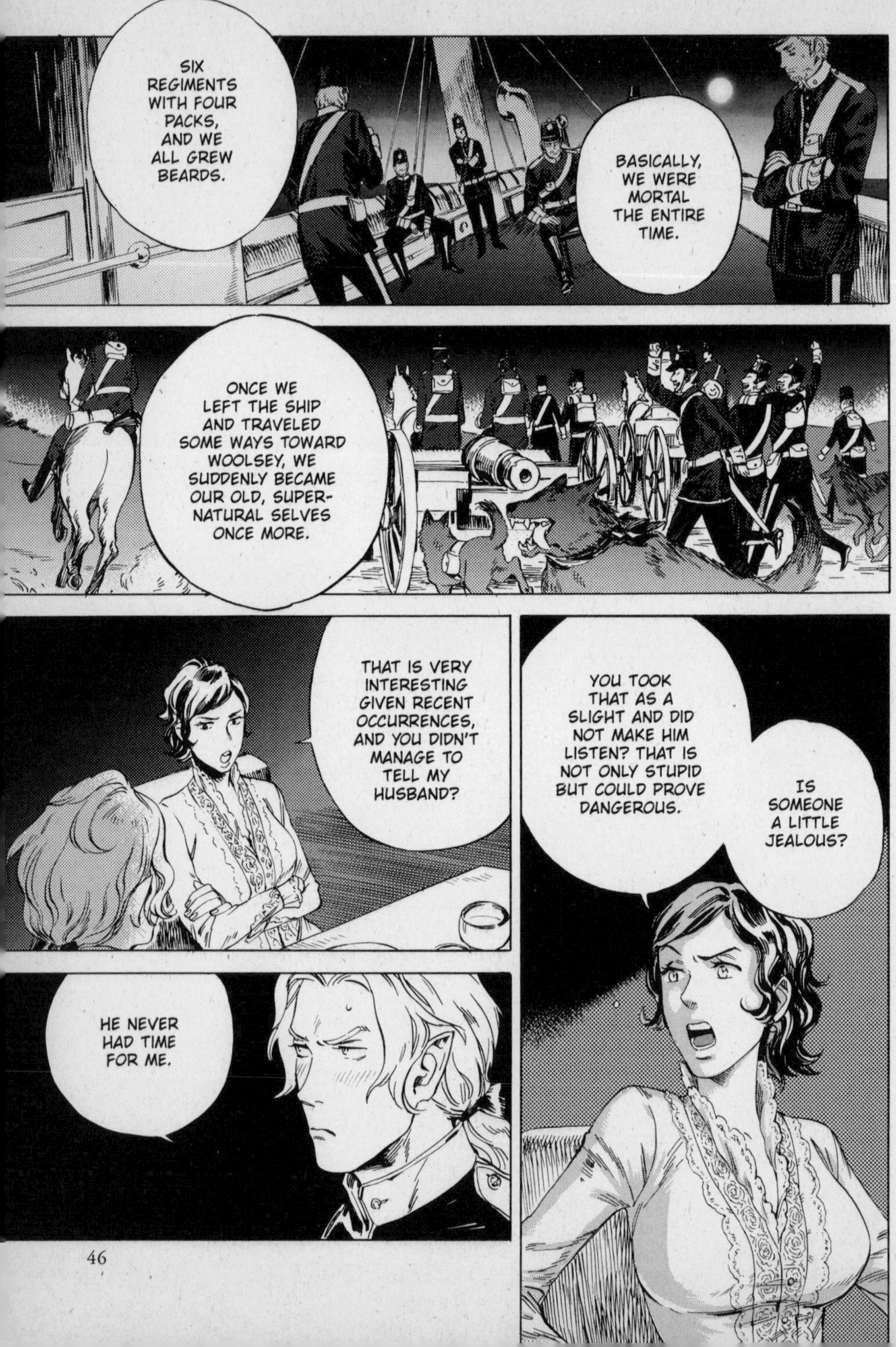
SIX REGIMENTS WITH FOUR PACKS, AND WE ALL GREW BEARDS.
BASICALLY, WE WERE MORTAL THE ENTIRE TIME.
ONCE WE LEFT THE SHIP AND TRAVELED SOME WAYS TOWARD WOOLSEY, WE SUDDENLY BECAME OUR OLD, SUPER-NATURAL SELVES ONCE MORE.
THAT IS VERY INTERESTING GIVEN RECENT OCCURRENCES, AND YOU DIDN'T MANAGE TO TELL MY HUSBAND?
HE NEVER HAD TIME FOR ME.
YOU TOOK THAT AS A SLIGHT AND DID NOT MAKE HIM LISTEN? THAT IS NOT ONLY STUPID BUT COULD PROVE DANGEROUS.
IS SOMEONE A LITTLE JEALOUS?

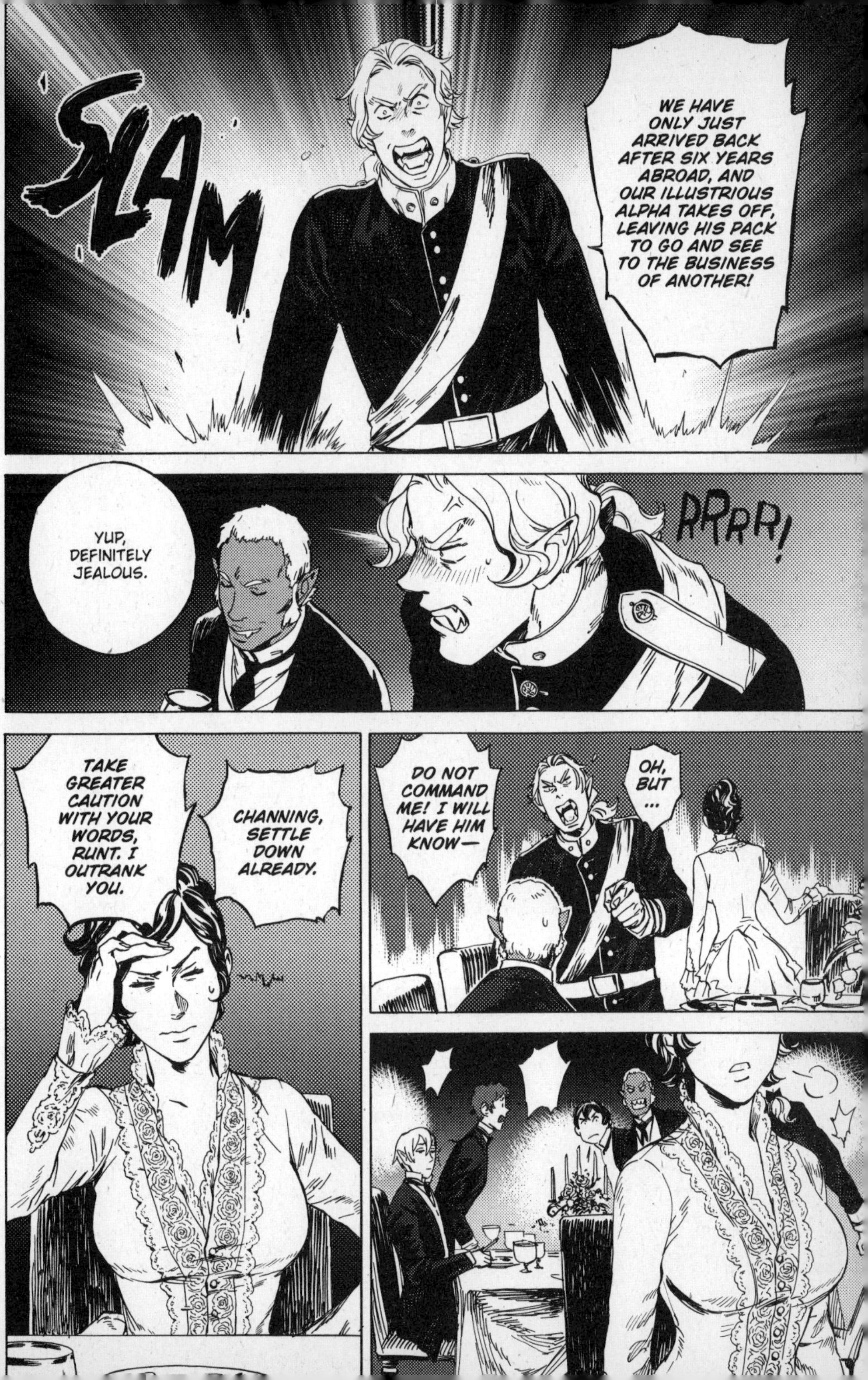
SLAM
WE HAVE ONLY JUST ARRIVED BACK AFTER SIX YEARS ABROAD, AND OUR ILLUSTRIOUS ALPHA TAKES OFF, LEAVING HIS PACK TO GO AND SEE TO THE BUSINESS OF ANOTHER!
YUP, DEFINITELY JEALOUS.
RRRR!
TAKE GREATER CAUTION WITH YOUR WORDS, RUNT. I OUTRANK YOU.
CHANNING, SETTLE DOWN ALREADY.
DO NOT COMMAND ME! I WILL HAVE HIM KNOW—
OH, BUT ...

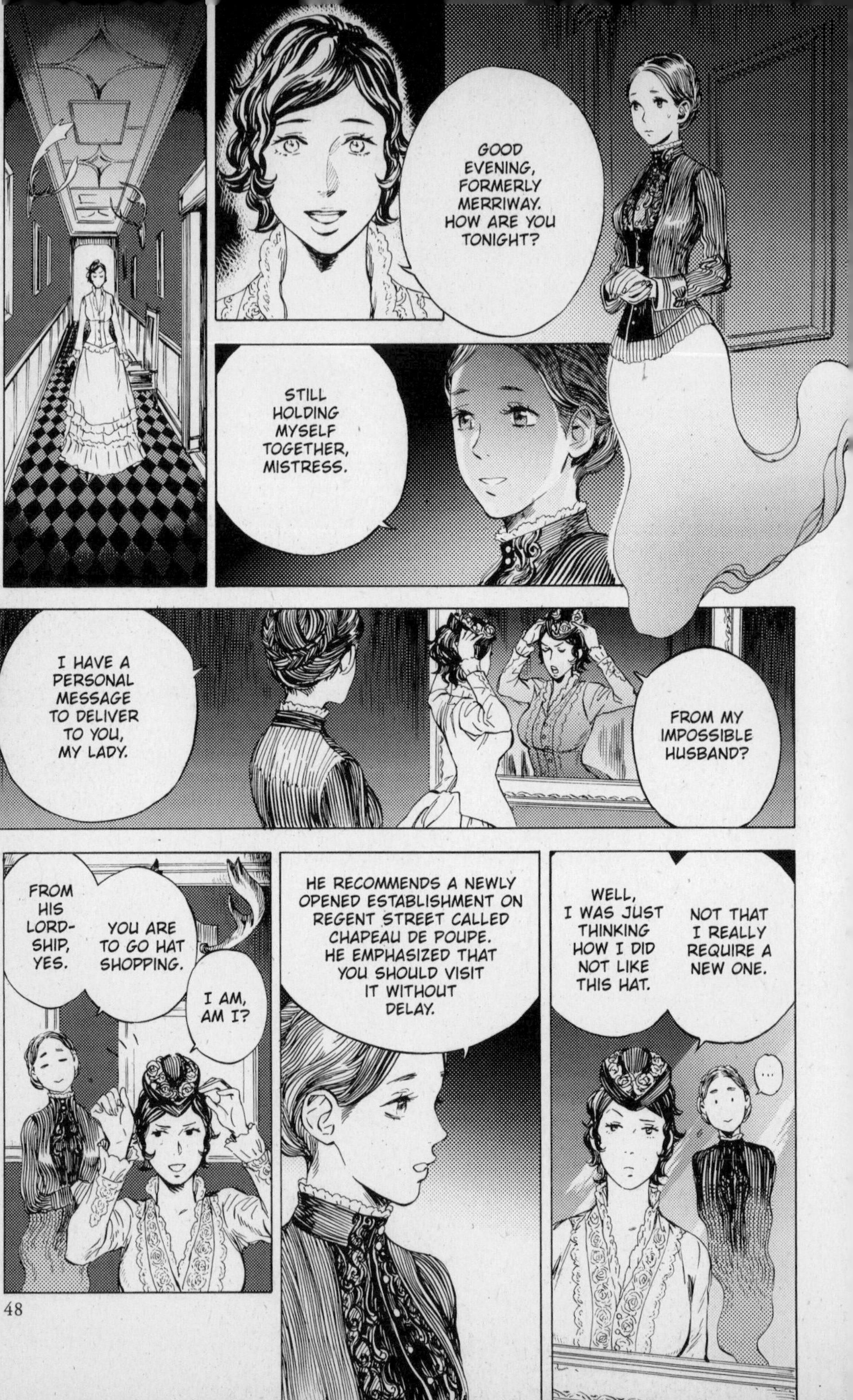
GOOD EVENING, FORMERLY MERRIWAY. HOW ARE YOU TONIGHT?
STILL HOLDING MYSELF TOGETHER, MISTRESS.
I HAVE A PERSONAL MESSAGE TO DELIVER TO YOU, MY LADY.
FROM MY IMPOSSIBLE HUSBAND?
FROM HIS LORD-SHIP, YES.
YOU ARE TO GO HAT SHOPPING.
I AM, AM I?
HE RECOMMENDS A NEWLY OPENED ESTABLISHMENT ON REGENT STREET CALLED CHAPEAU DE POUPE. HE EMPHASIZED THAT YOU SHOULD VISIT IT WITHOUT DELAY.
WELL, I WAS JUST THINKING HOW I DID NOT LIKE THIS HAT.
NOT THAT I REALLY REQUIRE A NEW ONE.
...

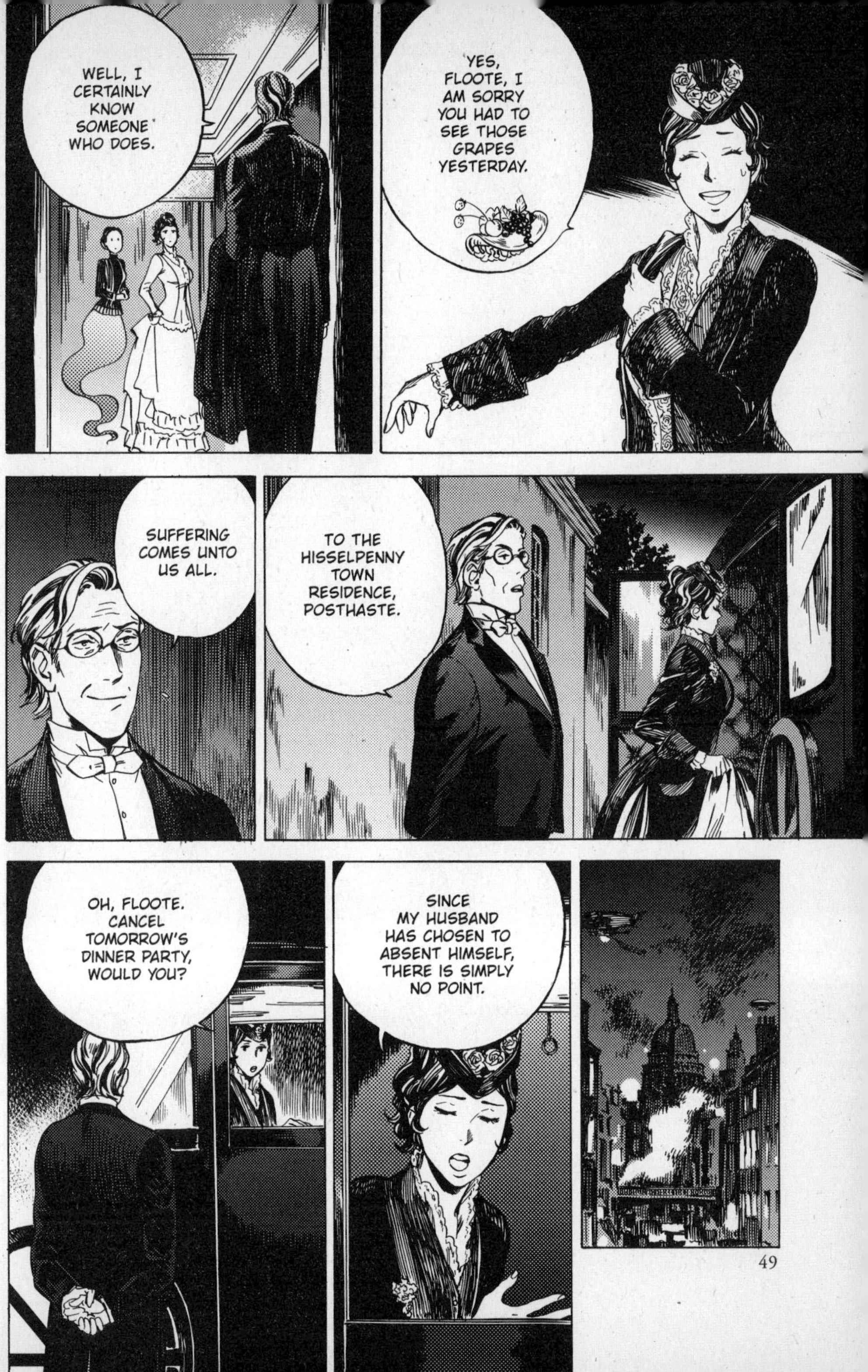
WELL, I CERTAINLY KNOW SOMEONE WHO DOES.
YES, FLOOTE, I AM SORRY YOU HAD TO SEE THOSE GRAPES YESTERDAY.
SUFFERING COMES UNTO US ALL.
TO THE HISSELPENNY TOWN RESIDENCE, POSTHASTE.
OH, FLOOTE. CANCEL TOMORROW'S DINNER PARTY, WOULD YOU?
SINCE MY HUSBAND HAS CHOSEN TO ABSENT HIMSELF, THERE IS SIMPLY NO POINT.

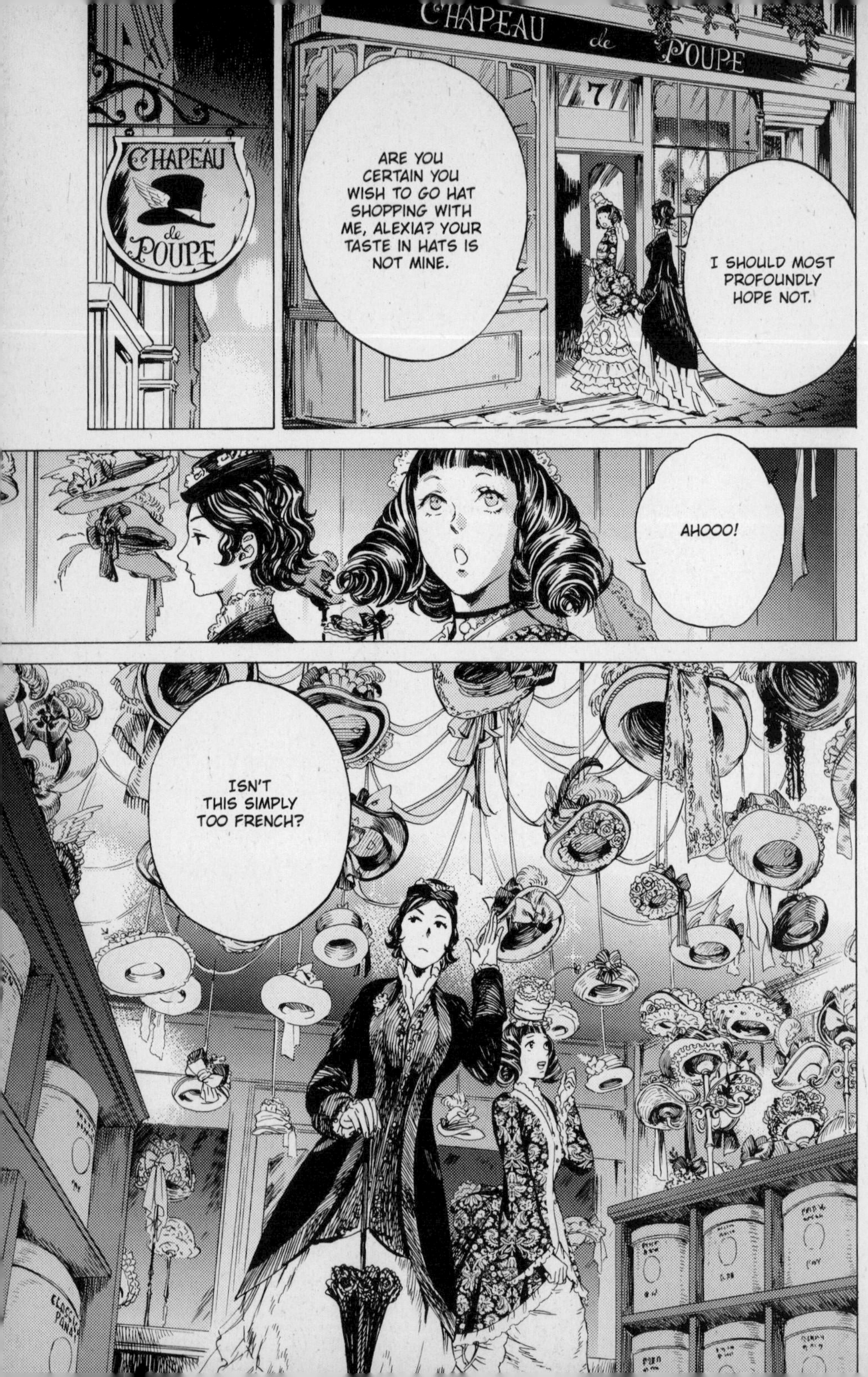
CHAPEAU de POUPE
CHAPEAU de POUPE
7
ARE YOU CERTAIN YOU WISH TO GO HAT SHOPPING WITH ME, ALEXIA? YOUR TASTE IN HATS IS NOT MINE.
I SHOULD MOST PROFOUNDLY HOPE NOT.
AHOOO!
ISN'T THIS SIMPLY TOO FRENCH?

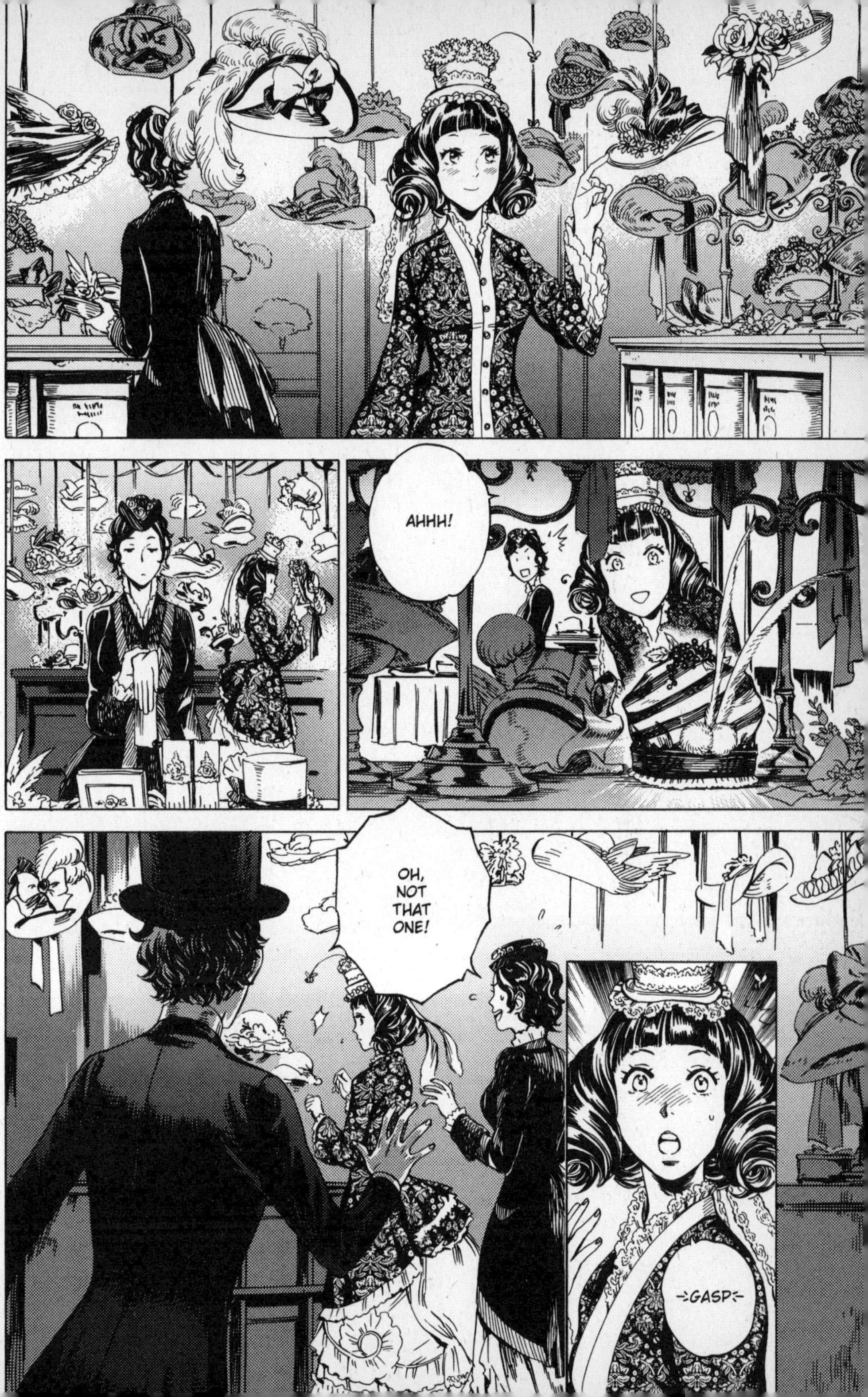
AHHH!
OH, NOT THAT ONE!
-GASP-

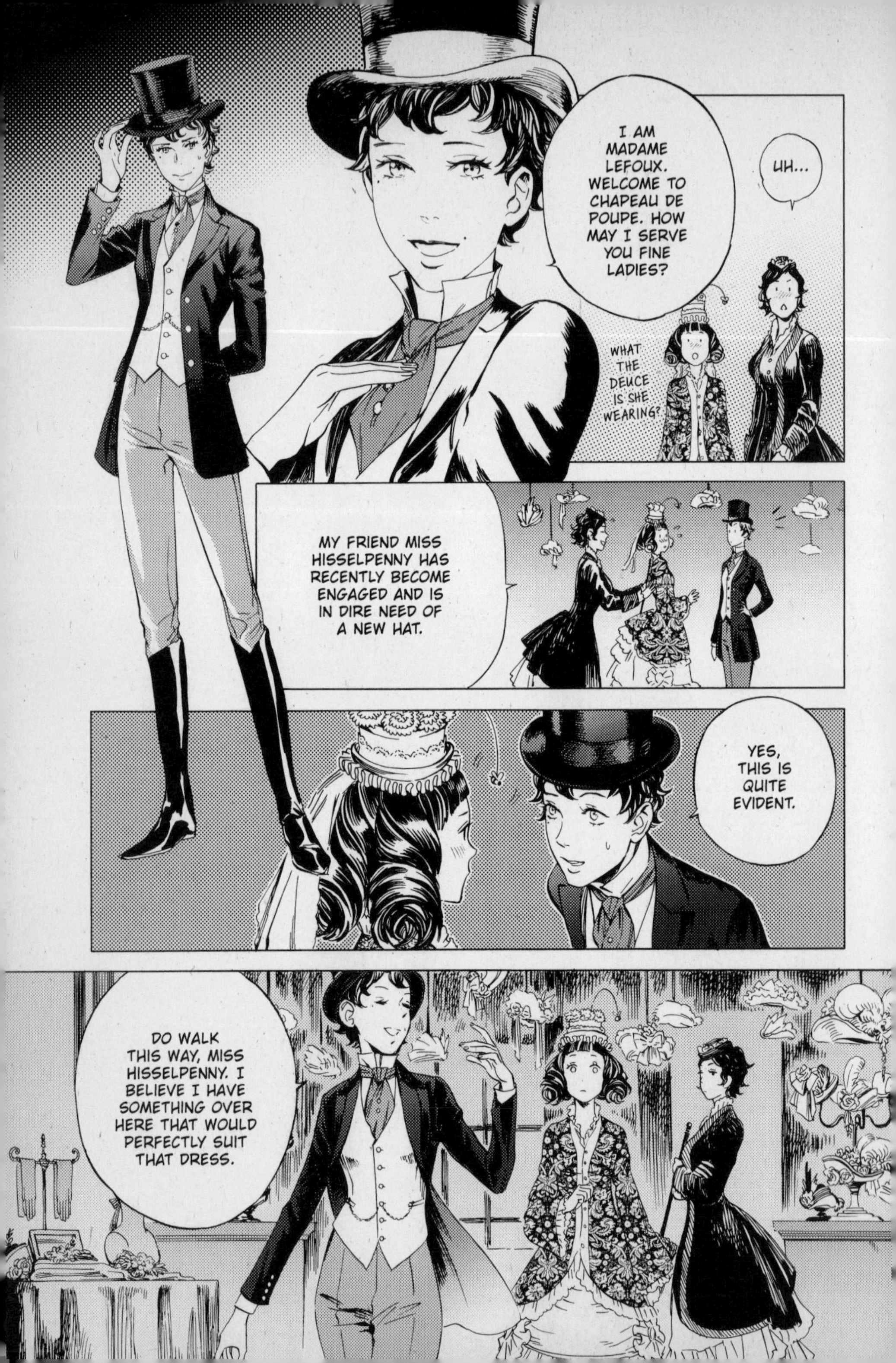
I AM MADAME LEFOUX. WELCOME TO CHAPEAU DE POUPE. HOW MAY I SERVE YOU FINE LADIES?
UH...
WHAT THE DEUCE IS SHE WEARING?
MY FRIEND MISS HISSELPENNY HAS RECENTLY BECOME ENGAGED AND IS IN DIRE NEED OF A NEW HAT.
YES, THIS IS QUITE EVIDENT.
DO WALK THIS WAY, MISS HISSELPENNY. I BELIEVE I HAVE SOMETHING OVER HERE THAT WOULD PERFECTLY SUIT THAT DRESS.

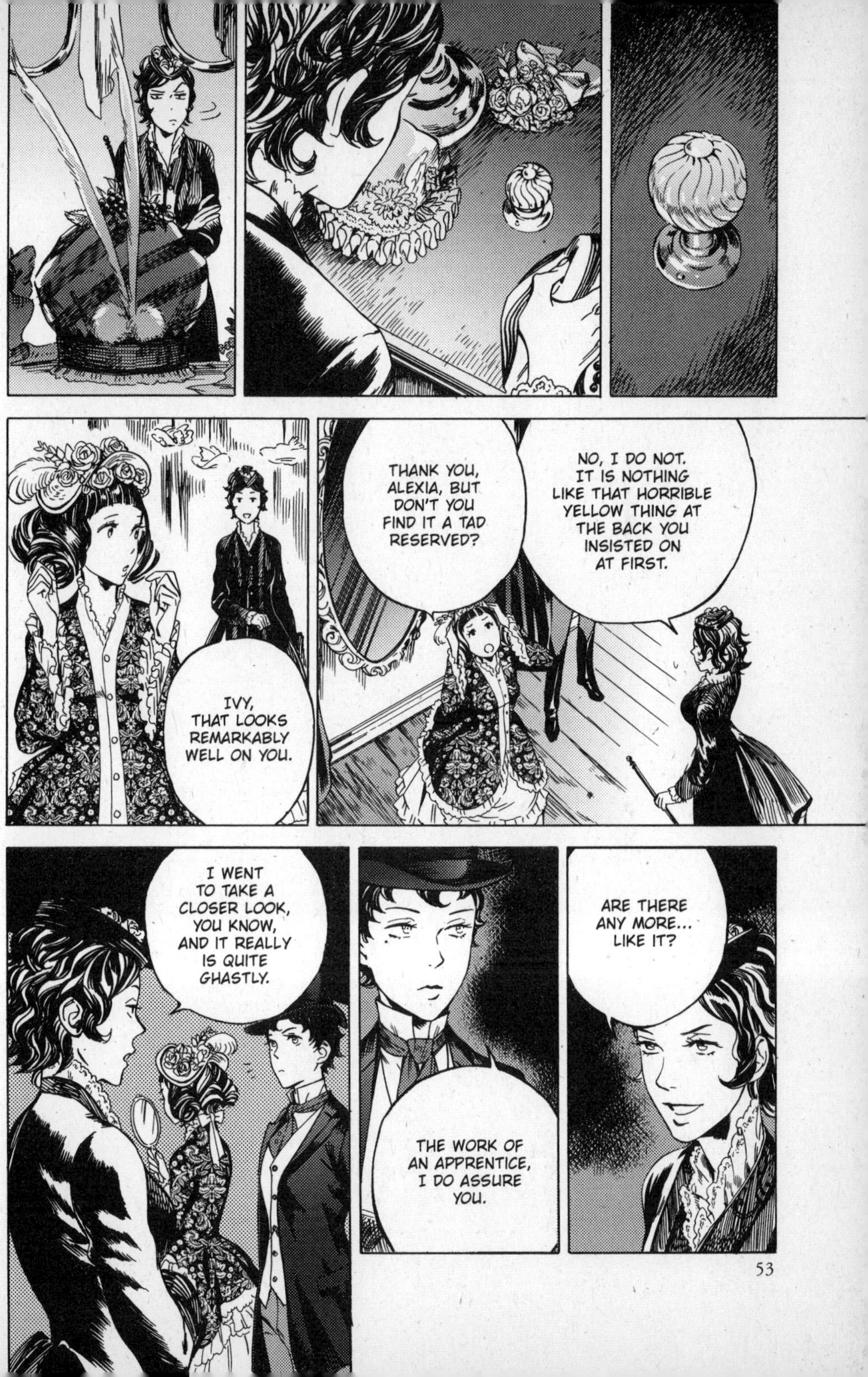
IVY, THAT LOOKS REMARKABLY WELL ON YOU.
THANK YOU, ALEXIA, BUT DON'T YOU FIND IT A TAD RESERVED?
NO, I DO NOT. IT IS NOTHING LIKE THAT HORRIBLE YELLOW THING AT THE BACK YOU INSISTED ON AT FIRST.
I WENT TO TAKE A CLOSER LOOK, YOU KNOW, AND IT REALLY IS QUITE GHASTLY.
THE WORK OF AN APPRENTICE, I DO ASSURE YOU.
ARE THERE ANY MORE... LIKE IT?

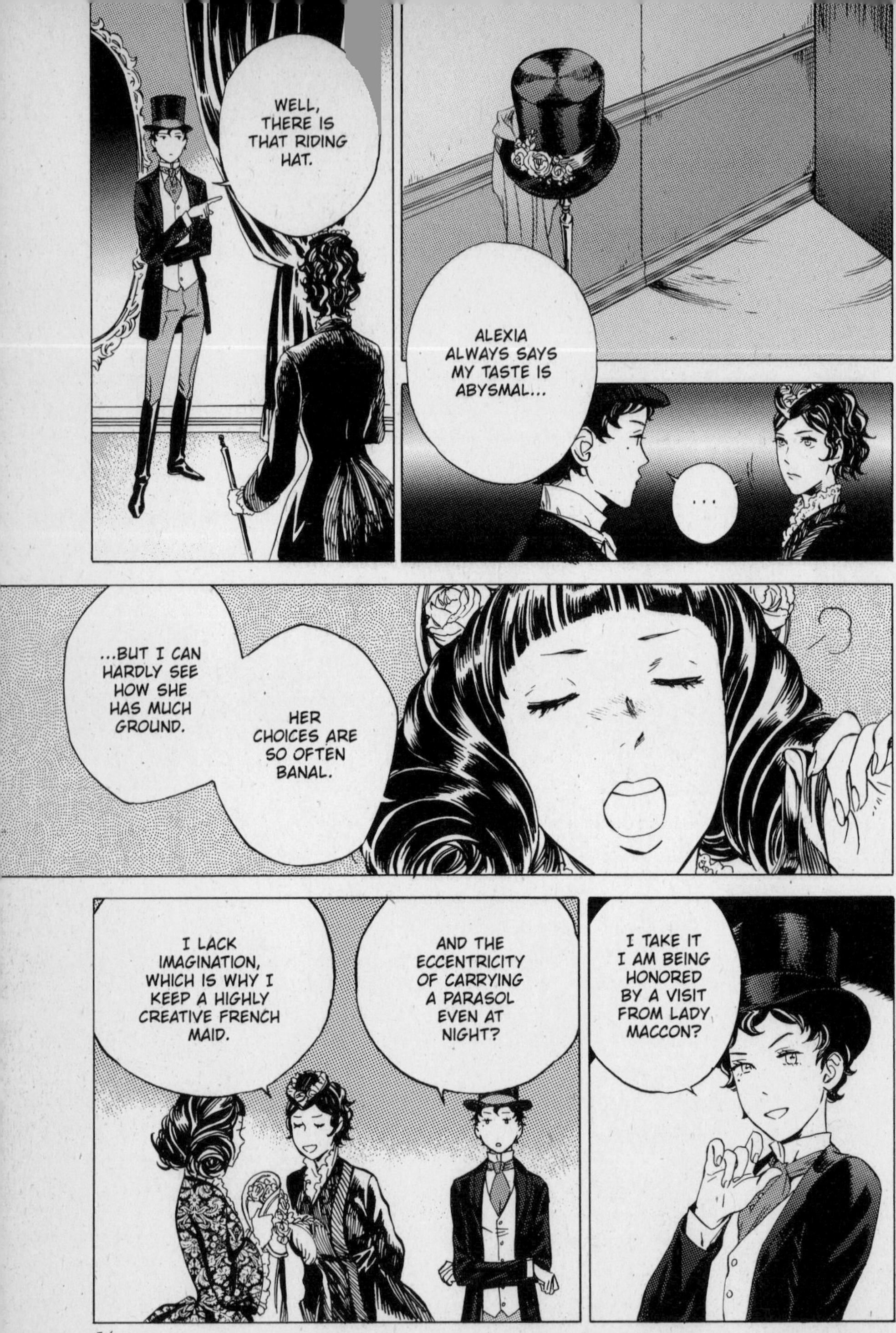
WELL, THERE IS THAT RIDING HAT.
ALEXIA ALWAYS SAYS MY TASTE IS ABYSMAL...
...
...BUT I CAN HARDLY SEE HOW SHE HAS MUCH GROUND.
HER CHOICES ARE SO OFTEN BANAL.
I LACK IMAGINATION, WHICH IS WHY I KEEP A HIGHLY CREATIVE FRENCH MAID.
AND THE ECCENTRICITY OF CARRYING A PARASOL EVEN AT NIGHT?
I TAKE IT I AM BEING HONORED BY A VISIT FROM LADY MACCON?

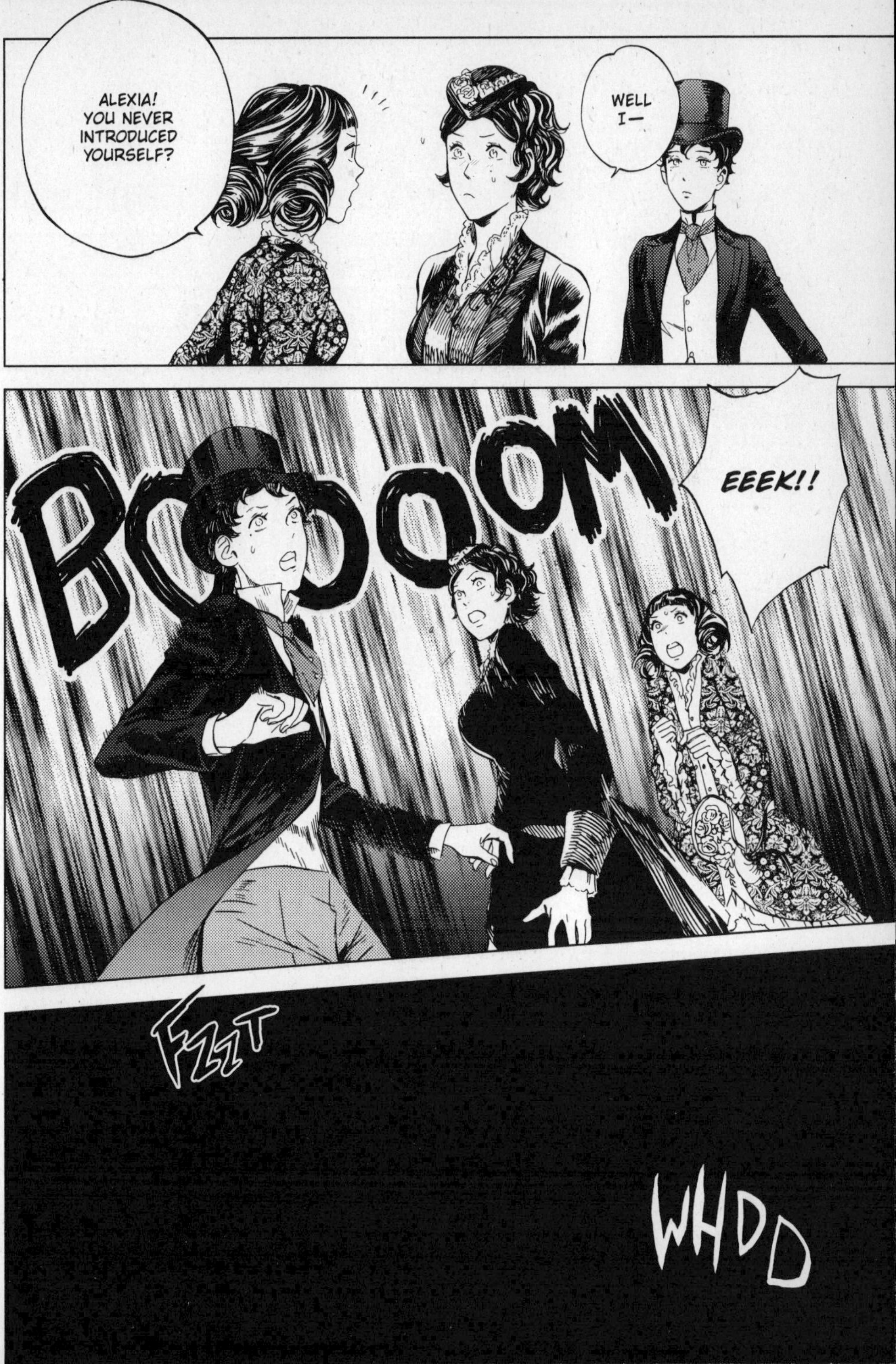
ALEXIA! YOU NEVER INTRODUCED YOURSELF?
WELL I—
BOOOOM
EEEK!!
FZZT
WHDD

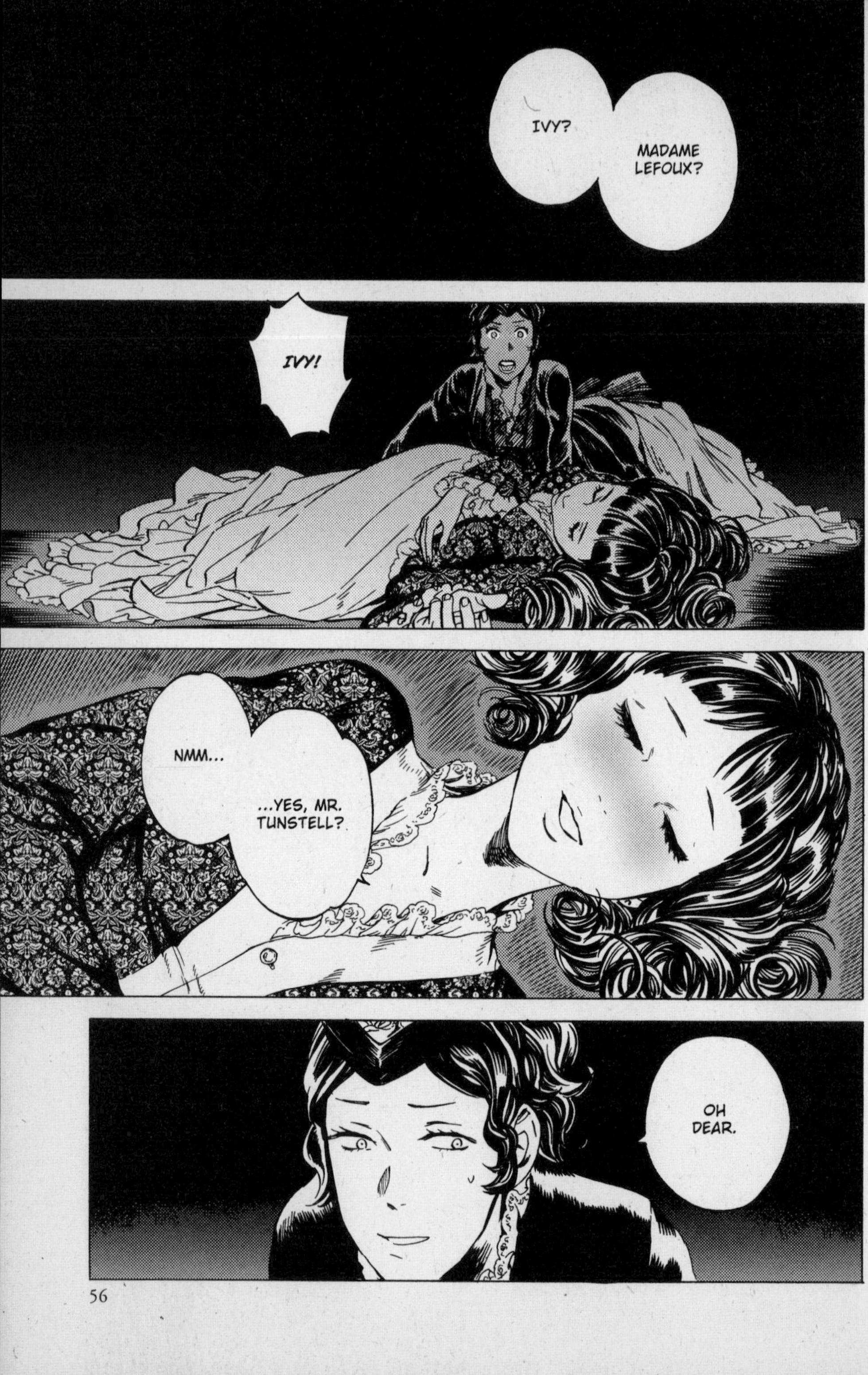
IVY?
MADAME LEFOUX?
IVY!
NMM...
...YES, MR. TUNSTELL?
OH DEAR.

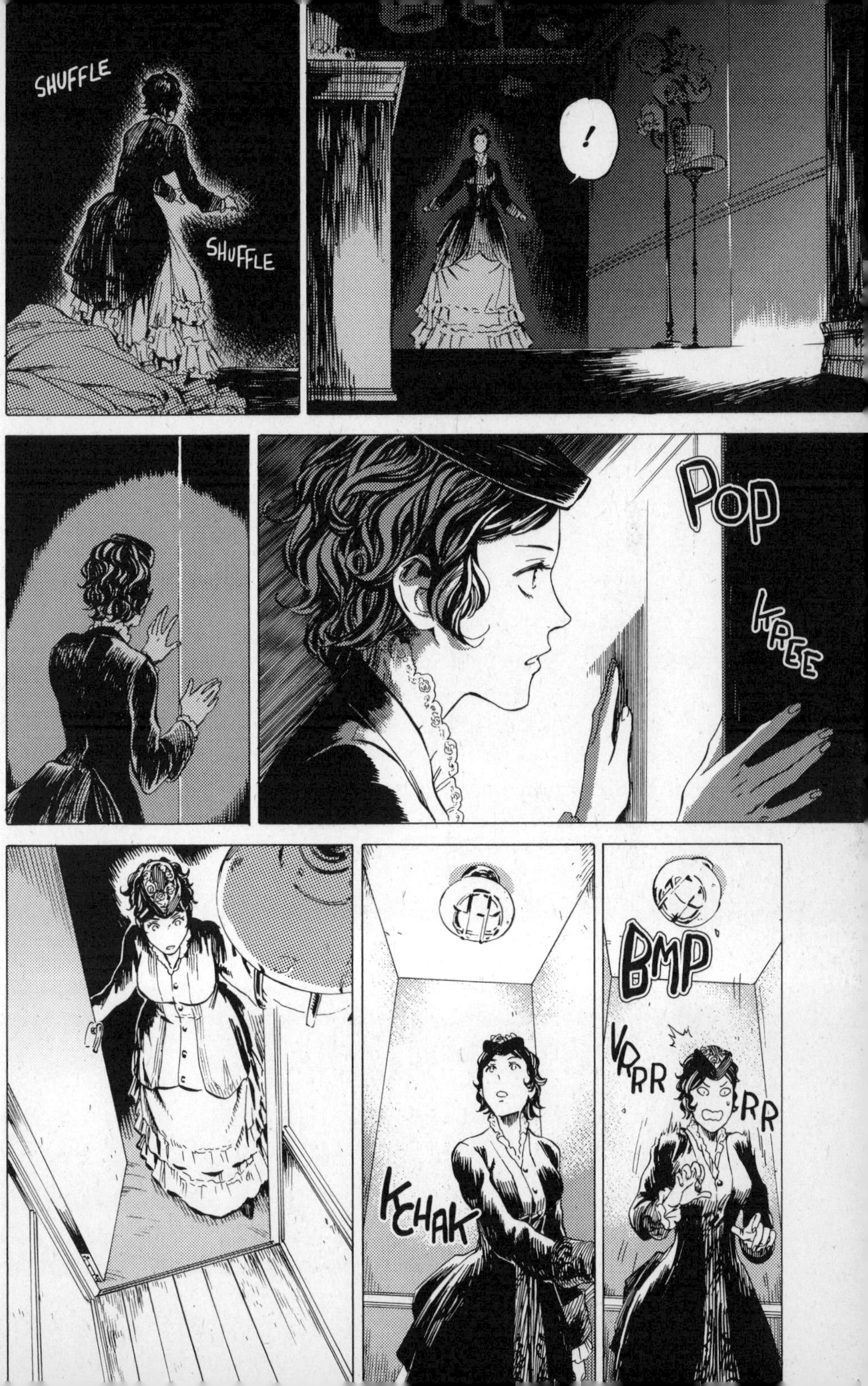
SHUFFLE
SHUFFLE
!
POP
KREE
KCHAK
BMP
VRRR
RR

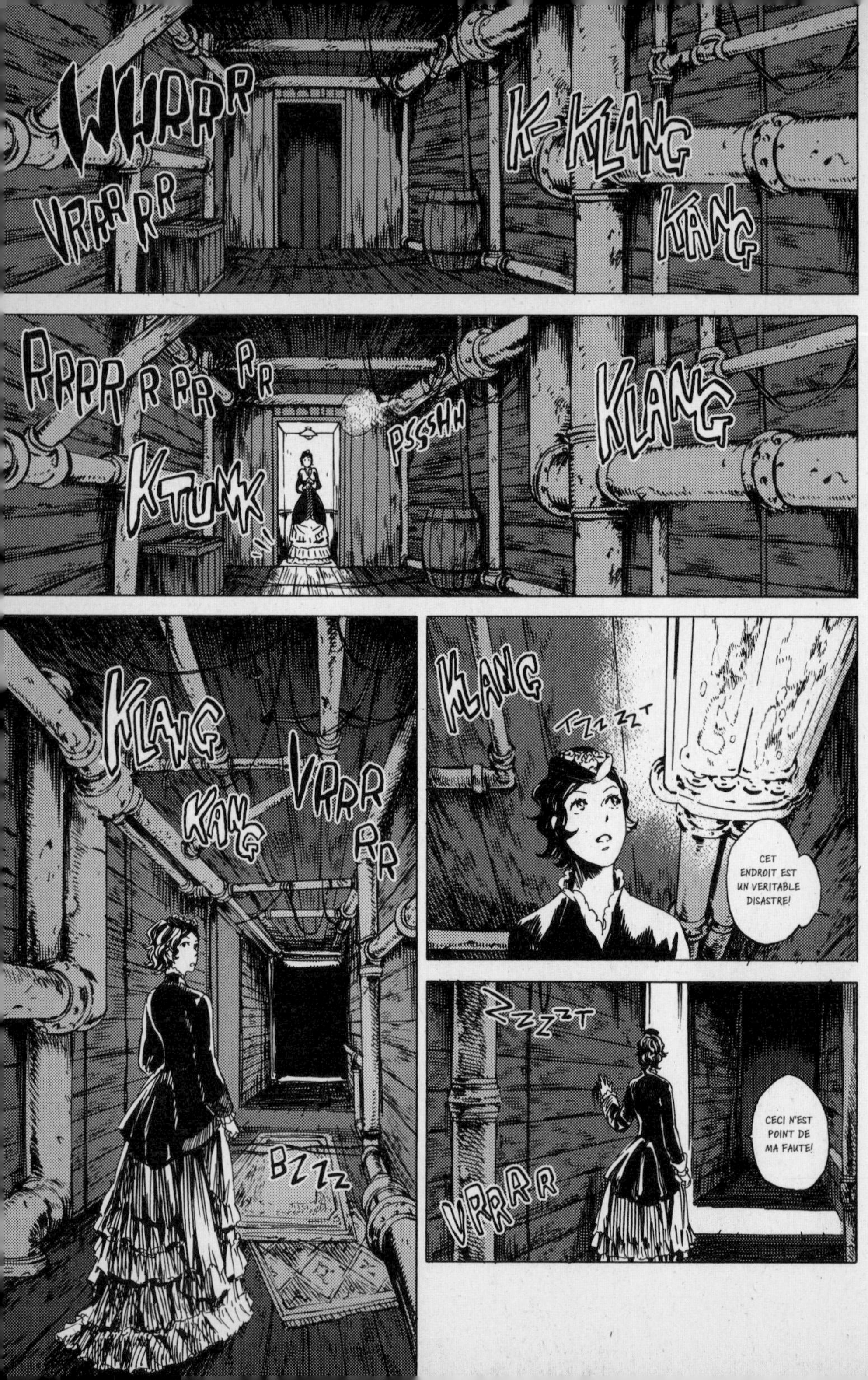
WHRRR
VRRRRR
K-KLANG
KANG
RRRRR RRR RR
KTUNK
PSSSHH
KLANG
KLANG
KANG
VRRR
RR
BZZZ
KLANG
TZZZZT
CET ENDROIT EST UN VERITABLE DISASTRE!
ZZZZT
CECI N'EST POINT DE MA FAUTE!
VRRRR

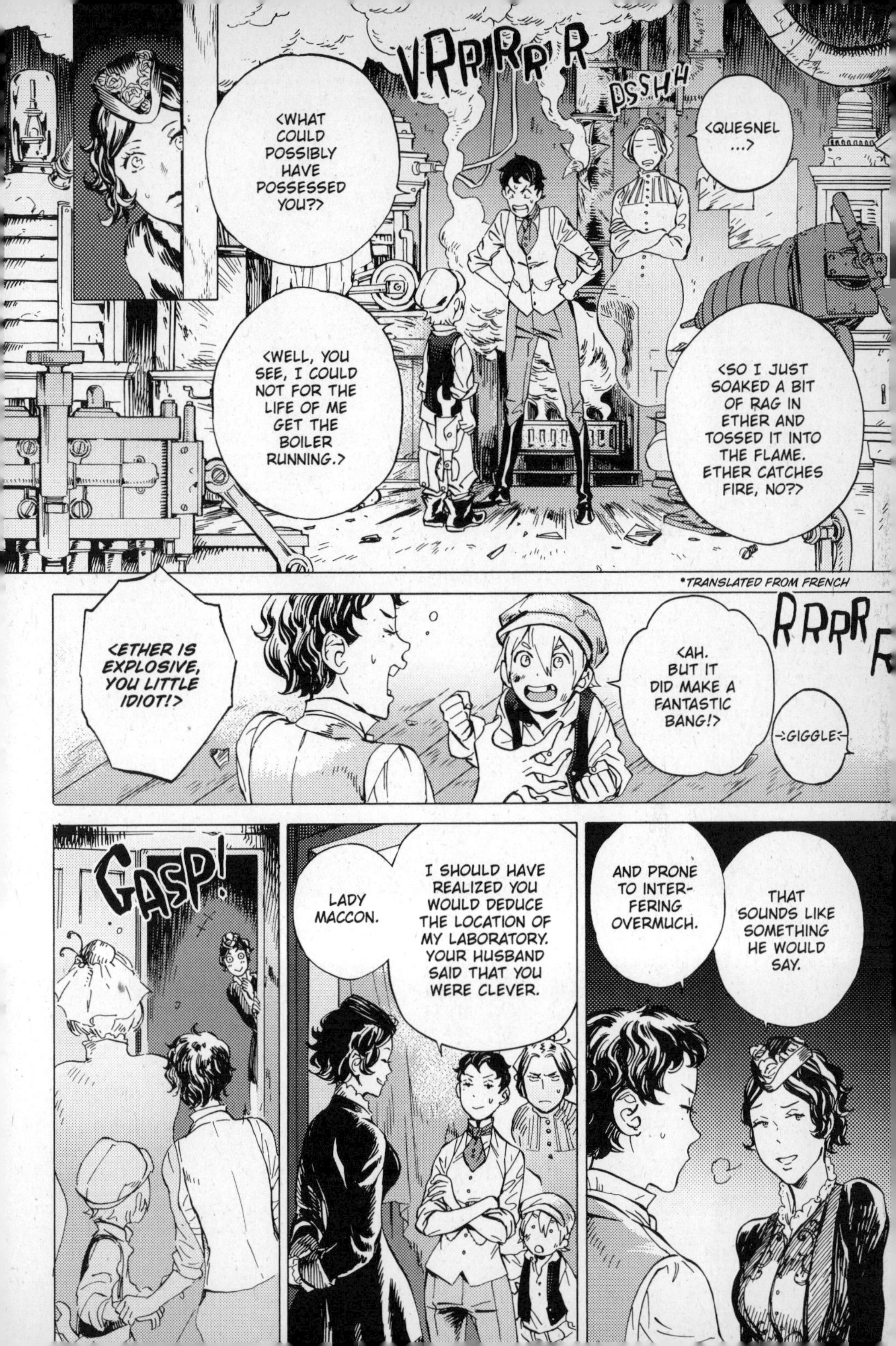
VRRRRR R
PSSHH
<WHAT COULD POSSIBLY HAVE POSSESSED YOU?>
<QUESNEL ...>
<WELL, YOU SEE, I COULD NOT FOR THE LIFE OF ME GET THE BOILER RUNNING.>
<SO I JUST SOAKED A BIT OF RAG IN ETHER AND TOSSED IT INTO THE FLAME. ETHER CATCHES FIRE, NO?>
*TRANSLATED FROM FRENCH
<ETHER IS EXPLOSIVE, YOU LITTLE IDIOT!>
<AH. BUT IT DID MAKE A FANTASTIC BANG!>
RRRR R
GIGGLE
GASP!
LADY MACCON.
I SHOULD HAVE REALIZED YOU WOULD DEDUCE THE LOCATION OF MY LABORATORY. YOUR HUSBAND SAID THAT YOU WERE CLEVER.
AND PRONE TO INTER-FERING OVERMUCH.
THAT SOUNDS LIKE SOMETHING HE WOULD SAY.

RR VRR RR B RRWHRR

HOW DO YOU DO? LADY MACCON, AT YOUR SERVICE.

QUESNEL LEFOUX.

THIS IS ALEXIA MACCON, LADY WOOLSEY.

SHE IS ALSO MUHJAH TO THE QUEEN.

YOU ARE ZE MUHJAH? NIECE, YOU ALLOW AN EXORCIST INTO MY VICINITY?

UNCARING, THOUGHTLESS CHILD! YOU ARE ZE WORSE THAN YOUR SON.

AUNT BEATRICE, DO NOT GET SO EMOTIONAL.

LADY MACCON CAN ONLY KILL YOU IF SHE TOUCHES YOUR BODY, AND ONLY I KNOW WHERE THAT IS KEPT.

I PREFER NOT TO PERFORM EXORCISMS IN ANY EVENT. DECOMPOSING FLESH IS VERY SQUISHY.

OH, WELL, THANK YOU FOR THAT.

SO, IN WHAT CAPACITY DID MY HUSBAND SEE FIT TO INFORM YOU OF MY NATURE AND MY POSITION?

AS ALPHA, AS EARL, OR AS THE HEAD OF B.U.R. INVESTIGA-TIONS?

WHRRR

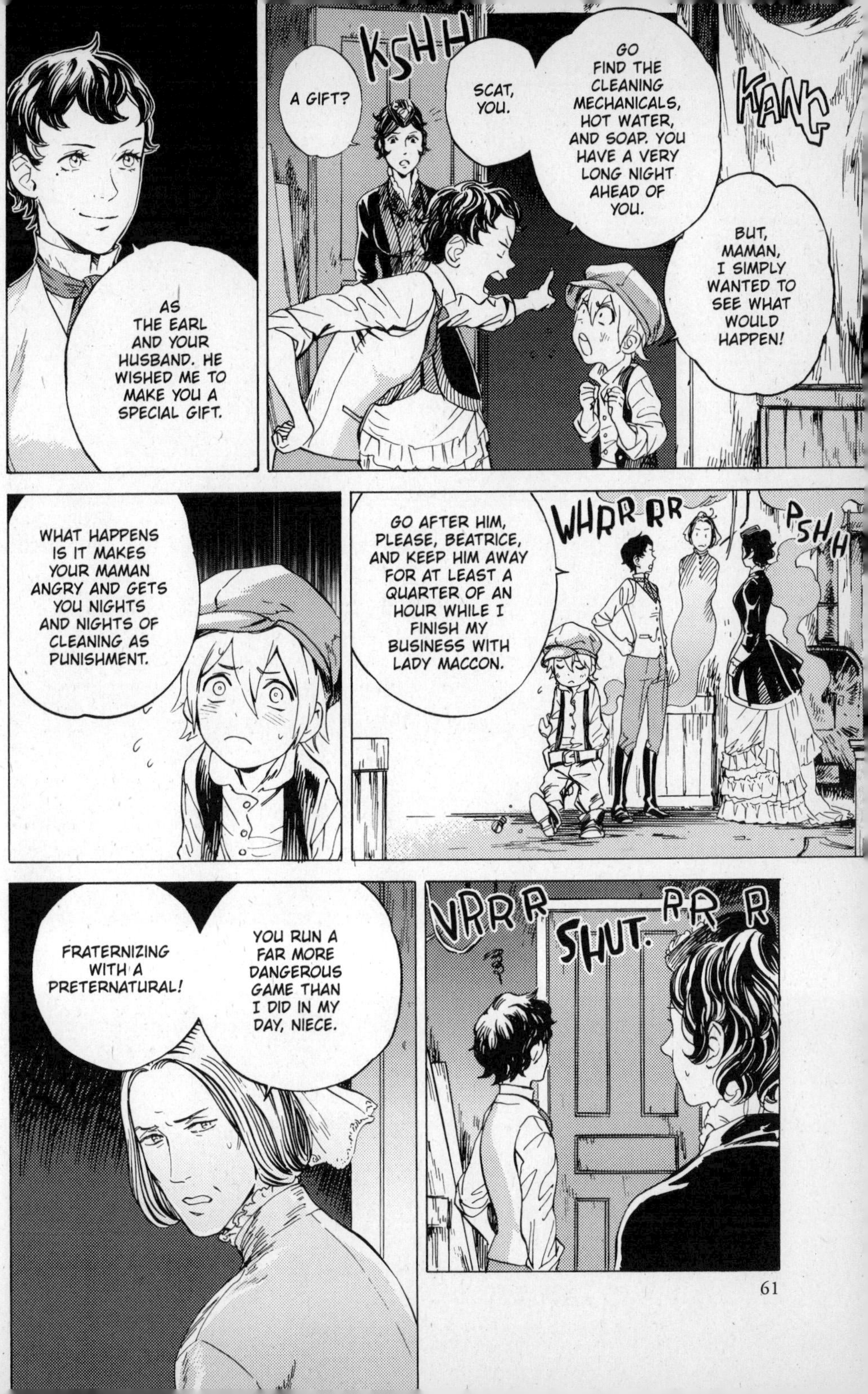
AS THE EARL AND YOUR HUSBAND. HE WISHED ME TO MAKE YOU A SPECIAL GIFT.
A GIFT?
KSHH
SCAT, YOU.
GO FIND THE CLEANING MECHANICALS, HOT WATER, AND SOAP. YOU HAVE A VERY LONG NIGHT AHEAD OF YOU.
KANG
BUT, MAMAN, I SIMPLY WANTED TO SEE WHAT WOULD HAPPEN!
WHAT HAPPENS IS IT MAKES YOUR MAMAN ANGRY AND GETS YOU NIGHTS AND NIGHTS OF CLEANING AS PUNISHMENT.
GO AFTER HIM, PLEASE, BEATRICE, AND KEEP HIM AWAY FOR AT LEAST A QUARTER OF AN HOUR WHILE I FINISH MY BUSINESS WITH LADY MACCON.
WHRRRR
PSHH
FRATERNIZING WITH A PRETERNATURAL!
YOU RUN A FAR MORE DANGEROUS GAME THAN I DID IN MY DAY, NIECE.
VRRRRRR
SHUT.

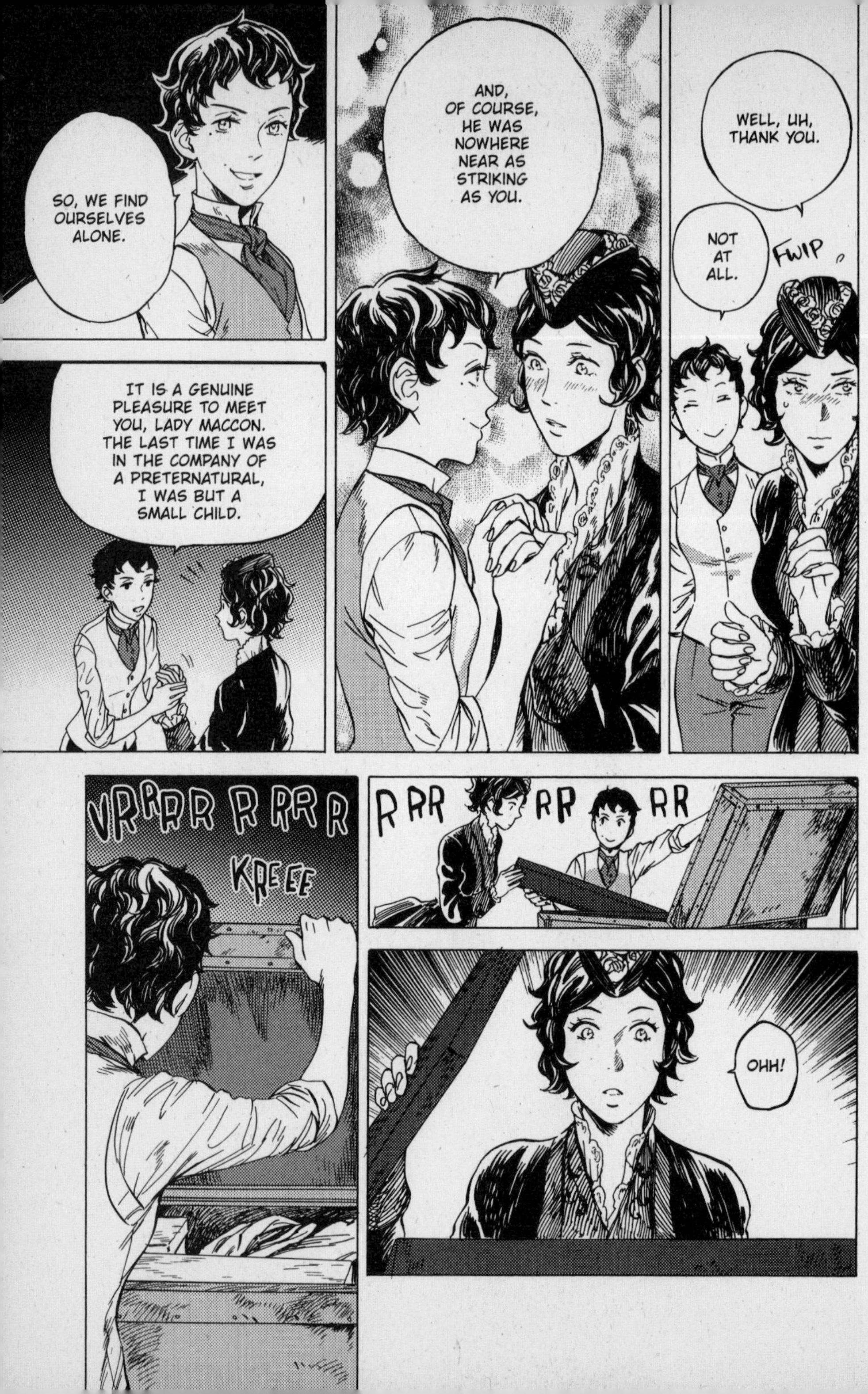

SO, WE FIND OURSELVES ALONE.
IT IS A GENUINE PLEASURE TO MEET YOU, LADY MACCON. THE LAST TIME I WAS IN THE COMPANY OF A PRETERNATURAL, I WAS BUT A SMALL CHILD.
AND, OF COURSE, HE WAS NOWHERE NEAR AS STRIKING AS YOU.
WELL, UH, THANK YOU.
NOT AT ALL.
FWIP
VRRRR R RRR R
KREEE
RRR
RR
RR
OHH!

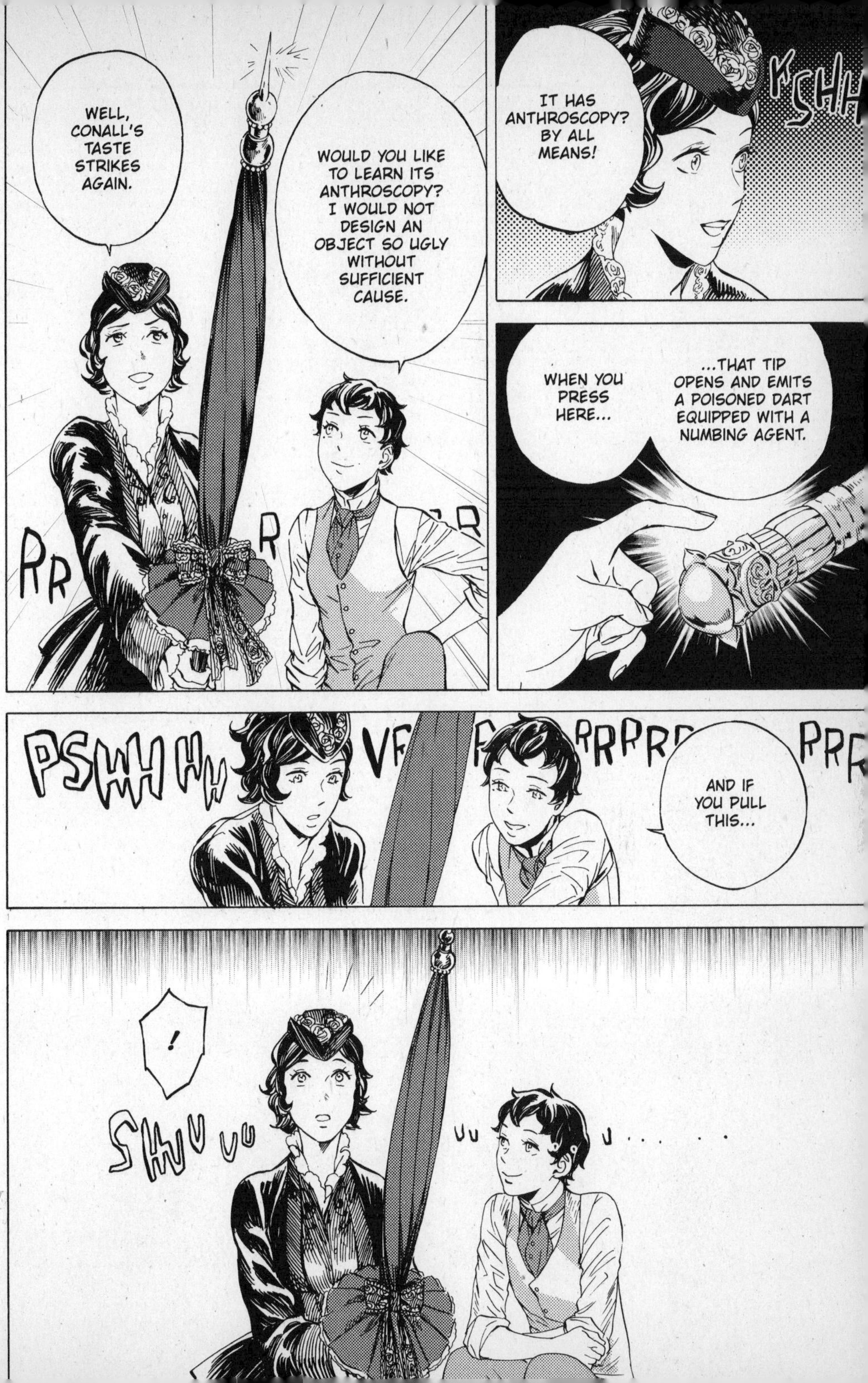
WELL, CONALL'S TASTE STRIKES AGAIN.
WOULD YOU LIKE TO LEARN ITS ANTHROSCOPY? I WOULD NOT DESIGN AN OBJECT SO UGLY WITHOUT SUFFICIENT CAUSE.
RR
R
IT HAS ANTHROSCOPY? BY ALL MEANS!
KSHH
WHEN YOU PRESS HERE...
...THAT TIP OPENS AND EMITS A POISONED DART EQUIPPED WITH A NUMBING AGENT.
PSHHHH
AND IF YOU PULL THIS...
!
SHUUU...

WHAT HAPPENED?

THE NODULE THERE EMITTED A MAGNETIC DISRUPTION FIELD.

IF YOU NEED TO SEIZE UP A STEAM ENGINE FOR ANY REASON, THIS WILL PROBABLY DO THE TRICK, BUT ONLY FOR A BRIEF AMOUNT OF TIME.

KTCH VRRRR RR WHRRR

REMARK-ABLE!

RR RRRRR

YOU CAN ALSO TURN IT THUS...

PAF

PSHHHH

...AND THE RIB CAPS WILL OPEN AND EMIT A FINE MIST. TWIST THE DIAL HERE, AND A MIXTURE OF LAPIS SOLARIS DILUTED IN SULFURIC ACID WILL SPRAY OUT.

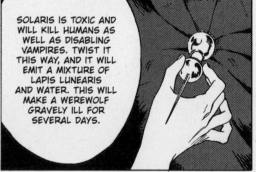

SOLARIS IS TOXIC AND WILL KILL HUMANS AS WELL AS DISABLING VAMPIRES. TWIST IT THIS WAY, AND IT WILL EMIT A MIXTURE OF LAPIS LUNEARIS AND WATER. THIS WILL MAKE A WEREWOLF GRAVELY ILL FOR SEVERAL DAYS.

TWIST IT FURTHER, AND IT WILL EMIT BOTH.

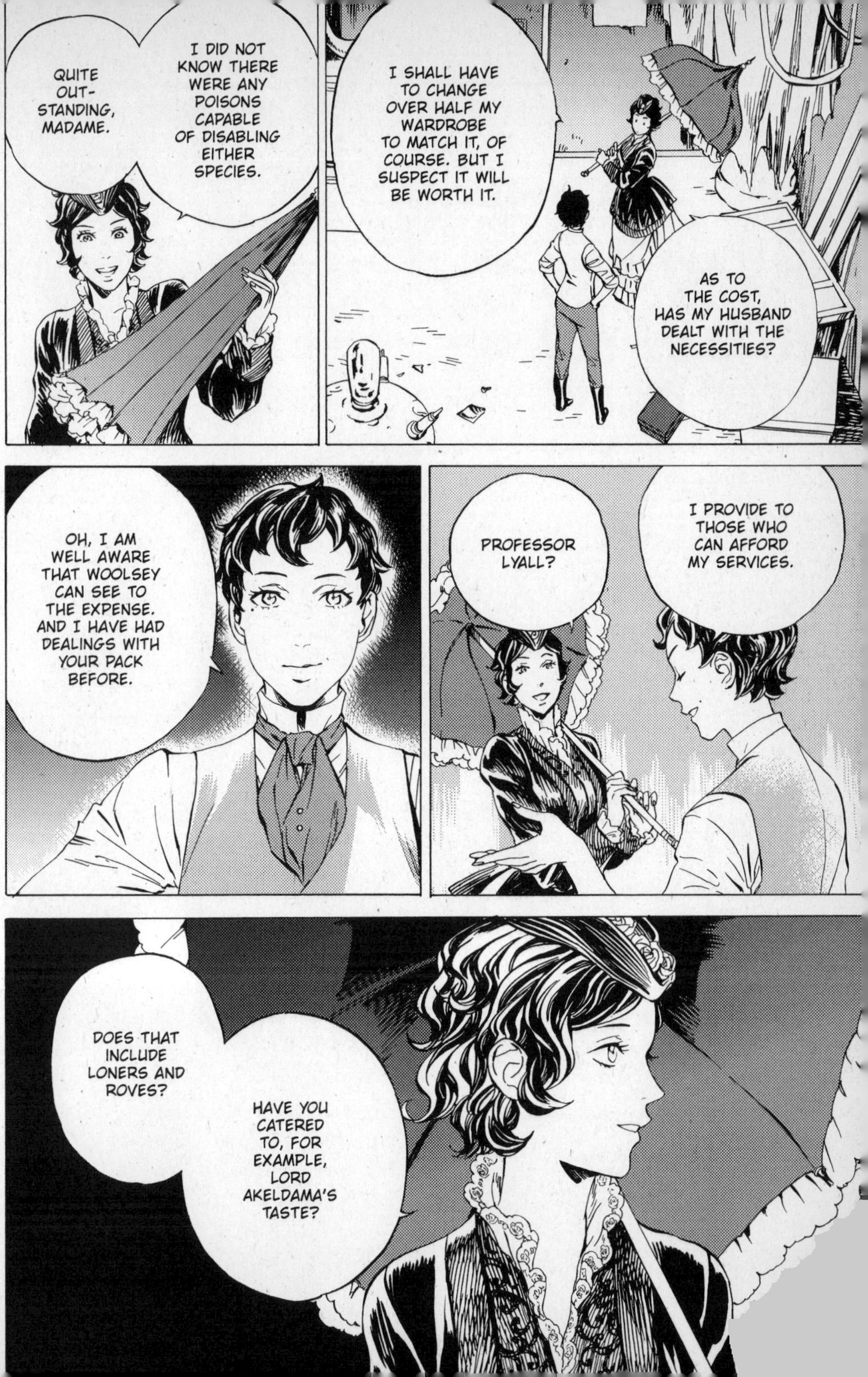
QUITE OUT-STANDING, MADAME.
I DID NOT KNOW THERE WERE ANY POISONS CAPABLE OF DISABLING EITHER SPECIES.
I SHALL HAVE TO CHANGE OVER HALF MY WARDROBE TO MATCH IT, OF COURSE. BUT I SUSPECT IT WILL BE WORTH IT.
AS TO THE COST, HAS MY HUSBAND DEALT WITH THE NECESSITIES?
OH, I AM WELL AWARE THAT WOOLSEY CAN SEE TO THE EXPENSE. AND I HAVE HAD DEALINGS WITH YOUR PACK BEFORE.
PROFESSOR LYALL?
I PROVIDE TO THOSE WHO CAN AFFORD MY SERVICES.
DOES THAT INCLUDE LONERS AND ROVES?
HAVE YOU CATERED TO, FOR EXAMPLE, LORD AKELDAMA'S TASTE?

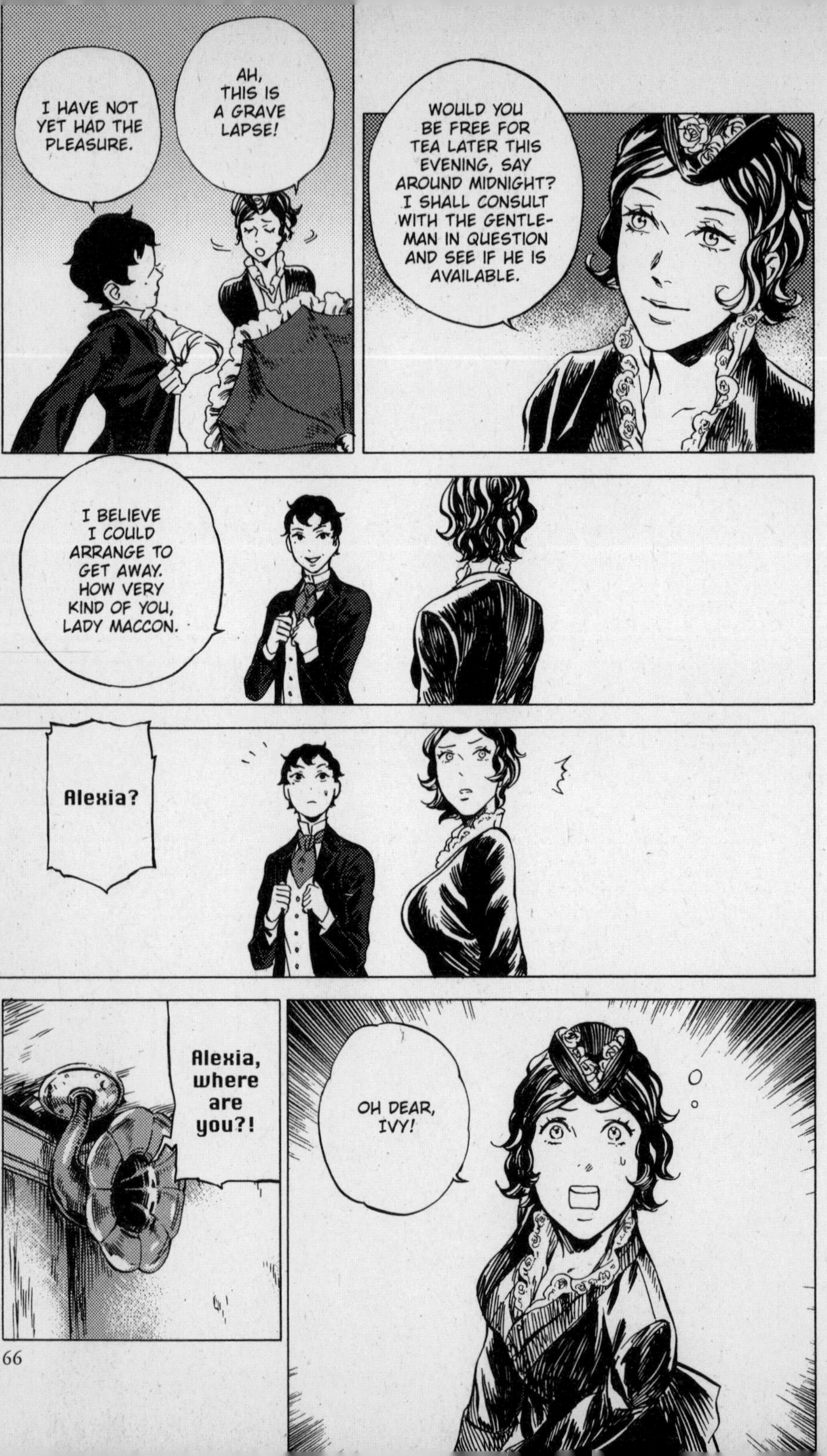
I HAVE NOT YET HAD THE PLEASURE.
AH, THIS IS A GRAVE LAPSE!
WOULD YOU BE FREE FOR TEA LATER THIS EVENING, SAY AROUND MIDNIGHT? I SHALL CONSULT WITH THE GENTLEMAN IN QUESTION AND SEE IF HE IS AVAILABLE.
I BELIEVE I COULD ARRANGE TO GET AWAY. HOW VERY KIND OF YOU, LADY MACCON.
Alexia?
Alexia, where are you?!
OH DEAR, IVY!

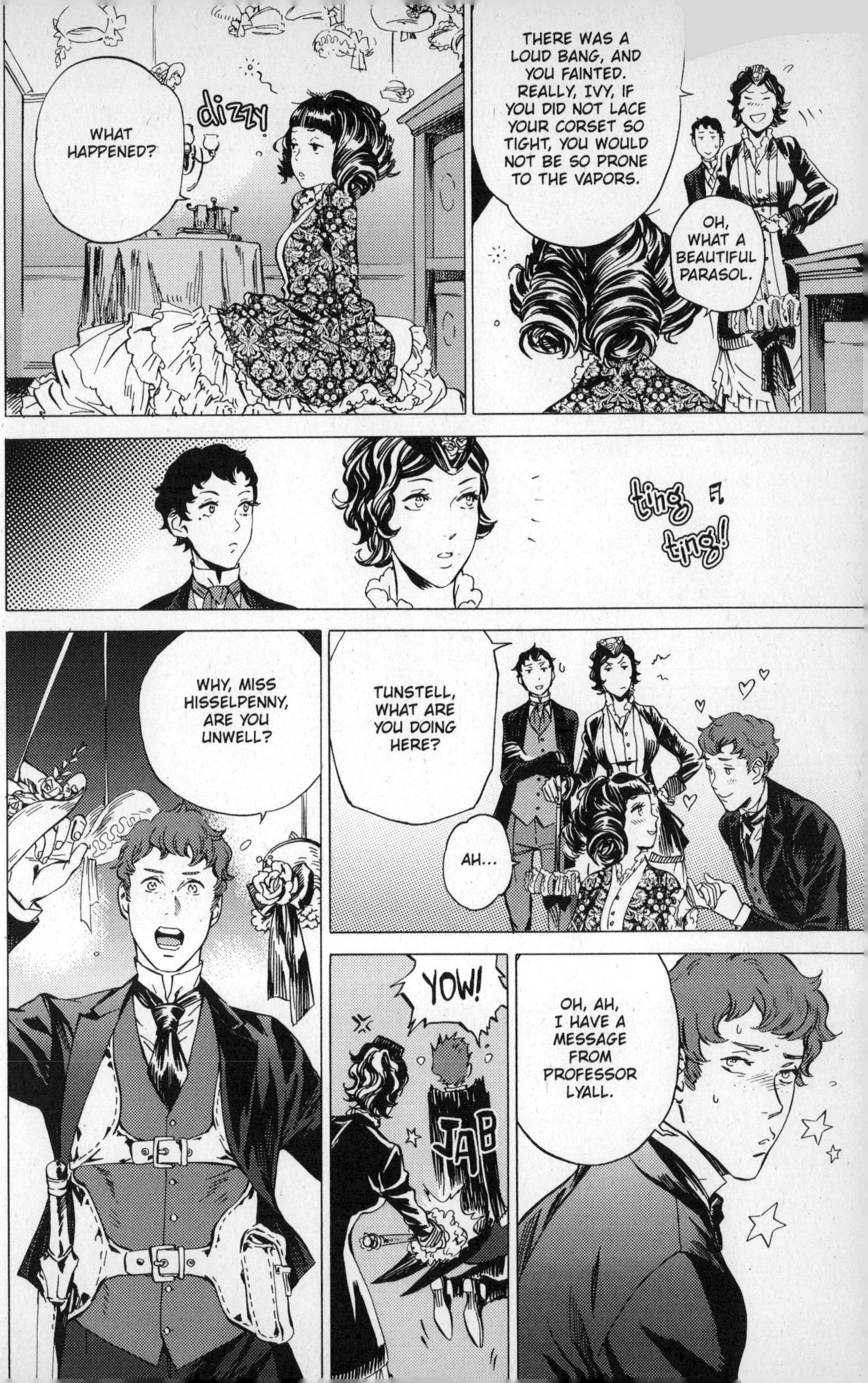
dizzy
WHAT HAPPENED?
THERE WAS A LOUD BANG, AND YOU FAINTED. REALLY, IVY, IF YOU DID NOT LACE YOUR CORSET SO TIGHT, YOU WOULD NOT BE SO PRONE TO THE VAPORS.
OH, WHAT A BEAUTIFUL PARASOL.
ting ting!
WHY, MISS HISSELPENNY, ARE YOU UNWELL?
TUNSTELL, WHAT ARE YOU DOING HERE?
AH...
YOW!
JAB
OH, AH, I HAVE A MESSAGE FROM PROFESSOR LYALL.

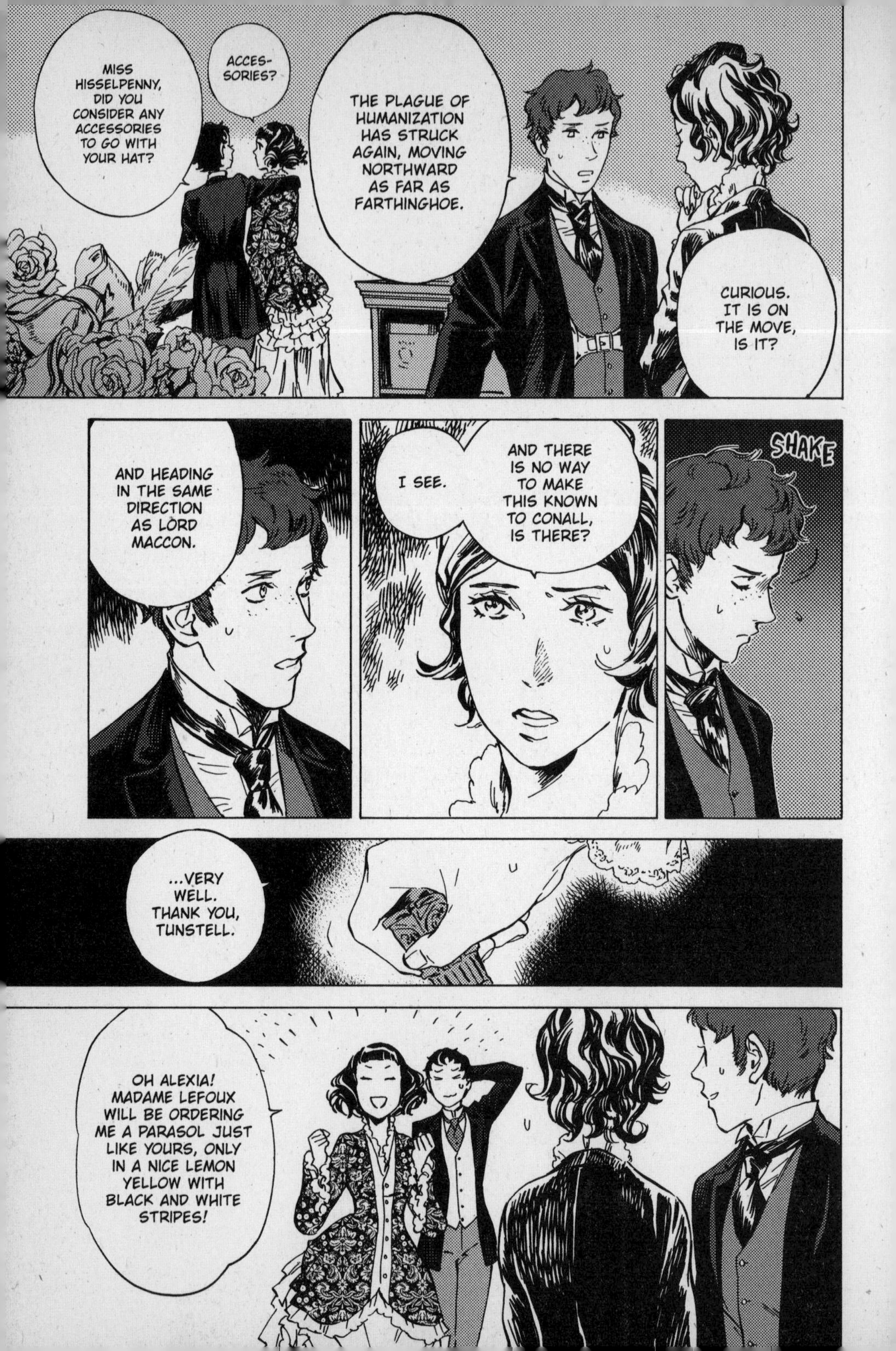
MISS HISSELPENNY, DID YOU CONSIDER ANY ACCESSORIES TO GO WITH YOUR HAT?
ACCES-SORIES?
THE PLAGUE OF HUMANIZATION HAS STRUCK AGAIN, MOVING NORTHWARD AS FAR AS FARTHINGHOE.
CURIOUS. IT IS ON THE MOVE, IS IT?
AND HEADING IN THE SAME DIRECTION AS LORD MACCON.
I SEE.
AND THERE IS NO WAY TO MAKE THIS KNOWN TO CONALL, IS THERE?
SHAKE
...VERY WELL. THANK YOU, TUNSTELL.
OH ALEXIA! MADAME LEFOUX WILL BE ORDERING ME A PARASOL JUST LIKE YOURS, ONLY IN A NICE LEMON YELLOW WITH BLACK AND WHITE STRIPES!

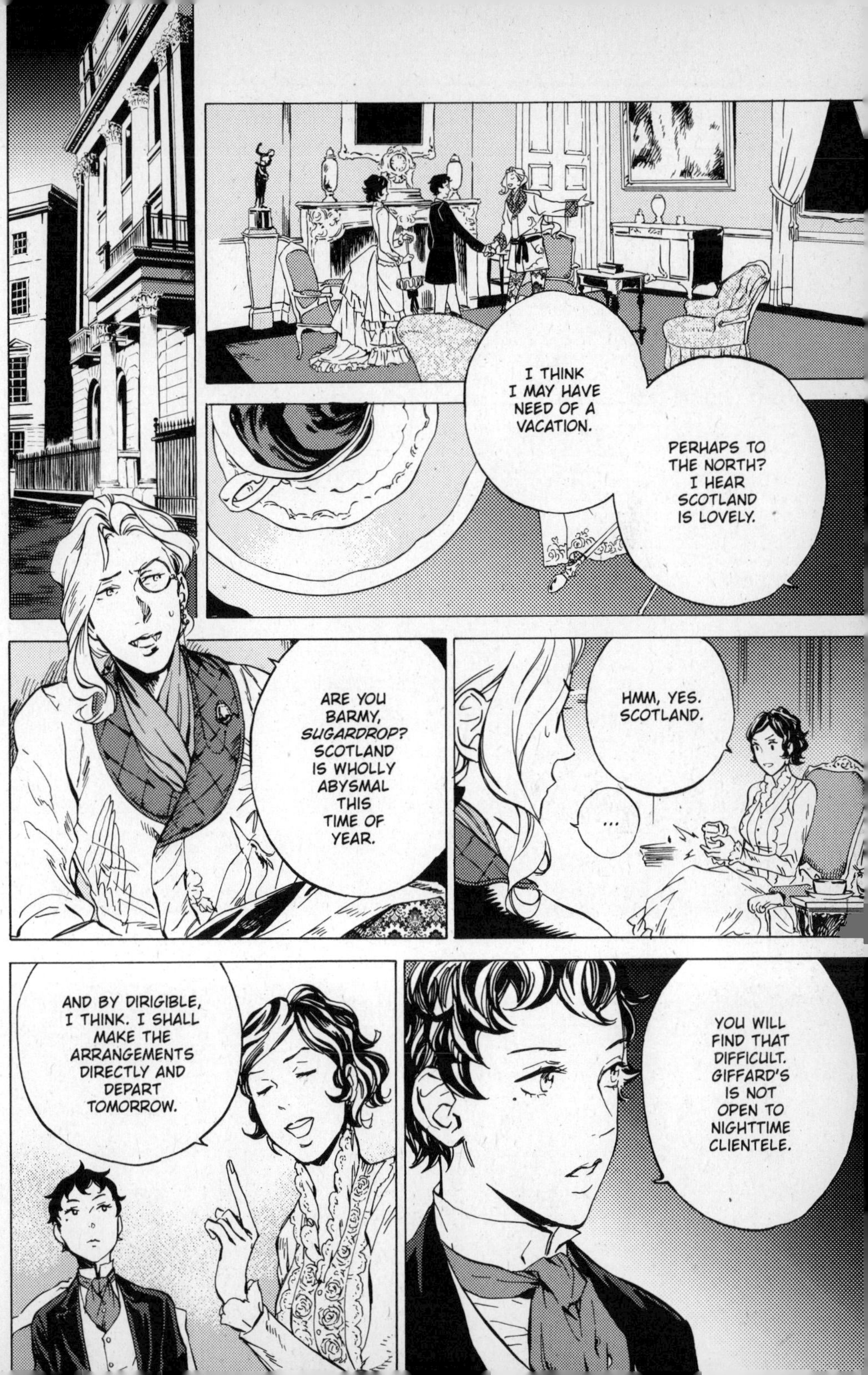

I THINK I MAY HAVE NEED OF A VACATION.
PERHAPS TO THE NORTH? I HEAR SCOTLAND IS LOVELY.
ARE YOU BARMY, *SUGARDROP?* SCOTLAND IS WHOLLY ABYSMAL THIS TIME OF YEAR.
HMM, YES. SCOTLAND.
...
AND BY DIRIGIBLE, I THINK. I SHALL MAKE THE ARRANGEMENTS DIRECTLY AND DEPART TOMORROW.
YOU WILL FIND THAT DIFFICULT. GIFFARD'S IS NOT OPEN TO NIGHTTIME CLIENTELE.

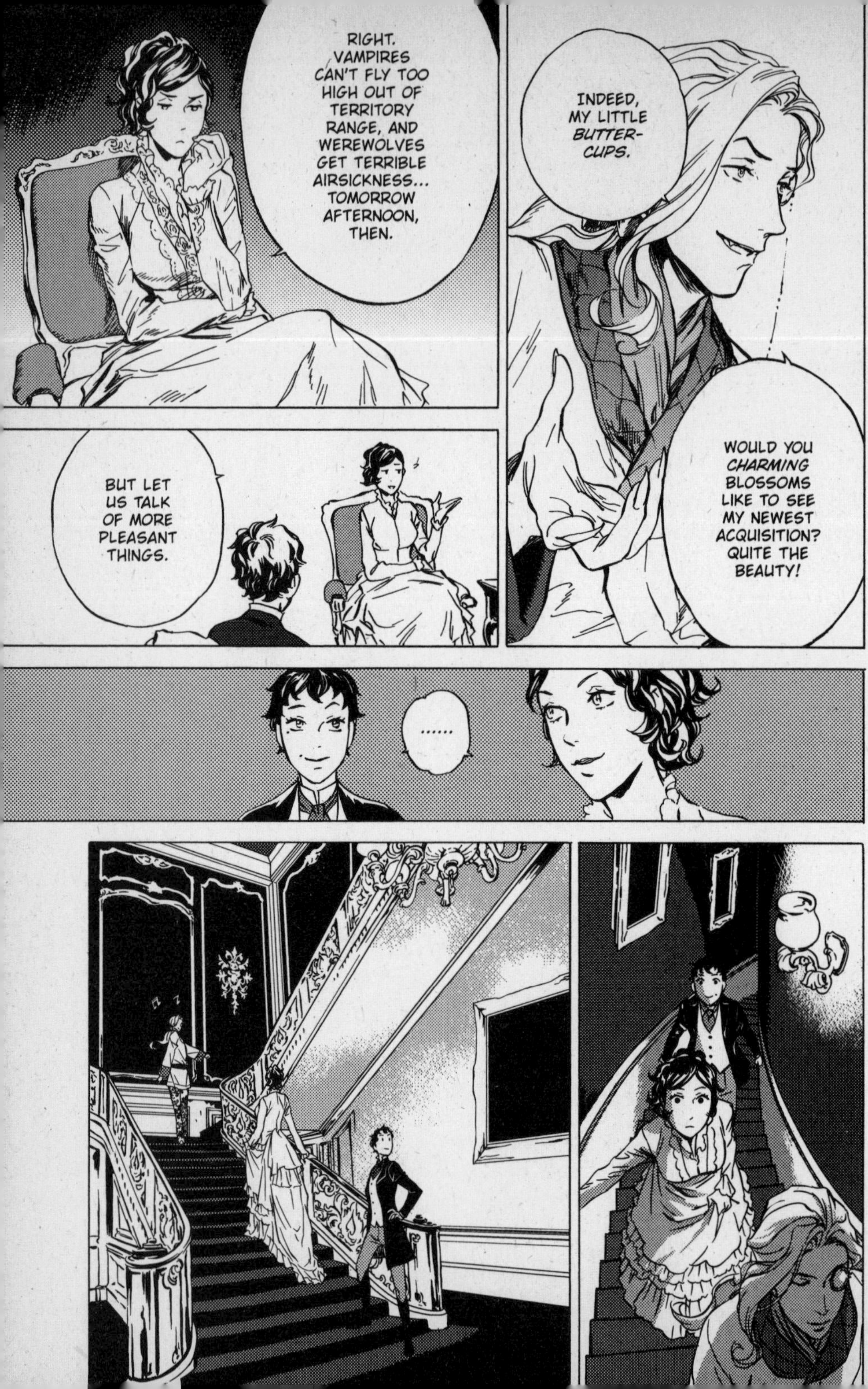
RIGHT. VAMPIRES CAN'T FLY TOO HIGH OUT OF TERRITORY RANGE, AND WEREWOLVES GET TERRIBLE AIRSICKNESS... TOMORROW AFTERNOON, THEN.
BUT LET US TALK OF MORE PLEASANT THINGS.
INDEED, MY LITTLE *BUTTER-CUPS.*
WOULD YOU *CHARMING* BLOSSOMS LIKE TO SEE MY NEWEST ACQUISITION? QUITE THE BEAUTY!
......

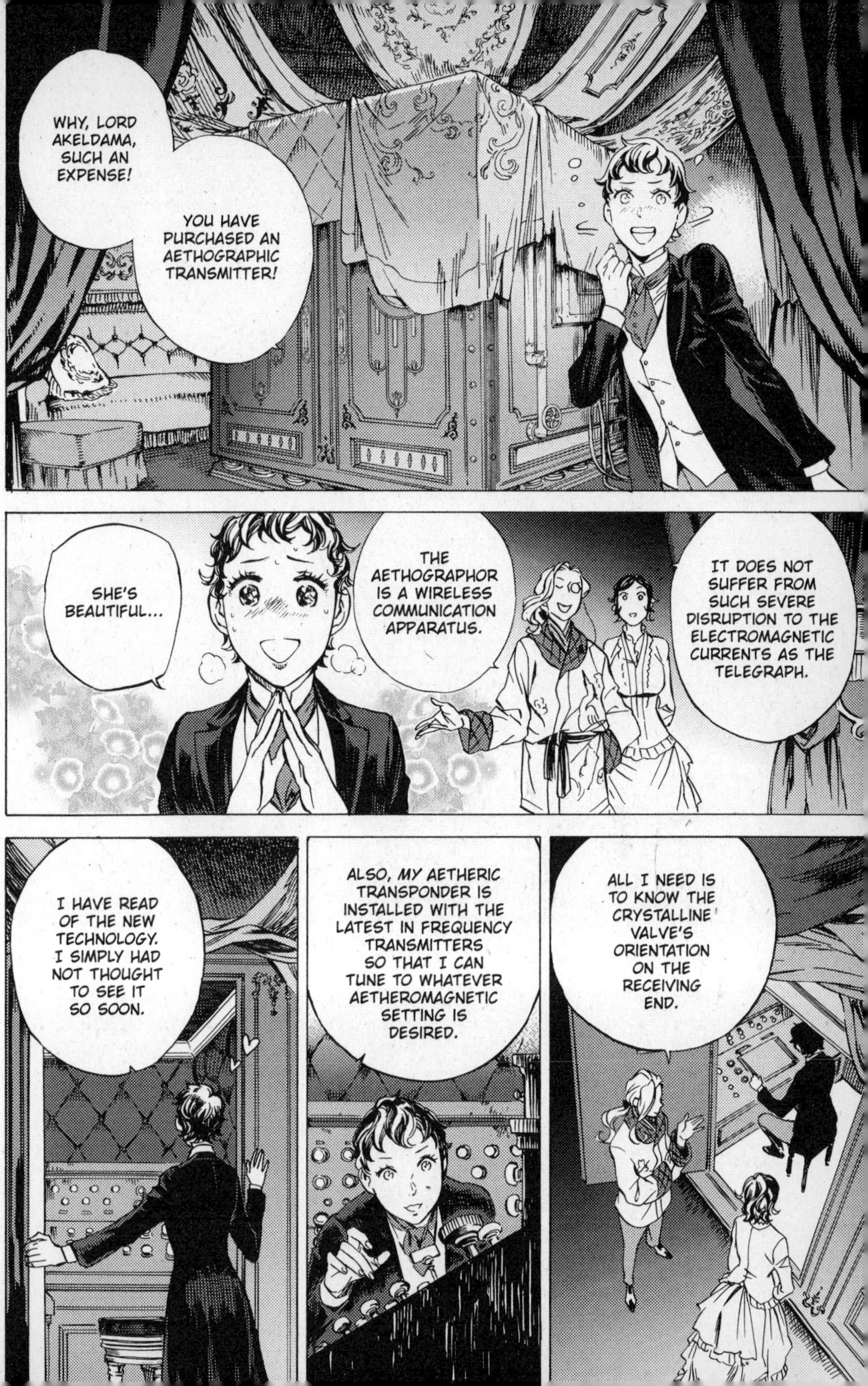
WHY, LORD AKELDAMA, SUCH AN EXPENSE!
YOU HAVE PURCHASED AN AETHOGRAPHIC TRANSMITTER!
SHE'S BEAUTIFUL...
THE AETHOGRAPHOR IS A WIRELESS COMMUNICATION APPARATUS.
IT DOES NOT SUFFER FROM SUCH SEVERE DISRUPTION TO THE ELECTROMAGNETIC CURRENTS AS THE TELEGRAPH.
I HAVE READ OF THE NEW TECHNOLOGY. I SIMPLY HAD NOT THOUGHT TO SEE IT SO SOON.
ALSO, *MY* AETHERIC TRANSPONDER IS INSTALLED WITH THE LATEST IN FREQUENCY TRANSMITTERS SO THAT I CAN TUNE TO WHATEVER AETHEROMAGNETIC SETTING IS DESIRED.
ALL I NEED IS TO KNOW THE CRYSTALLINE VALVE'S ORIENTATION ON THE RECEIVING END.

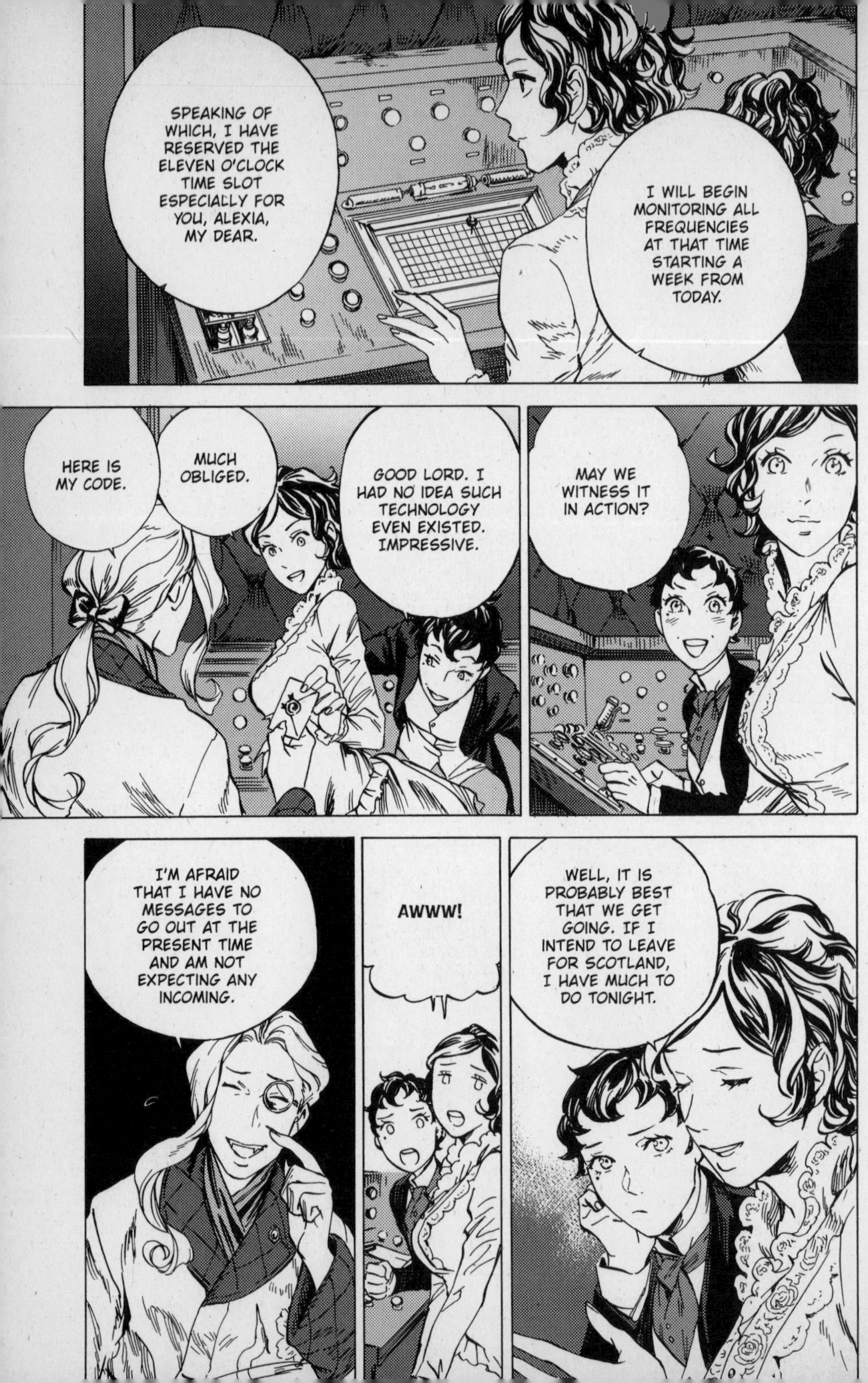
SPEAKING OF WHICH, I HAVE RESERVED THE ELEVEN O'CLOCK TIME SLOT ESPECIALLY FOR YOU, ALEXIA, MY DEAR.
I WILL BEGIN MONITORING ALL FREQUENCIES AT THAT TIME STARTING A WEEK FROM TODAY.
HERE IS MY CODE.
MUCH OBLIGED.
GOOD LORD. I HAD NO IDEA SUCH TECHNOLOGY EVEN EXISTED. IMPRESSIVE.
MAY WE WITNESS IT IN ACTION?
I'M AFRAID THAT I HAVE NO MESSAGES TO GO OUT AT THE PRESENT TIME AND AM NOT EXPECTING ANY INCOMING.
AWWW!
WELL, IT IS PROBABLY BEST THAT WE GET GOING. IF I INTEND TO LEAVE FOR SCOTLAND, I HAVE MUCH TO DO TONIGHT.

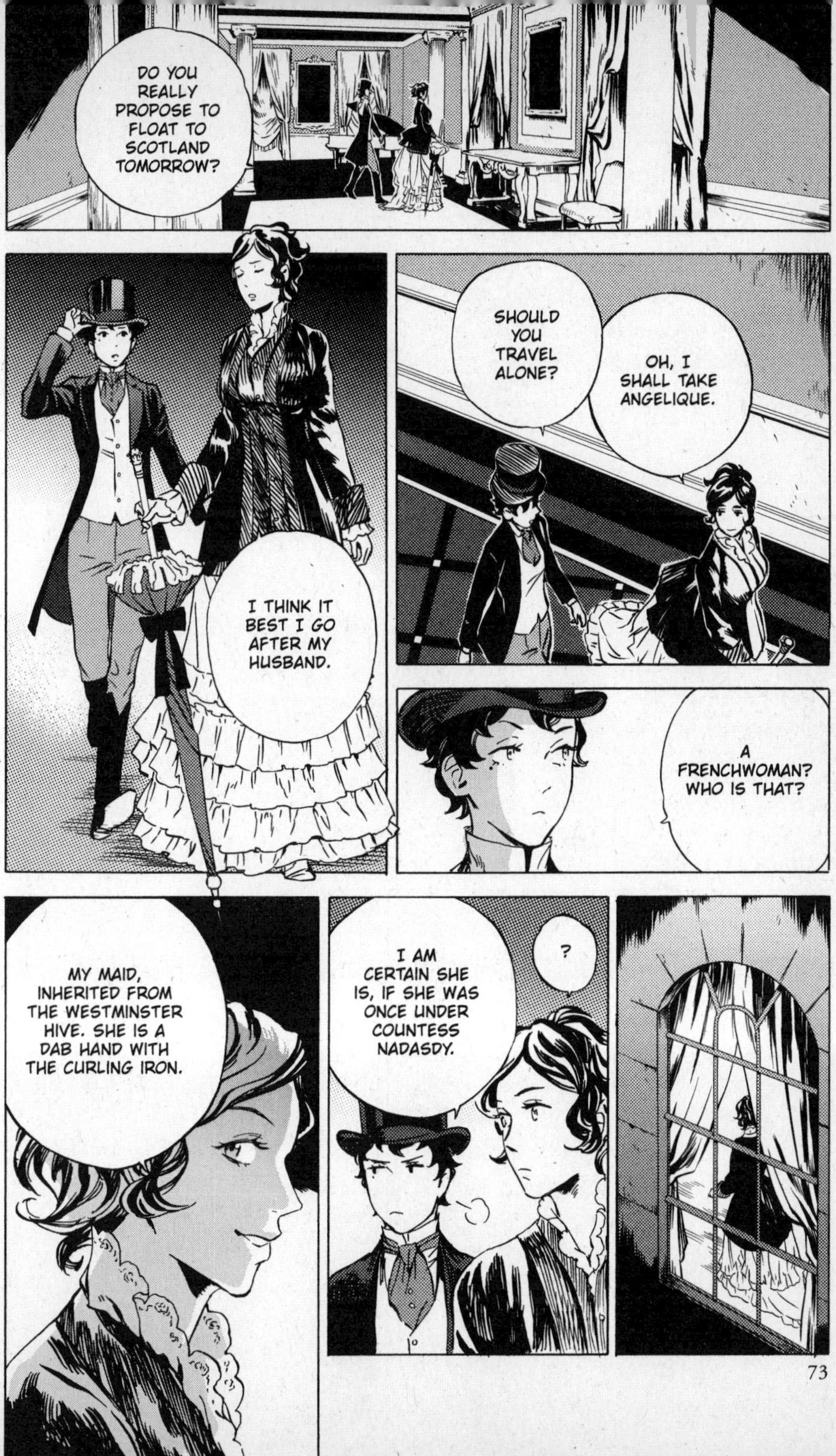
DO YOU REALLY PROPOSE TO FLOAT TO SCOTLAND TOMORROW?
I THINK IT BEST I GO AFTER MY HUSBAND.
SHOULD YOU TRAVEL ALONE?
OH, I SHALL TAKE ANGELIQUE.
A FRENCHWOMAN? WHO IS THAT?
MY MAID, INHERITED FROM THE WESTMINSTER HIVE. SHE IS A DAB HAND WITH THE CURLING IRON.
I AM CERTAIN SHE IS, IF SHE WAS ONCE UNDER COUNTESS NADASDY.
?

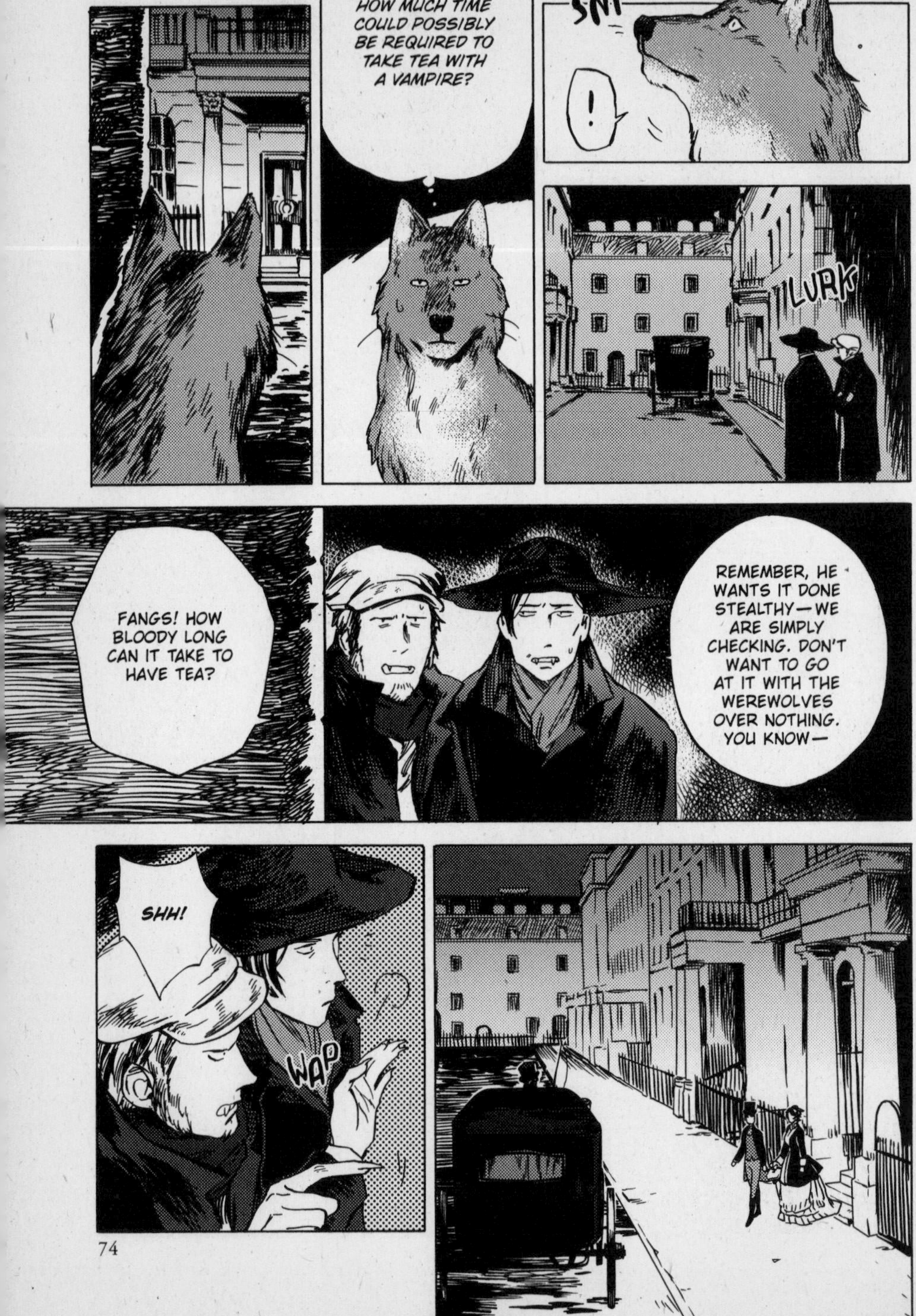
HOW MUCH TIME COULD POSSIBLY BE REQUIRED TO TAKE TEA WITH A VAMPIRE?
SNF
!
LURK
FANGS! HOW BLOODY LONG CAN IT TAKE TO HAVE TEA?
REMEMBER, HE WANTS IT DONE STEALTHY—WE ARE SIMPLY CHECKING. DON'T WANT TO GO AT IT WITH THE WEREWOLVES OVER NOTHING. YOU KNOW—
SHH!
WAP

CLIP
CLOP

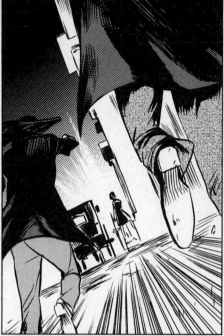

SOULLESS

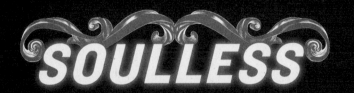

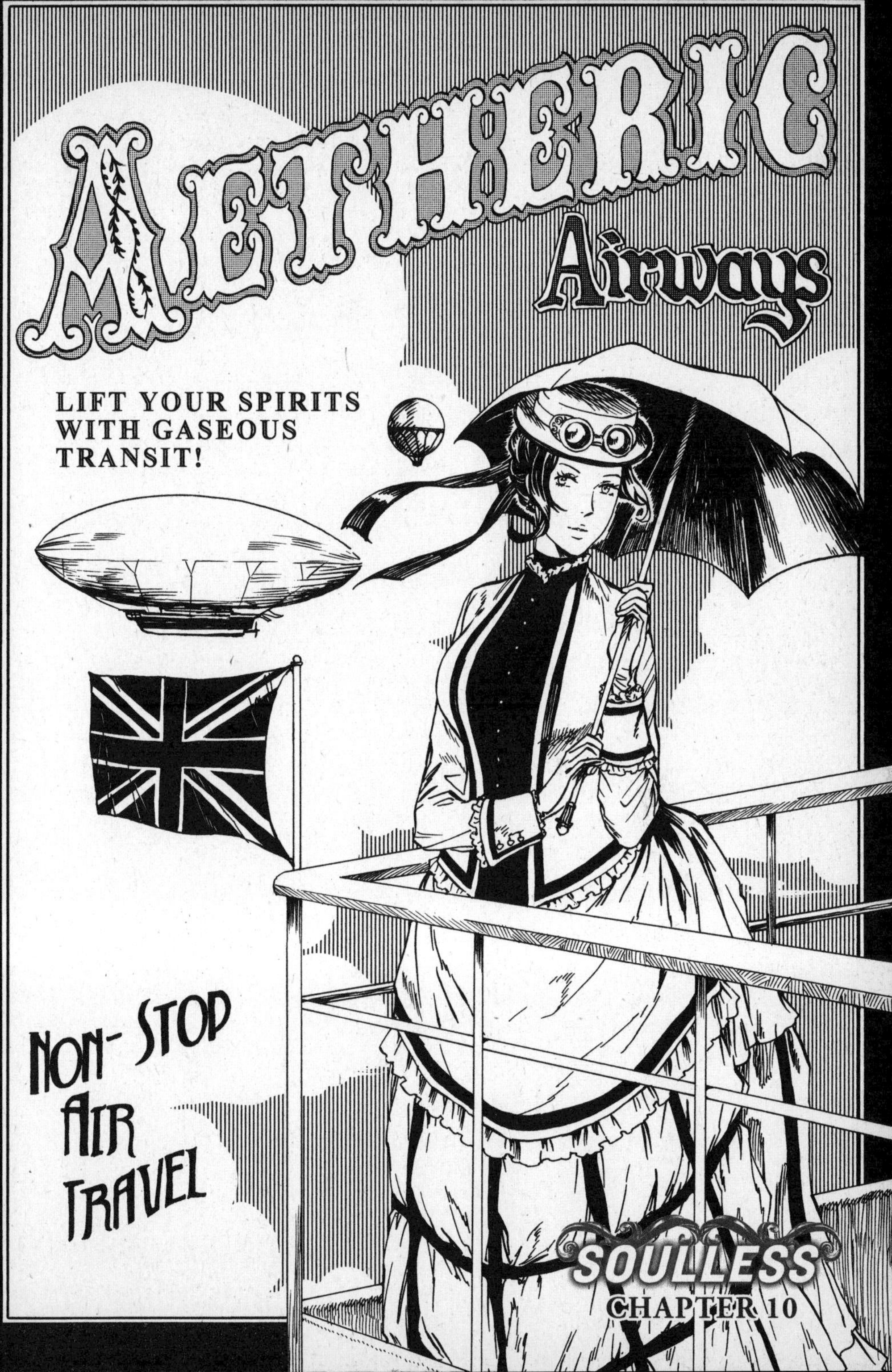

AETHERIC
Airways
LIFT YOUR SPIRITS WITH GASEOUS TRANSIT!
NON-STOP AIR TRAVEL
SOULLESS
CHAPTER 10

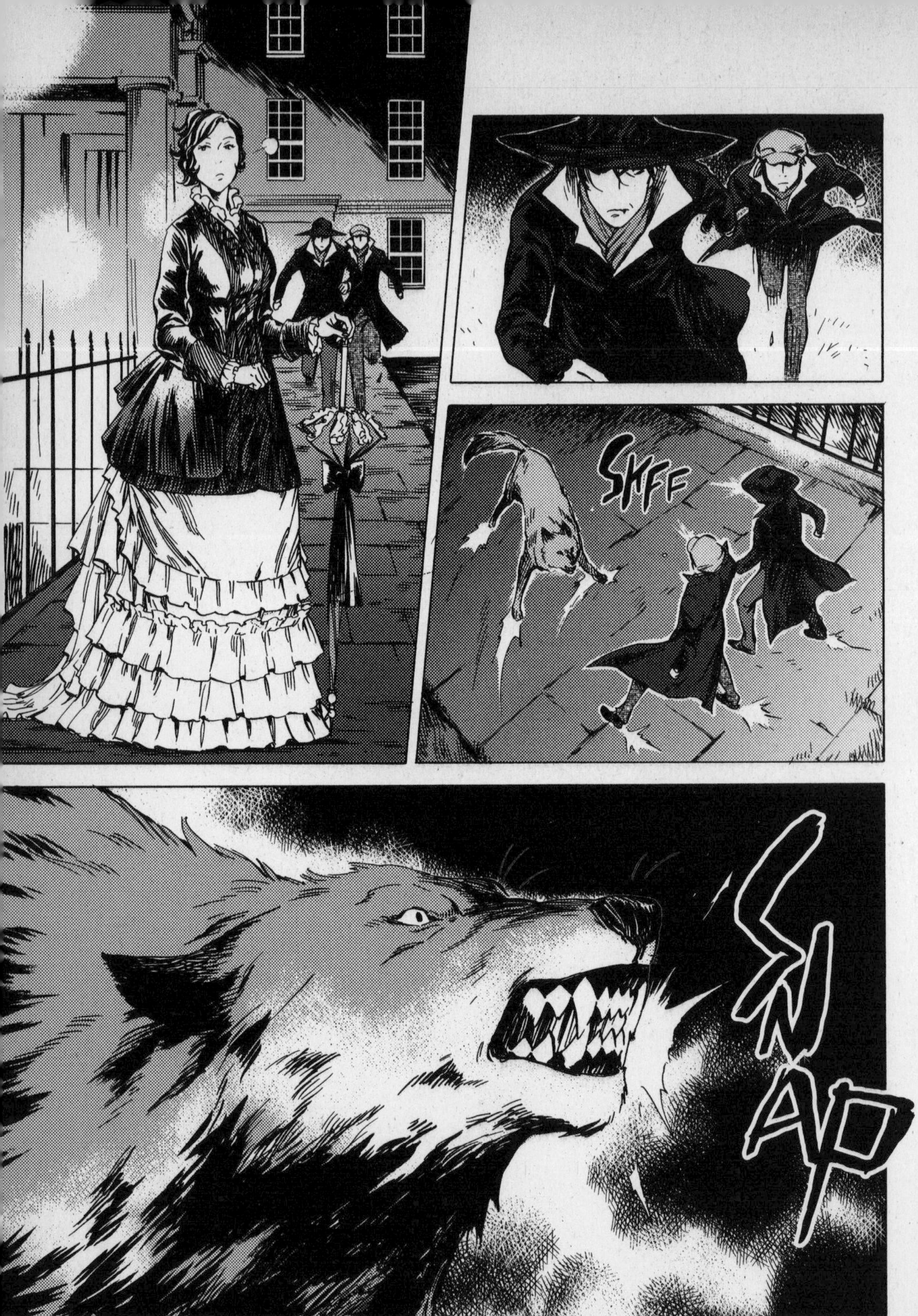
SKFF
SNAP

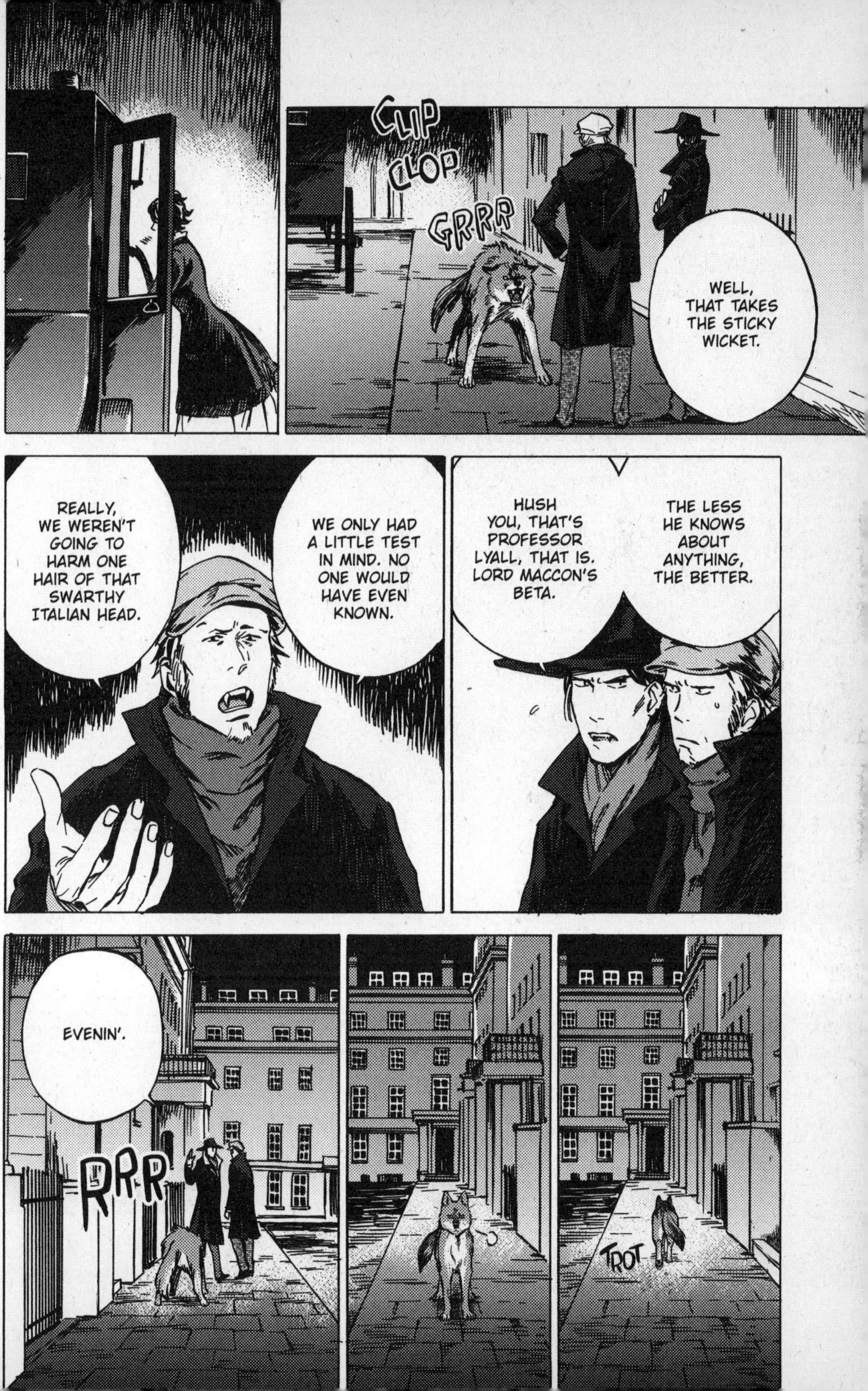
CLIP
CLOP
GRRR
WELL, THAT TAKES THE STICKY WICKET.
REALLY, WE WEREN'T GOING TO HARM ONE HAIR OF THAT SWARTHY ITALIAN HEAD.
WE ONLY HAD A LITTLE TEST IN MIND. NO ONE WOULD HAVE EVEN KNOWN.
HUSH YOU, THAT'S PROFESSOR LYALL, THAT IS. LORD MACCON'S BETA.
THE LESS HE KNOWS ABOUT ANYTHING, THE BETTER.
EVENIN'.
RRR
TROT

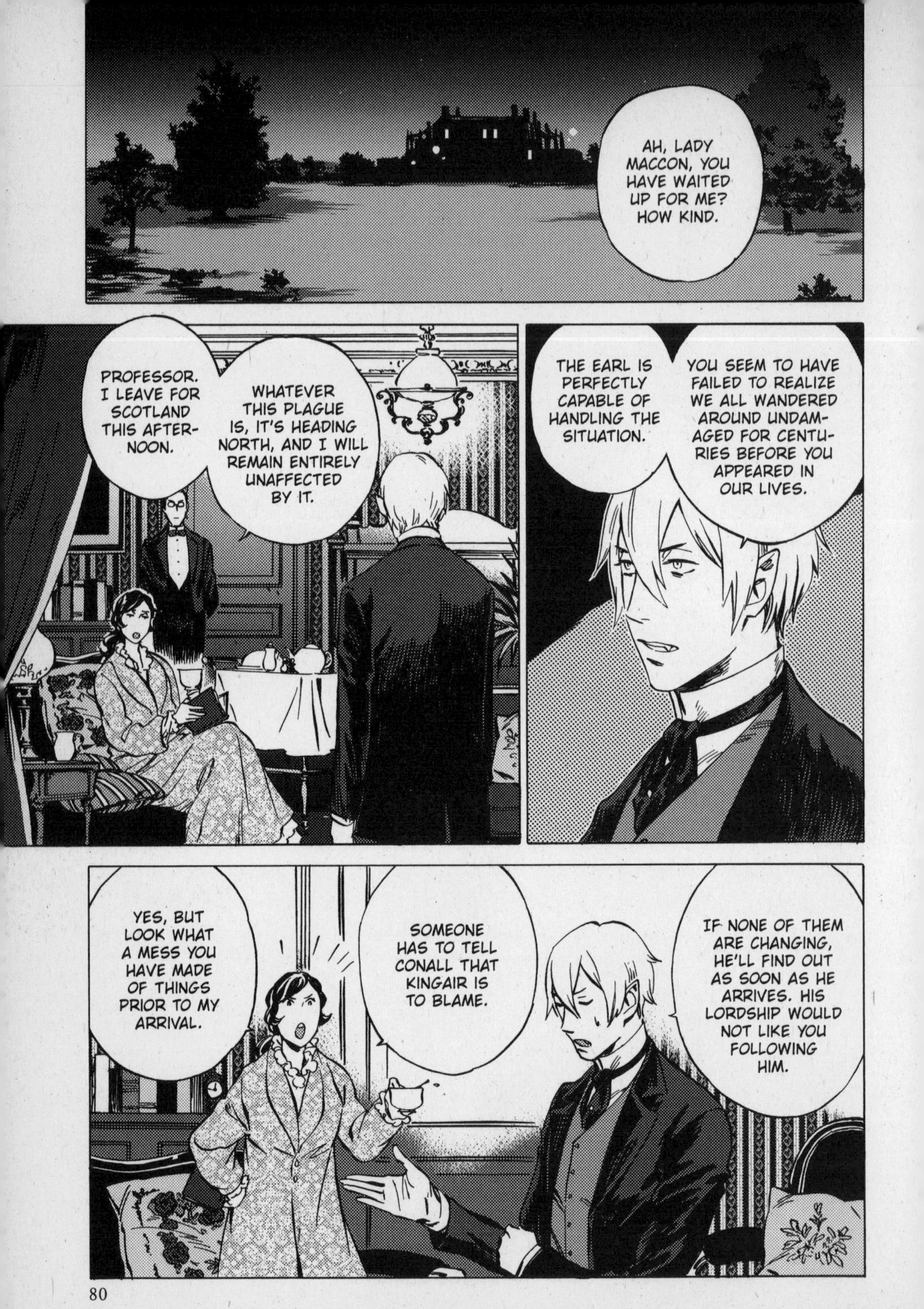

AH, LADY MACCON, YOU HAVE WAITED UP FOR ME? HOW KIND.
PROFESSOR. I LEAVE FOR SCOTLAND THIS AFTER-NOON.
WHATEVER THIS PLAGUE IS, IT'S HEADING NORTH, AND I WILL REMAIN ENTIRELY UNAFFECTED BY IT.
THE EARL IS PERFECTLY CAPABLE OF HANDLING THE SITUATION.
YOU SEEM TO HAVE FAILED TO REALIZE WE ALL WANDERED AROUND UNDAM-AGED FOR CENTU-RIES BEFORE YOU APPEARED IN OUR LIVES.
YES, BUT LOOK WHAT A MESS YOU HAVE MADE OF THINGS PRIOR TO MY ARRIVAL.
SOMEONE HAS TO TELL CONALL THAT KINGAIR IS TO BLAME.
IF NONE OF THEM ARE CHANGING, HE'LL FIND OUT AS SOON AS HE ARRIVES. HIS LORDSHIP WOULD NOT LIKE YOU FOLLOWING HIM.

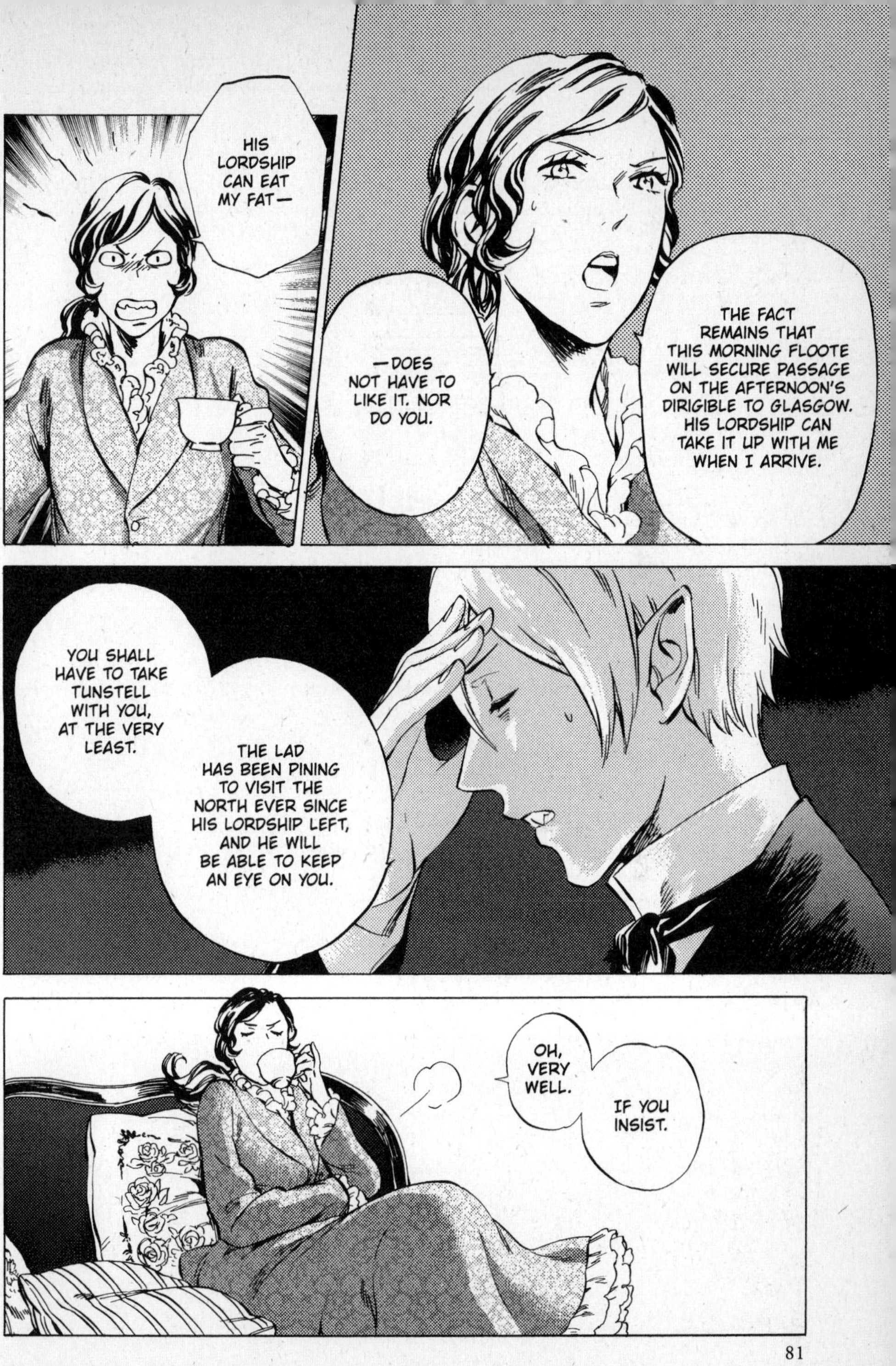
HIS LORDSHIP CAN EAT MY FAT—
—DOES NOT HAVE TO LIKE IT. NOR DO YOU.
THE FACT REMAINS THAT THIS MORNING FLOOTE WILL SECURE PASSAGE ON THE AFTERNOON'S DIRIGIBLE TO GLASGOW. HIS LORDSHIP CAN TAKE IT UP WITH ME WHEN I ARRIVE.
YOU SHALL HAVE TO TAKE TUNSTELL WITH YOU, AT THE VERY LEAST.
THE LAD HAS BEEN PINING TO VISIT THE NORTH EVER SINCE HIS LORDSHIP LEFT, AND HE WILL BE ABLE TO KEEP AN EYE ON YOU.
OH, VERY WELL.
IF YOU INSIST.

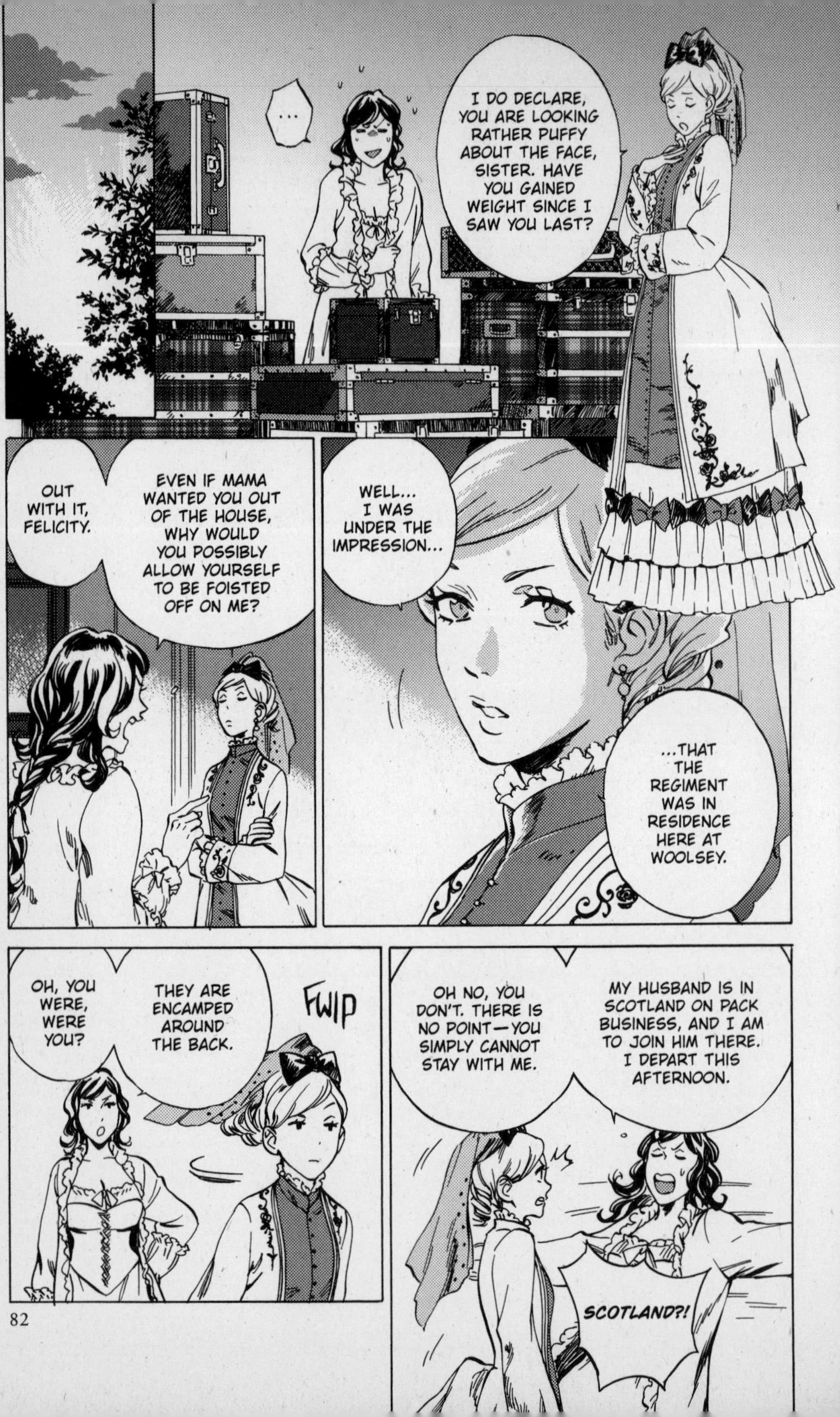
...
I DO DECLARE, YOU ARE LOOKING RATHER PUFFY ABOUT THE FACE, SISTER. HAVE YOU GAINED WEIGHT SINCE I SAW YOU LAST?
OUT WITH IT, FELICITY.
EVEN IF MAMA WANTED YOU OUT OF THE HOUSE, WHY WOULD YOU POSSIBLY ALLOW YOURSELF TO BE FOISTED OFF ON ME?
WELL... I WAS UNDER THE IMPRESSION...
...THAT THE REGIMENT WAS IN RESIDENCE HERE AT WOOLSEY.
OH, YOU WERE, WERE YOU?
THEY ARE ENCAMPED AROUND THE BACK.
FWIP
OH NO, YOU DON'T. THERE IS NO POINT—YOU SIMPLY CANNOT STAY WITH ME.
MY HUSBAND IS IN SCOTLAND ON PACK BUSINESS, AND I AM TO JOIN HIM THERE. I DEPART THIS AFTERNOON.
SCOTLAND?!

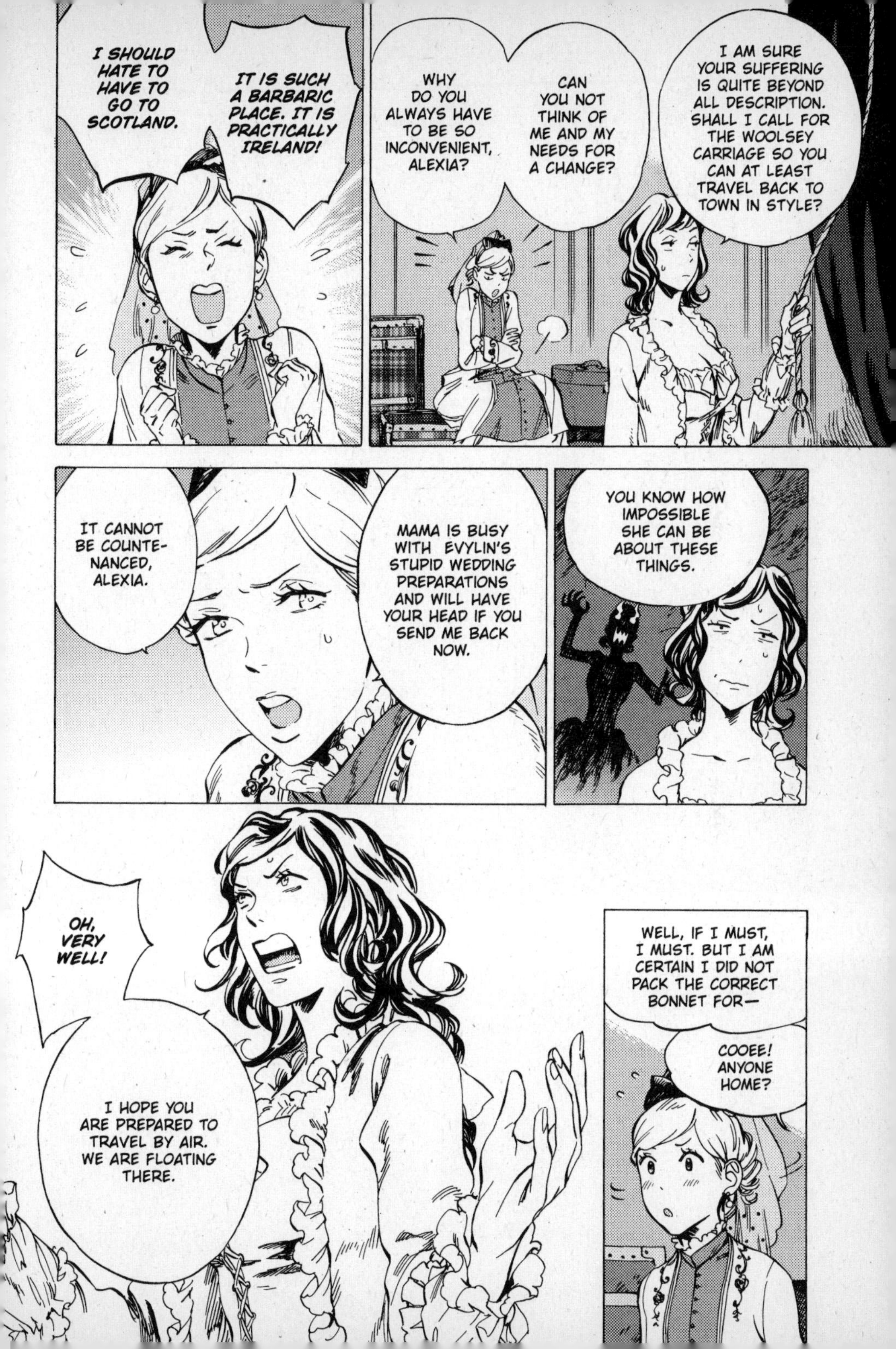
I SHOULD HATE TO HAVE TO GO TO SCOTLAND.
IT IS SUCH A BARBARIC PLACE. IT IS PRACTICALLY IRELAND!
WHY DO YOU ALWAYS HAVE TO BE SO INCONVENIENT, ALEXIA?
CAN YOU NOT THINK OF ME AND MY NEEDS FOR A CHANGE?
I AM SURE YOUR SUFFERING IS QUITE BEYOND ALL DESCRIPTION. SHALL I CALL FOR THE WOOLSEY CARRIAGE SO YOU CAN AT LEAST TRAVEL BACK TO TOWN IN STYLE?
IT CANNOT BE COUNTE-NANCED, ALEXIA.
MAMA IS BUSY WITH EVYLIN'S STUPID WEDDING PREPARATIONS AND WILL HAVE YOUR HEAD IF YOU SEND ME BACK NOW.
YOU KNOW HOW IMPOSSIBLE SHE CAN BE ABOUT THESE THINGS.
OH, VERY WELL!
I HOPE YOU ARE PREPARED TO TRAVEL BY AIR. WE ARE FLOATING THERE.
WELL, IF I MUST, I MUST. BUT I AM CERTAIN I DID NOT PACK THE CORRECT BONNET FOR—
COOEE! ANYONE HOME?

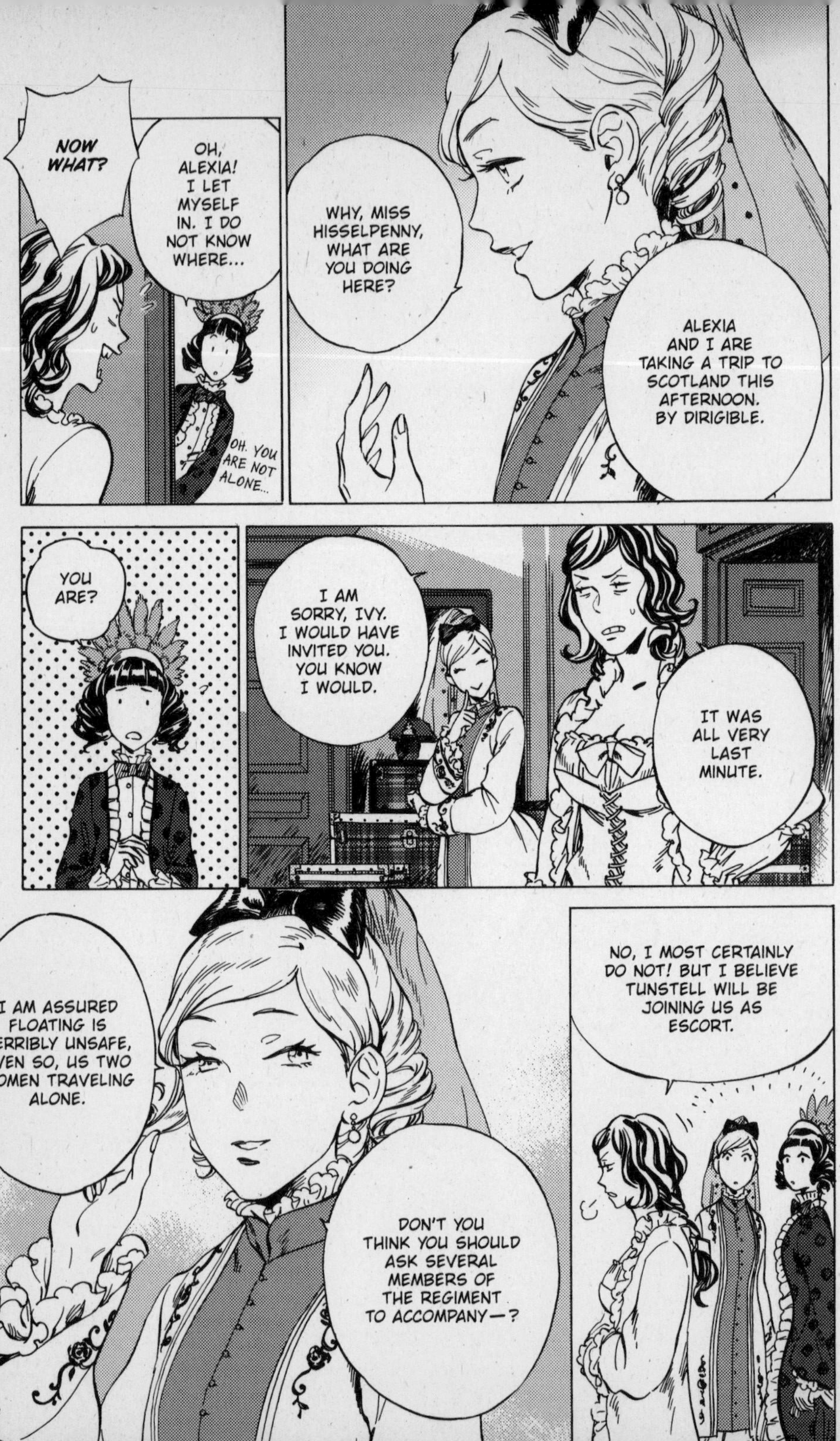
NOW WHAT?
OH, ALEXIA! I LET MYSELF IN. I DO NOT KNOW WHERE...
OH. YOU ARE NOT ALONE...
WHY, MISS HISSELPENNY, WHAT ARE YOU DOING HERE?
ALEXIA AND I ARE TAKING A TRIP TO SCOTLAND THIS AFTERNOON. BY DIRIGIBLE.
YOU ARE?
I AM SORRY, IVY. I WOULD HAVE INVITED YOU. YOU KNOW I WOULD.
IT WAS ALL VERY LAST MINUTE.
I AM ASSURED FLOATING IS TERRIBLY UNSAFE, EVEN SO, US TWO WOMEN TRAVELING ALONE.
DON'T YOU THINK YOU SHOULD ASK SEVERAL MEMBERS OF THE REGIMENT TO ACCOMPANY—?
NO, I MOST CERTAINLY DO NOT! BUT I BELIEVE TUNSTELL WILL BE JOINING US AS ESCORT.

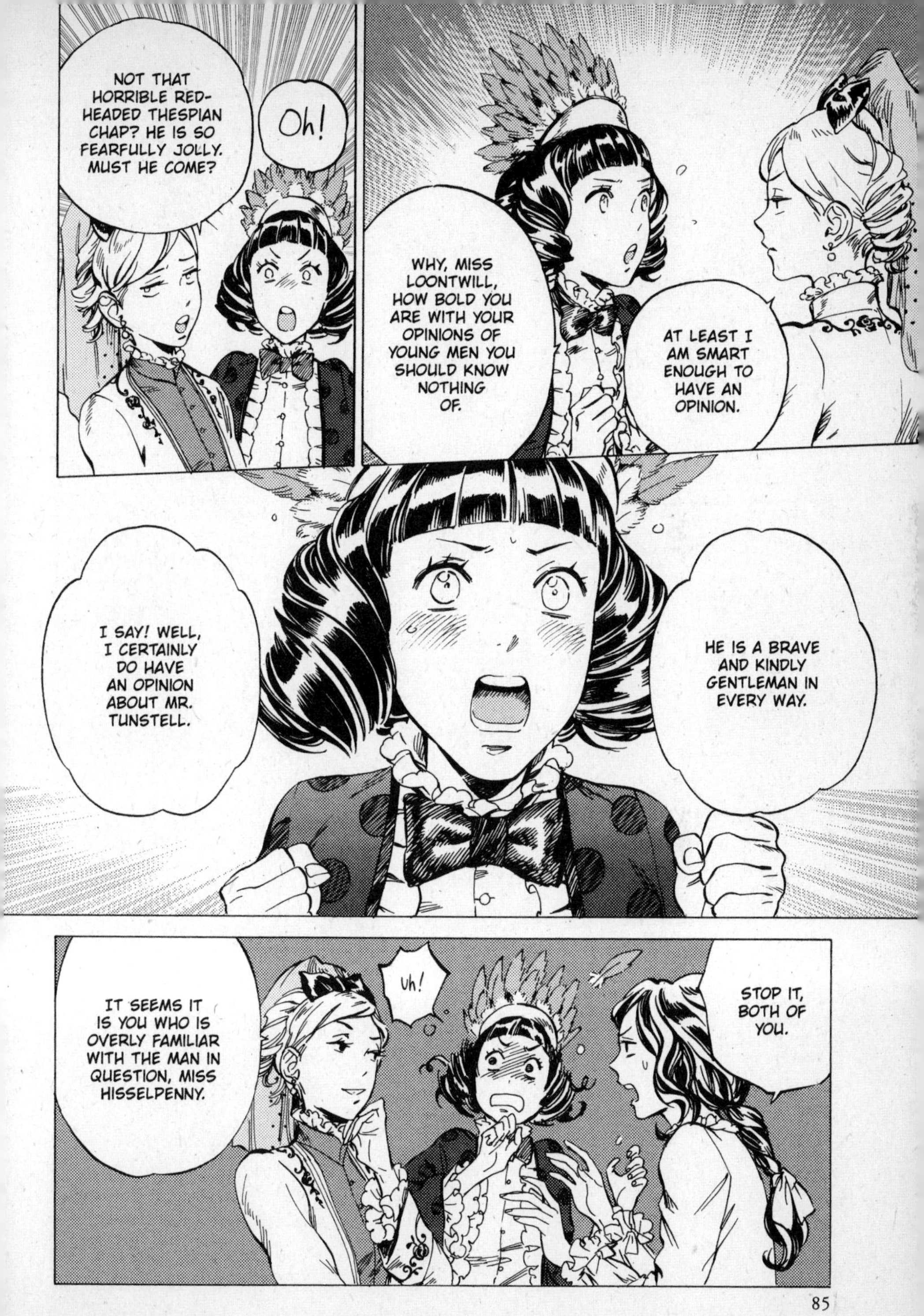

NOT THAT HORRIBLE RED-HEADED THESPIAN CHAP? HE IS SO FEARFULLY JOLLY. MUST HE COME?
Oh!
WHY, MISS LOONTWILL, HOW BOLD YOU ARE WITH YOUR OPINIONS OF YOUNG MEN YOU SHOULD KNOW NOTHING OF.
AT LEAST I AM SMART ENOUGH TO HAVE AN OPINION.
I SAY! WELL, I CERTAINLY DO HAVE AN OPINION ABOUT MR. TUNSTELL.
HE IS A BRAVE AND KINDLY GENTLEMAN IN EVERY WAY.
IT SEEMS IT IS YOU WHO IS OVERLY FAMILIAR WITH THE MAN IN QUESTION, MISS HISSELPENNY.
Uh!
STOP IT, BOTH OF YOU.

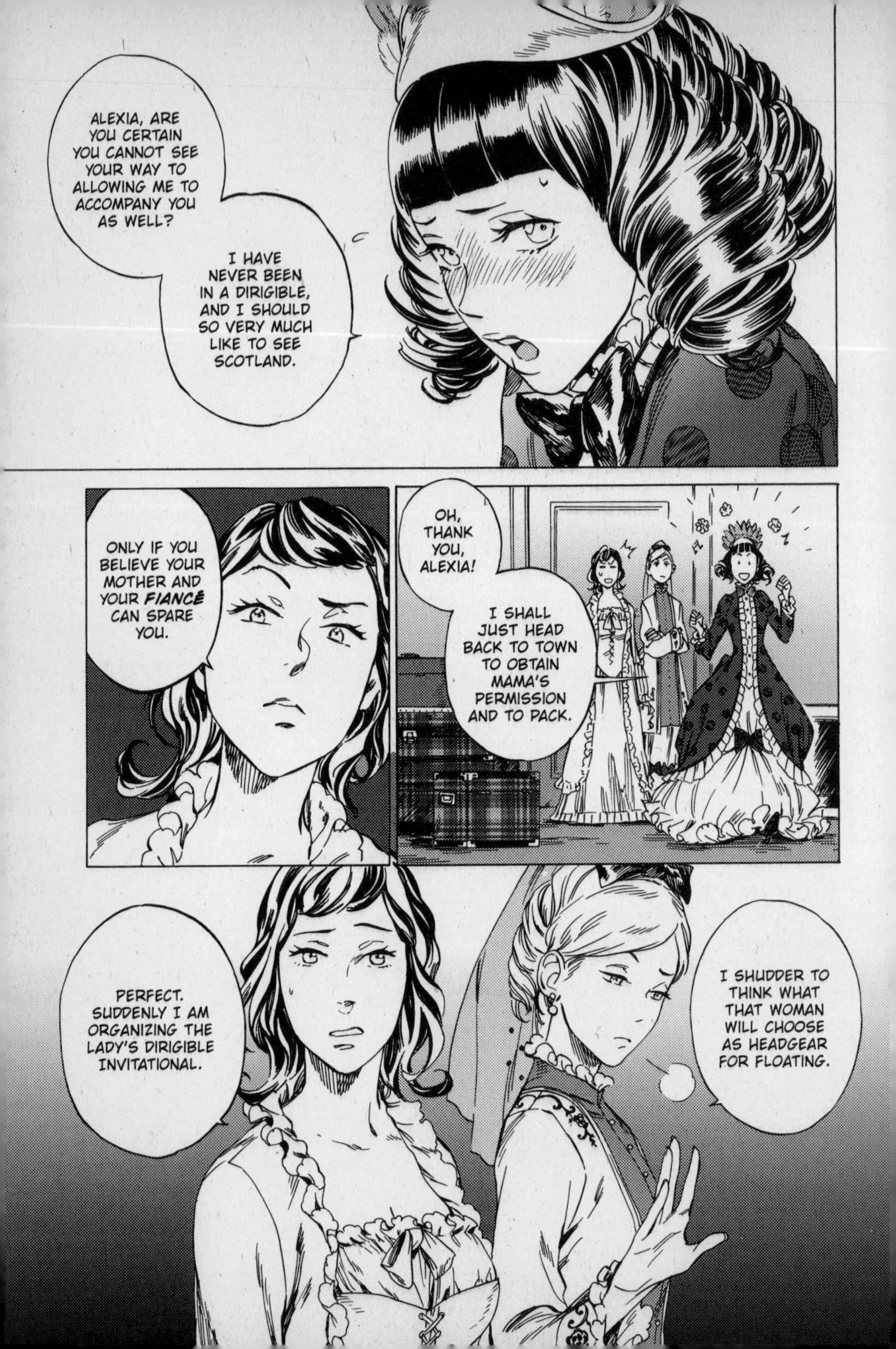
ALEXIA, ARE YOU CERTAIN YOU CANNOT SEE YOUR WAY TO ALLOWING ME TO ACCOMPANY YOU AS WELL?
I HAVE NEVER BEEN IN A DIRIGIBLE, AND I SHOULD SO VERY MUCH LIKE TO SEE SCOTLAND.
ONLY IF YOU BELIEVE YOUR MOTHER AND YOUR *FIANCÉ* CAN SPARE YOU.
OH, THANK YOU, ALEXIA!
I SHALL JUST HEAD BACK TO TOWN TO OBTAIN MAMA'S PERMISSION AND TO PACK.
PERFECT. SUDDENLY I AM ORGANIZING THE LADY'S DIRIGIBLE INVITATIONAL.
I SHUDDER TO THINK WHAT THAT WOMAN WILL CHOOSE AS HEADGEAR FOR FLOATING.

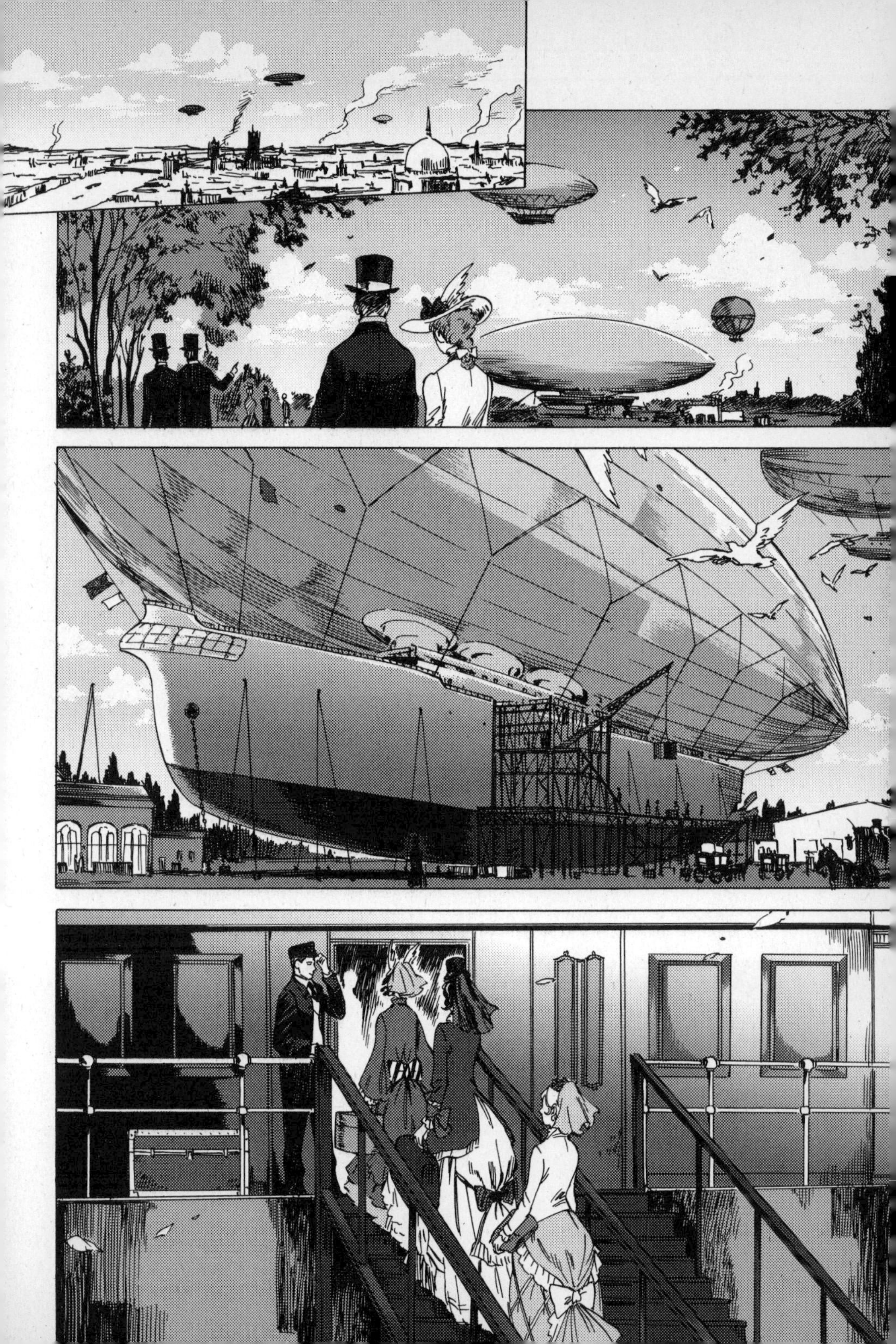

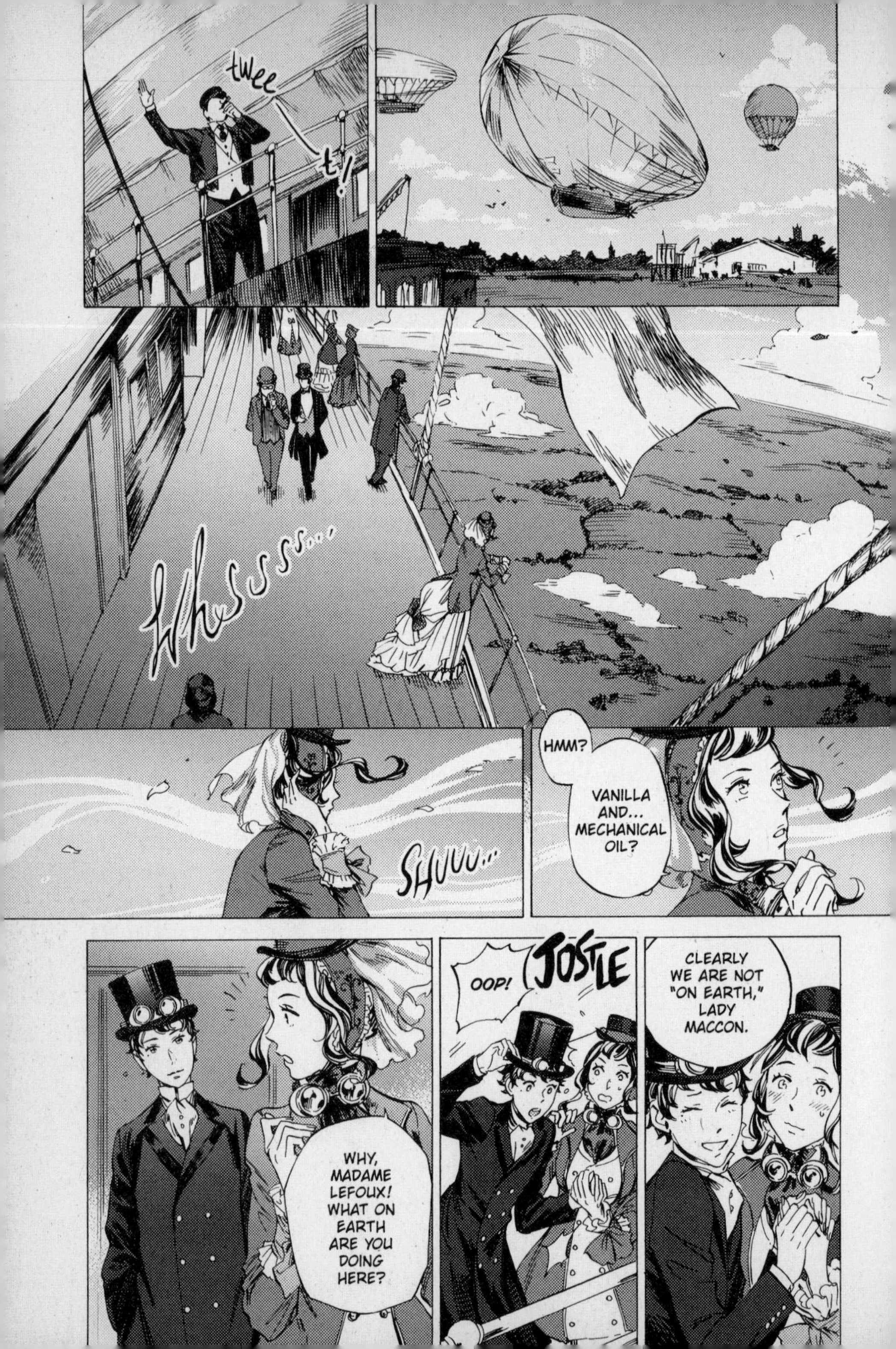

tweet!
Whsssss...
SHUUU...
HMM?
VANILLA AND... MECHANICAL OIL?
WHY, MADAME LEFOUX! WHAT ON EARTH ARE YOU DOING HERE?
OOP!
JOSTLE
CLEARLY WE ARE NOT "ON EARTH," LADY MACCON.

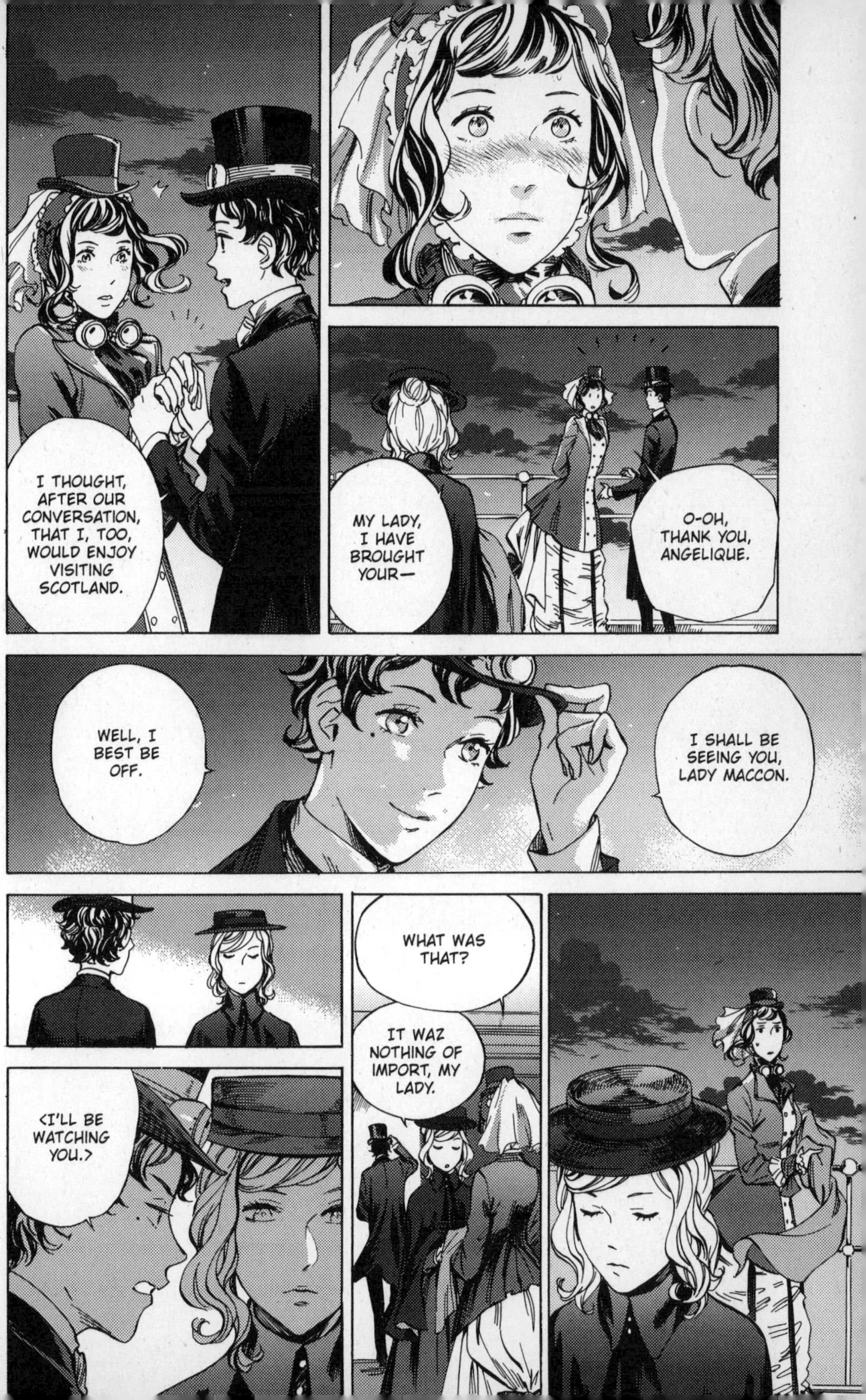
I THOUGHT, AFTER OUR CONVERSATION, THAT I, TOO, WOULD ENJOY VISITING SCOTLAND.
MY LADY, I HAVE BROUGHT YOUR—
O-OH, THANK YOU, ANGELIQUE.
WELL, I BEST BE OFF.
I SHALL BE SEEING YOU, LADY MACCON.
<I'LL BE WATCHING YOU.>
WHAT WAS THAT?
IT WAZ NOTHING OF IMPORT, MY LADY.

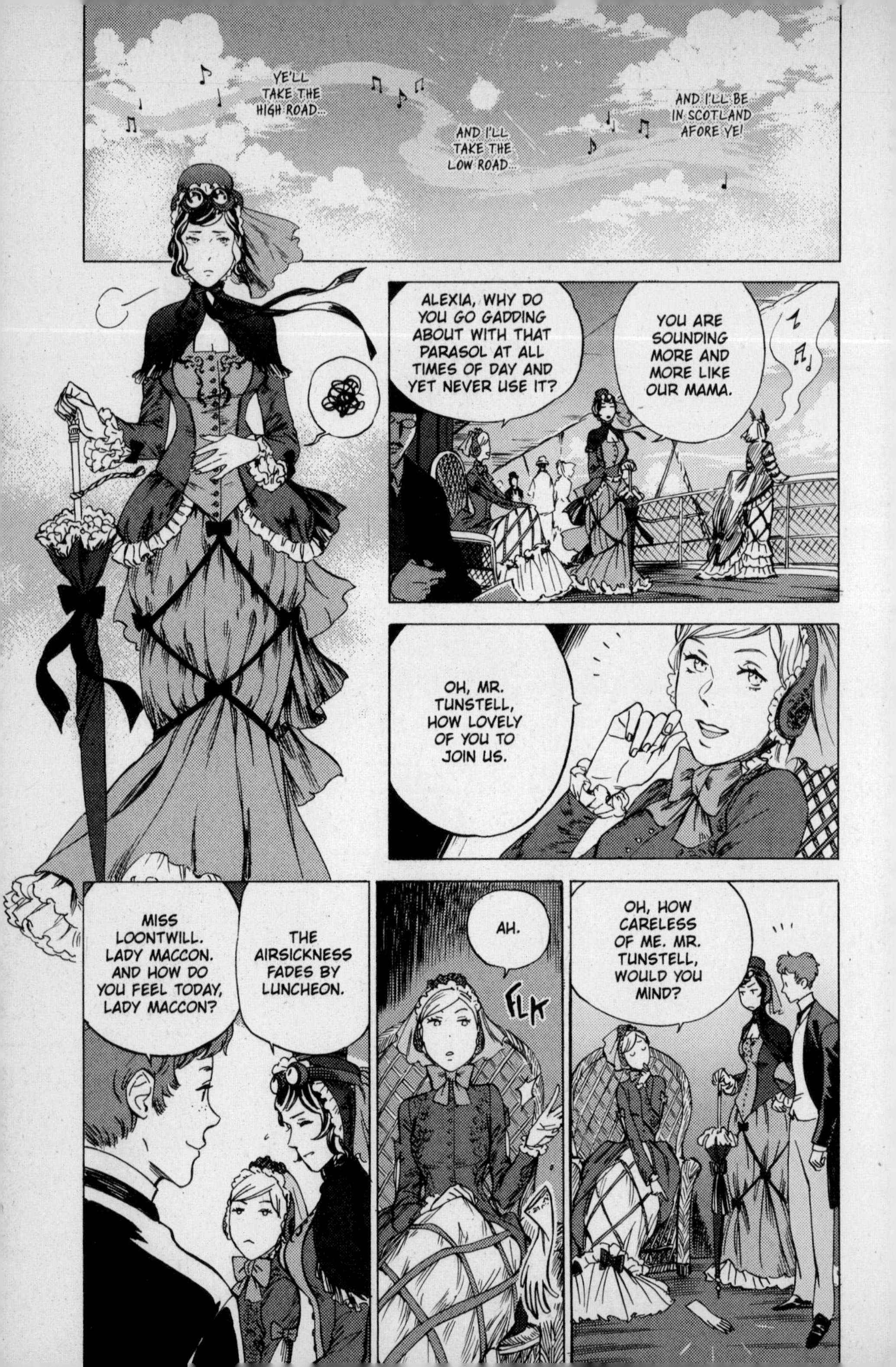
YE'LL TAKE THE HIGH ROAD...
AND I'LL TAKE THE LOW ROAD...
AND I'LL BE IN SCOTLAND AFORE YE!
ALEXIA, WHY DO YOU GO GADDING ABOUT WITH THAT PARASOL AT ALL TIMES OF DAY AND YET NEVER USE IT?
YOU ARE SOUNDING MORE AND MORE LIKE OUR MAMA.
OH, MR. TUNSTELL, HOW LOVELY OF YOU TO JOIN US.
MISS LOONTWILL. LADY MACCON. AND HOW DO YOU FEEL TODAY, LADY MACCON?
THE AIRSICKNESS FADES BY LUNCHEON.
AH.
FLK
OH, HOW CARELESS OF ME. MR. TUNSTELL, WOULD YOU MIND?

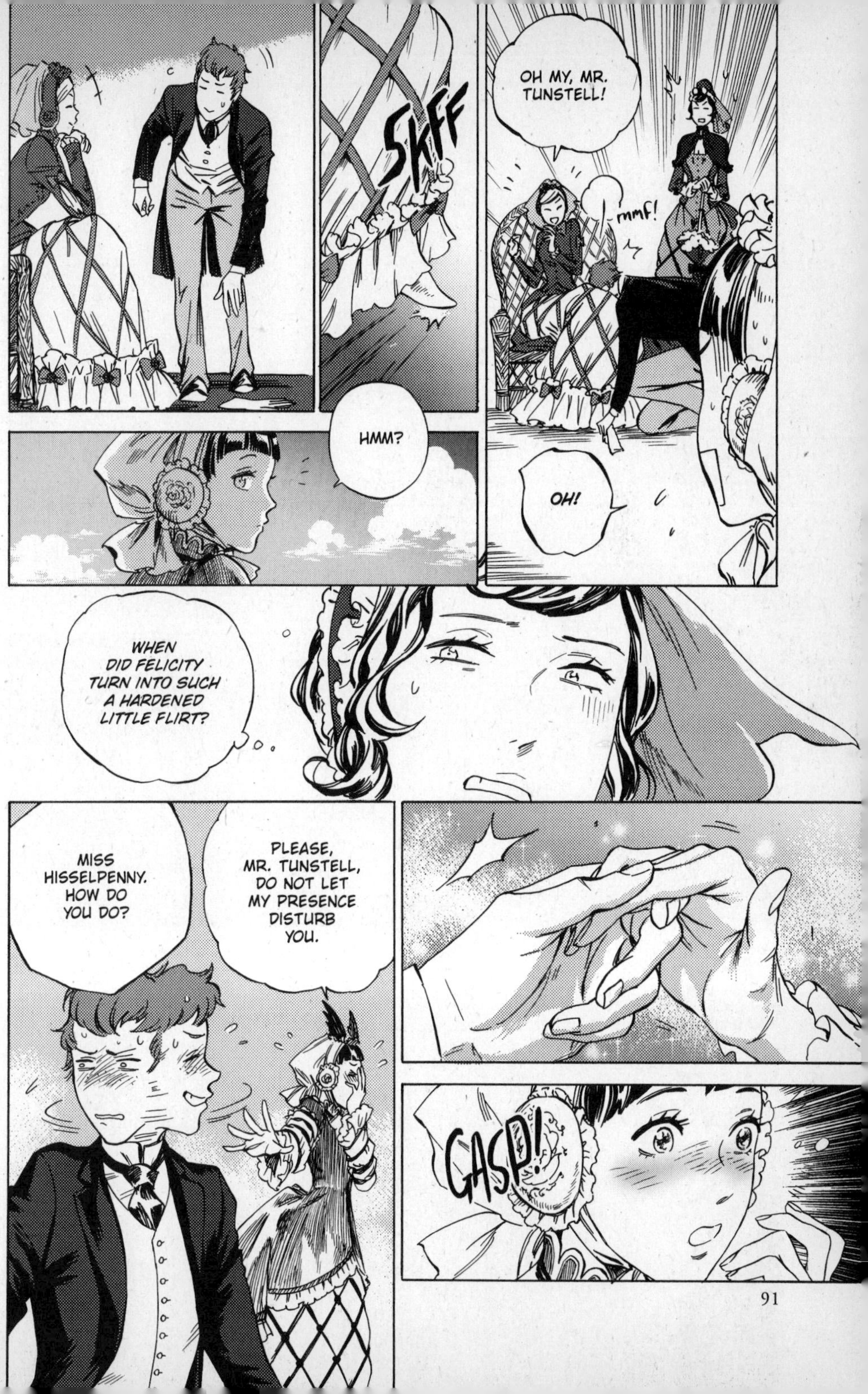
SKFF
OH MY, MR. TUNSTELL!
rmmf!
HMM?
OH!
WHEN DID FELICITY TURN INTO SUCH A HARDENED LITTLE FLIRT?
MISS HISSELPENNY. HOW DO YOU DO?
PLEASE, MR. TUNSTELL, DO NOT LET MY PRESENCE DISTURB YOU.
GASP!

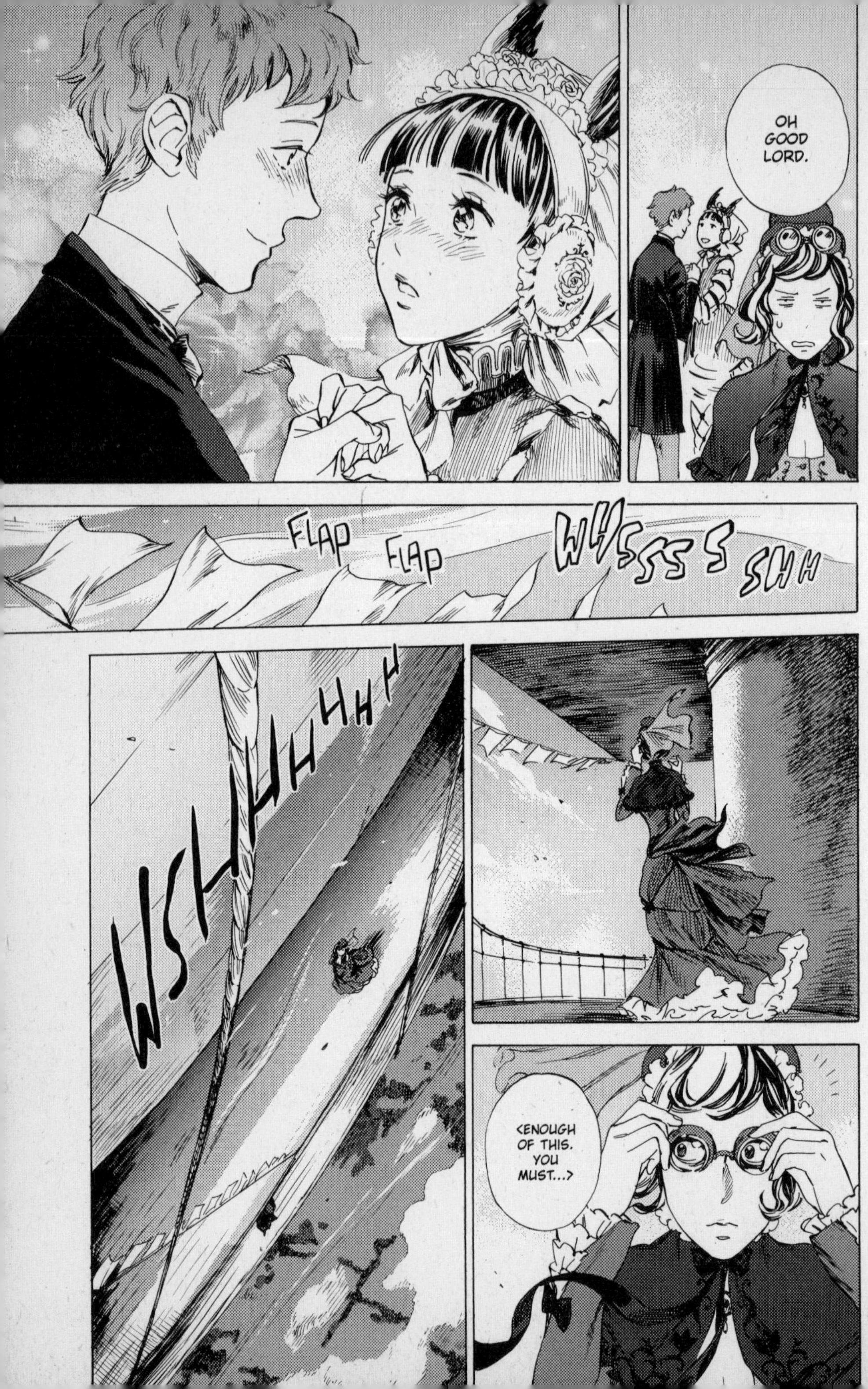
OH GOOD LORD.
FLAP FLAP
WHSSSS SHH
<ENOUGH OF THIS. YOU MUST...>
WSHHHHHHHH

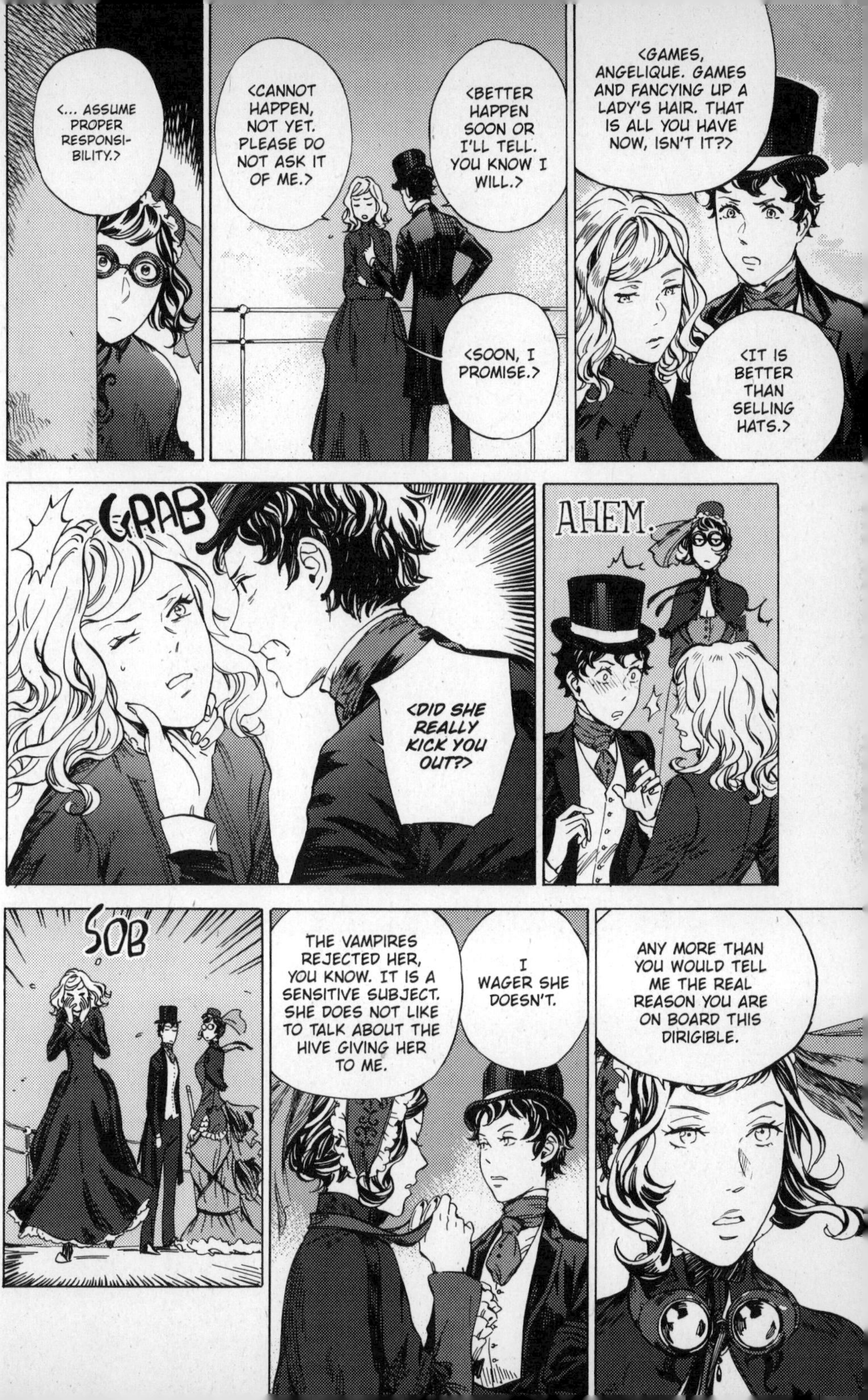

<... ASSUME PROPER RESPONSI-BILITY.>
<CANNOT HAPPEN, NOT YET. PLEASE DO NOT ASK IT OF ME.>
<BETTER HAPPEN SOON OR I'LL TELL. YOU KNOW I WILL.>
<SOON, I PROMISE.>
<GAMES, ANGELIQUE. GAMES AND FANCYING UP A LADY'S HAIR. THAT IS ALL YOU HAVE NOW, ISN'T IT?>
<IT IS BETTER THAN SELLING HATS.>
GRAB
<DID SHE REALLY KICK YOU OUT?>
AHEM.
SOB
THE VAMPIRES REJECTED HER, YOU KNOW. IT IS A SENSITIVE SUBJECT. SHE DOES NOT LIKE TO TALK ABOUT THE HIVE GIVING HER TO ME.
I WAGER SHE DOESN'T.
ANY MORE THAN YOU WOULD TELL ME THE REAL REASON YOU ARE ON BOARD THIS DIRIGIBLE.

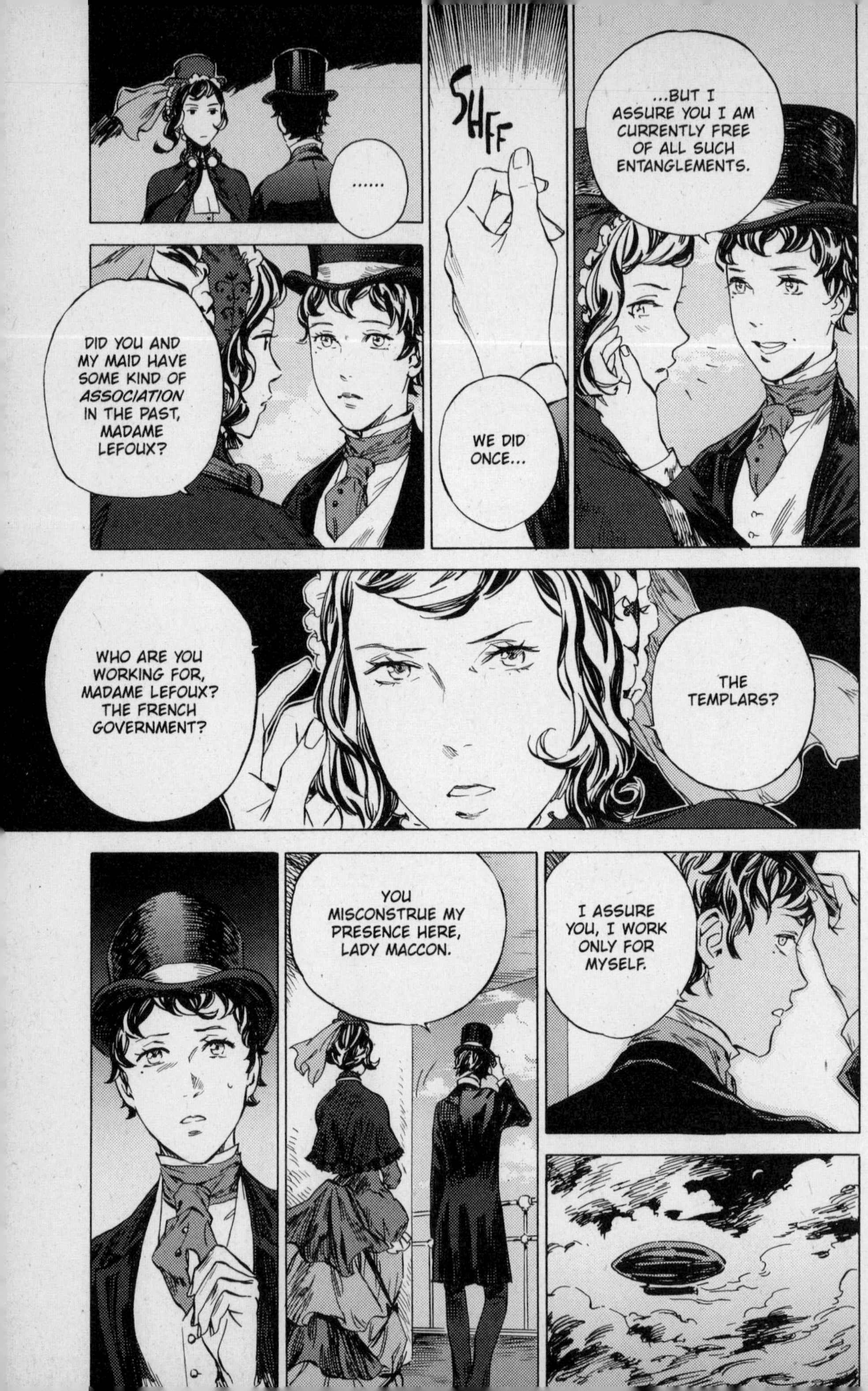
......
DID YOU AND MY MAID HAVE SOME KIND OF *ASSOCIATION* IN THE PAST, MADAME LEFOUX?
SHFF
WE DID ONCE...
...BUT I ASSURE YOU I AM CURRENTLY FREE OF ALL SUCH ENTANGLEMENTS.
WHO ARE YOU WORKING FOR, MADAME LEFOUX? THE FRENCH GOVERNMENT?
THE TEMPLARS?
YOU MISCONSTRUE MY PRESENCE HERE, LADY MACCON.
I ASSURE YOU, I WORK ONLY FOR MYSELF.

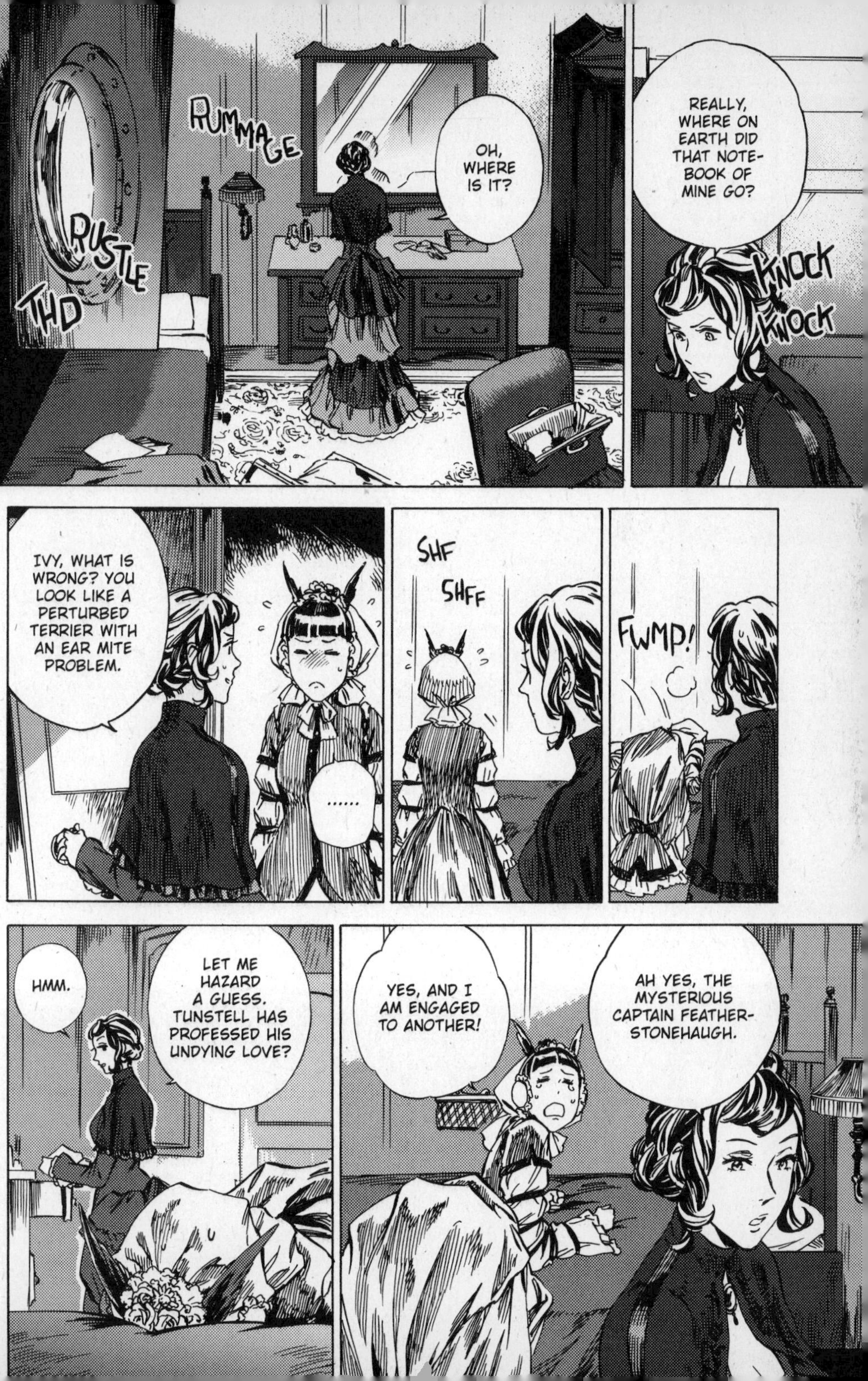
RUMMAGE
OH, WHERE IS IT?
RUSTLE
THD
REALLY, WHERE ON EARTH DID THAT NOTE-BOOK OF MINE GO?
KNOCK KNOCK
IVY, WHAT IS WRONG? YOU LOOK LIKE A PERTURBED TERRIER WITH AN EAR MITE PROBLEM.
......
SHF
SHFF
FWMP!
HMM.
LET ME HAZARD A GUESS. TUNSTELL HAS PROFESSED HIS UNDYING LOVE?
YES, AND I AM ENGAGED TO ANOTHER!
AH YES, THE MYSTERIOUS CAPTAIN FEATHER-STONEHAUGH.

WELL, WELL, WELL, YOU HAVE GOT YOURSELF INTO A PRETTY PICKLE.

OH, BUT, ALEXIA, I AM QUITE FEARFULLY AFRAID THAT I MIGHT JUST POSSIBLY, MAYBE A LITTLE ITTY-BITTY BIT, LOVE HIM BACK.

SHOULDN'T YOU BE CERTAIN OF A THING LIKE THAT?

I DO NOT KNOW. HOW DOES ONE DETERMINE ONE'S OWN STATE OF ENAMORMENT?

HAVE YOU KISSED HIM?

WELL, MAYBE, JUST A LITTLE.

AND?

OH, WELL, I THOUGHT IT WAS A LITTLE... DAMP.

MY HEAD IS POSITIVELY AWHIRL. DON'T YOU COMPREHEND MY CACOPHONY?

YOU MEAN CATASTROPHE?

DO I THROW OVER CAPTAIN FEATHERSTONE-HAUGH, AND HIS FIVE HUNDRED A YEAR, FOR MR. TUNSTELL AND HIS UNSTABLE... WORKING-CLASS STATION?

OR DO I CONTINUE WITH MY ENGAGEMENT? I SIMPLY DO NOT KNOW WHAT TO DO!

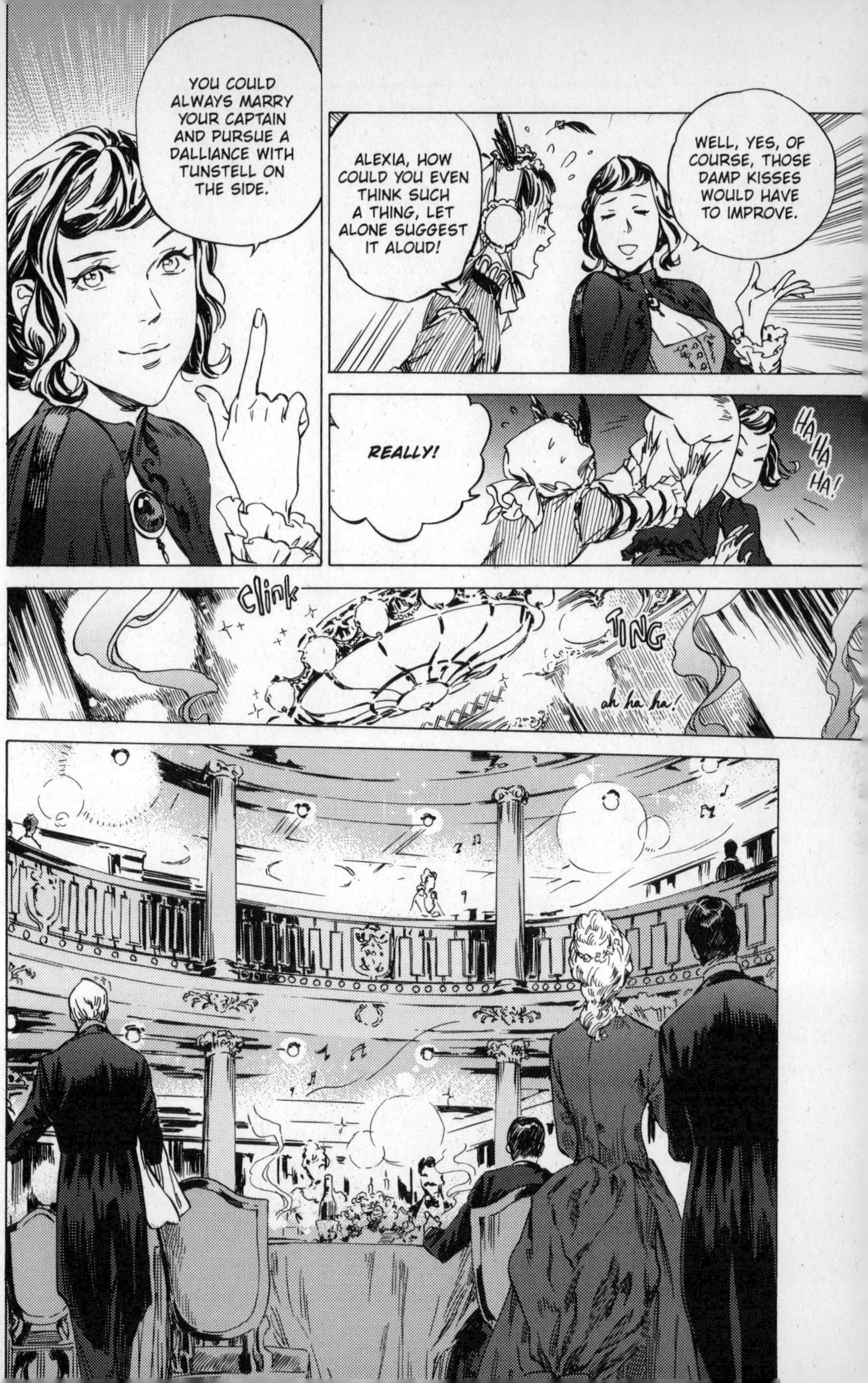
YOU COULD ALWAYS MARRY YOUR CAPTAIN AND PURSUE A DALLIANCE WITH TUNSTELL ON THE SIDE.
ALEXIA, HOW COULD YOU EVEN THINK SUCH A THING, LET ALONE SUGGEST IT ALOUD!
WELL, YES, OF COURSE, THOSE DAMP KISSES WOULD HAVE TO IMPROVE.
REALLY!
HA HA HA!
Clink
TING
ah ha ha!

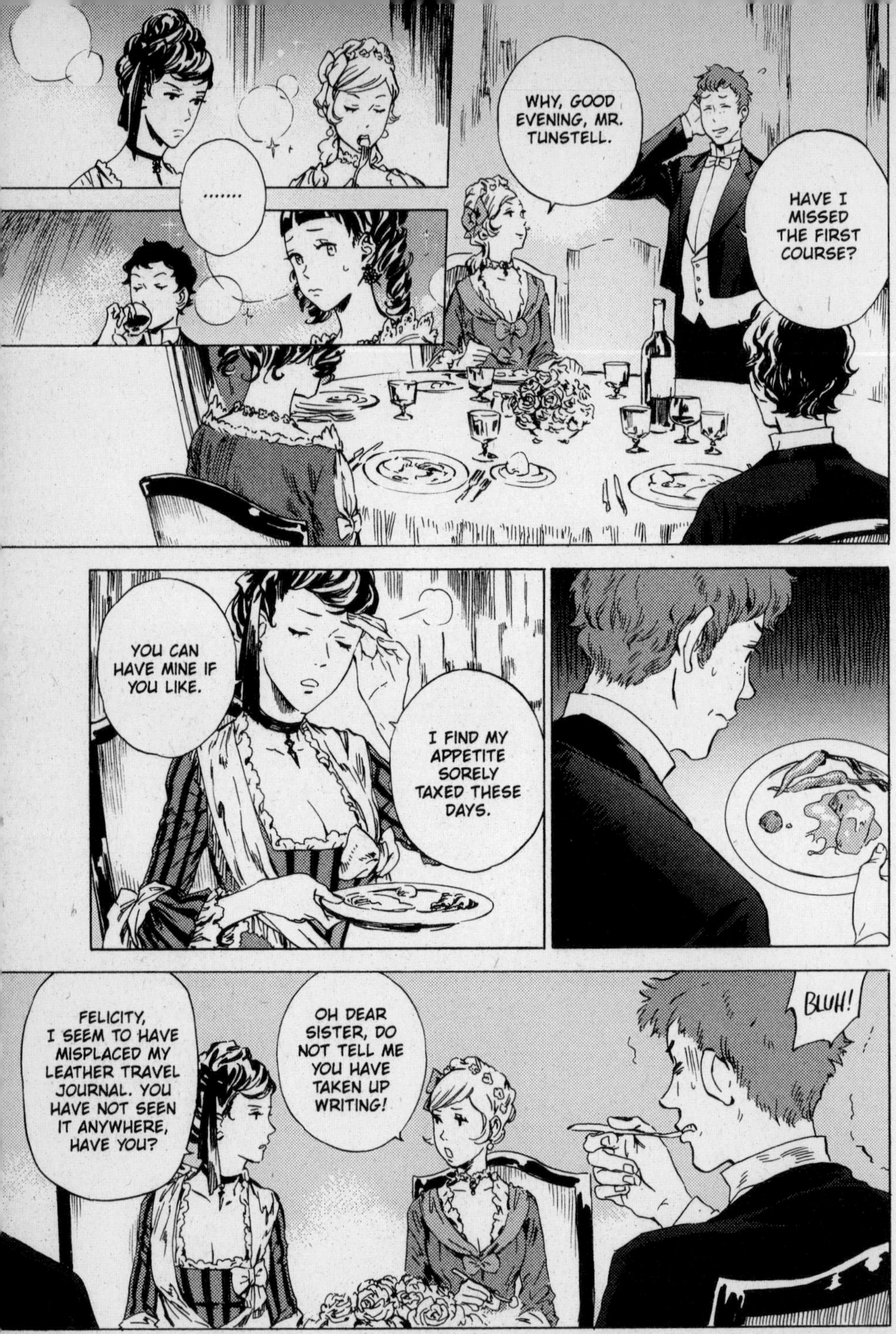
....
WHY, GOOD EVENING, MR. TUNSTELL.
HAVE I MISSED THE FIRST COURSE?
YOU CAN HAVE MINE IF YOU LIKE.
I FIND MY APPETITE SORELY TAXED THESE DAYS.
FELICITY, I SEEM TO HAVE MISPLACED MY LEATHER TRAVEL JOURNAL. YOU HAVE NOT SEEN IT ANYWHERE, HAVE YOU?
OH DEAR SISTER, DO NOT TELL ME YOU HAVE TAKEN UP WRITING!
BLUH!

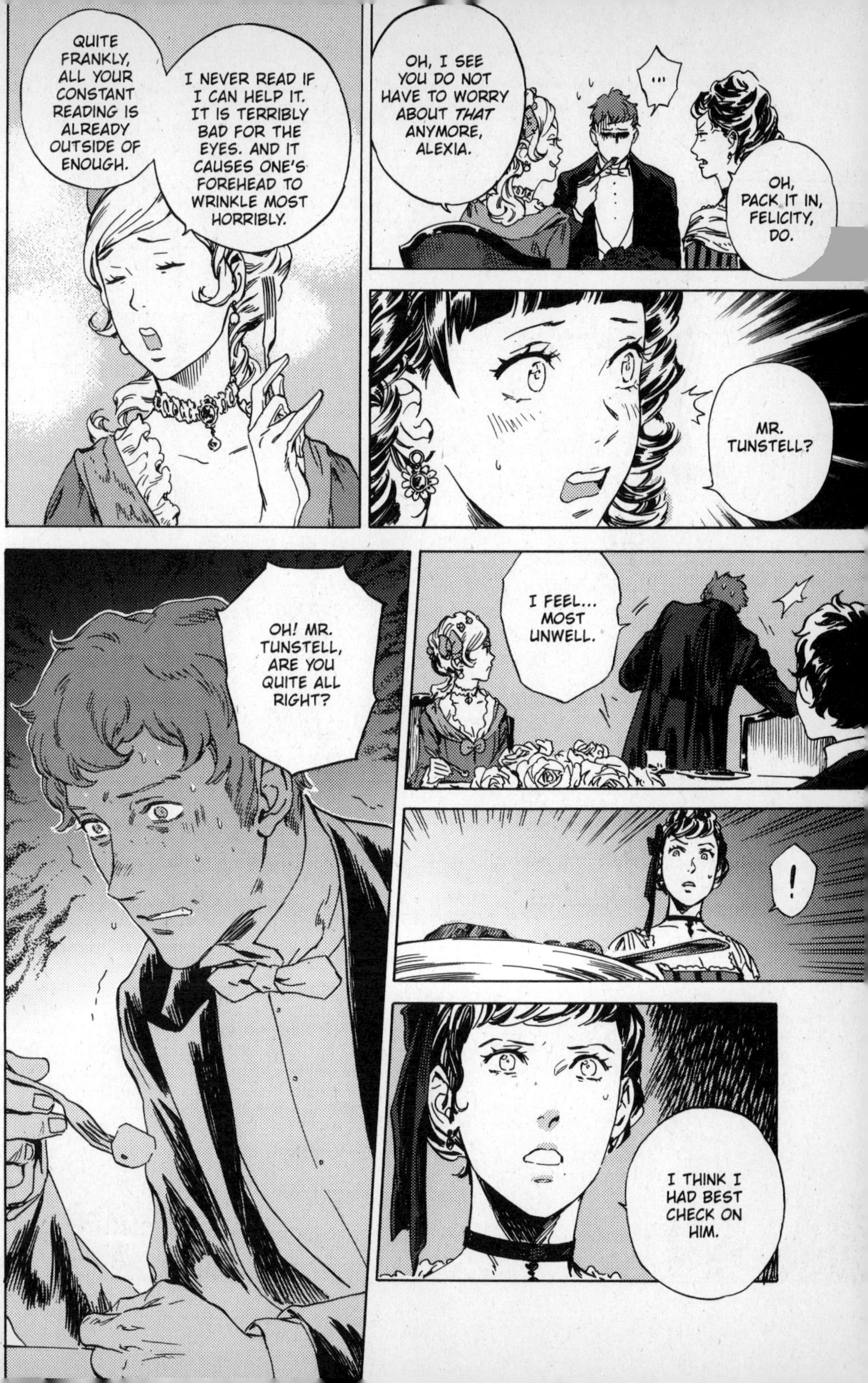
QUITE FRANKLY, ALL YOUR CONSTANT READING IS ALREADY OUTSIDE OF ENOUGH.
I NEVER READ IF I CAN HELP IT. IT IS TERRIBLY BAD FOR THE EYES. AND IT CAUSES ONE'S FOREHEAD TO WRINKLE MOST HORRIBLY.
OH, I SEE YOU DO NOT HAVE TO WORRY ABOUT *THAT* ANYMORE, ALEXIA.
...
OH, PACK IT IN, FELICITY, DO.
MR. TUNSTELL?
OH! MR. TUNSTELL, ARE YOU QUITE ALL RIGHT?
I FEEL... MOST UNWELL.
!
I THINK I HAD BEST CHECK ON HIM.

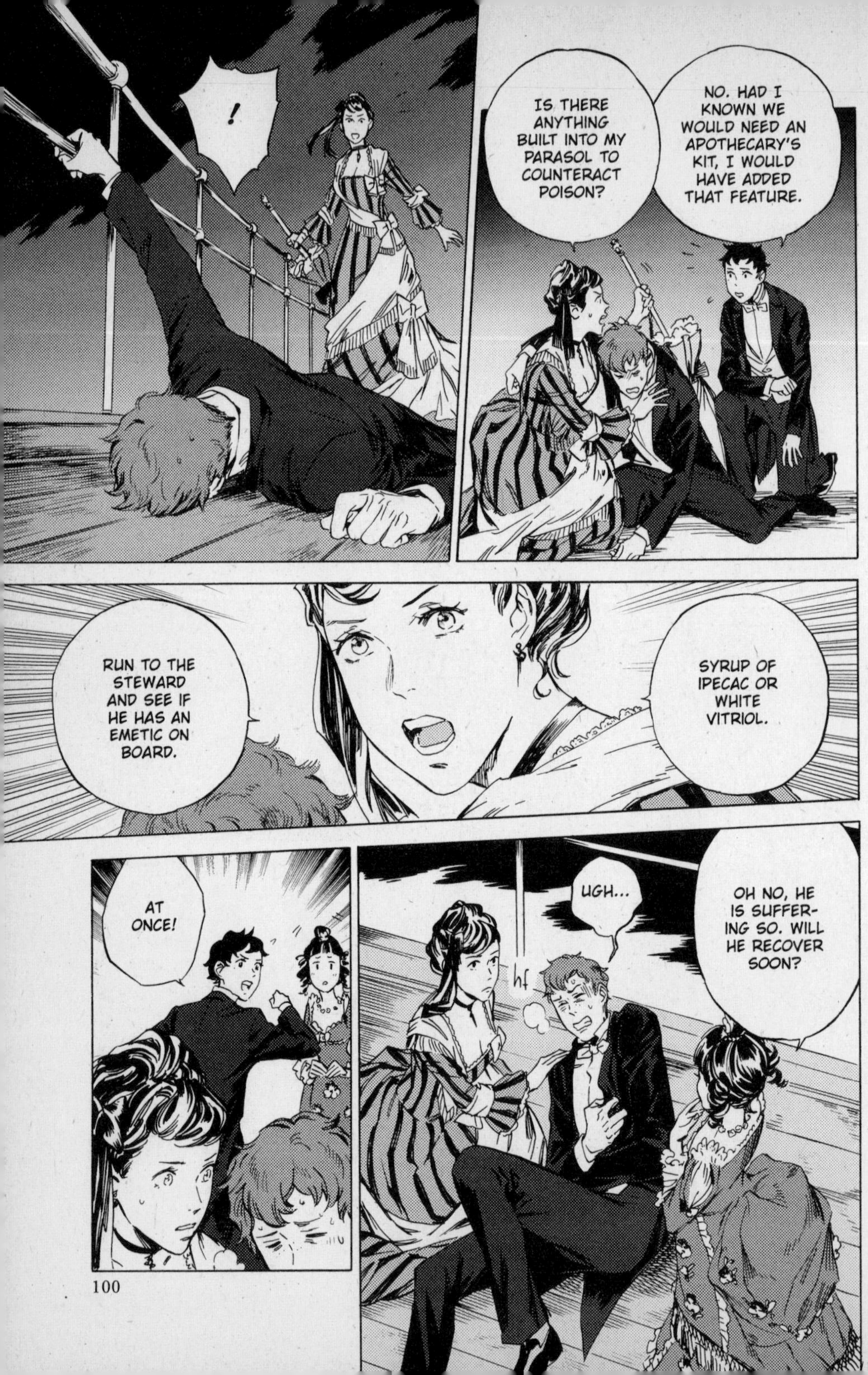
!
IS THERE ANYTHING BUILT INTO MY PARASOL TO COUNTERACT POISON?
NO. HAD I KNOWN WE WOULD NEED AN APOTHECARY'S KIT, I WOULD HAVE ADDED THAT FEATURE.
RUN TO THE STEWARD AND SEE IF HE HAS AN EMETIC ON BOARD.
SYRUP OF IPECAC OR WHITE VITRIOL.
AT ONCE!
UGH...
hf
OH NO, HE IS SUFFERING SO. WILL HE RECOVER SOON?

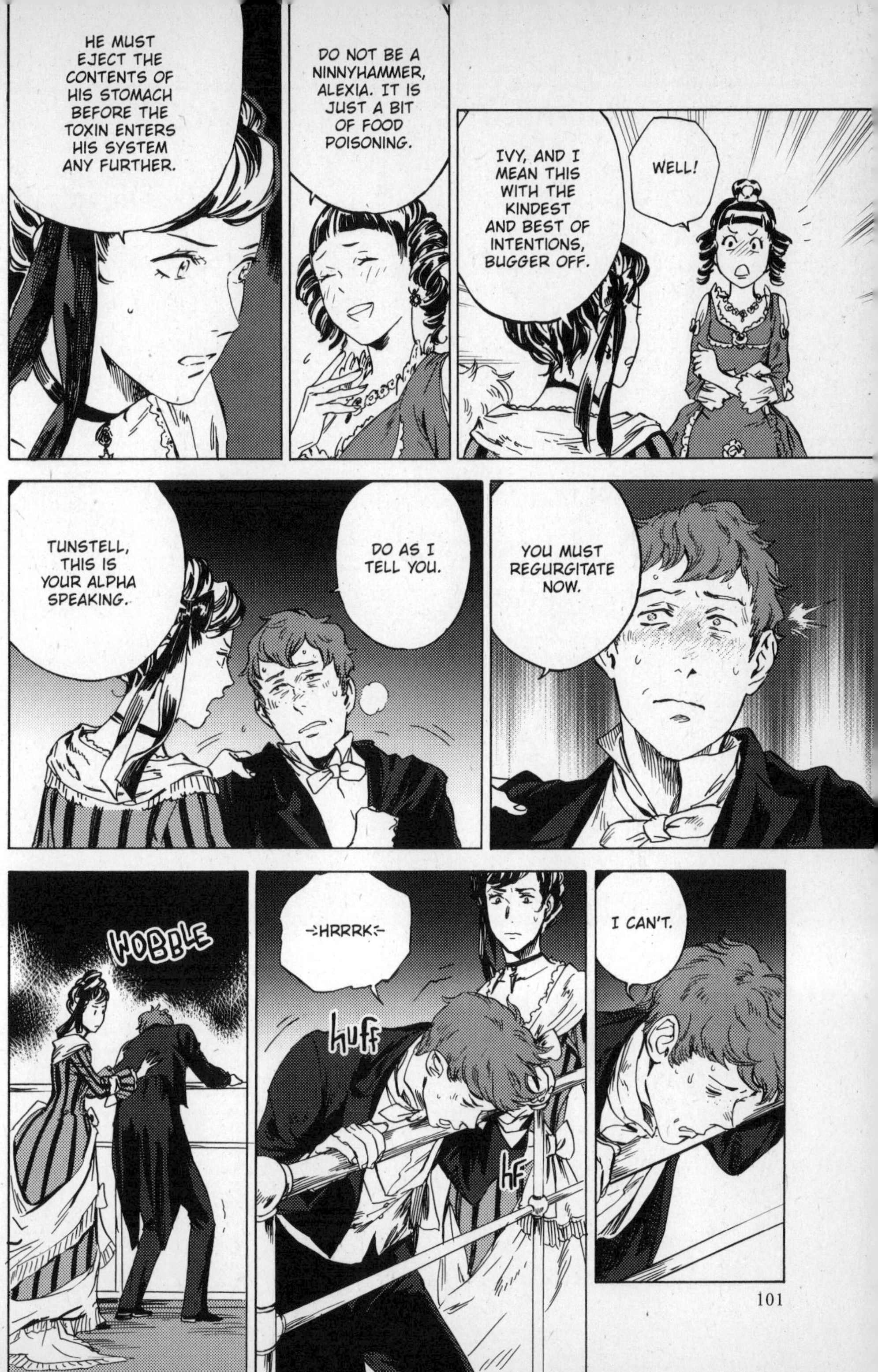
HE MUST EJECT THE CONTENTS OF HIS STOMACH BEFORE THE TOXIN ENTERS HIS SYSTEM ANY FURTHER.
DO NOT BE A NINNYHAMMER, ALEXIA. IT IS JUST A BIT OF FOOD POISONING.
IVY, AND I MEAN THIS WITH THE KINDEST AND BEST OF INTENTIONS, BUGGER OFF.
WELL!
TUNSTELL, THIS IS YOUR ALPHA SPEAKING.
DO AS I TELL YOU.
YOU MUST REGURGITATE NOW.
WOBBLE
-HRRRK-
huff
hf
I CAN'T.

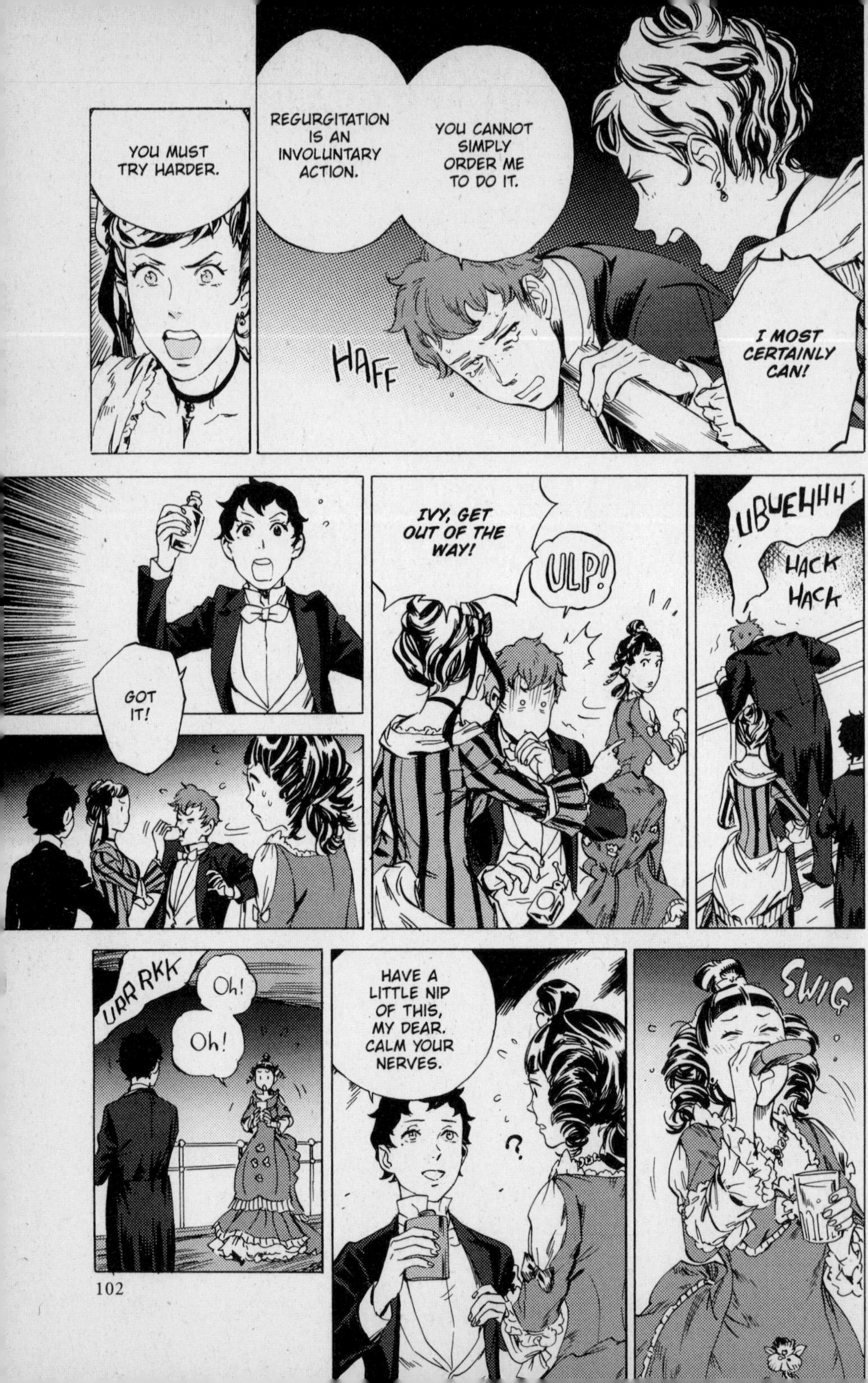
YOU MUST TRY HARDER.
REGURGITATION IS AN INVOLUNTARY ACTION.
YOU CANNOT SIMPLY ORDER ME TO DO IT.
HAFF
I MOST CERTAINLY CAN!
GOT IT!
IVY, GET OUT OF THE WAY!
ULP!
UBUEHHH
HACK HACK
URRRKK
Oh!
Oh!
HAVE A LITTLE NIP OF THIS, MY DEAR. CALM YOUR NERVES.
SWIG

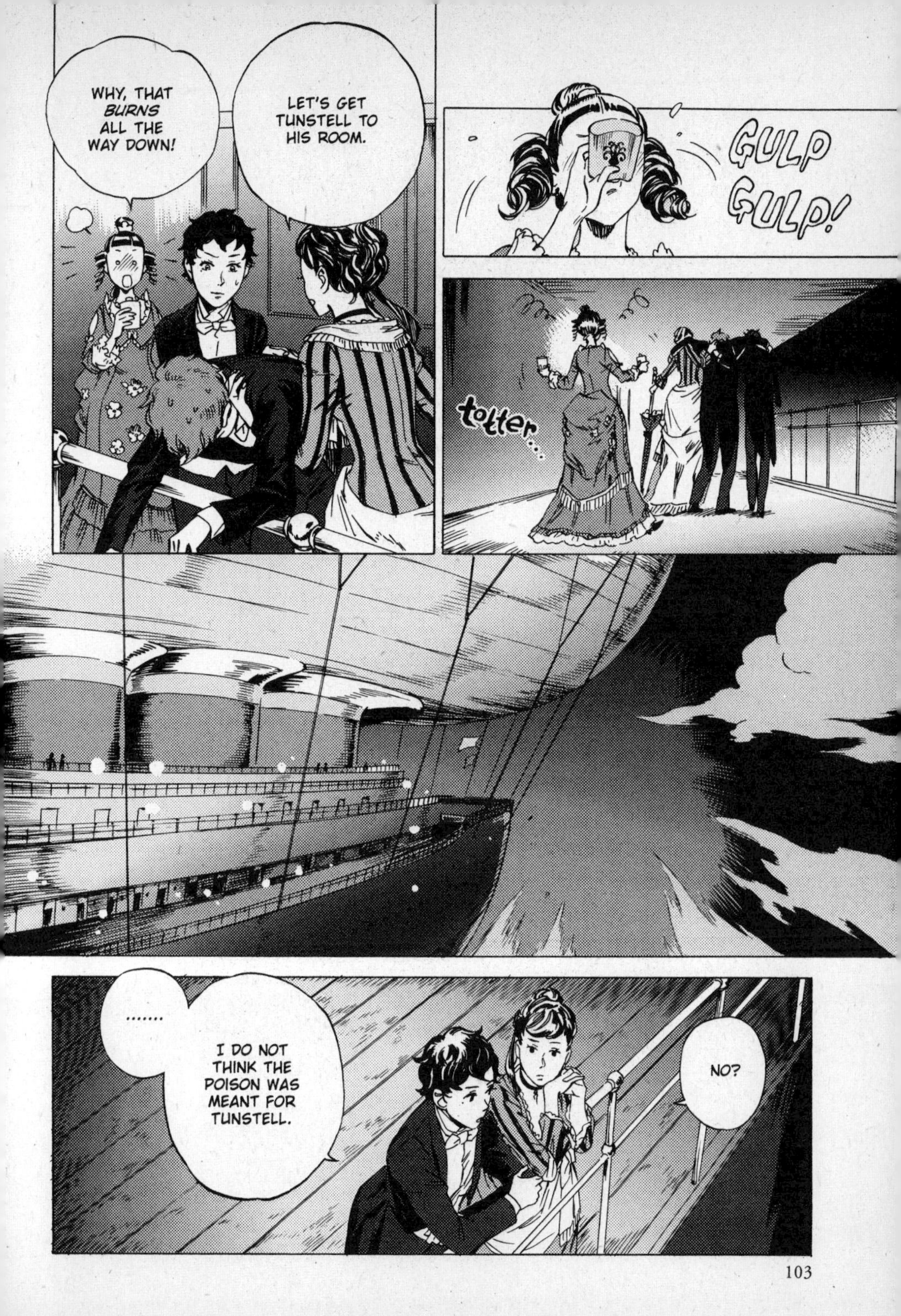

WHY, THAT *BURNS* ALL THE WAY DOWN!
LET'S GET TUNSTELL TO HIS ROOM.
GULP GULP!
totter...
......
I DO NOT THINK THE POISON WAS MEANT FOR TUNSTELL.
NO?

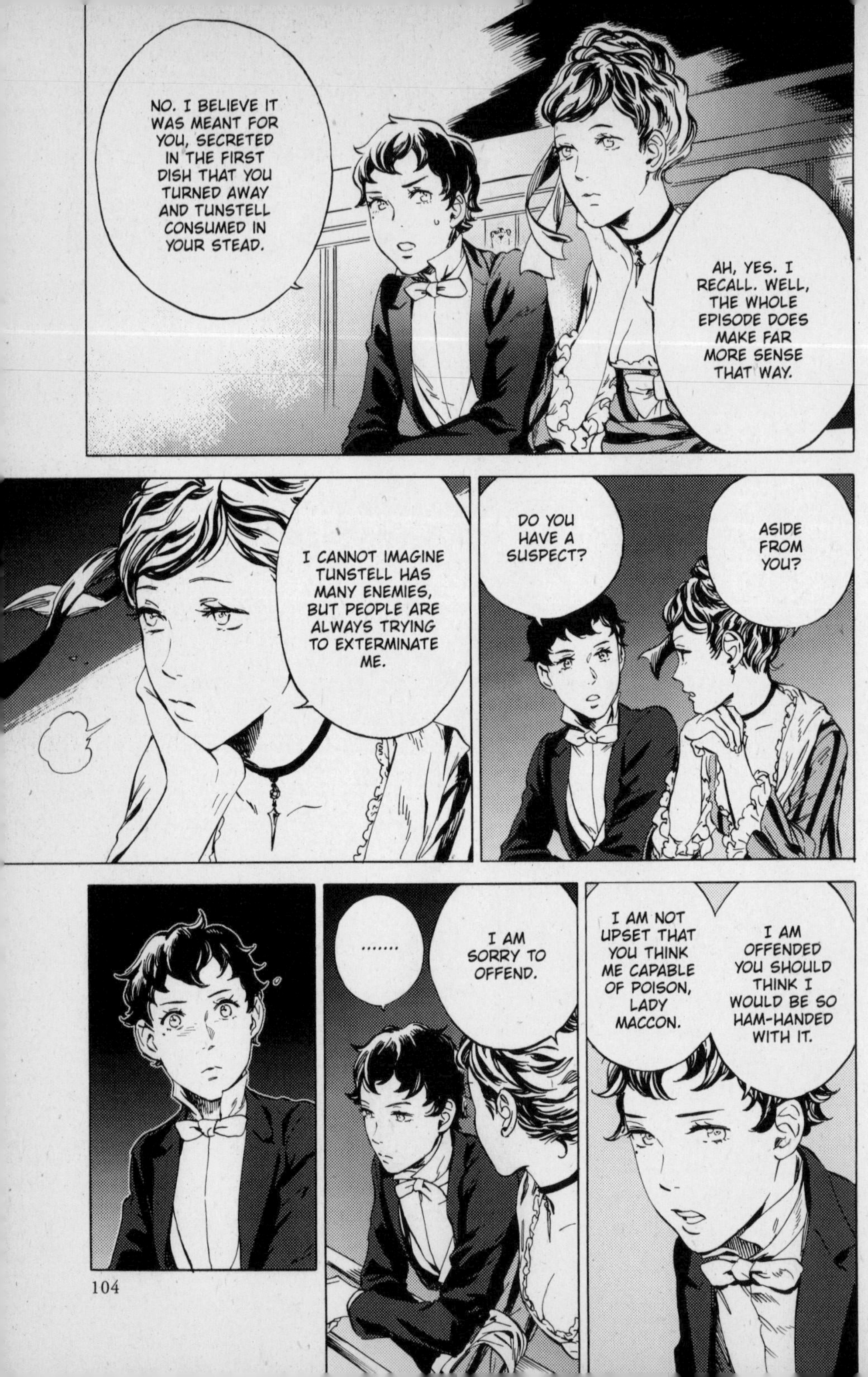
NO. I BELIEVE IT WAS MEANT FOR YOU, SECRETED IN THE FIRST DISH THAT YOU TURNED AWAY AND TUNSTELL CONSUMED IN YOUR STEAD.
AH, YES. I RECALL. WELL, THE WHOLE EPISODE DOES MAKE FAR MORE SENSE THAT WAY.
I CANNOT IMAGINE TUNSTELL HAS MANY ENEMIES, BUT PEOPLE ARE ALWAYS TRYING TO EXTERMINATE ME.
DO YOU HAVE A SUSPECT?
ASIDE FROM YOU?
....
I AM SORRY TO OFFEND.
I AM NOT UPSET THAT YOU THINK ME CAPABLE OF POISON, LADY MACCON.
I AM OFFENDED YOU SHOULD THINK I WOULD BE SO HAM-HANDED WITH IT.

HAD I WISHED YOU DEAD...

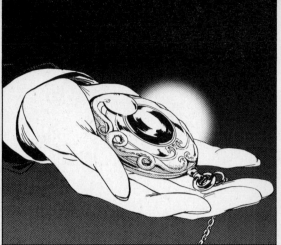

...I HAVE HAD AMPLE OPPORTUNITY.

FLK

....

TRUE, BUT THE PRIMITIVE NATURE OF THE ATTEMPT COULD BE TO THROW ME OFF THE SCENT.

YOU ARE OF A SUSPICIOUS INCLINATION, ARE YOU NOT, LADY MACCON?

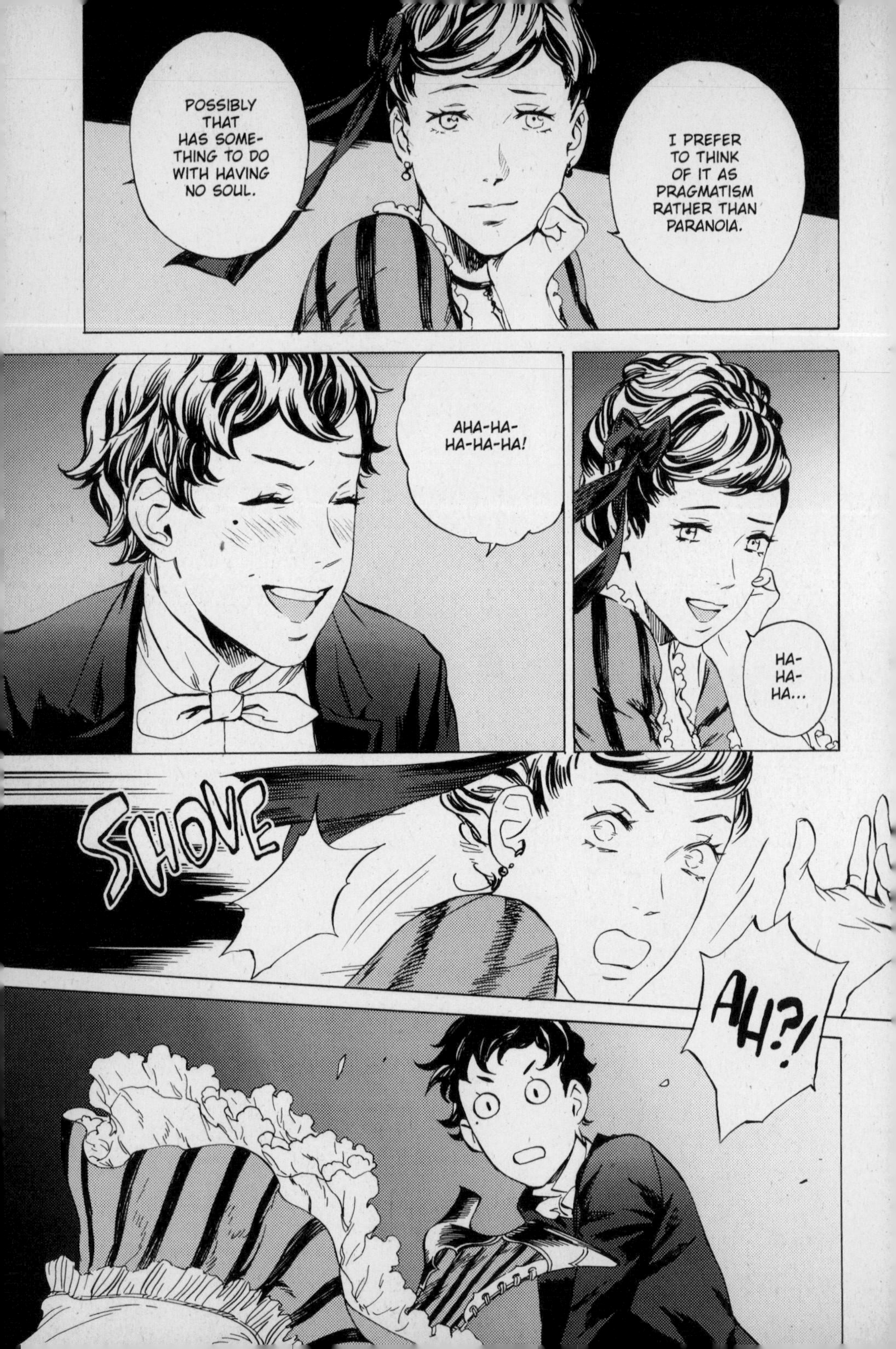
POSSIBLY THAT HAS SOME-THING TO DO WITH HAVING NO SOUL.
I PREFER TO THINK OF IT AS PRAGMATISM RATHER THAN PARANOIA.
AHA-HA-HA-HA-HA!
HA-HA-HA...
SHOVE
AH?!

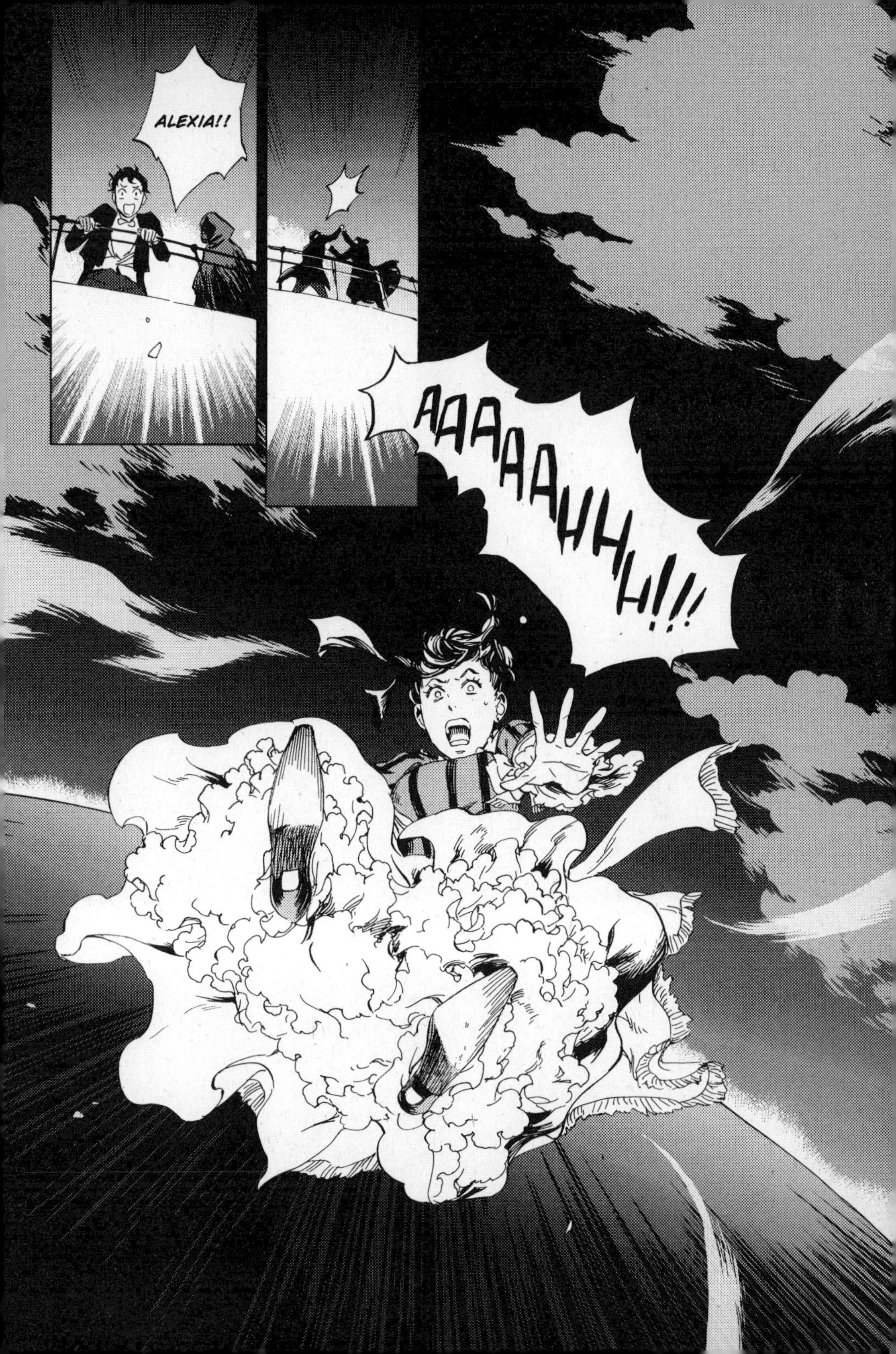
ALEXIA!!
AAAAAAHHHH!!!

SOULLESS

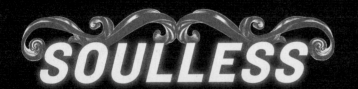

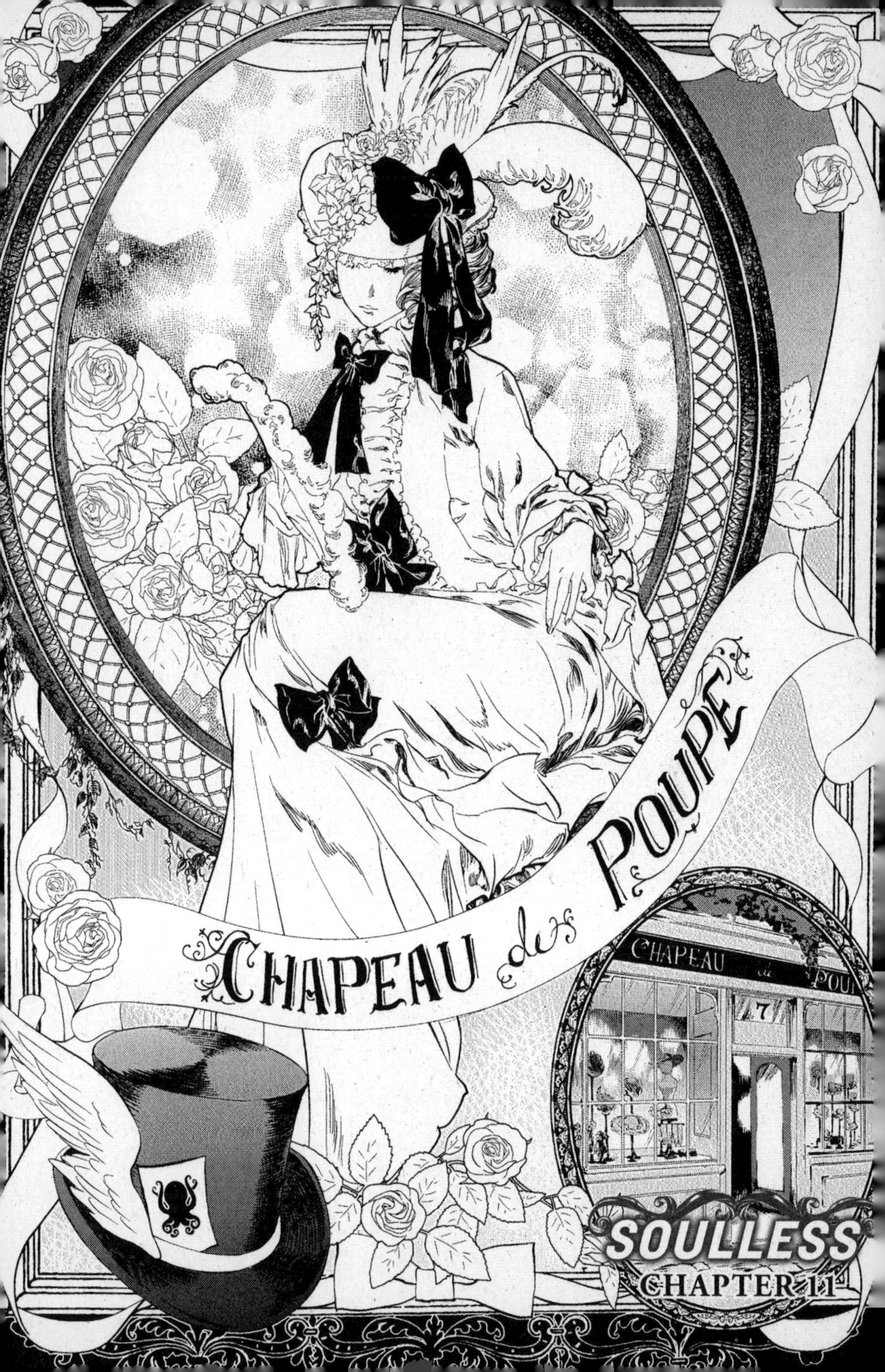
CHAPEAU de POUPE
CHAPEAU de POUPE
7
SOULLESS
CHAPTER 11

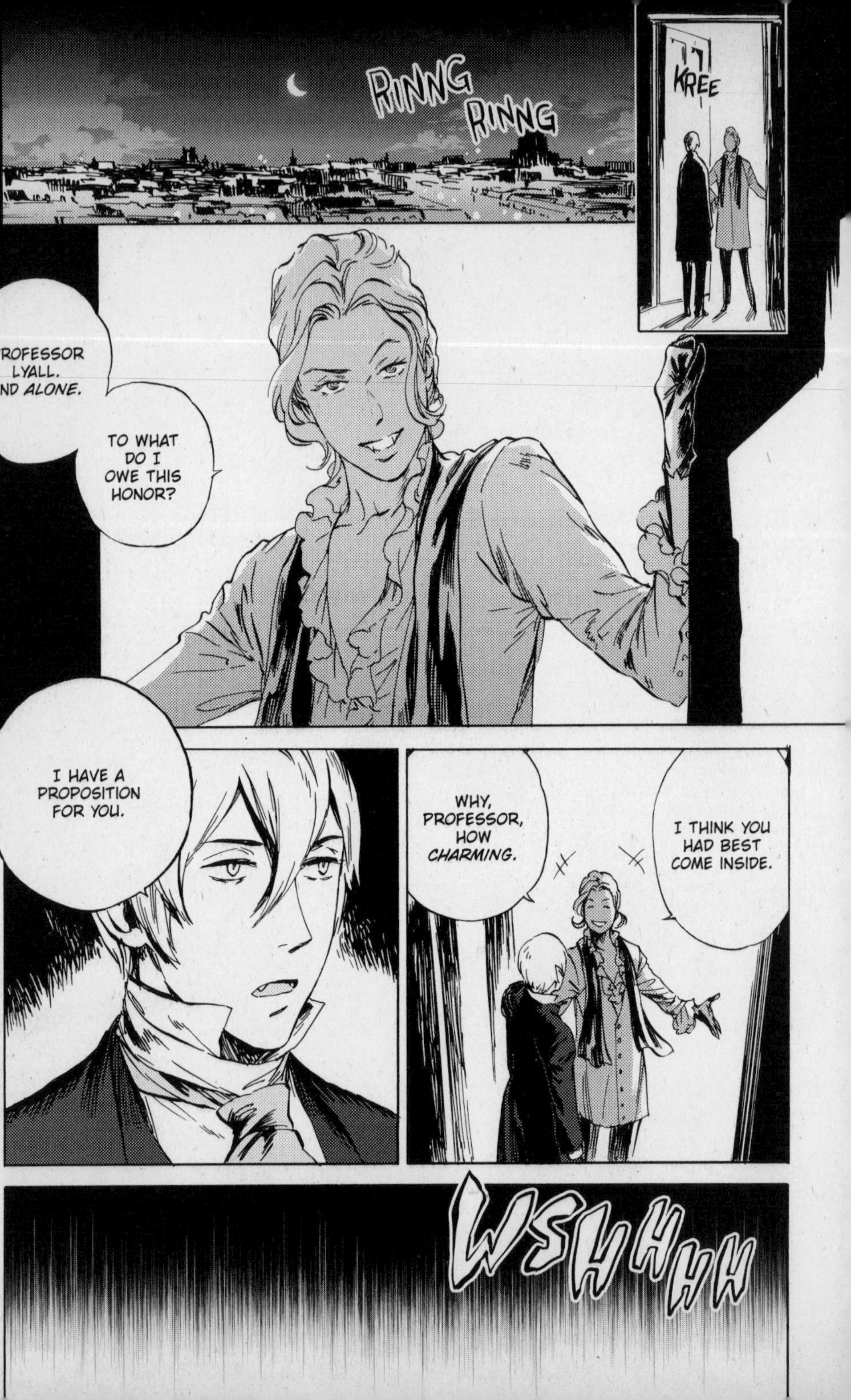
RINNG RINNG
KREE
PROFESSOR LYALL. AND *ALONE*.
TO WHAT DO I OWE THIS HONOR?
I HAVE A PROPOSITION FOR YOU.
WHY, PROFESSOR, HOW *CHARMING*.
I THINK YOU HAD BEST COME INSIDE.
WSHHHH

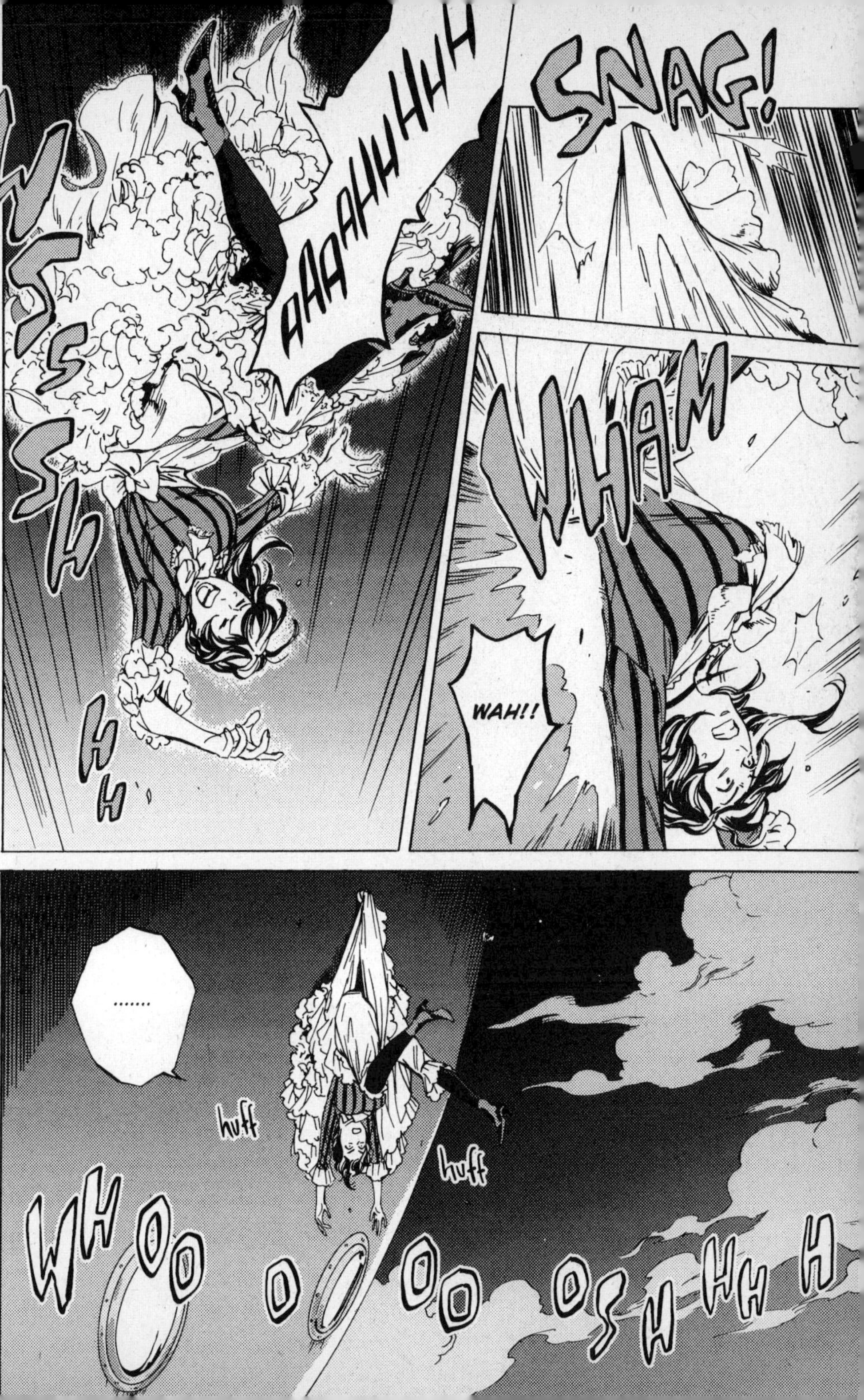
WHSSSHHH
AAAAHHHHHH
SNAG!
WHAM
WAH!!
......
huff
huff
WHOOOOOOOSHHHH

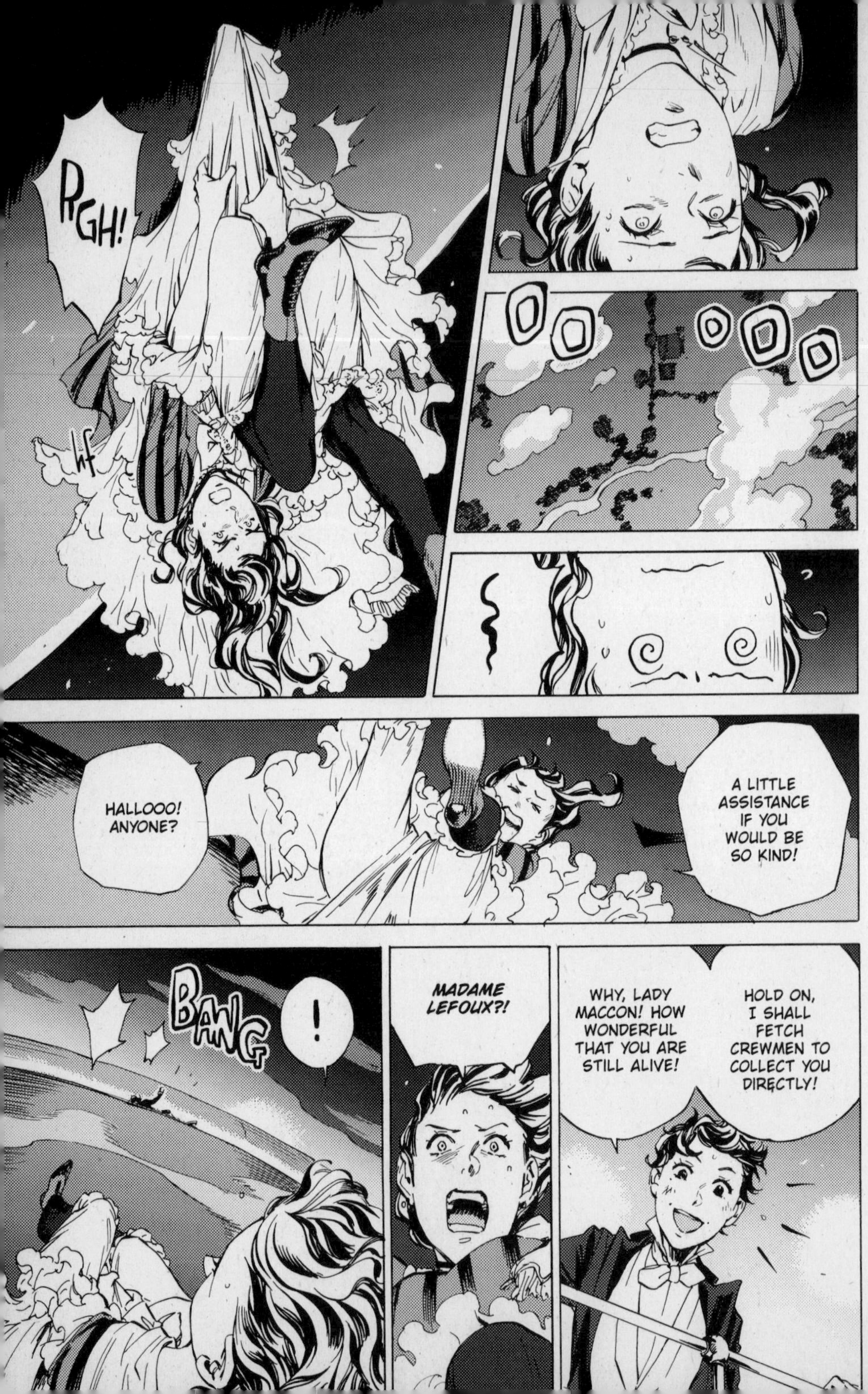
RGH!
hf
HALLOOO! ANYONE?
A LITTLE ASSISTANCE IF YOU WOULD BE SO KIND!
BANG
!
MADAME LEFOUX?!
WHY, LADY MACCON! HOW WONDERFUL THAT YOU ARE STILL ALIVE!
HOLD ON, I SHALL FETCH CREWMEN TO COLLECT YOU DIRECTLY!

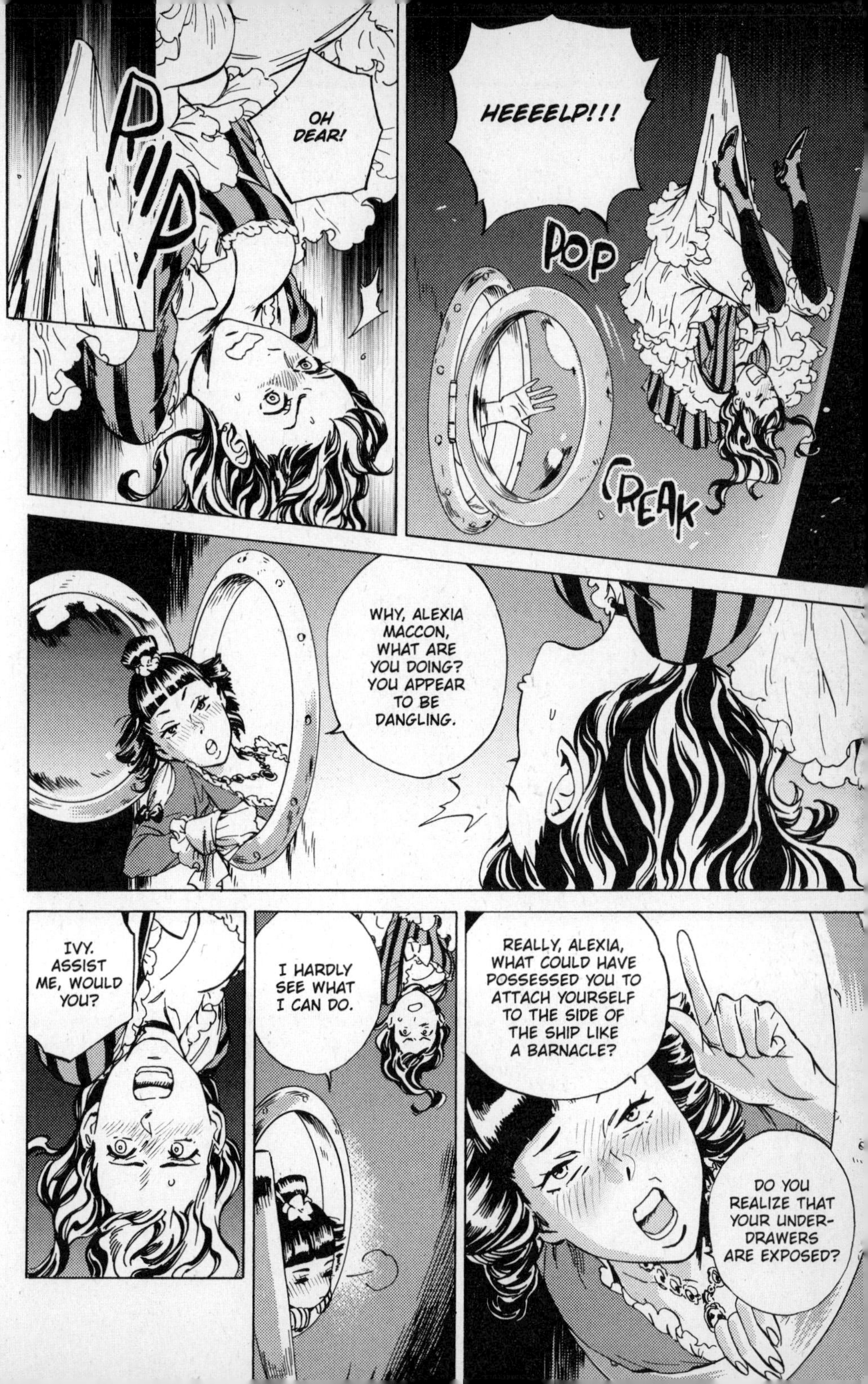
RIP
OH DEAR!
HEEEELP!!!
POP
CREAK
WHY, ALEXIA MACCON, WHAT ARE YOU DOING? YOU APPEAR TO BE DANGLING.
IVY. ASSIST ME, WOULD YOU?
I HARDLY SEE WHAT I CAN DO.
REALLY, ALEXIA, WHAT COULD HAVE POSSESSED YOU TO ATTACH YOURSELF TO THE SIDE OF THE SHIP LIKE A BARNACLE?
DO YOU REALIZE THAT YOUR UNDER-DRAWERS ARE EXPOSED?

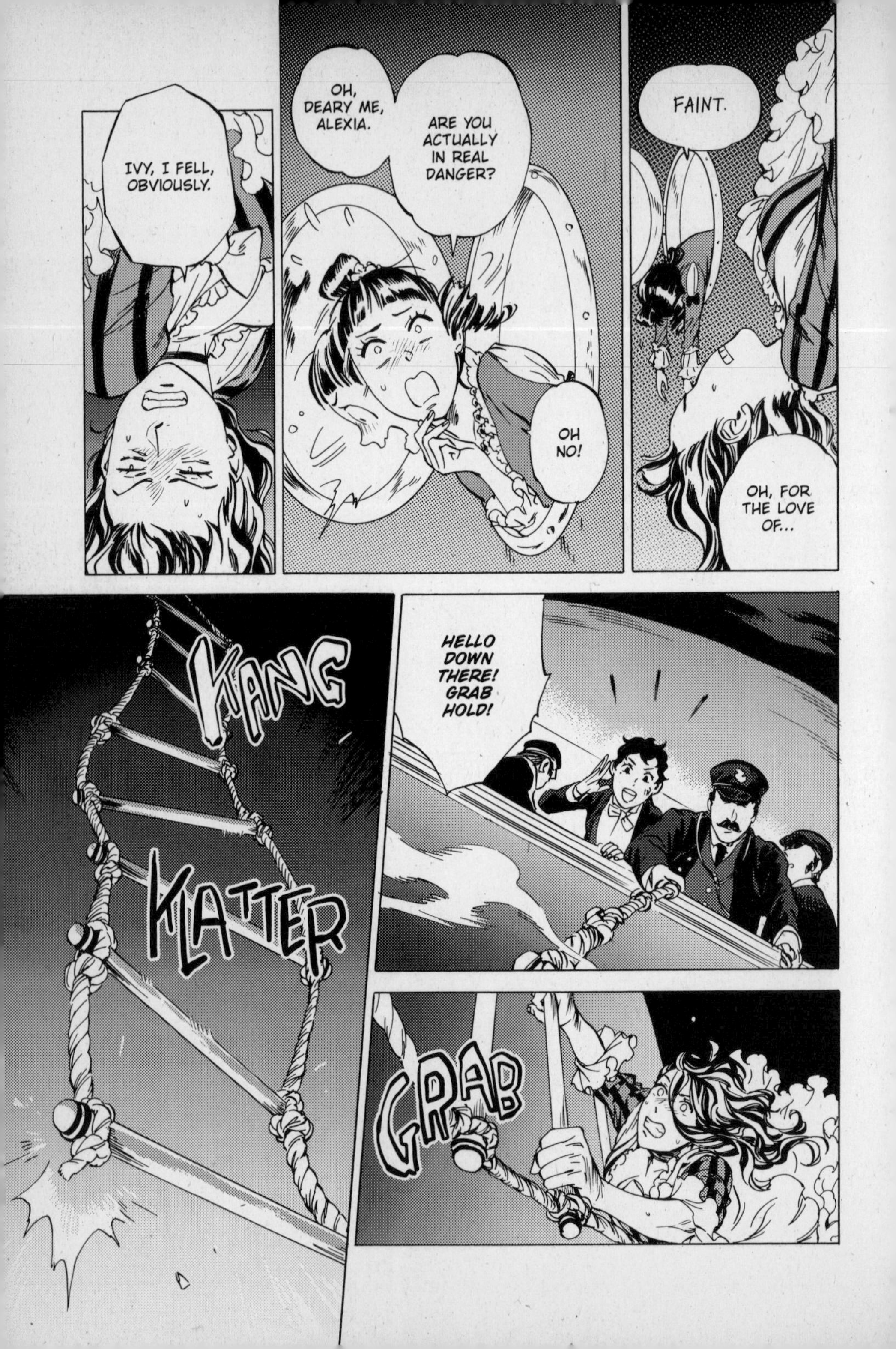
IVY, I FELL, OBVIOUSLY.
OH, DEARY ME, ALEXIA.
ARE YOU ACTUALLY IN REAL DANGER?
OH NO!
FAINT.
OH, FOR THE LOVE OF...
KANG
KLATTER
HELLO DOWN THERE! GRAB HOLD!
GRAB

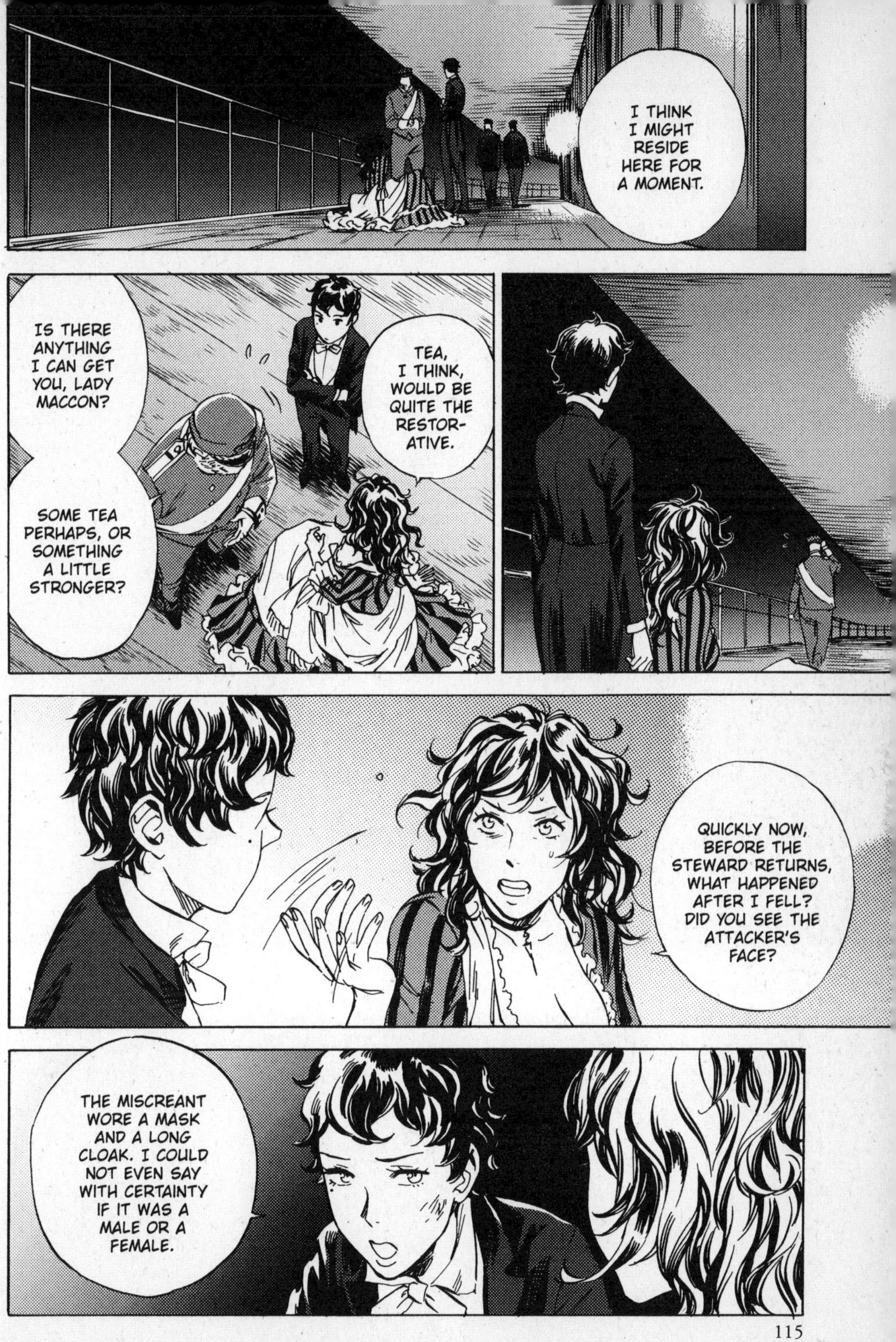
I THINK I MIGHT RESIDE HERE FOR A MOMENT.
IS THERE ANYTHING I CAN GET YOU, LADY MACCON?
SOME TEA PERHAPS, OR SOMETHING A LITTLE STRONGER?
TEA, I THINK, WOULD BE QUITE THE RESTORATIVE.
QUICKLY NOW, BEFORE THE STEWARD RETURNS, WHAT HAPPENED AFTER I FELL? DID YOU SEE THE ATTACKER'S FACE?
THE MISCREANT WORE A MASK AND A LONG CLOAK. I COULD NOT EVEN SAY WITH CERTAINTY IF IT WAS A MALE OR A FEMALE.

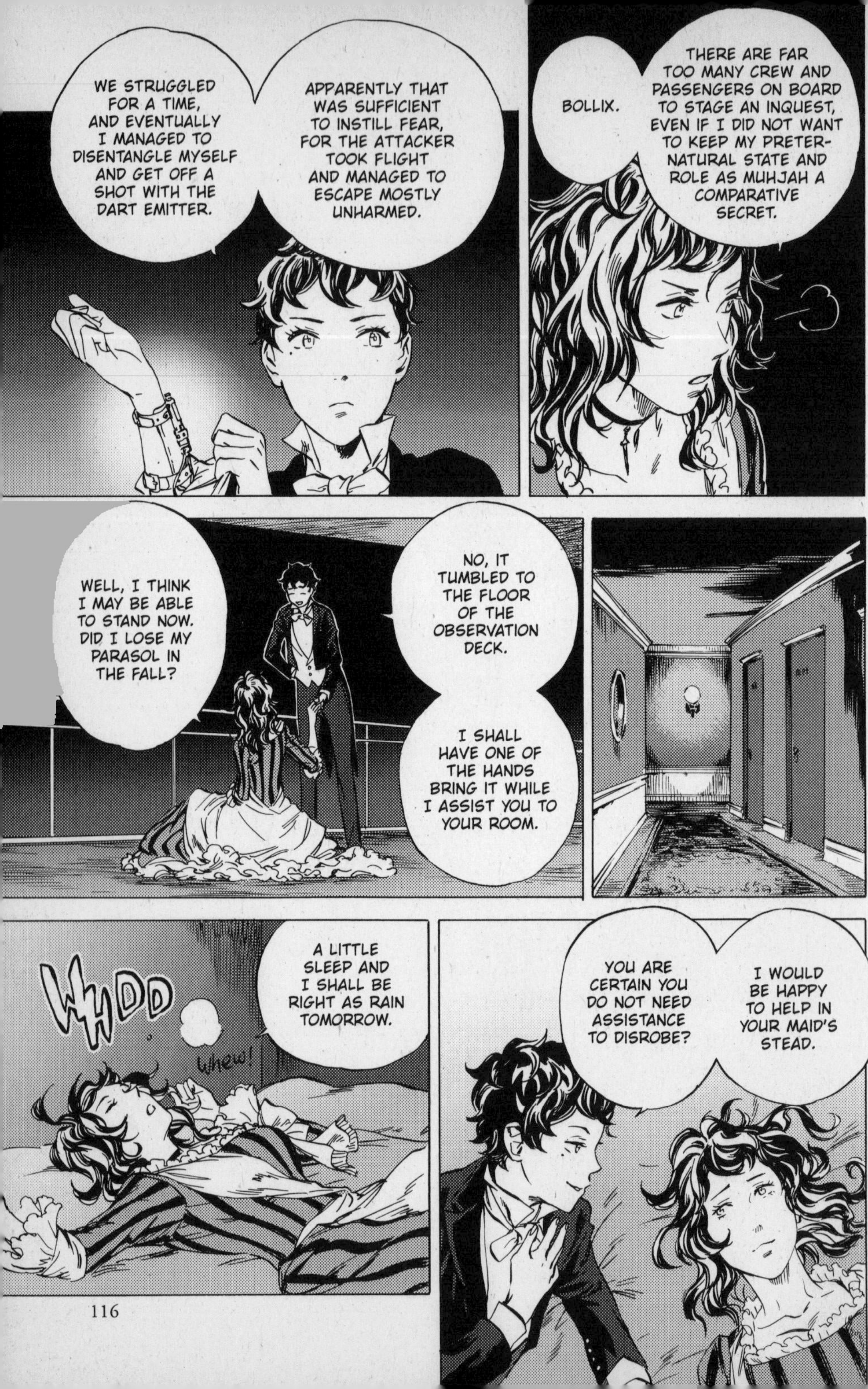
WE STRUGGLED FOR A TIME, AND EVENTUALLY I MANAGED TO DISENTANGLE MYSELF AND GET OFF A SHOT WITH THE DART EMITTER.
APPARENTLY THAT WAS SUFFICIENT TO INSTILL FEAR, FOR THE ATTACKER TOOK FLIGHT AND MANAGED TO ESCAPE MOSTLY UNHARMED.
BOLLIX.
THERE ARE FAR TOO MANY CREW AND PASSENGERS ON BOARD TO STAGE AN INQUEST, EVEN IF I DID NOT WANT TO KEEP MY PRETER-NATURAL STATE AND ROLE AS MUHJAH A COMPARATIVE SECRET.
WELL, I THINK I MAY BE ABLE TO STAND NOW. DID I LOSE MY PARASOL IN THE FALL?
NO, IT TUMBLED TO THE FLOOR OF THE OBSERVATION DECK.
I SHALL HAVE ONE OF THE HANDS BRING IT WHILE I ASSIST YOU TO YOUR ROOM.
WHDD
Whew!
A LITTLE SLEEP AND I SHALL BE RIGHT AS RAIN TOMORROW.
YOU ARE CERTAIN YOU DO NOT NEED ASSISTANCE TO DISROBE?
I WOULD BE HAPPY TO HELP IN YOUR MAID'S STEAD.

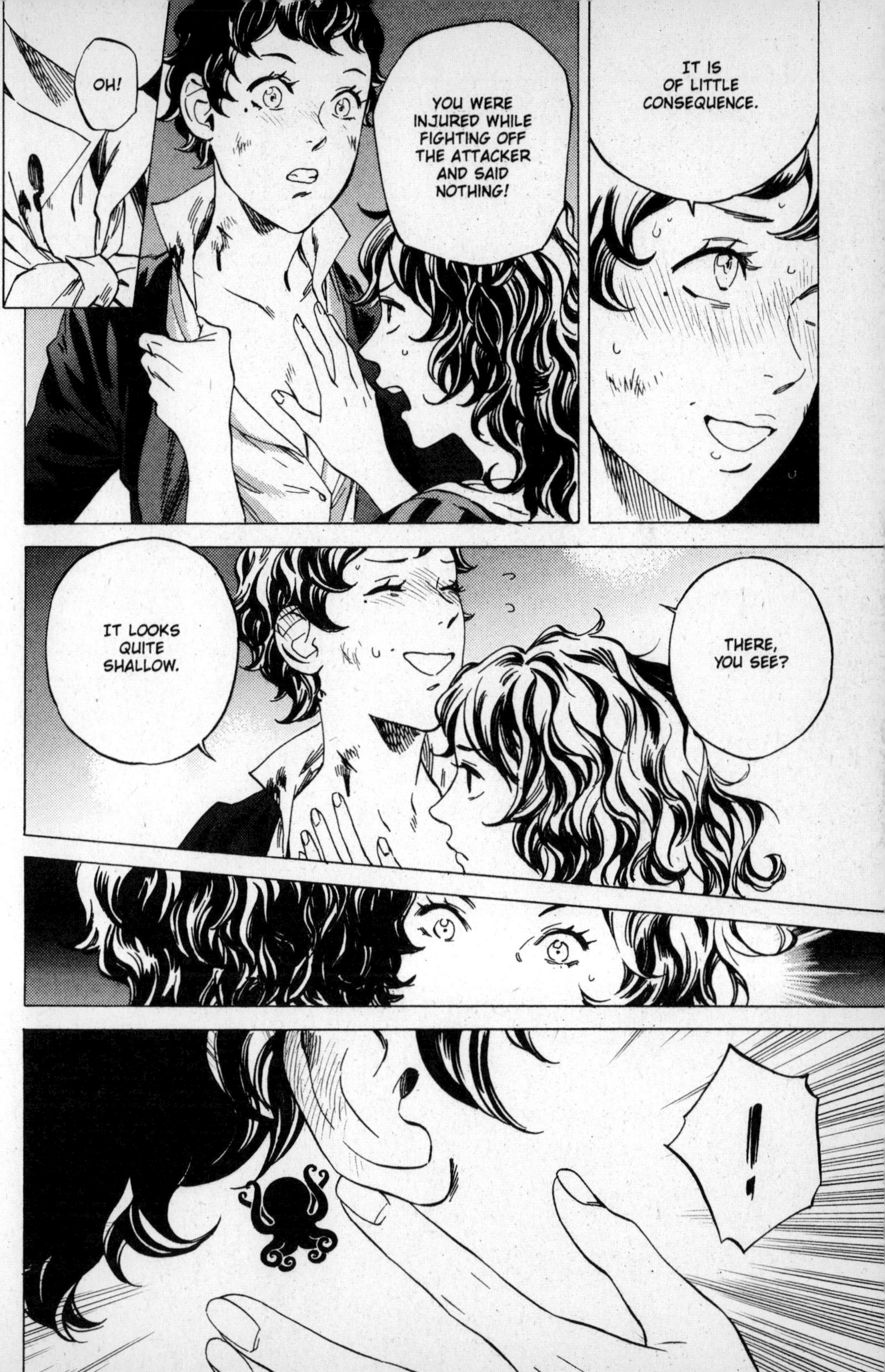
OH!
YOU WERE INJURED WHILE FIGHTING OFF THE ATTACKER AND SAID NOTHING!
IT IS OF LITTLE CONSEQUENCE.
IT LOOKS QUITE SHALLOW.
THERE, YOU SEE?
!

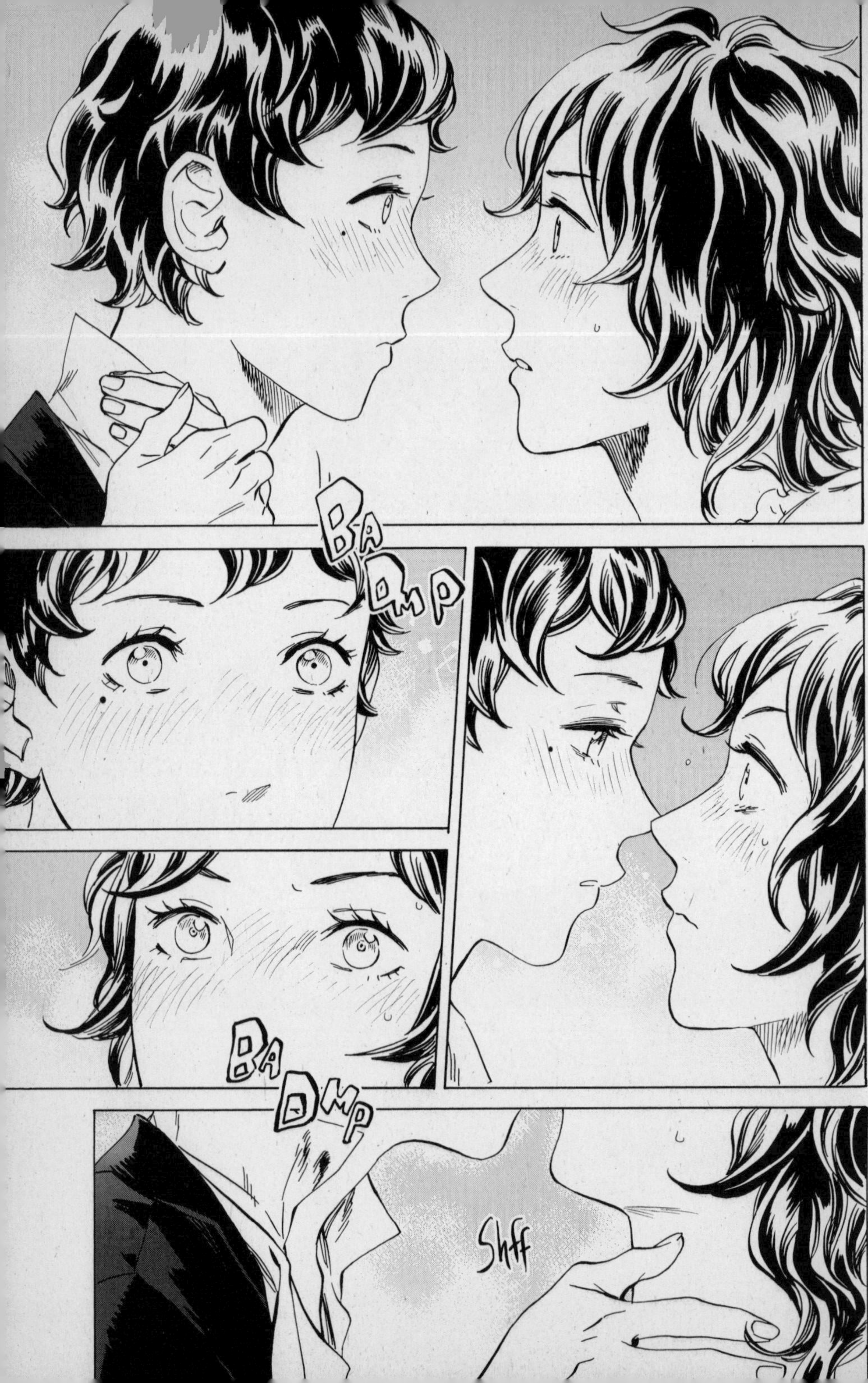
BADMP
BADMP
Shff

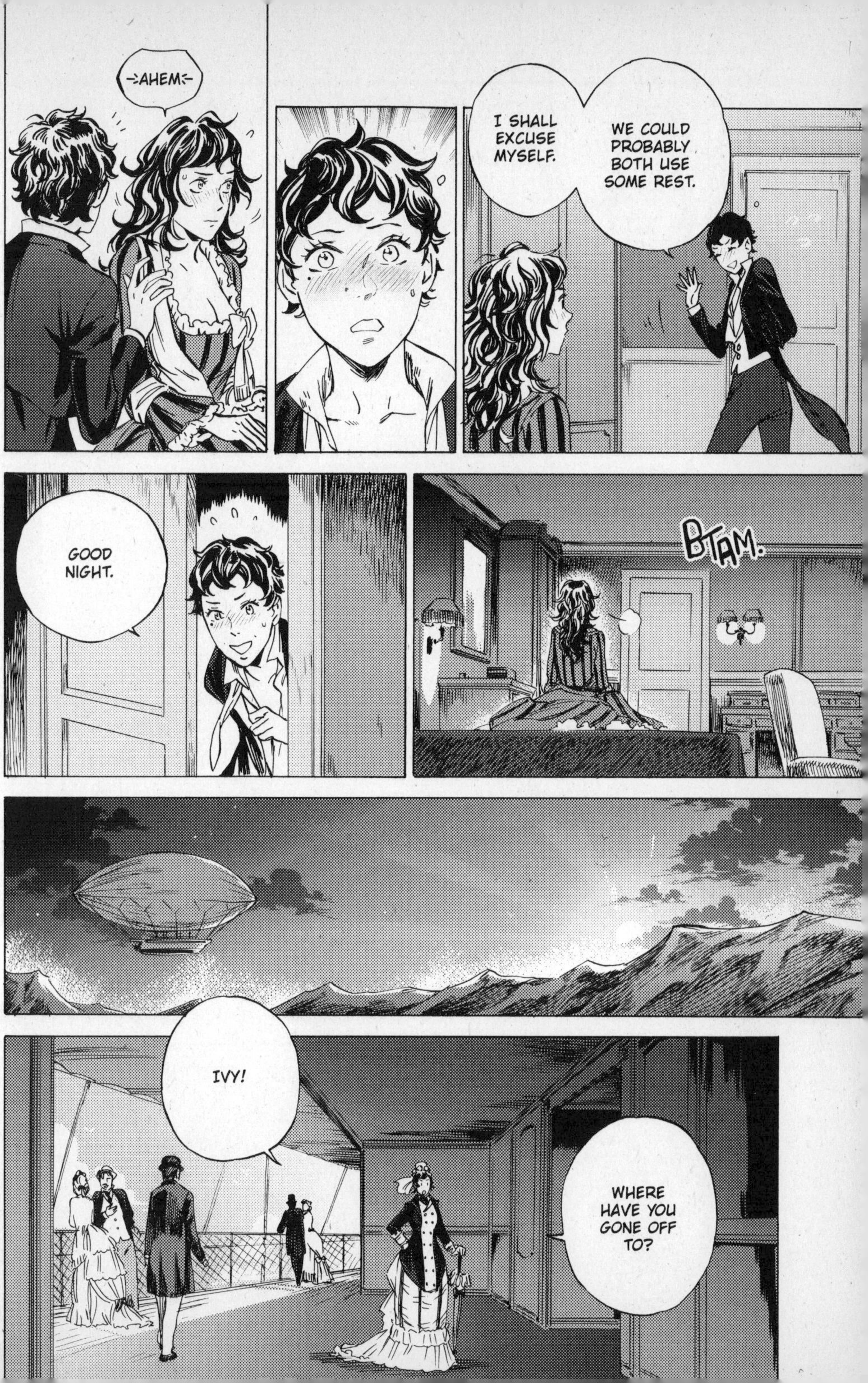
-AHEM-
I SHALL EXCUSE MYSELF.
WE COULD PROBABLY BOTH USE SOME REST.
GOOD NIGHT.
BTAM.
IVY!
WHERE HAVE YOU GONE OFF TO?

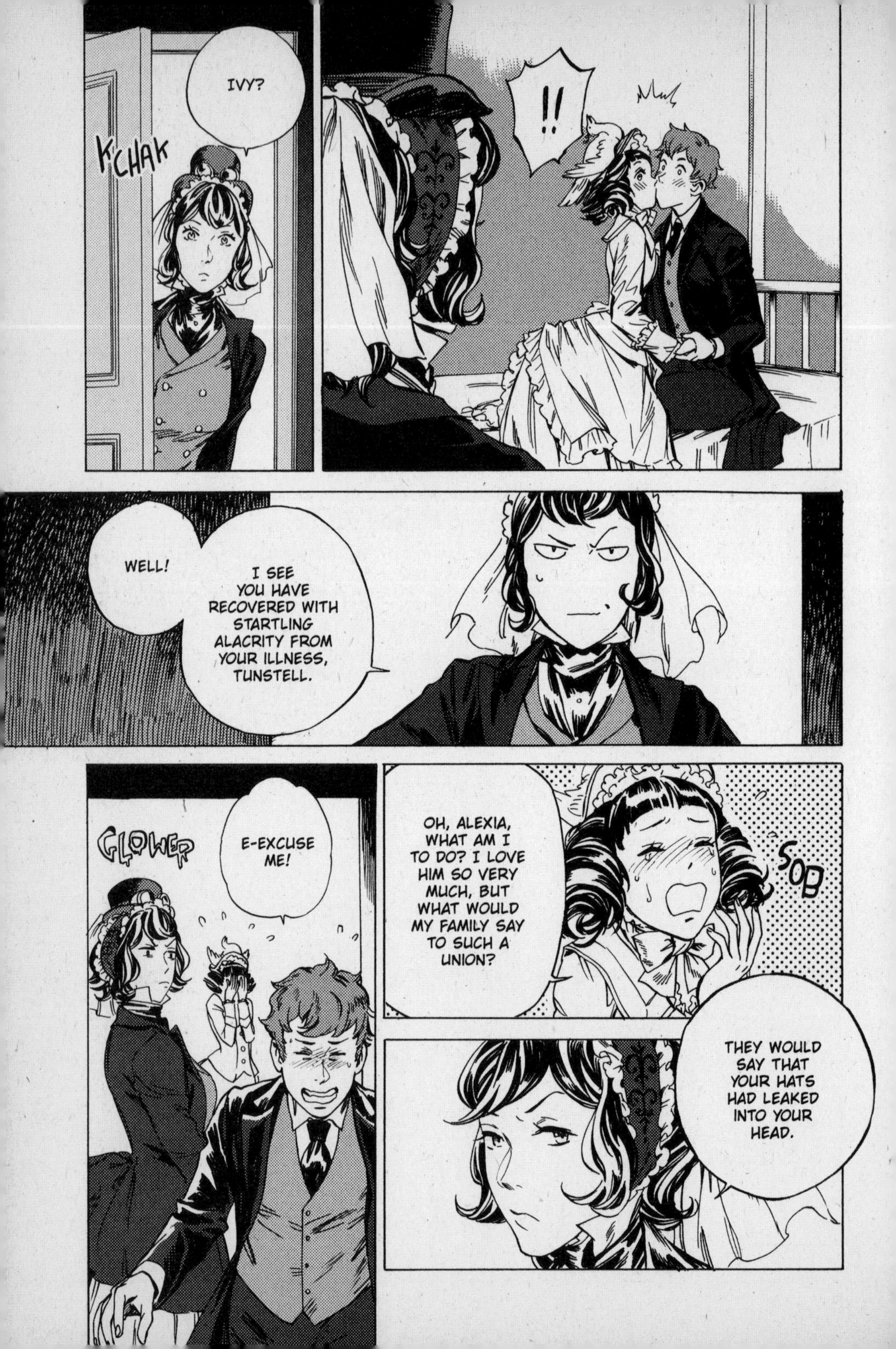
IVY?
K'CHAK
!!
WELL!
I SEE YOU HAVE RECOVERED WITH STARTLING ALACRITY FROM YOUR ILLNESS, TUNSTELL.
GLOWER
E-EXCUSE ME!
OH, ALEXIA, WHAT AM I TO DO? I LOVE HIM SO VERY MUCH, BUT WHAT WOULD MY FAMILY SAY TO SUCH A UNION?
SOB
THEY WOULD SAY THAT YOUR HATS HAD LEAKED INTO YOUR HEAD.

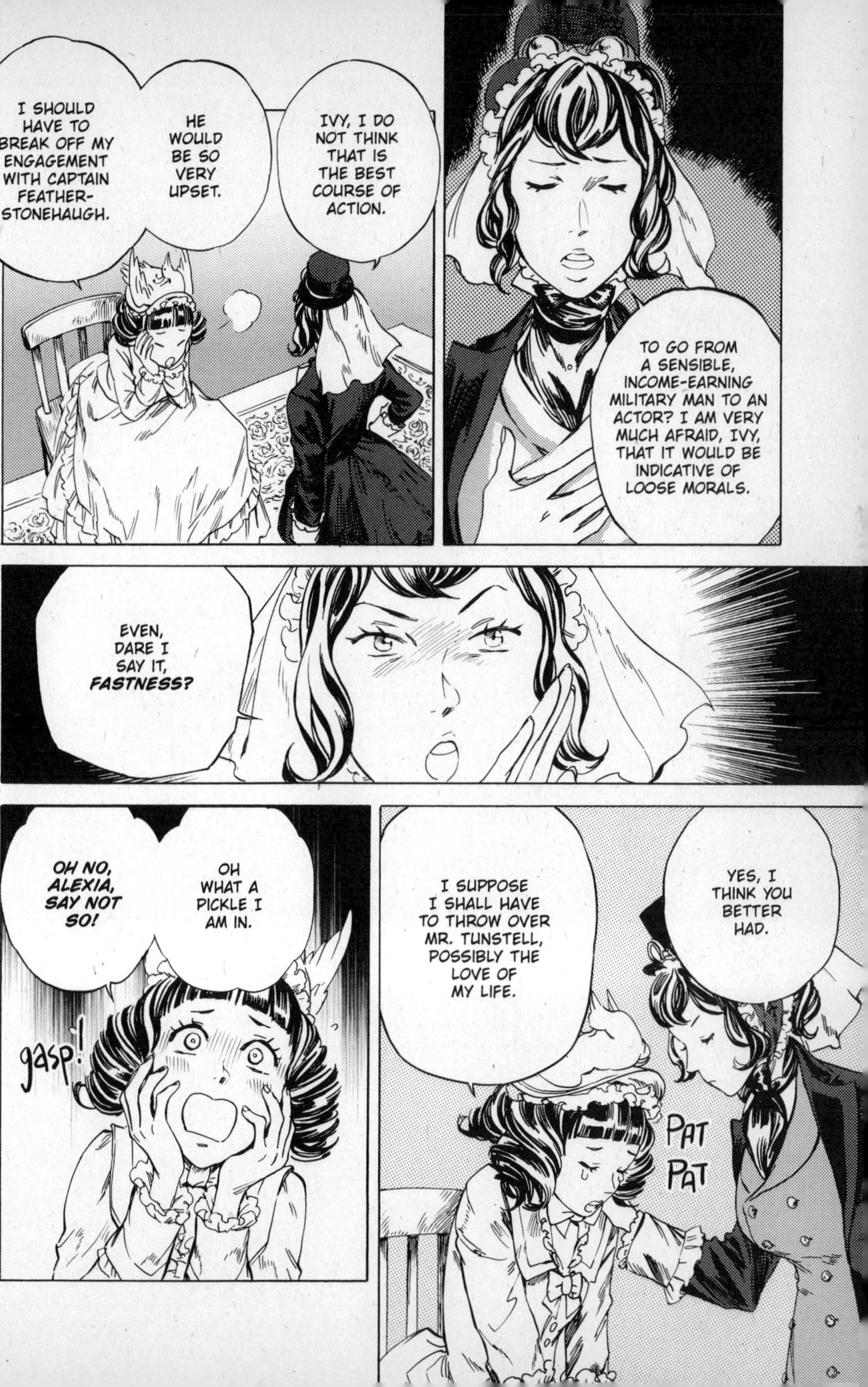
I SHOULD HAVE TO BREAK OFF MY ENGAGEMENT WITH CAPTAIN FEATHER-STONEHAUGH.
HE WOULD BE SO VERY UPSET.
IVY, I DO NOT THINK THAT IS THE BEST COURSE OF ACTION.
TO GO FROM A SENSIBLE, INCOME-EARNING MILITARY MAN TO AN ACTOR? I AM VERY MUCH AFRAID, IVY, THAT IT WOULD BE INDICATIVE OF LOOSE MORALS.
EVEN, DARE I SAY IT, ***FASTNESS?***
OH NO, ALEXIA, SAY NOT SO!
OH WHAT A PICKLE I AM IN.
gasp!
I SUPPOSE I SHALL HAVE TO THROW OVER MR. TUNSTELL, POSSIBLY THE LOVE OF MY LIFE.
YES, I THINK YOU BETTER HAD.
PAT PAT

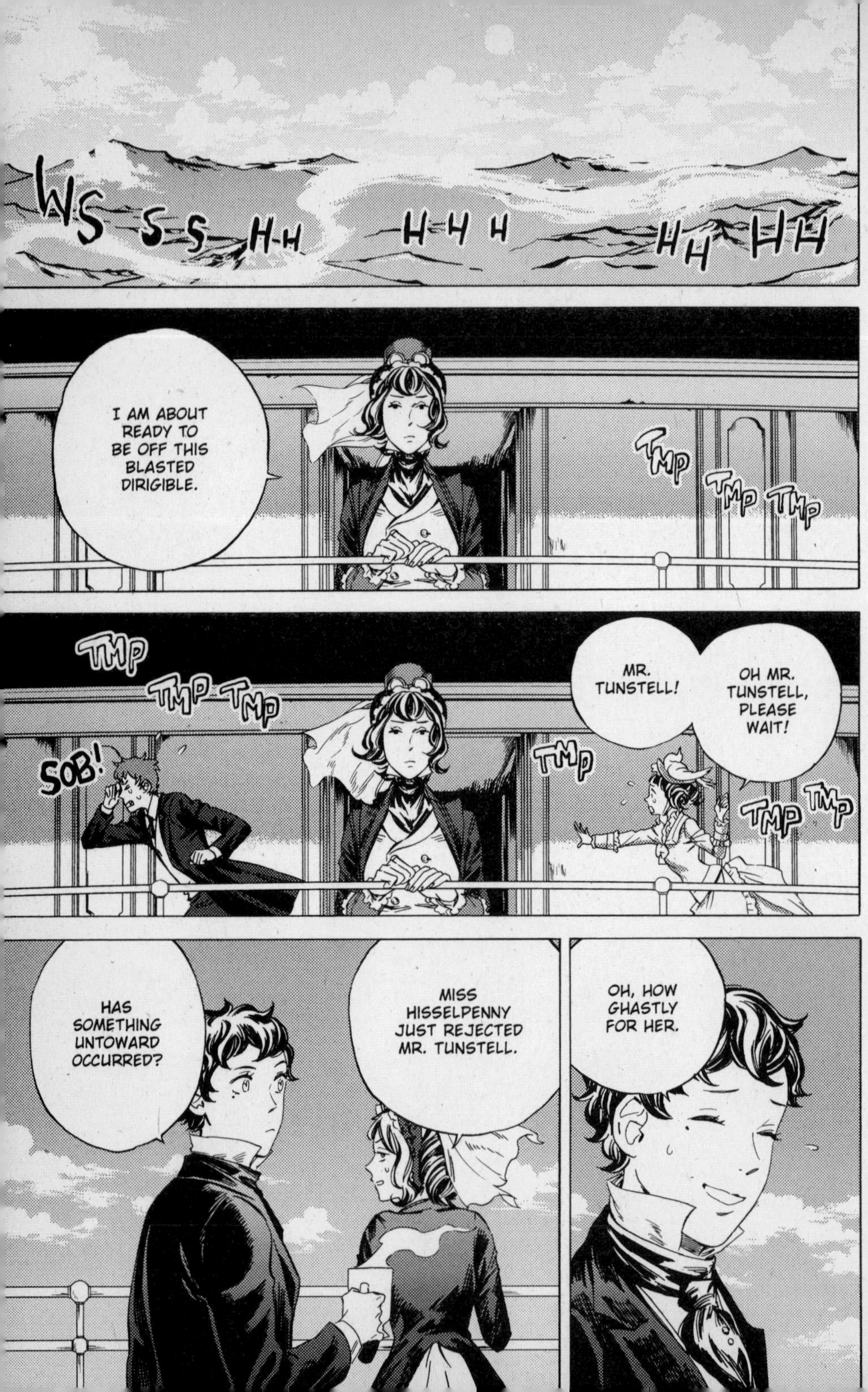
WSSSHH HHH HHHHH
I AM ABOUT READY TO BE OFF THIS BLASTED DIRIGIBLE.
TMP TMP TMP
TMP TMP TMP
SOB!
TMP
MR. TUNSTELL!
OH MR. TUNSTELL, PLEASE WAIT!
TMP TMP
HAS SOMETHING UNTOWARD OCCURRED?
MISS HISSELPENNY JUST REJECTED MR. TUNSTELL.
OH, HOW GHASTLY FOR HER.

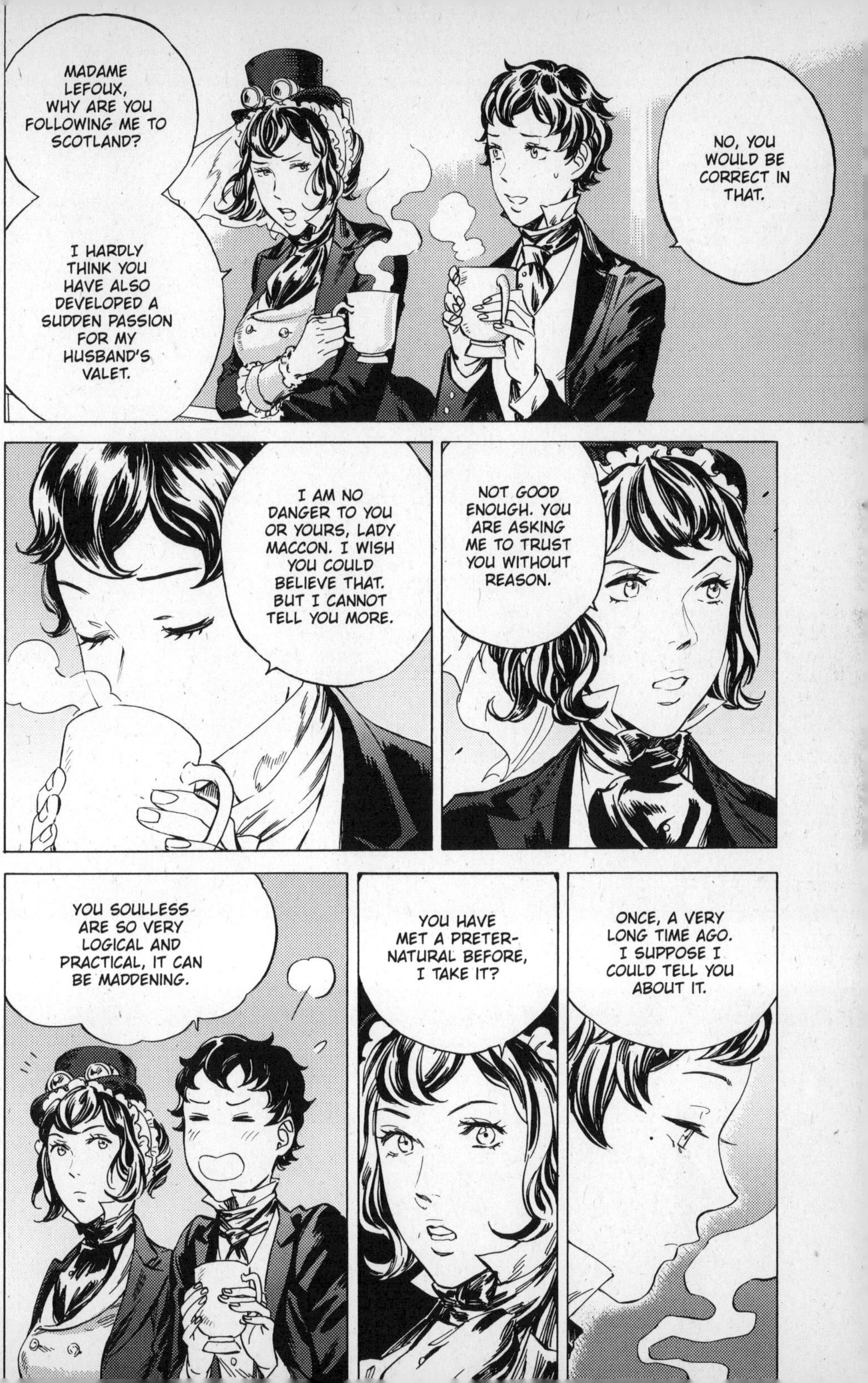
MADAME LEFOUX, WHY ARE YOU FOLLOWING ME TO SCOTLAND?
I HARDLY THINK YOU HAVE ALSO DEVELOPED A SUDDEN PASSION FOR MY HUSBAND'S VALET.
NO, YOU WOULD BE CORRECT IN THAT.
I AM NO DANGER TO YOU OR YOURS, LADY MACCON. I WISH YOU COULD BELIEVE THAT. BUT I CANNOT TELL YOU MORE.
NOT GOOD ENOUGH. YOU ARE ASKING ME TO TRUST YOU WITHOUT REASON.
YOU SOULLESS ARE SO VERY LOGICAL AND PRACTICAL, IT CAN BE MADDENING.
YOU HAVE MET A PRETER-NATURAL BEFORE, I TAKE IT?
ONCE, A VERY LONG TIME AGO. I SUPPOSE I COULD TELL YOU ABOUT IT.

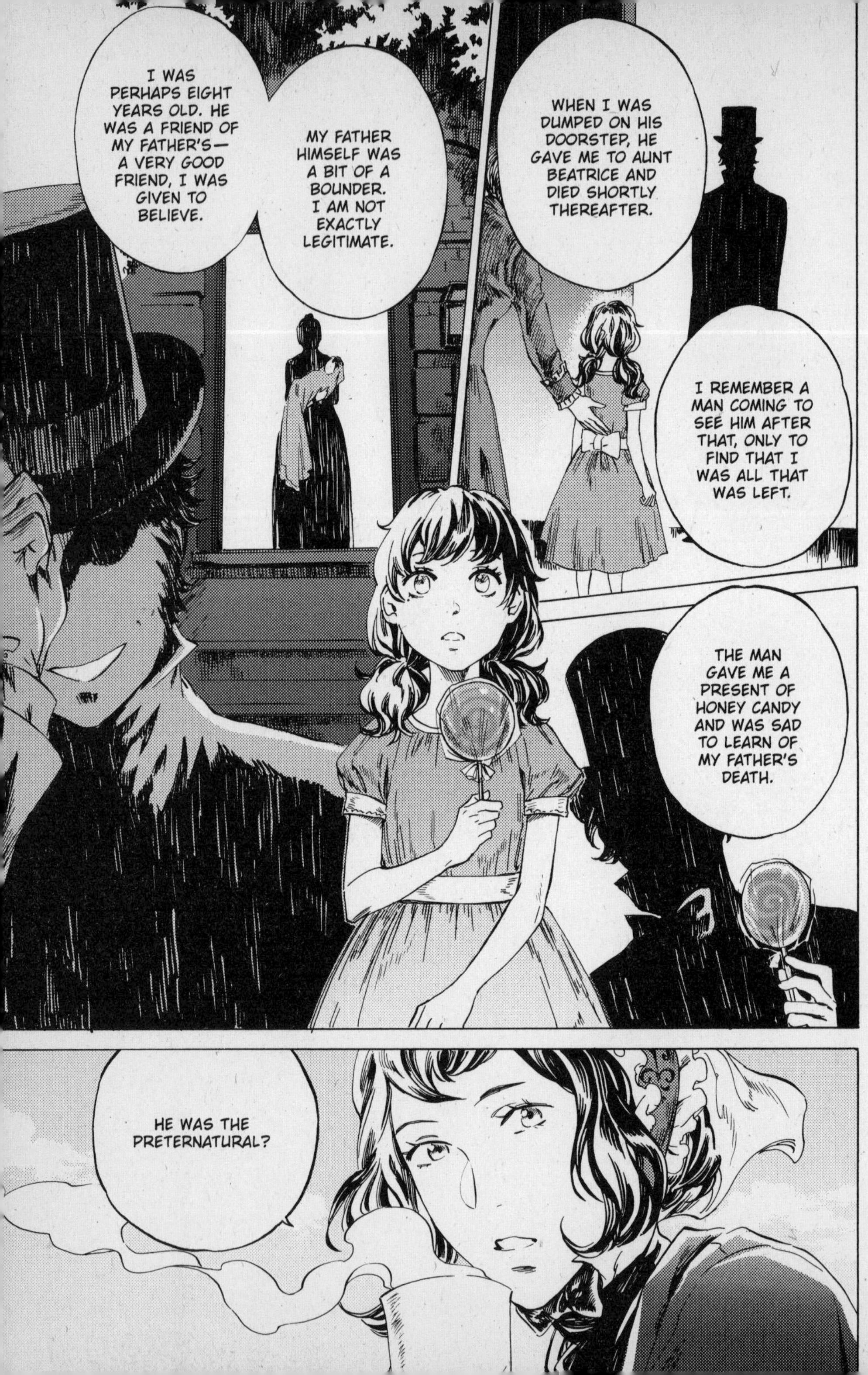
I WAS PERHAPS EIGHT YEARS OLD. HE WAS A FRIEND OF MY FATHER'S— A VERY GOOD FRIEND, I WAS GIVEN TO BELIEVE.
MY FATHER HIMSELF WAS A BIT OF A BOUNDER. I AM NOT EXACTLY LEGITIMATE.
WHEN I WAS DUMPED ON HIS DOORSTEP, HE GAVE ME TO AUNT BEATRICE AND DIED SHORTLY THEREAFTER.
I REMEMBER A MAN COMING TO SEE HIM AFTER THAT, ONLY TO FIND THAT I WAS ALL THAT WAS LEFT.
THE MAN GAVE ME A PRESENT OF HONEY CANDY AND WAS SAD TO LEARN OF MY FATHER'S DEATH.
HE WAS THE PRETERNATURAL?

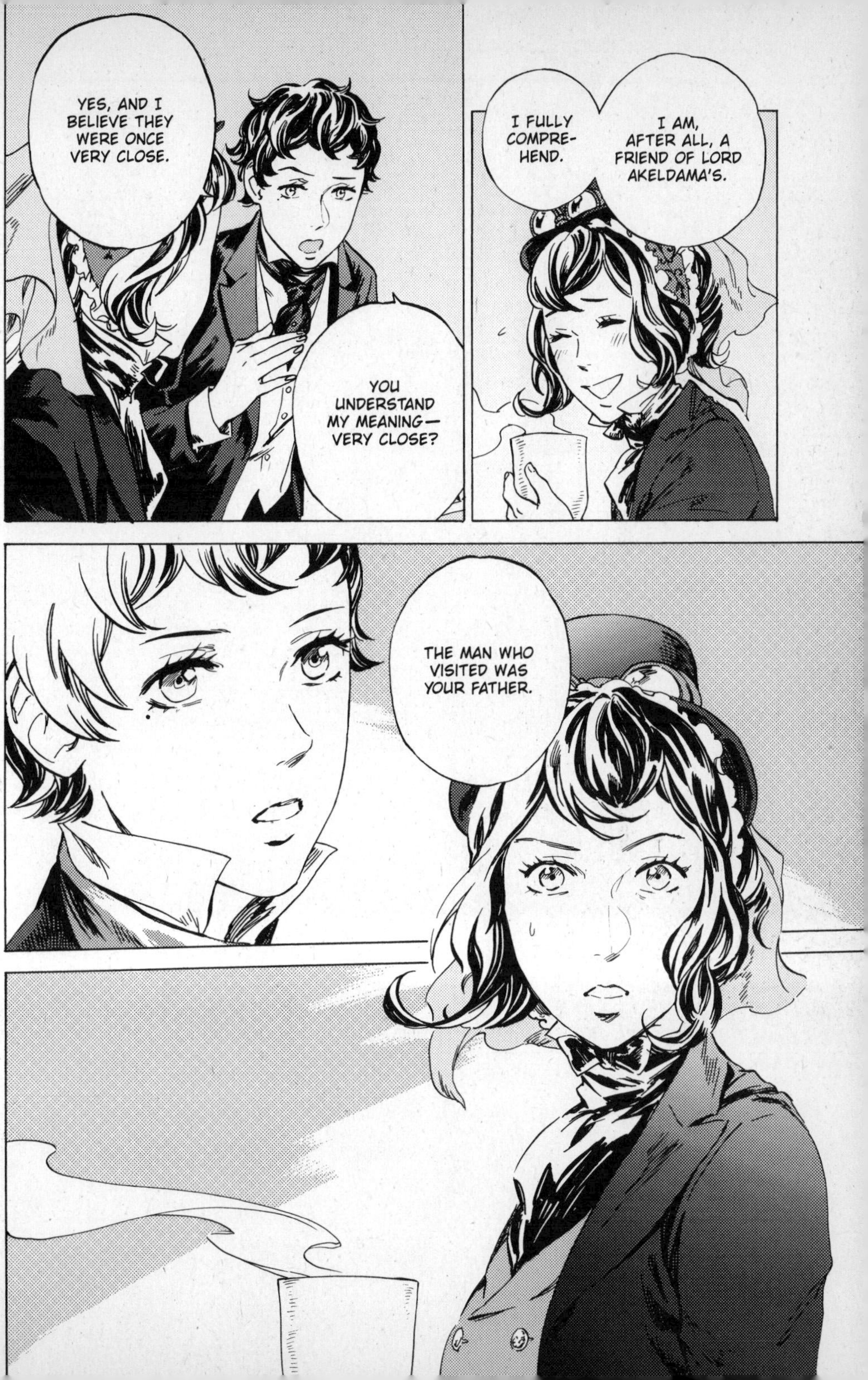
YES, AND I BELIEVE THEY WERE ONCE VERY CLOSE.
YOU UNDERSTAND MY MEANING— VERY CLOSE?
I FULLY COMPRE-HEND.
I AM, AFTER ALL, A FRIEND OF LORD AKELDAMA'S.
THE MAN WHO VISITED WAS YOUR FATHER.

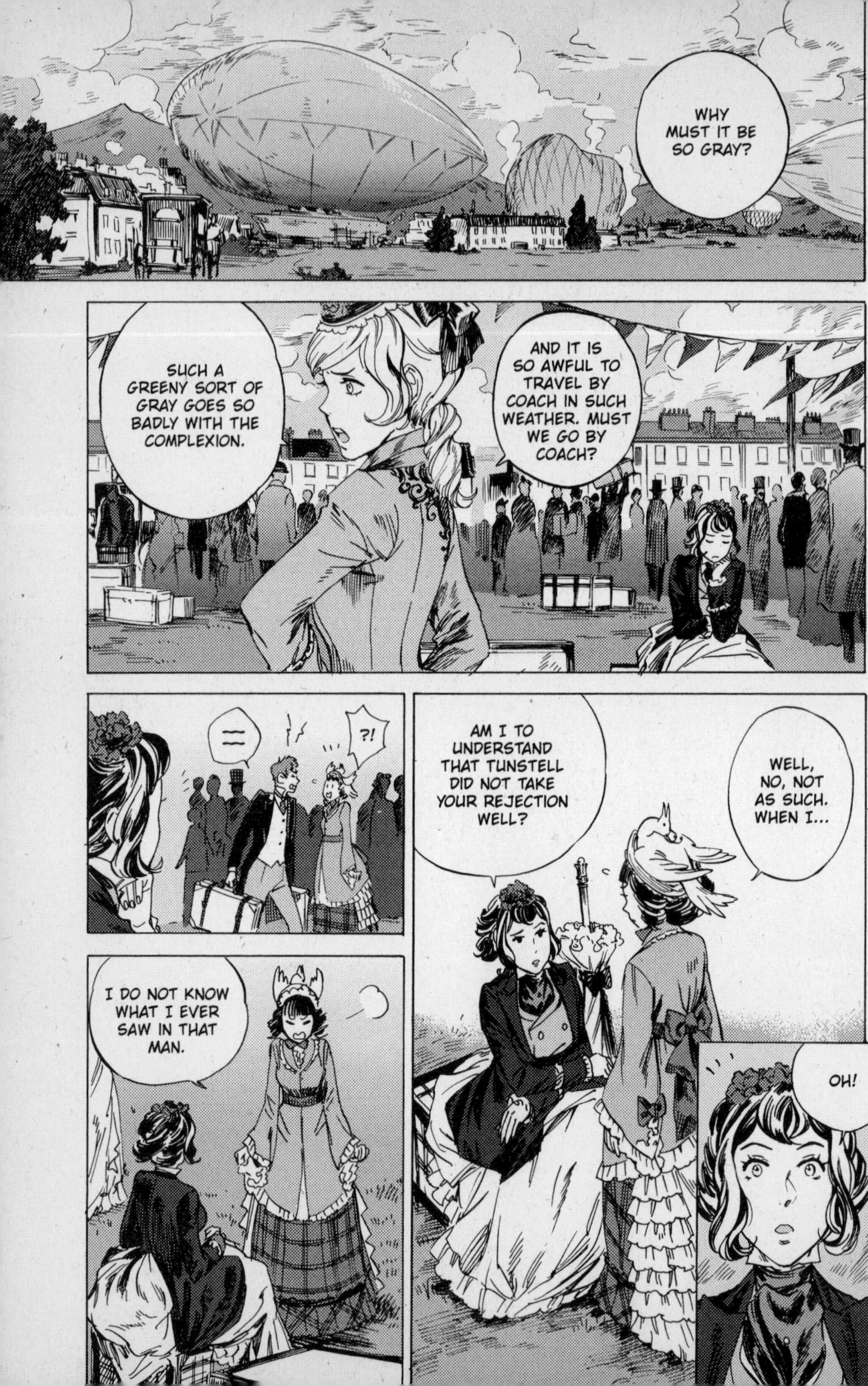
WHY MUST IT BE SO GRAY?
SUCH A GREENY SORT OF GRAY GOES SO BADLY WITH THE COMPLEXION.
AND IT IS SO AWFUL TO TRAVEL BY COACH IN SUCH WEATHER. MUST WE GO BY COACH?
——
?!
I DO NOT KNOW WHAT I EVER SAW IN THAT MAN.
AM I TO UNDERSTAND THAT TUNSTELL DID NOT TAKE YOUR REJECTION WELL?
WELL, NO, NOT AS SUCH. WHEN I...
OH!

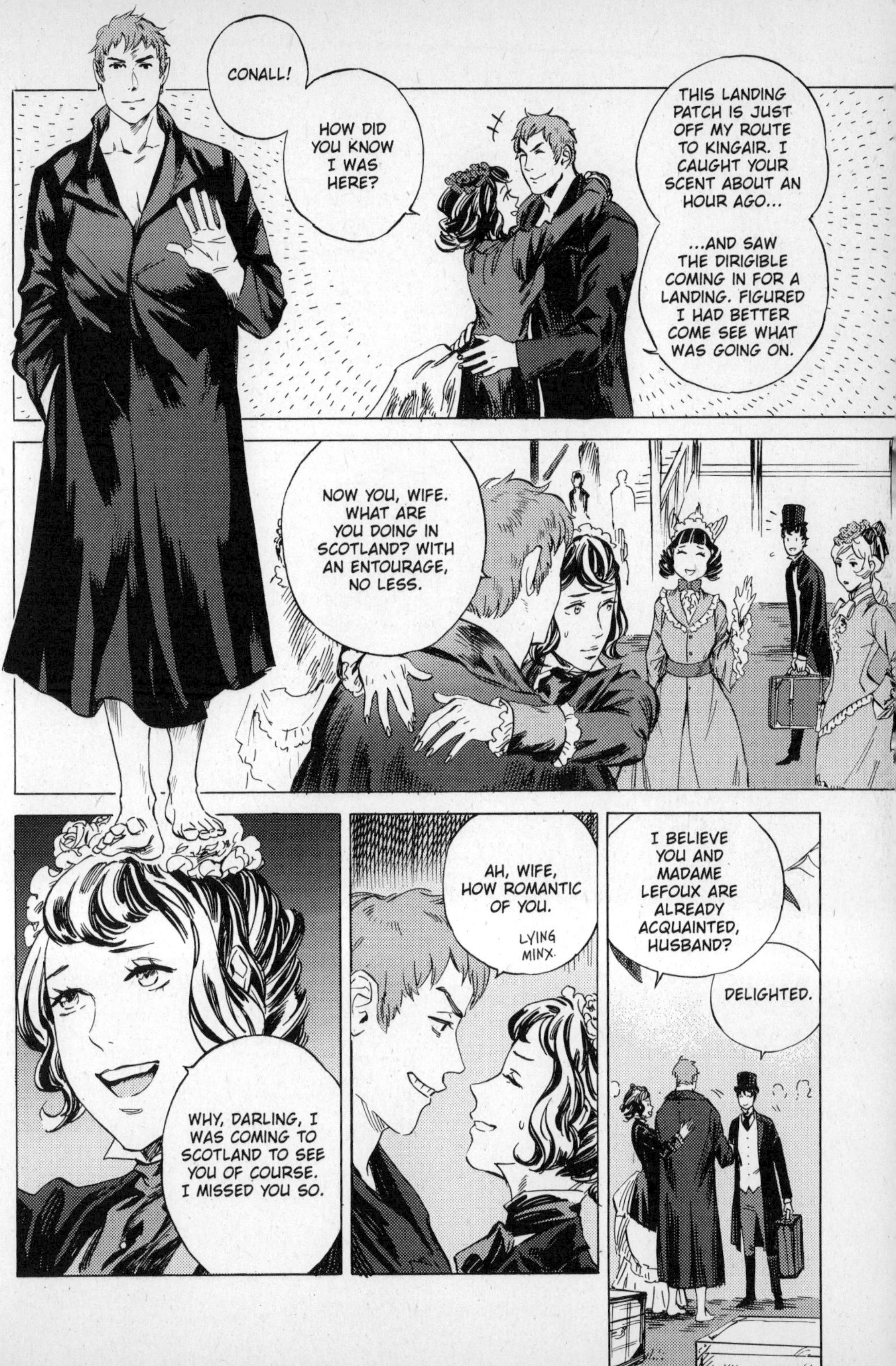
CONALL!
HOW DID YOU KNOW I WAS HERE?
THIS LANDING PATCH IS JUST OFF MY ROUTE TO KINGAIR. I CAUGHT YOUR SCENT ABOUT AN HOUR AGO...
...AND SAW THE DIRIGIBLE COMING IN FOR A LANDING. FIGURED I HAD BETTER COME SEE WHAT WAS GOING ON.
NOW YOU, WIFE. WHAT ARE YOU DOING IN SCOTLAND? WITH AN ENTOURAGE, NO LESS.
WHY, DARLING, I WAS COMING TO SCOTLAND TO SEE YOU OF COURSE. I MISSED YOU SO.
AH, WIFE, HOW ROMANTIC OF YOU.
LYING MINX.
I BELIEVE YOU AND MADAME LEFOUX ARE ALREADY ACQUAINTED, HUSBAND?
DELIGHTED.

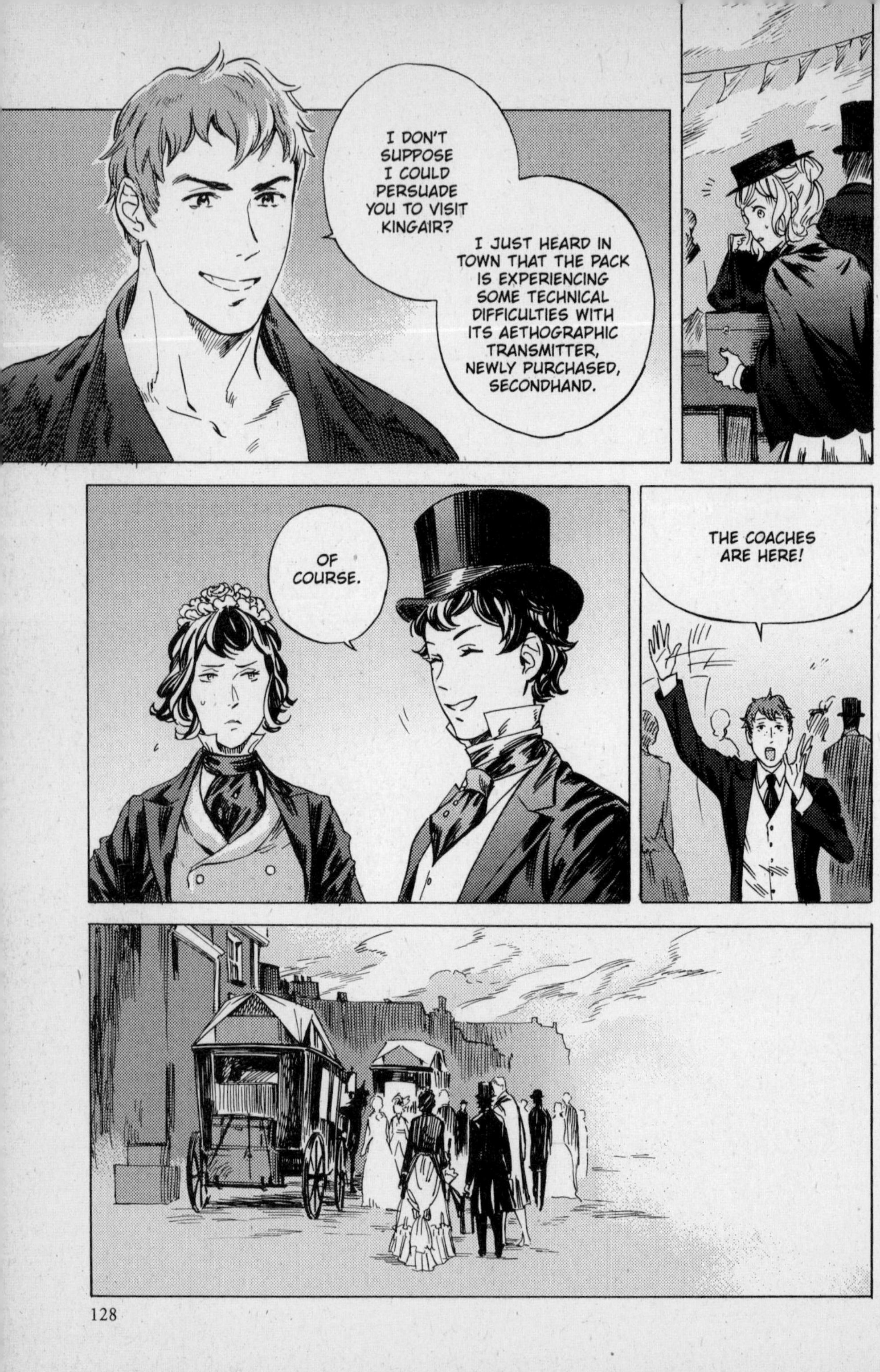
I DON'T SUPPOSE I COULD PERSUADE YOU TO VISIT KINGAIR?
I JUST HEARD IN TOWN THAT THE PACK IS EXPERIENCING SOME TECHNICAL DIFFICULTIES WITH ITS AETHOGRAPHIC TRANSMITTER, NEWLY PURCHASED, SECONDHAND.
OF COURSE.
THE COACHES ARE HERE!

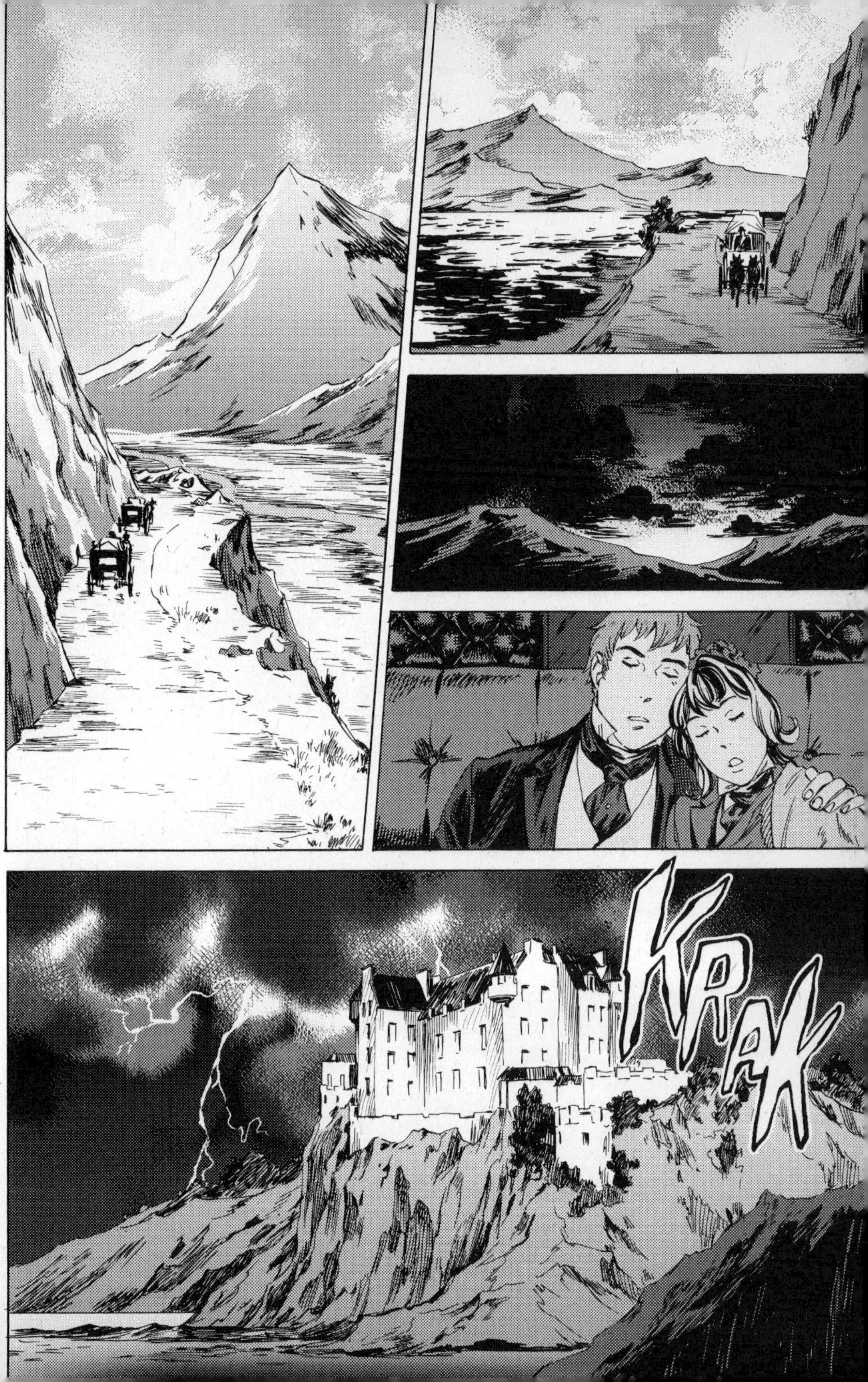
KRAK

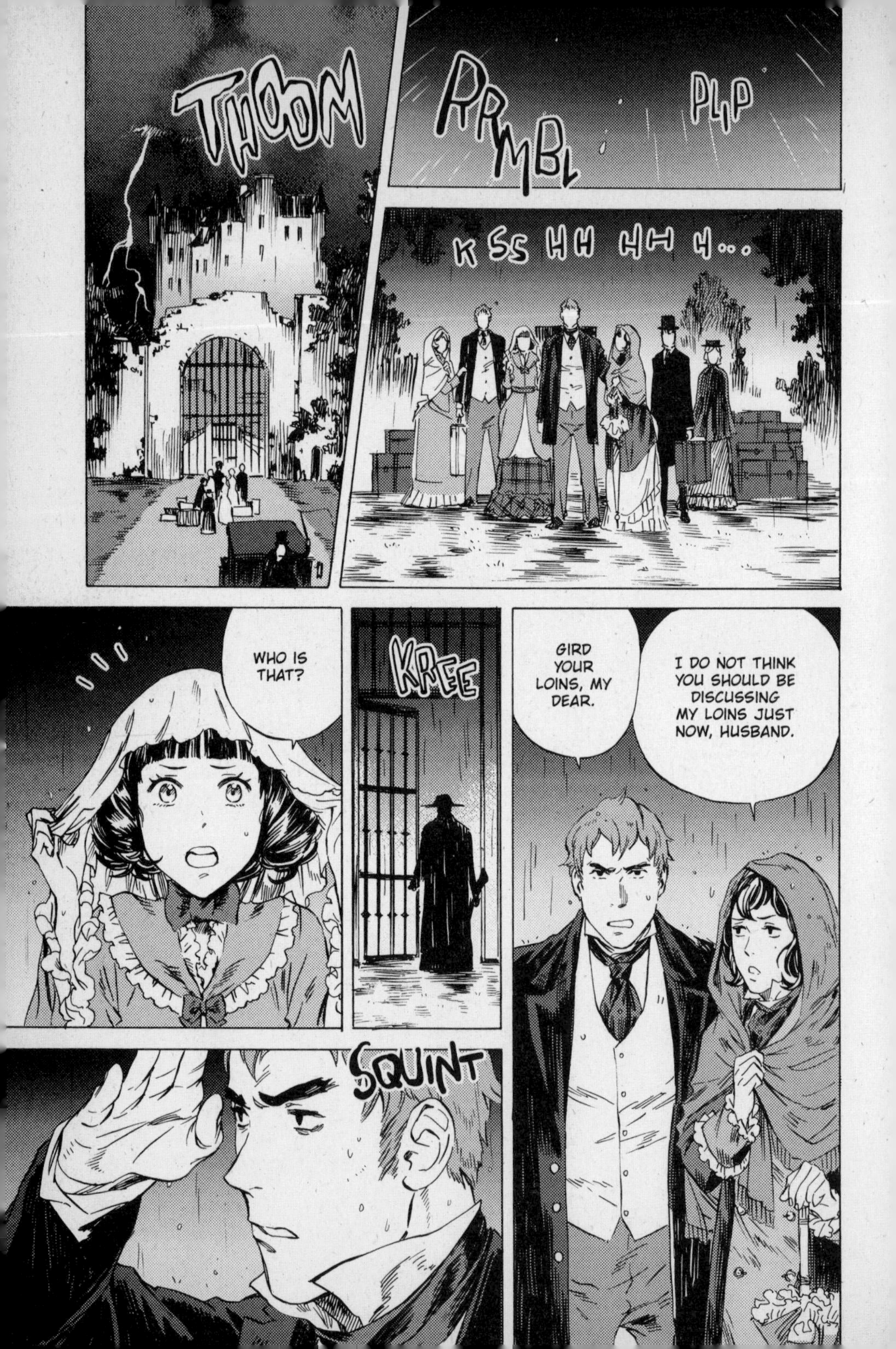
THOOM
PRRMBL
PLIP
KSS HH HH H...
WHO IS THAT?
KREE
GIRD YOUR LOINS, MY DEAR.
I DO NOT THINK YOU SHOULD BE DISCUSSING MY LOINS JUST NOW, HUSBAND.
SQUINT

YOU'RE NAE WELCOME HERE, CONALL MACCON, YOU KEN!

KCHAK

!

AND DINNA BE THINKING YOU CAN CHANGE ON ME!

PACK'S BEEN FREE OF YON WEREWOLF'S CURSE FOR MONTHS, SINCE WE STARTED OUT ACROSS THE SEA.

WHICH WOULD BE WHY I'M HERE.

WE HAVE COME TO HELP, SIDHEAG.

WHAT DO YOU CARE? YOU UP AND ABANDONED US.

I HAD NO CHOICE.

BOLLIX TO THAT, CONALL MACCON. 'TIS A COP-OUT, WELL AND TRULY, AND WE BOTH BE KNOWING IT.

YOU FIXING THE MESS YOU LEFT BEHIND THESE TWENTY YEARS GONE, NOW THAT YOU'RE BACK?

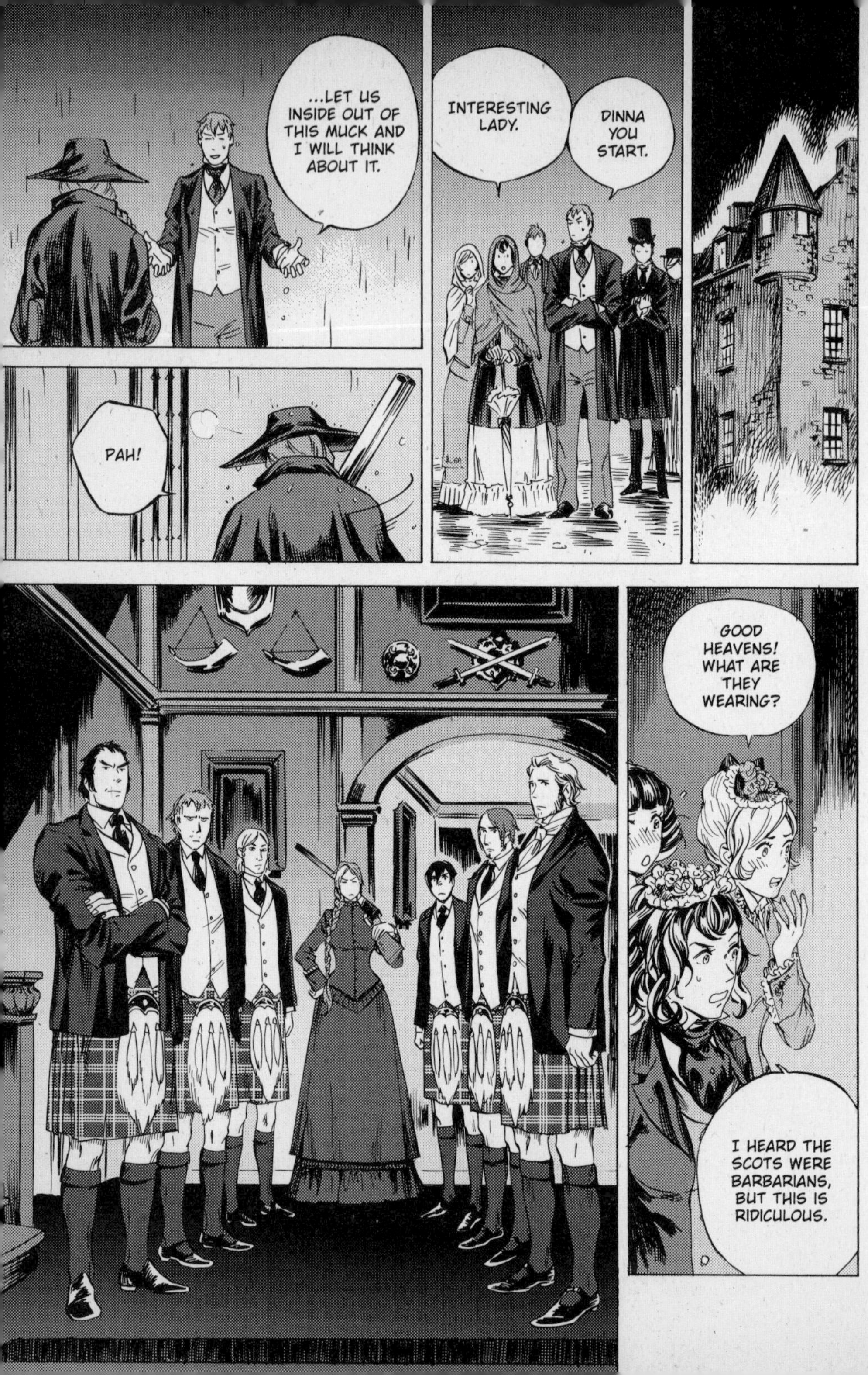
...LET US INSIDE OUT OF THIS MUCK AND I WILL THINK ABOUT IT.
INTERESTING LADY.
DINNA YOU START.
PAH!
GOOD HEAVENS! WHAT ARE THEY WEARING?
I HEARD THE SCOTS WERE BARBARIANS, BUT THIS IS RIDICULOUS.

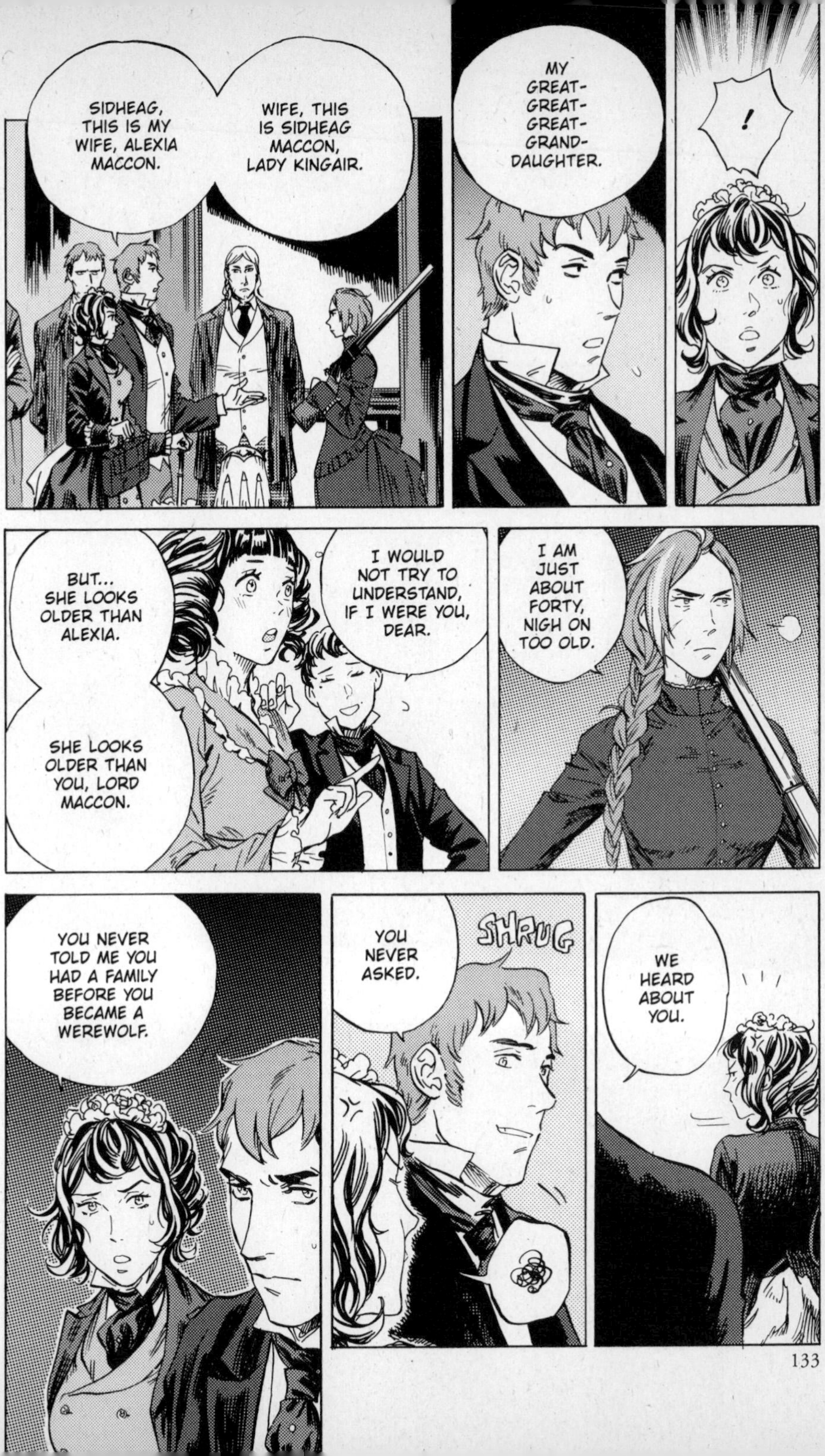
SIDHEAG, THIS IS MY WIFE, ALEXIA MACCON.
WIFE, THIS IS SIDHEAG MACCON, LADY KINGAIR.
MY GREAT-GREAT-GREAT-GRAND-DAUGHTER.
!
BUT... SHE LOOKS OLDER THAN ALEXIA.
SHE LOOKS OLDER THAN YOU, LORD MACCON.
I WOULD NOT TRY TO UNDERSTAND, IF I WERE YOU, DEAR.
I AM JUST ABOUT FORTY, NIGH ON TOO OLD.
YOU NEVER TOLD ME YOU HAD A FAMILY BEFORE YOU BECAME A WEREWOLF.
YOU NEVER ASKED.
SHRUG
WE HEARD ABOUT YOU.

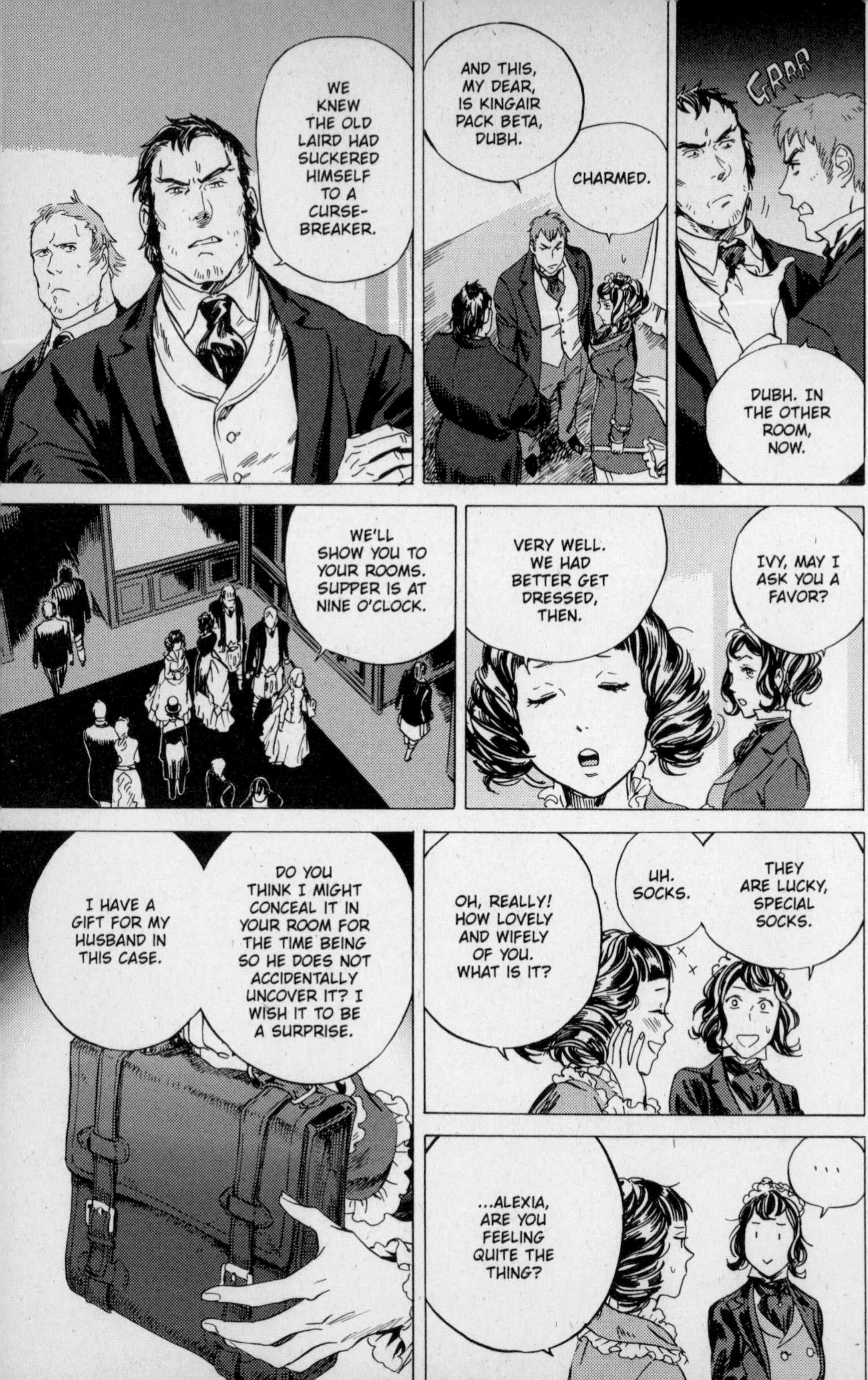

WE KNEW THE OLD LAIRD HAD SUCKERED HIMSELF TO A CURSE-BREAKER.
AND THIS, MY DEAR, IS KINGAIR PACK BETA, DUBH.
CHARMED.
GRAAR
DUBH. IN THE OTHER ROOM, NOW.
WE'LL SHOW YOU TO YOUR ROOMS. SUPPER IS AT NINE O'CLOCK.
VERY WELL. WE HAD BETTER GET DRESSED, THEN.
IVY, MAY I ASK YOU A FAVOR?
I HAVE A GIFT FOR MY HUSBAND IN THIS CASE.
DO YOU THINK I MIGHT CONCEAL IT IN YOUR ROOM FOR THE TIME BEING SO HE DOES NOT ACCIDENTALLY UNCOVER IT? I WISH IT TO BE A SURPRISE.
OH, REALLY! HOW LOVELY AND WIFELY OF YOU. WHAT IS IT?
UH. SOCKS.
THEY ARE LUCKY, SPECIAL SOCKS.
...ALEXIA, ARE YOU FEELING QUITE THE THING?
. . .

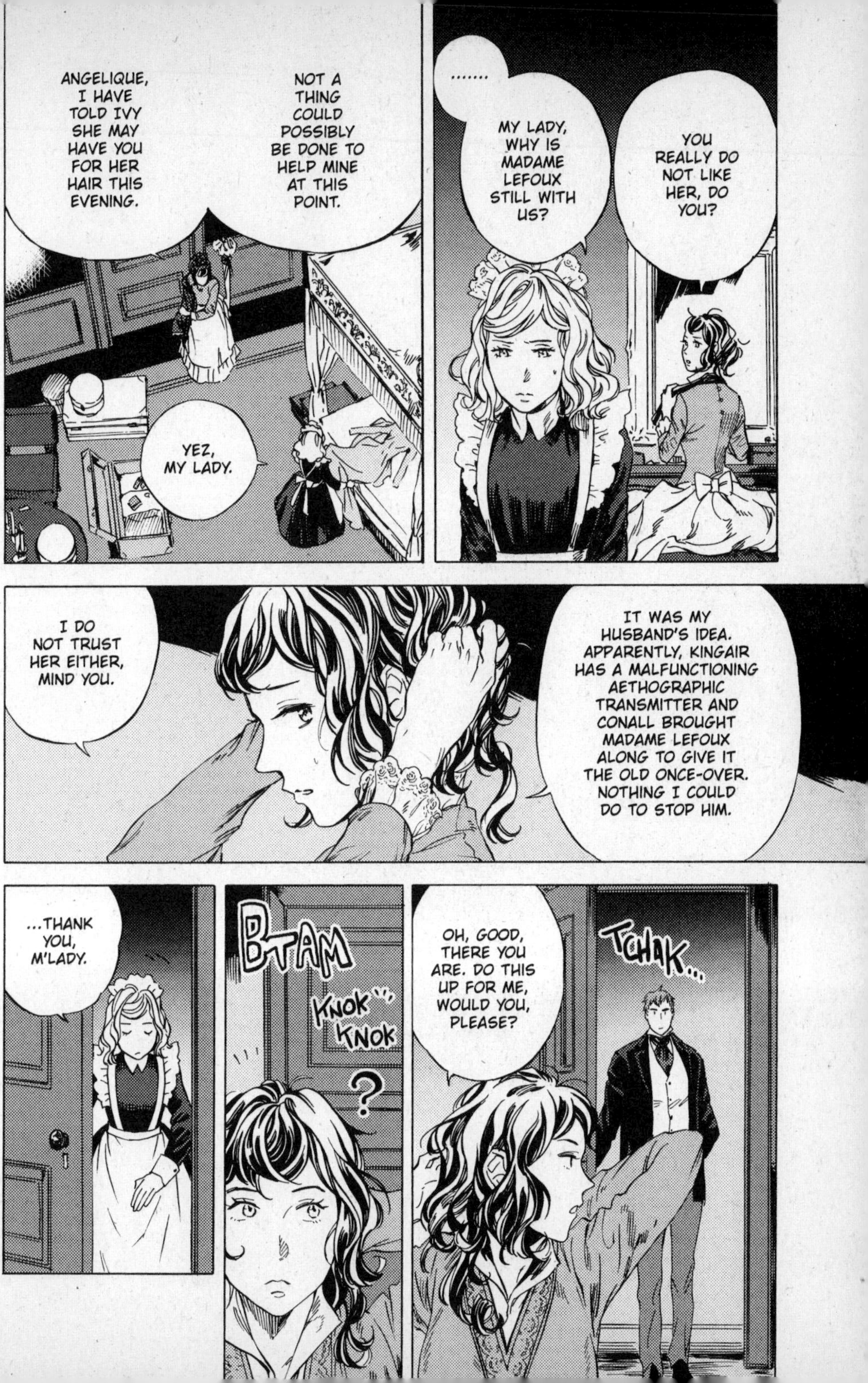
ANGELIQUE, I HAVE TOLD IVY SHE MAY HAVE YOU FOR HER HAIR THIS EVENING.
NOT A THING COULD POSSIBLY BE DONE TO HELP MINE AT THIS POINT.
YEZ, MY LADY.
......
MY LADY, WHY IS MADAME LEFOUX STILL WITH US?
YOU REALLY DO NOT LIKE HER, DO YOU?
I DO NOT TRUST HER EITHER, MIND YOU.
IT WAS MY HUSBAND'S IDEA. APPARENTLY, KINGAIR HAS A MALFUNCTIONING AETHOGRAPHIC TRANSMITTER AND CONALL BROUGHT MADAME LEFOUX ALONG TO GIVE IT THE OLD ONCE-OVER. NOTHING I COULD DO TO STOP HIM.
...THANK YOU, M'LADY.
BTAM
KNOK KNOK
?
OH, GOOD, THERE YOU ARE. DO THIS UP FOR ME, WOULD YOU, PLEASE?
TCHAK...

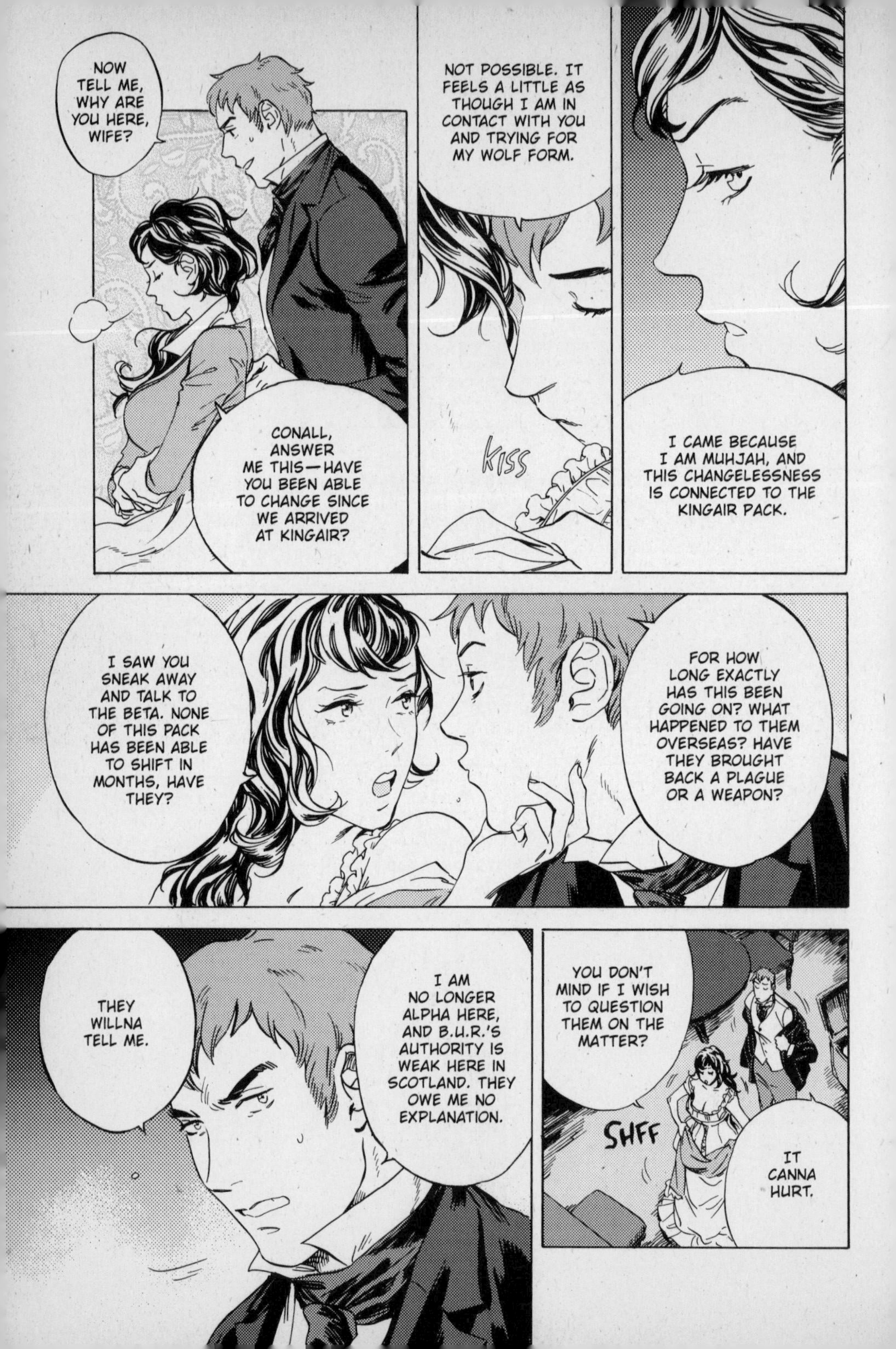
NOW TELL ME, WHY ARE YOU HERE, WIFE?
CONALL, ANSWER ME THIS—HAVE YOU BEEN ABLE TO CHANGE SINCE WE ARRIVED AT KINGAIR?
NOT POSSIBLE. IT FEELS A LITTLE AS THOUGH I AM IN CONTACT WITH YOU AND TRYING FOR MY WOLF FORM.
KISS
I CAME BECAUSE I AM MUHJAH, AND THIS CHANGELESSNESS IS CONNECTED TO THE KINGAIR PACK.
I SAW YOU SNEAK AWAY AND TALK TO THE BETA. NONE OF THIS PACK HAS BEEN ABLE TO SHIFT IN MONTHS, HAVE THEY?
FOR HOW LONG EXACTLY HAS THIS BEEN GOING ON? WHAT HAPPENED TO THEM OVERSEAS? HAVE THEY BROUGHT BACK A PLAGUE OR A WEAPON?
THEY WILLNA TELL ME.
I AM NO LONGER ALPHA HERE, AND B.U.R.'S AUTHORITY IS WEAK HERE IN SCOTLAND. THEY OWE ME NO EXPLANATION.
YOU DON'T MIND IF I WISH TO QUESTION THEM ON THE MATTER?
SHFF
IT CANNA HURT.

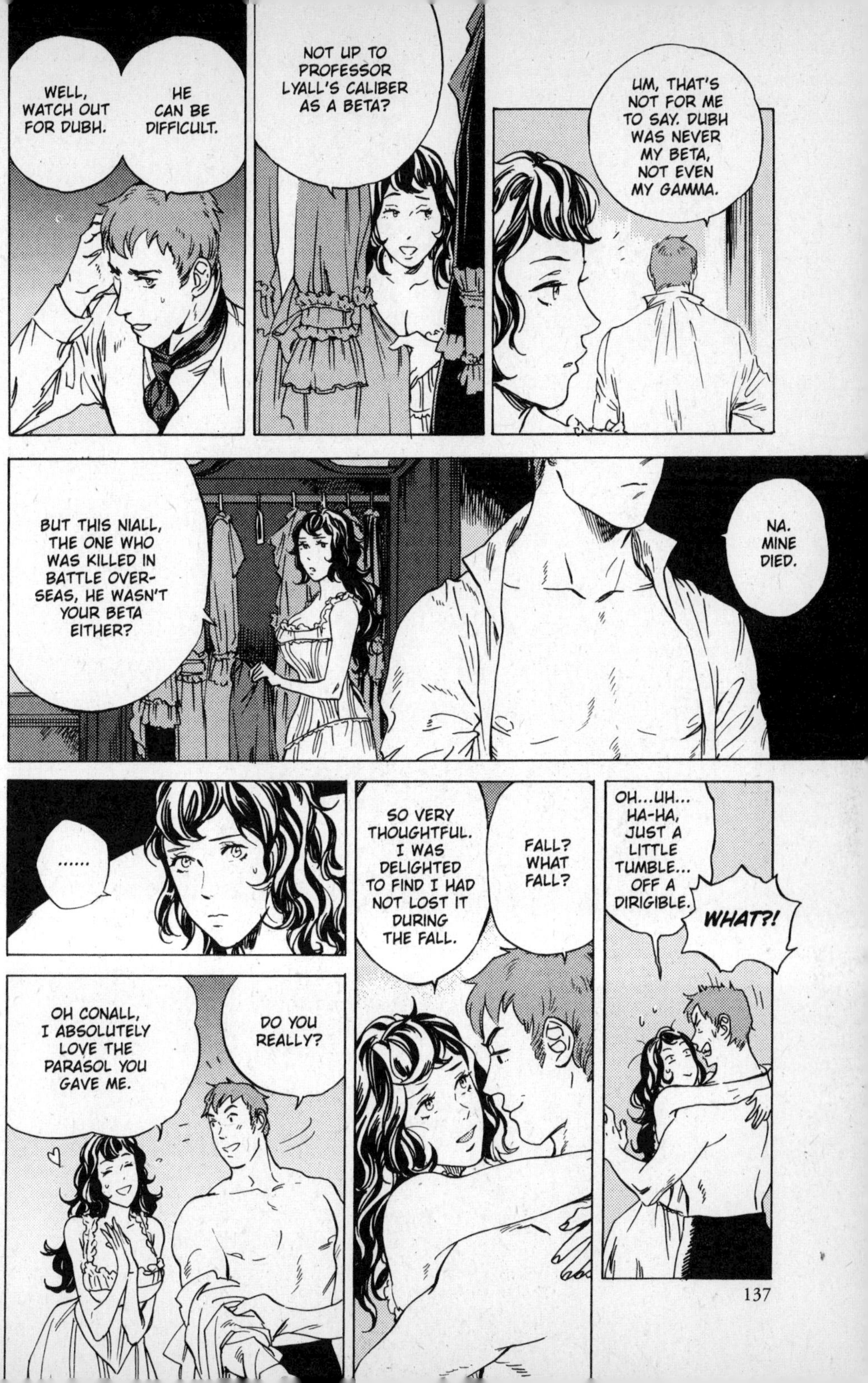
WELL, WATCH OUT FOR DUBH.
HE CAN BE DIFFICULT.
NOT UP TO PROFESSOR LYALL'S CALIBER AS A BETA?
UM, THAT'S NOT FOR ME TO SAY. DUBH WAS NEVER MY BETA, NOT EVEN MY GAMMA.
BUT THIS NIALL, THE ONE WHO WAS KILLED IN BATTLE OVER-SEAS, HE WASN'T YOUR BETA EITHER?
NA. MINE DIED.
......
OH CONALL, I ABSOLUTELY LOVE THE PARASOL YOU GAVE ME.
DO YOU REALLY?
SO VERY THOUGHTFUL. I WAS DELIGHTED TO FIND I HAD NOT LOST IT DURING THE FALL.
FALL? WHAT FALL?
OH...UH... HA-HA, JUST A LITTLE TUMBLE... OFF A DIRIGIBLE.
WHAT?!

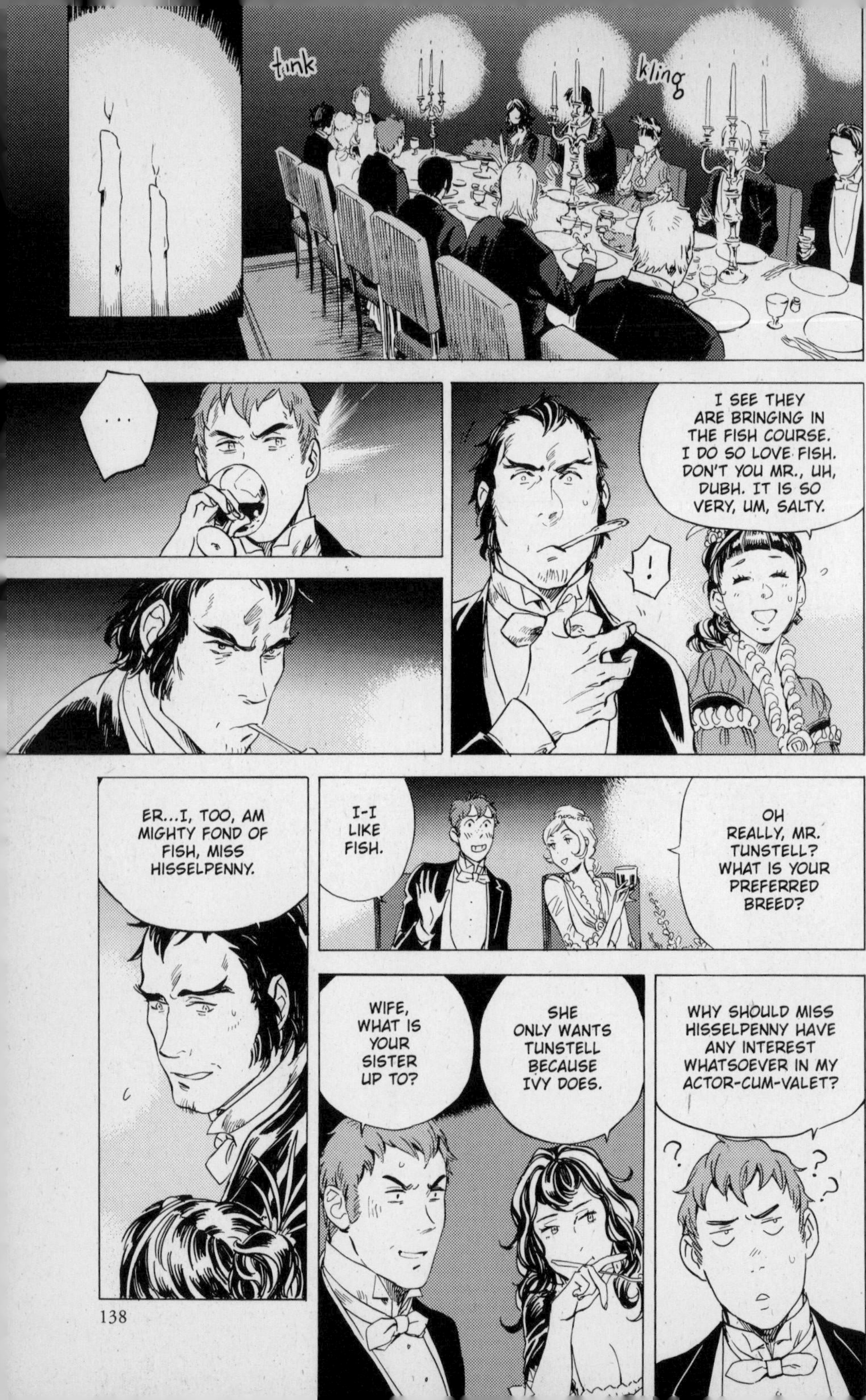
tink
kling
...
I SEE THEY ARE BRINGING IN THE FISH COURSE. I DO SO LOVE FISH. DON'T YOU MR., UH, DUBH. IT IS SO VERY, UM, SALTY.
!
ER...I, TOO, AM MIGHTY FOND OF FISH, MISS HISSELPENNY.
I-I LIKE FISH.
OH REALLY, MR. TUNSTELL? WHAT IS YOUR PREFERRED BREED?
WIFE, WHAT IS YOUR SISTER UP TO?
SHE ONLY WANTS TUNSTELL BECAUSE IVY DOES.
WHY SHOULD MISS HISSELPENNY HAVE ANY INTEREST WHATSOEVER IN MY ACTOR-CUM-VALET?
?
??

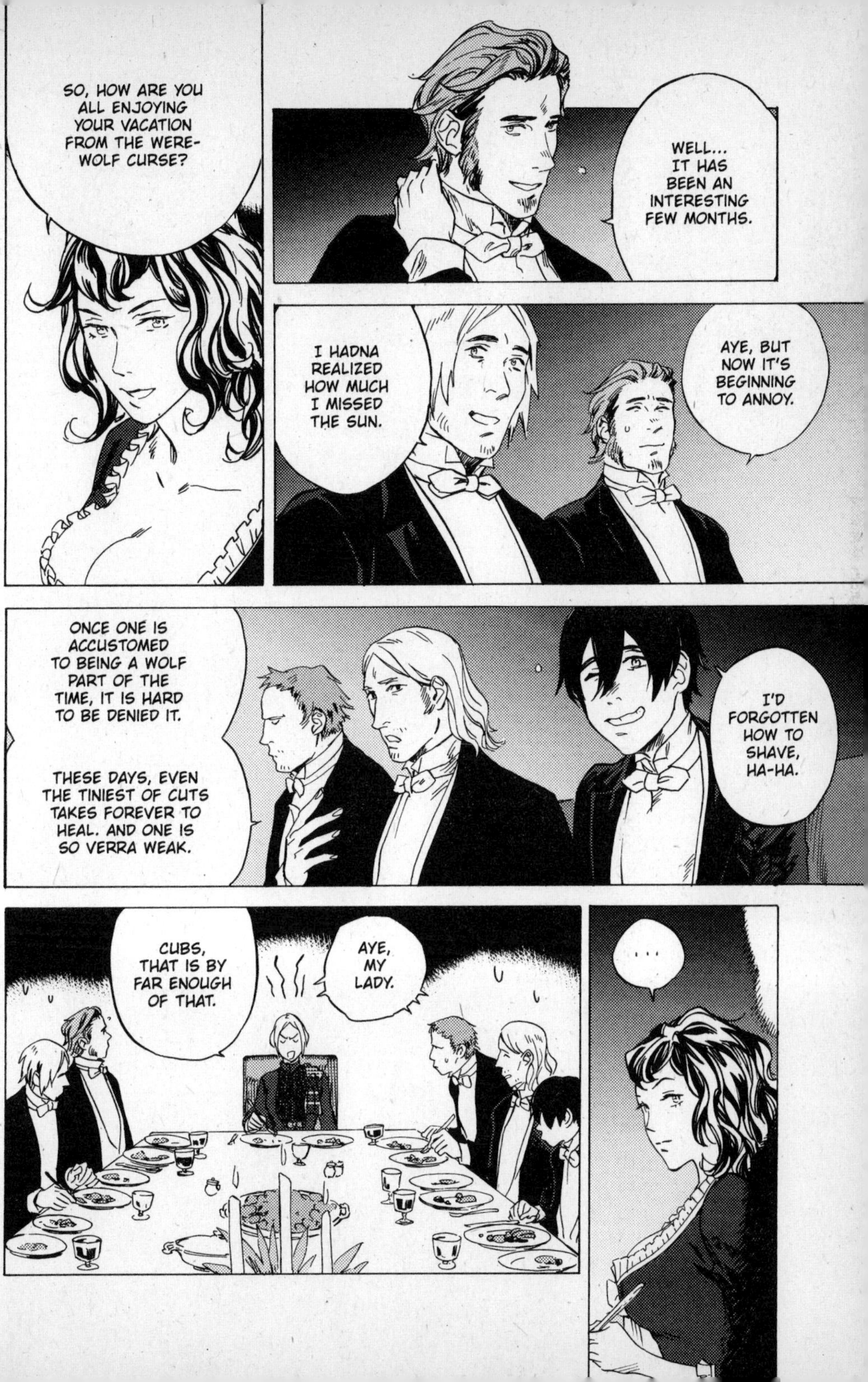
SO, HOW ARE YOU ALL ENJOYING YOUR VACATION FROM THE WERE-WOLF CURSE?
WELL... IT HAS BEEN AN INTERESTING FEW MONTHS.
I HADNA REALIZED HOW MUCH I MISSED THE SUN.
AYE, BUT NOW IT'S BEGINNING TO ANNOY.
ONCE ONE IS ACCUSTOMED TO BEING A WOLF PART OF THE TIME, IT IS HARD TO BE DENIED IT.
THESE DAYS, EVEN THE TINIEST OF CUTS TAKES FOREVER TO HEAL. AND ONE IS SO VERRA WEAK.
I'D FORGOTTEN HOW TO SHAVE, HA-HA.
CUBS, THAT IS BY FAR ENOUGH OF THAT.
AYE, MY LADY.
...

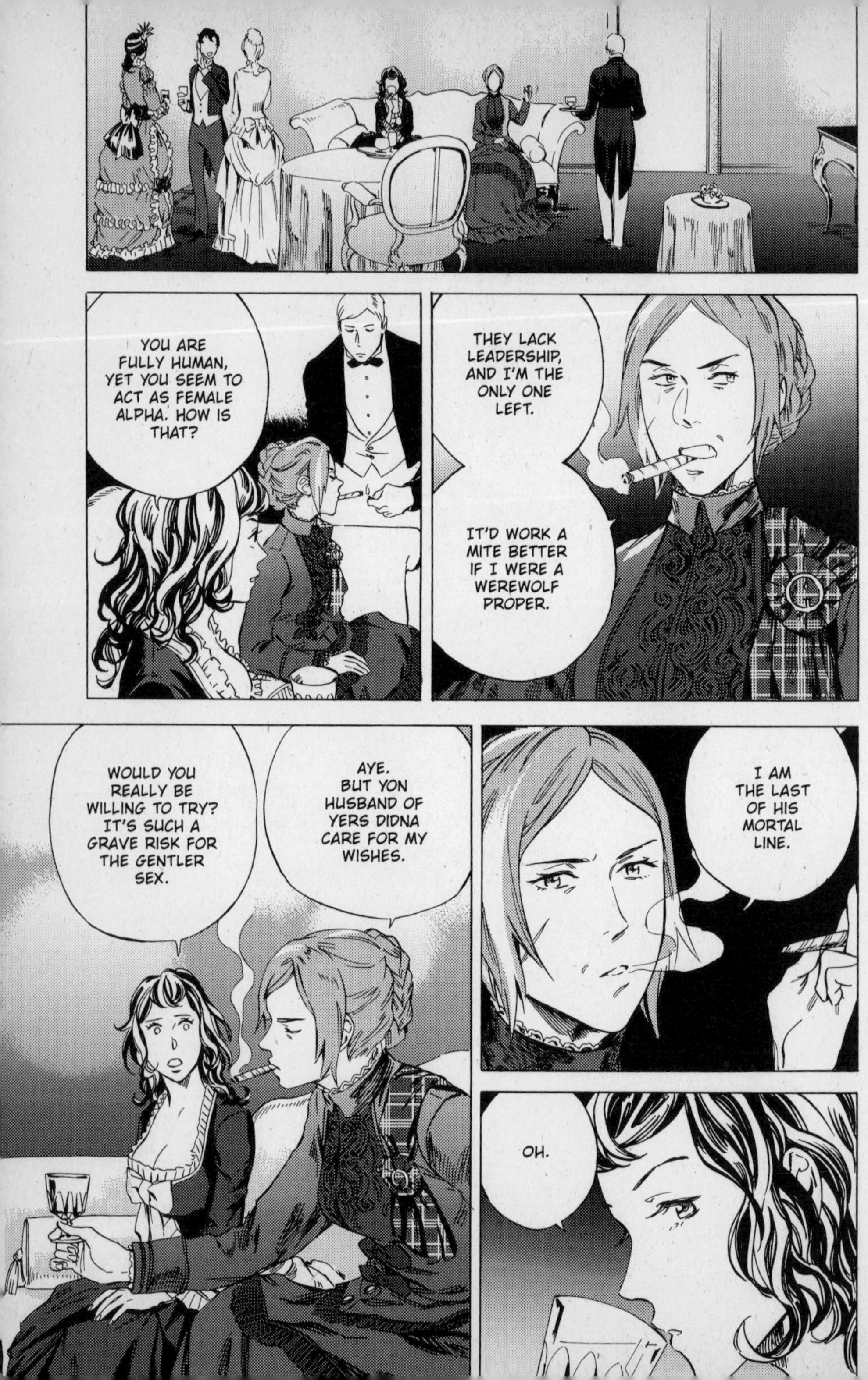

YOU ARE FULLY HUMAN, YET YOU SEEM TO ACT AS FEMALE ALPHA. HOW IS THAT?
THEY LACK LEADERSHIP, AND I'M THE ONLY ONE LEFT.
IT'D WORK A MITE BETTER IF I WERE A WEREWOLF PROPER.
WOULD YOU REALLY BE WILLING TO TRY? IT'S SUCH A GRAVE RISK FOR THE GENTLER SEX.
AYE. BUT YON HUSBAND OF YERS DIDNA CARE FOR MY WISHES.
I AM THE LAST OF HIS MORTAL LINE.
OH.

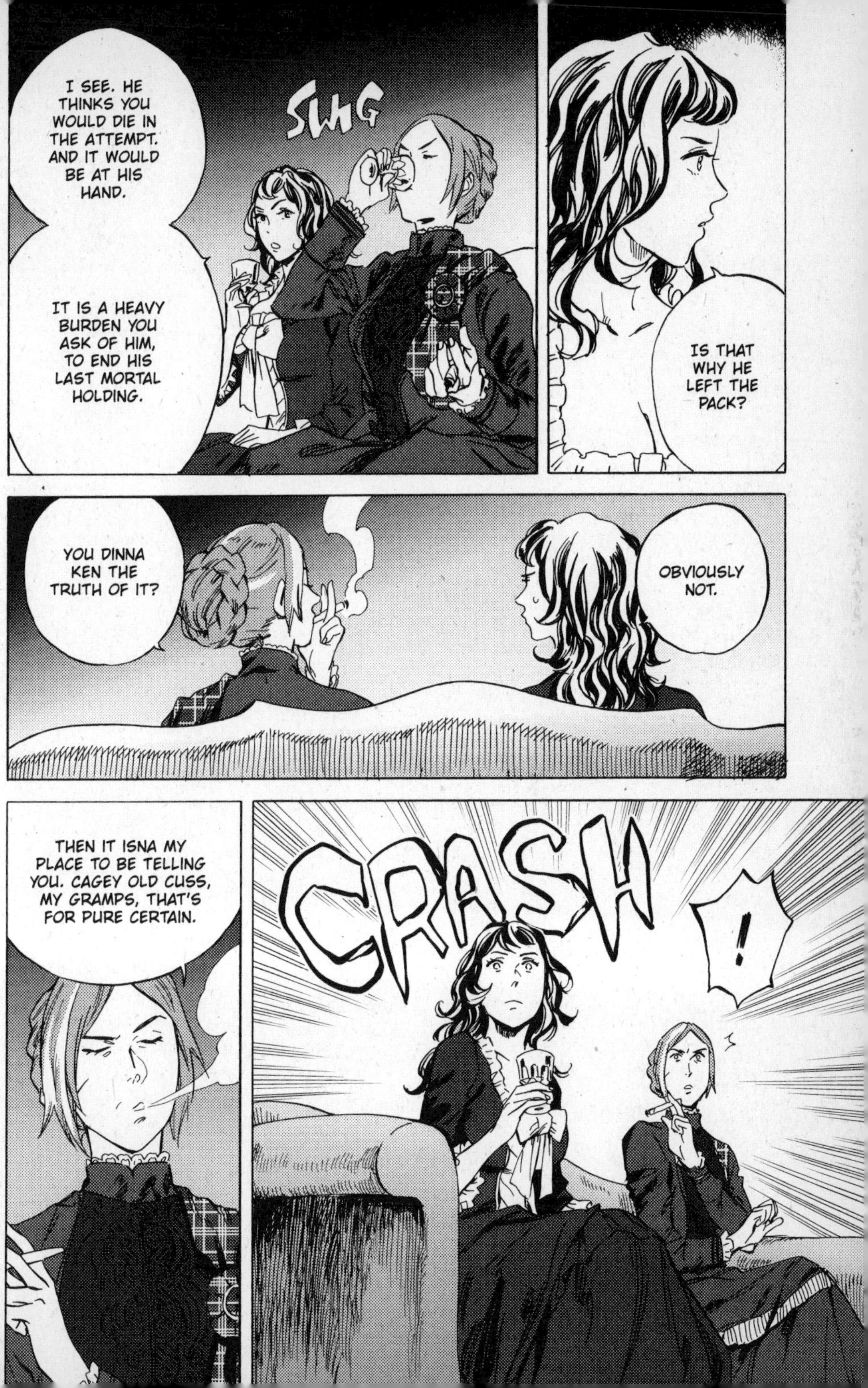
I SEE. HE THINKS YOU WOULD DIE IN THE ATTEMPT. AND IT WOULD BE AT HIS HAND.
SWIG
IT IS A HEAVY BURDEN YOU ASK OF HIM, TO END HIS LAST MORTAL HOLDING.
IS THAT WHY HE LEFT THE PACK?
YOU DINNA KEN THE TRUTH OF IT?
OBVIOUSLY NOT.
THEN IT ISNA MY PLACE TO BE TELLING YOU. CAGEY OLD CUSS, MY GRAMPS, THAT'S FOR PURE CERTAIN.
CRASH
!

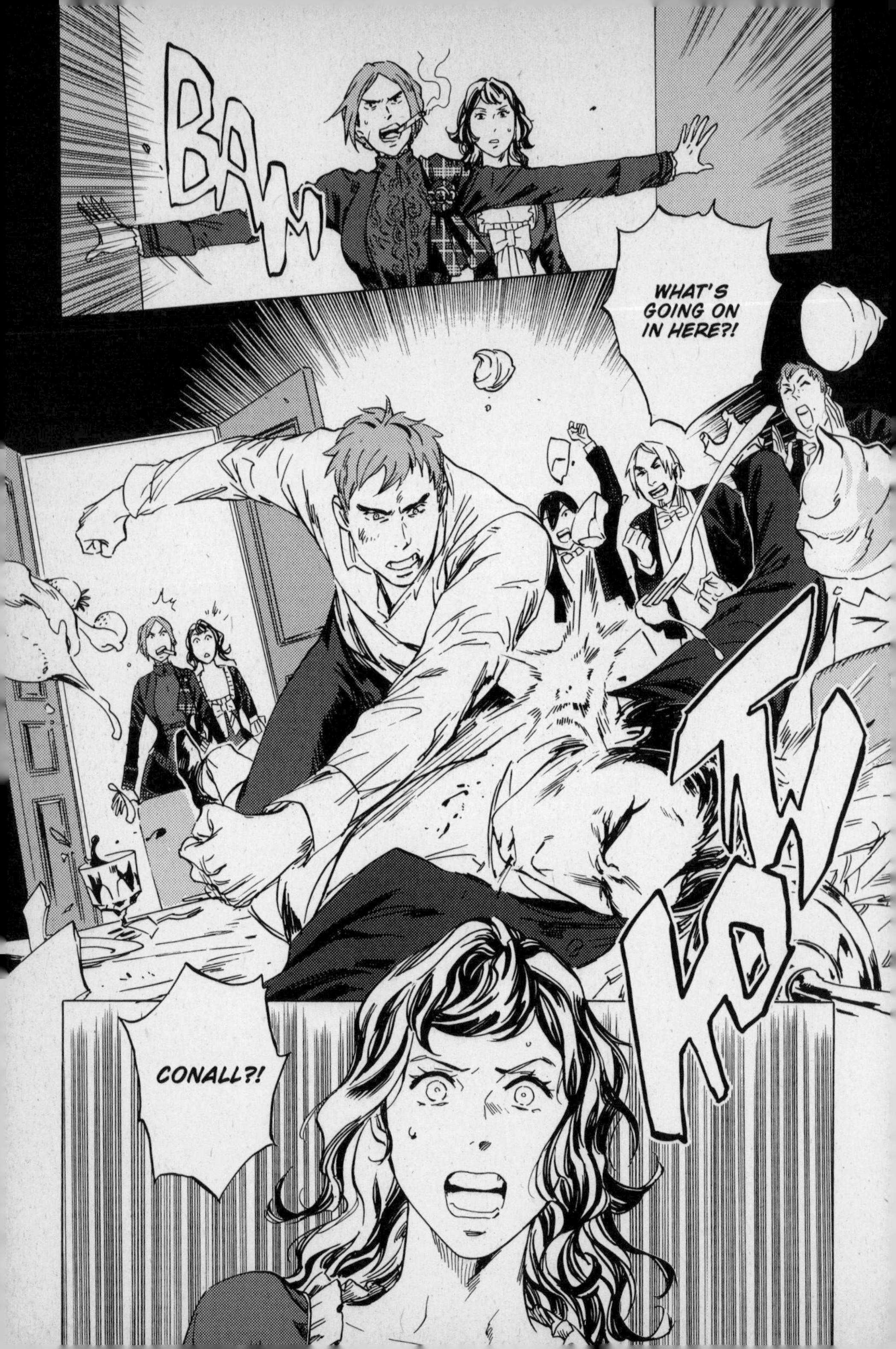
BAM
WHAT'S GOING ON IN HERE?!
CONALL?!
THWOK

SOULLESS

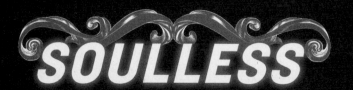

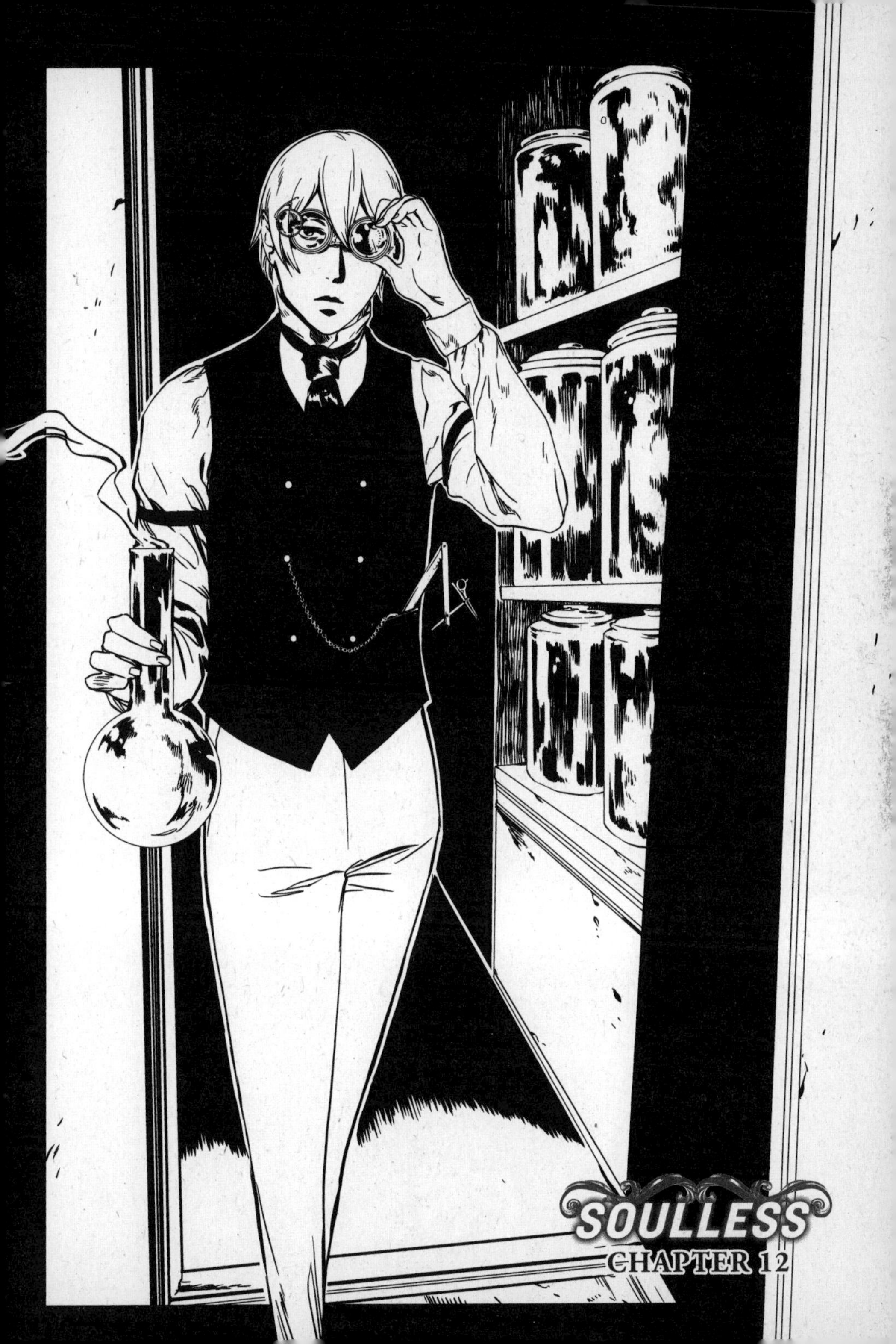
SOULLESS
CHAPTER 12

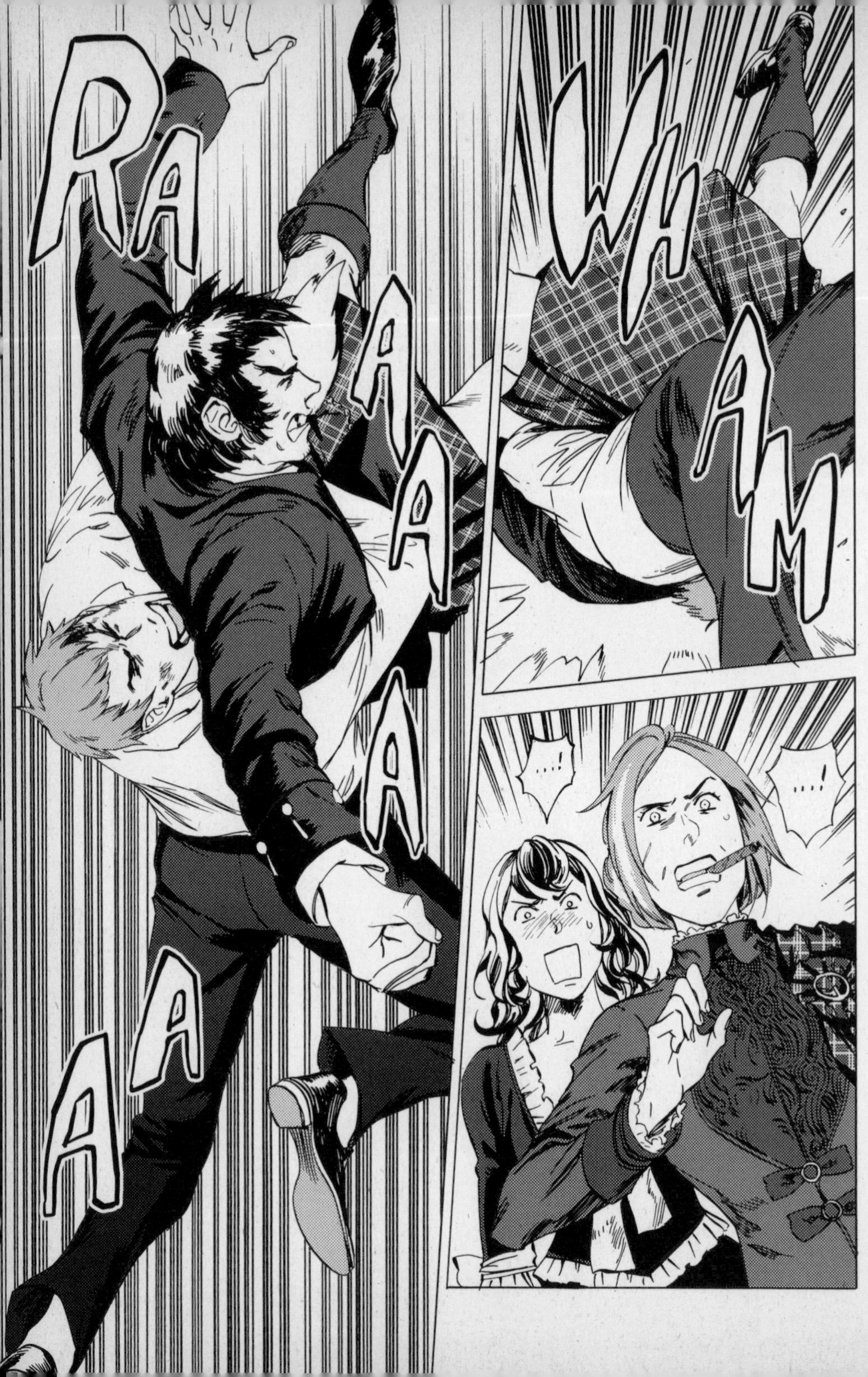

RAAAAAAAA
WHAAM
...!
...!

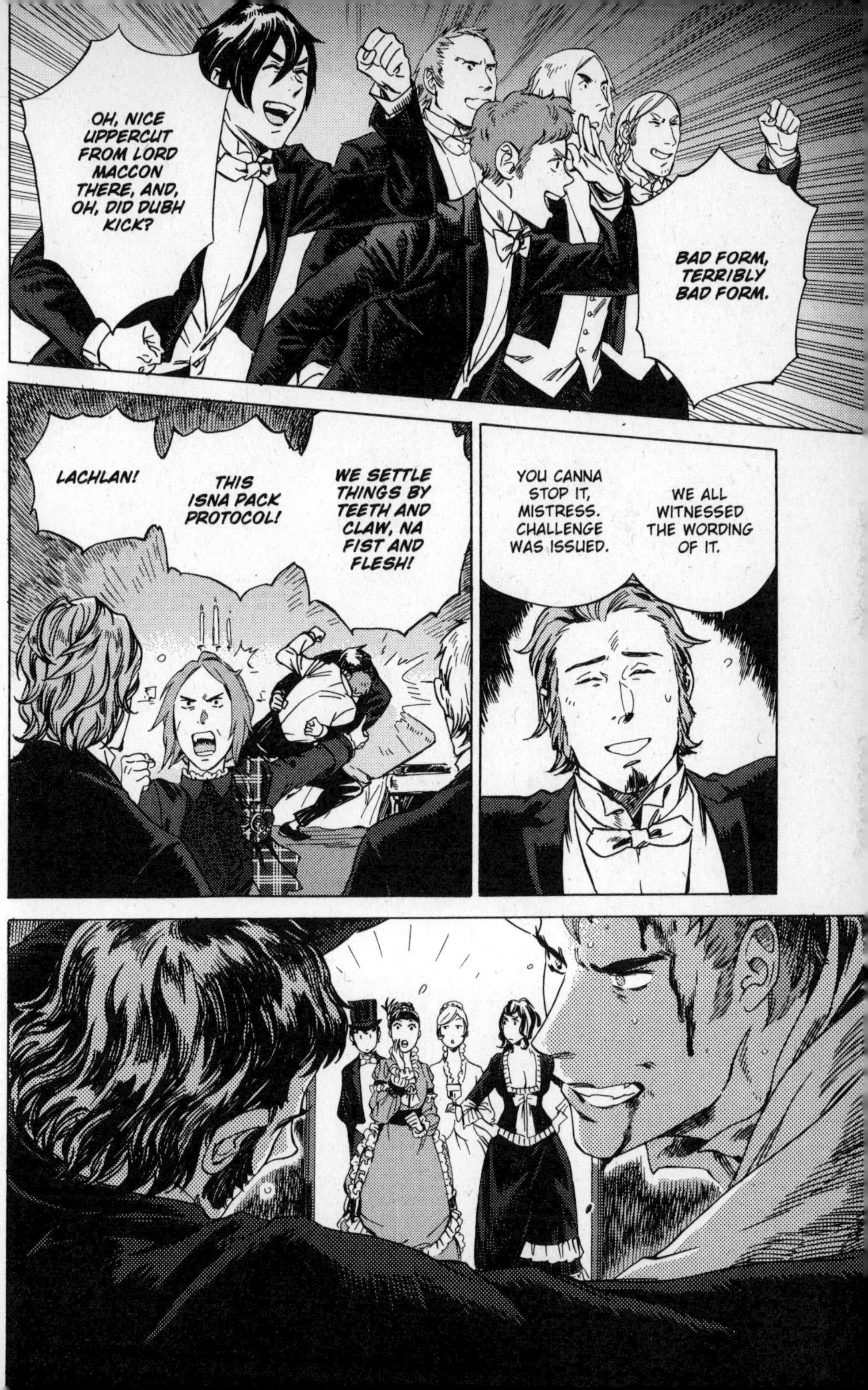
OH, NICE UPPERCUT FROM LORD MACCON THERE, AND, OH, DID DUBH KICK?
BAD FORM, TERRIBLY BAD FORM.
LACHLAN!
THIS ISNA PACK PROTOCOL!
WE SETTLE THINGS BY TEETH AND CLAW, NA FIST AND FLESH!
YOU CANNA STOP IT, MISTRESS. CHALLENGE WAS ISSUED.
WE ALL WITNESSED THE WORDING OF IT.

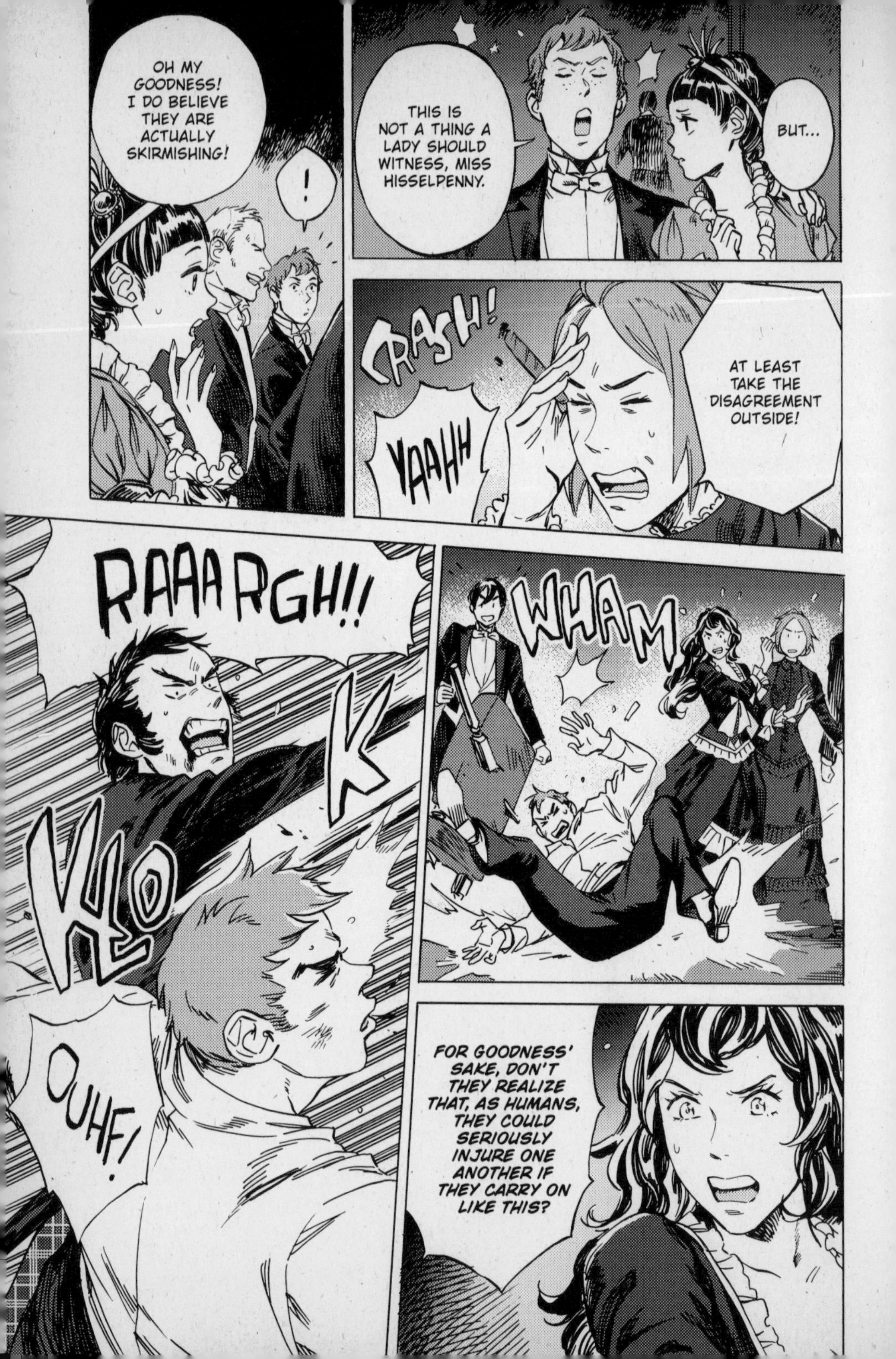
OH MY GOODNESS! I DO BELIEVE THEY ARE ACTUALLY SKIRMISHING!
!
THIS IS NOT A THING A LADY SHOULD WITNESS, MISS HISSELPENNY.
BUT...
CRASH!
YAAHH
AT LEAST TAKE THE DISAGREEMENT OUTSIDE!
RAAARGH!!
K
KO
OUHF!
WHAM
FOR GOODNESS' SAKE, DON'T THEY REALIZE THAT, AS HUMANS, THEY COULD SERIOUSLY INJURE ONE ANOTHER IF THEY CARRY ON LIKE THIS?

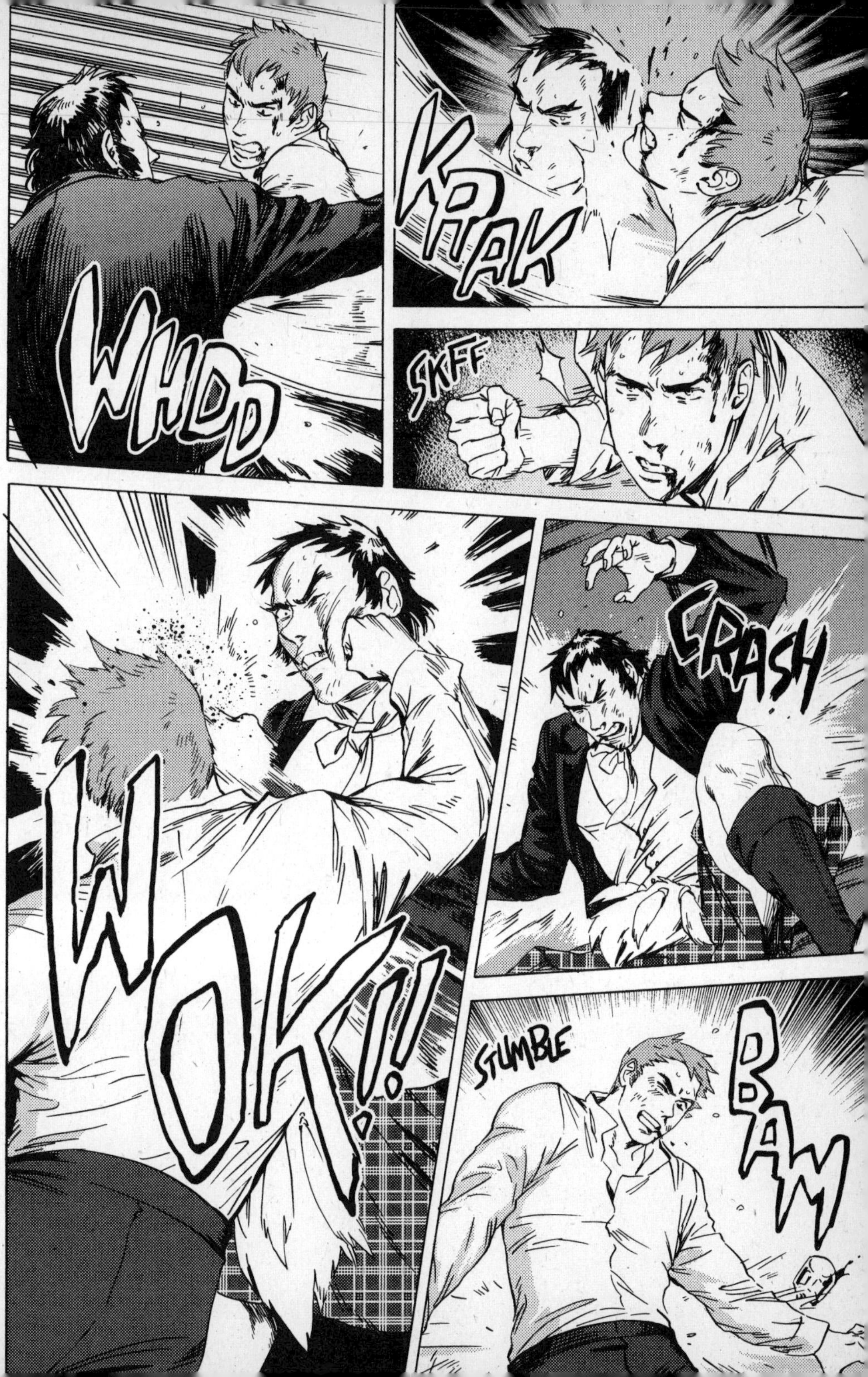
WHDD
KRAK
SKFF
WOK!!
CRASH
STUMBLE
BAM

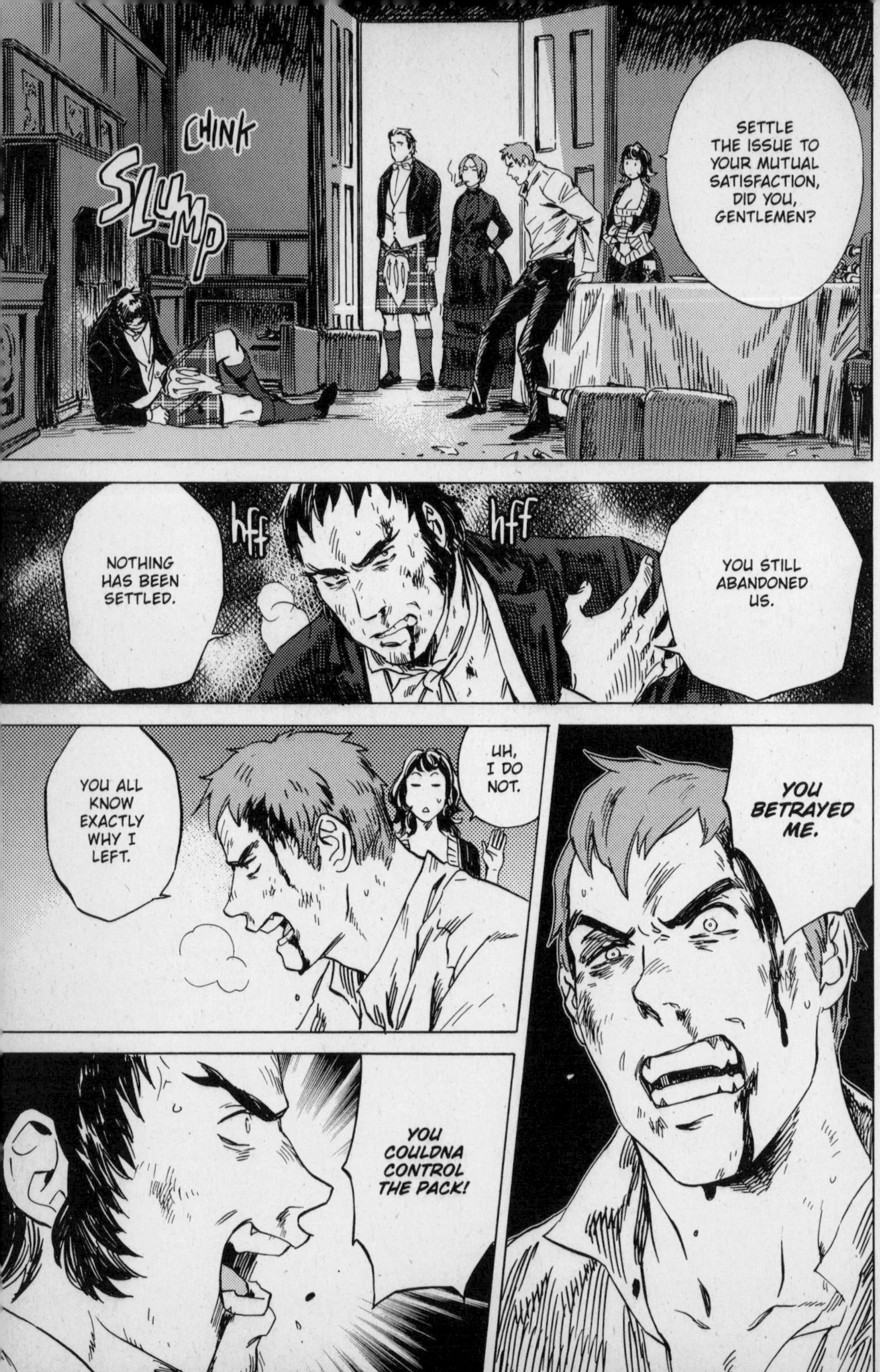
CHINK
SLUMP
SETTLE THE ISSUE TO YOUR MUTUAL SATISFACTION, DID YOU, GENTLEMEN?
NOTHING HAS BEEN SETTLED.
hff
hff
YOU STILL ABANDONED US.
YOU ALL KNOW EXACTLY WHY I LEFT.
UH, I DO NOT.
YOU BETRAYED ME.
YOU COULDNA CONTROL THE PACK!

AND YOU PAY US BACK IN KIND?

THE EMPTINESS YOU LEFT, WAS THAT FAIR?

THERE IS NAUGHT FAIR ABOUT PACK PROTOCOL. THERE IS SIMPLY PROTOCOL, AND THERE WAS NONE TO COVER WHAT YOU DID.

IT WAS ENTIRELY UNPRECEDENTED. SO I WAS CURSED WITH THE DUBIOUS PLEASURE OF HAVING TO MAKE IT UP MYSELF.

ABANDONMENT SEEMED TO BE THE BEST SOLUTION, SINCE I DIDNA WANT TO SPEND ANOTHER NIGHT IN YOUR PRESENCE.

......

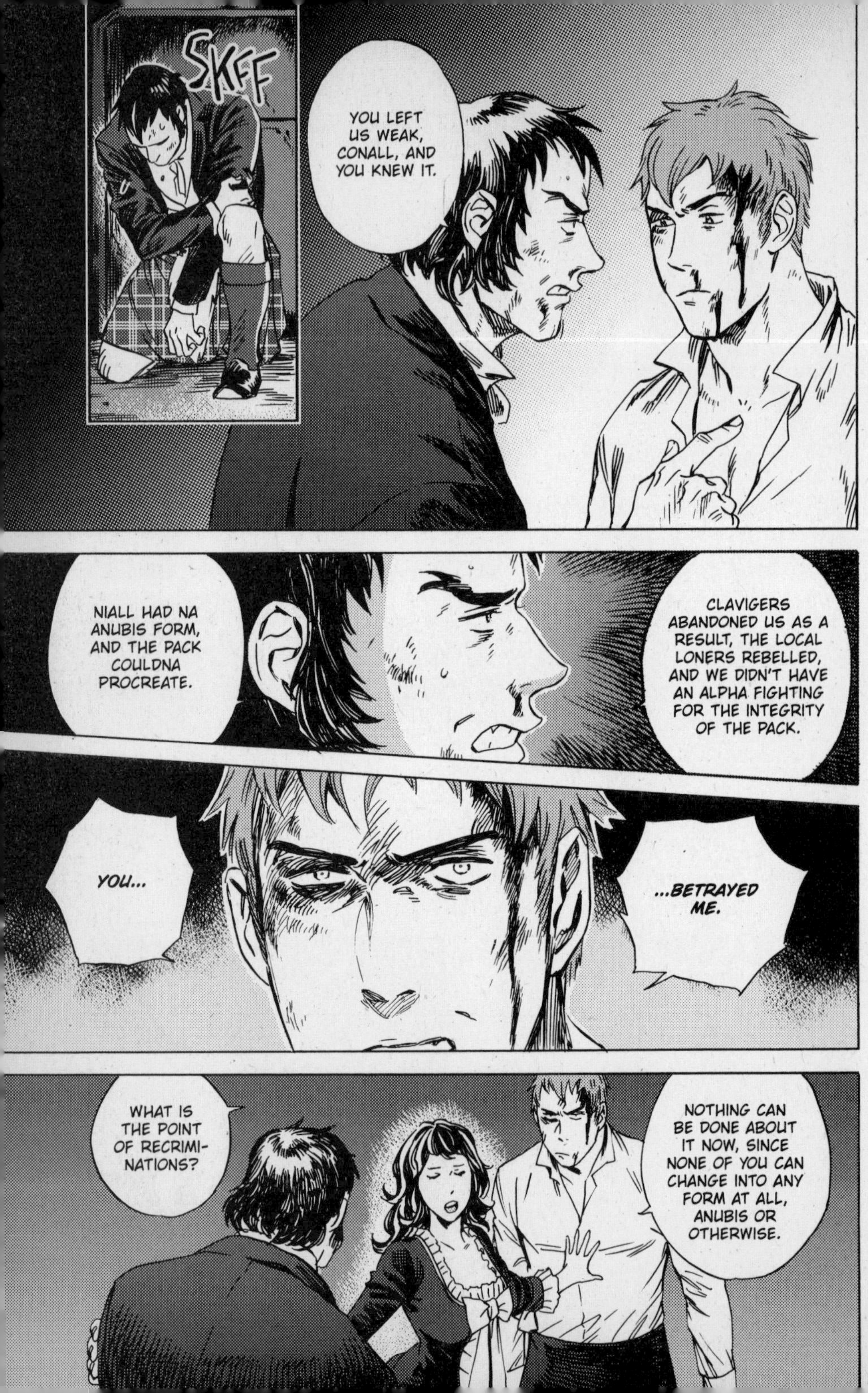
SKFF
YOU LEFT US WEAK, CONALL, AND YOU KNEW IT.
NIALL HAD NA ANUBIS FORM, AND THE PACK COULDNA PROCREATE.
CLAVIGERS ABANDONED US AS A RESULT, THE LOCAL LONERS REBELLED, AND WE DIDN'T HAVE AN ALPHA FIGHTING FOR THE INTEGRITY OF THE PACK.
YOU...
...BETRAYED ME.
WHAT IS THE POINT OF RECRIMINATIONS?
NOTHING CAN BE DONE ABOUT IT NOW, SINCE NONE OF YOU CAN CHANGE INTO ANY FORM AT ALL, ANUBIS OR OTHERWISE.

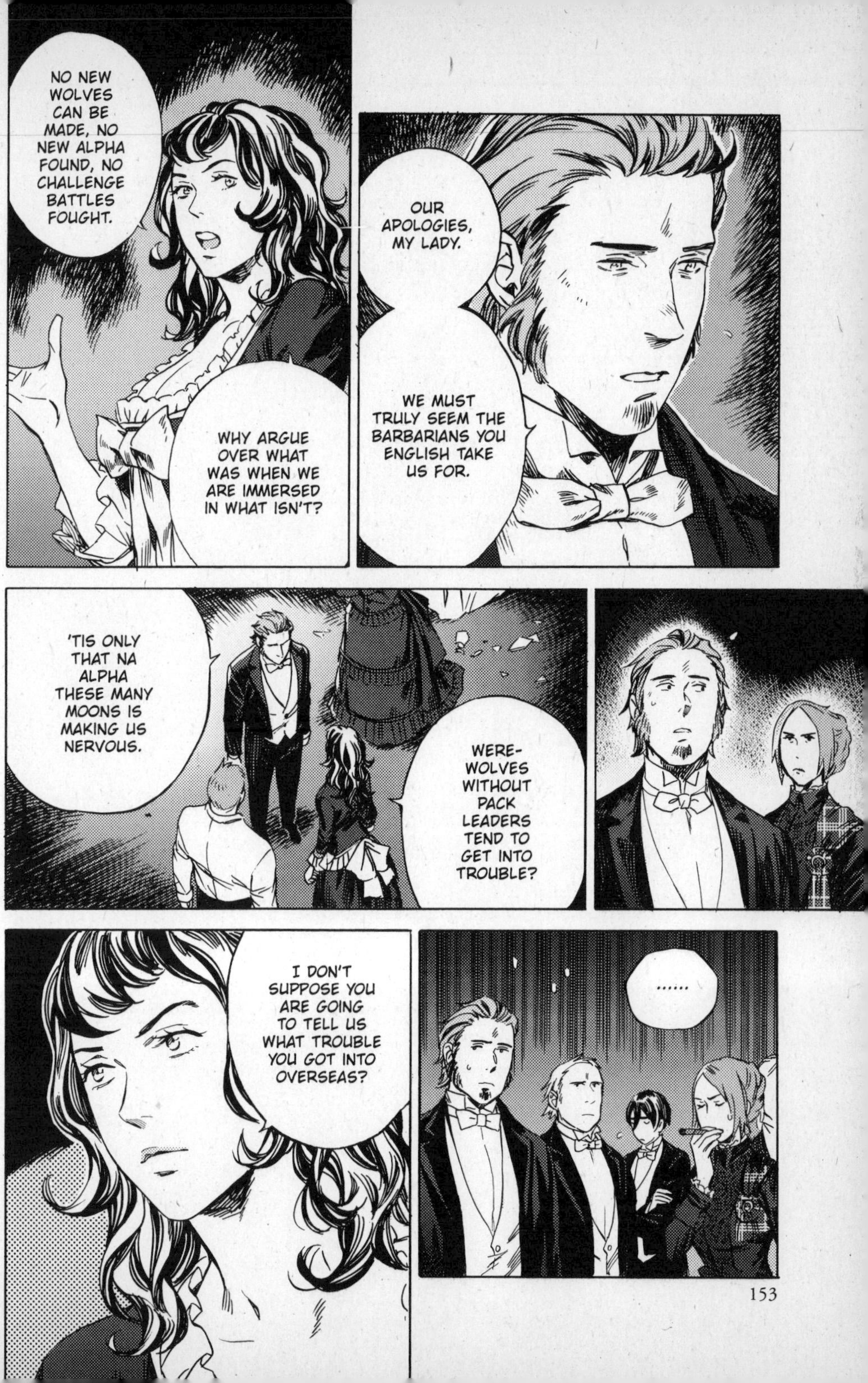
NO NEW WOLVES CAN BE MADE, NO NEW ALPHA FOUND, NO CHALLENGE BATTLES FOUGHT.
WHY ARGUE OVER WHAT WAS WHEN WE ARE IMMERSED IN WHAT ISN'T?
OUR APOLOGIES, MY LADY.
WE MUST TRULY SEEM THE BARBARIANS YOU ENGLISH TAKE US FOR.
'TIS ONLY THAT NA ALPHA THESE MANY MOONS IS MAKING US NERVOUS.
WERE-WOLVES WITHOUT PACK LEADERS TEND TO GET INTO TROUBLE?
I DON'T SUPPOSE YOU ARE GOING TO TELL US WHAT TROUBLE YOU GOT INTO OVERSEAS?
......

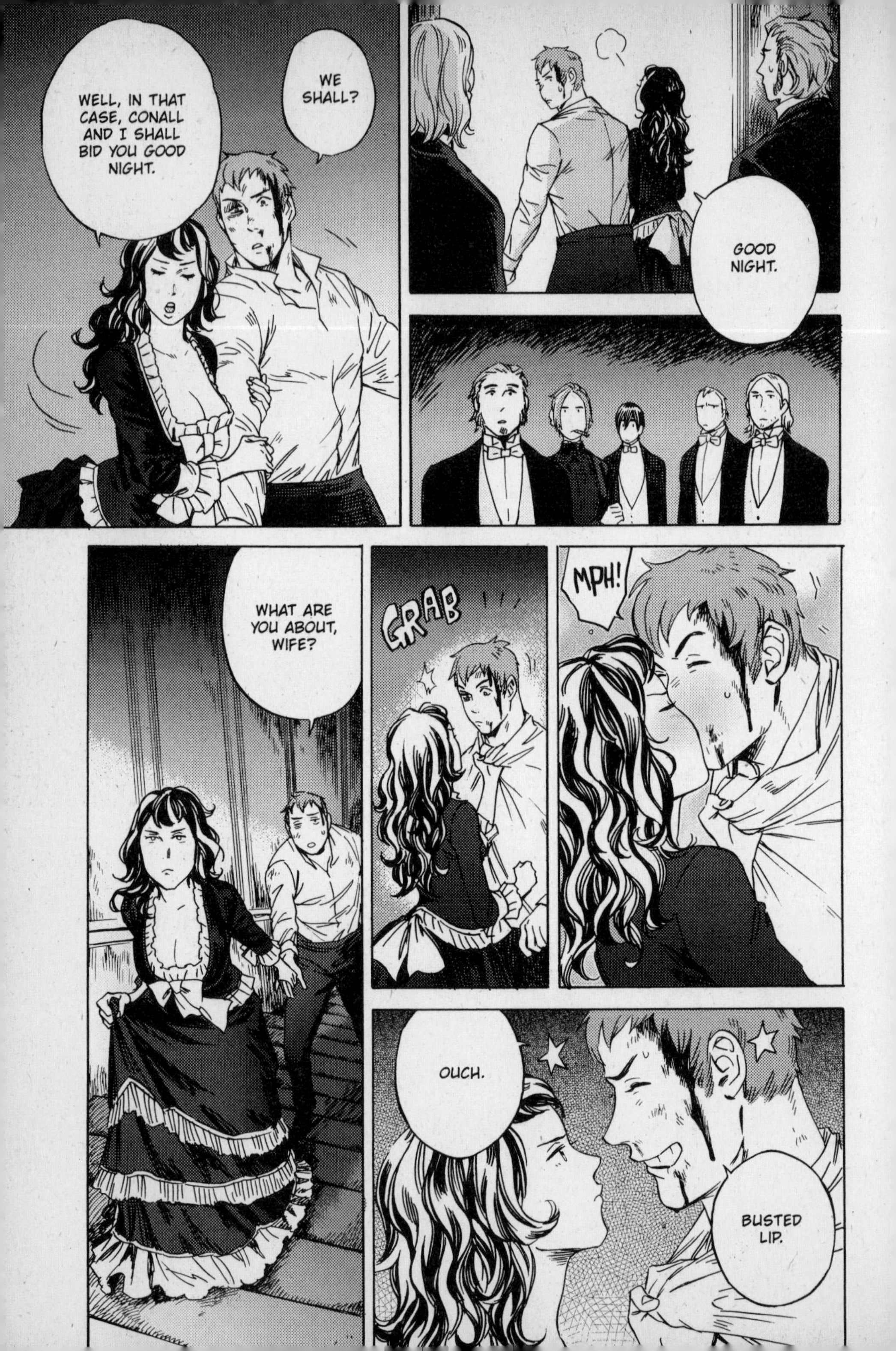
WELL, IN THAT CASE, CONALL AND I SHALL BID YOU GOOD NIGHT.
WE SHALL?
GOOD NIGHT.
WHAT ARE YOU ABOUT, WIFE?
GRAB
MPH!
OUCH.
BUSTED LIP.

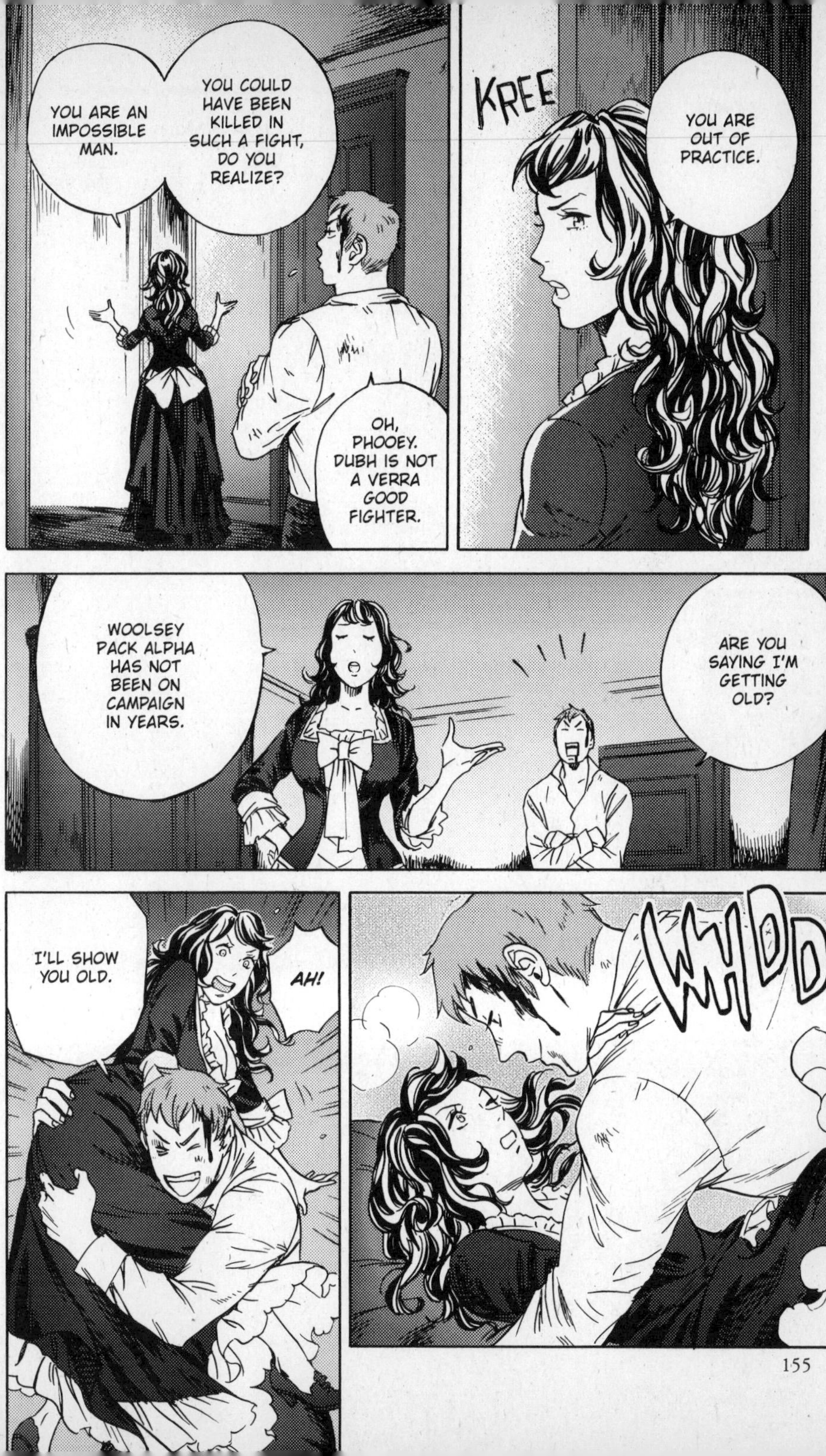

YOU ARE AN IMPOSSIBLE MAN.
YOU COULD HAVE BEEN KILLED IN SUCH A FIGHT, DO YOU REALIZE?
OH, PHOOEY. DUBH IS NOT A VERRA GOOD FIGHTER.
KREE
YOU ARE OUT OF PRACTICE.
WOOLSEY PACK ALPHA HAS NOT BEEN ON CAMPAIGN IN YEARS.
ARE YOU SAYING I'M GETTING OLD?
I'LL SHOW YOU OLD.
AH!
WHDD

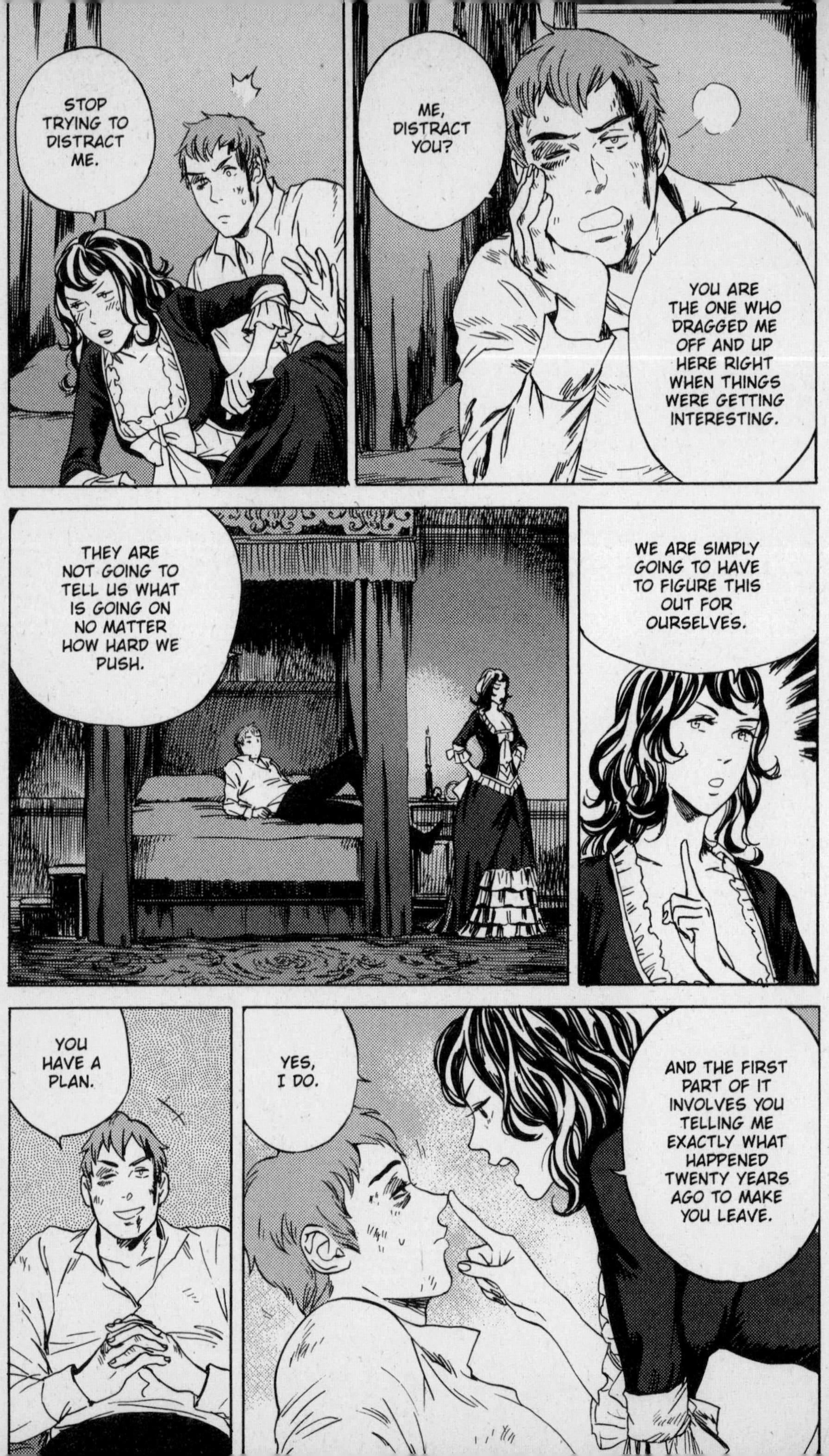
STOP TRYING TO DISTRACT ME.
ME, DISTRACT YOU?
YOU ARE THE ONE WHO DRAGGED ME OFF AND UP HERE RIGHT WHEN THINGS WERE GETTING INTERESTING.
THEY ARE NOT GOING TO TELL US WHAT IS GOING ON NO MATTER HOW HARD WE PUSH.
WE ARE SIMPLY GOING TO HAVE TO FIGURE THIS OUT FOR OURSELVES.
YOU HAVE A PLAN.
YES, I DO.
AND THE FIRST PART OF IT INVOLVES YOU TELLING ME EXACTLY WHAT HAPPENED TWENTY YEARS AGO TO MAKE YOU LEAVE.

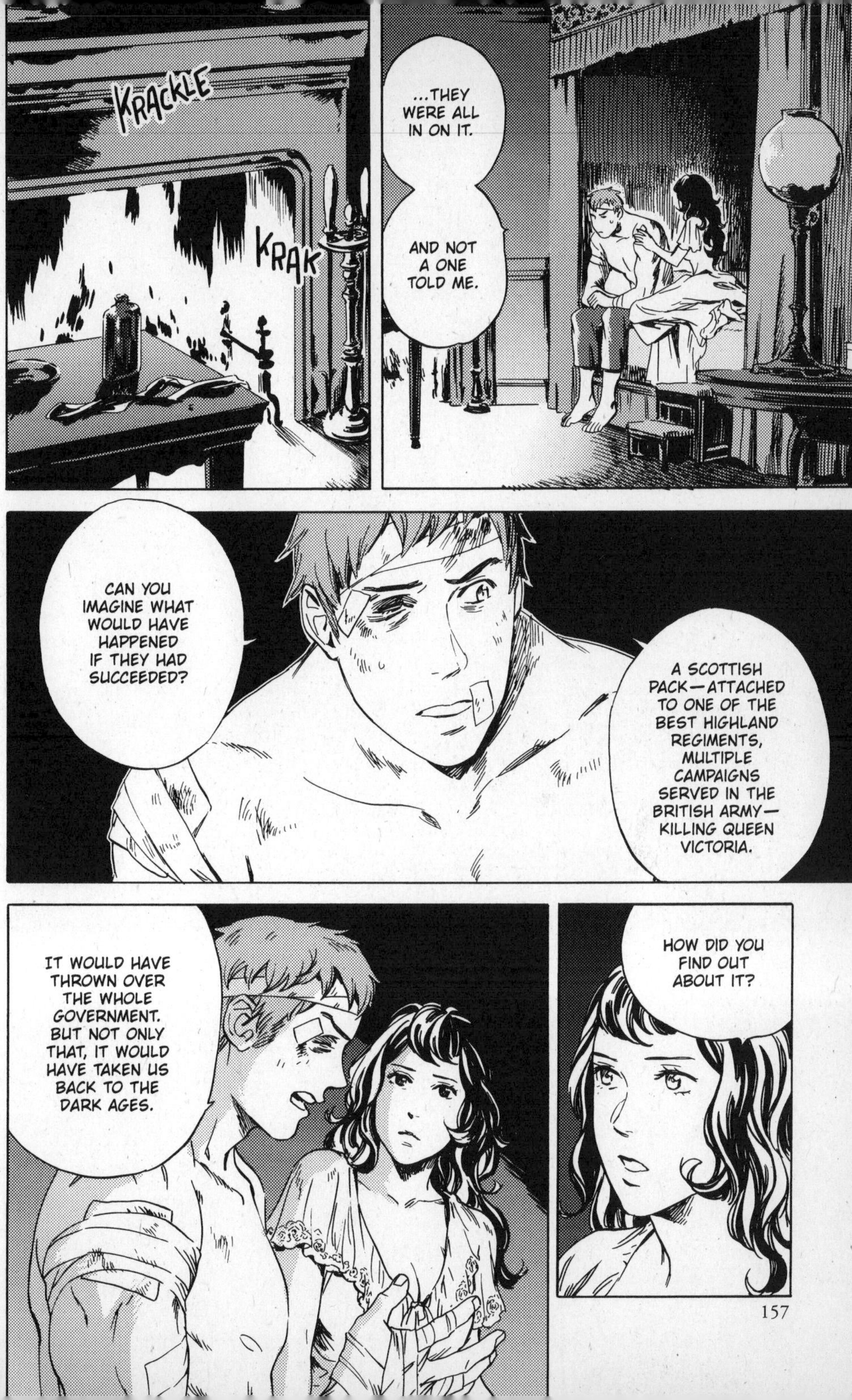
KRACKLE
KRAK
...THEY WERE ALL IN ON IT.
AND NOT A ONE TOLD ME.
CAN YOU IMAGINE WHAT WOULD HAVE HAPPENED IF THEY HAD SUCCEEDED?
A SCOTTISH PACK—ATTACHED TO ONE OF THE BEST HIGHLAND REGIMENTS, MULTIPLE CAMPAIGNS SERVED IN THE BRITISH ARMY—KILLING QUEEN VICTORIA.
IT WOULD HAVE THROWN OVER THE WHOLE GOVERNMENT. BUT NOT ONLY THAT, IT WOULD HAVE TAKEN US BACK TO THE DARK AGES.
HOW DID YOU FIND OUT ABOUT IT?

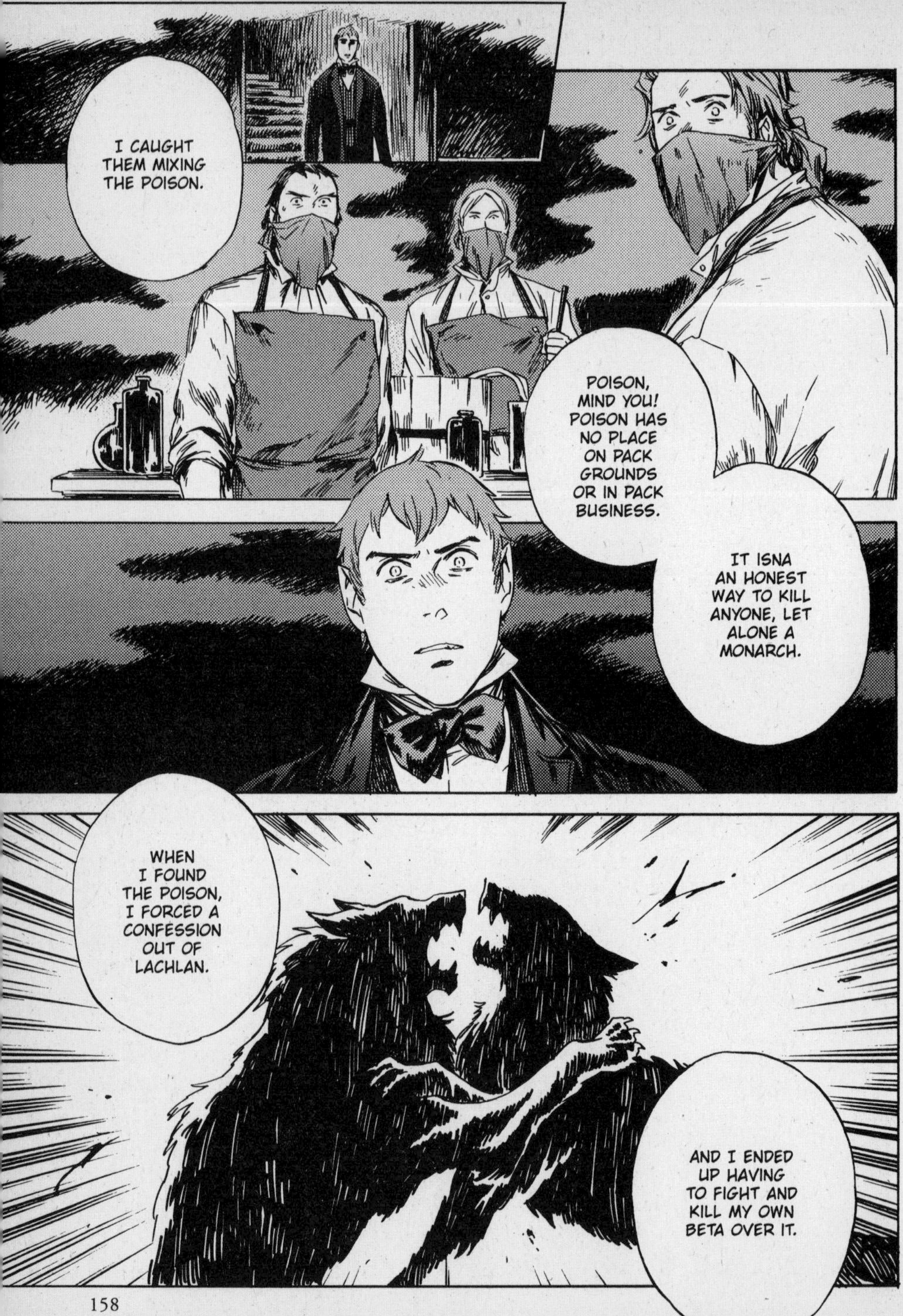
I CAUGHT THEM MIXING THE POISON.
POISON, MIND YOU! POISON HAS NO PLACE ON PACK GROUNDS OR IN PACK BUSINESS.
IT ISNA AN HONEST WAY TO KILL ANYONE, LET ALONE A MONARCH.
WHEN I FOUND THE POISON, I FORCED A CONFESSION OUT OF LACHLAN.
AND I ENDED UP HAVING TO FIGHT AND KILL MY OWN BETA OVER IT.

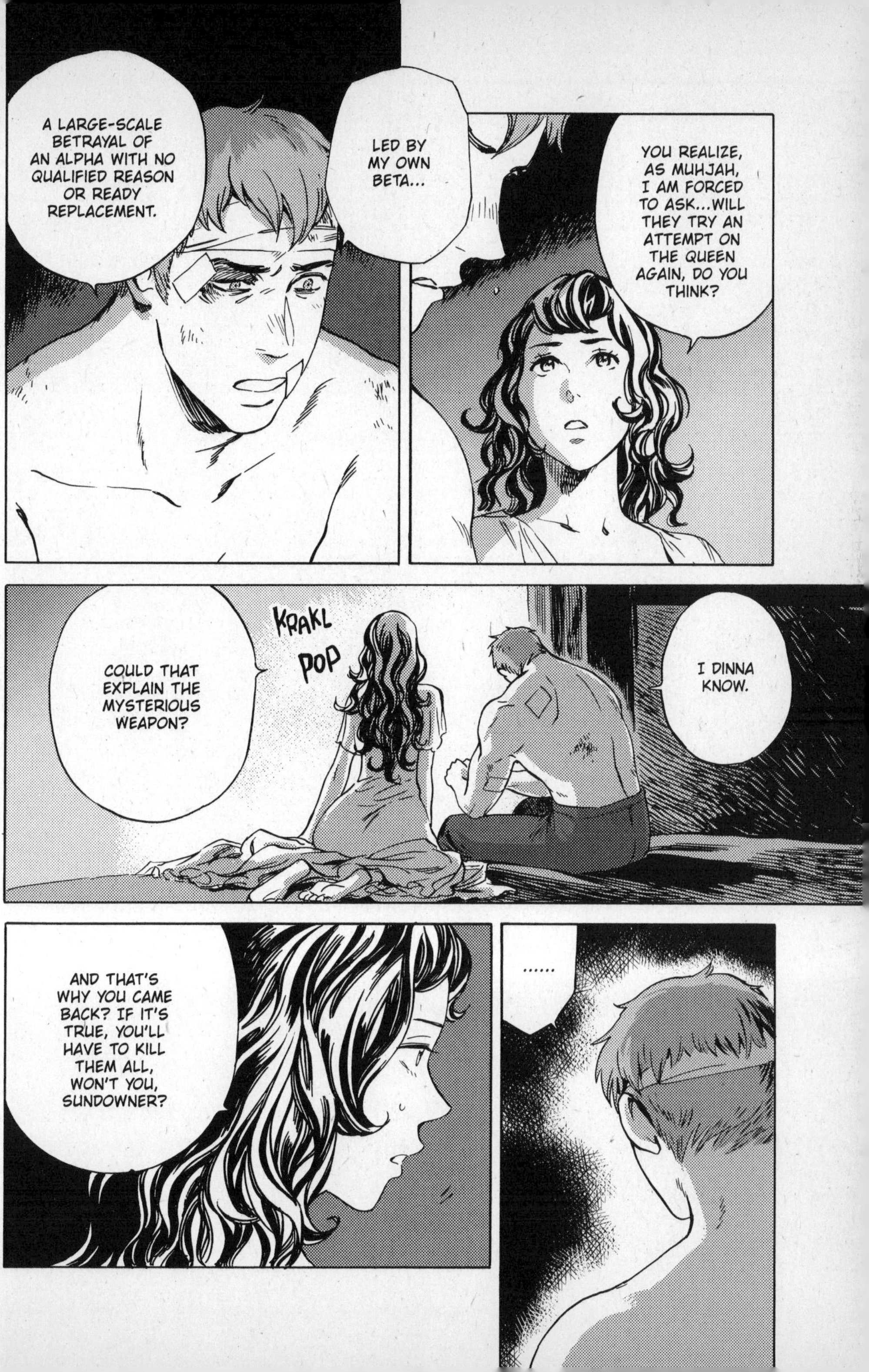
A LARGE-SCALE BETRAYAL OF AN ALPHA WITH NO QUALIFIED REASON OR READY REPLACEMENT.
LED BY MY OWN BETA...
YOU REALIZE, AS MUHJAH, I AM FORCED TO ASK...WILL THEY TRY AN ATTEMPT ON THE QUEEN AGAIN, DO YOU THINK?
COULD THAT EXPLAIN THE MYSTERIOUS WEAPON?
KRAKL
POP
I DINNA KNOW.
AND THAT'S WHY YOU CAME BACK? IF IT'S TRUE, YOU'LL HAVE TO KILL THEM ALL, WON'T YOU, SUNDOWNER?
......

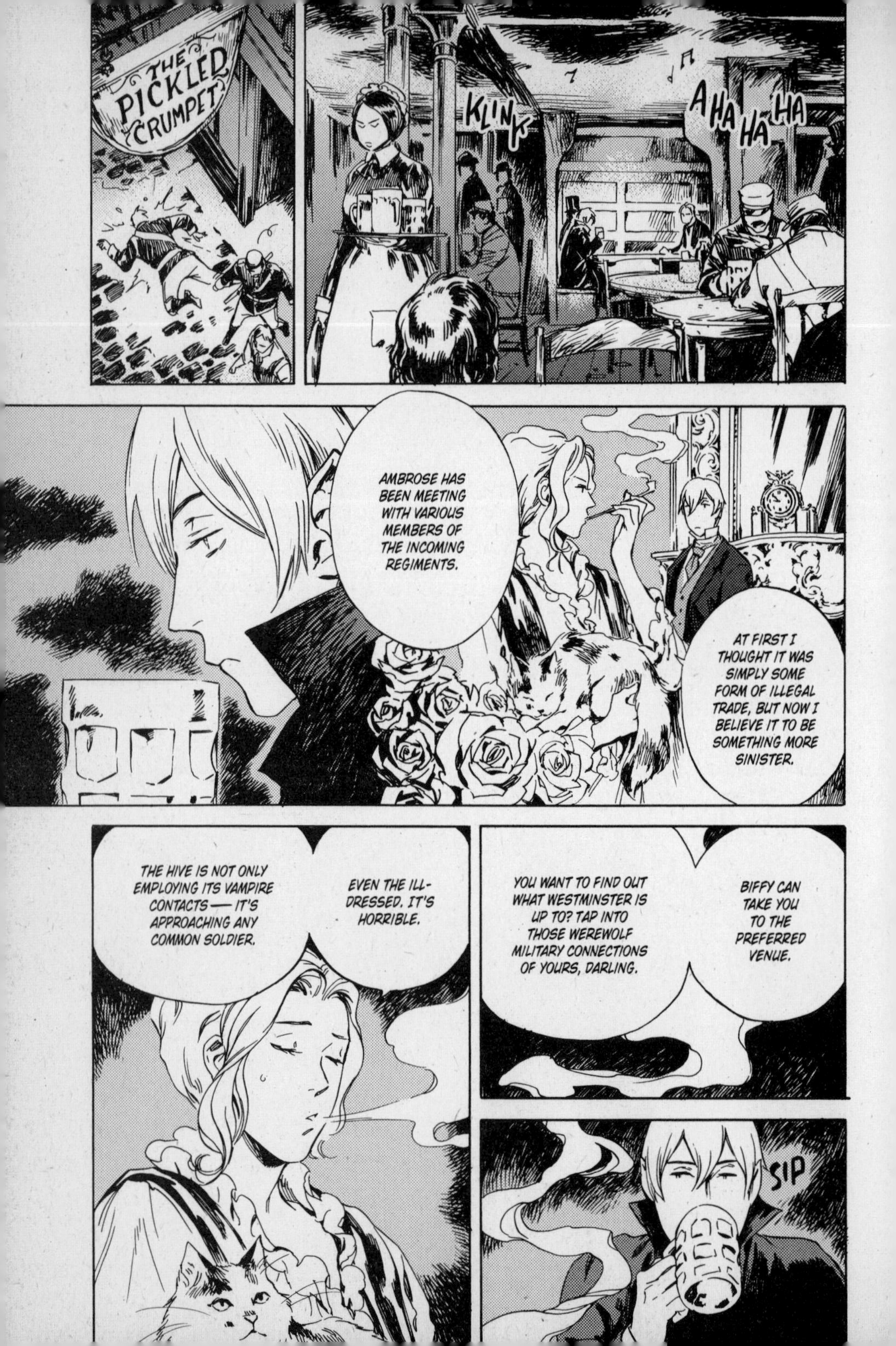
THE PICKLED CRUMPET
KLINK
AHAHAHA
AMBROSE HAS BEEN MEETING WITH VARIOUS MEMBERS OF THE INCOMING REGIMENTS.
AT FIRST I THOUGHT IT WAS SIMPLY SOME FORM OF ILLEGAL TRADE, BUT NOW I BELIEVE IT TO BE SOMETHING MORE SINISTER.
THE HIVE IS NOT ONLY EMPLOYING ITS VAMPIRE CONTACTS— IT'S APPROACHING ANY COMMON SOLDIER.
EVEN THE ILL-DRESSED. IT'S HORRIBLE.
YOU WANT TO FIND OUT WHAT WESTMINSTER IS UP TO? TAP INTO THOSE WEREWOLF MILITARY CONNECTIONS OF YOURS, DARLING.
BIFFY CAN TAKE YOU TO THE PREFERRED VENUE.
SIP

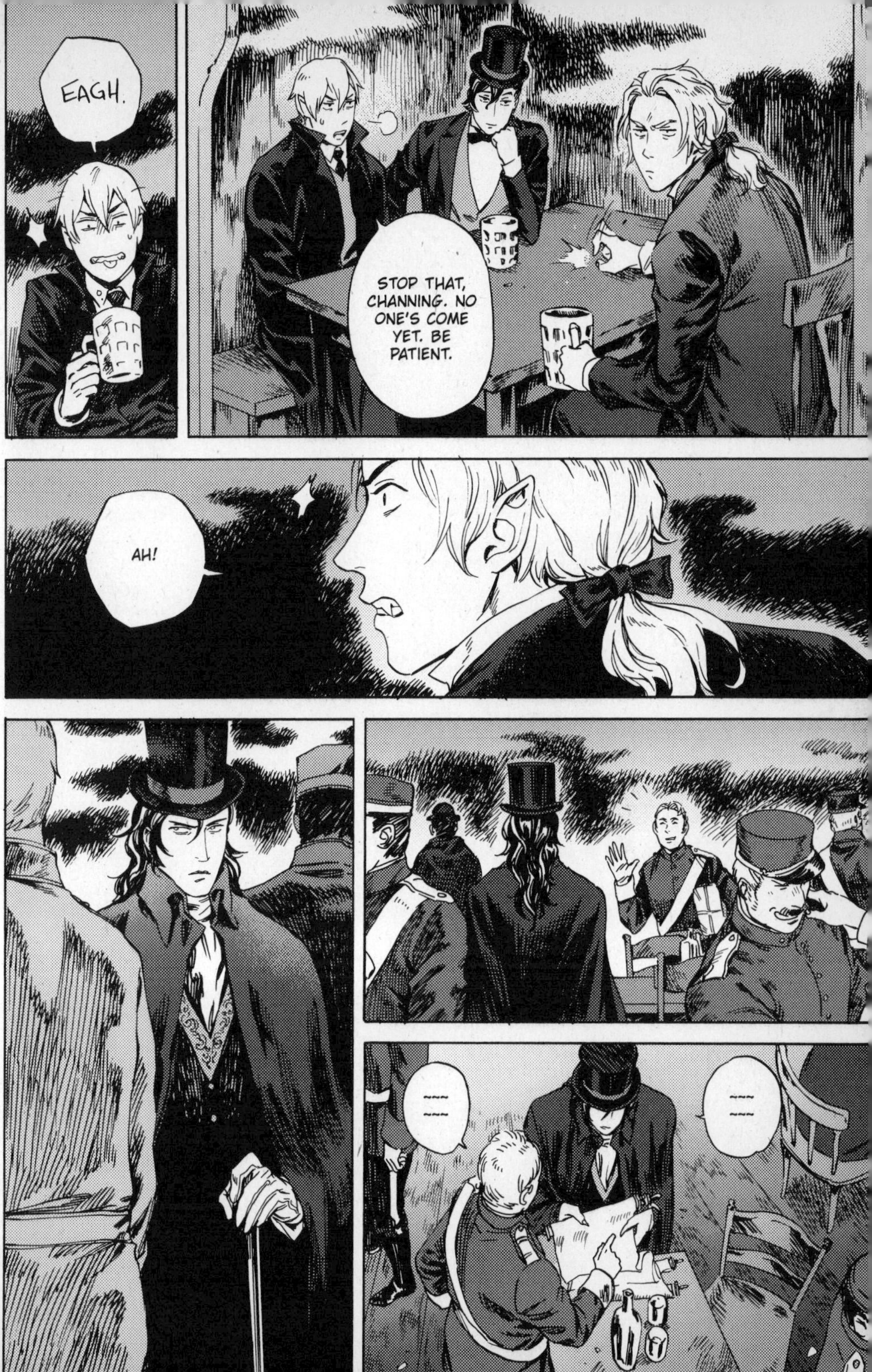
EAGH.
STOP THAT, CHANNING. NO ONE'S COME YET. BE PATIENT.
AH!
---- ----
---- ----

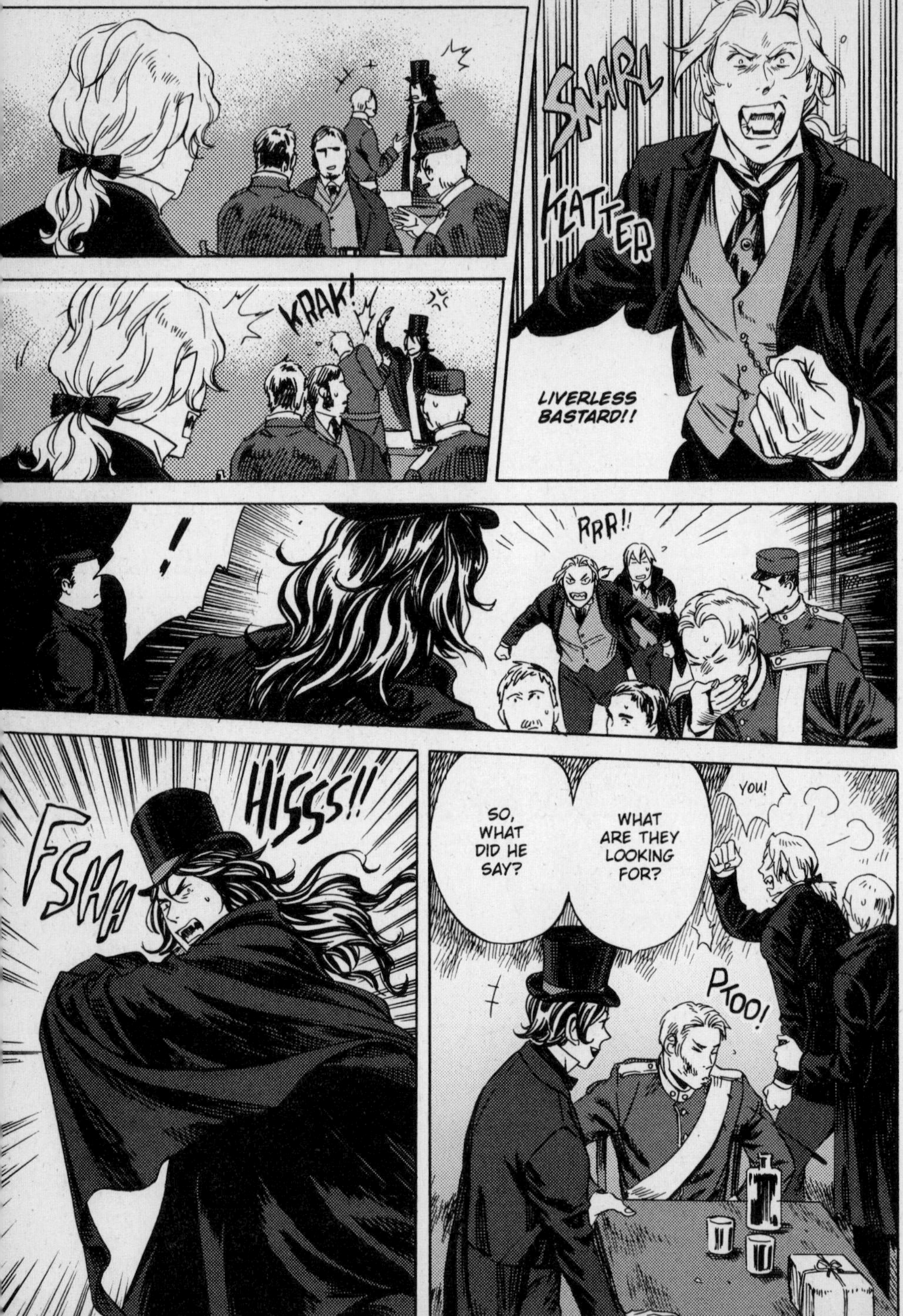
KRAK!
SNARL
KLATTER
LIVERLESS BASTARD!!
!
RRR!!
FSHH
HISSS!!
SO, WHAT DID HE SAY?
WHAT ARE THEY LOOKING FOR?
YOU!
PKOO!

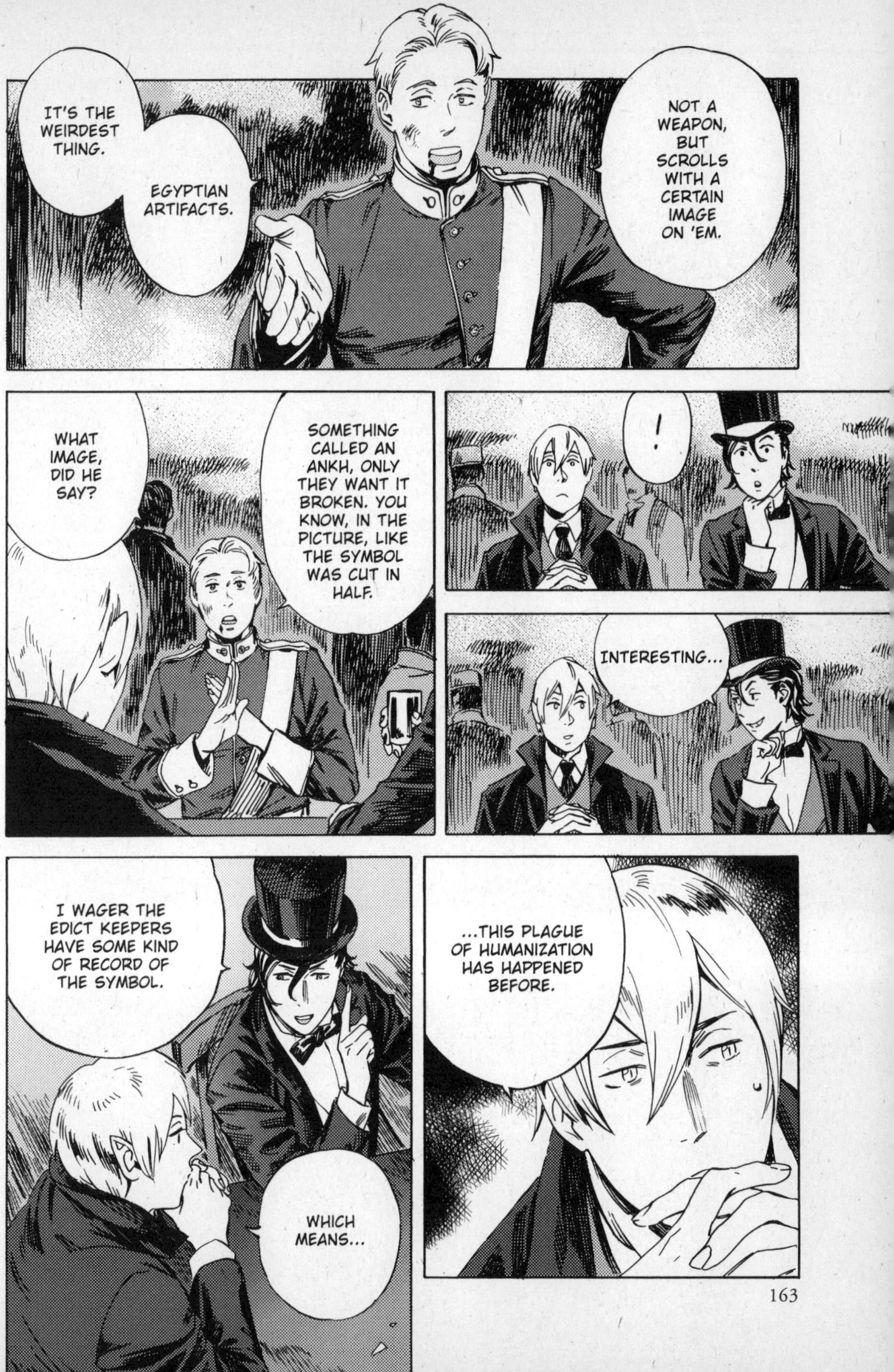
IT'S THE WEIRDEST THING.
EGYPTIAN ARTIFACTS.
NOT A WEAPON, BUT SCROLLS WITH A CERTAIN IMAGE ON 'EM.
WHAT IMAGE, DID HE SAY?
SOMETHING CALLED AN ANKH, ONLY THEY WANT IT BROKEN. YOU KNOW, IN THE PICTURE, LIKE THE SYMBOL WAS CUT IN HALF.
!
INTERESTING...
I WAGER THE EDICT KEEPERS HAVE SOME KIND OF RECORD OF THE SYMBOL.
WHICH MEANS...
...THIS PLAGUE OF HUMANIZATION HAS HAPPENED BEFORE.

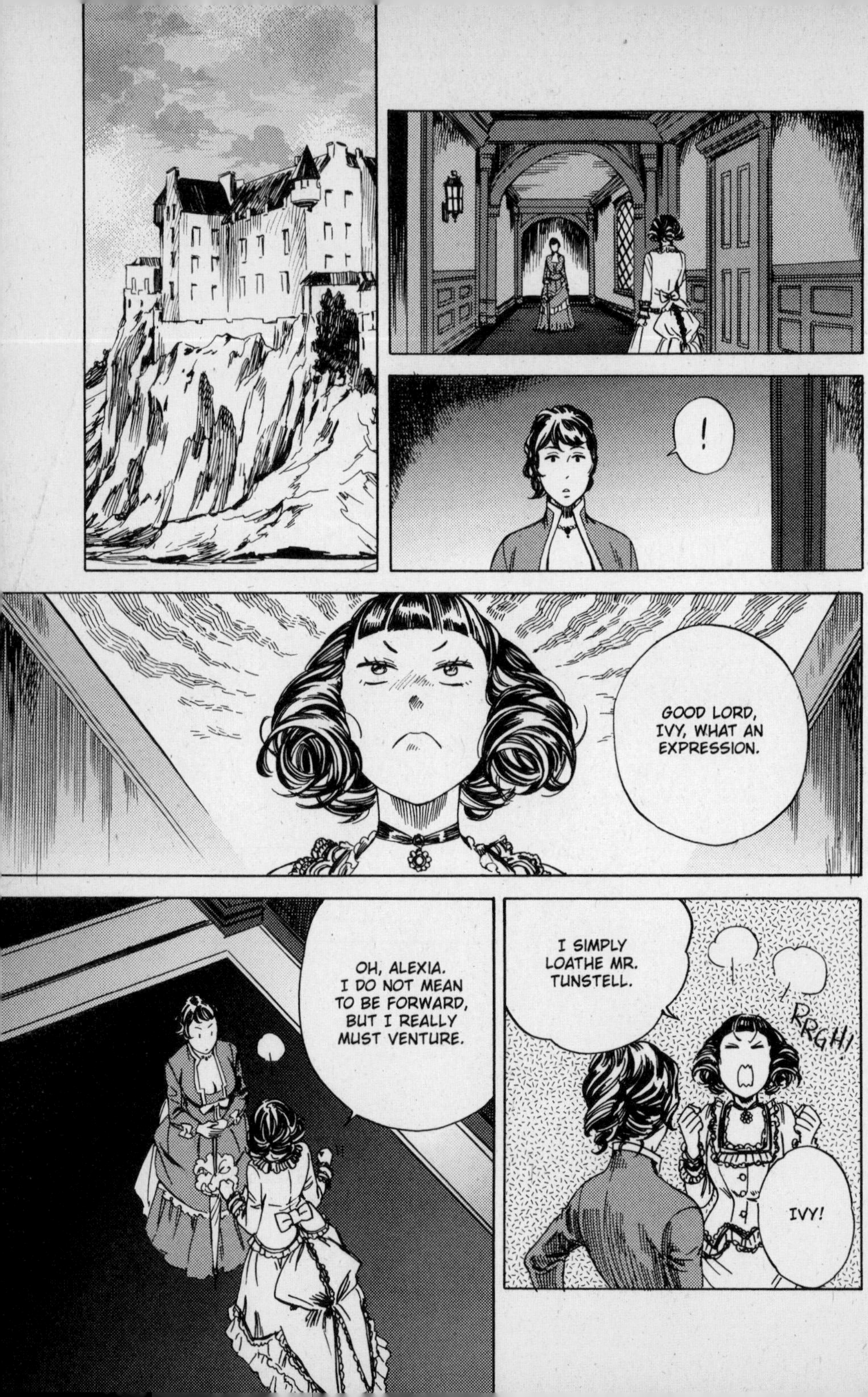
!
GOOD LORD, IVY, WHAT AN EXPRESSION.
OH, ALEXIA. I DO NOT MEAN TO BE FORWARD, BUT I REALLY MUST VENTURE.
I SIMPLY LOATHE MR. TUNSTELL.
RRGH!
IVY!

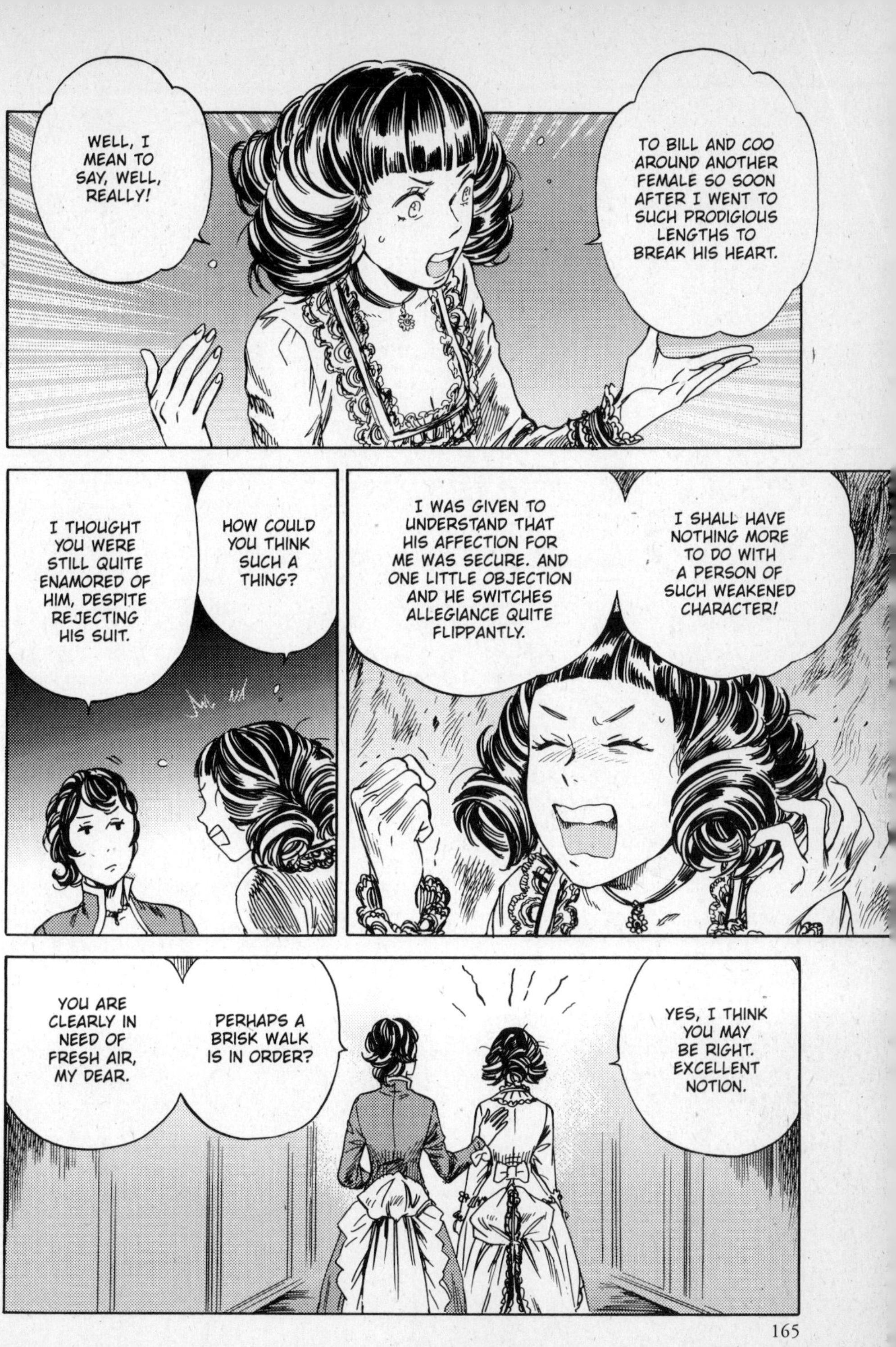
WELL, I MEAN TO SAY, WELL, REALLY!
TO BILL AND COO AROUND ANOTHER FEMALE SO SOON AFTER I WENT TO SUCH PRODIGIOUS LENGTHS TO BREAK HIS HEART.
I THOUGHT YOU WERE STILL QUITE ENAMORED OF HIM, DESPITE REJECTING HIS SUIT.
HOW COULD YOU THINK SUCH A THING?
I WAS GIVEN TO UNDERSTAND THAT HIS AFFECTION FOR ME WAS SECURE. AND ONE LITTLE OBJECTION AND HE SWITCHES ALLEGIANCE QUITE FLIPPANTLY.
I SHALL HAVE NOTHING MORE TO DO WITH A PERSON OF SUCH WEAKENED CHARACTER!
YOU ARE CLEARLY IN NEED OF FRESH AIR, MY DEAR.
PERHAPS A BRISK WALK IS IN ORDER?
YES, I THINK YOU MAY BE RIGHT. EXCELLENT NOTION.

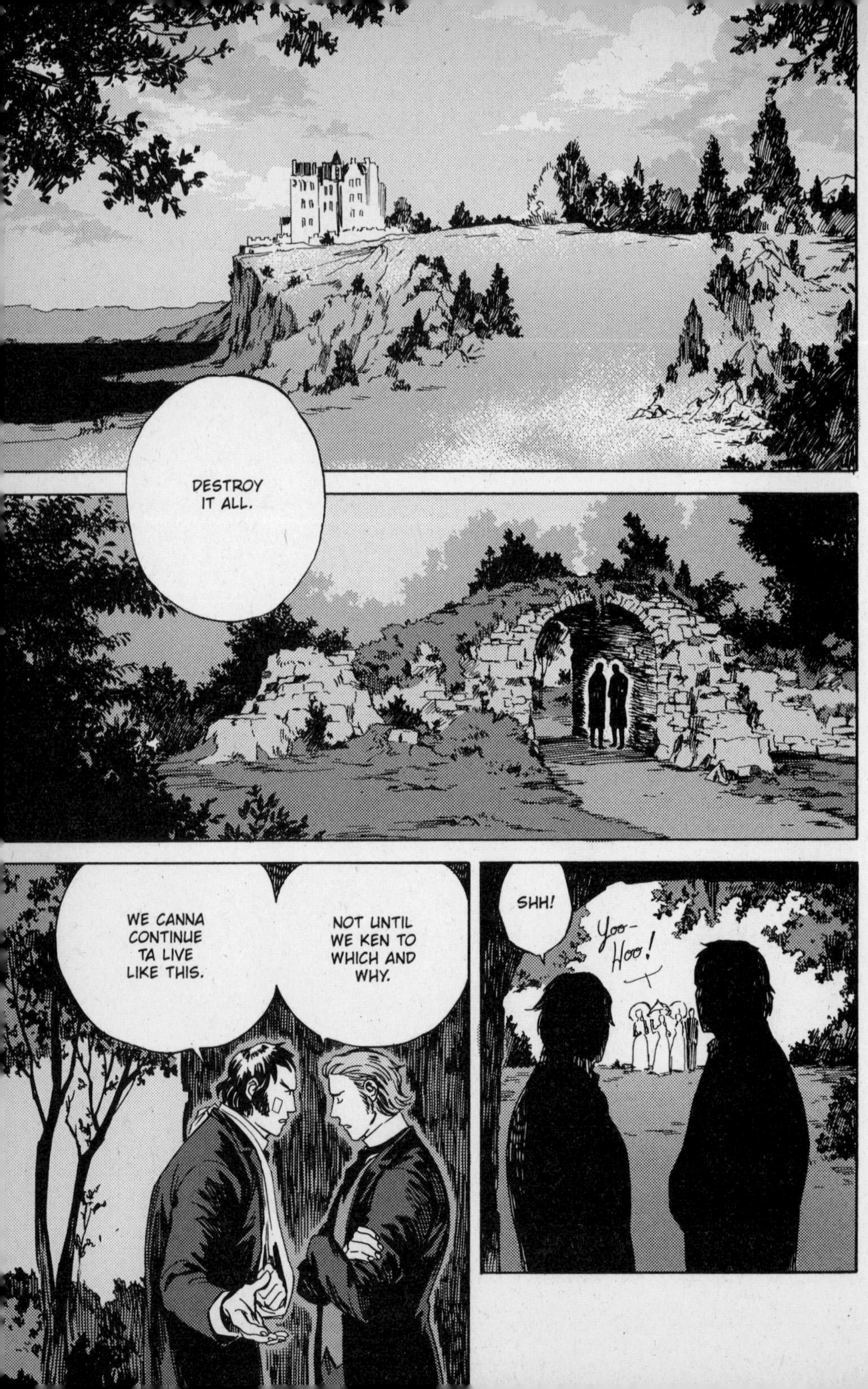
DESTROY IT ALL.
WE CANNA CONTINUE TA LIVE LIKE THIS.
NOT UNTIL WE KEN TO WHICH AND WHY.
SHH!
Yoo-Hoo!

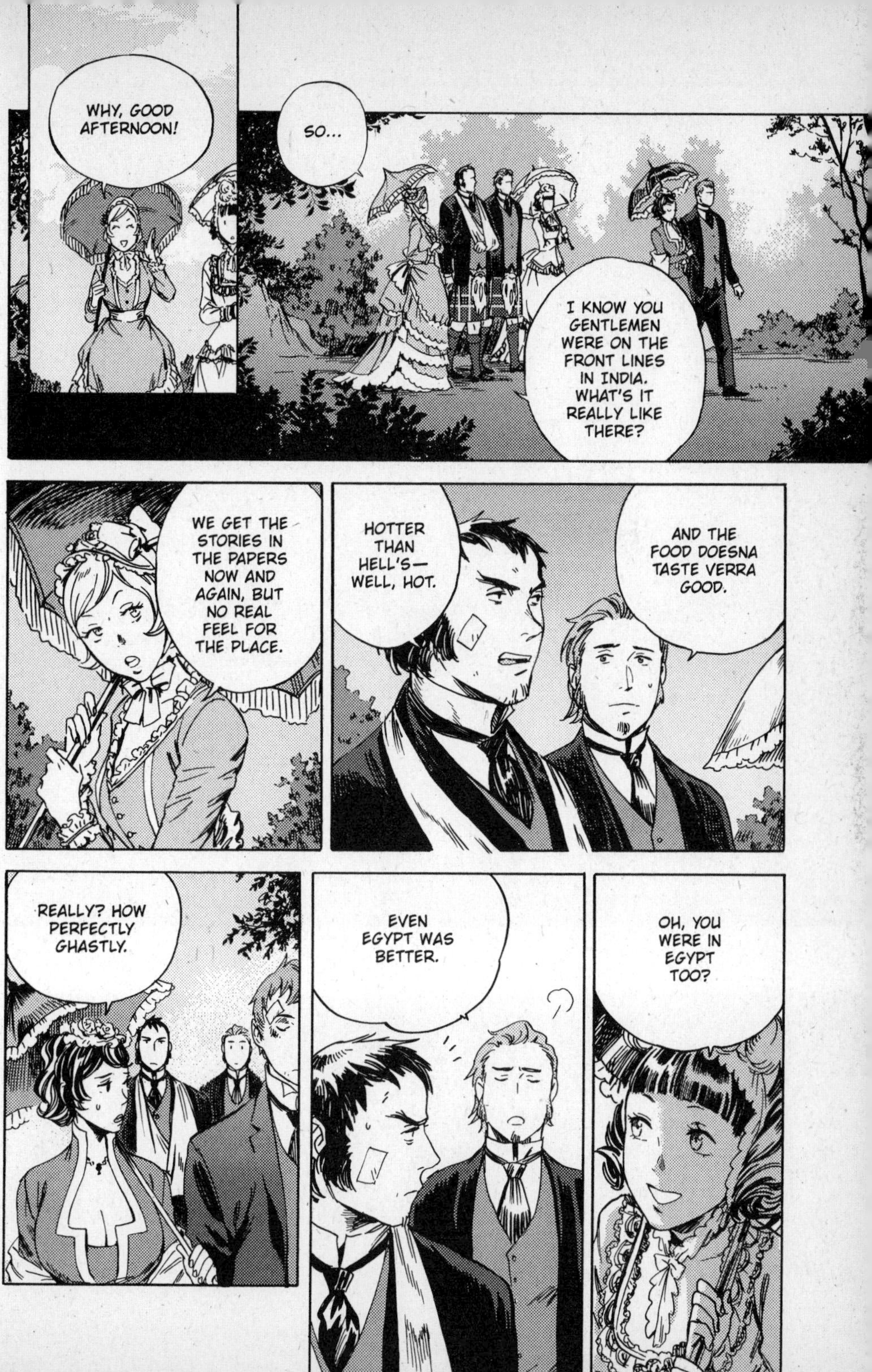
WHY, GOOD AFTERNOON!
SO...
I KNOW YOU GENTLEMEN WERE ON THE FRONT LINES IN INDIA. WHAT'S IT REALLY LIKE THERE?
WE GET THE STORIES IN THE PAPERS NOW AND AGAIN, BUT NO REAL FEEL FOR THE PLACE.
HOTTER THAN HELL'S—WELL, HOT.
AND THE FOOD DOESNA TASTE VERRA GOOD.
REALLY? HOW PERFECTLY GHASTLY.
EVEN EGYPT WAS BETTER.
OH, YOU WERE IN EGYPT TOO?

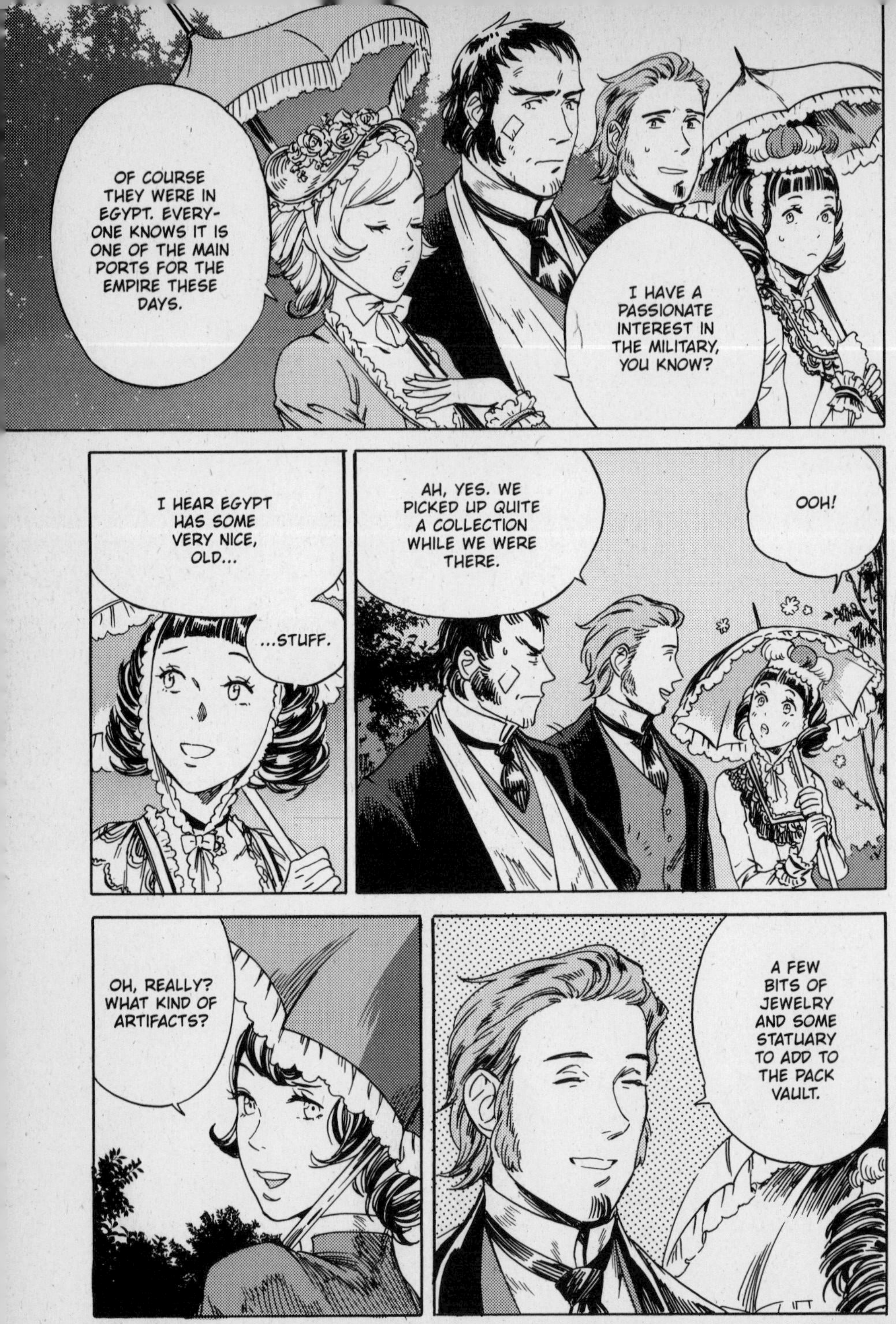
OF COURSE THEY WERE IN EGYPT. EVERY-ONE KNOWS IT IS ONE OF THE MAIN PORTS FOR THE EMPIRE THESE DAYS.
I HAVE A PASSIONATE INTEREST IN THE MILITARY, YOU KNOW?
I HEAR EGYPT HAS SOME VERY NICE, OLD...
...STUFF.
AH, YES. WE PICKED UP QUITE A COLLECTION WHILE WE WERE THERE.
OOH!
OH, REALLY? WHAT KIND OF ARTIFACTS?
A FEW BITS OF JEWELRY AND SOME STATUARY TO ADD TO THE PACK VAULT.

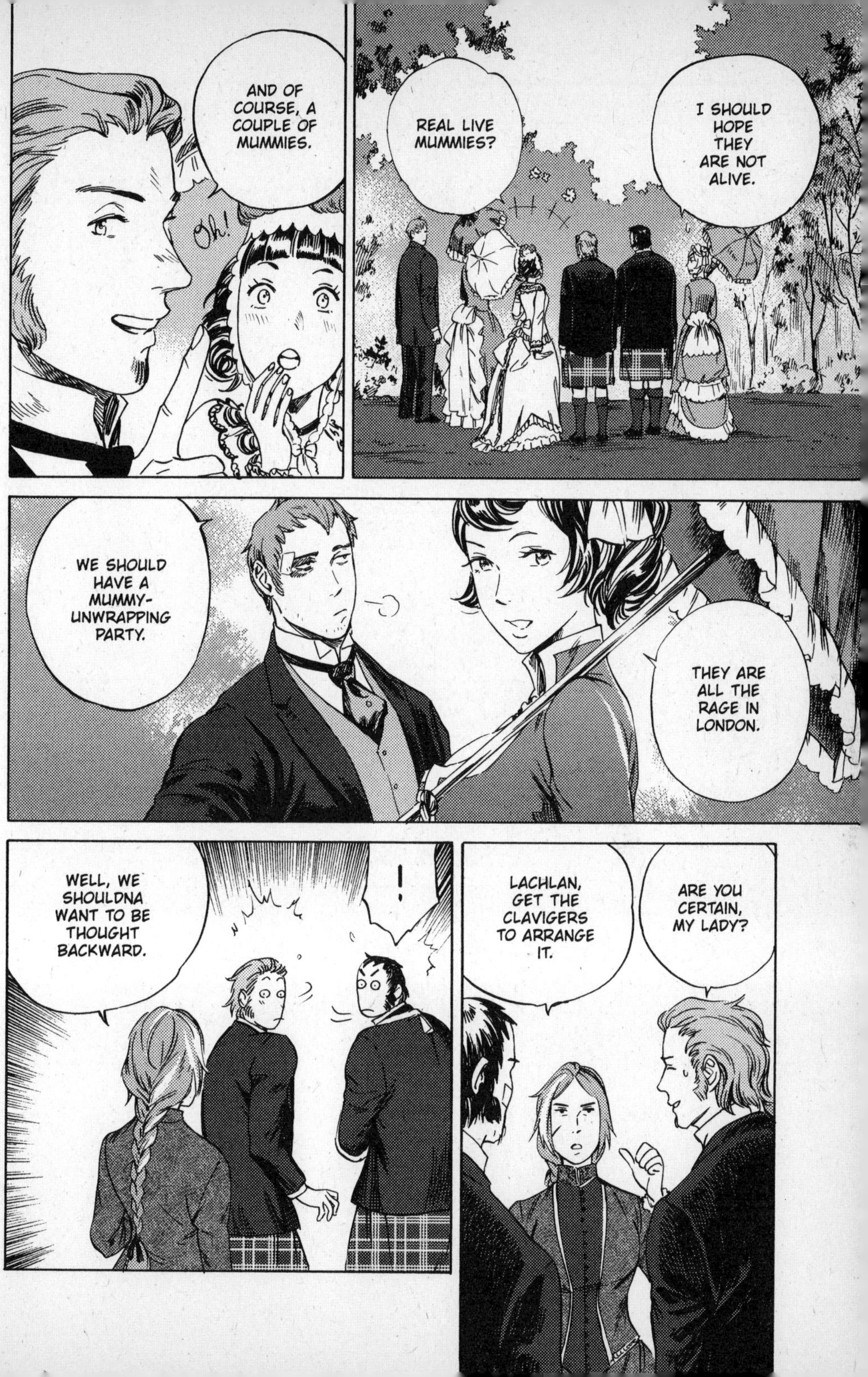
AND OF COURSE, A COUPLE OF MUMMIES.
OH!
REAL LIVE MUMMIES?
I SHOULD HOPE THEY ARE NOT ALIVE.
WE SHOULD HAVE A MUMMY-UNWRAPPING PARTY.
THEY ARE ALL THE RAGE IN LONDON.
WELL, WE SHOULDNA WANT TO BE THOUGHT BACKWARD.
!
LACHLAN, GET THE CLAVIGERS TO ARRANGE IT.
ARE YOU CERTAIN, MY LADY?

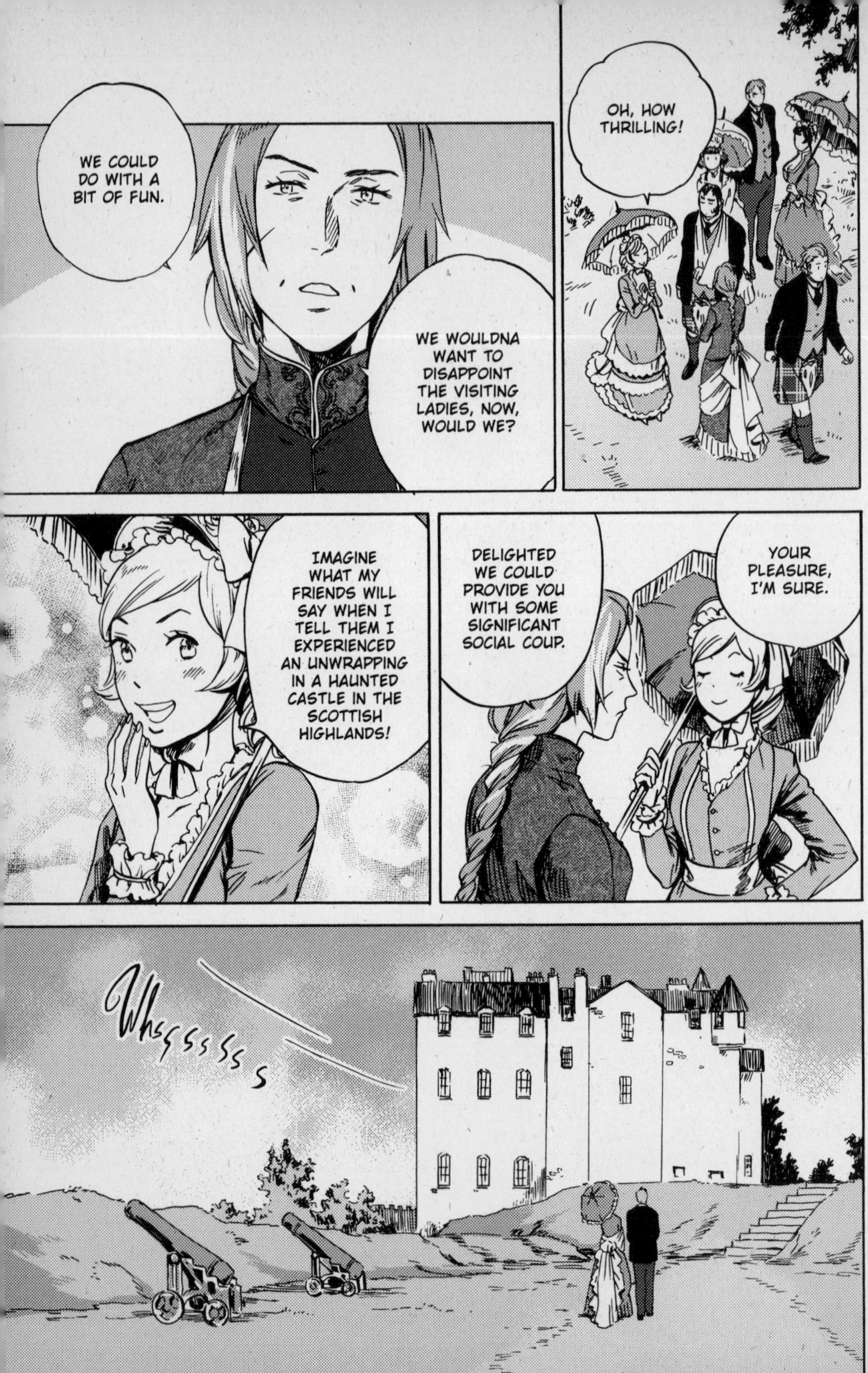
WE COULD DO WITH A BIT OF FUN.
WE WOULDNA WANT TO DISAPPOINT THE VISITING LADIES, NOW, WOULD WE?
OH, HOW THRILLING!
IMAGINE WHAT MY FRIENDS WILL SAY WHEN I TELL THEM I EXPERIENCED AN UNWRAPPING IN A HAUNTED CASTLE IN THE SCOTTISH HIGHLANDS!
DELIGHTED WE COULD PROVIDE YOU WITH SOME SIGNIFICANT SOCIAL COUP.
YOUR PLEASURE, I'M SURE.
Whsssssss

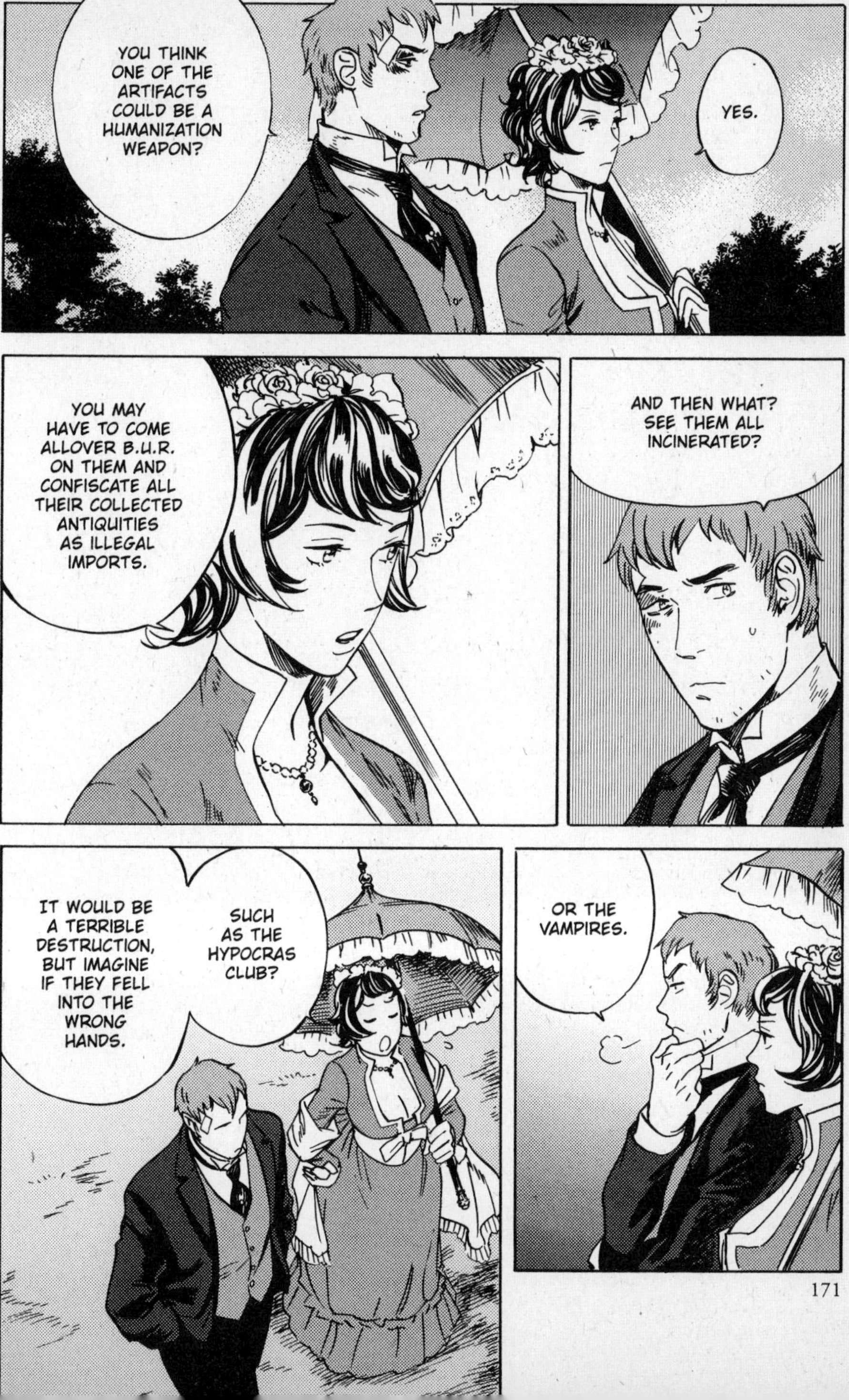
YOU THINK ONE OF THE ARTIFACTS COULD BE A HUMANIZATION WEAPON?
YES.
YOU MAY HAVE TO COME ALLOVER B.U.R. ON THEM AND CONFISCATE ALL THEIR COLLECTED ANTIQUITIES AS ILLEGAL IMPORTS.
AND THEN WHAT? SEE THEM ALL INCINERATED?
IT WOULD BE A TERRIBLE DESTRUCTION, BUT IMAGINE IF THEY FELL INTO THE WRONG HANDS.
SUCH AS THE HYPOCRAS CLUB?
OR THE VAMPIRES.

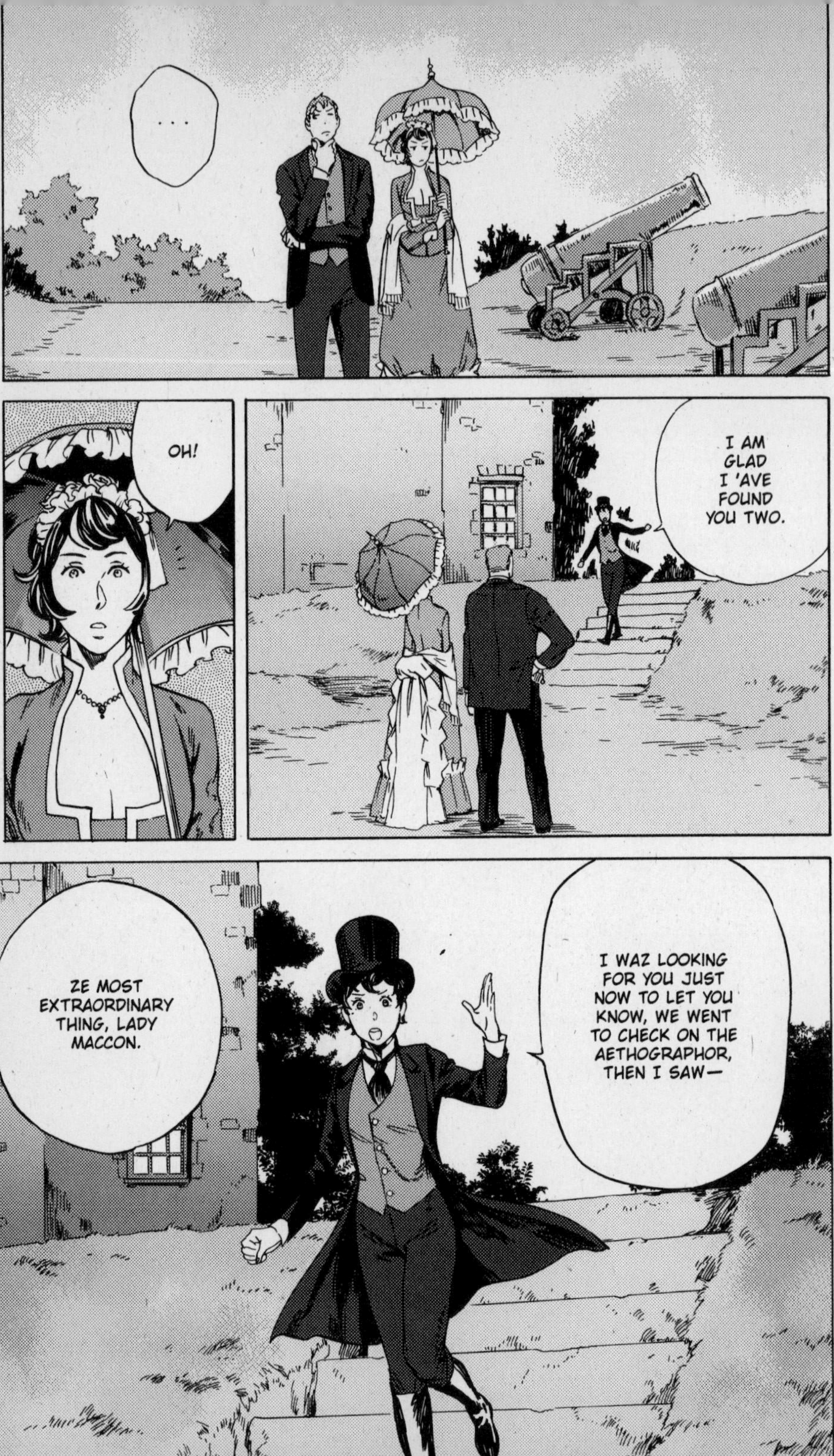
...
OH!
I AM GLAD I 'AVE FOUND YOU TWO.
ZE MOST EXTRAORDINARY THING, LADY MACCON.
I WAZ LOOKING FOR YOU JUST NOW TO LET YOU KNOW, WE WENT TO CHECK ON THE AETHOGRAPHOR, THEN I SAW—

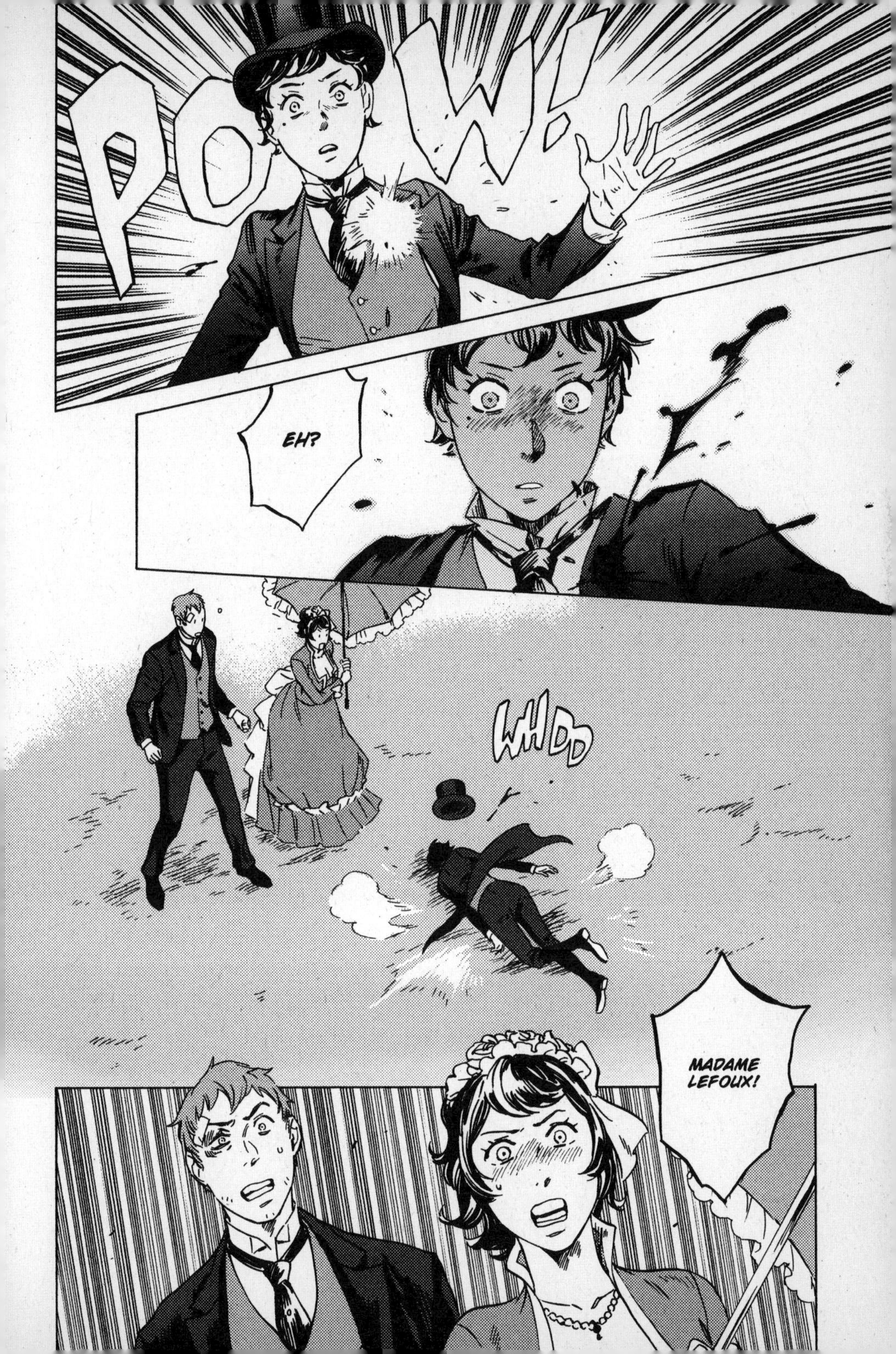
POW!
EH?
WHDD
MADAME LEFOUX!

SOULLESS

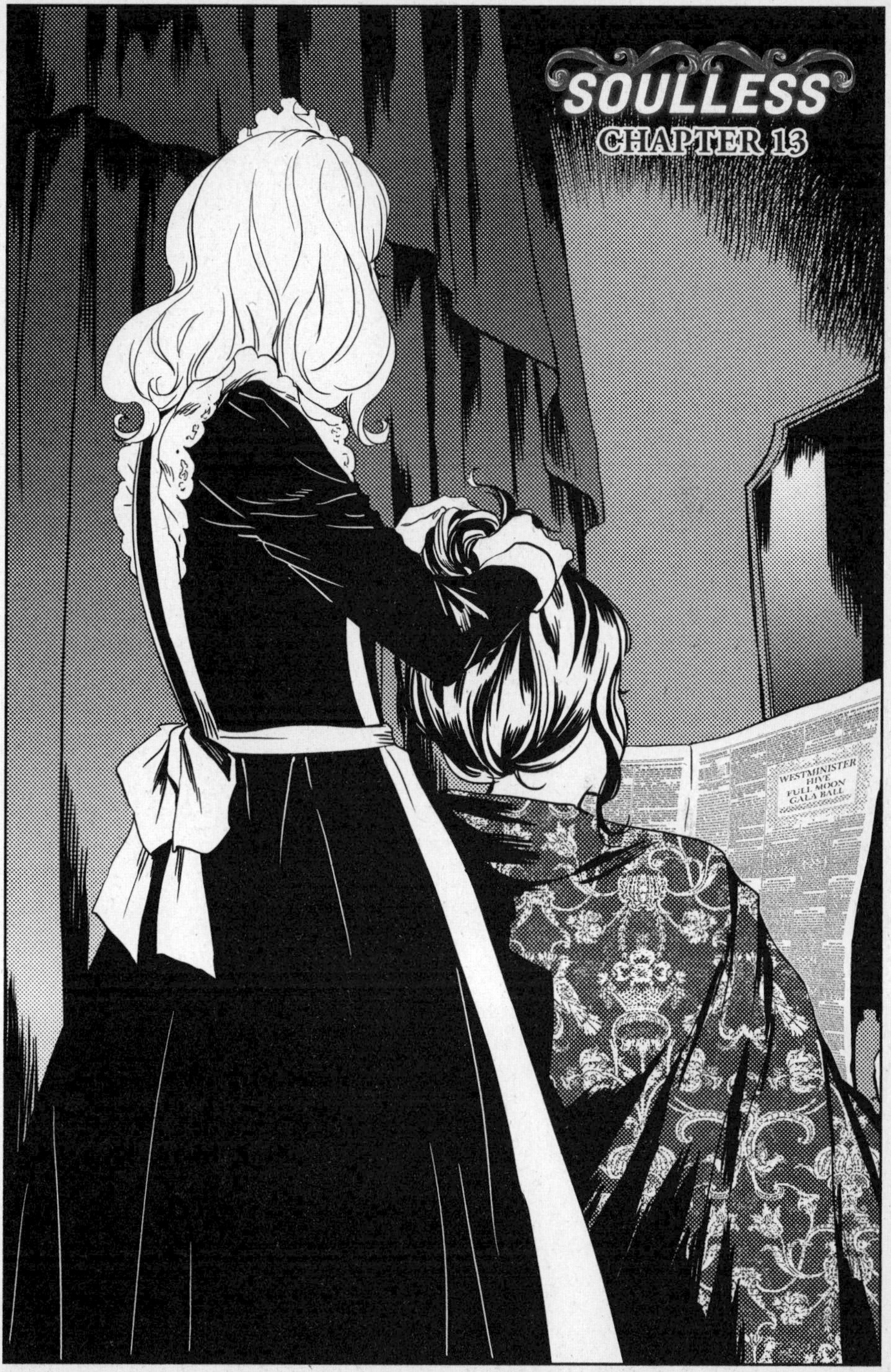
SOULLESS
CHAPTER 13
WESTMINISTER
HIVE
FULL MOON
GALA BALL

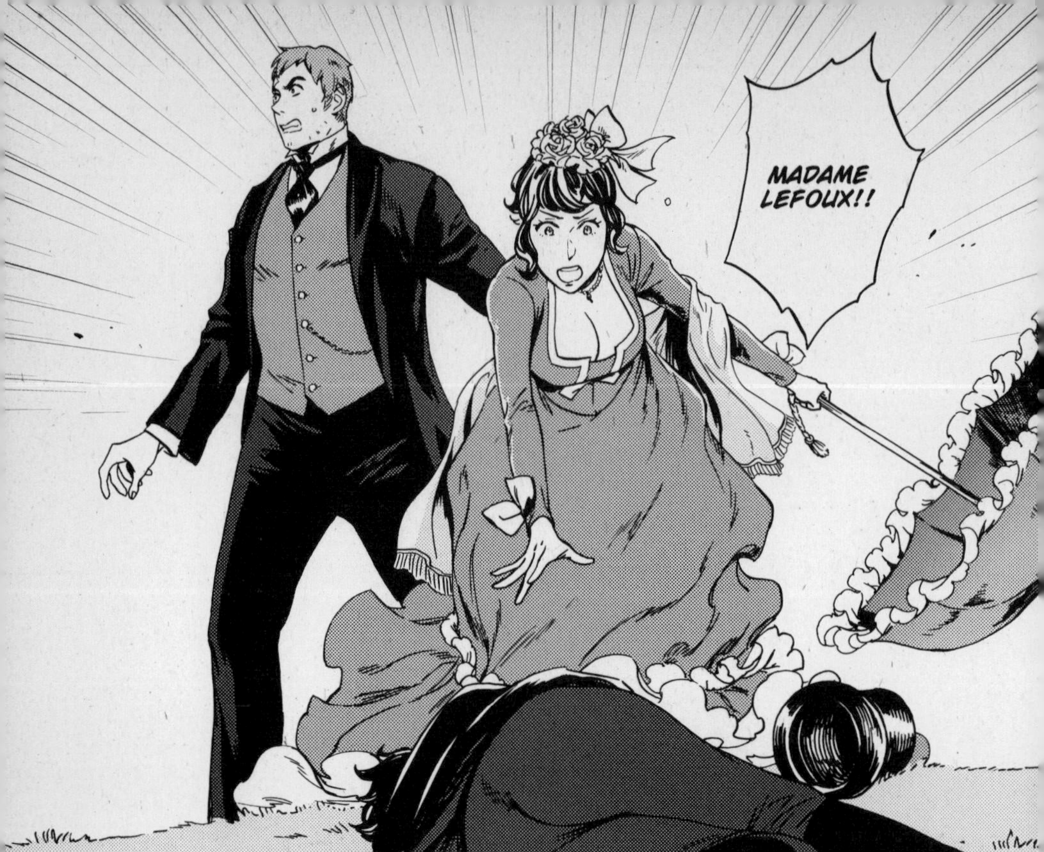
MADAME LEFOUX!!
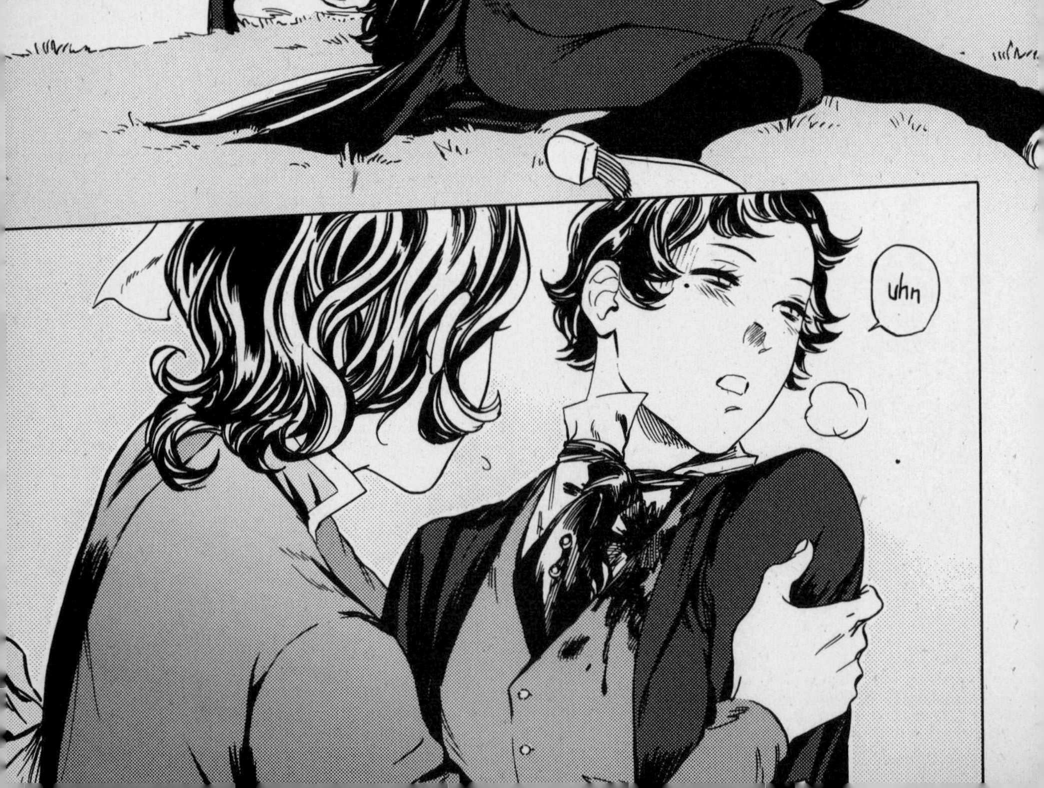
uhn

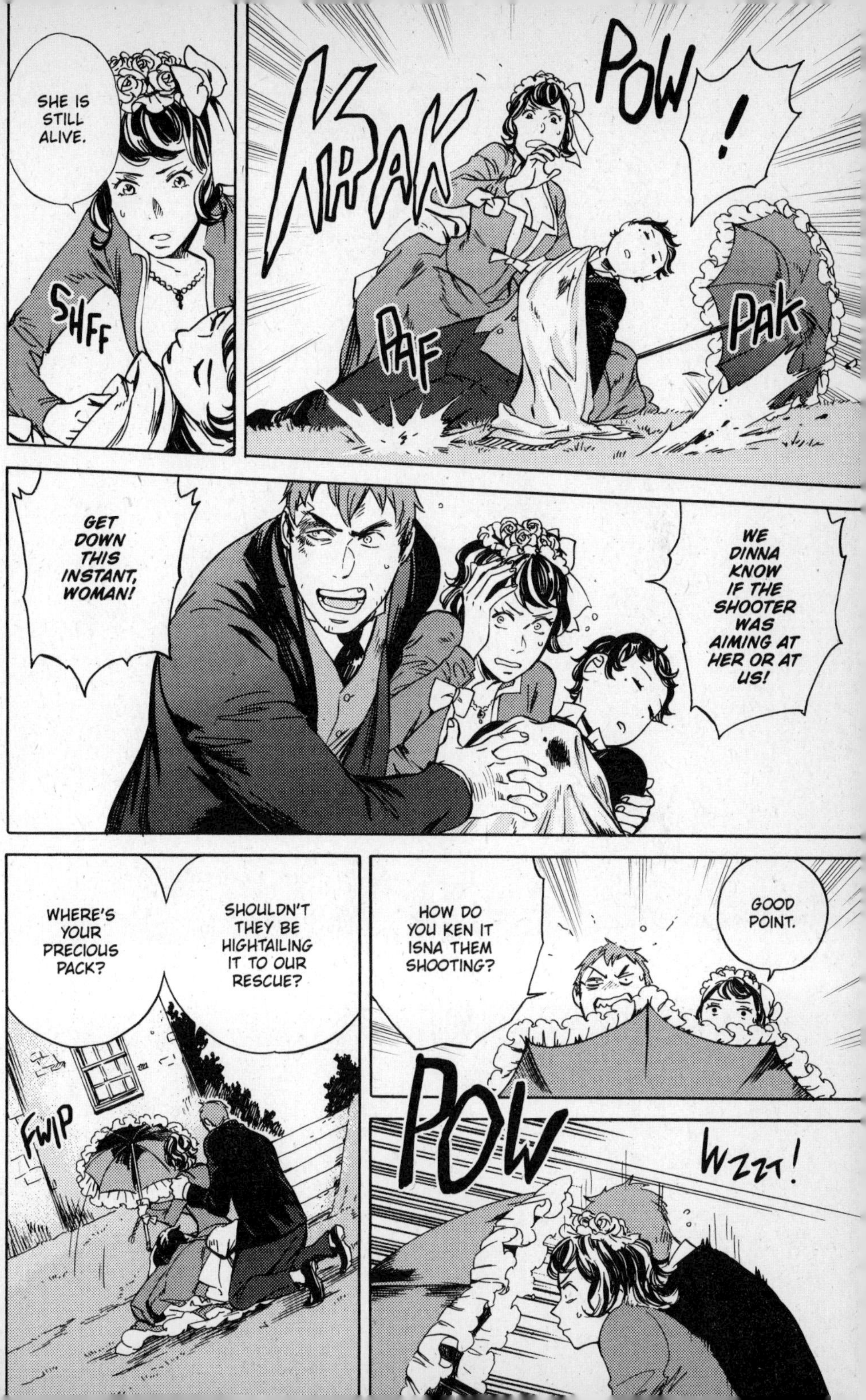
SHE IS STILL ALIVE.
SHFF
KRAK
POW
!
PAF
PAK
GET DOWN THIS INSTANT, WOMAN!
WE DINNA KNOW IF THE SHOOTER WAS AIMING AT HER OR AT US!
WHERE'S YOUR PRECIOUS PACK?
SHOULDN'T THEY BE HIGHTAILING IT TO OUR RESCUE?
FWIP
HOW DO YOU KEN IT ISNA THEM SHOOTING?
GOOD POINT.
POW
WZZT!

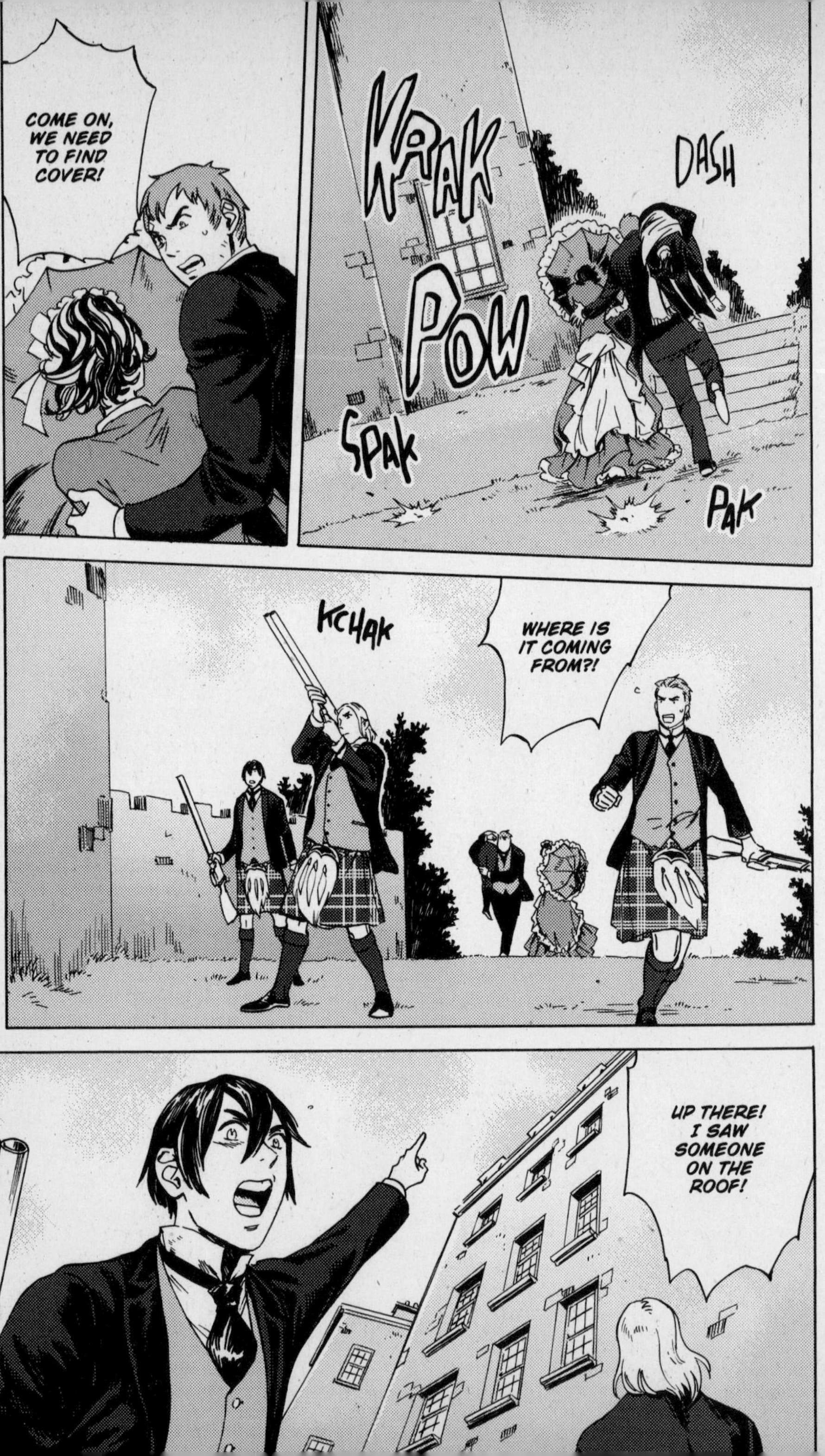
COME ON, WE NEED TO FIND COVER!
KRAK
POW
SPAK
DASH
PAK
KCHAK
WHERE IS IT COMING FROM?!
UP THERE! I SAW SOMEONE ON THE ROOF!

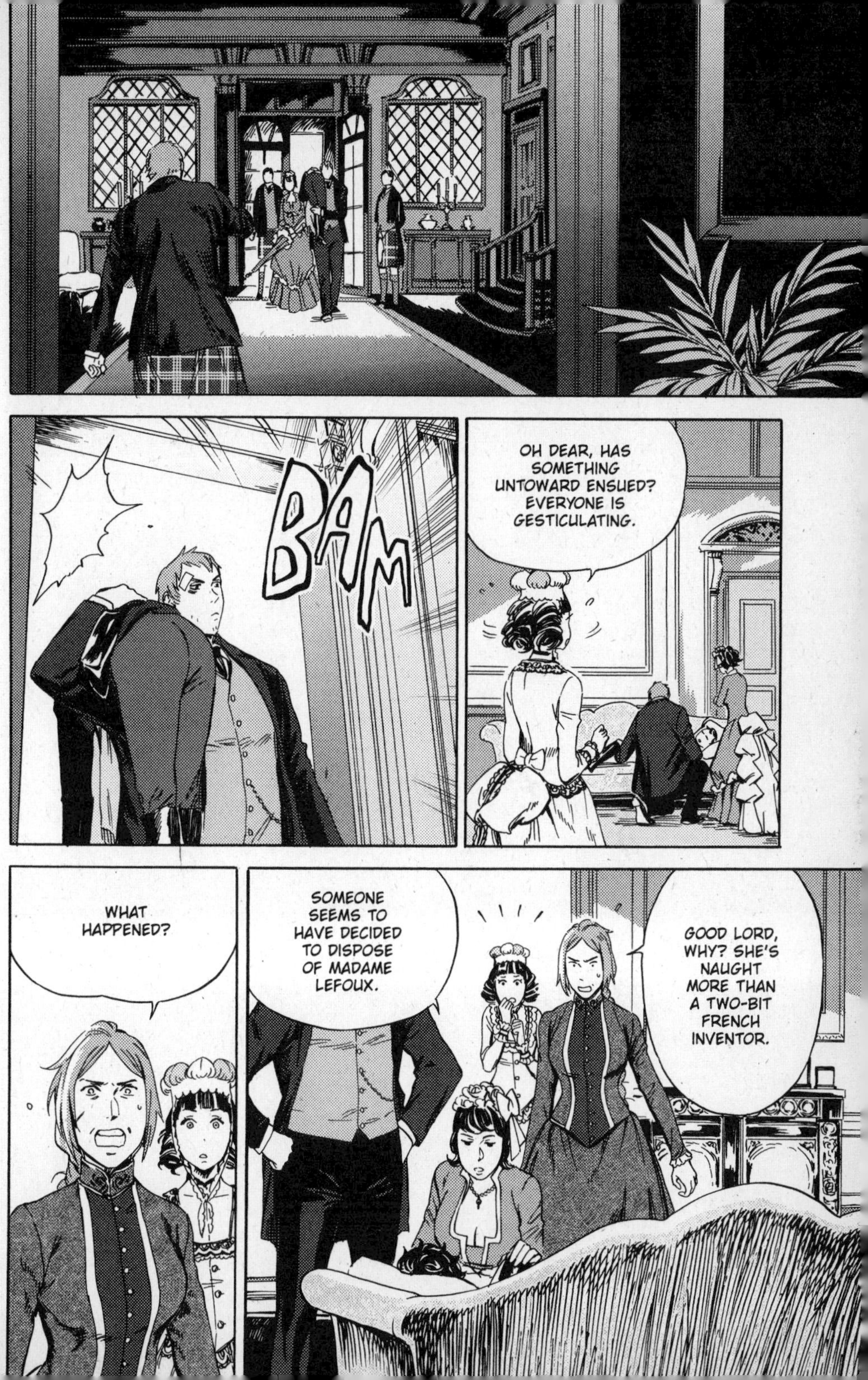
BAM
OH DEAR, HAS SOMETHING UNTOWARD ENSUED? EVERYONE IS GESTICULATING.
WHAT HAPPENED?
SOMEONE SEEMS TO HAVE DECIDED TO DISPOSE OF MADAME LEFOUX.
GOOD LORD, WHY? SHE'S NAUGHT MORE THAN A TWO-BIT FRENCH INVENTOR.

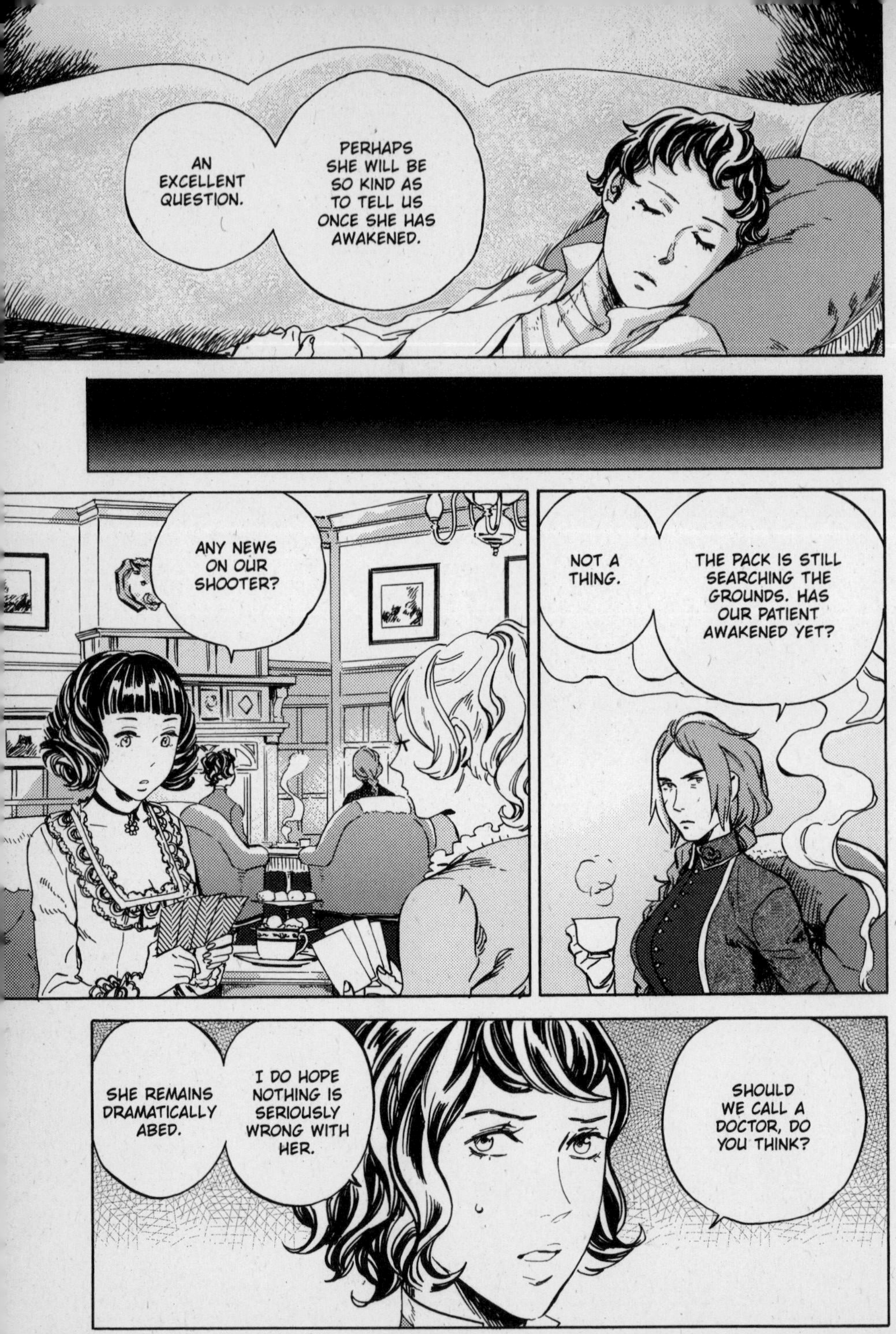
AN EXCELLENT QUESTION.
PERHAPS SHE WILL BE SO KIND AS TO TELL US ONCE SHE HAS AWAKENED.
ANY NEWS ON OUR SHOOTER?
NOT A THING.
THE PACK IS STILL SEARCHING THE GROUNDS. HAS OUR PATIENT AWAKENED YET?
SHE REMAINS DRAMATICALLY ABED.
I DO HOPE NOTHING IS SERIOUSLY WRONG WITH HER.
SHOULD WE CALL A DOCTOR, DO YOU THINK?

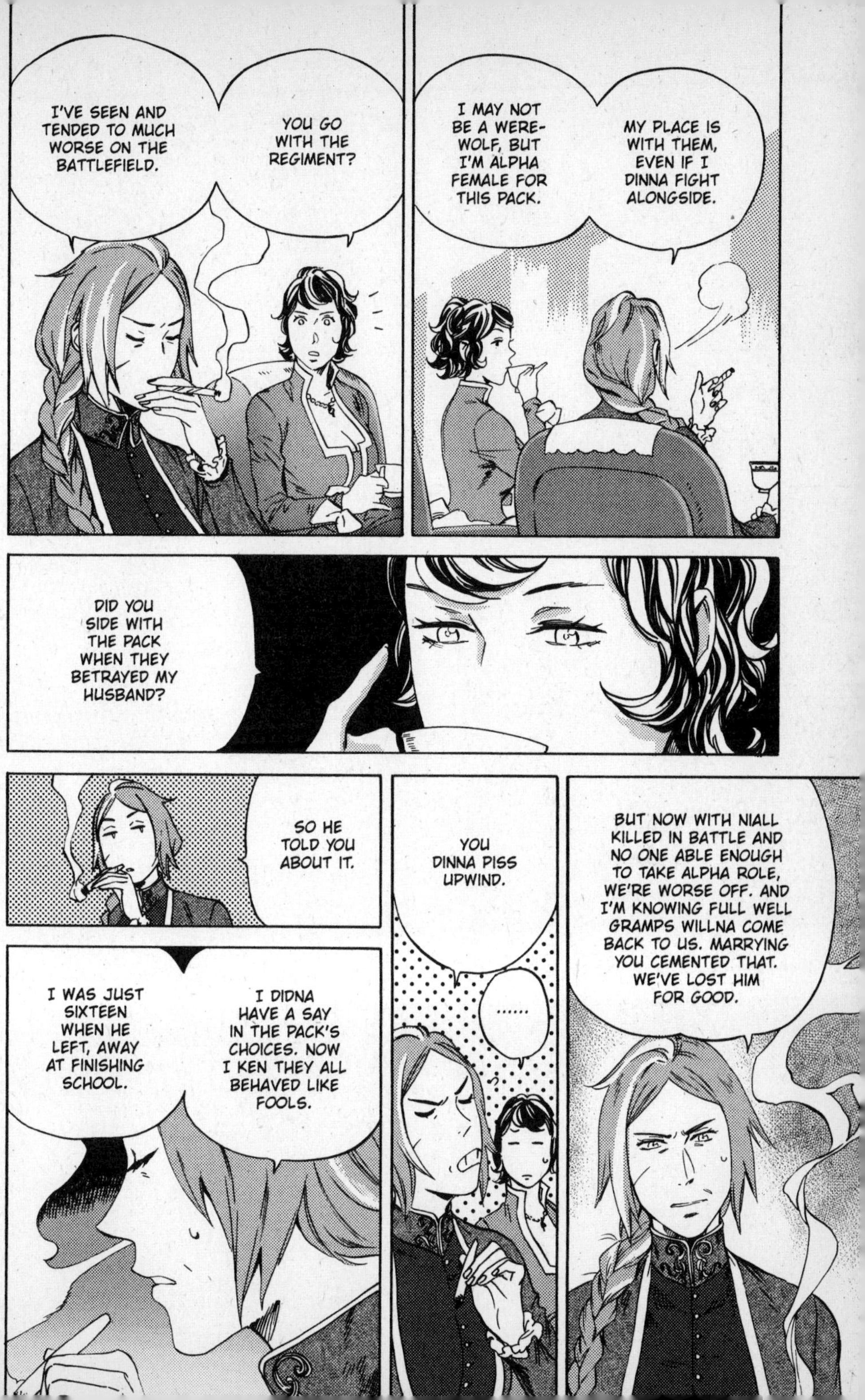
I'VE SEEN AND TENDED TO MUCH WORSE ON THE BATTLEFIELD.
YOU GO WITH THE REGIMENT?
I MAY NOT BE A WERE-WOLF, BUT I'M ALPHA FEMALE FOR THIS PACK.
MY PLACE IS WITH THEM, EVEN IF I DINNA FIGHT ALONGSIDE.
DID YOU SIDE WITH THE PACK WHEN THEY BETRAYED MY HUSBAND?
SO HE TOLD YOU ABOUT IT.
I WAS JUST SIXTEEN WHEN HE LEFT, AWAY AT FINISHING SCHOOL.
I DIDNA HAVE A SAY IN THE PACK'S CHOICES. NOW I KEN THEY ALL BEHAVED LIKE FOOLS.
YOU DINNA PISS UPWIND.
......
BUT NOW WITH NIALL KILLED IN BATTLE AND NO ONE ABLE ENOUGH TO TAKE ALPHA ROLE, WE'RE WORSE OFF. AND I'M KNOWING FULL WELL GRAMPS WILLNA COME BACK TO US. MARRYING YOU CEMENTED THAT. WE'VE LOST HIM FOR GOOD.

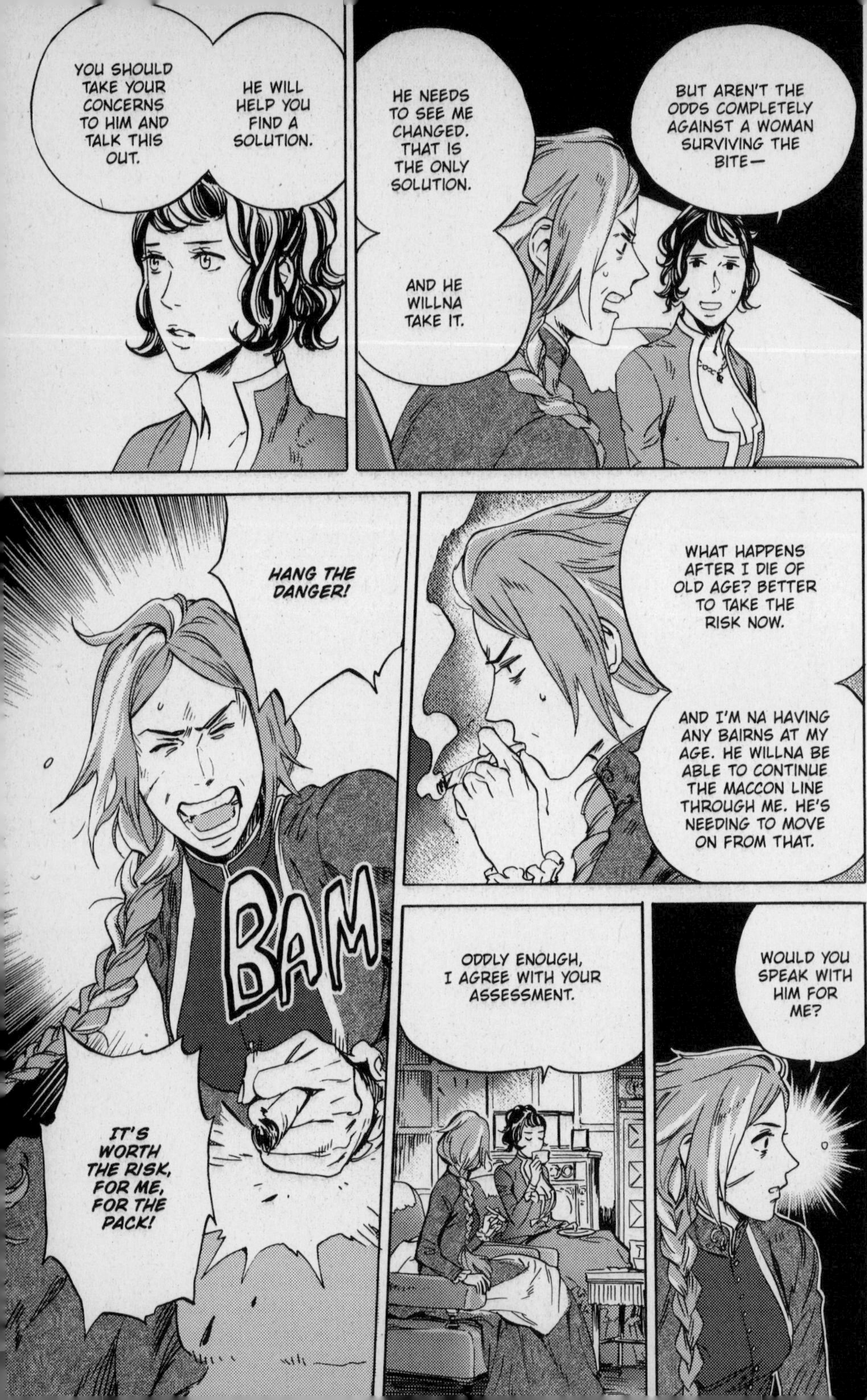
YOU SHOULD TAKE YOUR CONCERNS TO HIM AND TALK THIS OUT.
HE WILL HELP YOU FIND A SOLUTION.
HE NEEDS TO SEE ME CHANGED. THAT IS THE ONLY SOLUTION.
AND HE WILLNA TAKE IT.
BUT AREN'T THE ODDS COMPLETELY AGAINST A WOMAN SURVIVING THE BITE—
HANG THE DANGER!
BAM
IT'S WORTH THE RISK, FOR ME, FOR THE PACK!
WHAT HAPPENS AFTER I DIE OF OLD AGE? BETTER TO TAKE THE RISK NOW.
AND I'M NA HAVING ANY BAIRNS AT MY AGE. HE WILLNA BE ABLE TO CONTINUE THE MACCON LINE THROUGH ME. HE'S NEEDING TO MOVE ON FROM THAT.
ODDLY ENOUGH, I AGREE WITH YOUR ASSESSMENT.
WOULD YOU SPEAK WITH HIM FOR ME?

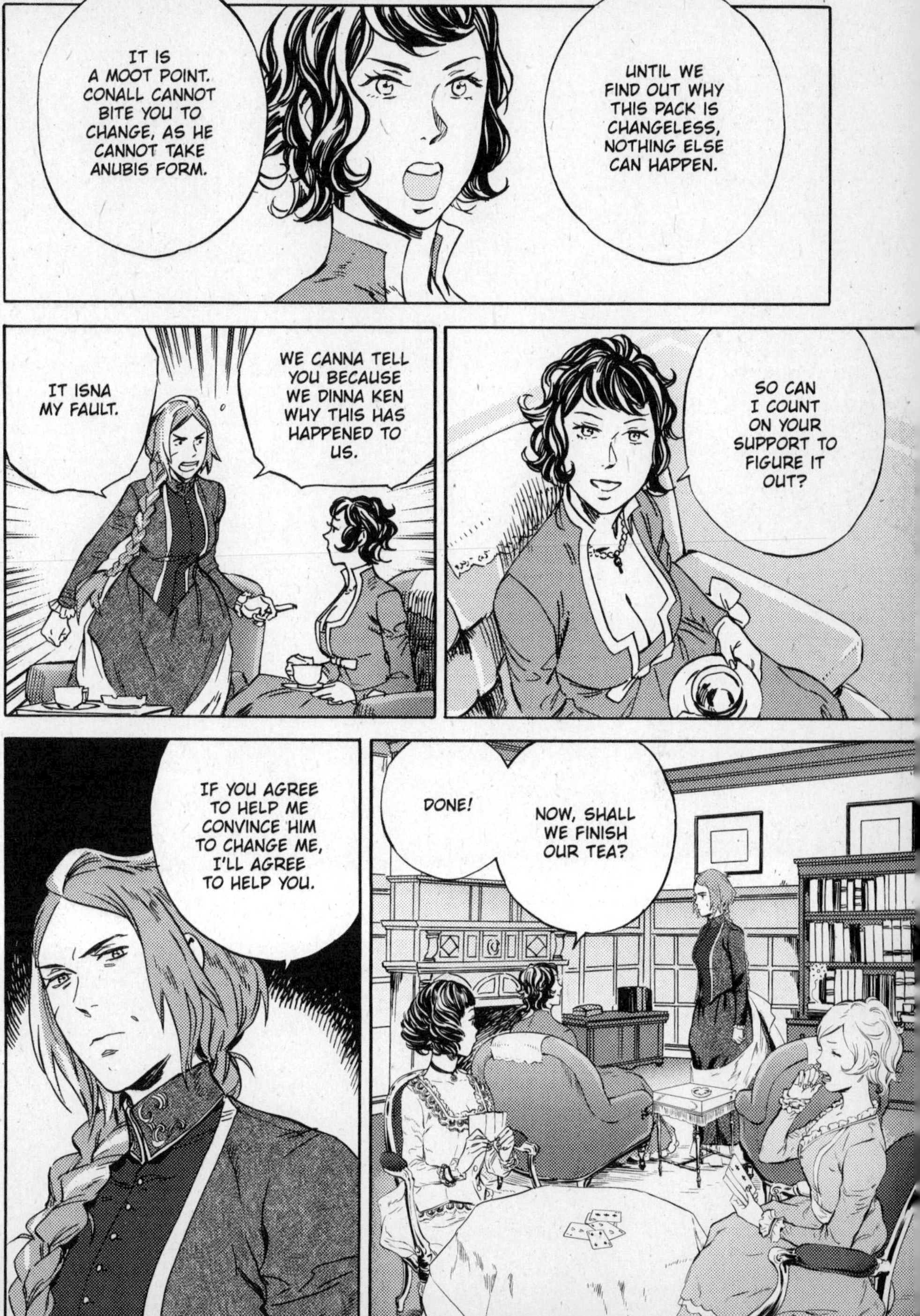

IT IS A MOOT POINT. CONALL CANNOT BITE YOU TO CHANGE, AS HE CANNOT TAKE ANUBIS FORM.
UNTIL WE FIND OUT WHY THIS PACK IS CHANGELESS, NOTHING ELSE CAN HAPPEN.
IT ISNA MY FAULT.
WE CANNA TELL YOU BECAUSE WE DINNA KEN WHY THIS HAS HAPPENED TO US.
SO CAN I COUNT ON YOUR SUPPORT TO FIGURE IT OUT?
IF YOU AGREE TO HELP ME CONVINCE HIM TO CHANGE ME, I'LL AGREE TO HELP YOU.
DONE!
NOW, SHALL WE FINISH OUR TEA?

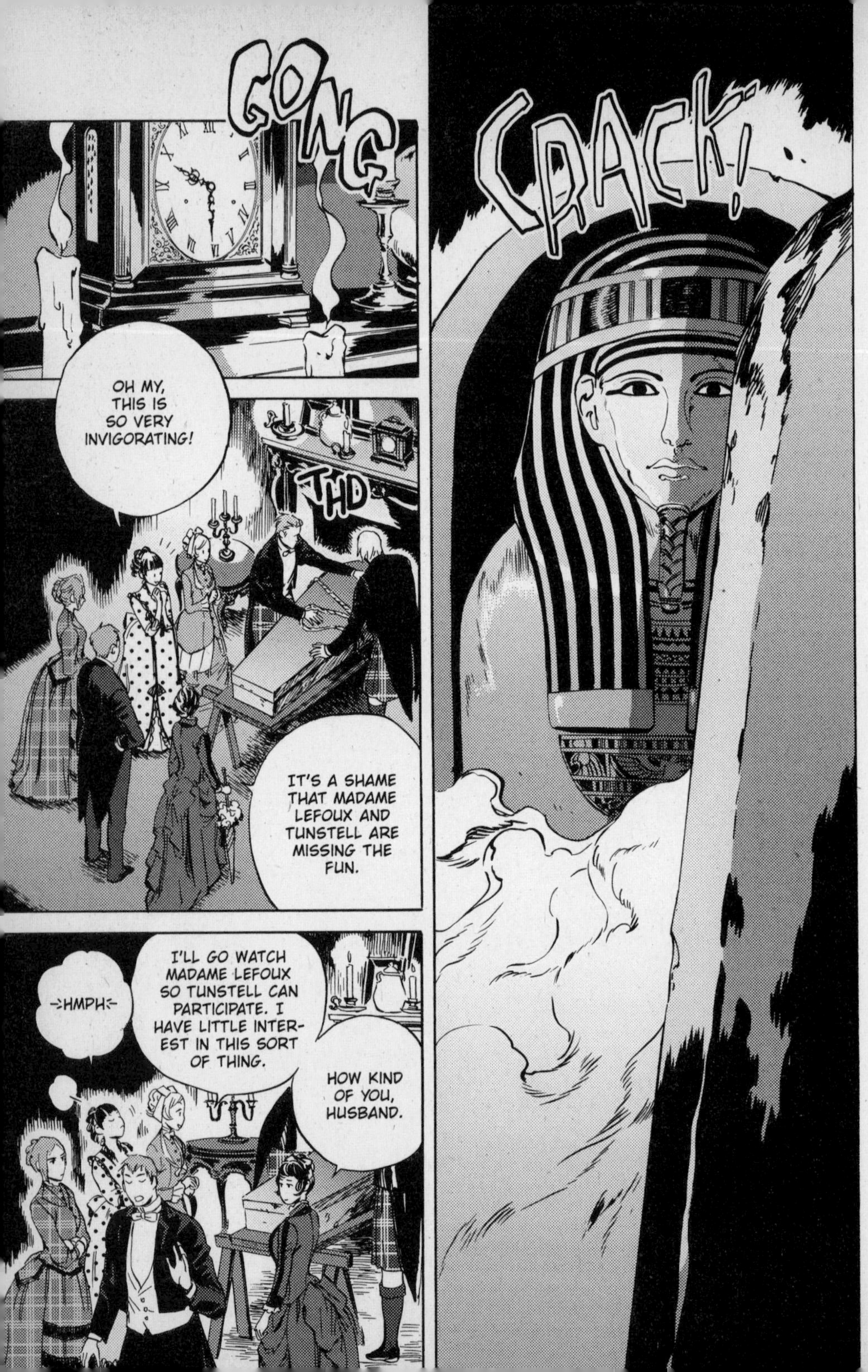
GONG
OH MY, THIS IS SO VERY INVIGORATING!
THD
IT'S A SHAME THAT MADAME LEFOUX AND TUNSTELL ARE MISSING THE FUN.
HMPH
I'LL GO WATCH MADAME LEFOUX SO TUNSTELL CAN PARTICIPATE. I HAVE LITTLE INTER-EST IN THIS SORT OF THING.
HOW KIND OF YOU, HUSBAND.
CRACK!

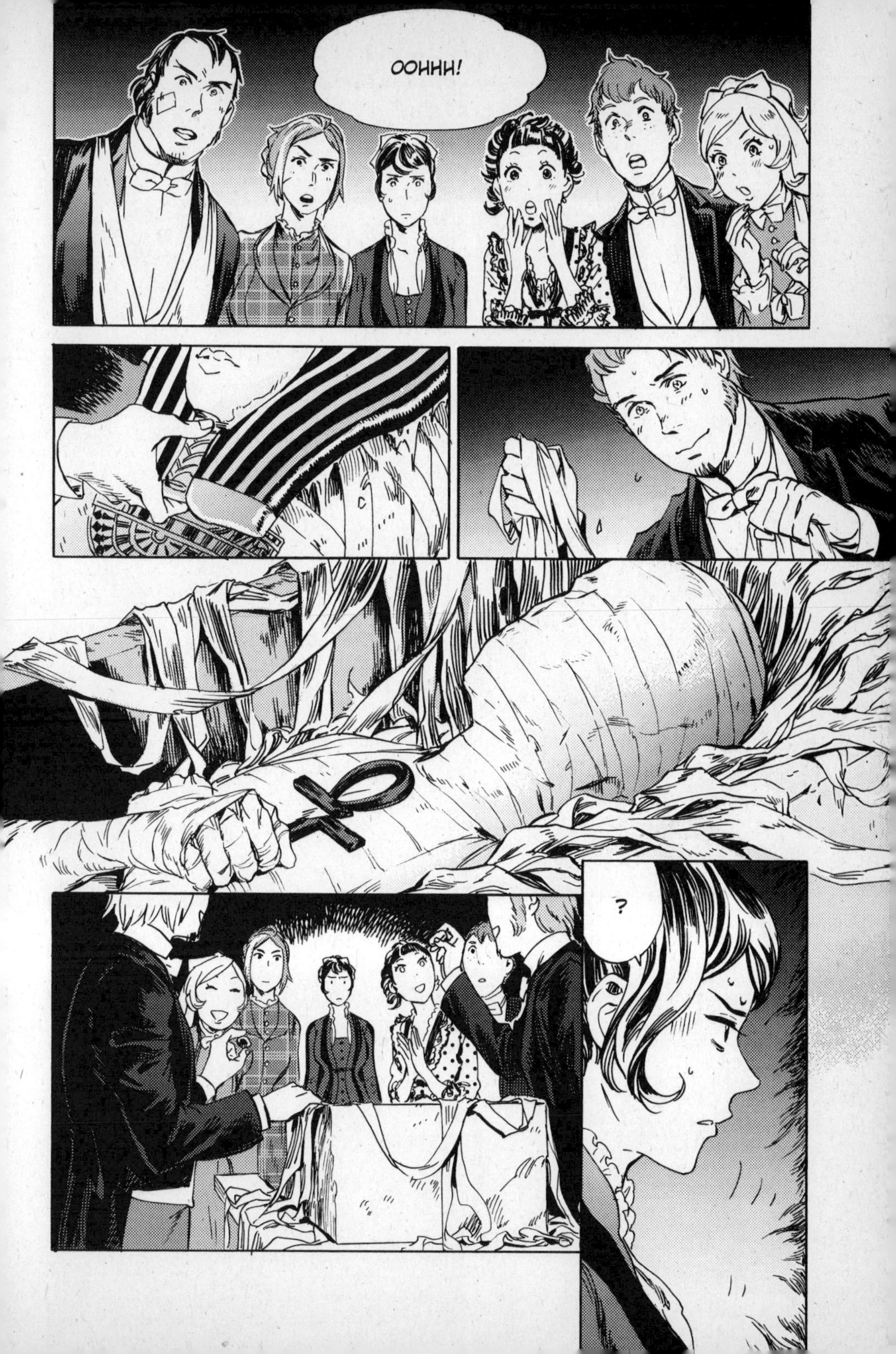
OOHHH!
?

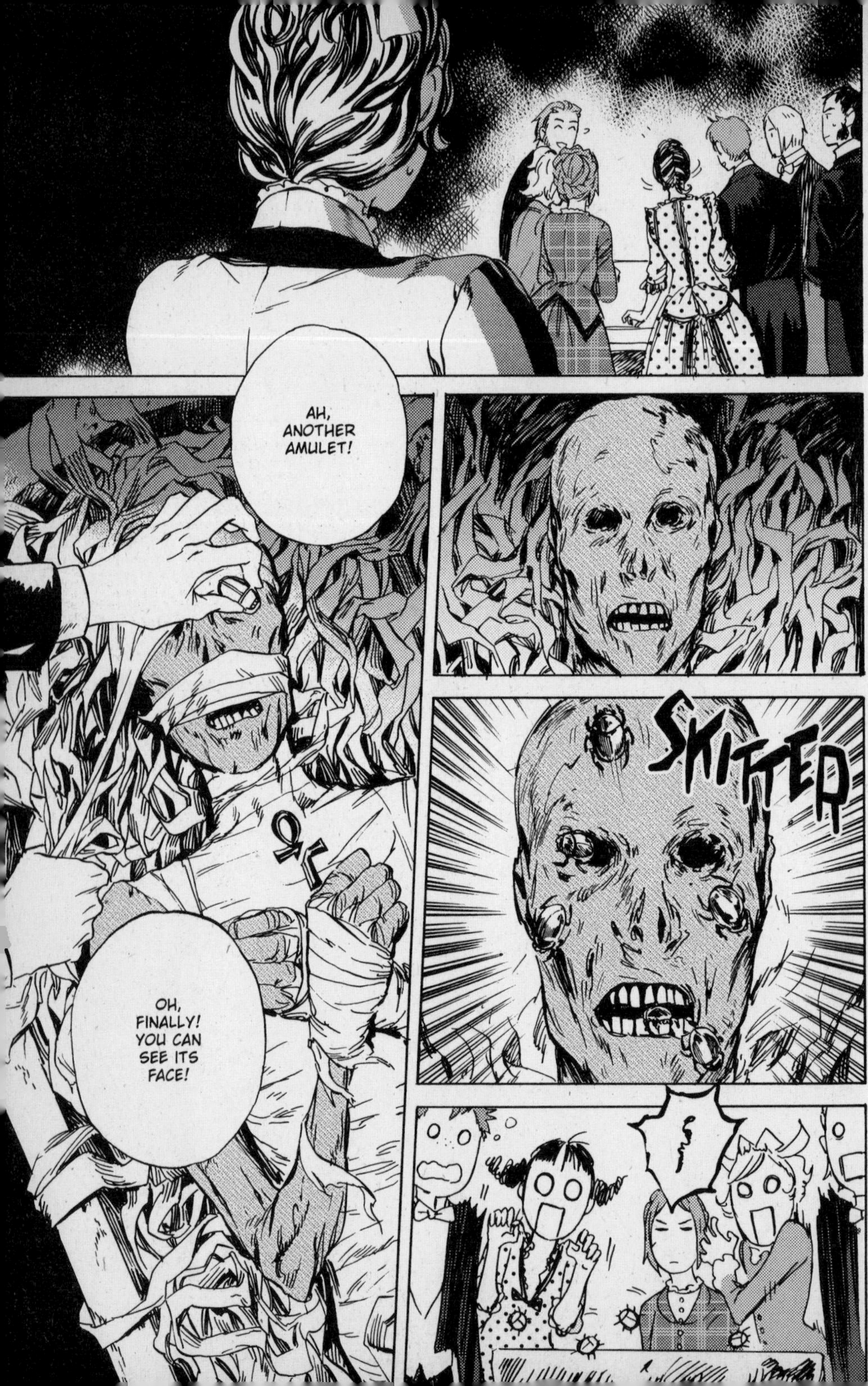
AH, ANOTHER AMULET!
OH, FINALLY! YOU CAN SEE ITS FACE!
SKITTER

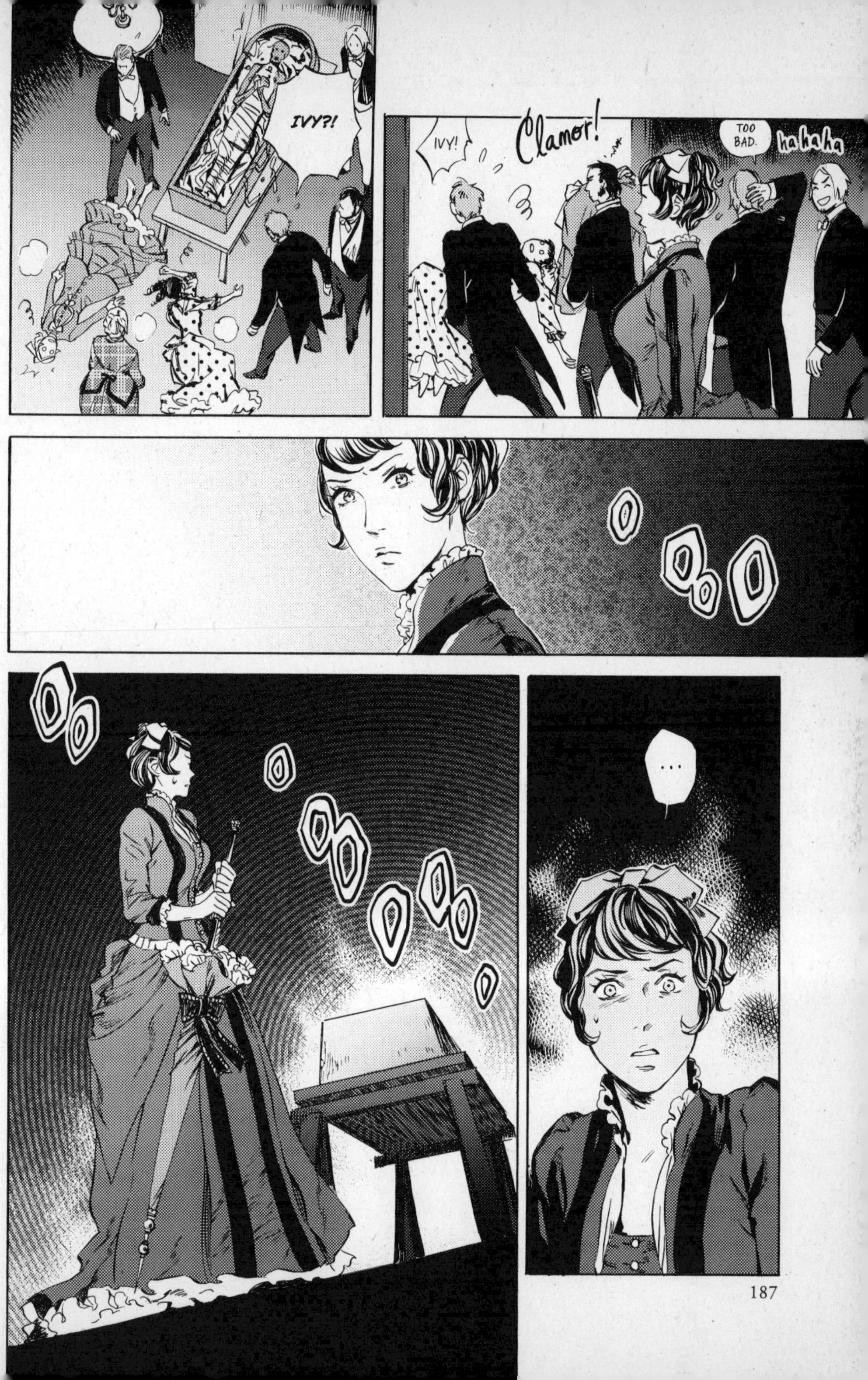
IVY?!
IVY!
Clamor!
TOO BAD.
ha ha ha
...

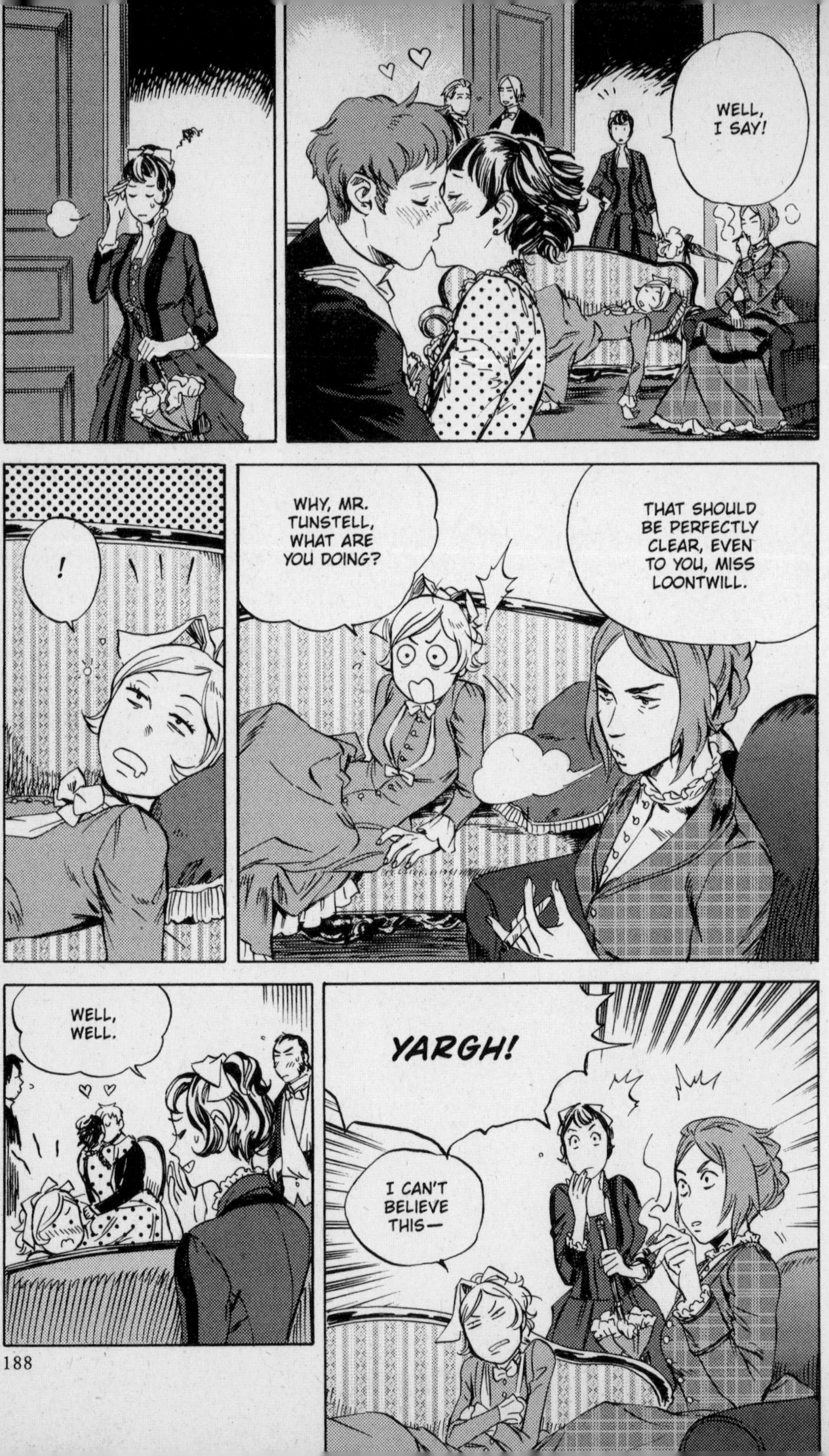
WELL, I SAY!
!
WHY, MR. TUNSTELL, WHAT ARE YOU DOING?
THAT SHOULD BE PERFECTLY CLEAR, EVEN TO YOU, MISS LOONTWILL.
WELL, WELL.
YARGH!
I CAN'T BELIEVE THIS—

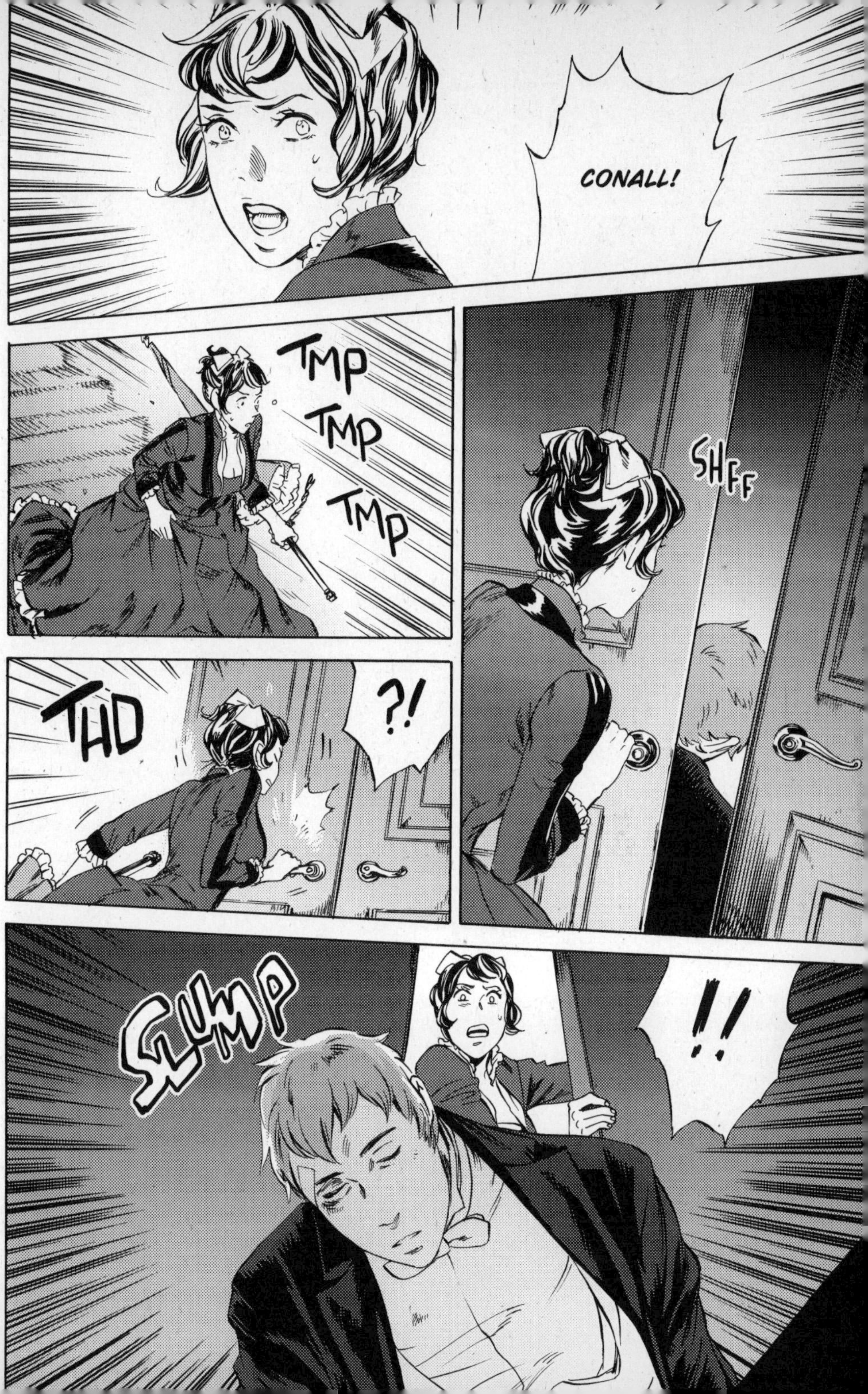
CONALL!
TMP
TMP
TMP
THD
?!
SHFF
SLUMP
!!

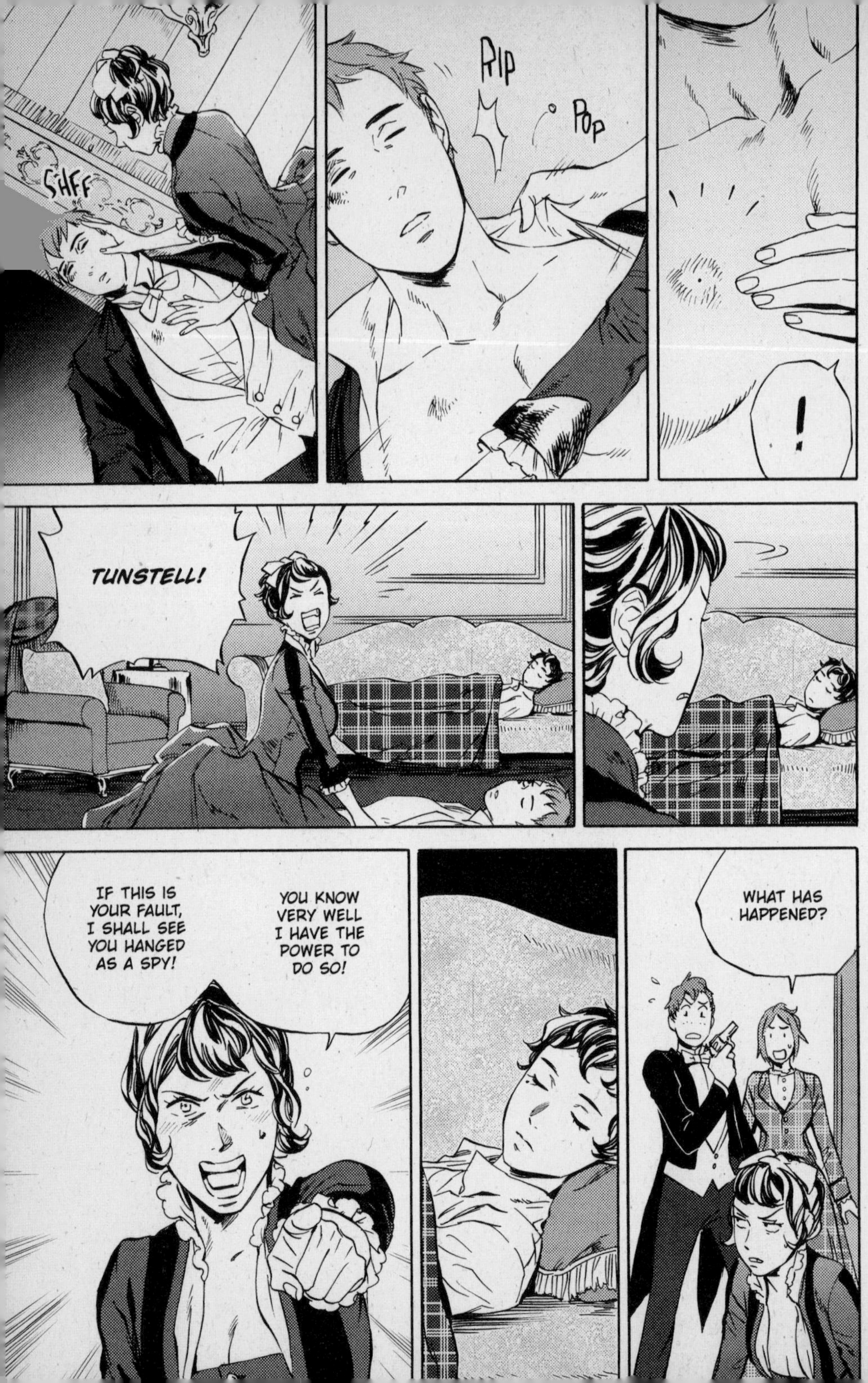
SHFF
RIP
POP
!
TUNSTELL!
IF THIS IS YOUR FAULT, I SHALL SEE YOU HANGED AS A SPY!
YOU KNOW VERY WELL I HAVE THE POWER TO DO SO!
WHAT HAS HAPPENED?

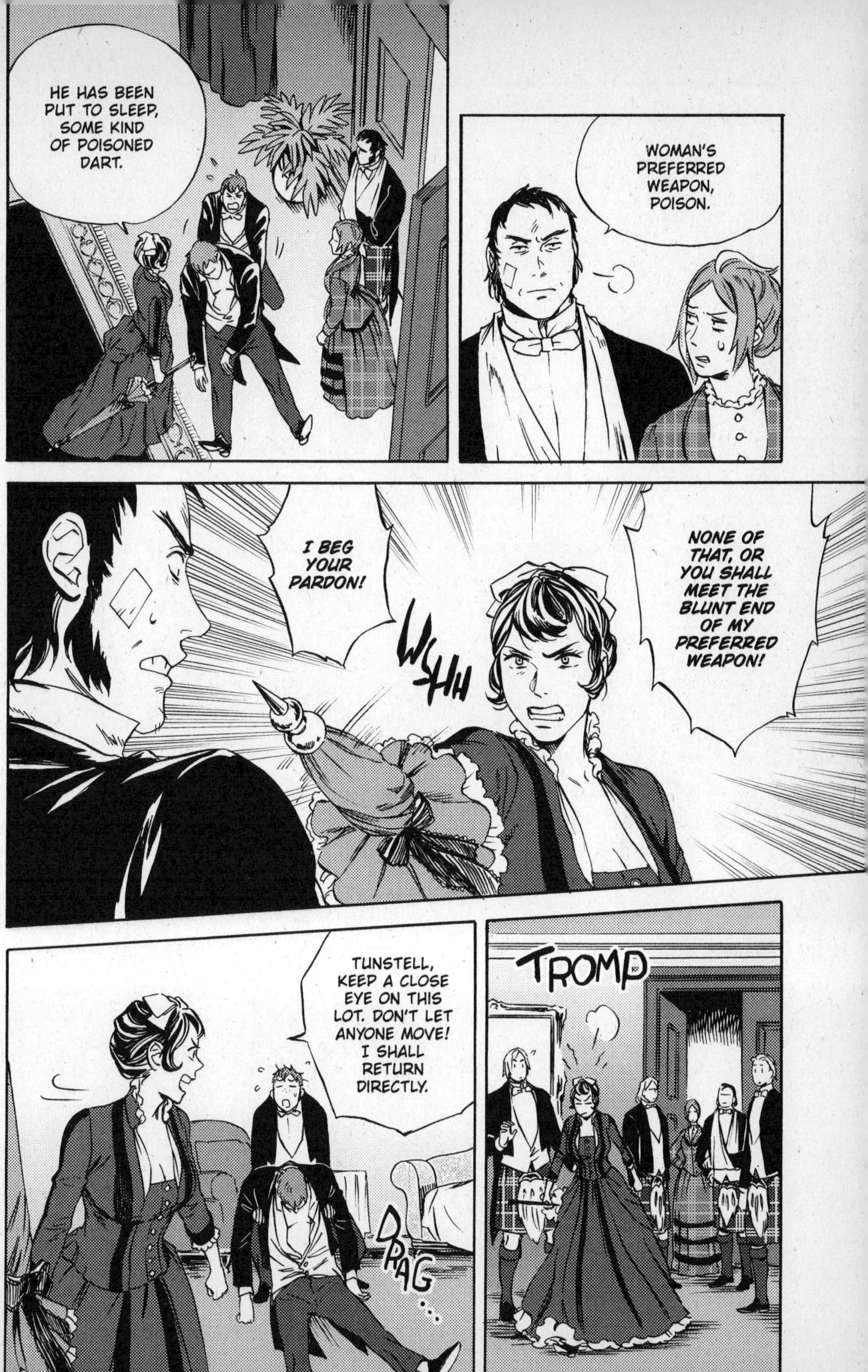
HE HAS BEEN PUT TO SLEEP, SOME KIND OF POISONED DART.
WOMAN'S PREFERRED WEAPON, POISON.
I BEG YOUR PARDON!
WSHH
NONE OF THAT, OR YOU SHALL MEET THE BLUNT END OF MY PREFERRED WEAPON!
TUNSTELL, KEEP A CLOSE EYE ON THIS LOT. DON'T LET ANYONE MOVE! I SHALL RETURN DIRECTLY.
DRAG...
TROMP

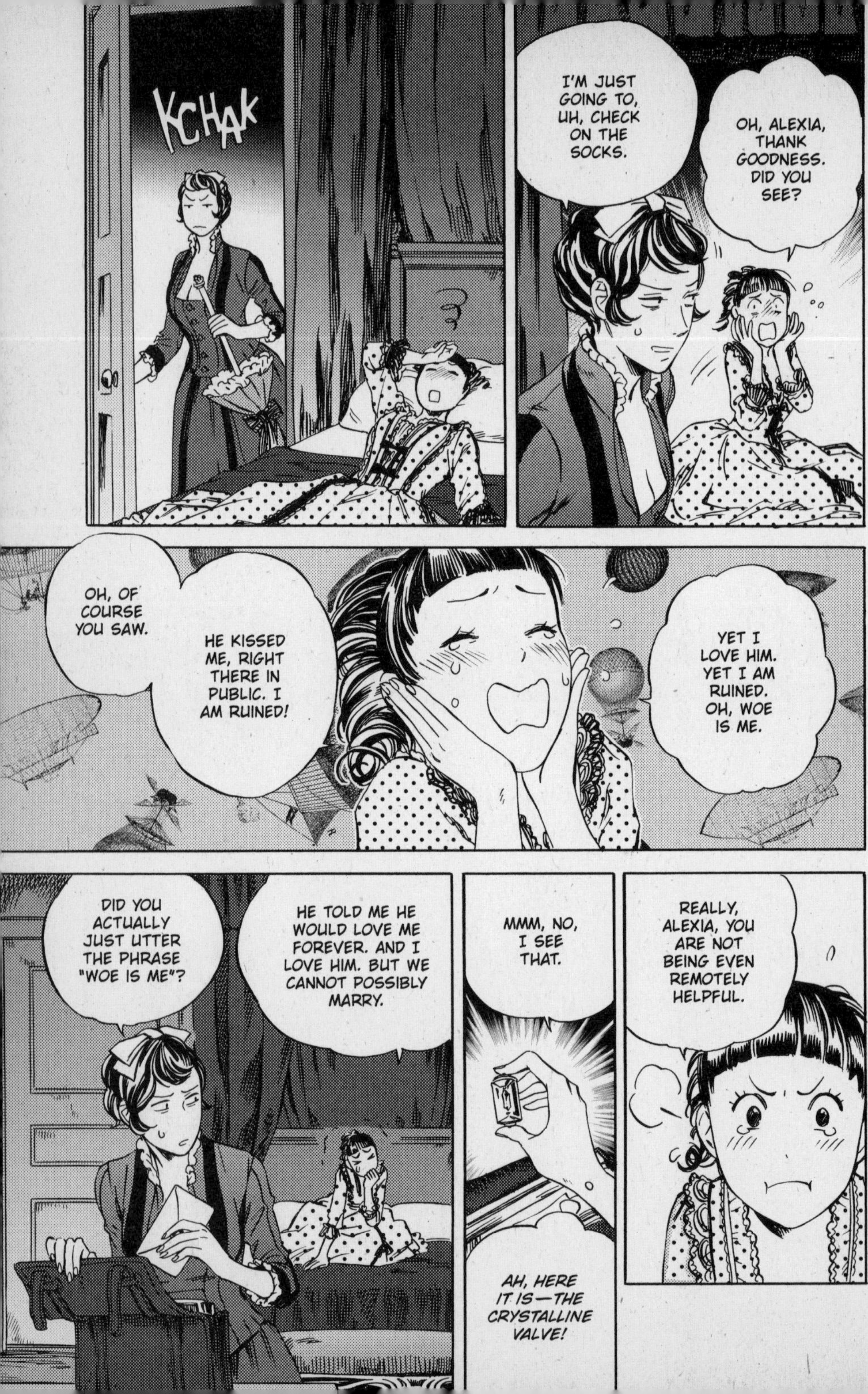
KCHAK
I'M JUST GOING TO, UH, CHECK ON THE SOCKS.
OH, ALEXIA, THANK GOODNESS. DID YOU SEE?
OH, OF COURSE YOU SAW.
HE KISSED ME, RIGHT THERE IN PUBLIC. I AM RUINED!
YET I LOVE HIM. YET I AM RUINED. OH, WOE IS ME.
DID YOU ACTUALLY JUST UTTER THE PHRASE "WOE IS ME"?
HE TOLD ME HE WOULD LOVE ME FOREVER. AND I LOVE HIM. BUT WE CANNOT POSSIBLY MARRY.
MMM, NO, I SEE THAT.
AH, HERE IT IS—THE CRYSTALLINE VALVE!
REALLY, ALEXIA, YOU ARE NOT BEING EVEN REMOTELY HELPFUL.

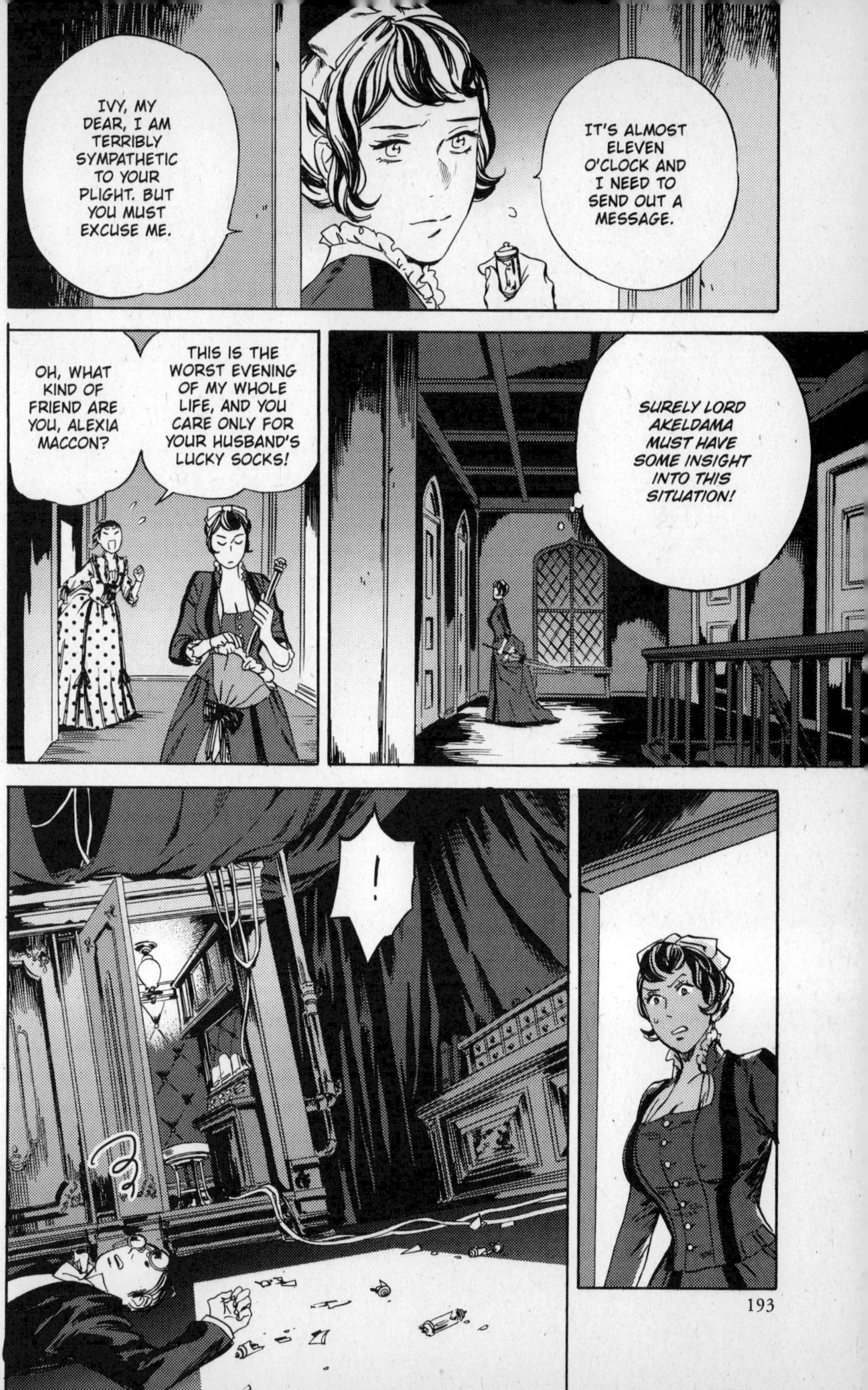
IVY, MY DEAR, I AM TERRIBLY SYMPATHETIC TO YOUR PLIGHT. BUT YOU MUST EXCUSE ME.
IT'S ALMOST ELEVEN O'CLOCK AND I NEED TO SEND OUT A MESSAGE.
OH, WHAT KIND OF FRIEND ARE YOU, ALEXIA MACCON?
THIS IS THE WORST EVENING OF MY WHOLE LIFE, AND YOU CARE ONLY FOR YOUR HUSBAND'S LUCKY SOCKS!
SURELY LORD AKELDAMA MUST HAVE SOME INSIGHT INTO THIS SITUATION!
!

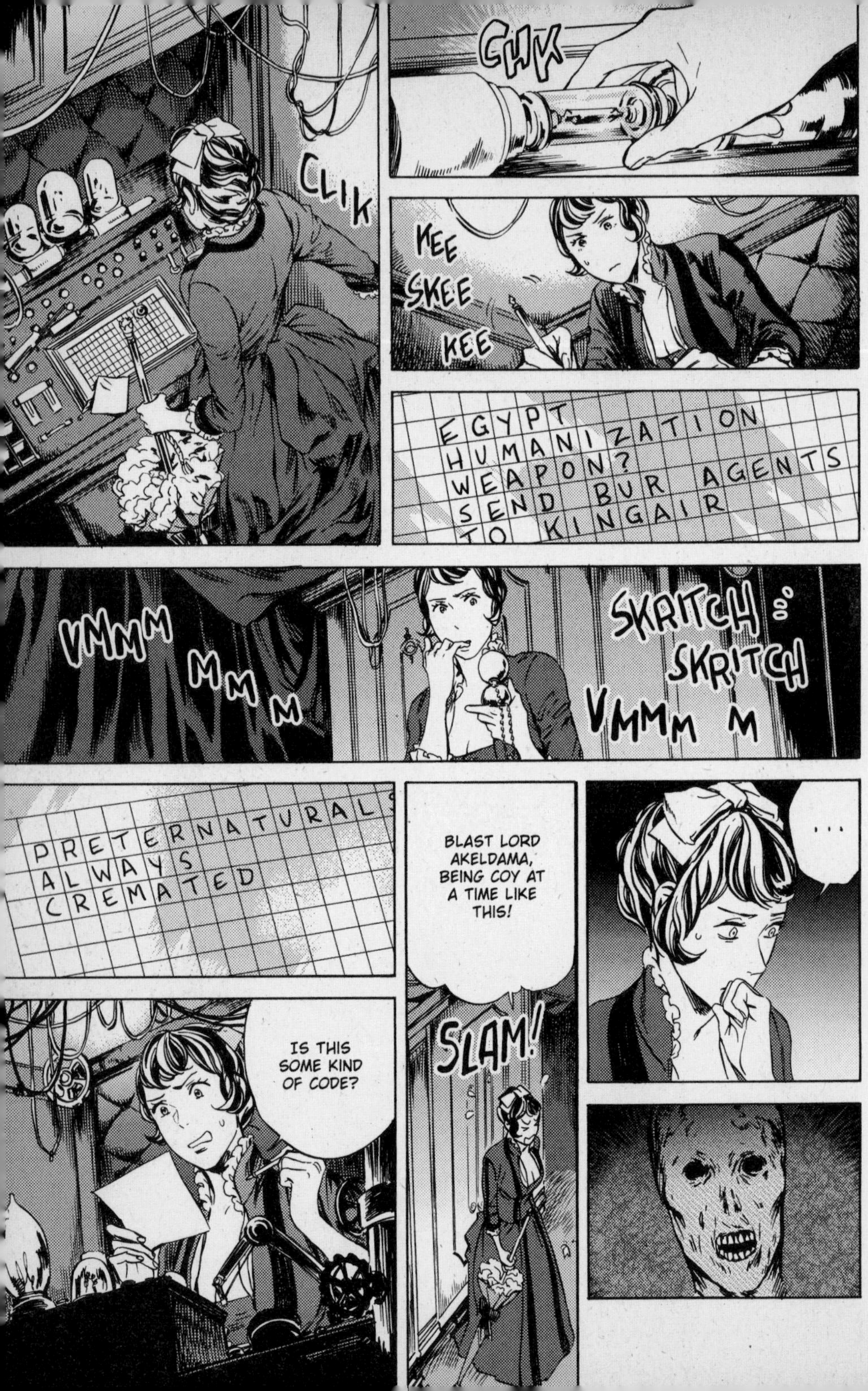
CLIK
CHK
KEE SKEE KEE
EGYPT
HUMANIZATION
WEAPON?
SEND BUR AGENTS
TO KINGAIR
VMMM MMM
SKRITCH SKRITCH
VMMM M
PRETERNATURALS
ALWAYS
CREMATED
IS THIS SOME KIND OF CODE?
BLAST LORD AKELDAMA, BEING COY AT A TIME LIKE THIS!
SLAM!
...

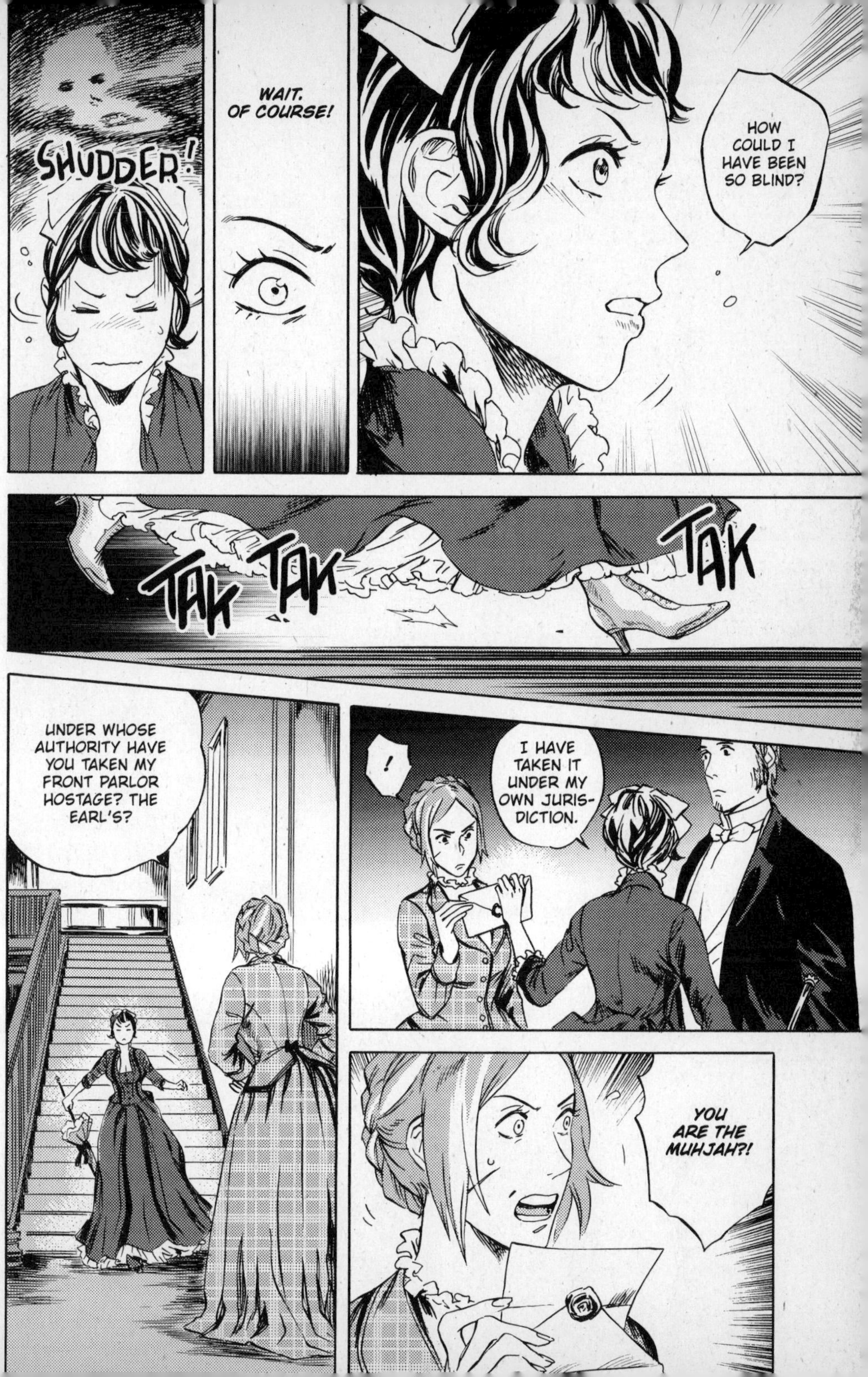
SHUDDER!
WAIT. OF COURSE!
HOW COULD I HAVE BEEN SO BLIND?
TAK
TAK
TAK
UNDER WHOSE AUTHORITY HAVE YOU TAKEN MY FRONT PARLOR HOSTAGE? THE EARL'S?
!
I HAVE TAKEN IT UNDER MY OWN JURISDICTION.
YOU ARE THE MUHJAH?!

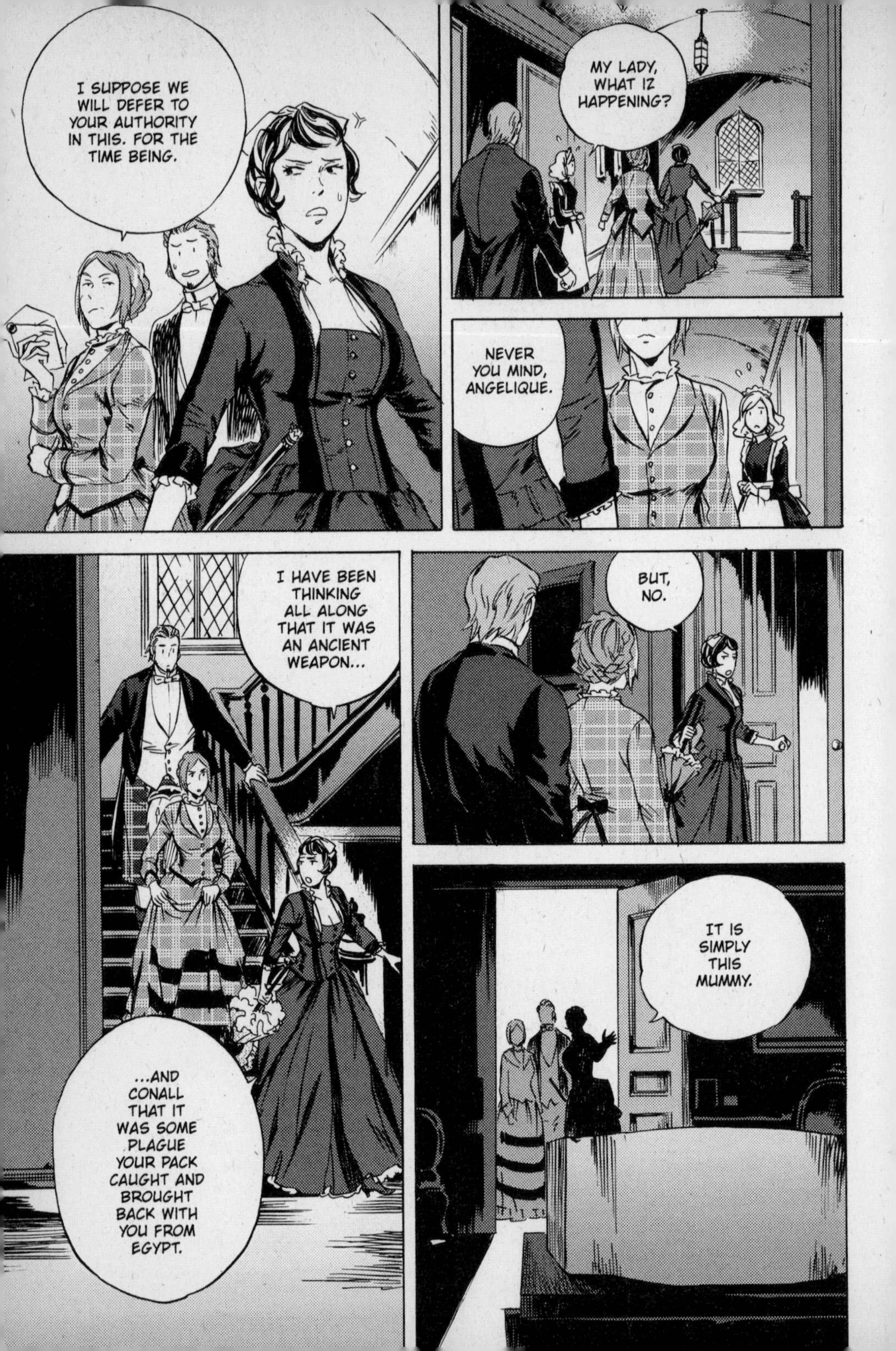
I SUPPOSE WE WILL DEFER TO YOUR AUTHORITY IN THIS. FOR THE TIME BEING.
MY LADY, WHAT IZ HAPPENING?
NEVER YOU MIND, ANGELIQUE.
I HAVE BEEN THINKING ALL ALONG THAT IT WAS AN ANCIENT WEAPON...
...AND CONALL THAT IT WAS SOME PLAGUE YOUR PACK CAUGHT AND BROUGHT BACK WITH YOU FROM EGYPT.
BUT, NO.
IT IS SIMPLY THIS MUMMY.

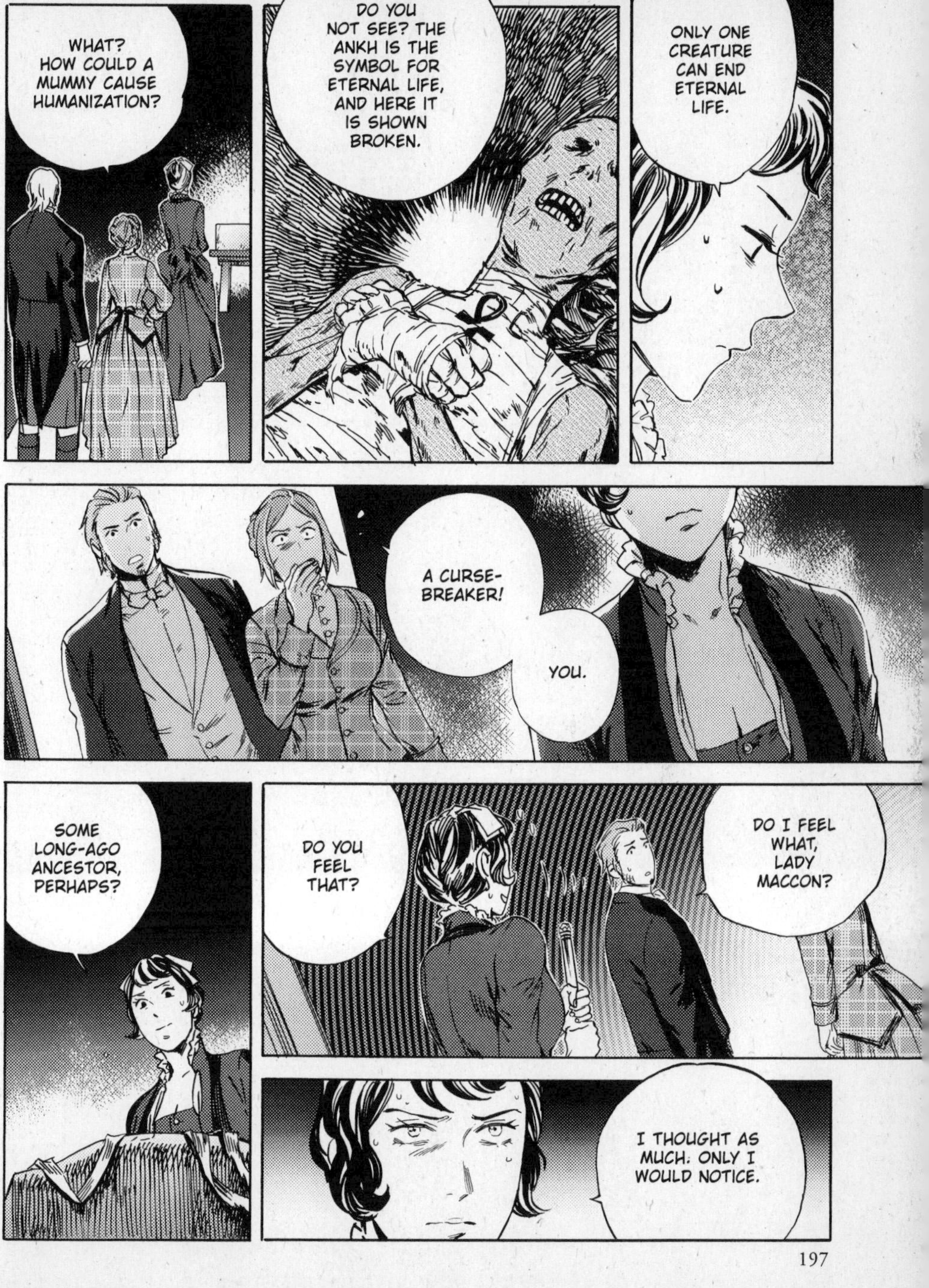
WHAT? HOW COULD A MUMMY CAUSE HUMANIZATION?
DO YOU NOT SEE? THE ANKH IS THE SYMBOL FOR ETERNAL LIFE, AND HERE IT IS SHOWN BROKEN.
ONLY ONE CREATURE CAN END ETERNAL LIFE.
A CURSE-BREAKER!
YOU.
SOME LONG-AGO ANCESTOR, PERHAPS?
DO YOU FEEL THAT?
DO I FEEL WHAT, LADY MACCON?
I THOUGHT AS MUCH. ONLY I WOULD NOTICE.

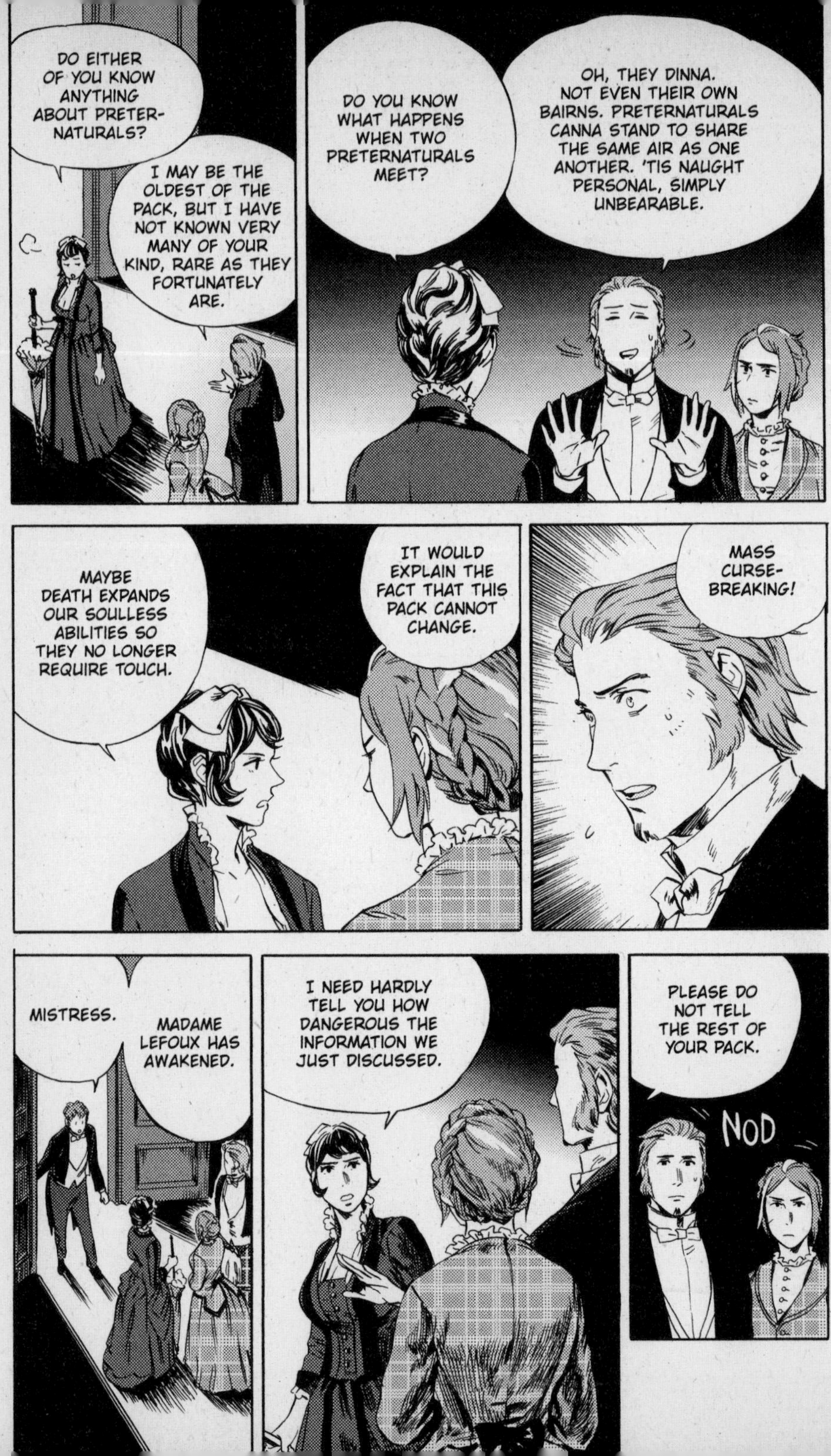
DO EITHER OF YOU KNOW ANYTHING ABOUT PRETER-NATURALS?
I MAY BE THE OLDEST OF THE PACK, BUT I HAVE NOT KNOWN VERY MANY OF YOUR KIND, RARE AS THEY FORTUNATELY ARE.
DO YOU KNOW WHAT HAPPENS WHEN TWO PRETERNATURALS MEET?
OH, THEY DINNA. NOT EVEN THEIR OWN BAIRNS. PRETERNATURALS CANNA STAND TO SHARE THE SAME AIR AS ONE ANOTHER. 'TIS NAUGHT PERSONAL, SIMPLY UNBEARABLE.
MAYBE DEATH EXPANDS OUR SOULLESS ABILITIES SO THEY NO LONGER REQUIRE TOUCH.
IT WOULD EXPLAIN THE FACT THAT THIS PACK CANNOT CHANGE.
MASS CURSE-BREAKING!
MISTRESS.
MADAME LEFOUX HAS AWAKENED.
I NEED HARDLY TELL YOU HOW DANGEROUS THE INFORMATION WE JUST DISCUSSED.
PLEASE DO NOT TELL THE REST OF YOUR PACK.
NOD

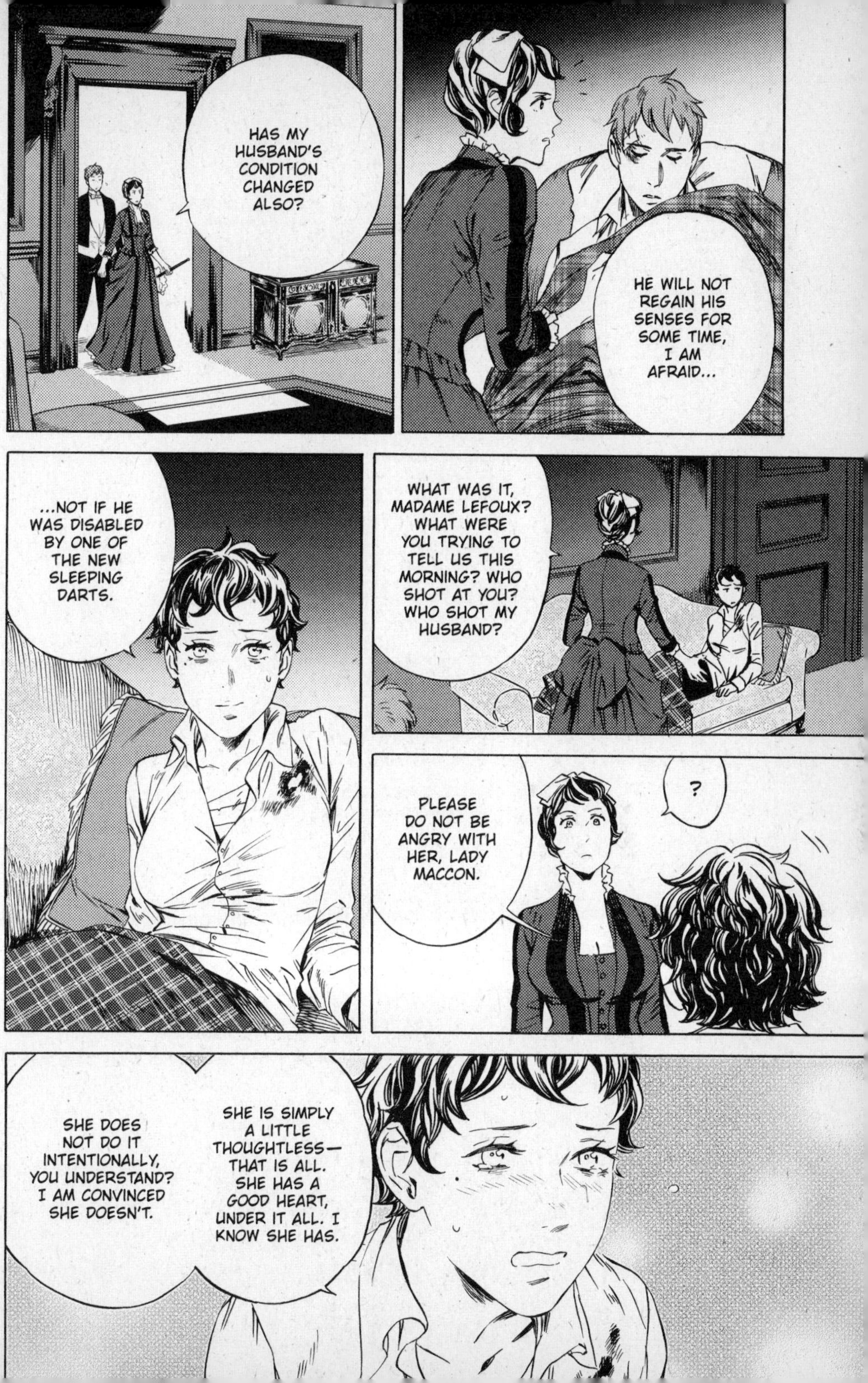
HAS MY HUSBAND'S CONDITION CHANGED ALSO?
HE WILL NOT REGAIN HIS SENSES FOR SOME TIME, I AM AFRAID...
...NOT IF HE WAS DISABLED BY ONE OF THE NEW SLEEPING DARTS.
WHAT WAS IT, MADAME LEFOUX? WHAT WERE YOU TRYING TO TELL US THIS MORNING? WHO SHOT AT YOU? WHO SHOT MY HUSBAND?
PLEASE DO NOT BE ANGRY WITH HER, LADY MACCON.
?
SHE DOES NOT DO IT INTENTIONALLY, YOU UNDERSTAND? I AM CONVINCED SHE DOESN'T.
SHE IS SIMPLY A LITTLE THOUGHTLESS— THAT IS ALL. SHE HAS A GOOD HEART, UNDER IT ALL. I KNOW SHE HAS.

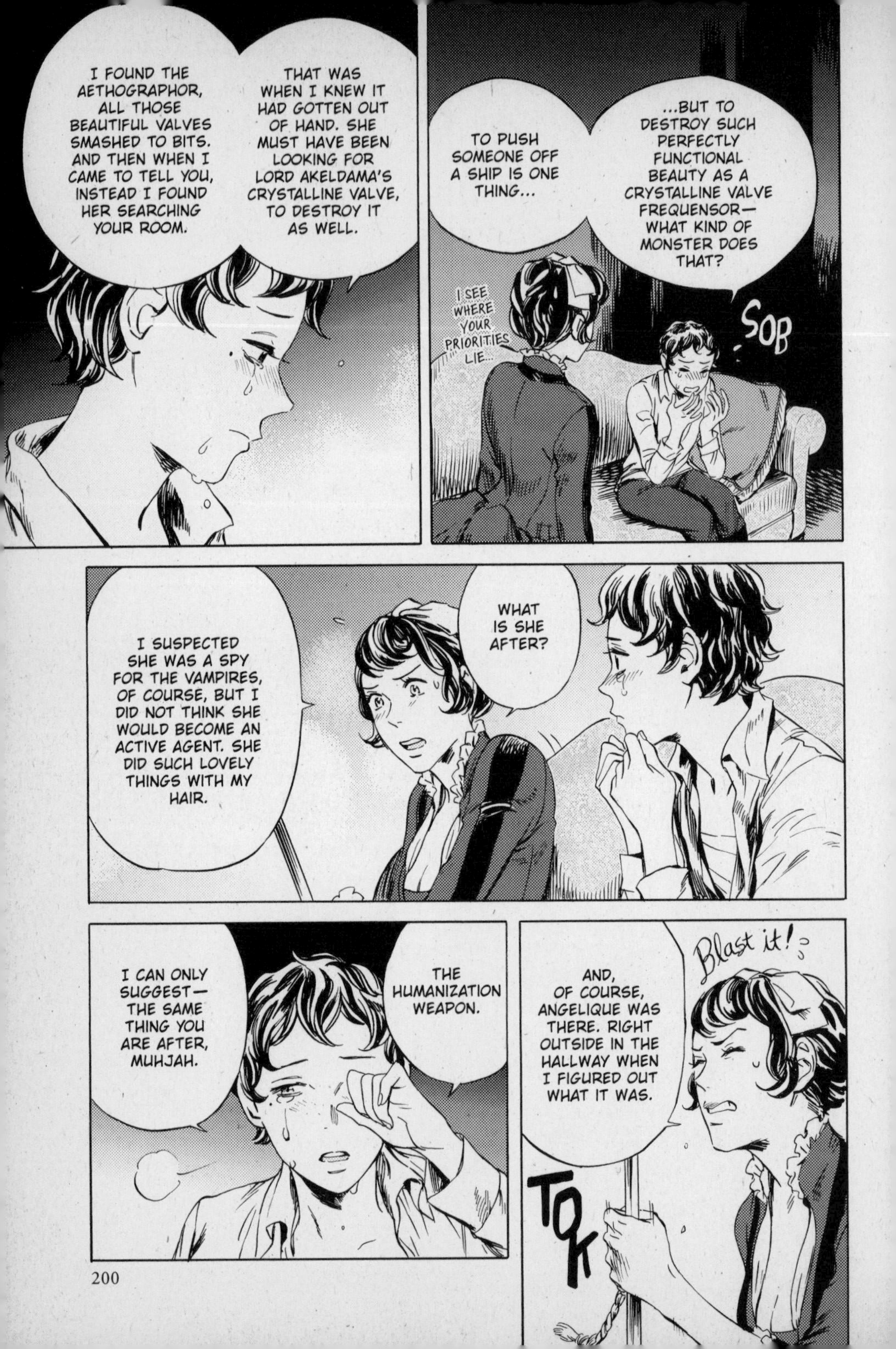
I FOUND THE AETHOGRAPHOR, ALL THOSE BEAUTIFUL VALVES SMASHED TO BITS. AND THEN WHEN I CAME TO TELL YOU, INSTEAD I FOUND HER SEARCHING YOUR ROOM.
THAT WAS WHEN I KNEW IT HAD GOTTEN OUT OF HAND. SHE MUST HAVE BEEN LOOKING FOR LORD AKELDAMA'S CRYSTALLINE VALVE, TO DESTROY IT AS WELL.
TO PUSH SOMEONE OFF A SHIP IS ONE THING...
...BUT TO DESTROY SUCH PERFECTLY FUNCTIONAL BEAUTY AS A CRYSTALLINE VALVE FREQUENSOR—WHAT KIND OF MONSTER DOES THAT?
I SEE WHERE YOUR PRIORITIES LIE...
SOB
I SUSPECTED SHE WAS A SPY FOR THE VAMPIRES, OF COURSE, BUT I DID NOT THINK SHE WOULD BECOME AN ACTIVE AGENT. SHE DID SUCH LOVELY THINGS WITH MY HAIR.
WHAT IS SHE AFTER?
I CAN ONLY SUGGEST—THE SAME THING YOU ARE AFTER, MUHJAH.
THE HUMANIZATION WEAPON.
AND, OF COURSE, ANGELIQUE WAS THERE. RIGHT OUTSIDE IN THE HALLWAY WHEN I FIGURED OUT WHAT IT WAS.
Blast it!
TOK

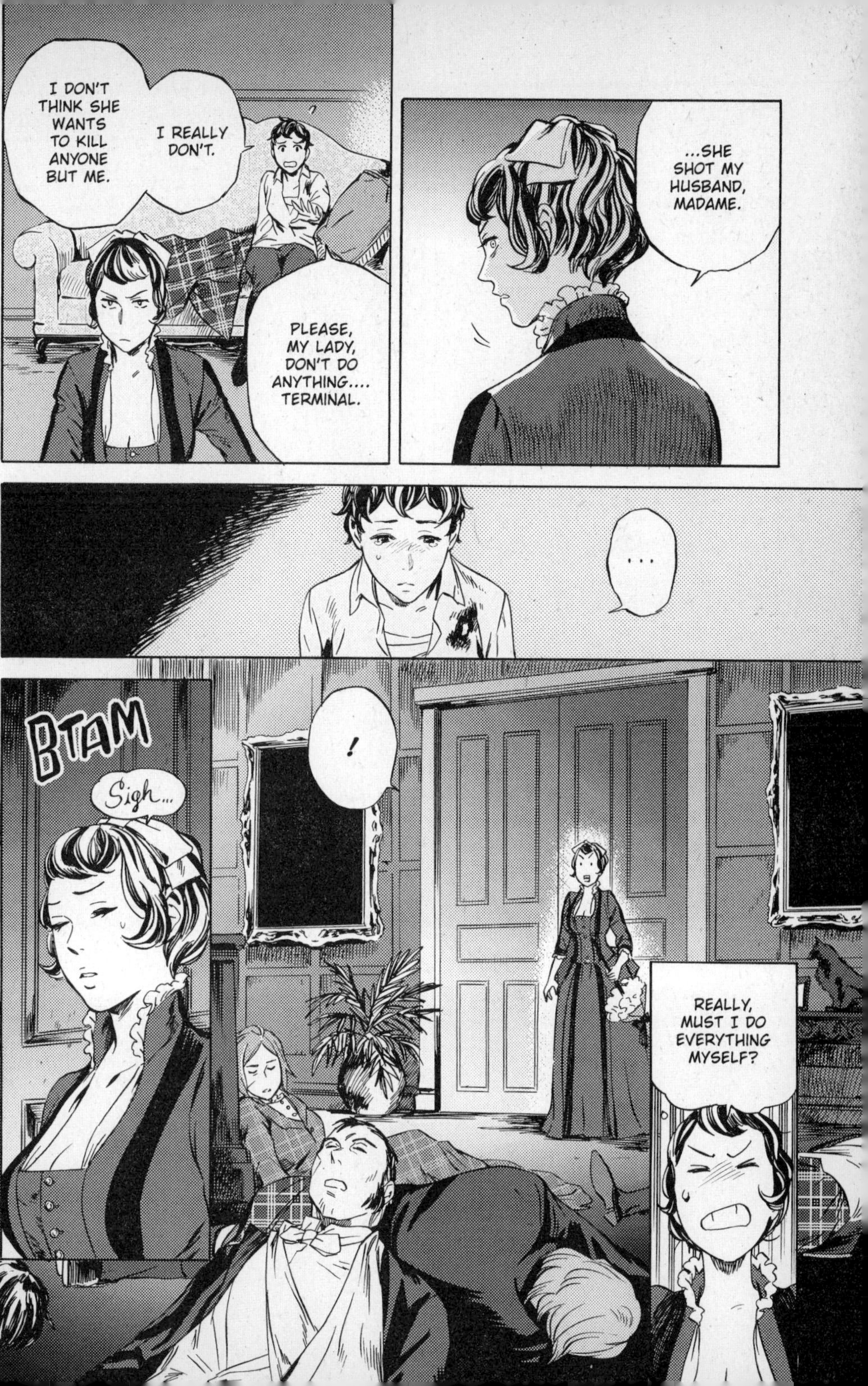
I DON'T THINK SHE WANTS TO KILL ANYONE BUT ME.
I REALLY DON'T.
PLEASE, MY LADY, DON'T DO ANYTHING.... TERMINAL.
...SHE SHOT MY HUSBAND, MADAME.
...
BTAM
Sigh...
!
REALLY, MUST I DO EVERYTHING MYSELF?

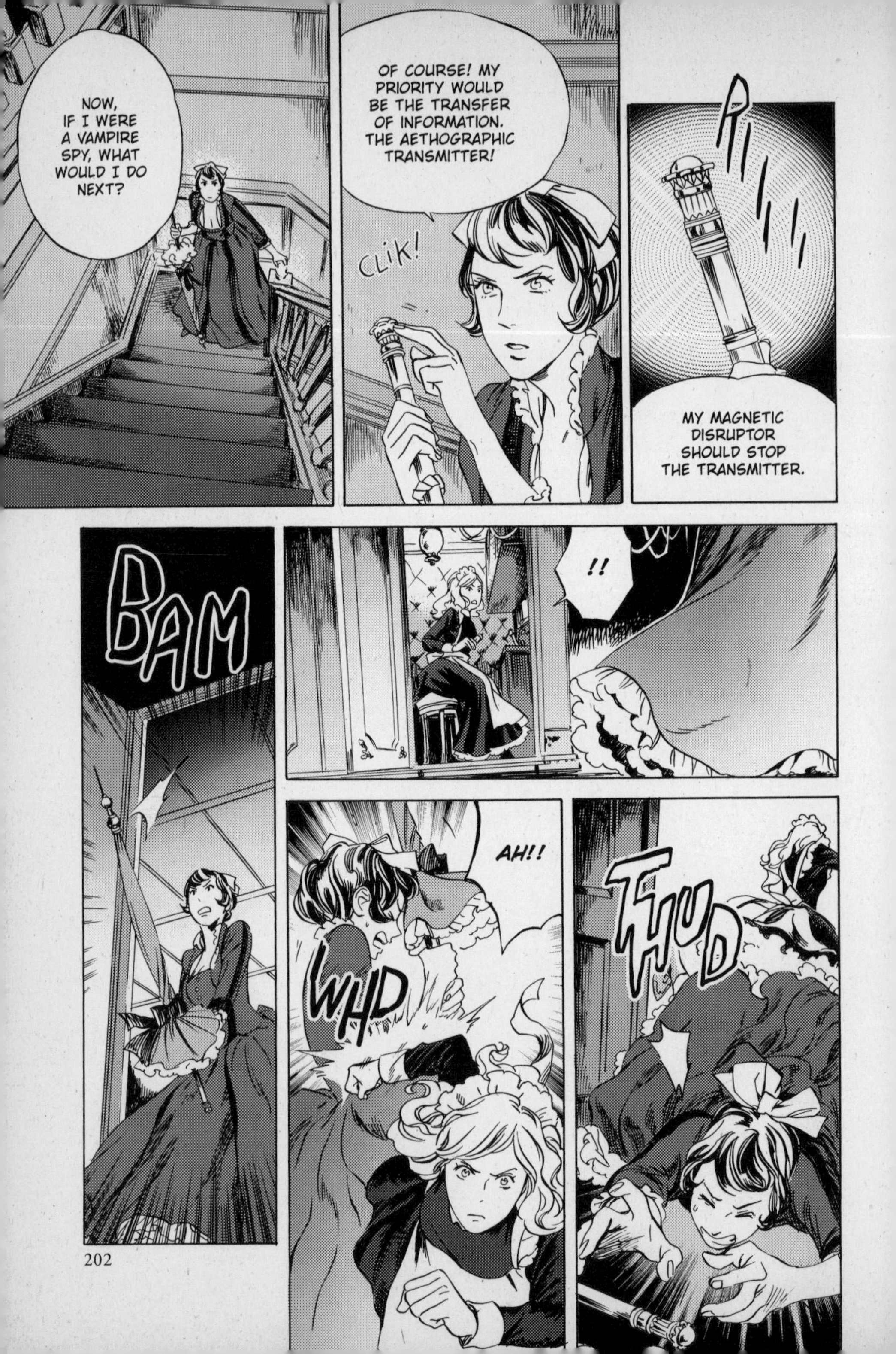
NOW, IF I WERE A VAMPIRE SPY, WHAT WOULD I DO NEXT?
OF COURSE! MY PRIORITY WOULD BE THE TRANSFER OF INFORMATION. THE AETHOGRAPHIC TRANSMITTER!
CLIK!
RI...
MY MAGNETIC DISRUPTOR SHOULD STOP THE TRANSMITTER.
BAM
!!
WHD
AH!!
THUD

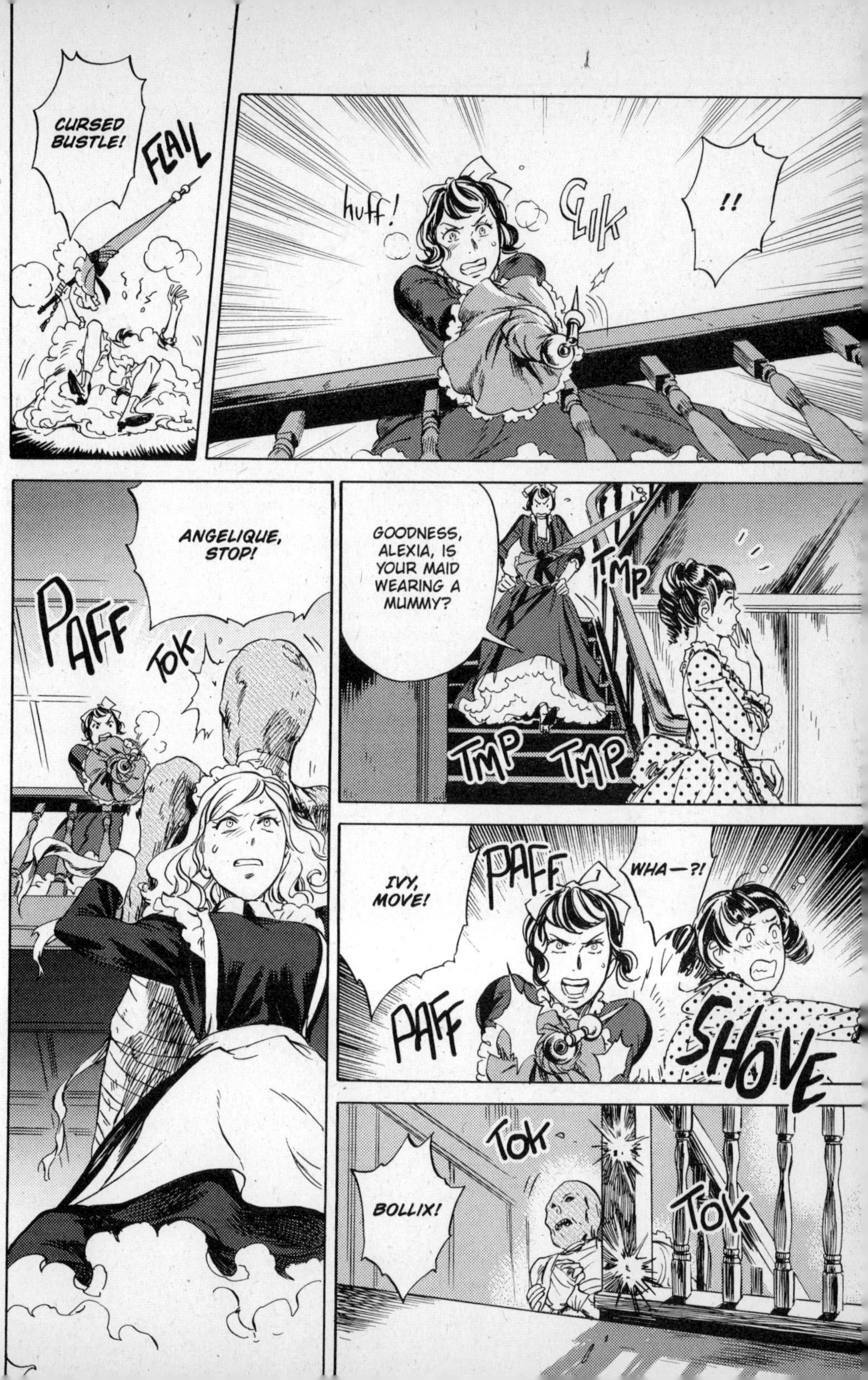
CURSED BUSTLE!
FLAIL
huff!
CLIK
!!
ANGELIQUE, STOP!
PAFF
TOK
GOODNESS, ALEXIA, IS YOUR MAID WEARING A MUMMY?
TMP
TMP
TMP
IVY, MOVE!
PAFF
WHA—?!
PAFF
SHOVE
TOK
BOLLIX!
TOK

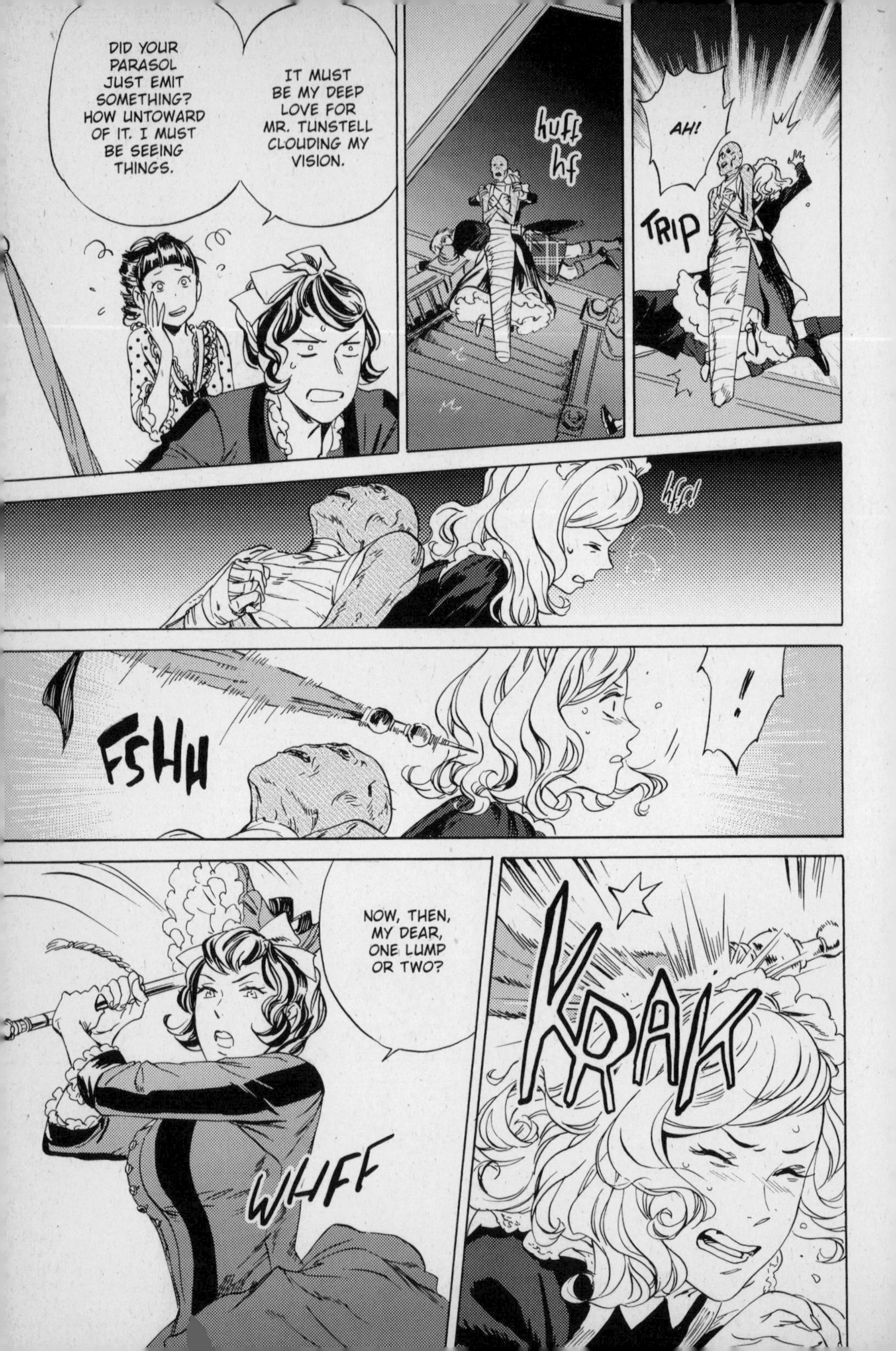
DID YOUR PARASOL JUST EMIT SOMETHING? HOW UNTOWARD OF IT. I MUST BE SEEING THINGS.
IT MUST BE MY DEEP LOVE FOR MR. TUNSTELL CLOUDING MY VISION.
huff hf
AH!
TRIP
FSHH
!
NOW, THEN, MY DEAR, ONE LUMP OR TWO?
WHFF
KRAK

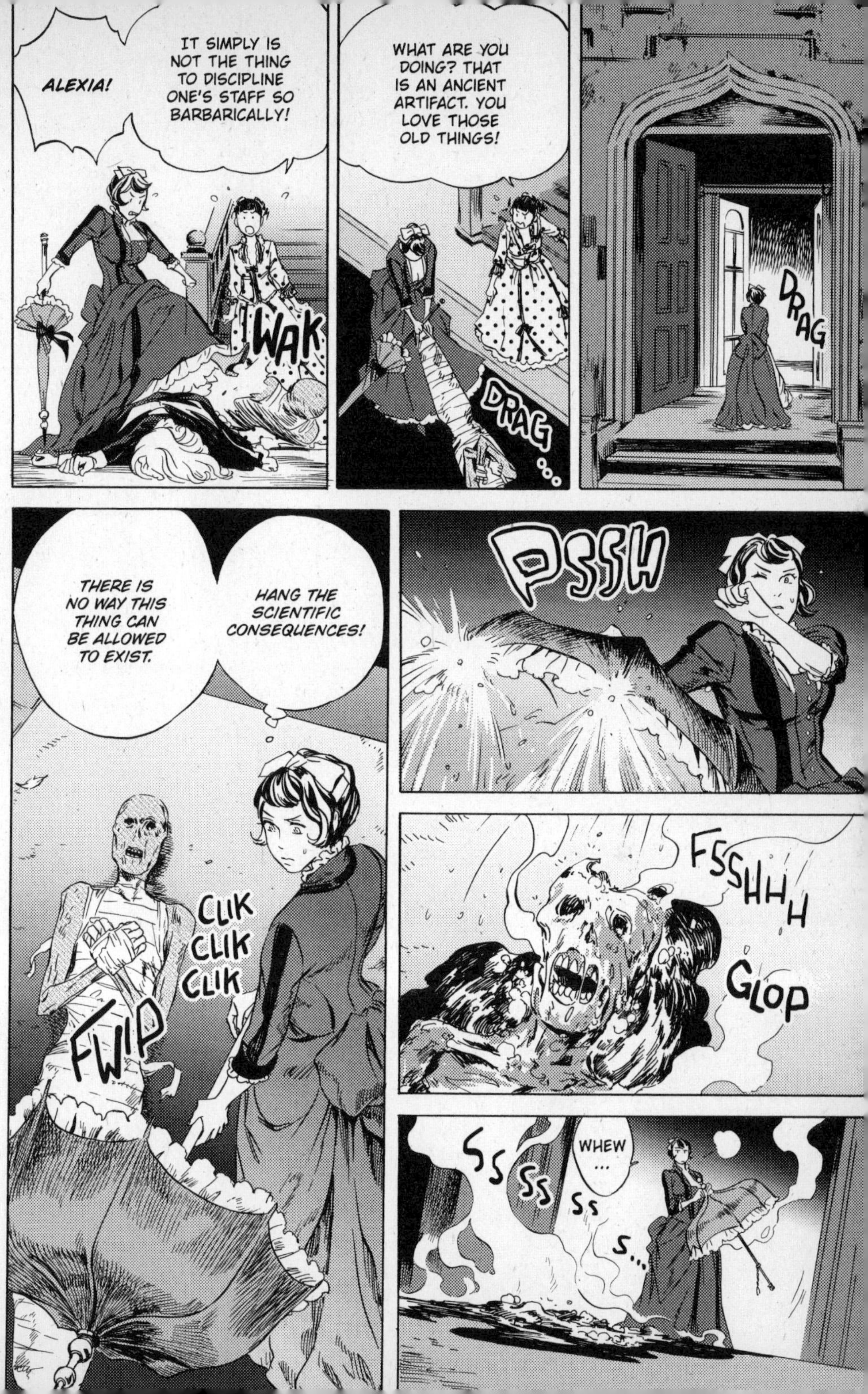
ALEXIA!
IT SIMPLY IS NOT THE THING TO DISCIPLINE ONE'S STAFF SO BARBARICALLY!
WAK
WHAT ARE YOU DOING? THAT IS AN ANCIENT ARTIFACT. YOU LOVE THOSE OLD THINGS!
DRAG...
DRAG
THERE IS NO WAY THIS THING CAN BE ALLOWED TO EXIST.
HANG THE SCIENTIFIC CONSEQUENCES!
CLIK CLIK CLIK
FWIP
PSSH
FSSHHHH
GLOP
SS SS SS S...
WHEW...

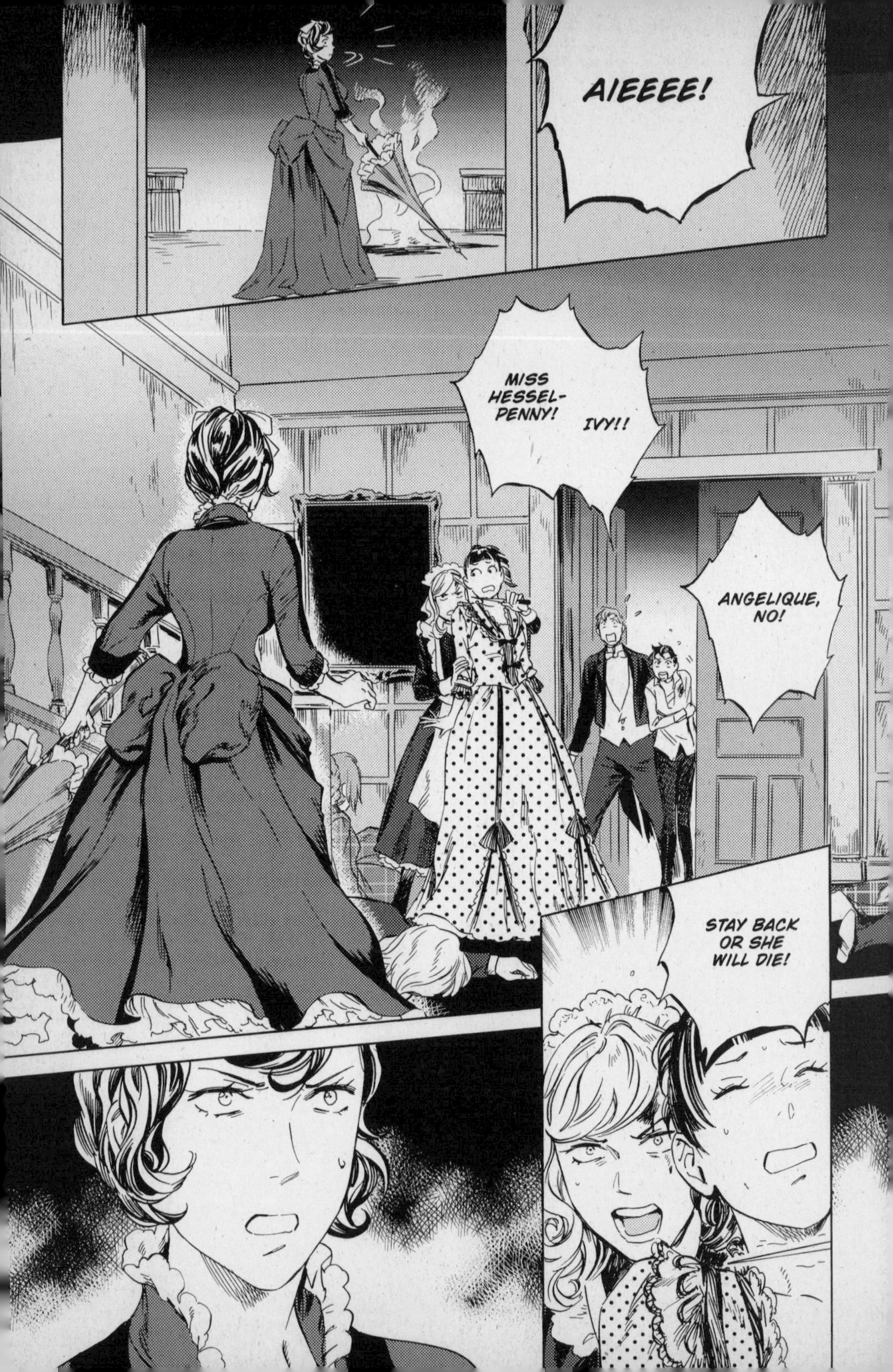

AIEEEE!
MISS HESSEL-PENNY!
IVY!!
ANGELIQUE, NO!
STAY BACK OR SHE WILL DIE!

SOULLESS

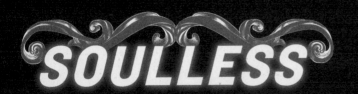

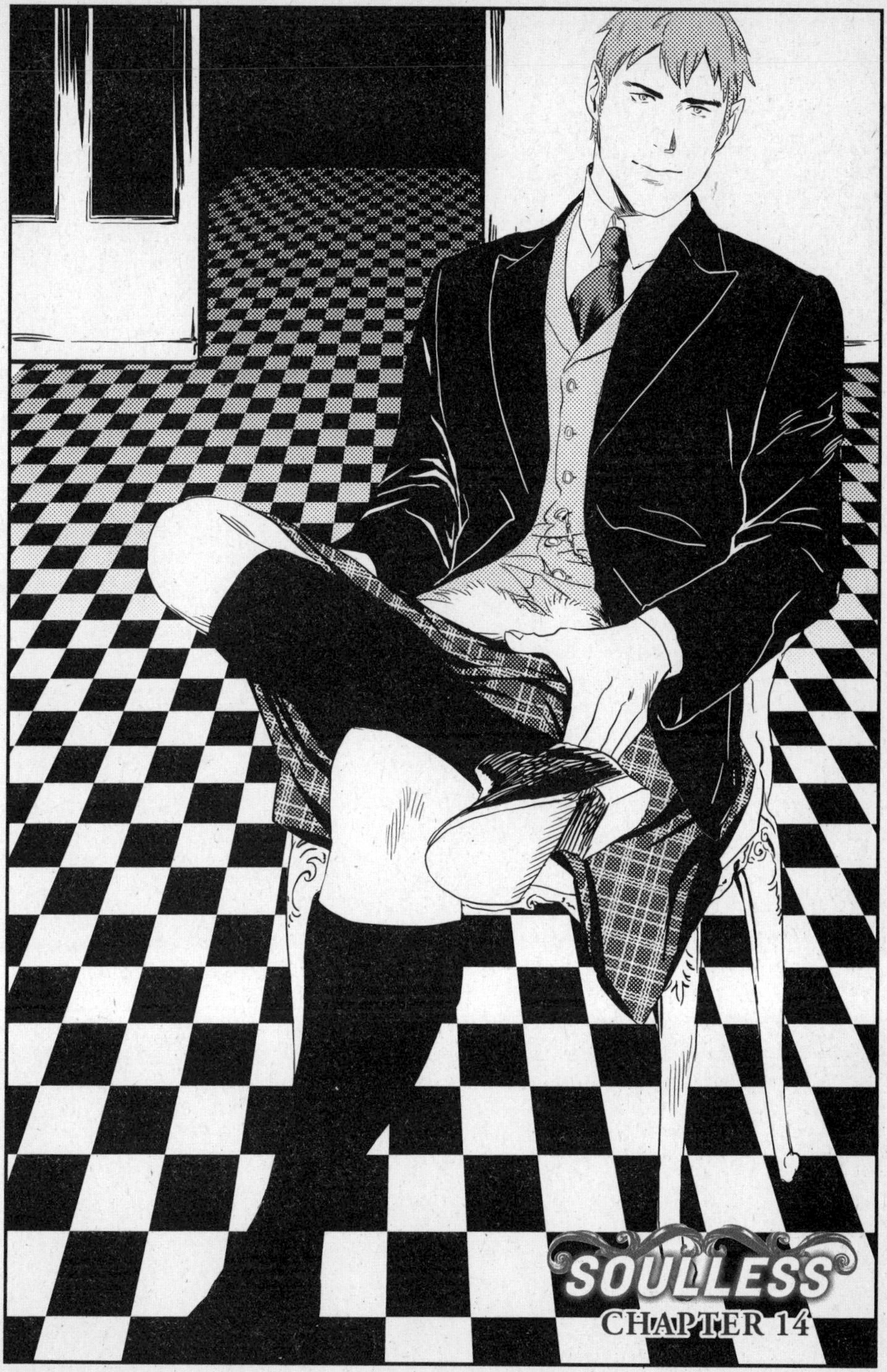
SOULLESS
CHAPTER 14

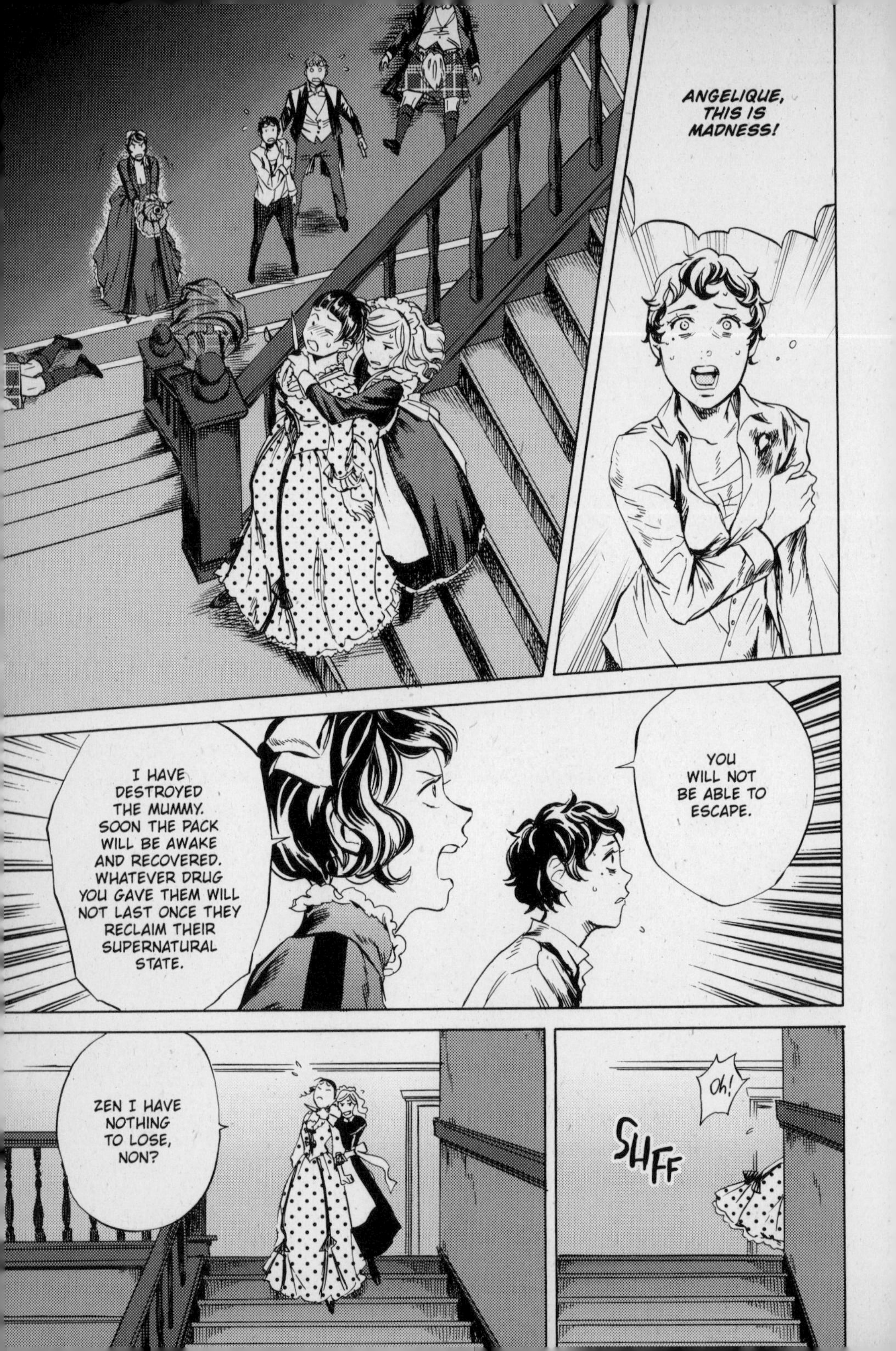
ANGELIQUE, THIS IS MADNESS!
I HAVE DESTROYED THE MUMMY. SOON THE PACK WILL BE AWAKE AND RECOVERED. WHATEVER DRUG YOU GAVE THEM WILL NOT LAST ONCE THEY RECLAIM THEIR SUPERNATURAL STATE.
YOU WILL NOT BE ABLE TO ESCAPE.
ZEN I HAVE NOTHING TO LOSE, NON?
Oh!
SHFF

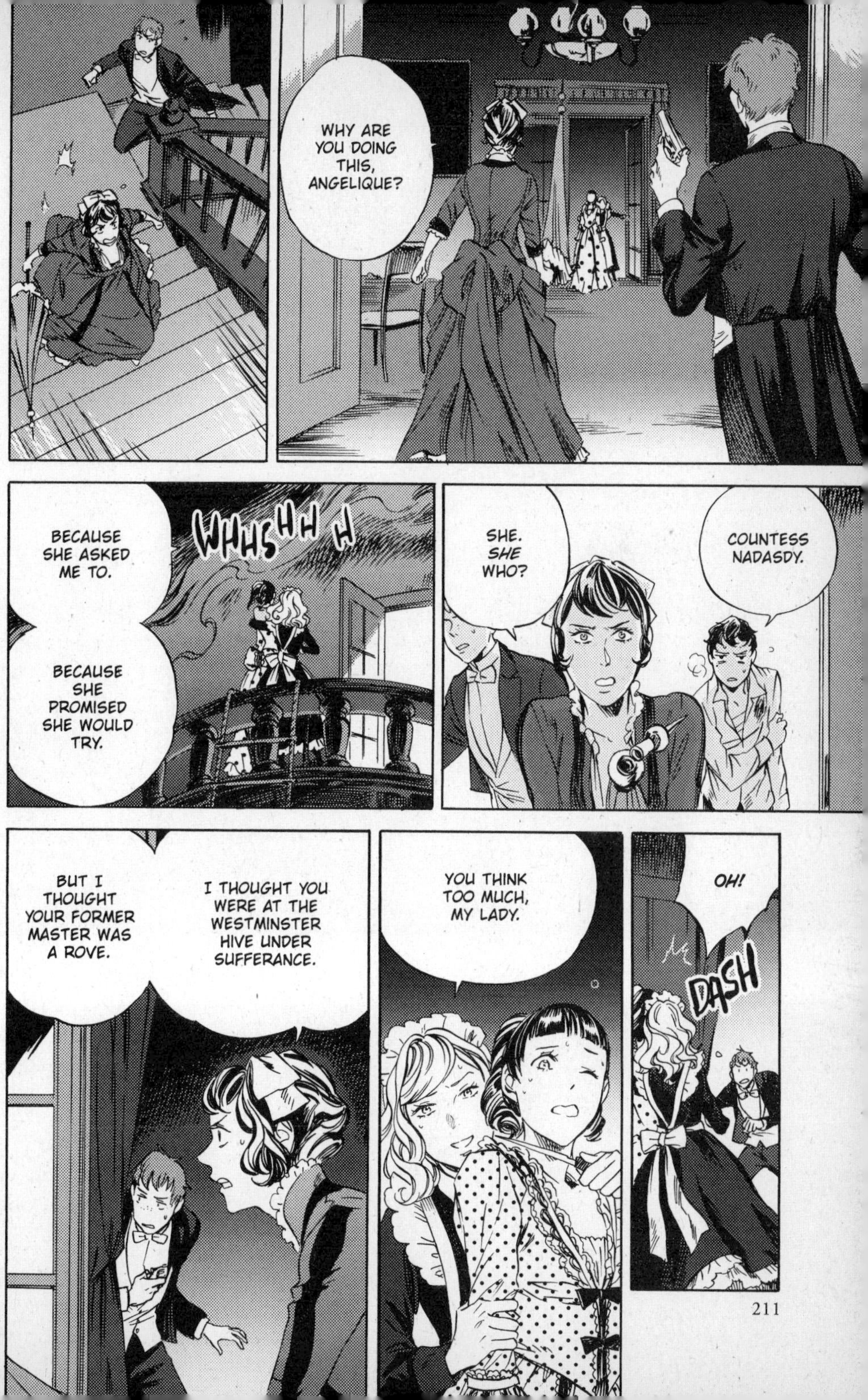
WHY ARE YOU DOING THIS, ANGELIQUE?
BECAUSE SHE ASKED ME TO.
WHHSHH H
BECAUSE SHE PROMISED SHE WOULD TRY.
SHE. SHE WHO?
COUNTESS NADASDY.
BUT I THOUGHT YOUR FORMER MASTER WAS A ROVE.
I THOUGHT YOU WERE AT THE WESTMINSTER HIVE UNDER SUFFERANCE.
YOU THINK TOO MUCH, MY LADY.
OH!
DASH

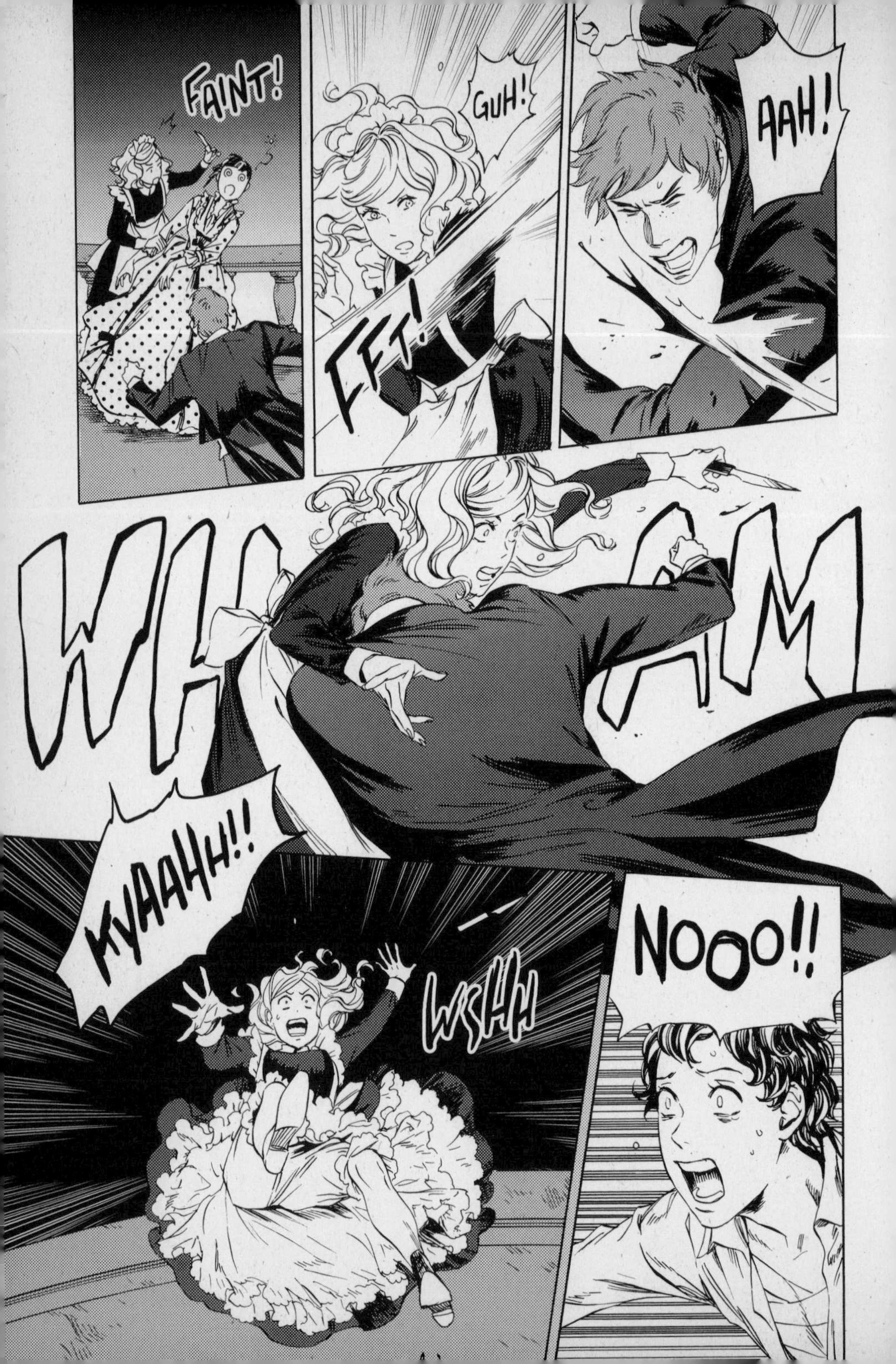
FAINT!
GUH!
FFT!
AAH!
WHAM
KYAAHH!!
WSHH
NOOO!!

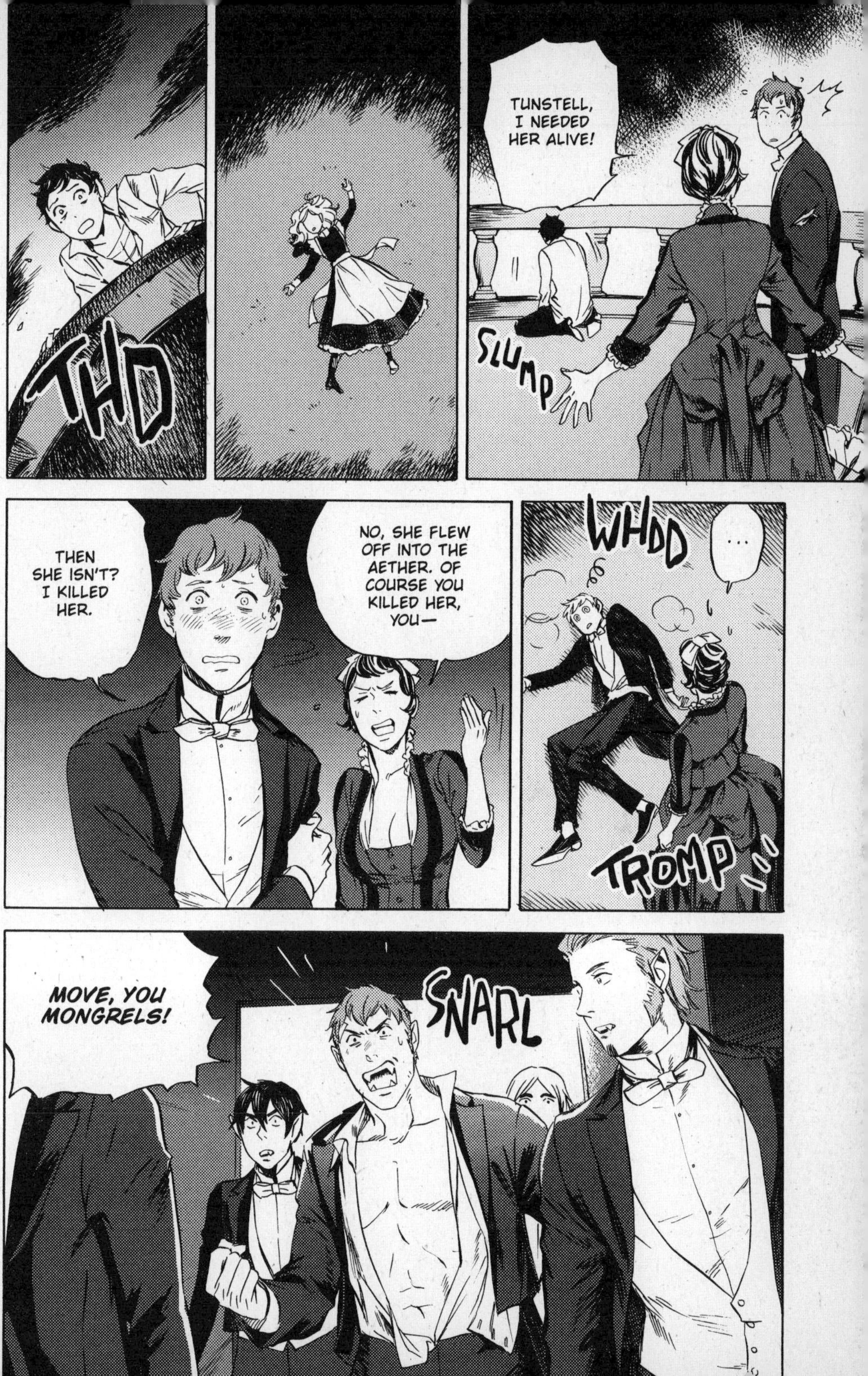
THD
TUNSTELL, I NEEDED HER ALIVE!
SLUMP
THEN SHE ISN'T? I KILLED HER.
NO, SHE FLEW OFF INTO THE AETHER. OF COURSE YOU KILLED HER, YOU—
WHDD
...
TROMP
MOVE, YOU MONGRELS!
SNARL

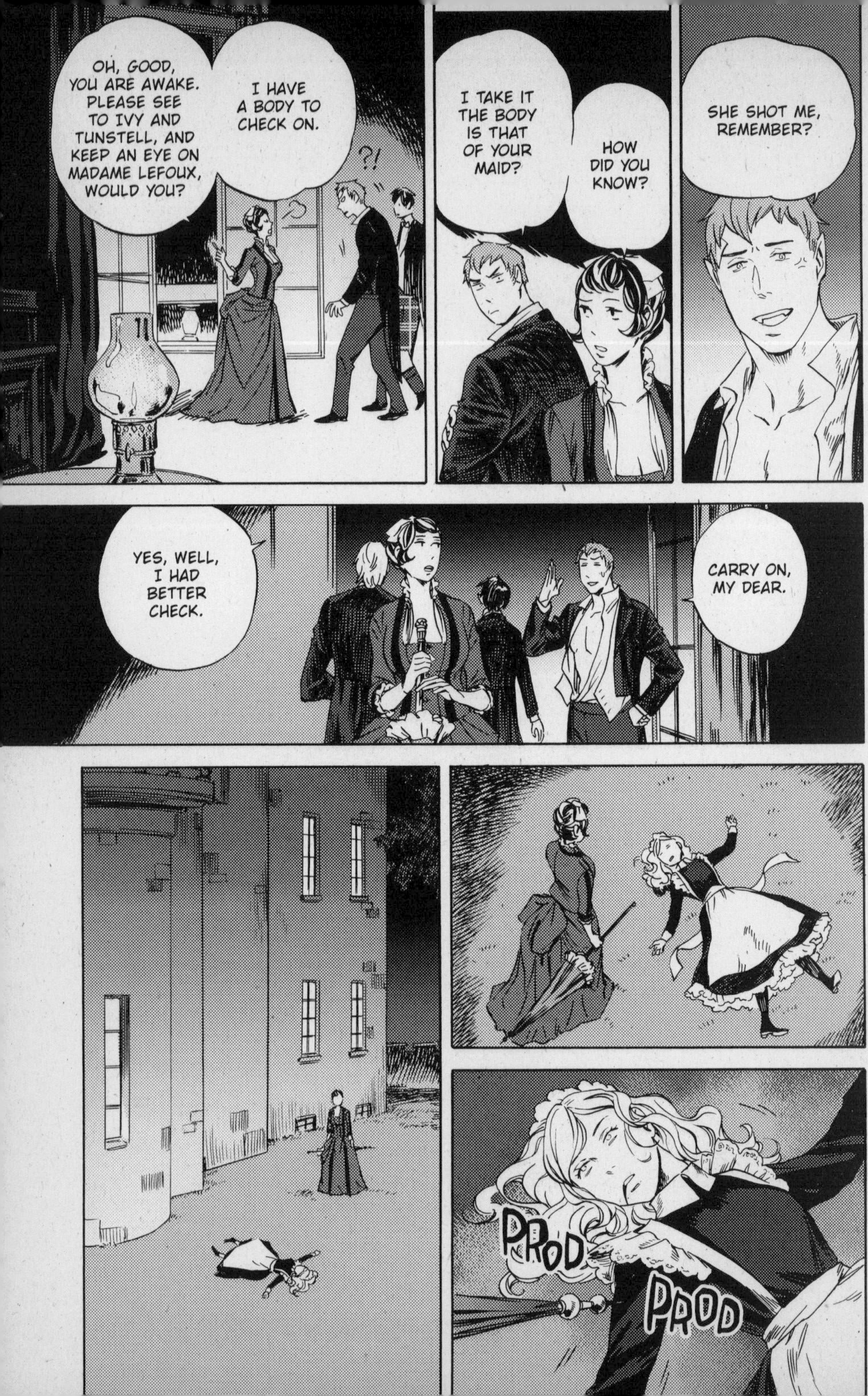
OH, GOOD, YOU ARE AWAKE. PLEASE SEE TO IVY AND TUNSTELL, AND KEEP AN EYE ON MADAME LEFOUX, WOULD YOU?
I HAVE A BODY TO CHECK ON.
?!
I TAKE IT THE BODY IS THAT OF YOUR MAID?
HOW DID YOU KNOW?
SHE SHOT ME, REMEMBER?
YES, WELL, I HAD BETTER CHECK.
CARRY ON, MY DEAR.
PROD
PROD

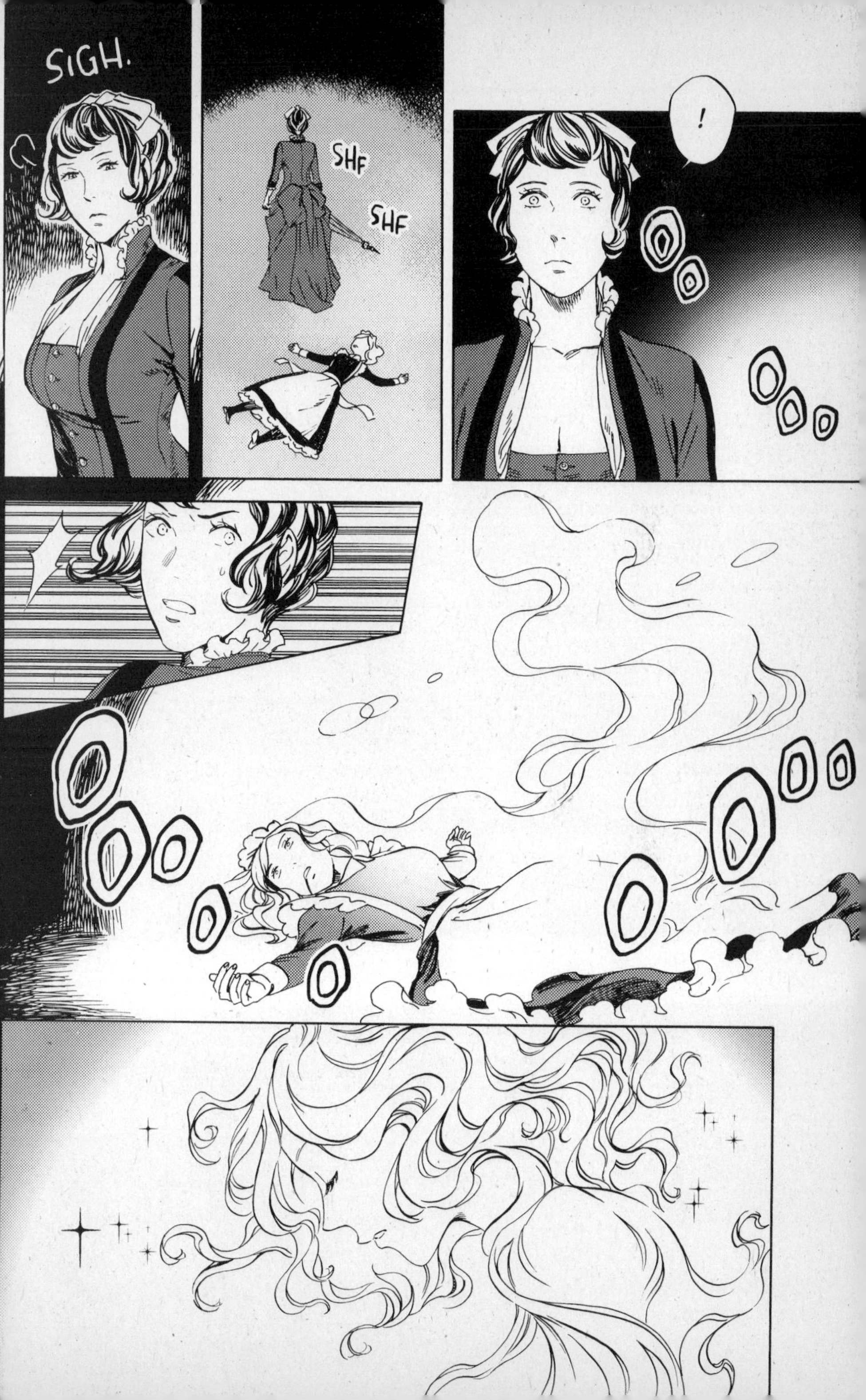
SIGH.
SHF
SHF
!

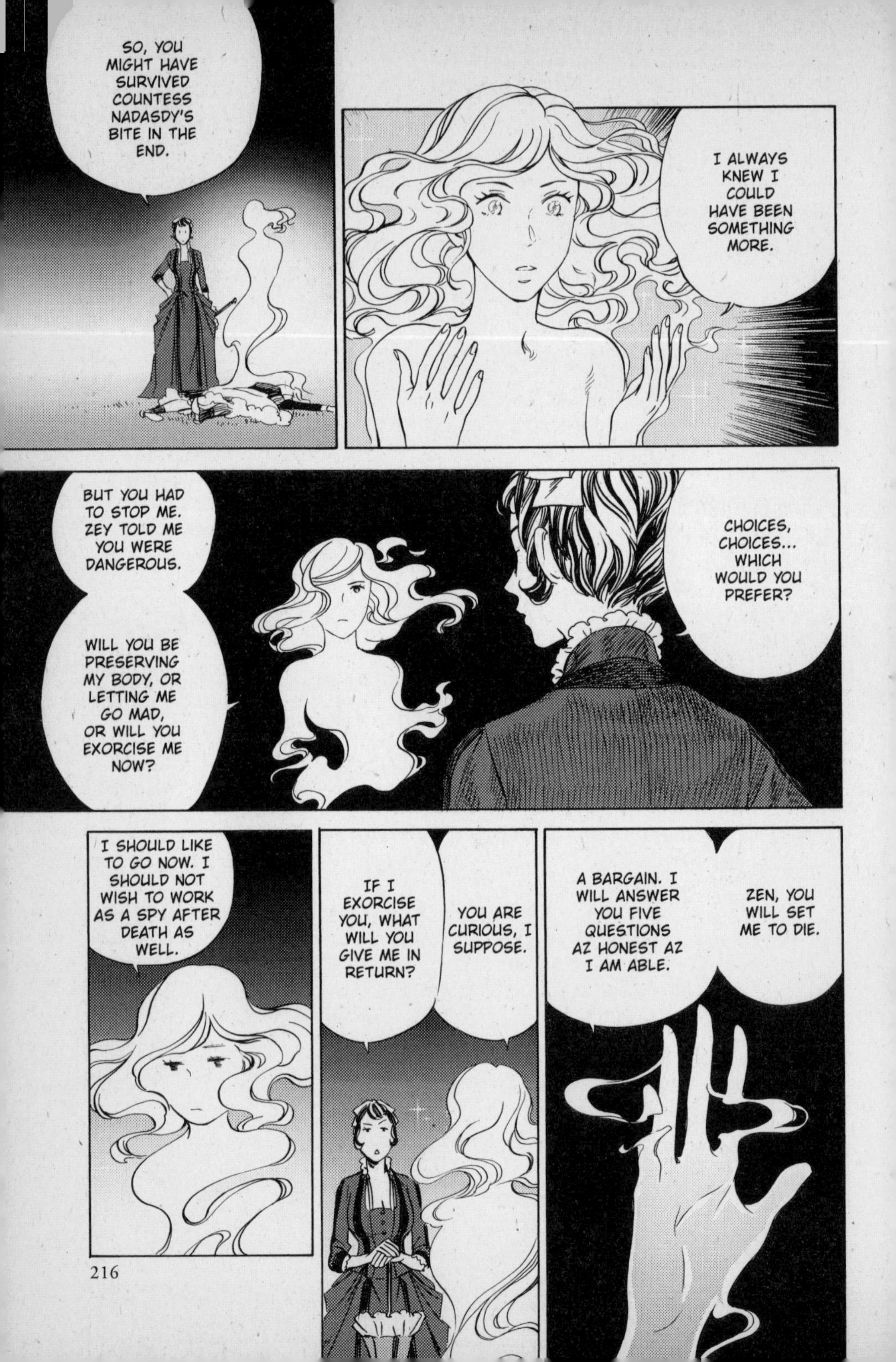
SO, YOU MIGHT HAVE SURVIVED COUNTESS NADASDY'S BITE IN THE END.
I ALWAYS KNEW I COULD HAVE BEEN SOMETHING MORE.
BUT YOU HAD TO STOP ME. ZEY TOLD ME YOU WERE DANGEROUS.
WILL YOU BE PRESERVING MY BODY, OR LETTING ME GO MAD, OR WILL YOU EXORCISE ME NOW?
CHOICES, CHOICES... WHICH WOULD YOU PREFER?
I SHOULD LIKE TO GO NOW. I SHOULD NOT WISH TO WORK AS A SPY AFTER DEATH AS WELL.
IF I EXORCISE YOU, WHAT WILL YOU GIVE ME IN RETURN?
YOU ARE CURIOUS, I SUPPOSE.
A BARGAIN. I WILL ANSWER YOU FIVE QUESTIONS AZ HONEST AZ I AM ABLE.
ZEN, YOU WILL SET ME TO DIE.

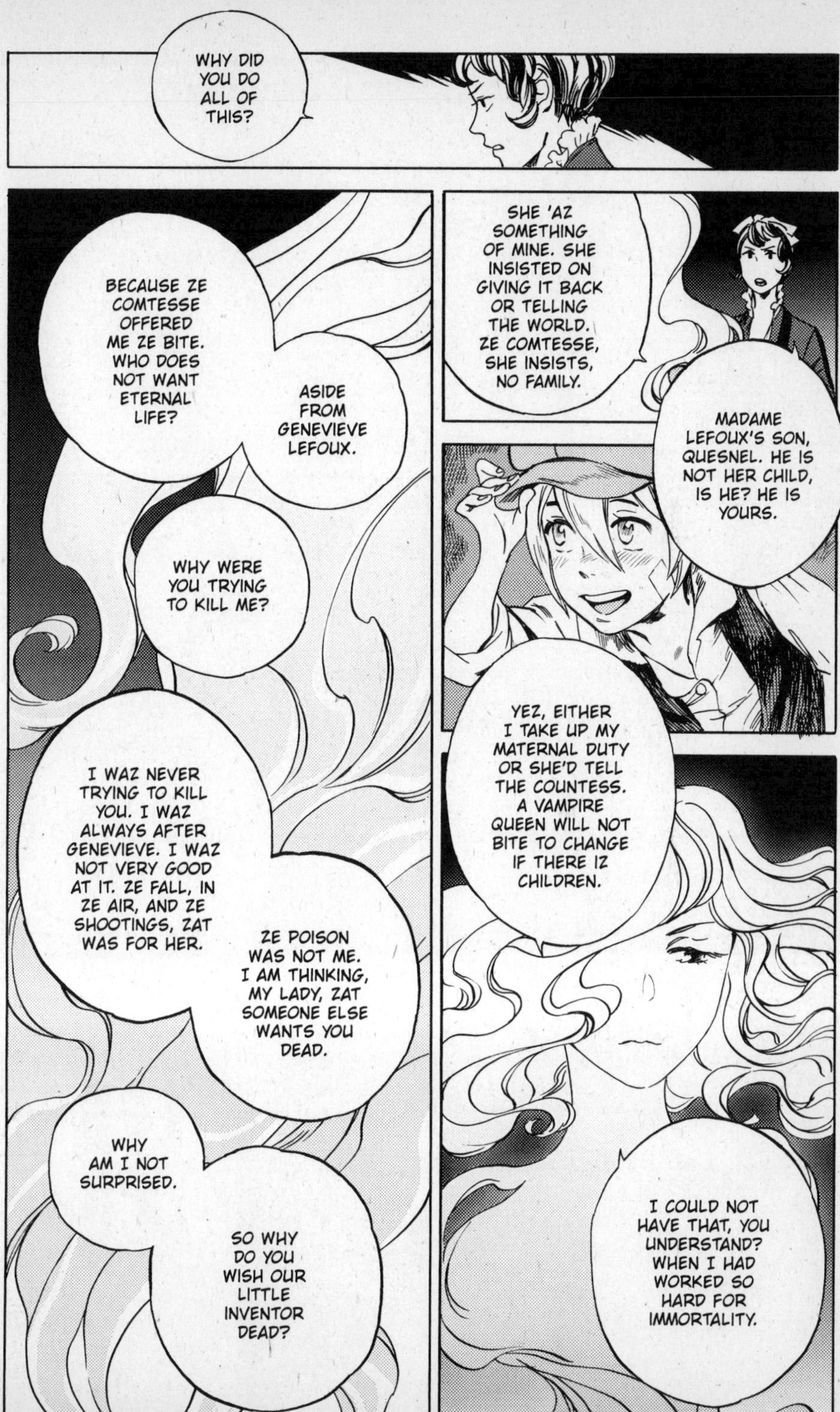
WHY DID YOU DO ALL OF THIS?
BECAUSE ZE COMTESSE OFFERED ME ZE BITE. WHO DOES NOT WANT ETERNAL LIFE?
ASIDE FROM GENEVIEVE LEFOUX.
WHY WERE YOU TRYING TO KILL ME?
I WAZ NEVER TRYING TO KILL YOU. I WAZ ALWAYS AFTER GENEVIEVE. I WAZ NOT VERY GOOD AT IT. ZE FALL, IN ZE AIR, AND ZE SHOOTINGS, ZAT WAS FOR HER.
ZE POISON WAS NOT ME. I AM THINKING, MY LADY, ZAT SOMEONE ELSE WANTS YOU DEAD.
WHY AM I NOT SURPRISED.
SO WHY DO YOU WISH OUR LITTLE INVENTOR DEAD?
SHE 'AZ SOMETHING OF MINE. SHE INSISTED ON GIVING IT BACK OR TELLING THE WORLD. ZE COMTESSE, SHE INSISTS, NO FAMILY.
MADAME LEFOUX'S SON, QUESNEL. HE IS NOT HER CHILD, IS HE? HE IS YOURS.
YEZ, EITHER I TAKE UP MY MATERNAL DUTY OR SHE'D TELL THE COUNTESS. A VAMPIRE QUEEN WILL NOT BITE TO CHANGE IF THERE IZ CHILDREN.
I COULD NOT HAVE THAT, YOU UNDERSTAND? WHEN I HAD WORKED SO HARD FOR IMMORTALITY.

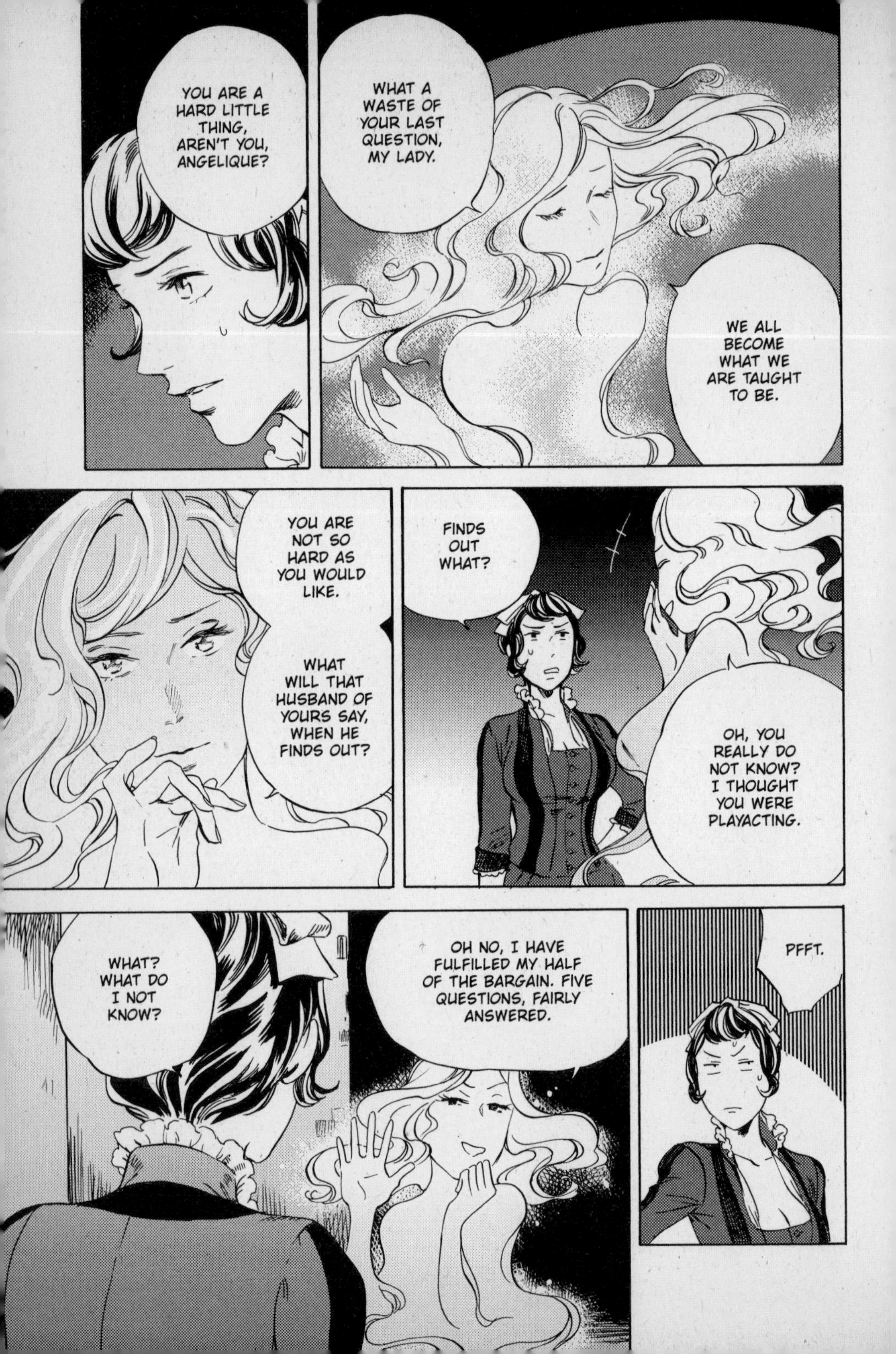
YOU ARE A HARD LITTLE THING, AREN'T YOU, ANGELIQUE?
WHAT A WASTE OF YOUR LAST QUESTION, MY LADY.
WE ALL BECOME WHAT WE ARE TAUGHT TO BE.
YOU ARE NOT SO HARD AS YOU WOULD LIKE.
WHAT WILL THAT HUSBAND OF YOURS SAY, WHEN HE FINDS OUT?
FINDS OUT WHAT?
OH, YOU REALLY DO NOT KNOW? I THOUGHT YOU WERE PLAYACTING.
WHAT? WHAT DO I NOT KNOW?
OH NO, I HAVE FULFILLED MY HALF OF THE BARGAIN. FIVE QUESTIONS, FAIRLY ANSWERED.
PFFT.

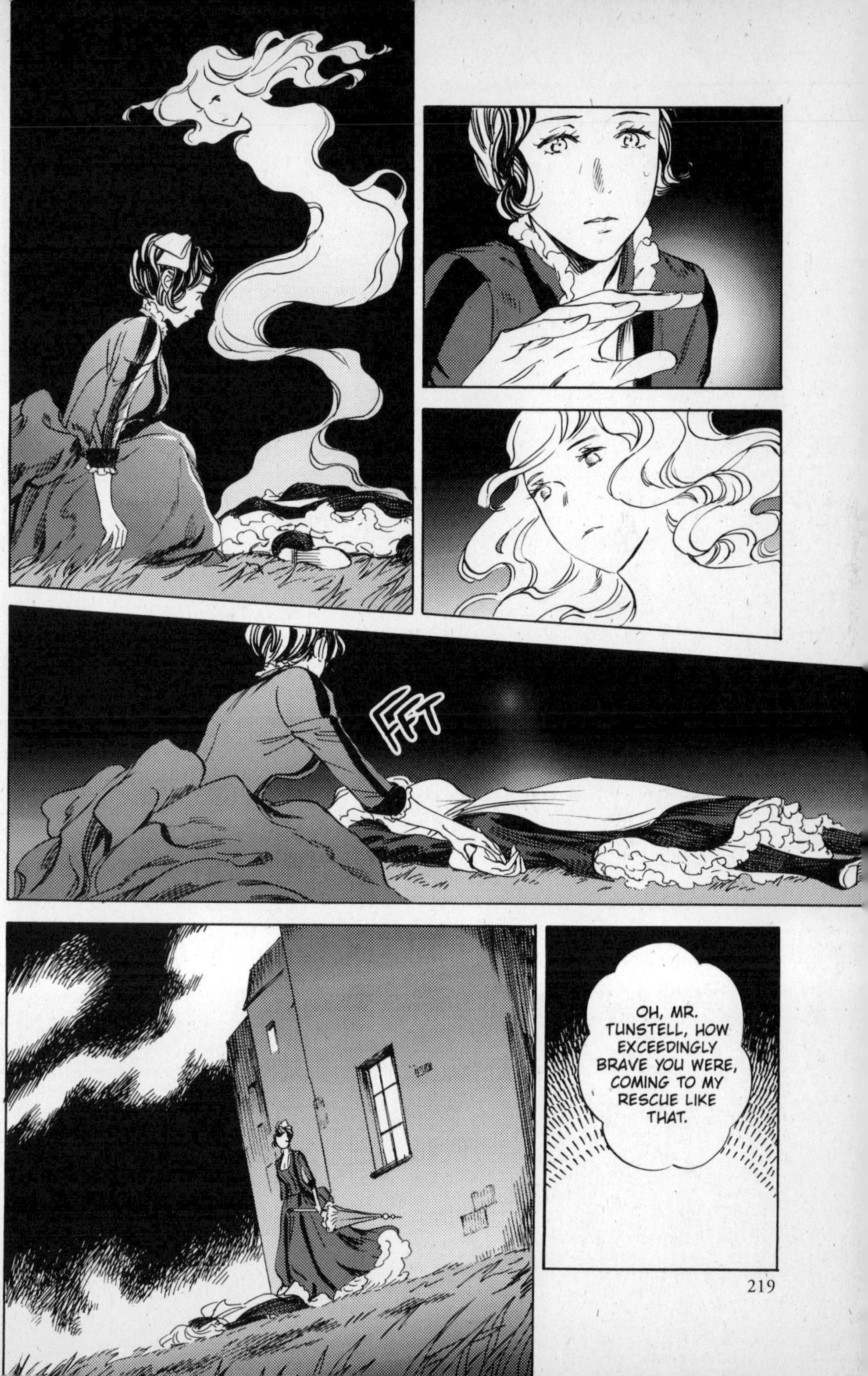
FFT
OH, MR. TUNSTELL, HOW EXCEEDINGLY BRAVE YOU WERE, COMING TO MY RESCUE LIKE THAT.

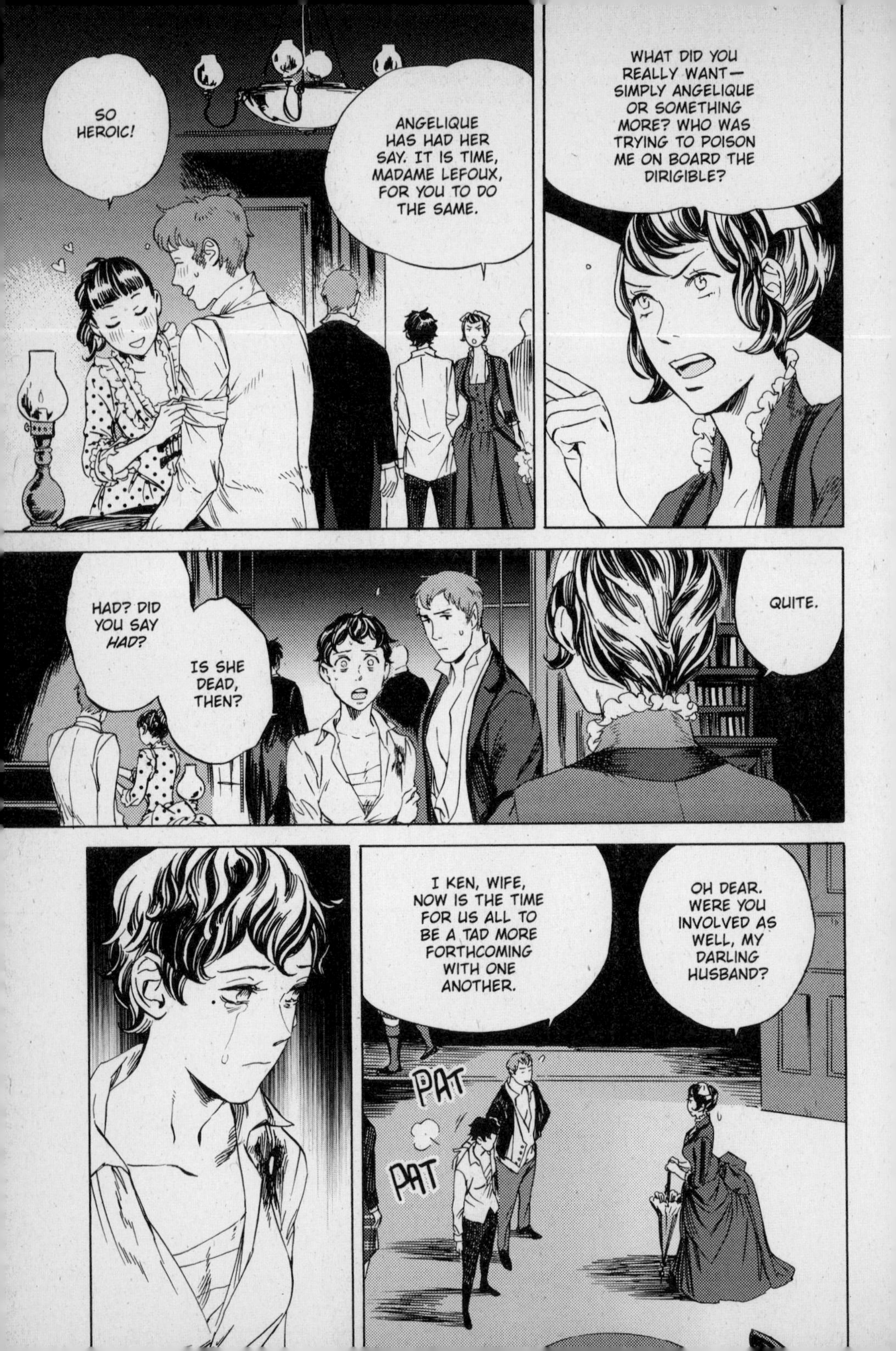
SO HEROIC!
ANGELIQUE HAS HAD HER SAY. IT IS TIME, MADAME LEFOUX, FOR YOU TO DO THE SAME.
WHAT DID YOU REALLY WANT— SIMPLY ANGELIQUE OR SOMETHING MORE? WHO WAS TRYING TO POISON ME ON BOARD THE DIRIGIBLE?
HAD? DID YOU SAY *HAD*?
IS SHE DEAD, THEN?
QUITE.
I KEN, WIFE, NOW IS THE TIME FOR US ALL TO BE A TAD MORE FORTHCOMING WITH ONE ANOTHER.
OH DEAR. WERE YOU INVOLVED AS WELL, MY DARLING HUSBAND?
PAT
PAT

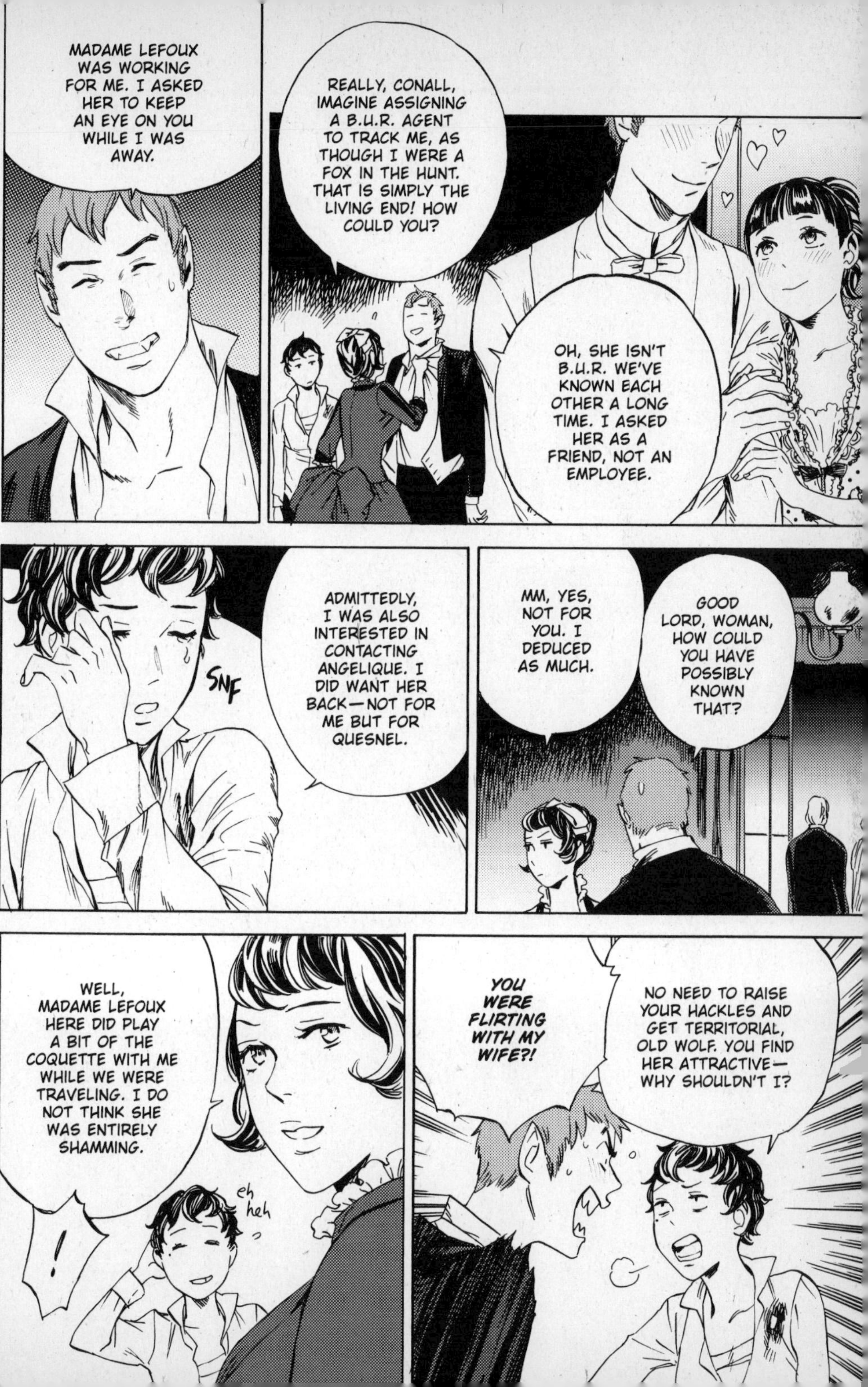
MADAME LEFOUX WAS WORKING FOR ME. I ASKED HER TO KEEP AN EYE ON YOU WHILE I WAS AWAY.
REALLY, CONALL, IMAGINE ASSIGNING A B.U.R. AGENT TO TRACK ME, AS THOUGH I WERE A FOX IN THE HUNT. THAT IS SIMPLY THE LIVING END! HOW COULD YOU?
OH, SHE ISN'T B.U.R. WE'VE KNOWN EACH OTHER A LONG TIME. I ASKED HER AS A FRIEND, NOT AN EMPLOYEE.
SNF
ADMITTEDLY, I WAS ALSO INTERESTED IN CONTACTING ANGELIQUE. I DID WANT HER BACK—NOT FOR ME BUT FOR QUESNEL.
MM, YES, NOT FOR YOU. I DEDUCED AS MUCH.
GOOD LORD, WOMAN, HOW COULD YOU HAVE POSSIBLY KNOWN THAT?
WELL, MADAME LEFOUX HERE DID PLAY A BIT OF THE COQUETTE WITH ME WHILE WE WERE TRAVELING. I DO NOT THINK SHE WAS ENTIRELY SHAMMING.
!
eh heh
YOU WERE FLIRTING WITH MY WIFE?!
NO NEED TO RAISE YOUR HACKLES AND GET TERRITORIAL, OLD WOLF. YOU FIND HER ATTRACTIVE—WHY SHOULDN'T I?

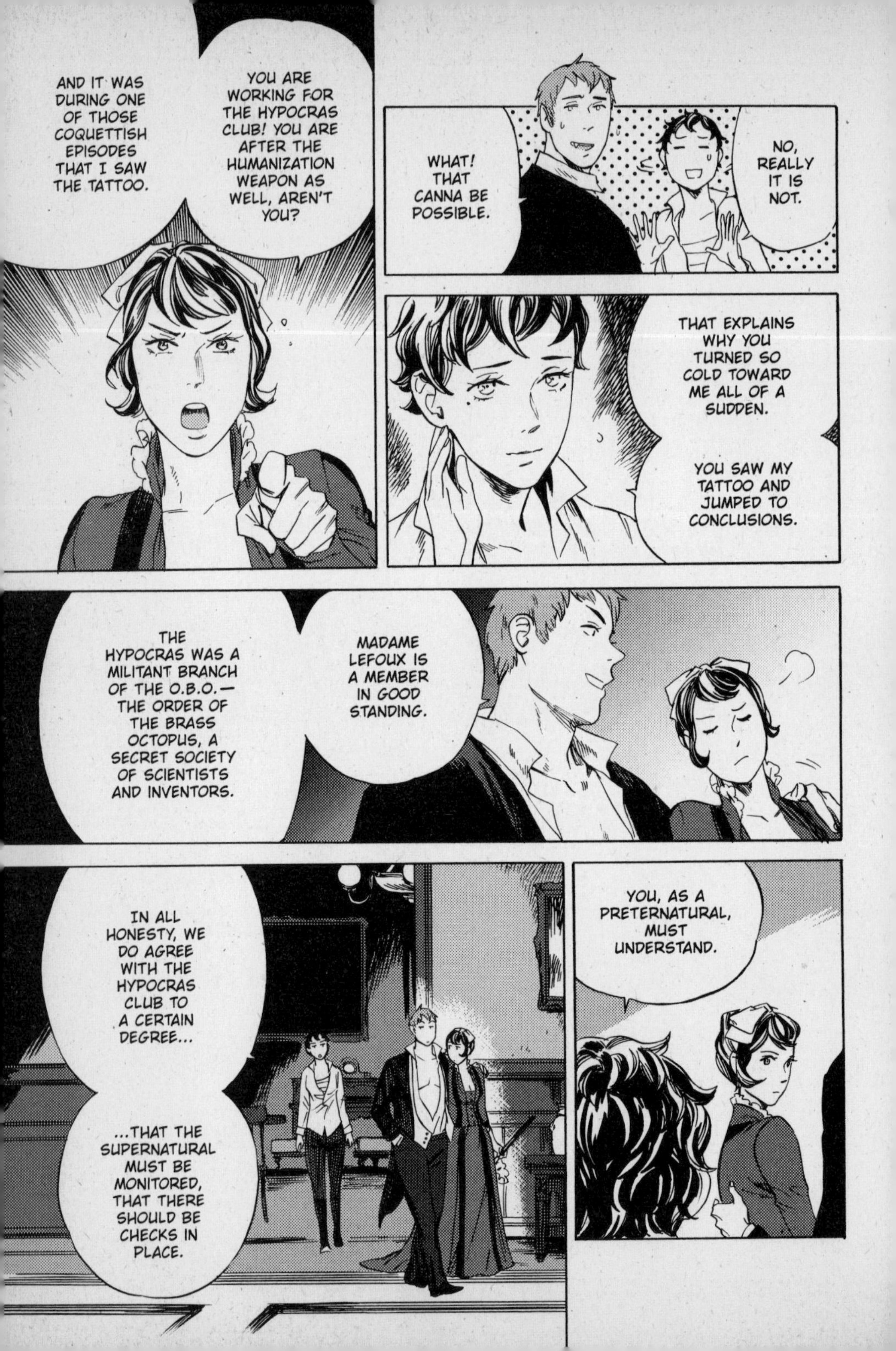
AND IT WAS DURING ONE OF THOSE COQUETTISH EPISODES THAT I SAW THE TATTOO.
YOU ARE WORKING FOR THE HYPOCRAS CLUB! YOU ARE AFTER THE HUMANIZATION WEAPON AS WELL, AREN'T YOU?
WHAT! THAT CANNA BE POSSIBLE.
NO, REALLY IT IS NOT.
THAT EXPLAINS WHY YOU TURNED SO COLD TOWARD ME ALL OF A SUDDEN.
YOU SAW MY TATTOO AND JUMPED TO CONCLUSIONS.
THE HYPOCRAS WAS A MILITANT BRANCH OF THE O.B.O.—THE ORDER OF THE BRASS OCTOPUS, A SECRET SOCIETY OF SCIENTISTS AND INVENTORS.
MADAME LEFOUX IS A MEMBER IN GOOD STANDING.
IN ALL HONESTY, WE DO AGREE WITH THE HYPOCRAS CLUB TO A CERTAIN DEGREE...
...THAT THE SUPERNATURAL MUST BE MONITORED, THAT THERE SHOULD BE CHECKS IN PLACE.
YOU, AS A PRETERNATURAL, MUST UNDERSTAND.

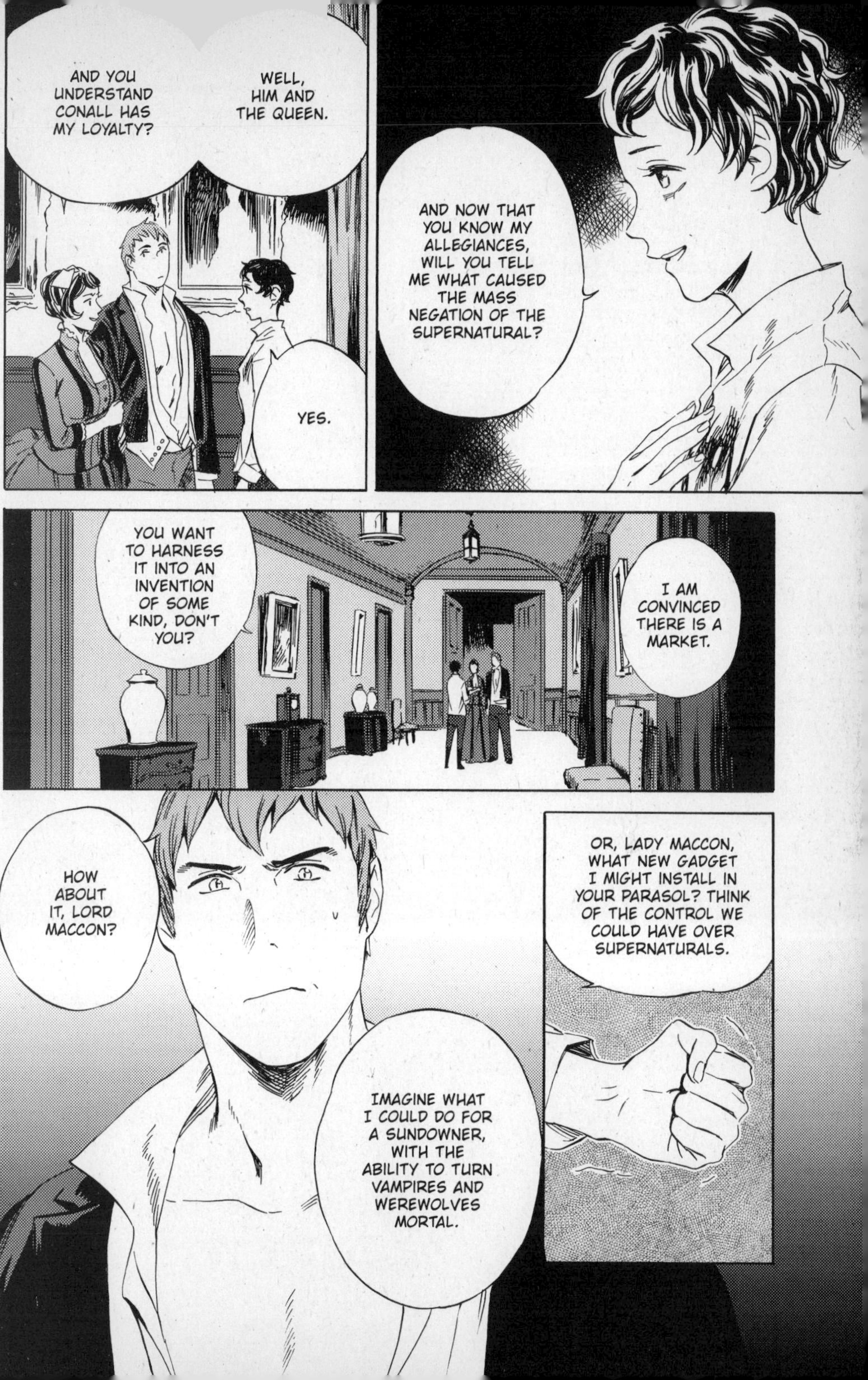
AND YOU UNDERSTAND CONALL HAS MY LOYALTY?
WELL, HIM AND THE QUEEN.
YES.
AND NOW THAT YOU KNOW MY ALLEGIANCES, WILL YOU TELL ME WHAT CAUSED THE MASS NEGATION OF THE SUPERNATURAL?
YOU WANT TO HARNESS IT INTO AN INVENTION OF SOME KIND, DON'T YOU?
I AM CONVINCED THERE IS A MARKET.
HOW ABOUT IT, LORD MACCON?
IMAGINE WHAT I COULD DO FOR A SUNDOWNER, WITH THE ABILITY TO TURN VAMPIRES AND WEREWOLVES MORTAL.
OR, LADY MACCON, WHAT NEW GADGET I MIGHT INSTALL IN YOUR PARASOL? THINK OF THE CONTROL WE COULD HAVE OVER SUPERNATURALS.

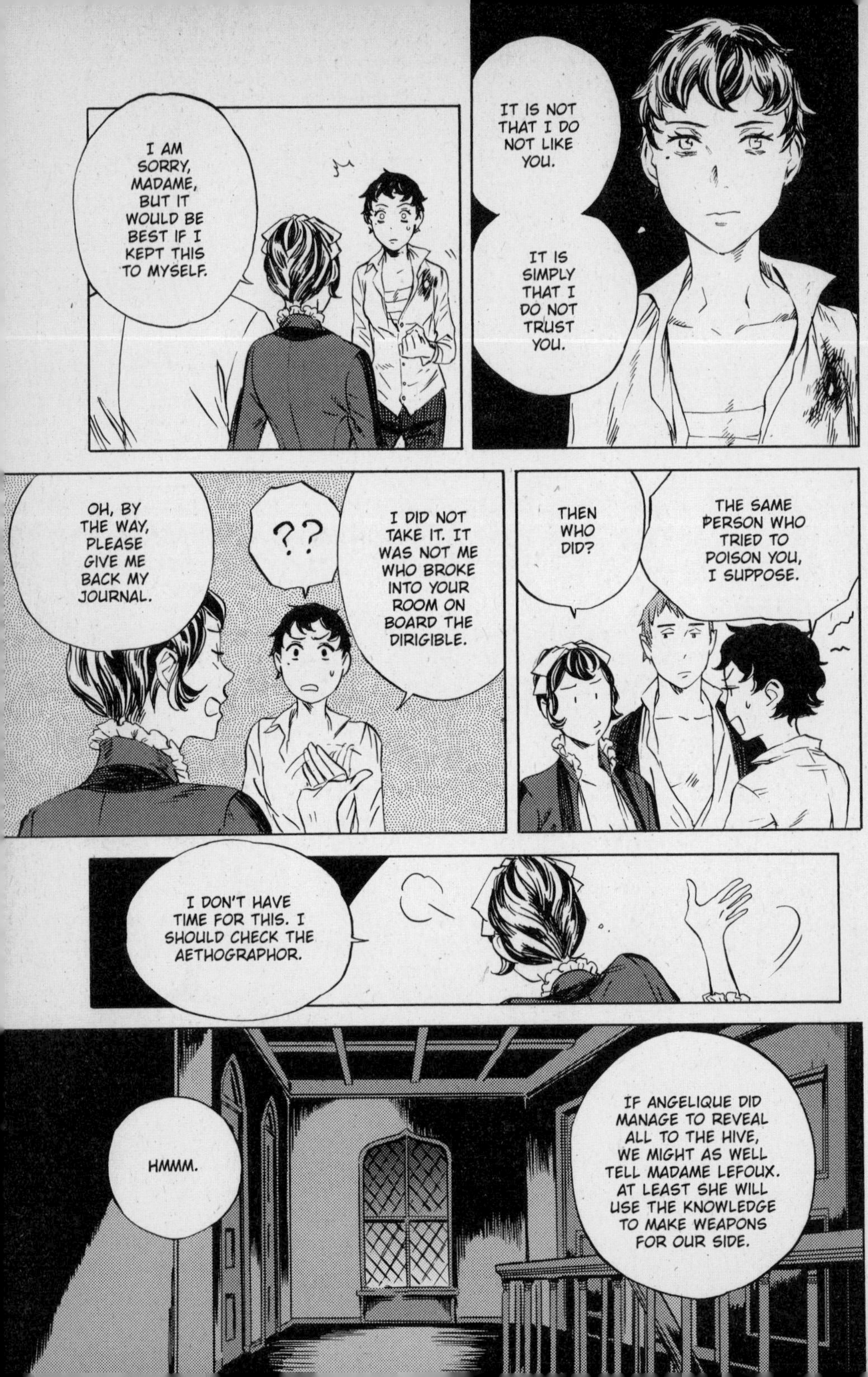
I AM SORRY, MADAME, BUT IT WOULD BE BEST IF I KEPT THIS TO MYSELF.
IT IS NOT THAT I DO NOT LIKE YOU.
IT IS SIMPLY THAT I DO NOT TRUST YOU.
OH, BY THE WAY, PLEASE GIVE ME BACK MY JOURNAL.
??
I DID NOT TAKE IT. IT WAS NOT ME WHO BROKE INTO YOUR ROOM ON BOARD THE DIRIGIBLE.
THEN WHO DID?
THE SAME PERSON WHO TRIED TO POISON YOU, I SUPPOSE.
I DON'T HAVE TIME FOR THIS. I SHOULD CHECK THE AETHOGRAPHOR.
HMMM.
IF ANGELIQUE DID MANAGE TO REVEAL ALL TO THE HIVE, WE MIGHT AS WELL TELL MADAME LEFOUX. AT LEAST SHE WILL USE THE KNOWLEDGE TO MAKE WEAPONS FOR OUR SIDE.

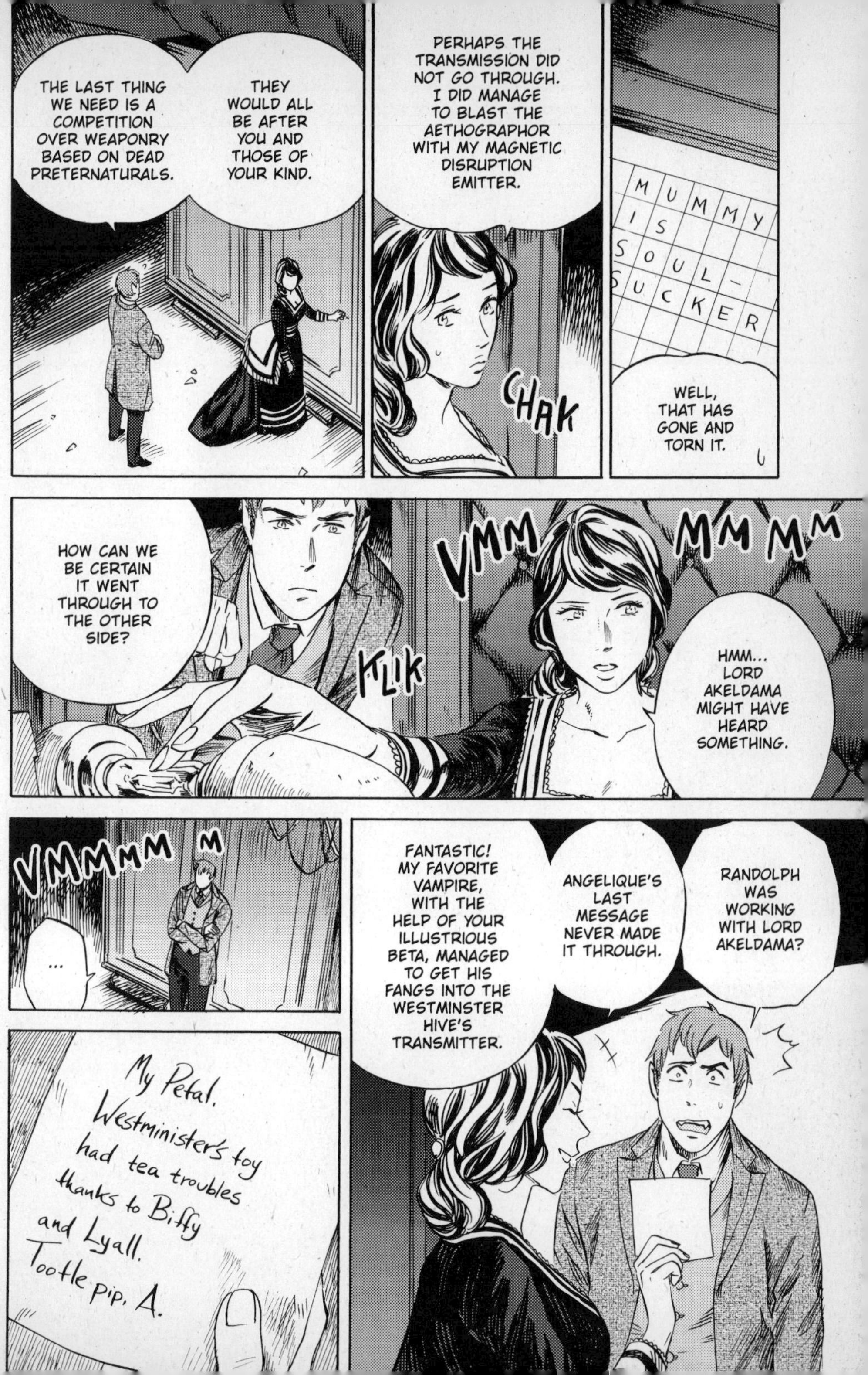
THE LAST THING WE NEED IS A COMPETITION OVER WEAPONRY BASED ON DEAD PRETERNATURALS.
THEY WOULD ALL BE AFTER YOU AND THOSE OF YOUR KIND.
PERHAPS THE TRANSMISSION DID NOT GO THROUGH. I DID MANAGE TO BLAST THE AETHOGRAPHOR WITH MY MAGNETIC DISRUPTION EMITTER.
CHAK
MUMMY IS SOUL-SUCKER
WELL, THAT HAS GONE AND TORN IT.
HOW CAN WE BE CERTAIN IT WENT THROUGH TO THE OTHER SIDE?
VMM
KLIK
MM MM MM
HMM... LORD AKELDAMA MIGHT HAVE HEARD SOMETHING.
VMMMM M
...
My Petal.
Westminister's toy had tea troubles thanks to Biffy and Lyall.
Tootle pip. A.
FANTASTIC! MY FAVORITE VAMPIRE, WITH THE HELP OF YOUR ILLUSTRIOUS BETA, MANAGED TO GET HIS FANGS INTO THE WESTMINSTER HIVE'S TRANSMITTER.
ANGELIQUE'S LAST MESSAGE NEVER MADE IT THROUGH.
RANDOLPH WAS WORKING WITH LORD AKELDAMA?

WELL... OTHER THAN THOSE THREE, WHO ELSE KNOWS ABOUT THE MUMMY?

LACHLAN AND SIDHEAG. AND IVY, BUT ONLY IN THAT WAY IVY KNOWS THINGS.

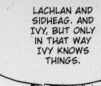

WHICH IS TO SAY, NOT WITH ANY REAL COGENCY?

EXACTLY.

Ha Ha Ha...

MISS HISSELPENNY HAS ELOPED.

WHAT?

WHY, YES, SISTER. SHE LEFT YOU A NOTE, WITH ME OF COURSE.

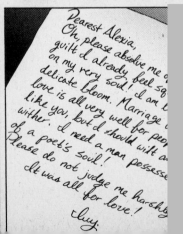

Dearest Alexia,
Oh, please absolve me o[f]
guilt I already feel sq[...]
on my very soul! I am [...]
delicate bloom. I am [...]
love is all very well for peo[ple]
like you, but I should wilt a[nd]
wither. I need a man possess[ed]
of a poet's soul!
Please do not judge me harshly.
It was all for love!

Ivy

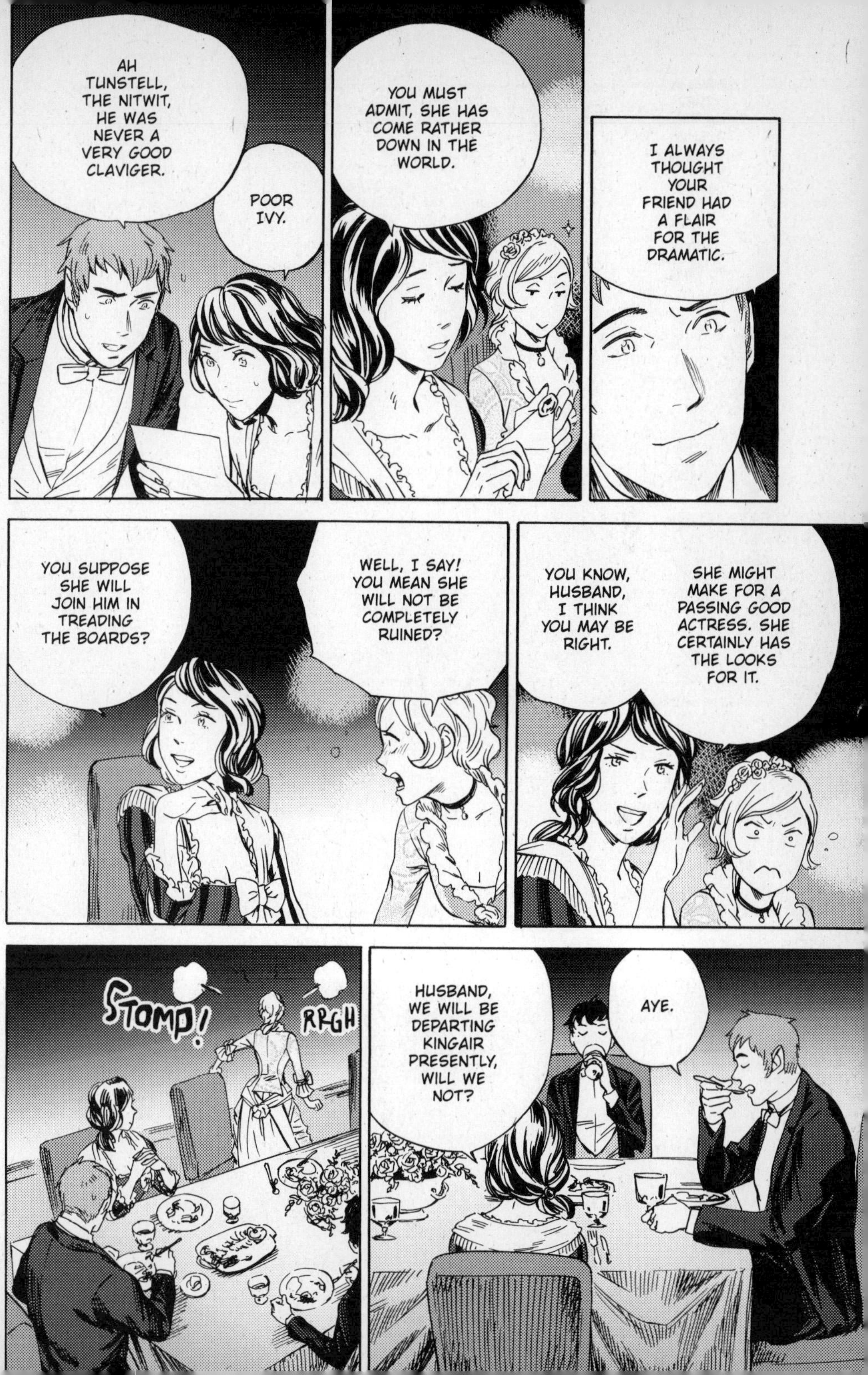
AH TUNSTELL, THE NITWIT, HE WAS NEVER A VERY GOOD CLAVIGER.
POOR IVY.
YOU MUST ADMIT, SHE HAS COME RATHER DOWN IN THE WORLD.
I ALWAYS THOUGHT YOUR FRIEND HAD A FLAIR FOR THE DRAMATIC.
YOU SUPPOSE SHE WILL JOIN HIM IN TREADING THE BOARDS?
WELL, I SAY! YOU MEAN SHE WILL NOT BE COMPLETELY RUINED?
YOU KNOW, HUSBAND, I THINK YOU MAY BE RIGHT.
SHE MIGHT MAKE FOR A PASSING GOOD ACTRESS. SHE CERTAINLY HAS THE LOOKS FOR IT.
STOMP!
RRGH
HUSBAND, WE WILL BE DEPARTING KINGAIR PRESENTLY, WILL WE NOT?
AYE.

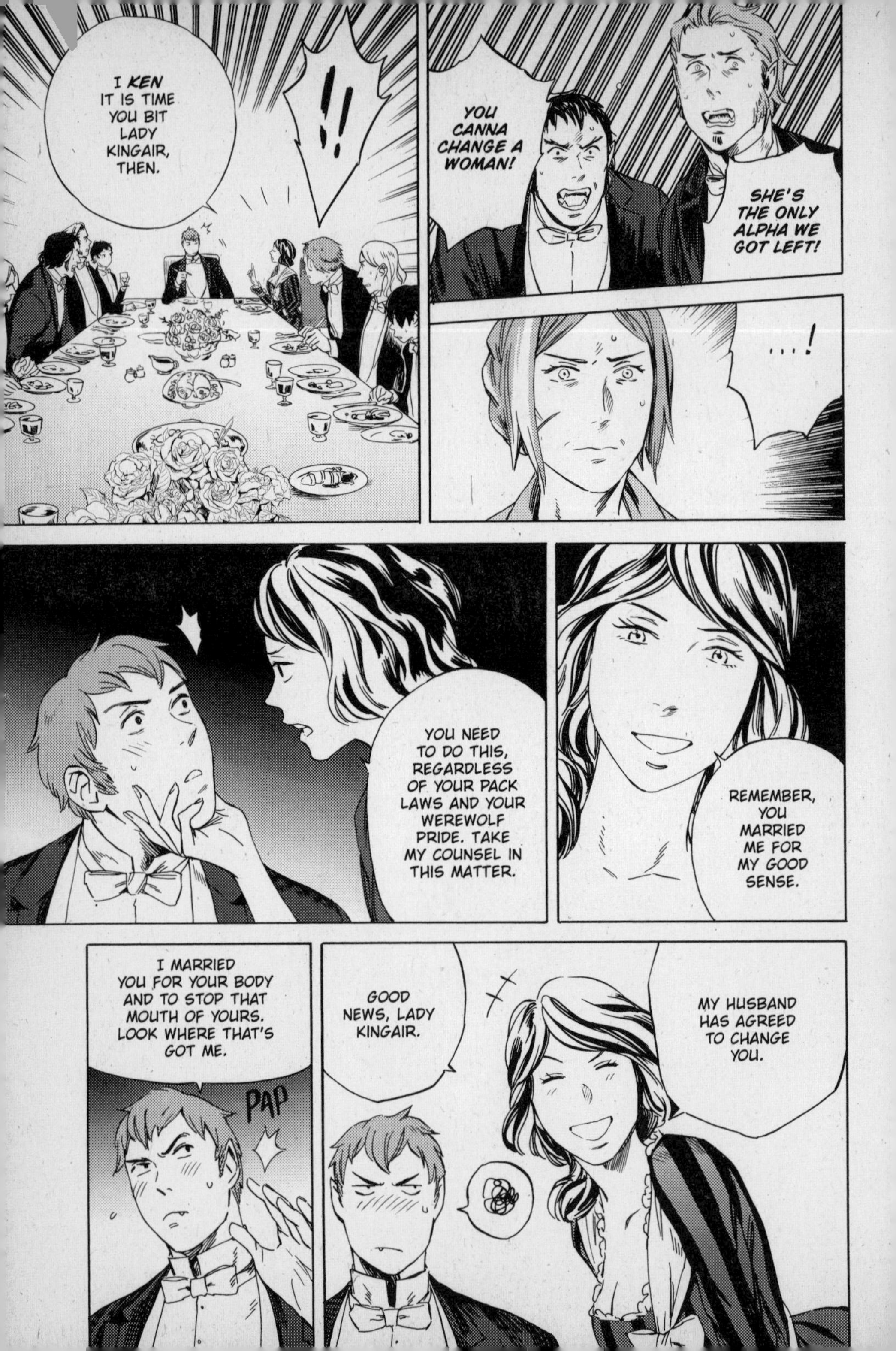
I KEN
IT IS TIME
YOU BIT
LADY
KINGAIR,
THEN.
!!
YOU
CANNA
CHANGE A
WOMAN!
SHE'S
THE ONLY
ALPHA WE
GOT LEFT!
...!
YOU NEED
TO DO THIS,
REGARDLESS
OF YOUR PACK
LAWS AND YOUR
WEREWOLF
PRIDE. TAKE
MY COUNSEL IN
THIS MATTER.
REMEMBER,
YOU
MARRIED
ME FOR
MY GOOD
SENSE.
I MARRIED
YOU FOR YOUR BODY
AND TO STOP THAT
MOUTH OF YOURS.
LOOK WHERE THAT'S
GOT ME.
PAP
GOOD
NEWS, LADY
KINGAIR.
MY HUSBAND
HAS AGREED
TO CHANGE
YOU.

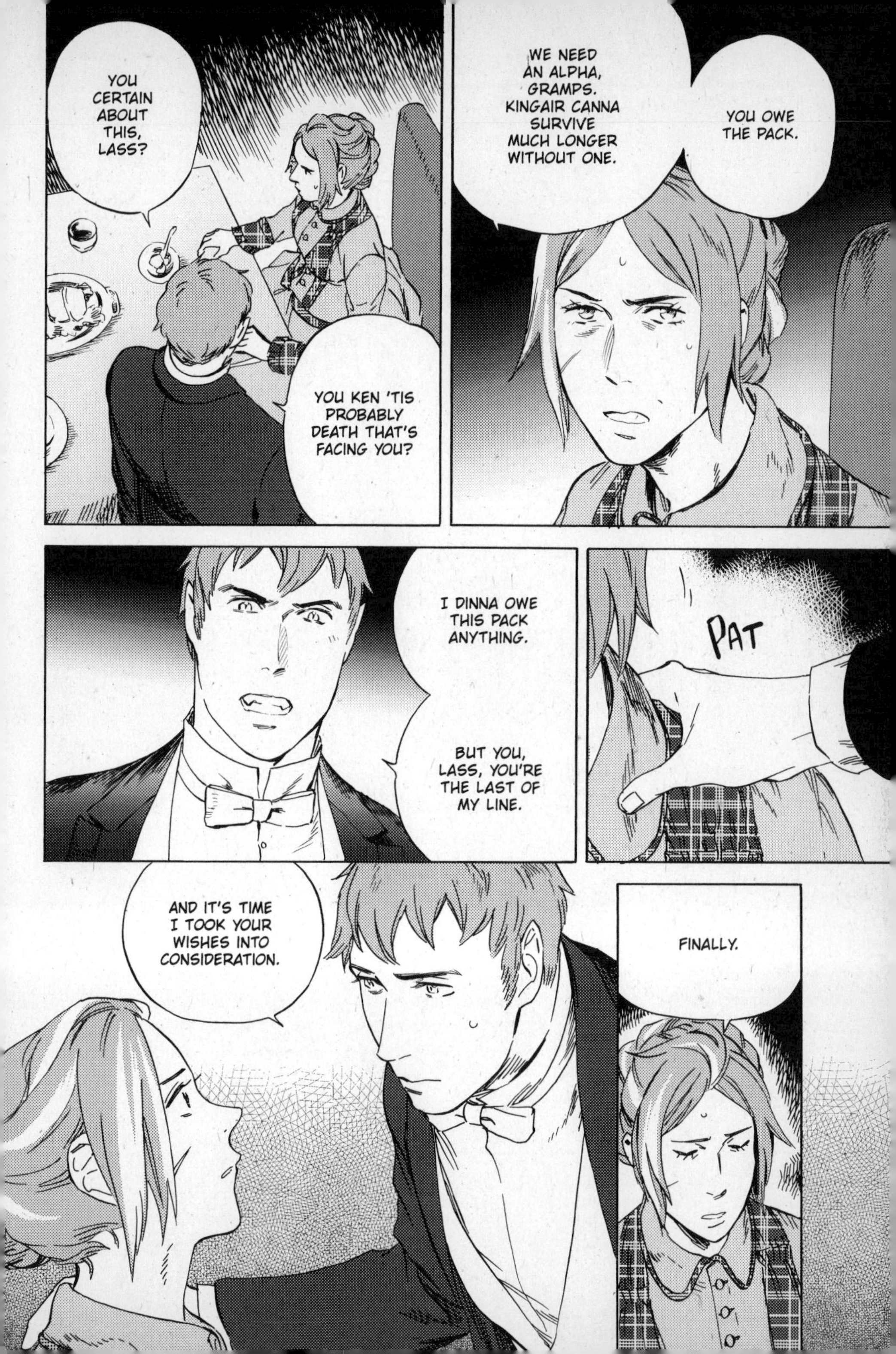
YOU CERTAIN ABOUT THIS, LASS?
YOU KEN 'TIS PROBABLY DEATH THAT'S FACING YOU?
WE NEED AN ALPHA, GRAMPS. KINGAIR CANNA SURVIVE MUCH LONGER WITHOUT ONE.
YOU OWE THE PACK.
I DINNA OWE THIS PACK ANYTHING.
BUT YOU, LASS, YOU'RE THE LAST OF MY LINE.
PAT
AND IT'S TIME I TOOK YOUR WISHES INTO CONSIDERATION.
FINALLY.

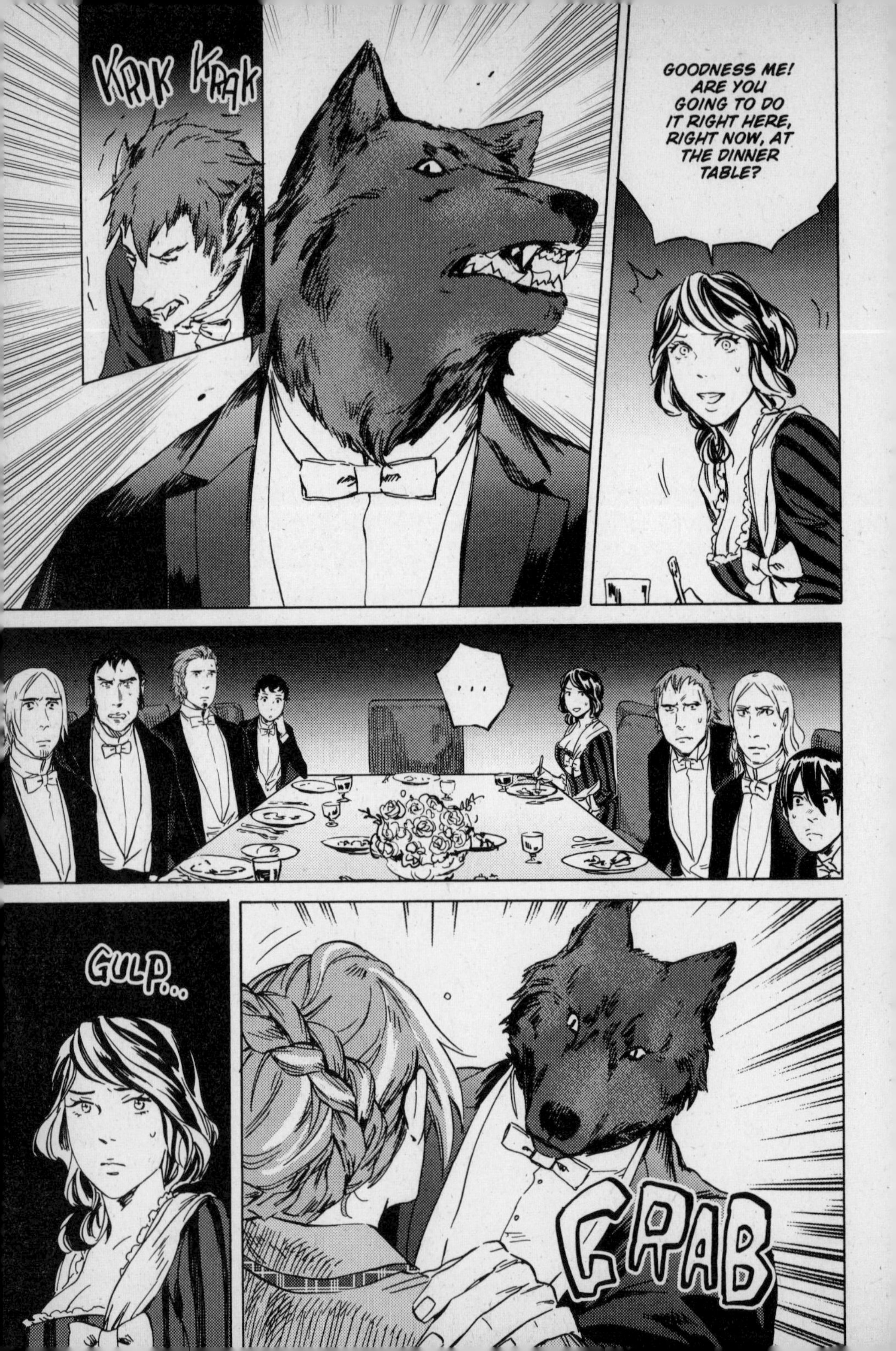
KRIK KRAK
GOODNESS ME! ARE YOU GOING TO DO IT RIGHT HERE, RIGHT NOW, AT THE DINNER TABLE?
...
GULP...
GRAB

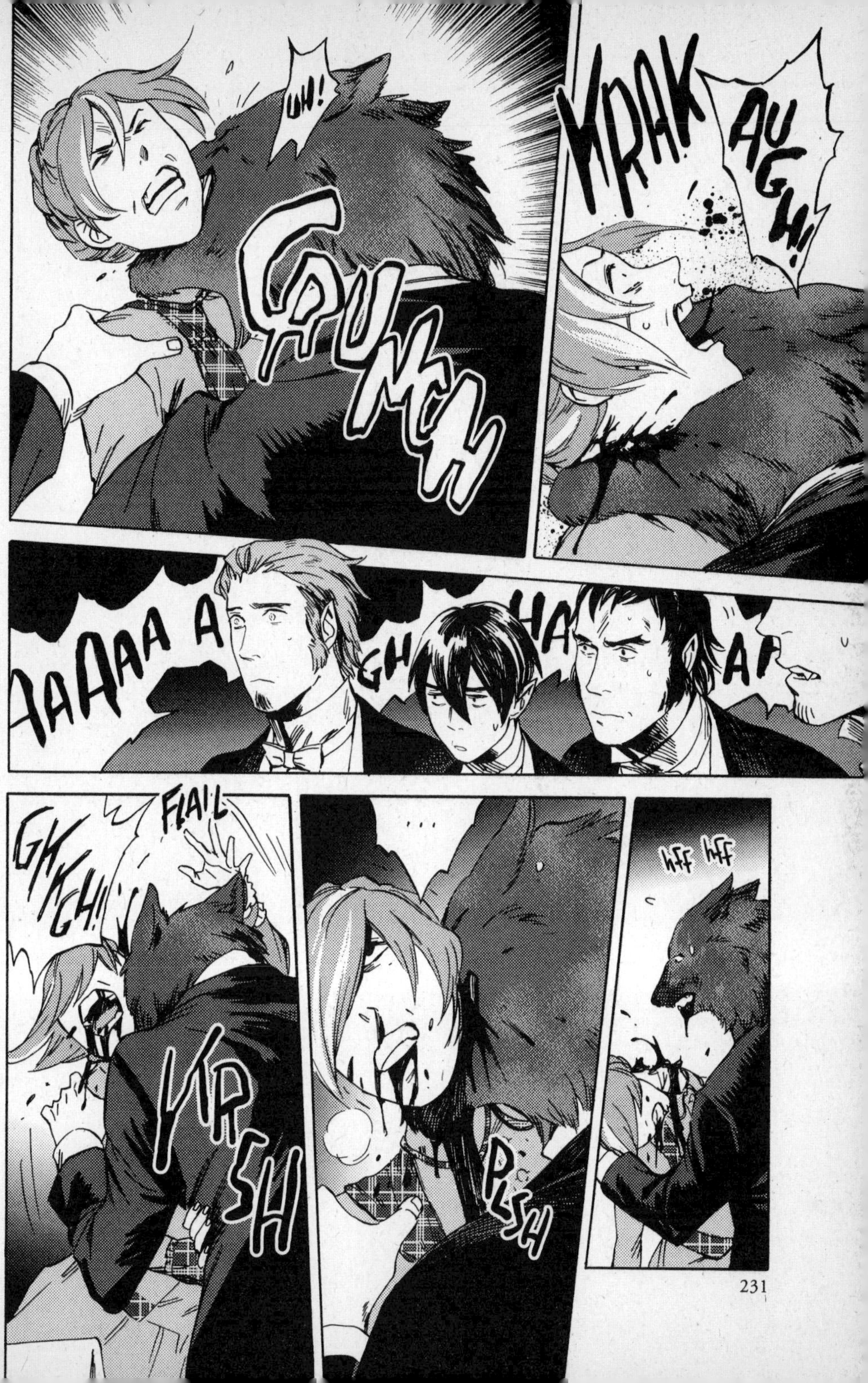
UH!
CRUNCH
KRAK
AUGH!!
AAAAAA A
GH
HA
AA
GKKGH!!
FLAIL
VRSH
...
PLSH
hff hff

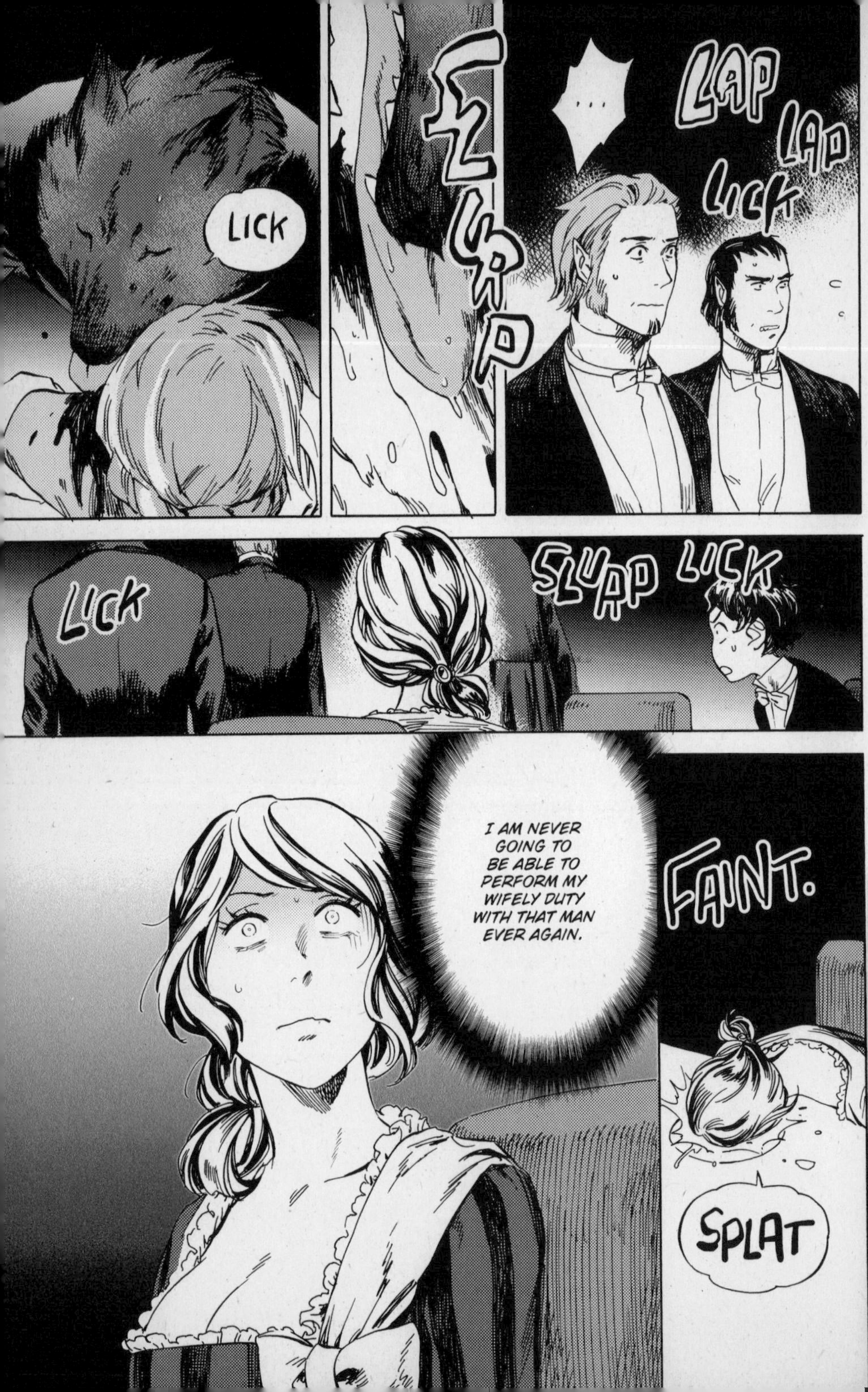
LICK
SLURP
...
LAP LAP LICK
LICK
SLURP LICK
I AM NEVER GOING TO BE ABLE TO PERFORM MY WIFELY DUTY WITH THAT MAN EVER AGAIN.
FAINT.
SPLAT

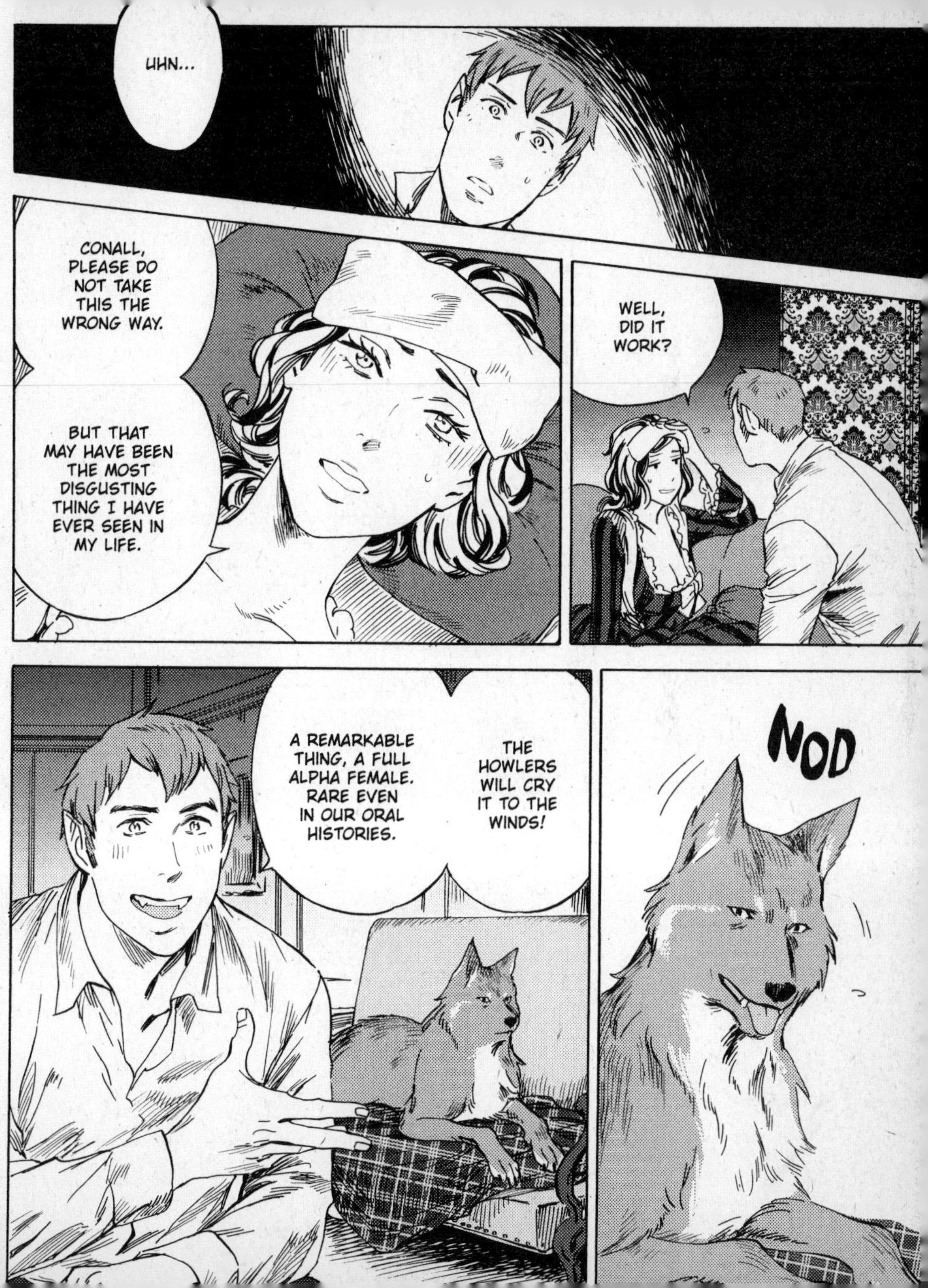
UHN...
CONALL, PLEASE DO NOT TAKE THIS THE WRONG WAY.
BUT THAT MAY HAVE BEEN THE MOST DISGUSTING THING I HAVE EVER SEEN IN MY LIFE.
WELL, DID IT WORK?
A REMARKABLE THING, A FULL ALPHA FEMALE. RARE EVEN IN OUR ORAL HISTORIES.
THE HOWLERS WILL CRY IT TO THE WINDS!
NOD

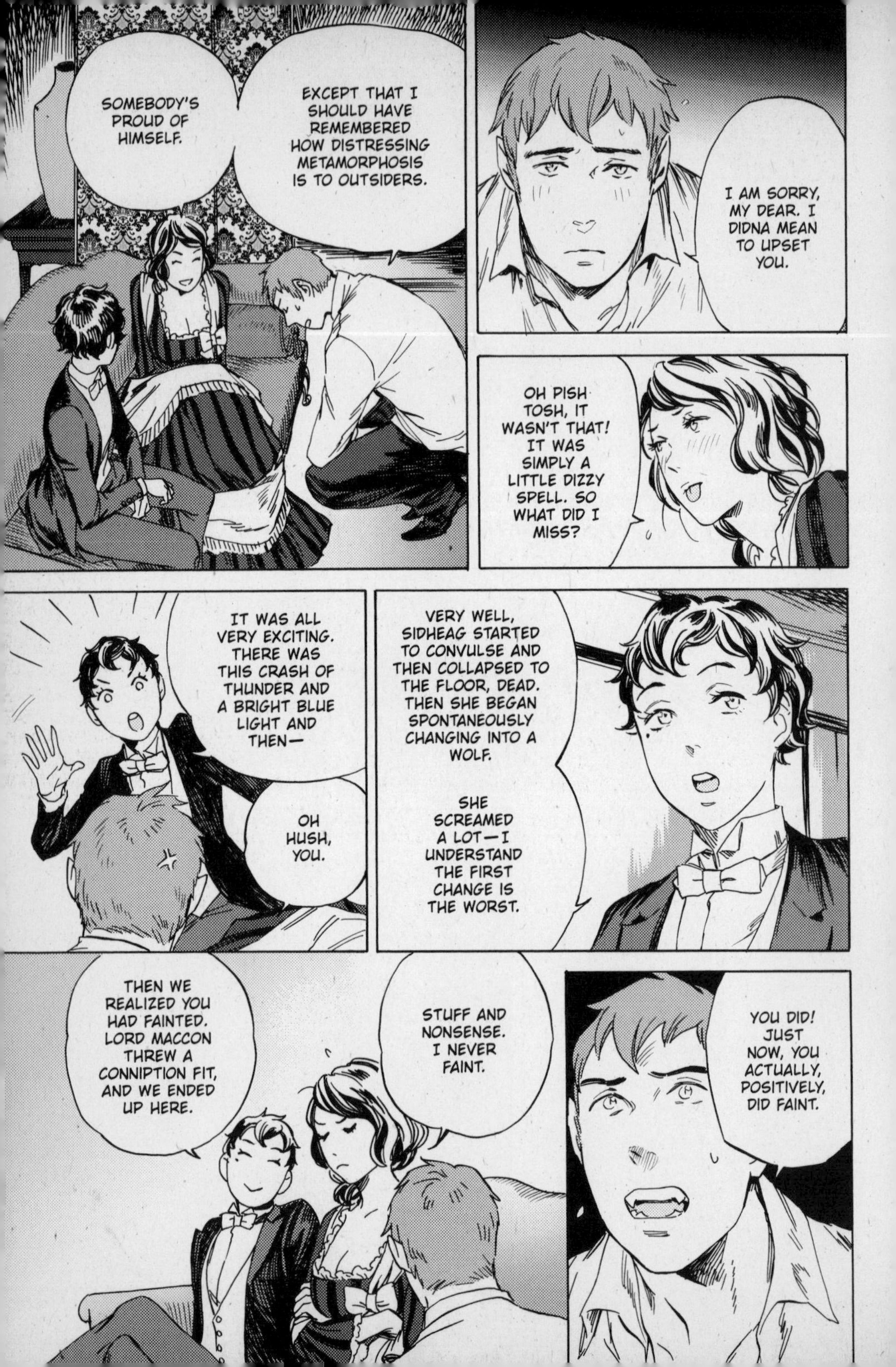
SOMEBODY'S PROUD OF HIMSELF.
EXCEPT THAT I SHOULD HAVE REMEMBERED HOW DISTRESSING METAMORPHOSIS IS TO OUTSIDERS.
I AM SORRY, MY DEAR. I DIDNA MEAN TO UPSET YOU.
OH PISH TOSH, IT WASN'T THAT! IT WAS SIMPLY A LITTLE DIZZY SPELL. SO WHAT DID I MISS?
IT WAS ALL VERY EXCITING. THERE WAS THIS CRASH OF THUNDER AND A BRIGHT BLUE LIGHT AND THEN—
OH HUSH, YOU.
VERY WELL, SIDHEAG STARTED TO CONVULSE AND THEN COLLAPSED TO THE FLOOR, DEAD. THEN SHE BEGAN SPONTANEOUSLY CHANGING INTO A WOLF.
SHE SCREAMED A LOT—I UNDERSTAND THE FIRST CHANGE IS THE WORST.
THEN WE REALIZED YOU HAD FAINTED. LORD MACCON THREW A CONNIPTION FIT, AND WE ENDED UP HERE.
STUFF AND NONSENSE. I NEVER FAINT.
YOU DID! JUST NOW, YOU ACTUALLY, POSITIVELY, DID FAINT.

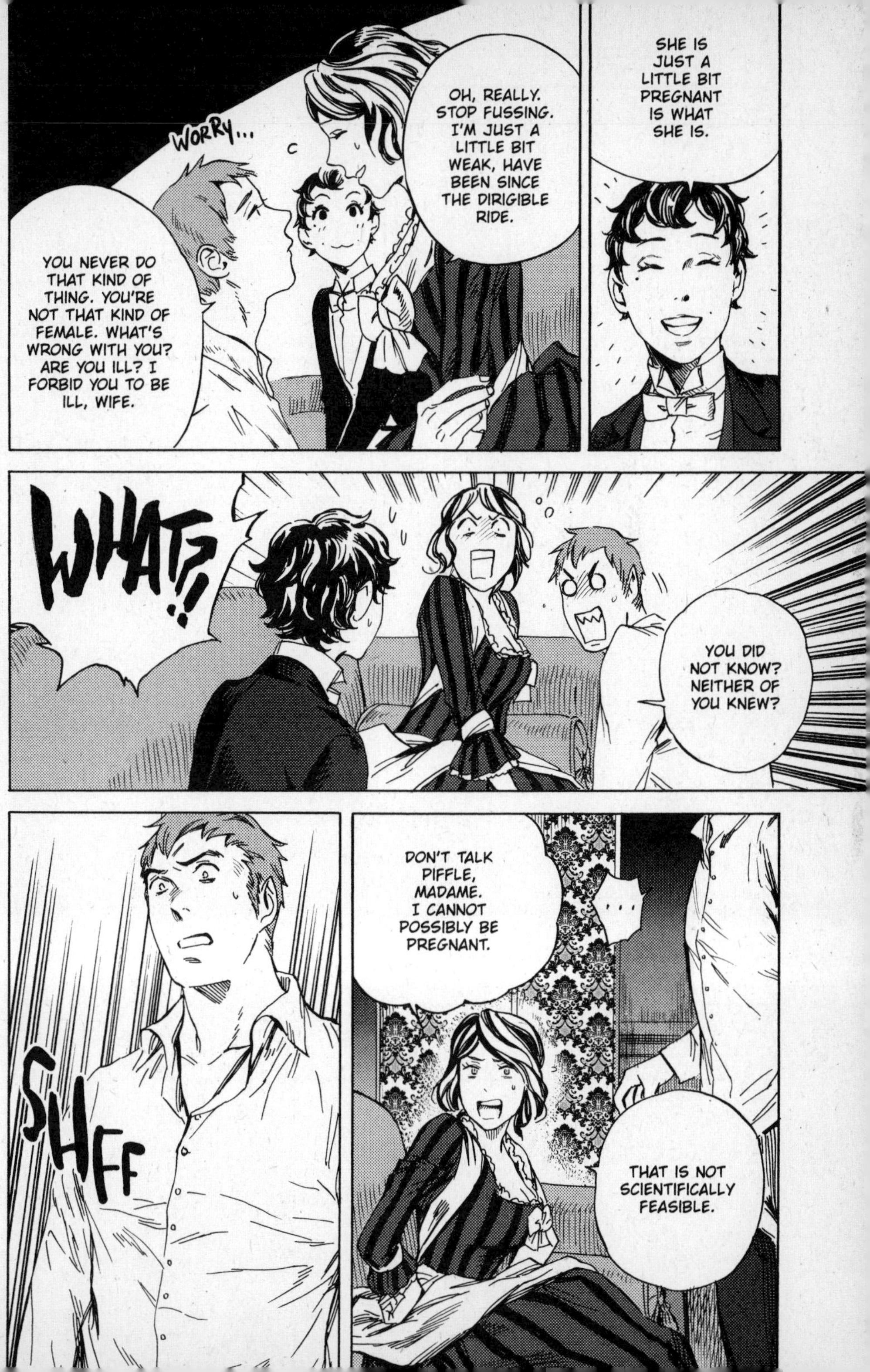
WORRY...
YOU NEVER DO THAT KIND OF THING. YOU'RE NOT THAT KIND OF FEMALE. WHAT'S WRONG WITH YOU? ARE YOU ILL? I FORBID YOU TO BE ILL, WIFE.
OH, REALLY. STOP FUSSING. I'M JUST A LITTLE BIT WEAK, HAVE BEEN SINCE THE DIRIGIBLE RIDE.
SHE IS JUST A LITTLE BIT PREGNANT IS WHAT SHE IS.
WHAT!?!!
YOU DID NOT KNOW? NEITHER OF YOU KNEW?
SHFF
DON'T TALK PIFFLE, MADAME. I CANNOT POSSIBLY BE PREGNANT.
...
THAT IS NOT SCIENTIFICALLY FEASIBLE.

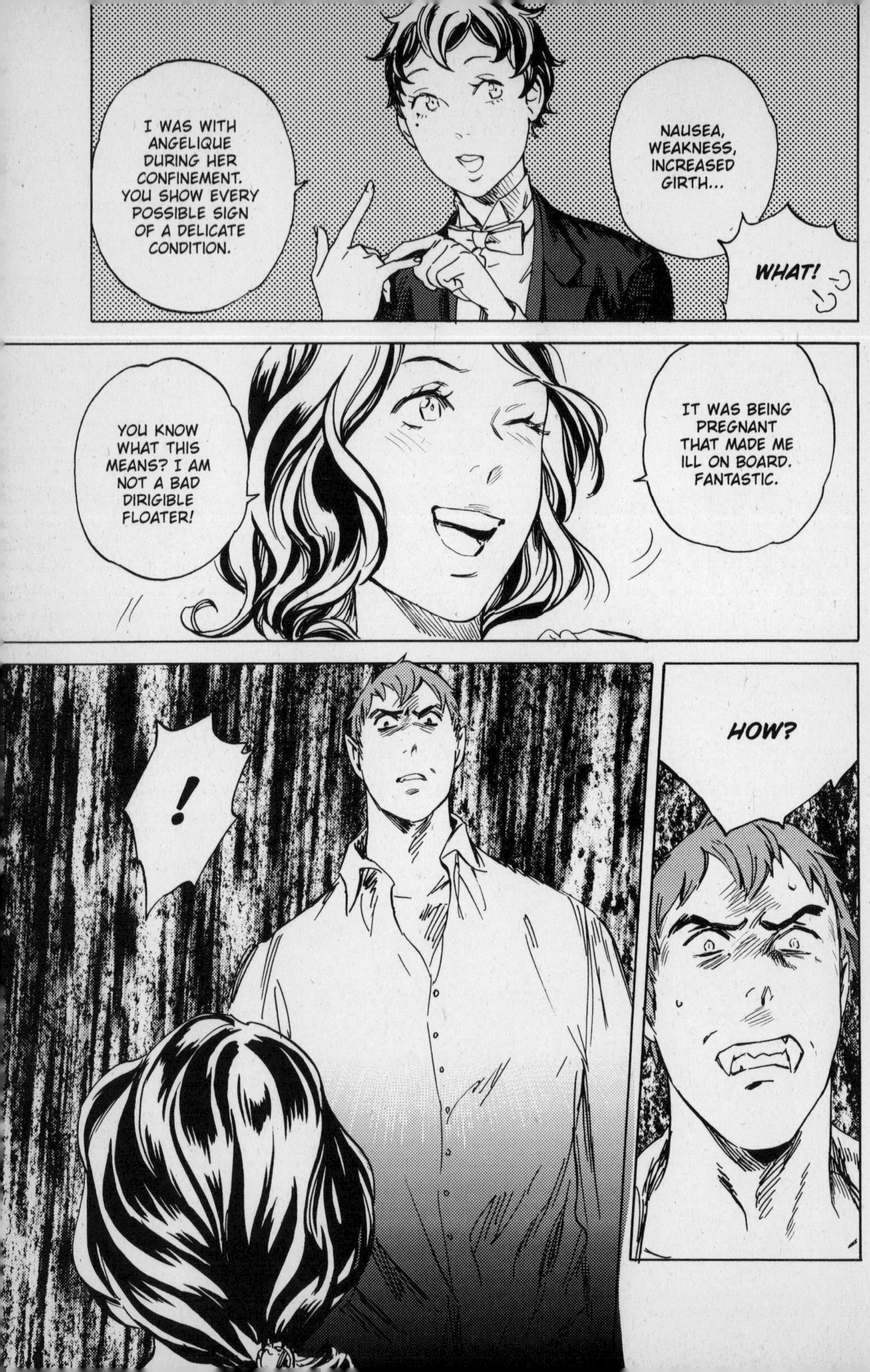
I WAS WITH ANGELIQUE DURING HER CONFINEMENT. YOU SHOW EVERY POSSIBLE SIGN OF A DELICATE CONDITION.
NAUSEA, WEAKNESS, INCREASED GIRTH...
WHAT!
YOU KNOW WHAT THIS MEANS? I AM NOT A BAD DIRIGIBLE FLOATER!
IT WAS BEING PREGNANT THAT MADE ME ILL ON BOARD. FANTASTIC.
!
HOW?

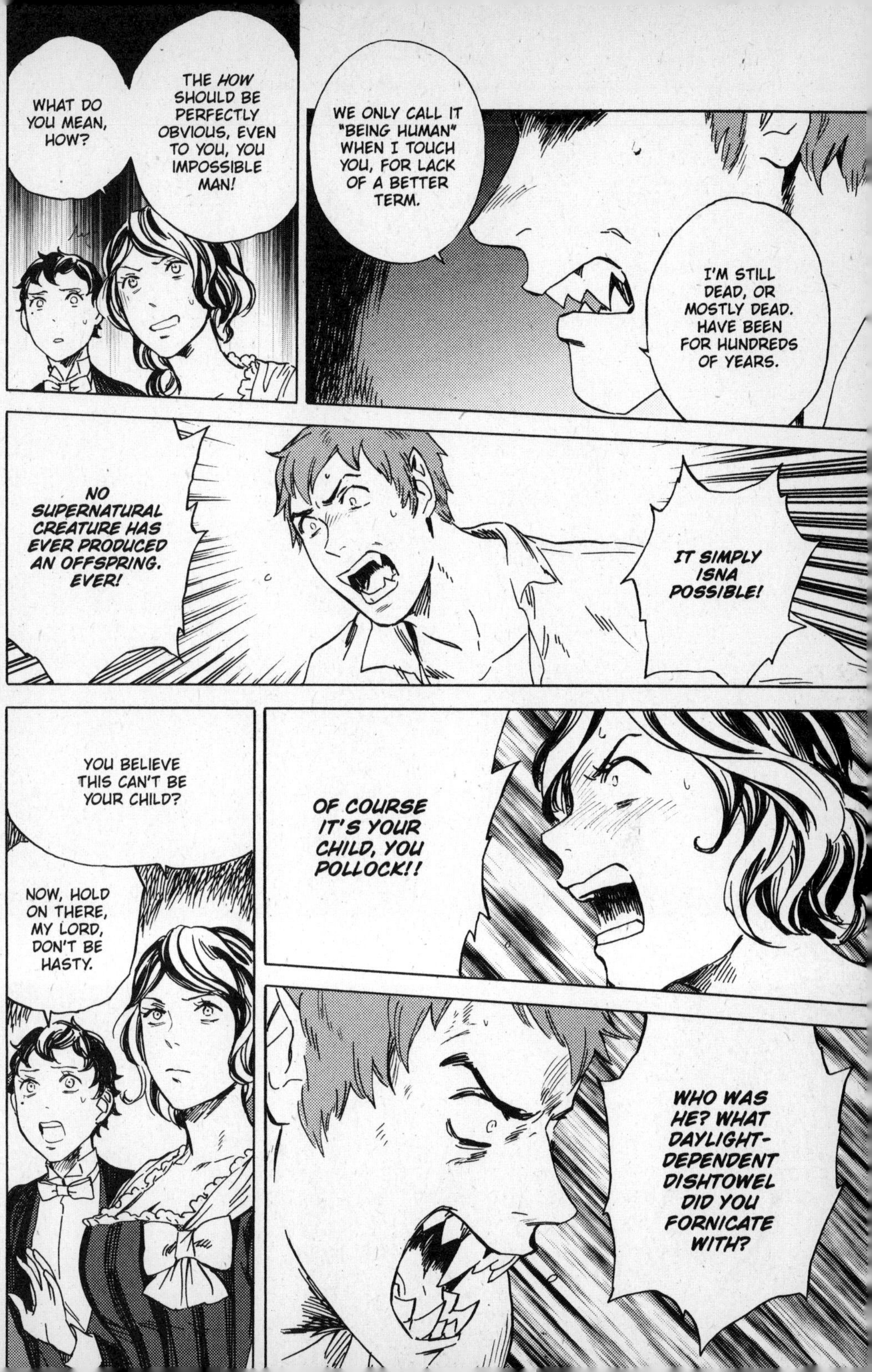
WHAT DO YOU MEAN, HOW?
THE *HOW* SHOULD BE PERFECTLY OBVIOUS, EVEN TO YOU, YOU IMPOSSIBLE MAN!
WE ONLY CALL IT "BEING HUMAN" WHEN I TOUCH YOU, FOR LACK OF A BETTER TERM.
I'M STILL DEAD, OR MOSTLY DEAD. HAVE BEEN FOR HUNDREDS OF YEARS.
NO SUPERNATURAL CREATURE HAS EVER PRODUCED AN OFFSPRING. EVER!
IT SIMPLY ISNA POSSIBLE!
YOU BELIEVE THIS CAN'T BE YOUR CHILD?
NOW, HOLD ON THERE, MY LORD, DON'T BE HASTY.
OF COURSE IT'S YOUR CHILD, YOU POLLOCK!!
WHO WAS HE? WHAT DAYLIGHT-DEPENDENT DISHTOWEL DID YOU FORNICATE WITH?

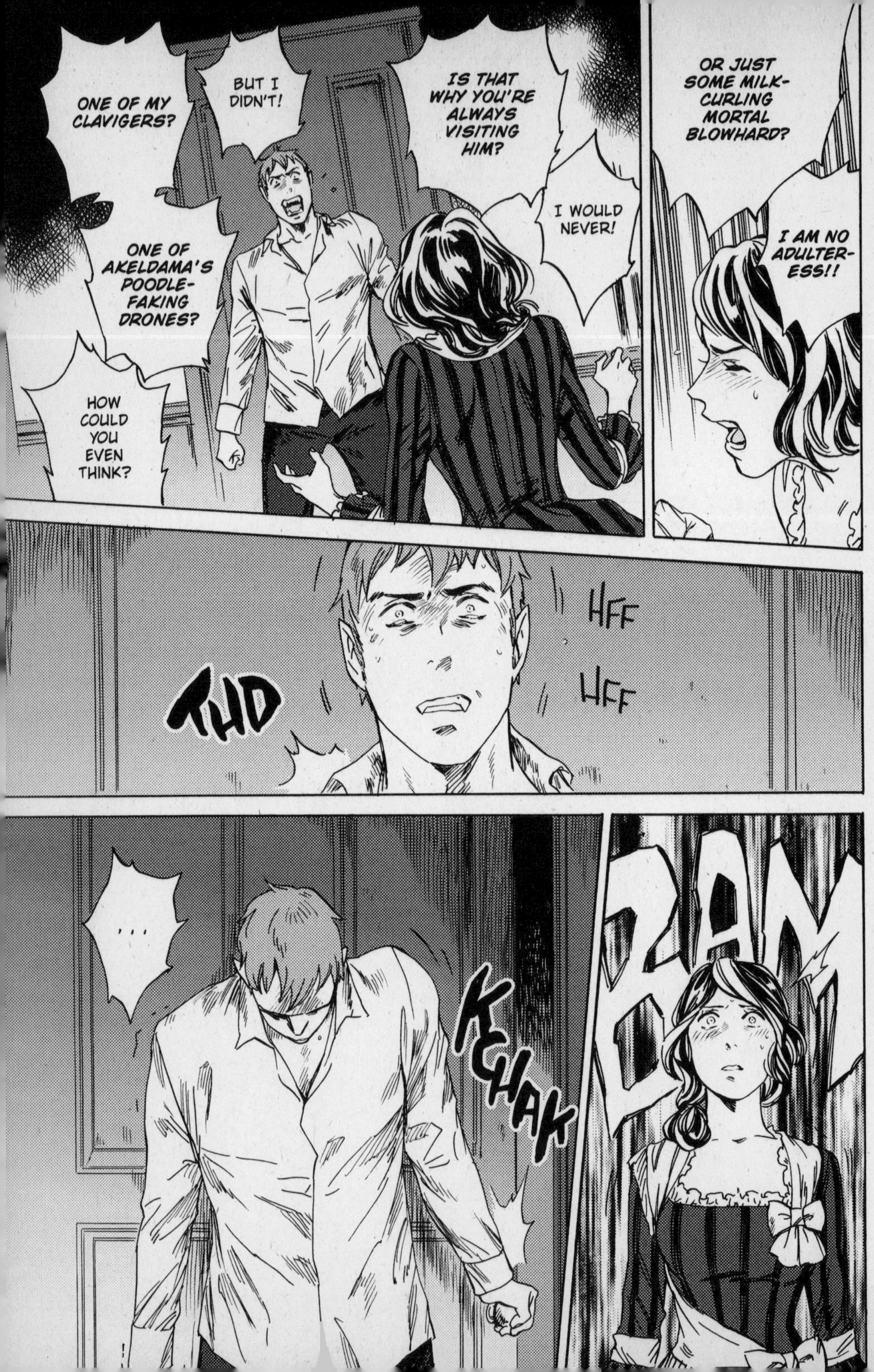
ONE OF MY CLAVIGERS?
BUT I DIDN'T!
IS THAT WHY YOU'RE ALWAYS VISITING HIM?
ONE OF AKELDAMA'S POODLE-FAKING DRONES?
I WOULD NEVER!
HOW COULD YOU EVEN THINK?
OR JUST SOME MILK-CURLING MORTAL BLOWHARD?
I AM NO ADULTER-ESS!!
THD
HFF
HFF
...
KCHAK
BAM

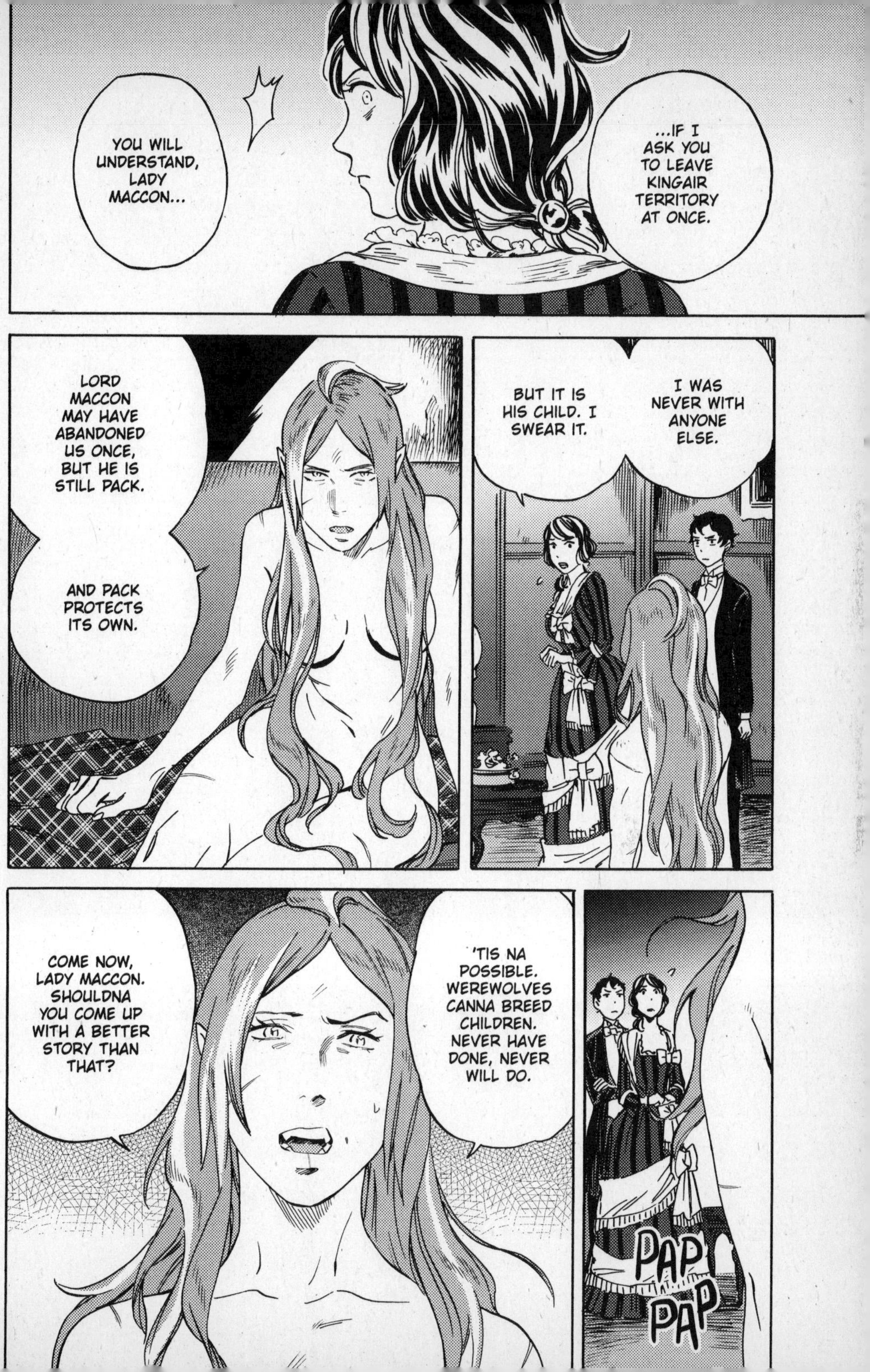
YOU WILL UNDERSTAND, LADY MACCON...
...IF I ASK YOU TO LEAVE KINGAIR TERRITORY AT ONCE.
LORD MACCON MAY HAVE ABANDONED US ONCE, BUT HE IS STILL PACK.
AND PACK PROTECTS ITS OWN.
BUT IT IS HIS CHILD. I SWEAR IT.
I WAS NEVER WITH ANYONE ELSE.
COME NOW, LADY MACCON. SHOULDNA YOU COME UP WITH A BETTER STORY THAN THAT?
'TIS NA POSSIBLE. WEREWOLVES CANNA BREED CHILDREN. NEVER HAVE DONE, NEVER WILL DO.
PAP
PAP

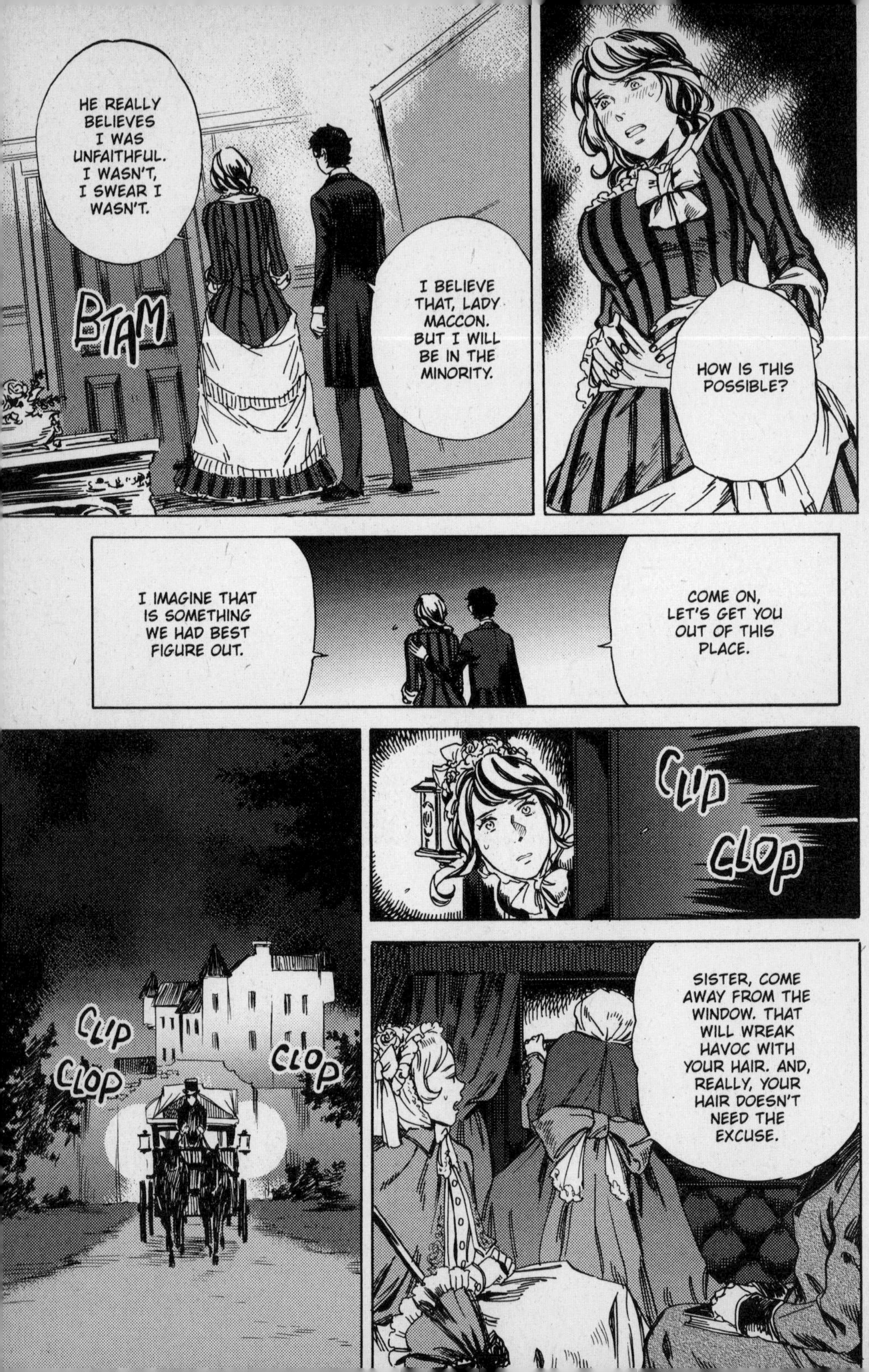
HE REALLY BELIEVES I WAS UNFAITHFUL. I WASN'T, I SWEAR I WASN'T.
BTAM
I BELIEVE THAT, LADY MACCON. BUT I WILL BE IN THE MINORITY.
HOW IS THIS POSSIBLE?
I IMAGINE THAT IS SOMETHING WE HAD BEST FIGURE OUT.
COME ON, LET'S GET YOU OUT OF THIS PLACE.
CLIP CLOP CLOP
CLIP CLOP
SISTER, COME AWAY FROM THE WINDOW. THAT WILL WREAK HAVOC WITH YOUR HAIR. AND, REALLY, YOUR HAIR DOESN'T NEED THE EXCUSE.

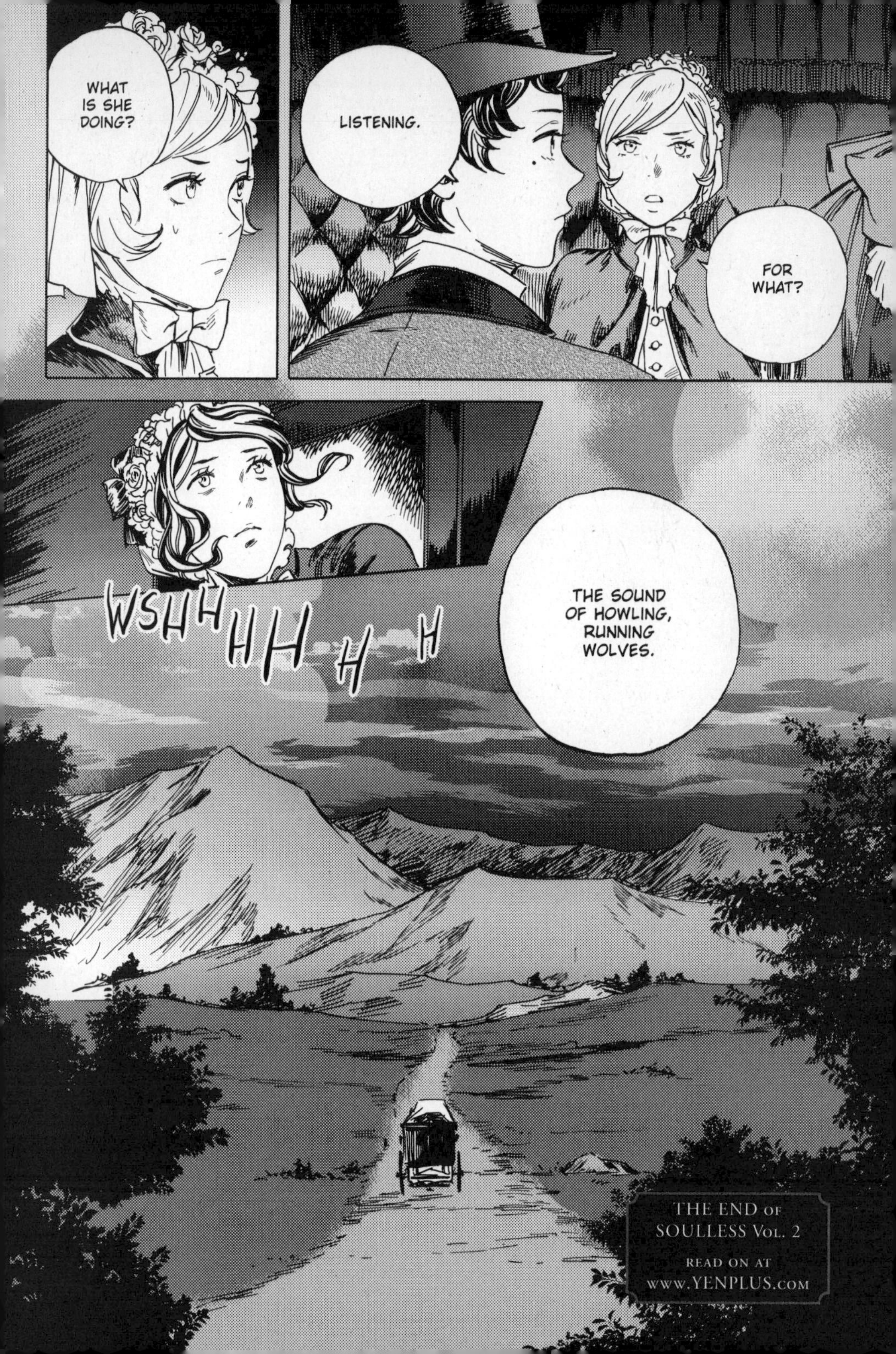
WHAT IS SHE DOING?
LISTENING.
FOR WHAT?
WSHHHHHH
THE SOUND OF HOWLING, RUNNING WOLVES.
THE END OF SOULLESS VOL. 2
READ ON AT www.YENPLUS.com

Westminster Hive's Tea Troubles

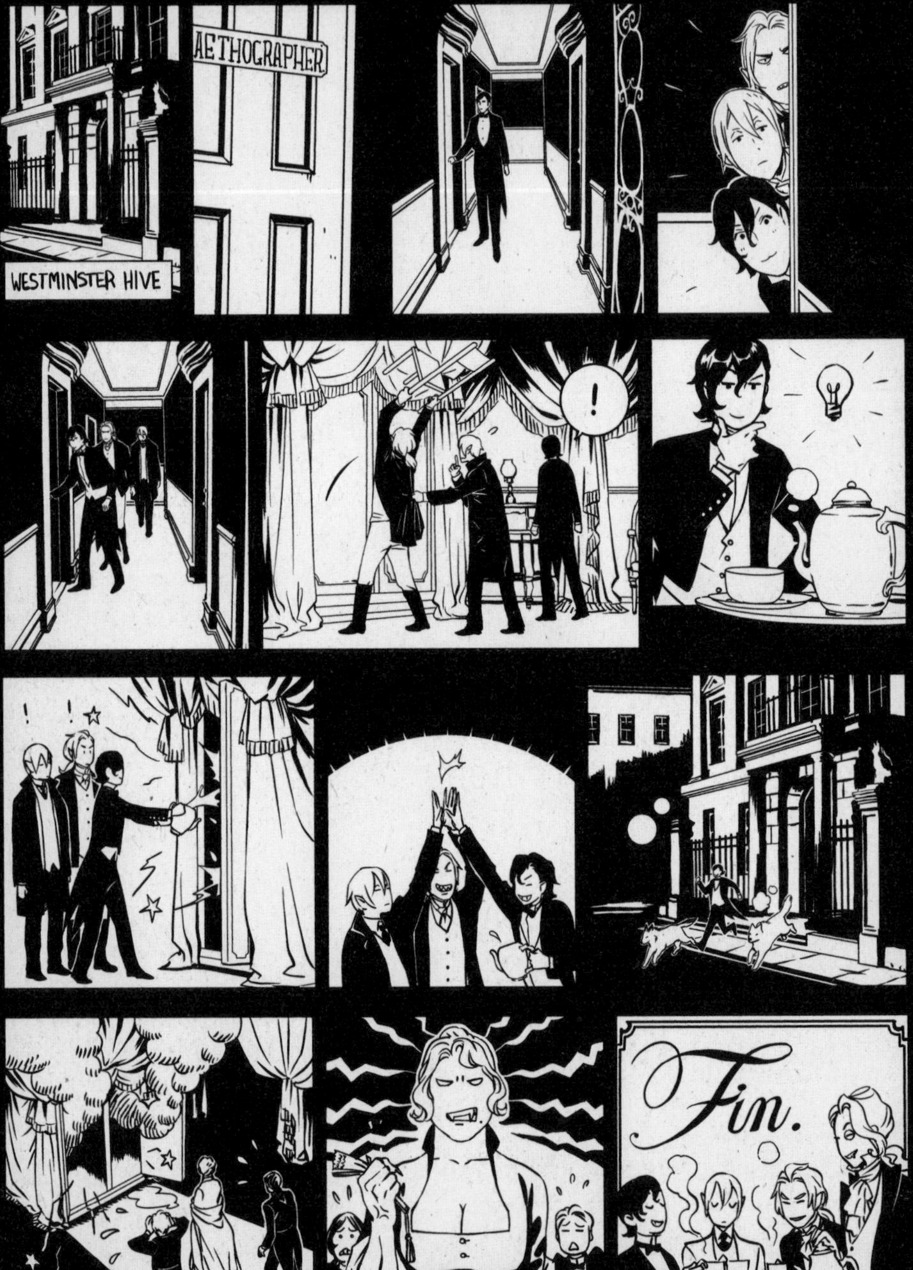
AETHOGRAPHER
WESTMINSTER HIVE
!
Fin.

SOUL EATER NOT!
READ IT THE SAME DAY AS JAPAN!
MAXIMUM RIDE
SOULLESS
WITCH & WIZARD
THE INFERNAL DEVICES
CLOCKWORK ANGEL

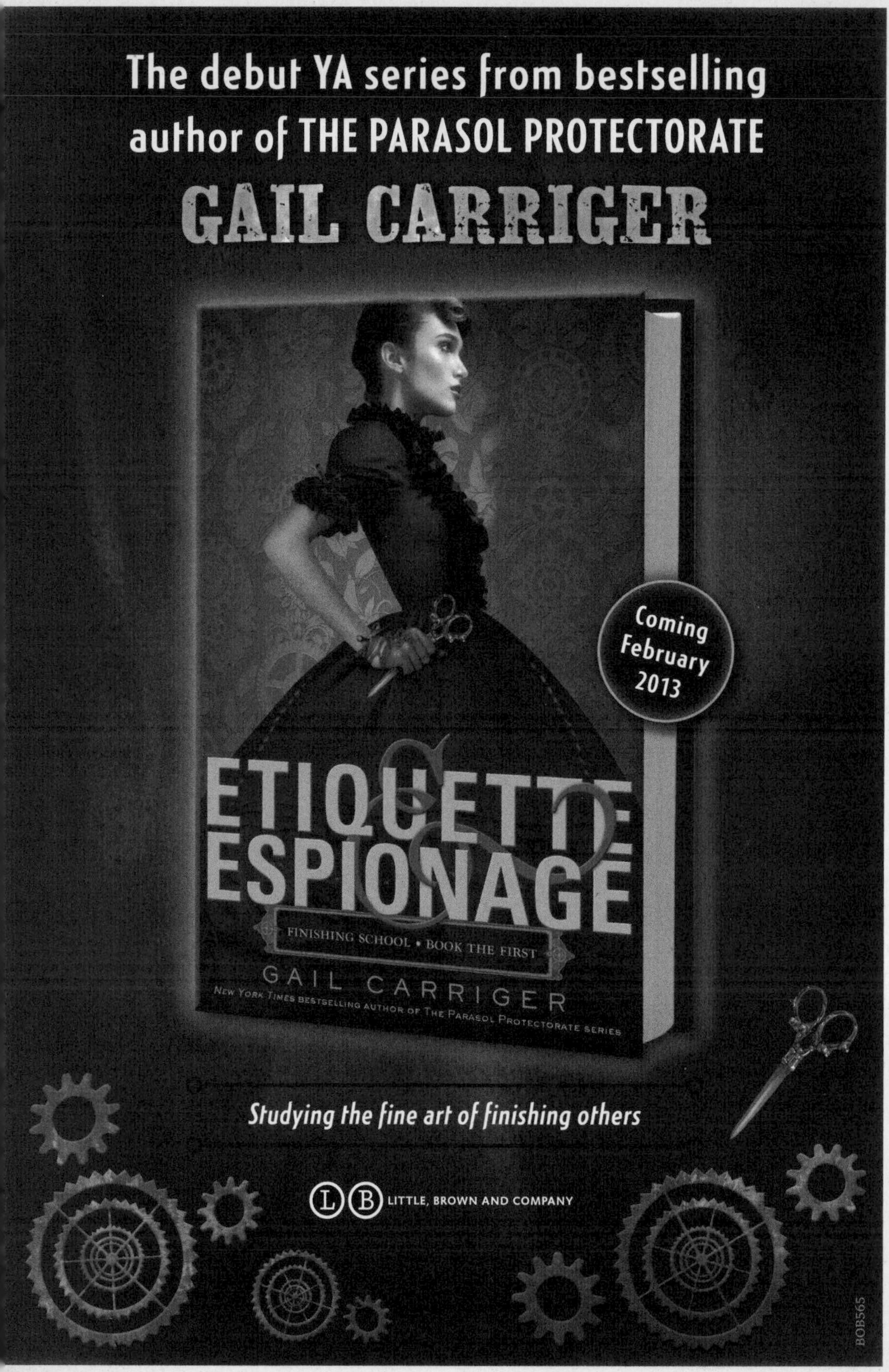
The debut YA series from bestselling
author of THE PARASOL PROTECTORATE
GAIL CARRIGER
ETIQUETTE & ESPIONAGE
FINISHING SCHOOL • BOOK THE FIRST
GAIL CARRIGER
NEW YORK TIMES BESTSELLING AUTHOR OF THE PARASOL PROTECTORATE SERIES
Coming February 2013
Studying the fine art of finishing others
LB LITTLE, BROWN AND COMPANY
BOB565

SOULLESS: THE MANGA ❷

GAIL CARRIGER
REM

Art and Adaptation: REM / Priscilla Hamby

Assistants: Maximo Lorenzo, Marcella Meyer, and Santos and Zara Gaitan
Lettering: JuYoun Lee

SOULLESS: THE MANGA, Vol.2 © 2012 by Tofa Borregaard

Illustrations © Hachette Book Group, Inc.

Yen Press
Hachette Book Group
237 Park Avenue, New York, NY 10017

www.HachetteBookGroup.com
www.YenPress.com

Yen Press is an imprint of Hachette Book Group, Inc. The Yen Press name and logo are trademarks of Hachette Book Group, Inc.

First Yen Press Edition: November 2012

ISBN: 978-0-316-18206-5

10 9 8 7 6 5 4 3 2 1

BVG

Printed in the United States of America